Grady's Tour

Sovereign Terrace Books
Mount Pleasant, South Carolina

Printed in the United States of America

This book is an historical novel. In part, it draws from historical records for the
strategic events of the Korean War and for some events in the Army-McCarthy
dispute, but real people have been used fictitiously, and many of the events,
conversations, and characters have been created for this story. Publications of the
CENTER OF MILITARY HISTORY, UNITED STATES ARMY were chiefly
relied upon for the history of the strategic events of the Korean War and for the maps
included herein.

ISBN: 0-9758992-1-X

To order additional copies, please contact us.
BookSurge, LLC
www.booksurge.com
1-866-308-6235
orders@booksurge.com

Grady's Tour

LIEUTENANT JOHN GRADY'S TOUR OF DUTY IN KOREAN WAR

JOHN H. GALLAGHER

John H. Gallagher

SOVEREIGN TERRACE BOOKS
858 Sovereign Terrace
Mount Pleasant, SC 29464

2005

GRADY'S TOUR

BOOK ONE

MANCHURIA

Hyesanjin
Hapsu
Manp'ojin
Kanggye
Kepsan
Kilchu
Ch'osan
Changjin
P'ungsan
Mup'yong-ni
Namsan-ni
Ch'ongsonjin
Hagaru-ri
CHANGJIN
(CHOSIN)
RES.
Songjin
Huich'on
Pukch'ong
Iwon
Uiju
Inch'o-ri
Sinuiju
Hamhung
Chongju
Tokch'on
Hungnam
Sinanju

SEA
OF
JAPAN

Yangdok
Wonsan

PYONGYANG

Chinnamp'o
Kosong

Sariwon
P'yonggang
Kansong
Namch'onjum
Ch'orwon
Kumhwa
Haeju
Yangyang
380
Yonan
Kaesong
380
Chumunjin
Paengnyong-do
Ongjin
Munsan-ni
Ch'unch'on
Kangnung
Uijongbu
Hongch'on

SEOUL

INCHON
Wonju
Samch'ok
Suwon
Chech'on
Tokchok-to
Osan
Ulchin
Ch'ungju
Yongju
Andong
Sangju
Yongdok
Taejon
P'ohang-dong
Kumch'on
Taegu
Yongch'on
Kunsan
Chonju
Kyongju
Ulsan
Miryang
Chinju
Masan
Kwangju
Chinhae
Pusan
Mokp'o
Yosu

KOREA STRAIT

YELLOW
SEA

KOREA

High Ground
Above 200 Meters

0   50 MILES

CHAPTER I. (29 SEPTEMBER 1950)

The new second lieutenant crammed his tall frame into the driver's seat of the jeep, shifted gears up to driving speed, and kept his eyes glued to the rutted road leading east from Sinsi-ri, a town south of the newly-liberated South Korean capital Seoul. Captain Phil Walker sat beside him and periodically looked down at the map on his lap and gave instructions to the lieutenant. When he wasn't reading the map, Walker closely scanned the adjacent terrain for North Korean troops waiting to ambush U.S. troops.

The lieutenant was relatively new in the army and was freshly arrived in the combat zone, but he was savvy enough to know that he was taking part in one of the most brilliant maneuvers in military history: the Inchon Landing. General Douglas MacArthur had conceived the idea of landing the United Nations X Corps (Tenth Corps) at Inchon, South Korea, one hundred fifty miles behind the attacking North Korean Army at the Pusan Perimeter, thereby to relieve the pressure on besieged U.N. Eighth Army troops within the Perimeter and to trap a major portion of the North Korean Army between the two U.N. forces.

As attentive as the lieutenant was to watching for ruts and evidence of land mines in the road, his mind grappled with the matter that had engaged his thoughts ever since he had received orders to FECOM (Far East Command). He had excelled in his training at The Signal School at Fort Monmouth, N.J., but he worried about what he would do in combat: did he have the manhood to perform his duties in a life and death combat situation? He rationalized that since he was in the Signal Corps maybe he wouldn't have to face life and death combat. His inner voice kept asking, "But if you do, are you up to it, John Grady, or will you live the remainder of your life in shame?"

Lieutenant John Grady was six feet one inch tall; weighed about one hundred eighty-five pounds; had good posture; and neatly trimmed, faded blond hair. He usually knew what he was doing and what he wanted to do next, and his approach to a task at hand projected confidence without suggesting cockiness. His height and build, together with his confidence, gave him a natural commanding bearing.

Thirty-one years old Captain Phil Walker was almost as tall as the lieutenant, but thinner and more wiry. He had broad and slightly rounded shoulders, and one thick tuft of his coal-black hair hung midway down on his forehead. He had a plain, honest-looking face that said, "You get what you see."

They arrived without incident at the 17th Infantry Regiment Com-Center located southeast of Seoul. Walker wanted to visit the 17th Regiment because it was the last regiment of the U.S. 7th Infantry Division to land at Inchon, and he wanted to see if they needed anything from Signal Section, Headquarters X Corps. Walker excused himself to go pay his respects to the senior officers of the regiment. ComCenter people briefed Grady on the local situation.

Walker inquired about the communications situation with the 17th Regiment, and the regimental executive officer told him that the 2nd Battalion reported that one of its platoons on a forward outpost couldn't establish telephone communications with its company command post or with its own firing positions and complained that its switchboard was bad.

The executive officer asked Walker, "You're Signal Corps, can you do something about that communications equipment."

"I don't know; that's not Signal Corps equipment, but we can take a look at it," Walker said, not wanting to say "No" to a combat unit. "But to be safe, go ahead and requisition a new switchboard right away."

An enlisted man guided the two Signal Corps officers about a mile and a quarter onto hilly terrain to the platoon command post (CP) where they met the platoon leader Second Lieutenant Tim Cavendish. He was young, just twenty-one, was tall and gangly, and a recent graduate of Infantry Officer Candidate School (OCS). He was disgusted with the telephone switchboard and with battalion headquarters for not getting him a new one. "How am I supposed to keep in touch with my firing positions?" Cavendish asked, not expecting an answer. "They issued us this crappy equipment just before we shipped out from Japan. It looked like it had been sitting in some warehouse ever since the end of World War II."

Walker said, "Let's have a look at it." He motioned to Grady to join him. Walker looked as if he were not sure of himself, and John wasn't either because he had not studied that equipment at The Signal School. Walker opened the back of the switchboard, looked in, jiggled some wire connections, tested the tightness of some nuts on threaded bolts, and stared at it. He didn't have a clue as to what the trouble was. He looked at Grady and said, "Take a look and see if you can see anything."

John moved into position and looked into the back of the switchboard. He saw that it was sturdily constructed, and from what was visible to him, he couldn't see a problem. He saw the fuse in its holder in the upper left side of the unit and thought about Sammy Figetti and the switchboard that had been struck by lightening during their field exercise at Fort Monmouth. Not knowing anything else to do, he reached in and pulled out the fuse. He turned around and held it up to the light and inspected it closely.

"This may be our trouble right here," he said. "Where are your spare fuses?"

One of the enlisted men replied, "I guess we should have some, but I've never seen one for that switchboard."

Grady turned to the platoon wireman and said, "Give me six inches of field wire and your wire cutters." John stripped the insulation from the wire, then held the bare wire next to the fuse holder and cut off a length of wire. He scraped clean the two ends of the wire and reached in and wrapped opposite ends of the wire around respective clips of the fuse holder to create a conductive path across the void space between the clips. "Try your circuits now," he told Cavendish.

The switchboard operator tried to contact a firing position. "Well, I'll be damned," he said, "I got them." He tried all the circuits and all were working.

"Thanks a million," Cavendish said. "You don't know what this means to me." They talked for a couple of minutes, then Cavendish said, "I'm going to check all the firing positions; do you want to go with me to see what our outpost looks like?"

"Sure," Captain Walker said. Cavendish and his platoon sergeant led the way and Walker and Grady followed them. All carried their weapons. The platoon position was a forward outpost around a broad ridge that overlooked lower hills that were sparsely covered with bushes and scrubby trees. The firing positions were foxholes that the men had dug after they had occupied the ridge without opposition. Cavendish talked with his men as he came to each firing position. Everything was quiet. The officers had visited about three-quarters of the positions when a volley of small-arms fire back to their right startled them.

"What the hell's that?" Cavendish bellowed as he and the platoon sergeant ran toward the firing. Walker and Grady followed behind them at a fast walk. They heard more firing. The Signal Corps officers approached the area where the firing was coming from and saw the platoon sergeant lying on the ground adjacent one of the foxholes and Cavendish kneeling adjacent another one talking on a telephone. GIs in both foxholes repeatedly fired their rifles. The platoon sergeant saw the Signal Corps officers and yelled, "Take cover. Take cover." Walker and Grady looked around and saw a slight depression in the ground behind the foxholes and ran to it and flopped onto their stomachs. One of the platoon's .30 caliber machine guns joined the intensified firing.

Walker said to Grady, "This is a hell of a situation. I don't like this one bit."

"I don't either," Grady replied, "and I don't think I want to stay where we are. I'm going up to Cavendish to see what's going on." He crawled on his stomach until he reached Cavendish.

"What is it?" he yelled to Cavendish.

"Hell's fire, it looks like a whole gook battalion in frontal assault."

Cavendish yelled into the telephone, "Get those guys in seven through ten to start firing. I haven't seen anything coming from them. Tell those positions on the right to keep the gooks from turning our flank. I'm going over there now."

"Where are positions seven to ten," Grady yelled to Cavendish.

"Over to the left. They have to start firing."

"I'll go over there," Grady yelled back.

"Go ahead; I have to go over to the right flank." Cavendish yelled to the platoon sergeant to stay and cover that section, then he ran toward the far side of the outpost.

Grady ran in a crouch to the foxholes to his left and hit the ground on his stomach behind the first one. Two young riflemen were cowered down in their foxhole and not firing their weapons.

"Fire! Fire!" Grady yelled at them, "Do you want to be killed in your foxhole? If you want to live, you have to beat them off with sustained fire. Get up and fire." Grady took a prone firing position beside the foxhole and saw the North Koreans advancing up the hill toward them. He fired a number of shots in rapid succession. He looked into the foxhole again and yelled, "If you don't defend yourselves you're going to die in that hole. Get up, pick a target, and fire!"

One of the GIs raised up in the foxhole and saw the North Koreans advancing toward him. He let out an oath and started shooting. He kicked at the other soldier in the foxhole and yelled at him, "Damn it, get the hell up here and help me—they're coming at us." The second man rose up, looked over the edge of the foxhole, and started shooting. Grady went on to the next foxhole where the situation was much the same. He got them up and firing and continued on and succeeded in getting the men in all four foxholes up and firing. He stopped several times and fired himself.

The Communist soldiers just kept coming. John was on high ground behind the foxholes and looked back to his right to see if he could see Captain Walker. He couldn't see him, but he did see that a small group of North Koreans had advanced near to the foxholes where the platoon sergeant was. "Holy hell," John exclaimed, "they're going to break through!" He ran toward the enemy intruders and inserted a new clip of cartridges into his MI carbine as he ran. The platoon sergeant jumped up and grappled with one enemy soldier and threw him to the ground. The intruders now were through the platoon's defense line but seemed scared and uncertain what to do next. They nervously swung their rifles about looking for someone to shoot. Grady ran dodging and weaving toward the enemy soldiers and fired his rifle until he expended all the rounds in his carbine. Several of the enemy intruders fell, but a standing one fired several times at Grady. A bullet glanced off Grady's steel helmet snapping his head back and knocking him off stride as he ran. He regained his stride and continued forward and swung the butt of his carbine as hard as he could against the side of the North Korean's head. The North Korean's cap flew off and blood splattered into the air and ran down his head as he collapsed onto the ground. Two remaining enemy soldiers who were nearby dropped their rifles and held up their hands with terrified looks on their faces. The platoon sergeant kicked their rifles away from them and motioned them to lay on the ground. He and Grady both crouched down.

John called loudly, "Captain Walker, Captain Walker, are you all right?"

Walker called from one of the foxholes, "I'm O.K. Take cover you damn fool."

Grady said to the sergeant, "What'll we do with the prisoners?"

"I'll have to pull one of my men to guard them, I guess. He can take them back to the CP area."

Grady said, "O.K. I'll take his place in his foxhole."

The Communists kept up their attack until late in the day, then they drifted away. John climbed out of his foxhole and found Walker, and the two of them went along the defense line doing everything they could to help. The platoon had suffered casualties, and the platoon medic was tending to the wounded. Walker and Grady met Cavendish who had a minor wound on his left hand, but he refused to let it stop him. He prepared his men to defend against a night attack—and it came. This time, however, U.S. artillery and mortar fire zeroed in on the attacking force and broke it up before it could do much more damage to the platoon. Cavendish maintained one hundred percent alert in the platoon: everyone remained in his foxhole until dawn.

Other platoons of the 2nd Battalion, 17th Infantry, also fought in the battle. In the morning, the battalion counted seventy-nine casualties. Dead GIs were laid aside, and medics treated the slightly wounded and sent the seriously wounded to the rear area. Walker and Grady helped out wherever they could. A sense of relief and survival settled in. The two Signal Corps officers found Cavendish and said, "Good-bye and good luck."

Cavendish responded, "Thanks for getting the switchboard operational and for helping us defend the outpost."

Walker and Grady returned to battalion headquarters and gave an account of the defense of the outpost to the battalion officers. They spoke highly of Lieutenant Cavendish. They said their farewells and drove off in their jeep. Both were in deep thought, and after they had driven about a quarter of a mile without conversation Grady asked, "Captain, where are we going?"

"Oh, let's get back to headquarters at Ascom City." They continued on in silence for a while, then Walker spoke up. "Can you believe it, we became involved in all that because of a blown fuse. I've been in the army a long time, and that's the first time I actually had to fight for my life. And all because of a lousy blown fuse."

"At least we get to walk away from it, Captain; those guys in the Infantry have to stay there. We're pretty lucky to be in the Signal Corps if you ask me."

"You're right about that; the Infantry earn their pay. By the way, I've never seen a Signal officer put on the show that you did yesterday. I'm glad you're on my side."

"Well, I don't know what happened," Grady replied. "It all happened so unexpectedly. I felt sorry for Cavendish and wanted to help him, and then when I saw those North Koreans inside our line I got mad as hell. That seems like a strange reaction."

"And a dangerous one. You were damned lucky."

When they returned to headquarters and had a meal of hot rations, Walker told Grady, "I have work to do, but there's no need for you to hang around so why don't you hit the pad."

"That sounds good to me," John said. He went upstairs, spread out his sleeping bag, stripped to his underwear and laid down, but he couldn't sleep. He tossed and turned from side to side, then onto his stomach, then onto his back. The more he tossed and turned the harder the floor seemed. As he lay on his back staring up at the ceiling his thoughts went back to the attack on the outpost. He had the answer to that gnawing question about his manhood: he hadn't run or hid but had stayed and fought.

The scenes of the attack on the outpost were burned into his memory and he played them over and over in his mind. He couldn't get out of his mind that scene where he had rushed the enemy soldiers who had broken through the platoon's defense line. Grady now knew that he had done a foolish thing—he could have gotten himself killed! He realized that he was fortunate to have gotten through it with nothing worse than a dent in his steel helmet. He lay in a cold sweat and was more frightened just thinking about it than he had been during the actual attack. "What the hell am I doing here?" he asked himself. "How did I get myself into this friggin mess?"

CHAPTER 2. (6 JUNE 1950).

The train rumbled out of the tunnel under the Hudson River and crossed the Jersey Meadowland in a light rain. As it continued south from Newark, patches of blue appeared in the sky and fast-moving white clouds pushed the dark-gray sky eastwardly across the Lower Bay of New York Harbor.

"This is good, I don't want to tromp around in the rain when I report in," John Grady said to himself. He had sat up all night on a bench in Pennsylvania Station waiting for a 8:15 a.m. train to Little Silver, New Jersey. He had shaved and brushed his teeth in the station washroom before boarding the train, and surprisingly, he felt fresh. He had removed his suit coat while he waited in Penn Station and had carefully folded it and placed it beside him on the bench. He had hung it on a hook under the overhead rack when he boarded the train, so both the coat and he looked good when the train arrived in Little Silver. John Grady usually looked good. When he was growing up, his father insisted that he take care of his clothes, wear a necktie, have a crease in his trousers, have a shine on his shoes, and admonished him, "Always look your best."

Grady considered his father to be a remarkable man. Both of his father's parents died when his father was a teenager, which compelled him to drop out of high school and go to work. He constantly tried to improve himself and tried to be the best in everything he did, and he constantly urged John to improve himself. His dad taught Sunday School and insisted that John attend Sunday School and church every Sunday. At his dad's urging, John played in the high school band and was drum major his senior year. His father loved sports, having boxed professionally when he was a young man. John shared that interest in sports and earned varsity letters in two high school sports. Grady also did fairly well in other high school activities: he sometimes was on the honor roll; he was class president one year; president of the leading boys' club; and he was a commencement speaker at high school graduation. John believed that he should try to do his best in everything he undertook. His dad died unexpectedly when John was eighteen years old and overseas in the U.S. Navy during World War II.

One of the greatest regrets of Grady's young life was that he had not told his dad that he appreciated everything that his dad had done for him.

John Grady stepped off the train at Little Silver with his big, old, heavy suitcase that contained all his worldly possessions. The station was deserted except for two women on the opposite north-bound platform. Commuters to "The City" were long gone. The air was warm and humid after the rain. Three older-model taxis were parked at the curb, and three overweight drivers in white shirts with open collars stood beside one of the cabs talking. None of them made a move toward John as he approached the cabs. "Can someone take me to Fort Monmouth?" he asked. The drivers looked him over, then one driver pointed to one of the cabs and said, "There." The driver went to the rear of the cab, opened the trunk, pushed a box and some tools to one side and said, "Here," as he pointed to John's suitcase and then to the cab trunk. He made no effort to help lift the big, old, heavy suitcase into the trunk of the cab.

The taxi left Little Silver and soon approached the tidal creek and marsh with Fort Monmouth on the far side. "Fort Monmouth—Home of the United States Army Signal Corps," the large sign at the side of the road proclaimed as they entered the grounds of the fort. The fort looked just as he remembered it from last summer. Most of the buildings were one or two-story, cream-colored, wooden buildings of World War I and early World War II vintage. Grady had spent a month there last summer in college Advanced ROTC summer camp, and he had been one of the few ROTC cadets selected to work another month in the Signal Corps Engineering Laboratories at Fort Monmouth after summer camp was over.

The driver turned the taxi into the Main Gate of Fort Monmouth and slowed down as he approached the military police guard shack. The driver mumbled something to the MP on duty, and the MP waived the cab through the gate. John saw the large American flag flapping at the top of the tall flagpole just inside the Main Gate.

"I'm not sure where I'm supposed to go," John said to the driver, "but let me try Russell Hall first." Russell Hall was the post headquarters building where the commanding general and his staff had offices. It was a substantial-looking, three-story, red brick building—the best looking military building on the post. Without turning his head, the driver said, "All new lieutenants report in at Russell Hall." With that statement the driver told John that he looked as if he were a new lieutenant, and that he, the driver, had driven dozens, or hundreds, of new lieutenants to Russell Hall.

The cab stopped in front of Russell Hall, and John and the driver went to the rear of the cab. The driver opened the lid of the trunk and stood aside without making a move to unload the suitcase. John looked at the driver, then reached in and pulled out his suitcase and set it down on the sidewalk. He asked the driver, "How much do I owe you?"

"Two fifty."

John counted out exactly two fifty and gave it to the driver. The driver looked at the two fifty and then looked at John. John said, "Thanks for your help." He turned, picked up his big, old, heavy suitcase and started up the steps to Russell Hall. Grady had spent two months at Fort Monmouth last summer but had never been inside Russell Hall. He went through the front door and into the lobby and looked around. A number of doors opened into the lobby, and each door had a name of an office on it. As John looked at the names trying to decide where to go, a sergeant walked out of an office at the far end of the lobby and turned toward him. John saw that the sergeant's stripes had three rockers on the bottom and a star between the chevrons and the rockers. "Ah, the post sergeant major in person," John said to himself.

The sergeant major saw John with his large suitcase and with a relaxed stride walked up to him and said, "May I help you?"

"Yes sir, I'm John Grady. I'm newly commissioned, and I'm reporting in for active duty."

The sergeant major smiled and said, "Yes, welcome to Fort Monmouth, Lieutenant Grady. I'm Sergeant Reimer. Please come this way and Sergeant Simpson will take care of you." The sergeant major led the way back through the door from which he had just come.

They entered a large, brightly lighted room containing several rows of precisely aligned desks at which army personnel and civilians worked. The clatter of typewriters was ceaseless. The sergeant major came to a desk at the head of one row and addressed a sergeant first class sitting there. "Sergeant Simpson, this is Lieutenant Grady reporting for duty; will you please take care of him." With that, Reimer turned to Grady, smiled and said, "If I can be of help to you while you're here, please let me know." He turned and walked away with his smooth, relaxed stride. "Dynaflow," John said to himself as he watched Reimer walk toward the door, "smooth as

Dynaflow." Still, John had a feeling that he wouldn't want to find himself on the wrong side of Sergeant Major Reimer.

Sergeant Simpson was tall and thin and was in his late thirties. He had half-a-dozen patches of long black hair tightly plastered to his white scalp. On his paper-cluttered desk, a burning cigarette was on an ashtray that already was full of butts, notwithstanding that it was just mid-morning.

John handed Simpson his orders directing him to report for active duty. Simpson explained that John needed to fill out a number of forms, and he went behind his desk to a large table that had many stacks of forms laid out in neat piles. He took one sheet from each of a number of the piles, then came back to John and pointed to an empty table and to his own desk and spoke to John in a way to be sure that there would be no confusion. "You can start with these. Go over to that empty table and fill these out and then bring them back to me." He wasn't brusque but seemed worried that John would not do what he was supposed to do. Sergeant Simpson was a worrier. Simpson lit another cigarette, and John went over to the table and began to look at the forms.

The army had a form for every aspect of John's life—past, present, and future. One requested family and biographical data, and one had to due with his pay. He learned that, for pay purpose, he was receiving credit for his months of service in the navy during World War II. That moved him higher up on the pay schedule for a second lieutenant. A medical form asked the usual questions about his medical history. John completed all the forms and walked back to Sergeant Simpson's desk. Simpson looked over the completed forms and John's orders for reporting for active duty and asked the question, "Regular Army?"

"Yes."

***

Grady received his army commission in the ROTC program at West Virginia University. He had been designated a Distinguished Military Graduate and had been awarded a medal as the Outstanding Signal Corps Cadet at West Virginia University. As a consequence, he had been offered the option of accepting a Regular Army commission or an Army Reserve commission. Grady had a strange feeling that he would be better off with the Regular Army commission even though it meant a four-year tour of duty. He couldn't explain why those strange feelings occurred, but they occurred every once in a while, and through the years he had learned to pay attention to them.

John Grady never expected to be in the army in the first place. His navy service during World War II made him exempt from the Selective Service draft, and he had no prior plan for a military career.

John had just turned seventeen years old when he graduated from high school. World War II was on at the time, but his father persuaded him to get some college education before he turned eighteen and entered the service. So, John attended the summer session and the fall semester at West Virginia University, College of Engineering, before he enlisted in the navy. He returned to WVU after World War II and earned a degree in Electrical Engineering, Communications Option. He went winter and summer, took a full schedule of courses each semester, and received his degree in three years. The GI Bill for World War II veterans paid for most of his college expenses in the post-war years.

Just before graduating from engineering school, Grady decided that he wanted to go to law school. He had used up all of his GI Bill eligibility in getting his engineering degree, and he had no money. Both of his parents were deceased and he was an only child, so there was no help available from family. The law school faculty frowned on a law student working at a part-time job, so that option was out of the question. ("You can't learn any law there," they preached.) The army paid Advanced ROTC cadets thirty dollars per month, and that looked like a lot of money to John. He knew where he could rent a room off-campus for twenty-four dollars per month, and he could make some money doing odd jobs around town during the summer and holidays. So, if he could get his meals taken care of he might be able to make it.

"What the hell," John declared, "nothing ventured, nothing gained." He applied for admission to law school—was accepted; applied for admission to the Signal Corps Advanced ROTC program—was accepted; and was able to keep his old job waiting tables at his fraternity house, which included his meals. (He had been president of his fraternity his last year and had been optimistic that "the brothers" would allow him to continue with the waiter job for the next year.) Everything fell into place and he entered law school in September.

At the conclusion of the two-year Advanced ROTC program the army said, in effect, "O.K., we paid you thirty dollars a month for two years and gave you a commission as a second lieutenant, now we want some return on our investment." Hence, his call to active duty. He had a year of law school to complete when he left for active duty.

***

Simpson went back to the table behind him and selected more materials from the piles of paper. He handed John a thick sheaf of stapled papers and a single sheet having a certification on it with a place for a signature at the bottom. Simpson said, "This is a portion of the Geneva Convention and instructions on what you're to do if you're captured by an enemy. Read them, sign the certificate that you read them, and return the certificate to me by next Tuesday."

Simpson handed him another slip of paper and said, "This is your appointment for your physical examination at the post dispensary tomorrow morning at 0900 hours."

He gave John another typed sheet of paper and told him, "There will be a Safety Meeting Thursday morning at 1100 hours in building 1529, and don't you dare miss this here meeting because the general will be speaking." Simpson handed him a map of Fort Monmouth and pointed out to him the location of building 1529. Simpson seemed worried that John would not show up for the meeting.

Simpson gave Grady another paper having the address of the Quartermaster Store and said, "This is where you can buy your uniforms." John received yet another sheet of paper authorizing him to draw bedding and get a room assignment in the Bachelor Officers Quarters (BOQ). Simpson asked him if he had a car. When John said "No," Simpson told him that he could catch a bus at the back entrance to Russell Hall that would take him to the BOQ Billeting Office.

John asked Simpsom, "What will I be doing?"

"You'll be going to the Basic Officers Course in The Signal School."

"How long does that last?"

"Three months."

"When do classes begin?"

"As soon as enough new people report in to form a couple of new classes."

"How long should that take?"

"It shouldn't be long: a lot of people will be reporting in this week and next. You report to this office every morning and every afternoon and check the bulletin board over there for announcements."

John carried the papers given him in one hand, picked up his big, old, heavy suitcase with the other hand, and walked to the back door of Russell Hall. He saw the sign outside identifying the bus stop and went there and waited. He was reviewing in his mind what had just happened when a stubby, school-bus type bus painted olive drab pulled up. John boarded the bus and told the civilian driver that he wanted to go to the BOQ Billeting Office. As he sat on the bus, he reviewed in his mind what he had to do when suddenly a shocking revelation came upon him—he had to buy his uniforms but didn't have money to pay for them! He had completely overlooked the fact that he had to buy uniforms. He felt his abdominal muscles tighten, and for the first time he noticed how hot it was on the bus.

The bus passed Squier Laboratory, one of the Signal Corps Engineering Laboratories, and stopped at the next side street. "You want the second building on the left," the driver announced. John thanked him, dismounted from the bus, and walked down the narrow side street to a one-story building that looked like a large shed. He went through the door and handed his billeting slip to an enlisted man behind a counter. The enlisted man greeted him and went to the back of the room and pulled blankets, linens, and a pillow from shelves along the walls. He brought them up to the counter, opened a large ledger book and made some entries in it, then spun the book around and asked John to print his name, rank, and serial number, and sign at indicated places. The billeting clerk assigned him to room 208 in BOQ 5 and pointed through the screen door to show him where BOQ 5 was located.

The BOQ area housed junior officers, most of whom were students in the Basic Officers Course in The Signal School. The area was comprised of a long asphalt parking area with six two-story wooden barracks on each side. The narrow ends of the barracks faced the parking area. BOQ 5 was on the far side. The area didn't show much elegance.

John walked through the front door of BOQ 5, past a pay telephone, and up the stairs to the second floor. His room was on the left at the far end of the hall overlooking the parking lot. He was not happy to be on the second floor because that type of building was not insulated, it was not air conditioned, and when the hot sun beat down on the roof the temperature on the second floor escalated to uncomfortable levels. He had been in that type of building in the navy.

A metal army cot was along the front wall and another one was along the back wall of the room, and two smallish field desks and straight chairs were against the side wall opposite the door. A clothes locker was on each side of the door. The cot along the front wall was made up and there were personal items on the desk on that side of the room. Obviously, he had a roommate.

John unpacked his suitcase and arranged his civilian clothes in the clothes locker and in the foot locker on the floor at the end of the bunk. He picked up a towel that he had brought with him and his toilet article kit and set out to find the "head," or as they call it in the army, the "latrine." He found it at the other end of the hall near the top of the stairs. He washed up and returned to his room. The door opened as he was stowing his towel and kit, and a tall, thin man in civilian clothes walked in. He saw John and stopped short, not expecting to find someone in his room. John saw his surprise and stuck out his hand and said, "Hi, I'm John Grady. I've been assigned to this room; I assume you live here also."

The man recovered his composure and said, "Yes. I'm Dan Hurley." Hurley was older than John.

"Are you just reporting in also?" John asked.

"No. I've been here seven weeks. I'm with the Federal Aviation Administration. I'm in the teletype school learning to service and repair teletype machines for the FAA."

"Oh, I didn't know that civilians were here also."

"Yes. I guess it's cheaper to run one school for all government agencies rather than each one run its own."

"That makes sense," John replied.

"Have you had lunch?" Dan asked.

"No. Where do you eat around here?"

"The officers' mess is just behind us here. I'm going over there as soon as I wash up; do you want to join me?"

"Sure. Thanks."

John liked Dan. He was from a small community outside Nashville, Tennessee, and seemed bright and good-natured.

The mess hall was a long, one-story wooden building with the entrance on the side. It served cafeteria style, and the lunch included a fried pork chop, mashed potatoes and gravy, whole kernel corn, and a slice of apple pie. It cost John $1.25.

Dan left for his class, and John returned to his room and to his problem about uniforms and the lack thereof. He said to himself, "What a hell of pickle this is: I can't afford to join the army." He picked up the literature on the Geneva Convention and began reading. He had heard about the Geneva Convention all his life but had never read any of the actual text. He found it quite interesting. He then read the material on what an American soldier should do, and not do, if he were captured by an enemy. The material instructed that it was a soldier's *duty* to try to escape if he were captured. It advised that the best time to try to escape was as soon after capture as possible and before removal to a rear area of the enemy. John hadn't received instruction on this type of thing in the navy. He signed and dated the certificate that he had read the material.

John ate breakfast with Dan the next morning, then walked to Russell Hall to report to Sergeant Simpson's office for any new announcements. Simpson noticed that John still wore his civilian suit, but he said nothing. There were no new announcements.

Grady walked over to the post dispensary for his physical examination. The medical people were not ready for him when he arrived, and when they finally started he thought that they were rather casual about it. "I guess this is the peacetime army," John thought to himself.

Grady reported back to Sergeant Simpson's office at 1330 hours and there were no new notices. Young-looking second lieutenants in their summer khaki uniforms milled around the bulletin board. Simpson saw John still wearing his civilian suit and came over to him and said, "Get in uniform." John said nothing. He was at a complete loss what to do. He usually could figure out some way to tackle a problem, but the simple fact was he was flat broke—period! He was lucky to be able to pay for his meals, and even that wouldn't last too much longer. John went back to his room, read the paper, had dinner, and listened to Dan's radio. He went to bed worrying about uniforms.

The next morning as John walked to Russell Hall in his civilian suit he dreaded having to face Sergeant Simpson. John was reading notices on the bulletin board when Simpson walked up to him and said with obvious impatience, "I told you to get in uniform."

John turned around and said, "Sergeant, I have a problem. I ... I don't have any uniforms, and I don't have money to buy uniforms."

"Well, why didn't you say so," Simpson replied. "Come over to my desk and I'll give you a voucher for a clothing allowance." Simpson sat down at his desk, opened a drawer and pulled out a pad of voucher forms. He filled out one for John and told him, "Take this over to the Finance Office and they'll give you two hundred dollars. They'll deduct money from your pay each month until it's paid back."

The weight of the world was lifted from John's shoulders. He practically floated out of Russell Hall and walked several blocks to the Finance Office building. He signed his name, rank, and serial number on the voucher and handed it to a civilian man behind the counter. The man counted out two hundred dollars and handed it to John. That's all there was to it.

John had to be at the Safety Meeting in Building 1529 at 1100 hours. He walked over there and arrived early. The door to the square, creme-colored, wooden building was locked, so he stood in the shade of a tree about twenty feet to the left of the door. Lieutenants and captains in pairs and singles straggled up to the front door. Most tried the door, found it locked, and sheepishly joined others standing outside. Grady was the only one in civilian clothes. At 1055 hours an olive drab Buick staff car flying a red flag with two white stars on it pulled up to the front walk. A two-star general and his first-lieutenant aide stepped out of the back seat of the car and started up the front walk. The general looked around as he walked and saw John in civilian clothes. The general stopped, exchanged salutes and talked with several groups of the officers, then he looked over to John again and started walking toward him. As the general approached him, John said, "Good morning, General," but he didn't salute because he was not in uniform.

The general replied, "Good morning. Are you here to attend the Safety Meeting?"

"Yes sir."

The general made small talk, and from what he was saying, John gained the impression that the general thought that he was a newspaper reporter. Suddenly, the front doors swung open and the general broke off the conversation and he and his aide were the first ones through the door. When the general entered, those waiting outside followed him in and quickly found seats. The inside of Building 1529 was an auditorium with a fairly large seating capacity in comfortable theater-type seats. Still,

John was the only person in civilian clothes. The general and his aide and a captain sat in chairs on the stage.

The captain arose and went to a lectern at the front of the stage. He tapped the microphone on the lectern. It was live. "Thank you for coming, gentlemen. This is the second in the series of Safety Meetings that General Lawrence has scheduled for personnel of the post. General Lawrence has some remarks, and then we will view a film on safe-driving habits. There will be attendance sheets to sign in the lobby as you exit the building. Gentlemen, I present Major General Karl J. Lawrence."

The general rose and strode to the lectern. He was over six feet tall and had a husky build. He probably was in his late-fifties, and his reddish, close-cropped hair was starting to turn gray. He spoke without notes.

"Last month, soldiers from Fort Monmouth were involved in eighty-seven highway accidents. That's too many and it has to stop. We're at Fort Monmouth to train and carry out a mission, and the time lost because of automobile accidents interrupts our training schedule and benefits no one. We never make up the loss of training time.

"Do you know that just to investigate an accident costs the government two hundred and eighty dollars. You can imagine what the costs of hospitalizations and medical treatments amount to, and on top of that are the personal suffering and financial loss out of the pockets of the soldiers. This can't go on, and I'm going to see to it that it changes."

Speaking slowly, and with emphasis on each word, the general continued. "These accidents are premeditated." He looked at individuals throughout the audience. "Yes, I said 'premeditated.' When a soldier goes into a bar at 2100 hours and drinks until 0100 hours in the morning, then goes out and gets into his car and tries to drive back to this post, his actions are premeditated. He knew before he went into that bar that he would have to drive on the highways back to his barracks before the night was over. Soldiers get a weekend pass and try to drive all night to get to Boston, or Richmond, Virginia, but fall asleep at the wheel and drive off the highway. They knew damn well that they get sleepy driving all night, particularly since they were up at 0500 in the morning. I don't care what you say, these accidents are premeditated.

"Many of you out there are troop commanders, or have military and civilian people working for you. I'm giving you the responsibility to take this message back to your people and make it a major priority in your training and in all your day-to-day activities. Don't take anything for granted. Don't assume that your people are any different from everyone else. I want you to start immediately to devote one of your weekly T.I.P. (Troop Information Program) sessions to safe driving. You will repeat it every month, and more often if you think it's necessary. I've appointed Major Wilbur Rodman Post Traffic Control and Safety Officer and he'll be getting educational material to all of you. But don't wait for Rodman; get moving on it immediately."

The general paused, shifted his weight, took his time looking throughout the audience, then resumed speaking. "Now, I've been accused by some people, including the local press, of being overzealous on this subject. But I—not they—have the responsibility for the lives and safety of eleven thousand soldiers on this post. I have the responsibility to write letters to Mothers and Fathers telling them, 'I regret to inform you that your son was killed in an automobile accident at 1:00 a.m. on Highway 35 while driving under the influence of alcohol.' Or, 'I regret to inform you that your son fell asleep at the wheel of his car, ran off the road, hit a telephone pole, and was instantly killed.' It's easy to be critical when you don't have the responsibility." He looked in the direction of the only civilian suit in the audience when he made that last statement. "That's all I have to say at this time."

The captain on the stage popped up from his chair and shouted, "Attention!" The audience rose to its feet, and the general and his aide left the stage and walked up a side aisle to the rear of the auditorium and exited the building.

An enlisted man came onto the stage and removed the lectern. A very large motor-controlled movie screen came down like a blind into position on the stage, and the captain introduced the safe driving film. It lasted about twenty minutes and was well done. The lights came on and the captain announced, "Gentlemen, that concludes the Safety Meeting. Be sure to sign the attendance sheets as you leave. Thank you." John was favorably impressed with the Safety Meeting. The general seemed to be a reasonable man trying to do his job.

***

John ate lunch, then went to the Quartermaster Store and picked out four sets of summer khaki uniforms, two sets of fatigue uniforms, ties, caps, socks, and belts. He also bought a pair of dress shoes and a pair of combat boots. He bought two sets of "brass," i.e., the gold (brass) bars of a second lieutenant, and a pair of the crossed signal flags insignia of the Signal Corps. He didn't have money to buy a summer dress uniform, or a raincoat, or winter uniforms. Hopefully, there would be no functions requiring a dress uniform. The final bill ate up a sizable portion of the two hundred dollars, but he had enough left over to assure that he could eat until payday.

John went back to his room, put brass on a set of khakis and put them on. They were a good fit and looked good on his tall frame. He wore the soft overseas cap down low on his forehead and absolutely centered side-to-side. He looked like a soldier. He went to Russell Hall to check for any news. There were more new lieutenants milling about each time he went there. Sergeant Simpson saw him but didn't say anything. John checked the bulletin board. There was nothing new for him there. He went over to Simpson's desk and said, "Sergeant Simpson, I want to thank you for helping me out." Simpson gave a quick nod but said nothing.

John checked in at Simpson's office the next morning and saw a crowd of young lieutenants gathered around the bulletin board. He walked over and looked over some shoulders and saw three new sheets of paper in the upper left corner of the bulletin board. They were class rosters for three new classes. John found his name on the first one, Class 329. The typed instructions at the top of the sheet informed that the class would meet at 0800 hours on 12 June 1950 in Building 302 for organization and orientation. John was pleased; he was eager to get started.

CHAPTER 3. (12 JUNE 1950)

Grady arrived at Building 302 at 0755 hours Monday morning. The inside was a tiered lecture hall with a seating capacity of probably seventy-five to ninety. Small booklets with orange covers were on the writing arms of each of thirty-five student chairs in the center portion of the room. He noticed two first lieutenants among the bevy of second lieutenants that were milling around the room. John went to a seat and opened the booklet. The first page indicated that the course would run from 12 June 1950 to 13 September 1950, and it included a message of greeting and a statement of the mission of The Signal School. The next page was a description of the Associate Signal Company Officers Course and set forth the twenty subjects that that they would study during the next three months.

At exactly 0800 hours, a major and a captain took their places at the lectern area, and the major commenced his welcoming and introductory speech. The captain then took over and went into detail about what the courses would cover and what the ground rules were for student-officers in The Signal School. He then referred to the last page in the booklet that showed the calendar for Class 329. John noticed that they would have several days off for Independence Day and for Labor Day. The next to last page was a class roster, by rank, alphabetically. A loose, folded sheet of paper in the booklet listed the first week's classes for Class 329. Their first class Electrical Fundamentals would commence at 0900 hours in Building 308. Before the captain dismissed them, he announced that individual grades and class standings would be published at the conclusion of each four weeks of classes. He also announced that First Lieutenant Kaspar Korjovic was the class leader for Class 329.

For the remainder of the day, Class 329 attended six different classes in six different buildings. Of the six instructors, one was a civilian and five were army officers. John was favorably impressed with the army instructors, three majors and two captains. They knew their subject matters, were well prepared, enthusiastic, made optimum use of class time, and conveyed a sense of importance to what the student-officers were there for.

During the first two weeks of classes, Grady learned more about his classmates, particularly his class leader Kaspar Korjovic. "Kas" had been a master sergeant before receiving a direct commission while serving in the Philippines near the end of World War II. He then spent time in the Army of Occupation in Okinawa and Japan and had just recently returned to the United States for the first time since the war. He was the oldest man in the class and he looked it. He was bald, wore thick glasses, and his teeth were slightly bucked. At first, John wondered about Kas, but as he knew him better his opinion of him changed considerably. Kas was outgoing, good-natured, intelligent and quick-witted, and he knew the army well. John liked him.

The other first lieutenant Bob Whatley was just the opposite of Kas. Whatley was not as old as Kas, had thick reddish-brown hair, fair complexion, and was quiet and reserved. He too had been a senior noncommissioned officer and had received a direct commission while serving in Germany. Whatley was an expert in cryptography and in signal intelligence. He didn't talk about his past experiences and was a serious student. Whatley and Korjovic both were married and had young children. They lived off-post with their families.

On the second Thursday of school, Class 329 had a test in Electrical Fundamentals, and on Friday had tests in Military Leadership and in Signal Organization, Theater of Operations. Grady was well prepared for the tests and felt that he had done well.

Grady had studied hard the first two weeks and was ready to relax on the weekend. Unlike his college experience, the Basic Officers Course did not have Saturday classes, so he didn't bother to get up for breakfast Saturday morning. He had a leisurely shower and shave, then dressed in civilian clothes and took some uniforms and other clothes to the post laundry. After lunch at the Officers Mess, he came back to his room and fell asleep on his bunk. He awoke about 1500 hours and studied until Dan came in just before dinner. They went to the mess hall together, and later that evening they walked over to Scrivner Hall, the on-post officers' club, for a couple of beers.

Scrivner Hall was an elongated, two-story, red-brick building that housed a barber shop, several meeting rooms, an informal dining room that specialized in hamburgers and various other types of sandwiches, pies, soft drinks, and chips. A small but comfortable lounge was at the far end of the first floor opposite the main entrance. An enclosed porch ran along the entire length of the front of the building, but it was not heated, was poorly furnished, and was seldom used. The main attraction of the club for most young officers was the large barroom whose main feature was a large oval-shaped bar with about thirty-five or forty barstools around it. The bartenders were noncommissioned officers who were moonlighting on their off-duty hours. Beer was the beverage of choice for most young officers.

CHAPTER 4. (24 JUNE 1950)

John woke up early Sunday morning, showered and shaved, and went to breakfast. He studied for an hour and then put on a civilian suit and walked to the post chapel for church services. On the way back to his room, he bought a copy of *The New York Times* from the newspaper vending machine outside the enlisted men's pool hall. Arriving back in his room, he tossed the newspaper onto his bunk, changed into some casual civilian clothes, and went to lunch at the mess hall. Many new lieutenants had arrived in the last two weeks and the mess hall was crowded.

Grady was hot when he returned to his room, so he stripped to his undershorts and began reading *"The Times"*. The feature article on the front page was about a new French cabinet crisis resulting in the Bidault Government's fall. Another article detailed the difficulty that the U.S. was having with the Soviet Union about a Japanese peace treaty. The Soviets were being obstinate, as usual, and there was talk that the U.S. might sign a separate peace treaty with Japan.

The headline above the article on the far left column of the front page was WAR IS DECLARED BY NORTH KOREANS; FIGHTING ON BORDER. The attack began before dawn on Sunday, 25 June 1950, Korean time, or about 2 p.m. on Saturday, 24 June 1950, eastern daylight time. The article contained sketchy reports of fighting and a report that a declaration of war had been announced on the North Korean radio. The article expressed the opinion that the invasion was a test of strength between Soviet Union-sponsored North Korea and United States-sponsored South Korea.

Grady went to THE NEWS OF THE WEEK IN REVIEW section of *"The Times"*, but there was nothing there about the Korean situation. He did read in that section an article about U.S. Senator Joseph McCarthy and his charges of Communist infiltration of the U.S. State Department. The article was of particular interest to John because McCarthy first made his charge of Communist infiltration of the State Department during a speech he made in Wheeling, West Virginia, John's hometown.

John turned on Dan's radio to hear the latest news. Radio station

WCBS in New York City was broadcasting a special news report. There seemed to be considerable uncertainty about what actually was going on in Korea. There had been many skirmishes in the past at the Thirty-eighth Parallel, the border between North Korea and South Korea, but now there were reports that North Korean tank-led forces broke through defenses at several points on the border and actually captured the town of Kaesong which was forty miles northwest of Seoul, the South Korean capital. A CBS correspondent from Tokyo reported that some U. S. officials in Japan were of the opinion that this was more than a border skirmish and probably was an all-out invasion. (United States intelligence agencies were completely blind and deaf with regard to the North Korean war preparations and attack. They had not uttered a word of warning!)

The news reported that president Harry Truman was spending a short vacation at his home in Independence, Missouri, but would cut it short and return to Washington, D.C., on Monday morning.

On Monday and Tuesday, Class 329 had more tests. John went to Scrivner Hall for a haircut during lunch break on Wednesday and read a copy of the *New York Daily News*. The news from South Korea was not good. Seoul had fallen to Communist forces, and North Korean tanks had broken through South Korean defenses at the Han River and proceeded south. South Korean forces were trying to establish a new defense line at the Kum River. President Truman ordered U.S. Air Force and U.S. Navy units to aid the South Koreans. General Douglas MacArthur, Supreme Commander Far East Command, announced from his headquarters in Tokyo that the air force and the navy were operating south of the Thirty-eighth Parallel. The U.S. Air Force had shot down four North Korean fighter planes.

Both houses of Congress supported President Truman, as did most nations in the United Nations. The U.S. House of Representatives ended what formerly had been a contentious debate on the Selective Service draft and voted three hundred fifteen to four to extend it for another year. The House bill also authorized the president to call to active duty the Reserves and the National Guard.

John headed back to the school area for his afternoon classes. A number of classmates were standing outside the classroom talking before their next class began. John walked up to Kas Korjovic and Bob Whatley and asked them if they had heard the latest on the Korean situation.

"Yes," Kas replied, "I heard the news on my car radio coming back from lunch."

"What do you think?" John continued.

"I think it's damn serious. Damn serious."

John asked Whatley, "What's your assessment, Bob?"

"I agree completely."

Just minutes after the final class of the day began, a corporal who worked in The Signal School office came into the classroom and handed a piece of paper to the instructor. The instructor read the paper and then said, "Lieutenant Whatley, bring all your gear and go with the corporal." Everyone in the class said to himself, "Now, what's this all about?"

The next morning John stood outside the classroom building having a smoke before the first class started. Kas Korjovic arrived with his usual fast-pace walk and came straight to John and said, "Did you hear about Whatley?"

"No. What?"

"They pulled him out of school and shipped his ass to FECOM."

"When?"

"He flies out of McGuire Air Force Base this morning. He's gone."

"Why did they do that?"

"He's a cryptographer and a specialist in signal intelligence. Those guys are in demand when things get hot."

"Wow. What a tough break for him and his family," John said.

"That's the army," Kas replied.

The South Korean news on Friday continued to be bad. The core of the North Korean Army was comprised of seasoned North Korean troops who had fought with the Communist Chinese Army in its conquest of mainland China after World War II. Some reports stated that the South Korean defenses were collapsing in the face of advancing North Korean tanks. President Truman ordered United States Army ground forces to Korea and authorized United States Air Force pilots to operate without restriction north of the Thirty-eighth Parallel.

Grady and Kas Korjovic were standing outside a building during an afternoon break between classes, and Kas said to John, "What did you get on the tests we had?"

John would rather not discuss his grades with anyone, but he didn't want to seem rude or unfriendly to Kas, so he said, "I got 100 in Electrical

Fundamentals, 96 in Signal Organization, and 98 in Military Leadership."

"You bastard you! You beat me. Those are the best I've heard so far." Kas's statement wasn't in anger or jealousy, it was just Kas. His vocabulary included a lot of cuss words; he was quite open; and he was competitive.

"Well, I should do well in Electrical Fundamentals," Grady replied, "I have a degree in electrical engineering and that test was designed for nonengineers.

"It sure looks as if we have a shooting war on our hands in Korea," John continued.

"You're right about that."

"Is there any chance that you'll be sent over there right away as Whatley was?" John asked.

"I don't think so. I'm not a specialist as Whatley is. **You** had better get ready, though. Once we finish here, you'll go over."

"Why do you say that?"

"You're Regular Army, right. Regular Army second lieutenants get sent where the action is. The army wants its Regular junior officers to have experience in a combat zone. You can count on it. You can say that you heard it first from me."

"How do you know I'm Regular Army?"

"I make it my business to know. You're also a World War II veteran, aren't you?" Kas seemed pleased that he had all that information about Grady.

"How come you know all this about me?"

"Like I said, I make it my business to know."

"Come on, Kas, don't play games with me, how do you know?" John moved his hands with a "come on" motion.

Kas smiled. "O.K. Major Bowen, Secretary of The Signal School, allowed me to look at the class records. I told him that as class leader I needed to know something about the class members. He's a good guy, so he let me see the records. They're not a complete 201 File on each individual, but they're an abstract of the important information."

Kas looked around them to see who was within listening distance. No one was. "Listen Grady, you and I are a little older than these kids in this class, and we've served before." Korjovic was quite serious now. "Chances are that most of these kids are going to be in a serious situation before long, and they're going to need as much help as they can get in the short time they're here. You and I ought to help them as much as we can."

"What do you have in mind?"

"I don't have anything particular in mind right now. Until something specific comes up, I guess the best we can do is be good examples to them what junior officers are supposed to be. If I get something specific, I'll talk to you about it. O.K.?"

"That's fine with me, Kas." John was impressed with Kas's concern and dedication. On his own initiative he was taking a leadership role. John said to himself, "I can see why Kas was given a direct commission from the enlisted ranks."

Despite the bad news from Korea and his concern for his immediate future, there was some good news for Grady. Friday was payday, and he immediately opened a checking account at the on-post branch office of the Eatontown National Bank. He had decided to save some money each payday so he would be able to buy a dress uniform and winter uniforms by the time his class graduated.

Saturday morning, 1 July 1950, John arose before breakfast and went over to the newspaper vending machine, dropped a nickel into the slot, and pulled out a copy of *The New York Times*. Things were bad and getting worse for the South Korean Army. Advance units of the U.S. 24th Infantry Division were flown from Japan to Pusan, South Korea, and rushed northward to aid the South Koreans in attempting to establish a line of resistance at the Kum river north of Taejon. It was not clear to John how many United States troops were involved. Some reports said that only a battalion was involved while others said that as many as a regiment had landed. In either case it sounded to John that there were not many U.S. troops to stop the advancing Communist army let by tanks.

Sunday's news was no better. U.S. Secretary of Defense Louis Johnson stated that a shooting war was on and that "American ground, air and naval forces were deeply engaged in a costly and hazardous campaign." James Reston, Washington Bureau Chief for *The New York Times*, reported that Washington was standing firm and that there would be "No more Munichs."

The next two weeks at school involved more classroom work. Class 329 started several new subjects, but John was getting impatient to do something more than study and sit in class.

Meanwhile, the situation in Korea continued to deteriorate. On Wednesday, 5 July, it was reported that Suwon, south of Seoul, fell to the Communists. Inchon, a port on the West Coast, also fell. The South Korean Army was in a rout. Several days later, the United Nations Security Council established a unified command for the troops of all nations that would contribute to the defense of South Korea. General Douglas MacArthur was placed in command of all forces. U.S. General Walton Walker was commander of Eighth Army which included all the ground combat troops in Korea. The situation in Korea never was far from the consciousness of the men in Class 329.

In mid-week of the fifth week of school for Class 329, class grades and standings for the first four weeks were posted. Grady stood first in his class with an average of 98.6. Korjovic was second with 97.9. Several others were close. There were no stragglers.

"Watch your ass, Grady, because I'm going to catch you," Korjovic said with a grin. Same old Kas.

**

The third and fourth weeks in July were bad for South Korean and United States troops. Taejon, the temporary capital of South Korea since the fall of Seoul, fell to the advancing Communist army. General William F. Dean, commander of the United States 24th Infantry Division, was missing in action. North Korean forces swept down the West Coast with little effective opposition and reached the southern end of the peninsula, then turned eastward. South Korean and U.S. forces retreated to a defensive area approximately ninety miles wide and ninety miles deep and anchored at the port of Pusan. The North Korean Army was in front of them and the Sea of Japan was behind them.

At home, support units of the Army Organized Reserves and the National Guard were ordered to active duty. The U.S. Marine Corps and the U.S. Navy called reservists to active duty, and Congress extended all military enlistments one year beyond their scheduled expiration dates. Department of Defense casualty lists, which were published in many newspapers, became longer. The army issued a call to three thousand doctors who were Reserve junior officers in the U.S. Army Medical Corps asking for volunteers for active duty. (The army had paid for the medical education of many of them.) Two hundred doctors replied—fifteen volunteered.

By the end of the month, the Pusan Perimeter had shrunk to a defense perimeter approximately sixty miles wide at the base and ninety miles out from Pusan. In addition to regular North Korean forces assaulting the Perimeter, armed Communist guerrilla forces harassed and engaged UN forces within the Perimeter. The Perimeter continued to shrink, and General Walker stated that the situation was critical and issued a "No Retreat" order to troops of Eighth Army. North Korean forces launched a major offensive on the last day of the month trying to eliminate the defenders of the Perimeter before more UN reinforcements could be brought in.

CHAPTER 5. (31 JULY 1950)

The coming week promised to be a welcomed change from Grady's classroom routine. Classes 329, 330 and 331 were to conduct a field exercise in which they would set up and operate the communications systems for a simulated army corps in a combat situation. Fort Monmouth had a large field-training area in a forest west of the main post where exercises were conducted. The training area had one-lane dirt roads running through the forest. Student-officers would establish and operate telephone, teletype, and radio communications between a simulated corps headquarters command post and the simulated command posts of three divisions. To simulate a combat environment, all command post locations would change several times during the exercise. Cryptography and other security measures would be standard operating procedures.

The men reported in at 0600 hours Thursday morning to a warehouse building where each man drew the personal field equipment needed for the exercise. They lined up by classes and marched a short distance down the road to a long line of waiting trucks that took them to the training area. They unloaded in a large cleared area where waiting officer-instructors gave them their final instructions.

Grady performed several different tasks during the first days of the exercise. At 0200 hours Friday morning, he was assigned to a pole-line crew whose job was to lay field wire between the next assigned locations of corps headquarters and Division C, and to pick up all the wire between the previous locations of those units. Kas was the crew chief. At about 0400 Kas came to the area where the crew was stretched out on the ground and shouted, "All right, get off your asses and gather 'round. We've just received orders to lay new telephone and teletype lines between the next locations of corps headquarters and Division C. I have the map coordinates. The lines have to be in place ready for hook up by 0530 hours when the next move takes place. That's not much time, so we have to get cracking. We'll pick up the old lines after the moves are made and the traffic on these roads dies down."

It was very dark, but the crew worked smoothly and was making good progress. To keep the field wire off the roads where it would get torn up by the trucks, Kas's crew tied the lines about fifteen to twenty feet high around the trunks of the large pine and oak trees that lined the roads. John had climbing irons strapped on his legs and a wide leather safety belt on his waist, as did several others, and was working as fast as he could climbing up the trees and tying wires around the tree trunks. He was not taking the time to secure his safety belt around the tree as he was taught to do. Grady was working fast and became careless. He was about twenty feet up the trunk of a large oak tree trying to tie the field wire around the thick trunk. He straightened up his body and moved closer to the trunk as he reached to pass the line around the back side of the thick trunk. As he did so, the implanted spikes of his climbing irons kicked out from the tree trunk and he dropped straight down with his arms still partially around the tree. "Holy Toledo! This can't be happening to me," John exclaimed. It is called "Skinning the pole," and they were warned about it repeatedly last summer in ROTC summer camp. About three feet from the ground, both of John's spikes caught and dug into the tree. His feet stopped but his rear end continued down and slammed into the backs of his boots, bringing his body to an abrupt halt.

Just as John came to the instant stop, Jeff Linder, a tall, freckle-faced redhead from Georgia Tech, trotted by and called with a chuckle, "Hey Grady, that was neat. Do it again so all the guys can see it."

"Thanks a lot, Linder; I almost killed myself and you make fun of me," John replied good-naturedly. With nothing injured but his dignity, John climbed back up the tree and tied in the lines. That was the first and last time he "Skinned the pole."

The field exercise ended mid-morning on Saturday. The students' performances in the exercise would be critiqued in classes Monday morning. The instructors worked through the weekend preparing for the critiques.

John was dead tired. He had managed only a couple of hours of fitful sleep the last two nights. He went back to his BOQ and showered, then went to the mess hall for lunch. He returned to his room, undressed, and went to bed with the intention of sleeping through the afternoon and night and getting up for breakfast Sunday morning. He slept about an hour and one-half, then he woke up wide awake. Grady put on civilian clothes and walked over to Scrivner Hall where he sat on a barstool and ordered a beer. He leaned both elbows on the bar and read the newspaper. He read that

President Truman had ordered to active duty four National Guard divisions and two National Guard Regimental Combat Teams (RCT). The quota for the Selective Service draft was increased by one hundred thousand men. The U.S. 2nd Infantry Division had landed at Pusan and immediately joined the 24th and 25th Infantry Divisions and the 1st Cavalry Division on the Pusan Perimeter. The U.S. 1st Provisional Marine Brigade was unloading from ships at Pusan.

Communist forces continued to press their assault on the Perimeter defenses trying to strike a victory before the defenses became too strong. The UN forces withdrew to a smaller perimeter to strengthen the defensive line. The U.S. Air Force, along with British and Australian planes, attacked the enemy throughout Korea.

As John placed aside the front section of the paper and picked up the sports section, he felt a hand on his shoulder. "Have you fallen out of any trees today?" a soft voice with a southern accent asked. John turned. It was his classmate Jeff Linder who had kidded him about "Skinning the pole." "What happened in the world while we were in the woods?" Jeff asked as he sat down on the barstool next to Grady.

"Not much that's good, except that the Pusan Perimeter is still holding. Here, take the front section of the paper."

They both read and sipped their beers. Linder read several pages and then said, "Police action? Like hell it is; that's an all-out war going on over there." He was quiet a moment, then said, "You and I could be over there in six weeks. You know that don't you Grady?"

"Yes, I know it. How do you feel about going over?"

Linder thought for a moment, then said, "I really haven't faced up to it yet. I'm not afraid to go, I think. If I do go, I'll do the best I can, but as I said, I really haven't faced up to it yet. How about you?"

"I figure I'll go to FECOM right out of school, and I think I'll be ready. I believe that we have to stand up to Communism to protect our freedom, and if it takes a fight to do it, then I guess I should take my turn at the barricades. We didn't start this war, and a lot of our guys over there are getting their butts shot off fighting Communism. If they need help, then I think I should help. Think of the alternative if we don't make a stand against Communism."

They read the paper and made small talk for a while, then John asked Linder "What do you do on weekends? I find that the weekends really drag."

"I go to the beach whenever I can. We don't have an ocean where I come from, and I go as often as I can. Most Sunday mornings I go to church in Red Bank."

"What church do you go to?"

"I go to the Methodist church."

"You're a 'Georgia Cracker' and you're a Methodist?" John teased. "I thought everyone from the deep South was a Baptist."

"Not everyone. My mom is a pillar of Aldersgate Methodist Church in Columbus, Georgia. If she weren't there, Aldersgate Methodist Church would fall down," he said with a grin. "I've been a Methodist all my life."

"Me too," Grady responded.

"Well, what do you know about that," Linder said. "You ought to go with me to the Methodist church tomorrow."

"Sounds good to me. What time is the service, and how will we get there? I don't have a car."

"I'll drive. Service is at 1100 hours." They continued talking until time for dinner, then walked to the mess hall together. They went to a movie theater in Asbury Park that night.

Sunday morning the two men met as arranged and attended services at the Methodist church. The minister was good, as evidenced by an overflowing sanctuary. John read in the church bulletin that a bible study class would be held on Wednesday evening at 7:30 p.m. He had not engaged in a formal bible study for a number of years and felt that he needed to get involved.

Wednesday evening, John took the post bus out to the West Gate on Highway 35 and then caught the public bus into Red Bank. Fourteen other people were at the church for bible study. The pastor was a good bible scholar and a good group leader and made the class interesting and worthwhile.

CHAPTER 6. (11 AUGUST 1950)

Friday afternoon of that same week, classes C 329, C 330 and C 331 went to the field exercise area on the west side of the post for a demonstration of the capabilities of the Signal Corps. Each class loaded onto a respective bus and went to a large cleared area about the size of a football field. The three buses parked directly behind a section of green-painted bleachers, and the students dismounted and took seats in the bleachers. Two captains in heavily starched khakis and several enlisted men in fatigues stood in the middle of the field behind the microphone of a public address system. One captain welcomed them and explained what the program of the day would be.

One of the demonstrations was of various ways to lay field wire in a hurry. First, enlisted men drove a jeep at high speed down the length of the field while paying out field wire from special wire reels on the back of the jeep. Next, the enlisted men erected a mortar at one end of the field, tied one end of a reel of field wire to a solid projectile, then slid an explosive charge and the projectile down the mortar tube. The charge exploded and the projectile arched up and over the length of the field, pulling the field wire behind it. In the concluding demonstration of this series, a helicopter swooped low along the length of the field paying out field wire as it went.

The instructors told the men to take a break and to assemble back in the bleachers in ten minutes. When the student-officers reassembled, a Signal Corps photographer and a Signal Corps pigeon handler were in the middle of the field. One of the captains explained that the photographer would take a picture of the assembled classes and then place the film negative into a capsule attached to the leg of a Signal Corps homing pigeon. The pigeon would be released and would fly back to the Signal Corps Pigeon Loft on the main post. People in the photography section would take the film from the pigeon and develop and print it. A driver would rush prints of the developed picture back to the field training site so that the students could see their picture before the exercise was over. The entire operation would be completed in twenty-five minutes.

The photographer, positioned in the middle of the field, took the picture of the assembled classes seated in the bleachers. He placed the negative in the capsule on the pigeon's leg, and the pigeon handler released the pigeon into the air. The bird flew up into the air, and then it circled, and it circled, and it circled. Suddenly, it took off directly to the west. The pigeon loft on the main post was to the east! Students called, "Hey, it's going in the wrong direction."

"Don't worry," one of the captains replied, "homing pigeons always find their way home."

The captains lectured on the history and role of pigeons in the Signal Corps and of the Signal Corps combat photographers. Combat photographers trained at Fort Monmouth took much of the movie and still photography of U.S. Army ground combat in World War II.

It appeared that the planned program was over, but the captains obviously were stalling for time. The photograph of the assembled classes had not been delivered within the promised twenty-five minutes. After more stalling and delay, an army pickup truck came racing down the dirt road with a cloud of swirling dust trailing behind it. It came to an abrupt stop behind the buses. The driver jumped out of the pickup and rushed a large manila envelope to the captains in the middle of the field. One of the captains opened the envelope and pulled out two 7x10 glossy photographs of a large group of young officers sitting in bleachers. The pictures were passed among the one hundred and five student-officers who now were standing in front of the bleachers. Facial features of the students were not clearly discernible because the picture had been taken from such a long distance.

John, Jeff Linder, and Kas Korjovic stood at the rear of the student-officers looking over many shoulders at one of the photographs when suddenly Kas became agitated and looked toward the bleachers behind them and then at the photograph. He repeated this several times. He reached through the crowd and snatched the photograph and said in a loud voice, "Those bastards are lying to us. Look at the buses in the photograph and look where our buses are parked today." Everyone within hearing distance did so and saw that the buses today were parked directly behind the bleachers, but the buses in the photograph were parked about twenty yards to the left of the bleachers.

Kas held the photograph above his head and started working his way through the crowd toward the middle of the field where the two captains were standing. "You bastards are lying to us," he kept shouting. "Who do you think you are?"

At first, John thought that Kas was kidding and cutting up as he sometimes did. Then he realized that Kas was serious. John hurriedly pushed forward through the crowd and positioned himself close against Kas to head him off from where the captains were standing . "Take it easy, Kas," John said. Still looking toward the captains, Korjovic tried to push John out of the way and tried to get around him. Grady was bigger than Kas and put his chest firmly against Kas's body and began pushing him to the rear. Kas continued to try to move forward, continued waiving the photograph over his head, and exclaimed in a loud voice, "You sons of bitches are phonies. You're lying to us. Who the hell do you think you are? You're supposed to be army officers."

John put an arm around Kas's waist and pushed his shoulder forcefully against him as he worked Kas toward the rear. "Cool it, Kas, you're out of line," John said in a stern voice. "You're right, but this is not the time or place to make a scene. They outrank you, and they hold the trump cards. They can put you on report for being disorderly and for conduct unbecoming an officer. You don't want that, so forget it; let it go."

John's stern admonitions caught Kas's attention. He relaxed somewhat and stopped pushing against John and dropped his arm that held the photograph. John kept his arm around Kas's waist and slowly walked him around beside the bleachers. Kas pulled away from John's arm and stood still looking at him. It was obvious that Kas was greatly embarrassed. He didn't say anything for a short while, then he said in a low voice, "Thanks, Grady, I owe you one."

The instructors and many of the students saw what had happened. The instructors said and did nothing; they were happy to let the matter die as soon as possible. They had tried to pull a fast one and got caught. They dismissed the students from the session, and the students loaded into their buses for the trip back to the school area.

***

Grady went over to Scrivner Hall Saturday night for a beer and to read the newspaper. The Marines and the 25th Infantry Division had made some slight gains on the southern side of the Pusan Perimeter. The army and air force called more reservists to active duty. The army issued a mandatory call to active duty to one thousand five hundred eighty-two doctors from the Army Medical Corps Reserves.

The newspaper contained another interesting item: Ethel Rosenberg, of New York City, was arrested on charges of conspiracy to commit espionage. Her husband Julius had been arrested 17 July on charges of unlawfully obtaining secret information on the atomic bomb and passing it to the Soviet Union. Julius Rosenberg was an electrical engineer who had worked briefly during World War II at the Squire Laboratory of the U.S. Army Signal Corps Engineering Laboratories at Fort Monmouth, N.J. "Very interesting indeed," John said. "Squire Laboratory is just around the corner from my BOQ. I pass it several times a day."

CHAPTER 7. (13 AUGUST 1950)

John awoke early Sunday morning and went to breakfast at the Officers Mess. At 1020 hours he met Jeff Linder in the parking lot and they drove to the Methodist church for morning services. After church and lunch, Grady went over to the enlisted men's pool hall, put three nickels into the newspaper vending machine, and pulled out a copy of the Sunday edition of The New York Times. He arrived back at his room where his roommate Dan Hurley was stretched out on his bunk reading a newspaper. It was hot in the room, so John stripped down to his shorts.

"I wish the army would provide an easy chair or something comfortable to sit in," John said to Dan. "It's not comfortable sitting on that hard straight chair at that undersized field desk, and it's impossible to get comfortable lounging on this army cot."

"You've got that right," Dan agreed.

John decided that the cot was the better option. He arranged the many sections of the paper in the order in which he usually read them. He put his pillow against the wall at the end of his steel cot and leaned against the pillow with his legs stretched out on the cot. He read in the front section of the paper that the situation in Korea continued as before. The North Koreans were attacking all along the Pusan Perimeter defenses trying to force a major breach, and communist guerrilla forces were fighting and harassing UN troops within the perimeter. Our forces were holding and inflicting heavy casualties on the enemy. Our casualty lists were growing. "Who knows, I might be over there in a little over a month," John thought to himself.

The paper also reported that the Communist Chinese had massed eight hundred thousand troops on the border of Tibet in preparation to "liberate" the Tibetans from the Dalai Lama.

John finished reading all the sections of the paper that he wanted to concentrate on, then he lit a cigarette and turned to the society section that had the wedding and engagement announcements. He sometimes looked at that section, somewhat as entertainment, to see how the other half lived. It seemed that only the wealthy families and the famous families made the society pages of *The New York Times*. It amused him how the blue bloods crammed their pedigrees, several residences, parental professions, prep schools, and private colleges into such a compact statement as one of those wedding or engagement announcements. He read one wedding announcement and sure enough, both families were wealthy, had several residences, etc. He wondered what it would be like to be rich.

He took a drag on the cigarette that he held between his lips, turned the page, and W-H-A-M! He just stared at the page—he couldn't move. A picture of a girl on the page jumped out at him. "H-o-l-y T-o-l-e-d-o!" he breathed. He ever-so-slowly took the cigarette butt from his lips, slowly swung his legs over the side of the cot, sat up straight, and without taking his eyes off the picture, ground the cigarette butt into the ashtray on the field desk next to his cot. "She is beautiful," he exclaimed to himself. "No, beautiful is not the correct word. She is something more than beautiful. Regal, maybe." John struggled to define her beauty. Despite the black-and-white photograph, she obviously was blond. She wasn't quite smiling, but it was a happy, intelligent-looking, self-confident face. John felt as though there were some force coupling him to that picture. Without taking his eyes off the picture, he felt around for his pack of cigarettes and Zippo® lighter and lit another one. "This is nuts," John said to himself as he looked over to see if Dan were watching him. He was not, thank goodness. John folded the paper and read the engagement announcement.

Hazlet, New Jersey. August 12 -
Mr. and Mrs. William R. Hazlet of Hazlet, New Jersey, and West Palm Beach, have made known the engagement of their daughter Rebecca June to Richard Newton Sowell of New York. A December wedding is planned.
Miss Hazlet attended Miss Crawford's School and has completed her third year at Smith College. She was introduced to society at the Grosvenor Ball in New York during the season of 1945 and at a supper dance given by her grandmother. Miss Hazlet is a Red Cross volunteer.
Mr. Sowell attended Lawrenceville School and is a graduate of Yale University. He is an account executive with the New York securities firm of Johnson, Price and Sheridan.
Miss Hazlet's paternal grandfather was Cyrus E. Hazlet, found-

ing partner of the investment banking house of Hazlet and Meyers. Her maternal grandfather was George R. Gregory, former chairman of Gregory Trust Co., Philadelphia. Her father is senior partner of Hazlet and Meyers.

Mr. Sowell's father is Dr. Gordon T. Sowell, a surgeon who practices in Philadelphia.

John looked at the picture again. He reread the engagement announcement. "Hazlet, New Jersey—that's not too far up Route 35," John thought to himself. "Her name is Hazlet and she lives in Hazlet—interesting."

"Hey, John, its getting hot in here," Dan called. "What do you say we go over to the club and get a cold beer."

"You talked me into it. Let me get some clothes on."

They walked over to Scrivner Hall where not more than half a dozen men were in the bar and on the enclosed front porch. They ordered beers and engaged in small talk. Another exciting Sunday afternoon in the army, John thought. They finished their second beers and John said, "Lets go get some chow."

"Uggh," Dan groaned, "Sunday night chow—cold cuts and potato salad. I don't know if it's worth going over to the mess hall."

"Where do you think you are, at the Ritz?" John joshed. "Come on, at least it'll keep body and soul together until breakfast tomorrow."

After the cold cuts and potato salad, and a square of yellow cake with white icing, while they walked back to the BOQ Dan said, "Do you want to go to the movie tonight?" John said that he had studying to do.

They returned to their room and Dan left when it was time for the movie. John retrieved the society page of the paper and reread the engagement announcement of Rebecca June Hazlet. He could not take his eyes off her. She seemed to be looking straight at him. "Crazy. Absolutely, positively crazy," he muttered to himself. "If I keep this up I'll be ready for a Section 8 discharge." But he had a strange feeling about that girl—one of those strange feelings of his. As he continued looking, a thought took form in his mind. He went to his footlocker and pulled out his stationery and then went to his small desk and began writing.

John H. Grady
2nd Lt. Sig C
Bachelor Officers Quarters 5
Fort Monmouth, New Jersey
August 13, 1950

Miss Rebecca Hazlet
Hazlet, New Jersey

Dear Miss Hazlet:

I am an army officer attending school at Fort Monmouth. I am twenty-four years old and unmarried. I have an electrical engineering degree and have completed two years of law school.

I read you engagement announcement in *The New York Times* and it had the most unusual effect on me. (You may find this weird, but please stay with me.) The feeling that I have tells me that we should meet. I understand that this is most unusual inasmuch as you are engaged, but I believe that we should meet before any more time goes by. Neither of us has much time remaining, so we should meet soon. I have a strange feeling that there may be something special here that we should not miss. After you are married, it will be too late.

Please be assured that my intentions are honorable. I shall treat you and your situation with respect and discretion.

You have absolutely nothing to lose now. If nothing more, perhaps we can talk on the telephone. My telephone number is 736-8985. Ask for me.

Respectfully yours,
John Grady

John read and reread the letter. He had never done anything like this before. "This is crazy. I should tear up this letter and forget this weird idea," he said as he read the letter again. Then he said, "What the hell, they can't put me in jail for sending it; let's see what happens." John had no address for her except Hazlet, N.J. He addressed and sealed the envelope and put it in his locker. "I don't believe I'm doing this," he said to himself as he shook his head in disbelief. He studied until Dan came home from the movie. They talked a short while, then hit the sack.

Grady dropped the letter into the mailbox in front of Russell Hall on his way to class Monday morning.

CHAPTER 8. (14 AUGUST 1950)

Grady was waiting for the first class of the afternoon on Monday when Kas Korjovic came up to him and said, "Grady, can I talk to you when school is out today?"

"Sure, Kas. What's up?"

"I don't know .... I've been doing some thinking about our incident with the pigeon and the photograph, and I'd like to talk with you about it, if you don't mind." Kas seemed subdued compared with his usual lively and exuberant demeanor.

After the last class, John waited outside the building. Kas came out and said, "Let's go over to my car and talk." They went to the parking lot and sat in Kas's late-model Dodge and rolled down all the windows.

"You seem troubled, Kas, what's up?" John tried to make it sound as casual as possible. He lit a cigarette.

"I've been giving a lot of thought to that incident with the pigeon. I lost my cool, and that bothers me a lot, but that's past history now. What really is bothering me, and what I can't seem to get over, is the fact that those two captains lied to us—they lied to over one hundred fellow officers. They lied to us and probably have been lying to other classes that went to that exercise. If you can't trust a fellow officer, who can you trust? What will the army be like if you can't trust anyone? I'm personally incensed that they lied to me, and I'm concerned for what they're doing to the army. I know I'm not perfect and not the best officer in the army, but by god I don't lie to my fellow officers. I've been trying to figure out why I'm so upset about it. I lost my cool over there, and I don't know if I'm being defensive about that by getting mad at the two captains. I thought about it all weekend and finally concluded that what those guys did was wrong and shouldn't continue.

"I made an appointment to see Major Bowen, Secretary of The Signal School, tomorrow after school. I intend to notify him what went on. The army can deal with it as it sees fit, but I've concluded that someone in authority should know about it. I don't like being a snitch, but I don't know any other way. What do you think?"

Initially, John was at a loss for words. He took a couple of puffs on his cigarette as he assessed the situation. "I'm like you, Kas, I don't like to be lied to, but while we don't like it we have to be realistic enough to know that it's going to happen. Obviously, you've concluded that the pigeon/photo incident is important enough to do something about it. You know, Kas, there may be consequences to face if you turn them in. It could affect your career. You're only a junior officer reporting on more senior officers. You have no guarantee that the army will deal with this objectively or fairly. Have you considered the possible consequences?"

"Hell yes I've considered the consequences. It wouldn't be a hard decision if there were no consequences to consider."

John figured that Kas didn't call him over to his car just to tell him that he was going to report the two captains. "Is there anything else on your mind, Kas?"

"Yeah, there is. I can report the incident, but maybe they won't pay any attention to me. After all, I'm not a college man and most of the other officers are. I'm up from the enlisted ranks, and they might think that I'm out to get senior officers. Who knows? Anyhow, I thought that if I had a witness to back me up it might make a better impression, and I was wondering if you would want to back me up when I see Major Bowen?

"Holy Toledo," John thought. He had come into the army to do his duty and to be as inconspicuous as possible doing it. What Kas was asking had the possibility of being anything but inconspicuous. John thought about it. He lit another cigarette.

Kas saw that John was in deep thought. "Look, John," he said, (It was the first time that Kas had called him "John"—it always had been "Grady.") "I had all weekend to think about it, and I'm springing this on you all of a sudden, so sleep on it and let me know tomorrow. O.K.?"

John didn't like to waffle on a moral decision. He hoped that he had character enough to face moral decisions and know what was right to do. As Kas was talking, a quote from Edmund Burke had come into John's thoughts: *All that is necessary for the triumph of evil is that good men do nothing.* John had given considerable thought to that phrase since he first read it several years ago. He had resolved that it would do him no good to get bogged down trying to decide whether he had the right to decide if something were evil, or how evil it was. Instead, he decided that he should concentrate on trying to do right and try to set things right when he saw what he thought was a wrong. John believed that God had given him a mind to make decisions with and that God expected him to use his mind to do just that. He decided that he should do something about the pigeon/photo matter and there was no need to delay.

"Sure, I'll go with you tomorrow," John said. After a pause, he continued, "Let me say this, Kas. I recommend that the statement, or presentation, or whatever you deliver to Major Bowen, be delivered in a calm, clear, rational manner, and that it be nothing but facts and truth. Be very professional about it. Do you intend to do this orally or in writing?"

"Right now, orally. And don't worry about me losing my cool. I'll be as professional as I know how."

All day Tuesday Grady was anxious about the meeting with Major Bowen. Finally, the last class was over and he and Korjovic walked over to Bowen's office where his civilian secretary directed them into the major's office. Major Arthur L. Bowen was of medium height and maybe just a little pudgy. He had a clear complexion and thick, shiny, black hair that had as straight a part in it as Grady had ever seen. He had a calm, quiet, and friendly manner. He smiled a lot. His title was Secretary, The Signal School, Officers Division, but he had considerable influence and authority for that position. It resulted from the fact that in his calm manner he did a prodigious amount of work. His superiors gave him much responsibility and authority because they knew that when they gave a job to Bowen it would be done—and done right. Those who knew him fully expected that one day he would reach the rank of general. He always did his homework and was on top of every situation. As an example of doing his homework, during that day he had read the personnel files of both Grady and Korjovic and had looked at their academic records in The Signal School. He knew that both men had prior service in World War II as enlisted men and that, academically, they stood first and second in their class.

Korjovic and Grady entered the office and saluted. Kas announced, "Lieutenants Grady and Korjovic reporting to Major Bowen for the requested meeting."

Bowen returned the salute, smiled, and said, "Please have a seat," as he motioned to two chairs in front of his desk. Still smiling, in his quiet manner he asked , "What can I do for you, gentlemen."

Kas commenced to relate the facts of the classes' experience with the captains in the pigeon/photo incident. He concluded by saying , "Sir, I don't like to make an unfavorable accusation against fellow officers, but I feel compelled to call your attention to this incident because I believe that our classes at that exercise were subjected to treatment that not only is personally offensive to me, but sets a bad example to the younger officers who were there. I don't want them to think that that kind of conduct is acceptable for an army officer."

Major Bowen nodded his head slightly to acknowledge that Korjovic had finished. He looked at Grady, smiled slightly, and said in a soft voice, "Lieutenant Grady, do you have anything to add?"

"Sir, I was present and personally witnessed all the events that Lieutenant Korjovic described. I believe that he described them truthfully and completely. I endorse his concluding personal note as well."

Bowen waited for Grady to continue his statement, but when he didn't continue, Bowen realized that Grady already had said everything that a corroborating witness needed to say. "Gentlemen, thank you for coming in," the major said in his usual slow and soft voice.

Neither man heard anything further from Major Bowen on the pigeon/photo matter. About three weeks later, Korjovic heard a rumor that the two captains involved in the incident had received orders for FECOM. He told Grady, but neither man tried to verify the rumor. They had done all they could do. (Grady figured that the rumor probably was true. He figured that Bowen, in his quiet and efficient style, had investigated the pigeon/photo incident, found that the report by Korjovic and Grady was true, and had the captains put on orders to FECOM. Bowen didn't get Korjovic or Grady involved any further because he didn't want anything about it on the records of the two promising junior officers.)

Grady was relieved that the meeting with Bowen was over. He went to dinner and then read the newspaper for a short time. UN forces in Korea were attacking at several points on the Pusan Perimeter trying to keep the North Korean forces off balance to prevent them from starting their anticipated great offensive to wipe out the Perimeter. Some U.S. commanders expressed optimism that the Perimeter would hold and that the Communists had lost their chance to eliminate it. Grady studied late into the night getting ready for a test the next day.

The test went well on Wednesday. Also on that day, the class grades and standings for the second month of school were posted on the Class 329 bulletin board. Again, Grady was first and Korjovic was second, with the spread between their grades being about the same as it was the first month. Several others in the class moved up close to them in averages.

"Damn you, you're a tough bastard to catch," Kas said to John.

"I'm not going to lay down and let you run over me, Kas," John replied with a grin.

CHAPTER 9. (18 AUGUST 1950)

John had a difficult assignment to prepare on Thursday night. The class was taking a course in teaching techniques, and each student-officer had to prepare and deliver an instructional lecture on a topic of the student's choosing. First of all, John had no inspiration for a topic on which to talk. After much indecision, he finally settled upon a description of several common military justice crimes that the officers might expect to come across. He had to study the Uniform Code of Military Justice to be sure that he fully understood them himself, then he had to present them in a manner that he was sure laymen would understand. It wasn't coming easily, and it was beginning to get late. It was raining, the windows were closed, and the room was warm and muggy.

About 2130 hours someone on the first floor of BOQ 5 let out a shout, "**Grady, telephone.**" John hurried along the length of the second floor hall and down the stairs to the pay phone that was just inside the entrance to the building.

"Hello," he puffed, "Lieutenant Grady speaking."

"John Grady?" a woman's voice asked.

"Yes ma'am."

"Lieutenant Grady, this is June Hazlet."

Grady stood there breathing heavily. His mind was a blank. He didn't know a woman by the name June. He was trying to think if he knew someone from college named June.

"Hello, are you there?"

"Yes ma'am, I am," John replied, feeling stupid.

"I'm June Hazlet; you wrote me the letter."

"Oh! Rebecca Hazlet, from Hazlet."

"I go by my middle name June. You know, I'm crazy to be replying to your letter."

"That makes two of us. I had to be crazy to write that letter." They both chuckled nervously. John couldn't believe it—it really was happening. He didn't know what to say. He had a ringing in his ears. "I really do appreciate you calling me." After a slight pause he continued, "Tell me, why did you call?"

"I don't know, curiosity I think."

That seemed like an honest-enough answer. The question didn't put her on the defensive; she knew why he asked the question.

Grady didn't want to ruin the situation before it began, but he just had to ask, "Do you have the same feeling I do that there may be something special here?"

"John Grady," she shot back, "I don't know you. I haven't even met you."

"Forgive me, Miss Hazlet, it's just that neither of us has much time, and I do think that we should meet."

"Why don't you have much time?"

"I'm in school here at Fort Monmouth, and school will be over soon and I'll be getting orders. I probably will be leaving here."

"When will you be leaving?"

"In about a month."

He felt that he had to be bold. "Can you meet me tomorrow evening for a drink and then dinner?"

After a short hesitation she said, "I can't have dinner. I have to be home by seven o'clock."

John caught his breath. Was she saying "Yes" to the drinks? He certainly wasn't going to give her a chance to say "No." "Good. You know this area better than I do, where do you suggest we meet for drinks?"

"I'm engaged; I can't be seen in public with you."

"Fine, I have the perfect place. None of your friends or neighbors will be there."

"Where?"

"The Fort Monmouth Officers Club. None of your friends or neighbors go there, do they?

After a pause she replied, "Probably not."

"Good enough. June, listen, because we have such little time, would it be possible for you to meet me tomorrow afternoon at 5:30 at the Officers Club?" (Not only did they have such little time, but he didn't have a car to pick her up.)

"Good lord! You expect me to ...." There was silence—a long, long silence. Then, "I suppose so. How do I get there?" she answered with hesitation and uncertainty in her voice. "What in the world am I getting my-self into?" she asked herself. "Why am I meeting this man? Why did I say 'Yes'?"

John gave her directions to Gibbs Hall, the Fort Monmouth Officers Mess Country Club on Tinton Avenue that was west from the West Gate of the main post. It was a very nice country club with an eighteen hole golf course, tennis courts, a swimming pool, and a nice clubhouse that had a particularly fine dance floor with a roll-back roof. It had much more class than Scrivner Hall that was on the main part of the post. "Pull past the canopy at the front entrance and go about twenty yards and you'll see the parking lot. I'll meet you there."

"All right, I'll see you tomorrow at 5:30, but I can't stay long. Don't you be late and make me wait around in a strange place," she commanded. "How will I know you?"

"I'll have on a khaki uniform and a dark green tie."

"Oh," she replied, missing completely his intended humor. There would be thousands of men at Fort Monmouth wearing a khaki uniform and a dark green tie.

"June, you don't know how much I appreciate this. Thanks so much." He couldn't think of anything else to say, so he said, "Good night."

Grady went upstairs and paced back and forth in the hallway trying to remember every word of the conversation. He analyzed the conversation: She was nervous; her voice had a nice pitch; she was direct in her state-ments and was responsive to my statements; she wasn't giddy; she didn't try to impress me with sophistication; and she probably is intelligent. But questions kept surfacing. If she's engaged, why did she call, and why is she going to see me?

The next morning John went to breakfast with his roommate and prevailed upon him to drive him over to Gibbs Hall after classes that afternoon.

The morning classes went well, but the afternoon dragged on and on. He thought it never would end. Finally it did, and he walked to the gate of the school area where he had arranged for Dan to pick him up. Dan arrived and drove John to Gibbs Hall. It was only 1715 hours, so John went into the clubhouse to the men's locker room and wiped the dust off his shoes, washed his hands and face, combed his hair, and straightened his tie. Then he went out to the front steps under the canopy and waited.

At 1727 hours a Chrysler convertible with the top up entered the driveway of the country club. The convertible was the model that had the fancy light-colored wood panels on the body. The guys in college called those cars "Woodys." John walked about twenty yards to the parking lot and waited. The convertible slowly came up the driveway and hesitated at the canopy, then proceeded to the parking lot. John saw that a woman was driving it, so he raised his arm and waived hoping that it was Miss Hazlet and not some senior officer's wife. The convertible pulled into a parking space near to where Grady was standing. It was she!

John walked up to the car, looked through the open window and said, "Hello, Miss Hazlet, I'm John Grady. Thank you for coming."

"Hello," she replied. She rolled up the window and began to open the door to get out of the car. John turned partially around and walked away so as not to watch her getting out of the car. She noticed it and was appreciative and impressed with his thoughtfulness. She closed the door of the car and stood there looking at Grady. He stood about twelve feet away looking at her. Neither one said anything or made a move. Each one, unashamedly, was sizing up the other.

She saw that he was tall and erect, with broad shoulders. She thought to herself, "I probably could wear heels if I went out with him." He had a slight smile on his face which she thought was becoming. She even would say that he was handsome. "So far, so good," she thought to herself, but she would be looking for more than looks.

He saw that she was tall. Her thick hair was natural golden blond—or at least it appeared to be natural. She wore it cut under her ears and slightly curled at the bottom. Every strand was in place. Her face was tanned and unblemished, and her eyes were blue. She had broad shoulders, a trim figure, and good posture. She wore a dark tan sport coat that had a subdued design that looked like tweed and a tan skirt that had deep pleats in the front. She had a white collared blouse under her coat, and she wore hose and highly polished penny loafer shoes. He was not sure how old she was, but it didn't matter—she was absolutely stunning! John had never seen a more beautiful woman.

"Miss Hazlet, we can go inside and have a drink if you like. We'll go in the front door under the canopy."

"Please call me June. What should I call you, 'Lieutenant Grady,' 'Mr. Grady,' or what? I've never known an army officer."

He smiled. "Call me John."

He held the front door open as she entered and asked, "Have you ever been in this clubhouse?"

"No."

"Let me show you around." He gave her a brief tour of the rooms on the main floor. "The golf pro shop and the locker rooms are downstairs. We can sit in the lounge, or bar, over there, if that's all right with you."

"That will be fine, John."

No one else was in the lounge at the time. Only the bartender was at the bar, and it appeared that he was just setting up for the evening. They sat in a booth making small talk about whether she had any difficulty finding the place. The bartender made no move to come over to take their order, so John said, "It looks as if I'll have to go over to the bar to get the drinks. What would you like?"

"A Cocoa-Cola®, please."

John went over to the bar and ordered a Coke® for June and a beer for himself. He returned to the booth, set the drinks down, and slid in on the seat. "Here's to your health," he toasted. She smiled and took a sip of her drink.

"June, as we said in our phone conversation, this is kind of a crazy situation, and it might even get crazier. But I hope you'll be patient and tolerant so we might get to know each other. For some reason that I can't explain, I have a feeling that we should. If we do get to know each other better, maybe the situation will take care of itself. Maybe we'll shake hands and say good-bye, or maybe we won't want to say good-bye. I understand that I'm imposing on you and that this is a difficult situation for you. I have no right to ask you to do this, but I'll appreciate it greatly if you'll give us some time." He smiled and said, "We shall not pass this way again."

She looked squarely at him all the time he was talking. She said nothing for a short while, but never took her eyes off him. She appeared to be in deep thought. John figured that she was trying to decide whether she wanted to continue with this or cut out now. Finally, she said, "What do you have in mind?"

"We can start by me telling you about my life thus far, and you telling me about yours. We can start there and see where it leads us. What do you think?"

"Right now I think that it's awfully warm in here. Don't they have air conditioning?" Would you mind if I take off my jacket?

"Go ahead. They probably haven't turned the air conditioning on yet because they're just opening up for the evening."

She took off her jacket and placed it beside her. John noticed that she wore a chemise under her blouse so that her slip and brassiere, and their straps, were not visible through her blouse. He liked this. In his opinion it showed class. He never understood why women allow their underwear, or the outlines of them, to be visible through their outer clothing. It looked tacky to him.

She opened her purse and took out a handkerchief and wiped her forehead.

"Grab your coat. Let's get out of here," Grady said as he stood up.

She looked up at him with surprise. "Why? Where are we going? What about our drinks?"

"Forget the drinks. Follow me."

Somewhat annoyed, she stood up and wondered what this strange guy was up to. They went back out the front door. He led her to the left along the driveway and onto the lawn and then up onto a grassy knoll overlooking the first tee of the golf course where they sat on a wood bench. Indeed, the fresh air and slight breeze were a welcome relief after the warm bar.

"We should have come here to begin with," she said.

John thought that she was rather haughty in the way she said it. He didn't know if she were annoyed with him, or couldn't deal with a little discomfort, or whatever. "Is she just a spoiled rich kid?" he wondered.

"Well," she said, "I have to be home by seven. Are you going to tell me about yourself?"

"There she goes again," John said to himself. He wasn't sure he liked the way she said it. Grady was thinking, "Maybe this whole thing has been a big mistake on my part. She's from a different world, and maybe she should stay in her world and I should stay in my world. Well, I started this thing with that letter I wrote, so I ought to follow through with it—at least for today."

"Sure. Please understand that I'll say some things that perhaps I wouldn't include the first time I met a girl." John began a well-organized recitation of his life up to the present. He was in deep thought as he recalled his personal history. She watched him intently all the while he spoke. Both were silent for a short time after he finished speaking.

"Do you have a girlfriend back home?" June asked.

"No. I never had time in college to get serious about anyone."

"Did you date at all?"

"Oh sure. I had dates for the fraternity parties and dances, and on some Saturday nights when we brought dates to the fraternity house, but I didn't go steady with anyone. I guess you could say that I had girlfriends but no sweetheart."

"How can I know that you're telling me the truth?"

"You'll just have to believe me, I guess. If you get to know me, you'll know that I don't lie. I work awfully hard to be truthful in everything I do. But as you say, you don't know that now."

"Oh, 'Honest John,' are you?" In fact, she did believe him, and she was impressed. "You seemed to have been a leader in almost everything you were involved in," she said. "Isn't that true?"

"Well, in some things. Now, tell me about you, and don't be modest; we don't have time for modesty."

" I ... I've never done anything like this before." She looked embarrassed and self-conscious. "Well, anyway ... I've lived all my life in the same house in Hazlet. When I was young we lived in the north wing of the house and my grandfather and grandmother lived in the main part of the house. Grandfather Hazlet bought the house and developed the things on the property. After my grandparents passed away, we moved into the main part of the house. I went to a private grade school in Rumson, N.J., and went two years to high school at a boarding school in Pennsylvania. I went to college one year at Bryn Mawr, near Philadelphia, but didn't go back. I spent most of the next year in Europe with my uncle and aunt. I came back and went to Smith College for two years, but I'm not going back this year. And that's about it. I haven't had the exciting life that you have."

"Why did you leave Bryn Mawr?"

"I wasn't comfortable there. I didn't seem to fit in with the rest of the girls or the faculty. Everyone there seemed too occupied with being a woman and insisting on their feminine rights. I'm just not interested in that."

"What did you major in at Smith?

She blushed and had a sheepish grin. "I didn't really get into a major. I was taking courses trying to find something that I liked. My advisor kept trying to push me into the social sciences, but I didn't think that I wanted to end up there so I didn't make a commitment to a major."

"Tell me about your family."

"My father is in the private investment banking business in New York. He's very busy, and sometimes I don't get to see too much of him. He has a couple of outside interests which the family enjoys and which we get to do together.

"My mother is a housewife, I guess you would say. She grew up outside of Philadelphia. Her family owns a big bank there. She spends her time running the house and playing golf and bridge at the country club."

"Do you have any siblings?" John asked.

"Oh, yes, I have a sister." She didn't volunteer any more information about her sister.

"Does your sister live at home? Is she younger then you or older?"

"She's older than I am. She lives in Maine." That was all she said about her sister.

"You said that your grandfather developed things on the property. What kind of things did he develop?"

" Oh, the barn, the stables, the orchard, the gardens, the polo field, and the steeplechase course.

"It sounds as if your grandfather was a horseman."

"He was. He played polo until he was 75. He was quite a man. He had many diverse interests. He started the business that Daddy runs."

John had to ask this question. "Tell me about your fiancé."

June looked at him as if to say, "Did you have to ask that question?" After a short pause she said, "I've known him most of my life. His mother and my mother were college roommates at Bryn Mawr. Our families have visited back and forth ever since I can remember, and we've vacationed together several times."

John wanted to ask a follow up question on the subject of her fiancé, but he figured that he shouldn't press the matter too much. It probably didn't matter anyhow because he was thinking right then that he would not see any more of Miss June Hazlet. She was a rich kid, and she was far out of his league. But he really didn't know too much about her yet, so he asked, "What do you like to do? How do you spend your time?"

"In good weather I play golf and I ride. I read some, and I do volunteer work at Riverview Hospital a day or two a week when I'm home. "

"Where do you ride?"

"At home. We have a couple of horses."

"What do you read?"

"Mostly fiction, but I enjoy historical novels." John avoided both of those.

"Do you attend church? If so, where do you go?"

"Mother and I attend Trinity Episcopal Church in Red Bank. Golly, you really are grilling me! You'll make a good prosecuting attorney."

"As I said, we don't have much time to get acquainted."

Neither one knew what to say next. They watched a foursome of golfers hit from the first tee.

"Have you played this course?" June asked.

"I played it once last summer with a couple of the guys I was with in summer camp." Grady had played golf only twice in his life.

"I've played most of the courses in this area, but I've never played this one. It might be interesting to play," June said matter-of-factly.

"Now, what does she mean by that statement?" Grady asked himself. "Is she asking for an invitation to play golf here?" He didn't know her well enough to know what to make of the situation. At this point, John concluded that he would not pursue the June Hazlet matter any further, but he didn't want to be rude to her. After all, she replied to that weird letter that he sent, and at his urging she did consent to meet with him. It wouldn't hurt to try to be polite to her, so he said, "If you would like to play here, we can anytime you want to. But again, it will have to be soon."

She looked at him with surprise. She was not fishing for an invitation to play golf there; she was just making idle conversation. The two of them were not on the same "wavelength" throughout most of their conversation. She was nervous and not sure of this situation and was not her usual self. Grady also was nervous. He just wasn't sure how to deal with meeting a rich engaged girl. And, he was too suspicious. He was looking for things that were not actually present. He could not understand why she came.

June had not thought past this first meeting with Grady. She was curious to see what he looked like and what he was like, but she hadn't thought beyond that. She did think that he was kind of interesting. Finally, she said, "Oh, all right. When do you want to play?"

"Tomorrow is Saturday; can you play tomorrow? I'm not very good, so I would prefer to play late in the day when the course is not crowded. What time do you have to be home tomorrow?"

She mulled the matter over in her mind. "Tomorrow the hospital is having a charity bazaar and I've volunteered to work there from 10:00 until 4:00 o'clock. I could be here by 4:20, if that would that be O.K.? May I change clothes here?"

"Sure. Yes, you can change clothes in the ladies' locker room downstairs. What time do you have to be home?"

"Actually, I don't have to worry about that tomorrow. Mother and Daddy are going to Pound Ridge, New York, to spend the weekend with a friend of Daddy's who's also involved in steeplechase racing, and they won't be home until Sunday evening."

John smiled, "It sounds good to me. That settles it. Now, if you're going to get home by 7:00 o'clock you had better be getting on your way. June, I want to thank you again for coming. It was a pleasure to meet you."

John assessed his meeting with June Hazlet as he rode the shuttle bus back to his BOQ. He concluded that he had been foolish to even consider contacting her. He wished he hadn't. About golf tomorrow, he reasoned that he could manage for a couple of hours. He figured he'll thank June and wish her happiness in her marriage. There should be no regrets on either side: you win some and you lose some—she surely understands that.

Grady read the Saturday morning newspaper after a leisurely breakfast. The Pusan Perimeter was holding, and the fighting around Taegu and to the northwest of the Perimeter was fierce. Eighth Army shifted some troops from the south of the Perimeter to the north of Taegu to hold the North Koreans. The casualties were high on both sides. John studied several of his courses the remainder of the morning and into early afternoon.

About 1430 hours he dressed in some casual clothes and went to the bus stop and boarded the shuttle bus to Gibbs Hall. He arrived early, selected his rented clubs, paid the fees, and carried the clubs to the bag rack. He then went to the front of the building to await June Hazlet.

She pulled up in her Woody, and he went out and greeted her. She stepped out of the car, smiled, and greeted him. She wore her starched, gray hospital uniform with a broad white collar, white stockings, and highly polished black oxford shoes. No matter what he thought of her, she was a beautiful woman. She reached into the back of the car and brought out a suit bag with a couple of hangers extending through the top.

"Where's the locker room? When is our starting time?" she asked.

"We have to go to the other side of the building to get to the locker rooms. We have a 4:30 starting time, so we'll have a couple of minutes to loosen up."

"Right. While I'm changing clothes, would you mind getting my clubs out of the car trunk for me? Here are my keys." John led her into the pro shop and directed her to the ladies' locker room. He went to her car and lifted out her clubs, then secured each bag onto a pull cart.

June came out of the pro shop looking for him. She wore a pleated tan skirt that was below her knees and a white collared polo shirt with a Navesink Country Club crest on the pocket. Her clothes were loose on her but not sloppy. She did not expose her body features by wearing tight clothes. Her brown and white golf shoes were highly polished. She exuded class.

"We can go over by the first tee to loosen up," John said. "Here, let me pull your cart."

"No, thank you, I'll pull my own cart."

"Who shines your shoes?" John asked with a grin. "You could pass inspection any day with the highly polished shoes I've seen you wear."

"I polish my own shoes, just as you do," she replied returning his smile.

"You do good work."

They did some stretching exercises and some practice swings, and then they were next up on the tee box. John dreaded this. He was sure that he would make a fool of himself. He placed his ball on the tee, took his stance, stared at the ball, and swung the club. The ball started down the middle of the fairway and then drifted to the right and landed in high grass in the rough.

As they walked up to the ladies' tee box, John said to her, "You see that I left the fairway uncluttered for you. I didn't want you to have to hit through debris on the fairway."

"You're all heart, John. A true gentleman." They both grinned.

She placed her ball on the tee, backed away and looked down the fairway, then took her stance. She drew back her club and came through with a relaxed but forceful swing that sent the ball streaking down the center of the fairway. It hit the ground and rolled fifteen yards more. Her ball was easily thirty yards beyond John's ball.

"Hey," John said, "you've played this game before."

She smiled. "I've played it a few times."

They walked together to John's ball in the high grass. He selected a three iron and gave a mighty swing. The ball started down the right side of the fairway and then sliced to the right and landed deep into the rough about twenty-five feet short of the green.

"I don't want to wear out the fairway," John said.

"You'll never get the chance with shots like that," June said. They both laughed.

June took out a fairway wood, and with the same relaxed swing she hit the ball down the middle of the fairway. Her ball hit the ground about ten yards in front of the green, went up a slight incline and onto the green. It stopped about twenty feet from the cup.

"Great shot," John called from the rough. For his next shot, John chose a pitching iron. He sculled the ball and it went streaking about two feet off the ground toward the green. It crossed the green and finally stopped about twenty feet beyond. "I'm a little off on my distance there," John said as they walked up to the green.

"You might say so."

John landed onto the green with his next shot, but it took him three putts to put the ball into the cup. He finished up with a score of seven for the hole and was lucky to get that. June put her ball into the cup with two putts to par the hole. As they walked to the second tee box John said with a grin, "Well, because you're the guest I wanted you to have the honors on the first hole, but don't expect me to be so benevolent on the rest of the holes."

"You must have found it difficult to hold back and hide your talent," she teased, " but I must say that you did a wonderful job of it." They laughed. Her good sense of humor surprised John.

They played two more holes with pretty much the same results as far as the scores went. They continued their good-natured kidding and became more relaxed with each other. She showed that she had a quick mind.

At the beginning of the fifth hole June said, "Would you mind if I give you a couple of tips on your grip and swing."

"I won't mind a bit. I'm happy to get any free instruction I can get. It is free, isn't it?"

"For you it's free; I hate to see you suffer. Seriously, try to keep your left elbow straight as you swing through." She demonstrated with a practice swing. "Also, turn your left hand over more in your grip."

John tried to change his grip as he thought she had told him to do, but he did it incorrectly. She came over in front of him and took his hands and began moving them around the club. She gave him instructions and looked down at his hands as she moved them. Her head was directly in front of his and no more than eighteen inches away. He looked at her face and not at his hands.

She looked up and saw him looking at her face. "You're not paying attention," she said.

"Oh, I'm paying attention to you, Miss Hazlet."

She blushed.

His next drive was a great improvement; it had just a slight fade to the right. "You're a good teacher; that drive was almost straight," he said to her. They continued to talk and kid each other as they walked the next two holes. Both seemed to enjoy it. The sky had become overcast, and it began to sprinkle when they arrived at the tee box that was in front of the clubhouse. They waited under a tree beside the tee box to see if the rain would stop. It became worse.

"What do you say we call it a day and go into the grill," John said.

"Is the air conditioning on?" June said with a grin.

"That was uncomfortable yesterday, wasn't it. I apologize for that."

"It wasn't your fault. Yes, let's quit. Get the umbrella here on my bag and open it up. Let's go to my car and put my bag into the trunk, then I'll go to the locker room and get my clothes." He opened the umbrella and held it over them as they walked .

They took care of their business in the clubhouse and were about to leave when John said to June, "Wait here will you please; I want to check on something. Excuse me for a minute." He went upstairs to the club office and inquired whether there would be dancing at the club that night. The answer was that there would be dancing starting at 2000 hours. He returned to June and said, "Miss Hazlet, will you accompany me to a dance here at the club tonight? It starts at eight o'clock, and none of your friends or neighbors are allowed in."

She studied John as if she were trying to read his mind. And, she was trying to make up her own mind.

"We shall not pass this way again," he said with a serious look on his face.

"Eight o'clock," she said as she looked at her watch. "Golly, that doesn't give much time, and I haven't eaten dinner."

"I haven't either, and I have a recommendation. We can grab a hamburger at the diner outside the West Gate. Hardly anyone goes there except soldiers, so it'll be safe for us to eat there. Then you can go home and shower and change clothes, and I'll go to my BOQ and shower and change. It won't matter if we don't get there exactly at eight. What do you say?

She looked at him and shook her head. "John Grady, I don't know how you get me into these things. Four days ago I had never heard of you. I've seen you twice since then, and now you want me to go dancing with you. I can't believe this is happening to me." She paused. "John, I'll be happy to accompany you to the dance tonight. Let's get going."

They went to the diner and ordered hamburgers and milkshakes. They worked out a time schedule for getting back together later in the evening. It pleased John that June was very much a participant in the planning. Some facts then occurred to June. "You need a ride to your dorm, don't you? And, you have no transportation for tonight, isn't that right?"

"I'm afraid you're right. I can catch the shuttle bus to my BOQ, and I can meet you at the club later. I'm sorry that I can't take you home and pick you up, but that's the way it is. I'm just a poor hillbilly from West Virginia. June, please don't feel that you have to go tonight. It'll be O.K. with me if you don't."

"I said I will. I'll take you to your BQ, or whatever you call it, and I'll pick you up later. Just show me how to get there."

"You are some kind of girl, you are," Grady said.

She blushed.

They arrived at the club sometime after 2100 hours. June wore a conservative dress and a single strand of pearls around her neck. She wore shoes with medium-high heels. As was her custom, except for a light touch of lipstick, she wore no makeup. She didn't need it because she had a healthy All-American-Girl look that didn't need additional coloring. John wore a brown, double-breasted, summer-weight suit.

"You look great tonight," John told her as they entered the club.

They went to the ballroom which was at ground level on the west side of the club. The room was rectangular and had several tiers around the dance floor where tables for two, and for four, were arranged. A nine-piece orchestra played at one end of the dance floor. A young man in civilian clothes directed them to a table for two on the second tier, and a waiter promptly appeared and took their order for two Cokes. June said that she didn't partake of alcohol, and Grady didn't want to order an alcoholic drink if she didn't. They looked around taking in the scene and made small talk. The band began playing a popular ballad and John said, "Shall we dance?"

"Fine," June replied, and they descended the few steps to the dance floor. John pulled the folded white handkerchief from his outside breast pocket, placed it across his left palm, then place June's right hand on it. He placed his right hand on her side and kept her at arm's length as they proceeded to dance.

"Oh my," she said, "you're quite formal and proper, aren't you."

"I promised you in my letter that I'd treat you with respect and decorum." They made a round of the dance floor getting familiar with each other's dance style. On the second round they began to work together more smoothly. The music ended and they lightly applauded the orchestra. Another slow piece began, and they again danced at arm's length. The music ended and they returned to their table.

The rain had ended and the sky had cleared, so the club manager opened the sliding roof of the ballroom to reveal the star-filled sky. "This really is quite lovely," June said.

"It makes a nice effect, doesn't it," John replied.

After a short break, the orchestra began playing again. "Oh, that's one of my favorites," June said. "May we dance this one?" They again danced in John's formal manner. They danced the second slow piece of the set, and then the orchestra began a fast piece. "Shall we?" John asked.

"Why not," June replied with a perky smile. John put away his handkerchief and they danced to the swing of the music. They both enjoyed it. At the conclusion of the music they returned to their table.

"You're a good dancer," June said. "You're very easy to follow."

"You're an excellent dancer," he responded. "It's no effort at all to dance with you." They continued talking and seemed completely at ease with each other.

The orchestra began the next set, and as they started down to the dance floor June said, "Keep your handkerchief in your pocket." They assumed their dancing positions and she moved in closer than arms length. Neither said much as they danced. Each found it pleasant to be in the company of the other. At the conclusion of the fast piece of that set, the orchestra leader announced that the orchestra would take a fifteen minute break.

"Let's step outside and get a breath of fresh air," John said. He led her the short distance to the tee box where they had ended their golf game that afternoon.

"Thank you for coming, June; I really am enjoying this evening with you."

"Thank you for inviting me; I'm enjoying it too."

They talked for a short time, then John said, " June, I don't want to be rude or stick my nose into your affairs, but I have to ask you, where is your fiancé this weekend?"

"His firm is holding a weekend retreat out at East Hampton with some of their best clients and he has to be there. Why do you ask?"

"I just wondered."

They strolled back to the ballroom and danced several more sets. They went back to the table and became involved in conversation and sat out the next set. June did much of the talking, usually in response to John's queries. He discovered that she had a good head on her shoulders and expressed herself well. He completely changed the opinion of her that he had yesterday. She would be an interesting date even if she weren't the best-looking woman in the ballroom.

As she talked away in response to something that John had said, he put his elbow on the table and rested his chin in the palm of his hand. He looked at June, interrupted her and said, "No, no, it's all wrong."

June sat up startled, and said, "What's wrong?"

"It's all wrong. It doesn't fit."

"What doesn't fit?" she asked with a quizzical look on her face.

" 'June'. It's wrong. It doesn't fit."

"What in the world are you talking about?" she demanded.

"You're not 'June,' you're 'Rebecca,'" he replied. He had a devilish grin on his face.

"I don't understand what you're talking about," she repeated.

"You. 'Rebecca' fits your personality much better than 'June' does. From now on you are 'Rebecca.'"

She looked at him quizzically and didn't know what to say.

"Come on, Rebecca, let's dance," he said as he arose from his chair. They went to the dance floor and danced the next set. By the second piece in the set, she had moved in closer to him. At the end of the evening she was dancing with her head resting on his shoulder.

At 11:30 John said, "Rebecca, if you're alone in your house this week-end, we should leave now so you can get home before it gets much later."

"I'm not alone. We have a couple who works for us and has an apartment in the south wing; they'll be home. But I'm ready to go if you are."

They drove back to his BOQ, and before Grady said good night he asked, "Are you going to church tomorrow?"

"Yes."

"Are you planning to go to the Episcopal church in Red Bank?"

"Yes. Why?"

"I wonder if you would join me in going to the service at the chapel here at Fort Monmouth? It starts at 11:00 o'clock, and it's a full Protestant service. None of your friends or neighbors will be there," he said with a grin.

"John Grady, there you go again!"

"What? What did I do?"

"You're trying to get me to go out with you again, that's what." Her pretense of being peeved with him was not too convincing.

"That's your fault, not mine," he replied. They looked at each other. "Thanks for a wonderful evening, Rebecca."

"John, for some reason you're able to get your way even though I know I shouldn't go out with you." They made plans to meet for morning services at the post chapel.

Sunday morning she showed up in her Woody at the chapel parking lot where Grady was waiting. She said to herself, "Never in my life have I supplied the transportation and chauffeured my date around. That's all I've done since I met this man. Why am I doing this?"

"Good morning, Rebecca."

"Good morning. Are you going to continue to call me Rebecca?"

"Yes ma'am. You are Rebecca, but unfortunately your parents got it all wrong when they started calling you June."

She shook her head at him. "You're hopeless."

"You look great this morning, Rebecca," he said as they walked into the chapel.

Each had a worshipful experience throughout the service. As they walked out of the chapel at the conclusion of the service, Rebecca asked herself, "How many men have I dated who invited me to worship with them? None, except John Grady. Is this guy for real?" She could not deny that she was hoping that he was.

"What do you have planned for the remainder of the day," John asked as they walked down the sidewalk from the chapel.

"Nothing. Mother and Daddy will be home about supper time."

"Rebecca, I'd like to take you to lunch somewhere, but you can't be seen with me in public, so I don't know what to suggest. If you don't have any other plans, we can grab a little something to eat at Scrivner Hall, the officers club here on the main post. They don't have a formal dining room, just a kind of lunch arrangement. It doesn't open until 12:30 on Sunday. We could go over to the club and wait in the lounge until it opens. This isn't much to offer, but I'd enjoy being with you. I don't want to impose on you, so please don't feel that you have to stay."

They walked a little farther, then she said, "I'll enjoy having lunch with you, John."

"It isn't far over to the club; can you walk over there in those shoes?" He was referring to the high-heel shoes that she had on.

"Oh yes."

They ambled over to Scrivner Hall and John showed her around the interior of the club. They went to the far corner of the lounge and sat in adjacent, dark leather chairs. They were alone in that part of the club. "This is very nice," Rebecca told him as she looked around. "You know, John, Fort Monmouth pretty much has been our hideaway these past three days. It's my fault that we've had to see each other 'on the sly.' I'm sorry."

"Please don't apologize. I invited you, I urged you, to meet with me and to do things with me, so I'm the one who started it. I knew that you were engaged.

"Rebecca, at our first meeting I thought that we wouldn't be seeing any more of each other. Then things between us started to improve at the golf game and I wanted to see you again. At first, I felt guilty asking you to go out with me, but after last night I don't feel guilty at all. I want to continue seeing you, Rebecca, but before any more time goes by you should decide whether you want to see me. If we need to stop this, let's do it now."

She leaned forward and looked at him with a troubled look on her face. "John, I'm just a 'dumb blond' who's getting things all mixed up. I don't want to be dishonest with anyone, and I'm uncomfortable having to be sneaky. I'd prefer that we could have met another way at a much earlier time. I'm not married yet, so I don't think I've committed any sin in seeing you. John, I try to be honest, just as you said you do." She paused and looked him in the eyes. " Yes, I want to see you in the future. I know it doesn't make sense, being engaged as I am." She sat back in the chair and looked at her hands on her lap. "Now this 'dumb blond' has spoken. And John, I don't know what to do next or how to go about it."

"Rebecca, I don't know what to tell you. You might want to tell your fiancé that you've met me. You could tell him that neither of you should make a mistake about marriage. Tell him to put the engagement on hold for a couple of weeks. You and I have to have some resolution of this, one way or another, in a couple of weeks. What do you think?"

"Oh, both our mothers would be hysterical if I tell them now. I just can't tell them now. I don't want to be deceptive, John, but you don't know them."

"Well then, I don't have enough imagination to think of anything for us to do except what we've been doing. I don't like it, but if you can't tell anyone I don't know what else we can do." He paused, then continued. "This much I'm sure of: I don't feel guilty about us seeing each other, and I really think that you have a right to see me if you want to. This situation didn't exist when you became engaged."

The lunch counter opened and John went over and ordered a couple of sandwiches and Cokes. He took them to a table and motioned for Rebecca to join him.

After a period of silence while they ate, Grady said, "Rebecca, let me tell you something, and you listen carefully. You are not a 'dumb blond,' and don't you let anyone treat you as though you are. Do you understand what I'm saying?"

She remained silent for a period of time, then she asked him, "John, you said you thought that we wouldn't be seeing each other after our first meeting. Why did you say that?"

He smiled at her. "I thought you were a spoiled rich kid."

"And what do you think now?"

"I think I was wrong."

"That doesn't tell me much."

"I want to spend as much time with you as I can. Does that tell you anything? Which brings up the subject of when we'll see each other again. I'll be in the field most of next week and won't be able to do anything. I'll be back to my BOQ about noon on Saturday."

She didn't know what "in the field" meant. He explained it to her.

"Will you be shooting guns and cannons and all those things," she asked.

"No, no. The Signal Corps is a support service. We mostly provide communication services to the higher headquarters of the units that do the shooting." He continued. "May I call you about 1:30 Saturday afternoon?"

"Oh no, don't call me; I'll have to call you."

"Do you still have my BOQ telephone number?"

She blushed. "Yes."

They finished their sandwiches and returned to the lounge and talked for a short while, then they leisurely strolled back to the post chapel and Rebecca's Woody.

"Thanks for coming, Rebecca. You are some kind of girl, you are."

CHAPTER 10. (22 AUGUST 1950)

At school on Tuesday, Grady's class and a number of other classes had preparatory instructions for the field exercise that would begin early Wednesday morning. The exercise was to provide communications for a simulated army command comprised of three corps engaged in a combat situation. It would be similar to the exercise that they had earlier in the summer except that this one would be about three times larger.

The first day and one-half of the field exercise were similar to the earlier exercise, except that more people were involved and Grady seemed to be busier than he had been in the first exercise. No one was getting much sleep. He had drawn the duty to be corporal-of-the-guard in the area security detail starting at 2200 hours Thursday night and continuing until 0200 hours Friday morning. He had free time from 1500 hours Thursday until his security detail started. A thunder storm had begun about 1530. Because he would be up with his security detail during the middle of the night, John decided to get some sleep. He wrapped himself in his shelter half and went under a large pine tree and tried to sleep. He got wet, so he went into the large army command-center tent and looked for a place where he could squeeze in among the many stretched-out student-officers who had arrived there before he did.

Many wires from other command posts to communications equipment in the tent entered the tent from various directions and ran along the ground under the mass of bodies. John spotted a void space in the mass of bodies and started for it just as a thunderous crash of lightening struck the ground just outside the tent. Electricity from that lightening bolt ran to the wires in the tent, and the men laying on the wires received electrical shocks. They popped straight up in the air. To John, they looked like popping kernels of popcorn in a hot skillet. A loud BANG came from a switchboard in the tent and a flash of light went off in the face of the switchboard operator. Men rose to standing positions with dazed looks and shook their heads.

John called out, "Is anyone hurt?" Some mumblings came back, "I'm O.K." None of those who had been lying on the ground was injured. John went over to the switchboard operator Clyde Williams, a classmate, who seemed dazed and immobile. "Are you all right Clyde?" Williams didn't answer. He was looking straight ahead with a frightened look on his face. Grady bent down and looked closely at Williams's face and bare chest. There were a number of red patches on his face and neck and around his eyes. John put his hand on Clyde's shoulder, looked at him face to face, and again asked, "Are you O.K., Clyde?" Williams looked at Grady and slowly worked out the words, "Yeah, I guess so." The red marks on Williams's face and neck seemed to be burn marks. A couple of other student-officers had come over to the switchboard by then. "Where are those medics and that ambulance parked?" John asked. "It's on the edge of that field down the road beyond the intersection," someone said. "Let's get Williams down there to have the medics look at his face," John directed. One of the student-officers volunteered to take him down. Another student-officer who was on the same detail with Williams sat down at the switchboard and inspected it closely.

"Check all your circuits to see if you still have contact with your command posts," John said. The new operator tried to make contact on each of the circuits. All circuits were dead. Grady stood up full height, turned toward the men milling about in the middle of the large tent and looked around until he spotted the man he was looking for. "Hey Sammy, we need your magic touch over here," he called. A short, muscular student-officer with black wavy hair turned around and came over to Grady. Sam Figetti and Grady had met at Fort Monmouth last summer, and both were among the few ROTC cadets selected to work in the Signal Corps Engineering Laboratories after ROTC summer camp was over. Sam was in the class behind Grady's in The Signal School. He had graduated in electrical engineering at Carnegie Tech and was a real fanatic about electricity and electronics. He would rather talk about electronics and amateur radio than eat—and he knew what he was talking about. He was a "ham" radio operator, and when he established his amateur radio station he didn't use store-bought equipment. He studied many circuit diagrams, decided what features he wanted, then designed and built his own radio transmitter and receiver.

"Sammy," Grady said as he put his hand on Figetti's shoulder, "it looks like this switchboard took a hit from that lightning bolt. All circuits to the command posts are out. Take a look at it and see what you can find."

Figetti's eyes lit up with anticipation. That was the kind of thing that he found challenging. He went behind the switchboard and took off the wooden back. He was oblivious to everyone around him. He didn't move a muscle as he studied the inside of the switchboard. He reached in and pulled out the fuse cartridge and examined it thoroughly. "This is an easy one," he said with a look of satisfaction on his face. "The fuse element has been vaporized by the lightning bolt. It did its job, though, it blew and protected the remainder of the equipment." Two spare fuses were inside the switchboard, so Sammy put a new fuse cartridge in the fuse holder. "Try your circuits now," he said to the operator. The operator ran his check; all circuits were live.

The field exercise ended late Saturday morning and the troops returned to the main post shortly after noon. John rushed to his BOQ, showered, and sat on the barracks front steps near the pay phone inside to await Rebecca's telephone call. He hoped that she would call at 1330 hours, as she had promised. At 1333 the pay phone rang, and Grady went inside and answered it. "BOQ 5. Lieutenant Grady speaking."

"John, it's me," she said in a hushed voice. "I can't talk long, and I can't see you this weekend. Dick is here until Sunday evening."

That news disappointed him. He had to think fast. "Rebecca, I'm going to the bible study class at the Methodist church in Red Bank on Wednesday evening. Can you meet me there at 7:00 o'clock? We can talk before and after the class. Please try to make it."

"I'll try. If I can't get there, I'll let you know. I really have to go now, John. Good-bye."

Grady went back to his room, laid down on his bunk and fell asleep. He woke up when Dan came into the room just before supper. They talked, then went to the mess hall.

After dinner, Grady went to his room and read the newspaper that Dan had brought with him. A front-page story reported that President Truman, acting as Commander in Chief of the armed forces, issued an order that the federal government would take over and operate the nation's railroads, effective at 4:00 p.m., Sunday, 27 August 1950. Two railroad workers' unions, The Brotherhood of Railroad Trainmen and the Order of Railway Conductors, had called a strike for 6:00 a.m. Monday morning. Steel mills had started to shut down in anticipation of the strike by the railroad workers. President Truman issued the takeover order "to protect the nation's security, defense and health."

"Good for Truman," John thought to himself. "I wonder how many GIs on the front line on the Pusan Perimeter have threatened to strike because they don't like the pay or the working conditions." He didn't care much for railroad conductors, anyhow. They had treated him like dirt when he was a teenage sailor traveling on railroads in World War II.

***

In Korea, Communist forces were making a major attack at Pohang in the north and at several other points on the Perimeter. The North Koreans still had an advantage in manpower, but UN forces were gaining strength. Our air force and navy were active. Navy destroyers were coming in close to shore and directing effective shellfire against North Korean forces trying to move down the East Coast toward Pusan.

There were reports that Communist China had massed two armies on the Manchuria-North Korea border.

CHAPTER 11. (30 AUGUST 1950)

Wednesday seemed a long time arriving. After the last class, John rushed through dinner, showered, put on civilian clothes that included a sport coat and tie, and rode the post shuttle bus to the West Gate and Highway 35 where he caught the public bus to Red Bank. He stepped off the bus at the Methodist church and waited at the front of the driveway for Rebecca. She drove the Woody onto the driveway and motioned for him to get in. She continued to the parking lot behind the church and parked at the far corner of the lot. They rolled down the windows and remained in the car.

"You look great tonight," he said with a smile. She wore a gray skirt and white blouse. As usual, she looked as though she had just stepped out of a fashion magazine. Grady didn't know how to continue the conversation. "What does one say to an engaged girl who works you in between visits by her fiancé," he thought. "How was your weekend?" he finally said. He couldn't think of anything else to say to her.

She completely ignored his question. "John, how much time do you have left?"

"We graduate two weeks from today. Chances are that I'll get orders that will take me from Fort Monmouth. Why do you ask?"

"Do you have plans for this weekend?" That weekend would be a long weekend because of the Labor Day holiday on Monday.

"No."

"John, my fiancé Dick will be spending the weekend at Toms River. My parents are going to a steeplechase event this weekend and will be staying with a college friend of Daddy's over near Princeton, and they expect me to go with them. But if we can see each other this weekend I'll stay home."

"Why aren't you going to Toms River with your fiancé?"

"He said that it was an investment seminar on alternative investments and he'll have very little free time. He said I would be bored to death."

"To answer your question, yes, you know I want to see you."

"I'm going to stay home."

"Rebecca, you are some kind of girl, you are."

"Oh John, you keep saying that. You embarrass me."

"I wouldn't say it if it weren't true," he said with a smile.

"John, I'm afraid to go into the church with you. There might be someone in there who knows me. What should we do?"

"Rebecca, there are worse places to be caught than in a bible study class. Let's go in and see what happens.

John led the way to a classroom and introduced Rebecca to the pastor and to the other bible students. Rebecca and John took seats at the table, and he whispered to her, "Do you see anyone you know?"

"No, thank goodness."

The pastor began the class with a prayer, and then they all took turns reading a paragraph or two of scripture starting at the thirteenth chapter of First Corinthians which is Saint Paul's famous lecture on Christian love. Rebecca and John sat close together sharing his small testament. After the reading, the pastor commented on the scripture and asked questions to stimulate discussion about it. Most class members participated in the discussion. Rebecca had a comment to contribute, but John was silent. After a little over an hour the pastor closed the discussion with a prayer. As they stood up to leave, the pastor and several class members invited Rebecca to join them again. The pastor said, "Would you like to join us for coffee and cookies in the kitchen.?"

"No thank you, we have to be on our way," John quickly replied. He said to Rebecca in a hushed voice, "Let's get out of here. Follow me."

As Rebecca and John walked to the Woody, Rebecca said, "That was good John, thank you for inviting me." She put her arm around his arm as they walked. She slid onto the driver's seat when they arrived at the car, but he stayed outside and said, "About the weekend, would you like to go to the movie at the post on Friday night? They show first-run movies. Then we can go over to Scrivner Hall and have some refreshments. We'll use our hideaway at Fort Monmouth," he joshed. "We can make plans there for the remainder of the weekend. How does that sound?"

"That sounds good."

"You shouldn't be too late getting home, so you had better leave now."

She agreed and drove off. Grady went out to the road and waited for a bus.

Friday evening John waited at the post theater for Rebecca to arrive. She showed up just about the time the movie was to start. She saw the billboard advertising the current feature and exclaimed, "Oh wonderful. Bob Hope in *Fancy Pants*. I've wanted to see that." Rebecca noticed the sign on the box office window that informed that the ticket price was twenty-five cents. "You can't beat that price," she said.

"You're a cheap date," he told her. "Two bits for this movie, and Wednesday it didn't cost anything to take you to the bible study class." She gave him a playful push with her shoulder as they walked into the theater.

They thoroughly enjoyed the movie and were in good spirits when they left the theater. They drove to Scrivner Hall and went into the lounge and sat in adjacent leather chairs in the far corner where they had sat during their earlier visit. John went to the bar and brought back two Cokes and a basket of snacks.

"You know, John, I didn't know a thing about the army before I met you. I must say that I'm favorably impressed with what I've seen so far."

"Fort Monmouth is a good post. It's a permanent post and an important one because it's the Home of the Signal Corps. You're seeing the best side of the army, but there are other places that are not so nice: Korea right now, for example"

"I was thinking about the people as much as the camp," she said.

"What about tomorrow?" he asked her. "What are your plans?

"I plan to spend tomorrow with you," she said without hesitation. "Let's get an early start. The time I spend with you seems to go by so quickly. What would you like to do?"

John was pleasantly surprised at her forwardness—and he continued to be confused. "Do you want to go to one of the beaches? They probably will be crowded because of the holiday, but the swimming and surfing still are good."

"John, I hate to be a wet blanket about going to any place in public, but I really have to be careful right now. I'm sorry to be like that."

"Rebecca, I'm confused. You seem to want to do things with me, but because you insist on preserving and protecting your engaged status I don't know what to think. I enjoy being with you, but if it doesn't mean anything more than just putting in time with you when your fiancé has other things to do, then I really ought to move on."

She put her hand on his arm. "Oh John, don't do that." She didn't know what to say further. Finally she said, "John, meeting you and getting to know you has happened so quickly and so unexpectedly that I'm confused also, and probably more than you are. It's been only two weeks since we met, and things have happened faster than I can sort them out. I never expected anything like this to happen to me." She was silent for a while. "John, I was engaged when we met, but you were completely free. We didn't begin our relationship from the same starting line, and I have hurdles to confront that you don't." She kept her hand on his arm and gripped it tighter. "John, I hope you never feel that you're just putting in time when we're together. I value our time together very much."

John put his hand over her hand. "Rebecca, forgive me, I'm impatient. I'm obsessed with time. I know that I probably have less than two weeks left, and I want everything to happen NOW. I'm like you: I never expected anything like this to happen to me, and I was not prepared to deal with it. Your analysis of our situation is absolutely correct: you do face hurdles that I don't. You did a wonderful job in analyzing our relationship." He paused and gently rubbed his hand over hers. "Rebecca, I don't know how our situation is going to work itself out, but let's not let it die because we're afraid to be bold."

Both were silent for a time. "Grab you coat. Let's get out of here," John said.

"Where are we going?"

"Follow me." He led her out to her Woody. "Do you mind going down to Ocean Grove?"

She looked at her watch. "No, I guess not. What are we going to do down there?"

Ocean Grove was a town, really mostly a summer community south of Asbury Park, that had some connection with the Methodist Church. The laws and regulations that governed the town would make John Wesley and Francis Asbury proud. For example, Ocean Grove prohibited the sale of alcoholic beverages and prohibited all automobile traffic on Sunday. Because of the restrictions, not too many young people hung out there when they went to the Jersey shore. But last summer Grady and a WVU friend he was with in summer camp found a small upscale summer hotel that had a lounge and dance floor. It usually was not crowded, and it had a juke box with all the current hits, so it was a good place to take a pick-up date to dance. It didn't have the "action" of some of the dance spots in Bradley Beach, for example, but it was nice.

Rebecca said, "Why don't you drive." On the drive down John told her where they were going. They arrived at 2230 hours and found the lounge fairly crowded due to the holiday weekend. John paid the modest cover charge, and they sat at a small table and ordered their usual Cokes. The music began and they started toward the small dance floor. "No hand-kerchief, please," Rebecca said. They danced several slow ones, then a fast one came up and they stayed on the floor and danced it. Both were good dancers and they worked well together and enjoyed it. They went back to their table, sipped their drinks, and talked. John found that as they became better acquainted Rebecca became more of a talker, and she didn't babble or talk nonsense. She had an active mind and seemed eager to talk with someone who seemed intelligent and responsive. And she wanted to know what Grady was thinking, and why.

They danced several more dances, fast ones and slow ones, then returned to the table. "We still haven't made plans for the remainder of the weekend," John said. "Tell me what you would like to do."

"I've been thinking," Rebecca said slowly. "You said, 'let's be bold,' then let's be bold. Let's spend the day at my house. How's that for boldness?"

"Wait a minute—hold the phone!" John exclaimed. "What are you talking about? You're the girl who's afraid to be seen with me, and now you're proposing going into the lion's den, so to speak."

"We'll be all right, John, trust me. Mother and Daddy are away; Sally and Harold Scott, the couple who works for us and lives there, will be visiting relatives this weekend; the maid won't be working tomorrow; and no one else will be there after the stable chores are completed about 9:00 o'clock. Otherwise, I'm all alone this weekend."

"What about your neighbors?"

"We'll be all right, believe me."

"Do you really want to do this, Rebecca?"

"Yes. I can show you around our property. I'll fix us lunch. We can have a walk in the woods, and we can ride if you want to. Let's do it. I'll pick you up at 10:00 o'clock."

John responded, "It's your neck that'll get wrung if we get caught. I'm game if you are."

"Then it's settled."

They danced several more dances. During a slow dance, Rebecca rested her cheek against John's.

They left the lounge at 2330 hours, and John drove them back to Fort Monmouth. He stepped out of the Woody at his BOQ, and Rebecca slid over to the driver' side. "I'm excited about tomorrow," she said.

Rebecca arrived at BOQ 5 at the appointed time on Saturday morning. Grady wore a pair of khaki trousers, polo shirt, and his combat boots under his trouser legs—the attire recommended by Rebecca last night. She wore a similar outfit, except for the combat boots. Again she asked him to drive. They traveled north on Highway 35, through Red Bank, across the Navesink River bridge, and north through Middletown. At an unmarked side road on the right, she told him to turn off onto a narrow, two-lane county road. They traveled a mile or so on the level winding road and then up and down low hills in the heavily wooded countryside. As they approached the crest of one hill, Rebecca said, "Slow down and turn in at the gate on the right." In front of them appeared a large gate of fancy ironwork extending between tall pillars of a stone wall that extended about ten yards on each side of the gate. A heavy growth of large rhododendron and mountain laurel bushes grew behind the stone wall, and tall evergreen and maple trees rose up from among the bushes. White fencing that enclosed much of the property joined the stone wall.

Rebecca stepped out of the car and went to a green post on the side of the driveway and inserted and turned a key in a key-operated electrical switch. The gates slowly parted. She returned to the Woody and said, "Go ahead, drive through and follow the road around to the right." The gates slowly closed behind them. Another grove of large rhododendron and laurel bushes grew among evergreens and maples a short distance in front of them. That grove blocked the view from the gate to the interior of the property. Grady drove about thirty yards to the right, and then the road made a sharp turn to the left around the growth of trees and shrubs that shielded the interior of the property. He turned to the left at a low speed and they came out into the open. "Will you look at that!" Grady said as he turned off the engine, opened the car door, and walked forward about ten feet. Immediately in front of him was one hundred and fifty to two hundred yards of green, closely-mowed hay or native grass, and sitting on a rise above that field was a large mansion house built of gray granite blocks and a slate roof. The mansion house had a large center section with transverse wings on each end. The landscaping around the house gave evidence of considerable thought having gone into it—it fit perfectly. To the left of the field of hay or grass was another large field that had a race course around it. Several types of horse jumps were in the infield of the race course. There were other things up by the mansion house, but he could not make out the details. He stood there with his hands on his hips staring and trying to take in all that was before him. Rebecca sat in the Woody. He shook his head slowly, then returned to the car. "Rebecca … I had no idea that—"

She interrupted him. "We can talk when we get up to the house. Let's go on."

The road continued along the right side of the green field and up a rise to the level of the house. As they came around the side of the house John realized that what he had seen from a distance was the rear of the house. The front of the house faced east toward the ocean and the rising sun. The front was elegant and had a circular driveway up to the covered front entrance. "Stop in front of the porch," she told him.

They stepped out of the car and walked onto the porch. She asked for the keys and opened the front door. They went inside and Grady looked around. "Rebecca," he said sheepishly, "I don't know what to say. This is magnificent; I'm out of my league."

"John, don't say that. A house doesn't determine what kind of person someone is. I don't think I'm the type of person who judges another person by the type of house he or she lives in. I hope you aren't."

"I can see why you weren't worried about neighbors seeing us here. There isn't another house for miles."

"Not quite. Come on, I'll show you the house." She took his hand and led him through the rooms on the first floor and explained how the family used each room if it was not apparent. They went outside and she told him, "Our property really is located in Middletown, but Grandfather always used the Hazlet post office for old times sake because his ancestors were the first settlers there and his father was postmaster there for decades. We've continued the custom."

Beyond the house on the north side was a formal garden with roses and other seasonal flowers in bloom. Two tennis courts and a swimming pool were beyond the garden, and beyond them was an orchard of fruit and nut trees. Rebecca led him to the front of the house where the land was cleared to afford an unobstructed view to the east.

"This is a magnificent home," John said. "I imagine that it was a wonderful place to grow up."

"It really was. I feel so fortunate to be able to live here."

"If you're hungry we can go in and fix a sandwich. After lunch, we'll go out to the barn and then take a walk."

"That sounds good to me."

They went to the large and well-equipped kitchen. Grady could see that it was well suited for entertaining. Rebecca went to the refrigerator and brought out a cooked ham, some sliced cheese, a head of lettuce, a tomato, a loaf of bread, and a quart of milk. "John, will you cut some ham for our sandwiches. Get one of those sharp knives in the holder over there on the counter." They worked together quite well preparing the sandwiches. When the sandwiches and milk were ready, Rebecca said, "Let's eat in the sun room." It was a bright, cheery room, and Rebecca talked while they ate.

After lunch they went out to the stable which was beyond the orchard and overlooked the race course. The stable included eight stalls, a large tack room, a feed storage area in addition to the hay stored overhead, and an office. The floor was concrete. Everything looked first class. Two good-looking horses were in adjacent stalls.

"They need some exercise," Rebecca said. "Help me get them out to the pasture." She talked him through the procedure of putting a halter and lead line on one horse while she did the same to the other one. They led the horses out of the barn, through one pasture and into another one. They turned the horses loose, closed the gate, and leaned against the rail as they watched the horses. "This was the polo field when Grandfather and Daddy played," she informed him. "Let's walk up to the woods; it's pretty up there." They walked through the pasture and entered a wooded area. Rebecca led him along a faint trace of a path to the highest elevation where they sat on a rock outcropping. Rebecca pointed to the east and said, "When the leaves are off the trees and on a very clear day you can see the ocean from here. Grandfather used to bring my sister and me up here when we were small."

"You've mentioned your grandfather several times; you must have been fond of him."

"Yes, he was an exceptional man. His family was all-important to him. He was a good businessman and had hundreds of friends. He bought the half-finished house and this undeveloped land for a song from a stock broker who went broke at the beginning of the depression, and he spent most of the remainder of his life improving it. You would have liked him if you knew him.

"Let's go around the side of the hill; I want to show you a cliff over there where my sister and I used to climb and play." They went about fifty yards and stood on the edge of a cliff about fifteen or twenty feet high. Their hands found each other and they held hands.

"It sounds as if you were a tomboy growing up," John said.

"Oh, I was. Mother used to get so upset with me. She tried to make me into a little lady, but you can see from the way I ended up that she failed."

"Someone did a good job rearing you, Rebecca: you're a fine person."

"Thank you, John, it's nice of you to say that." Each put an arm around the other's waist as they walked back to the rock outcropping where they talked a long time. They were on the same "wavelength" and talked about their lives, their beliefs, and their relationship. They were directly responsive to each other in their conversation—no babbling, no fluff, and neither one tried to impress the other with her/his worldliness or intelligence. They were two honest and intelligent people who were quite interested in each other. Each on her/his own came to the conclusion that, yes indeed, there just might be something very special here.

"Rebecca, do you want to go somewhere for a quiet dinner?" She seemed unenthused. "You don't want to go out in public, do you?"

"I really don't. I'm sorry. Why don't we stay here. Sally always has some surprises to eat in the refrigerator. But I warn you, I'm not much of a cook."

"I make a mean omelet," John said. "How about that? If you have some eggs, I can cut up some of that ham, and we can use the tomatoes and the cheese. You probably have an onion somewhere, and we can see what else we can find to throw in."

"That sounds great," she said enthusiastically.

Rebecca, I want to be away from here before dark. I don't like to see you here alone, but I shouldn't be in the house with you after dark. I wish you didn't have to drive me back to Fort Monmouth and then drive back home alone. I didn't know that you have had such a long drive to Fort Monmouth to meet me, and then drive back home after our date—and at night. I'm chagrined."

"I did it because I wanted to. Well, let's get moving; we have to get the horses back into their stalls first. "

They took care of the horses, washed up, and fixed two delicious omelets with toast and blackberry jelly. Again, they worked well together and enjoyed it. They left the house before dark.

On the drive back to Fort Monmouth John said, "Beck, I have a proposal for tomorrow. How about going to church at the post chapel again and then getting a bite to eat at Scrivner Hall. You can bring some casual clothes with you and change in the ladies lounge after we eat. We can drive out to old Fort Hancock on Sandy Hook and explore the old gun emplacements and then take a walk down on the beach. We'll be pretty much away from public places."

They spent Sunday as planned. It was not an exciting itinerary, but they enjoyed being together and never ran out of something to talk about. The day was hot and sultry—the Jersey coast at its worst in late summer. The only partial relief they had during the afternoon was the walk on the ocean beach where there was some slight movement of the hot humid air. It was after 1800 hours when they returned to the car from their walk. "Beck, we haven't planned for dinner; do you have any suggestions?"

"I would enjoy some Italian food tonight. There's a small Italian restaurant in Long Branch that I've been to once or twice. They used to have good food, and it's kind out of the way. Just the locals go there, mostly. Let's go there."

Grady drove to Long Branch, and Rebecca guided him to the restaurant after directing him down a couple of wrong streets. It was a one-story, wooden structure on the side of a tidal creek. They entered and whiffed the aroma of spices and strong cheese. The ambiance was more homey than one might have expected for an Italian-American restaurant on the Jersey shore. It had three rows of booths with high backs, rather subdued lighting, and a small dance floor in one corner overlooking the creek. The proprietress Momma Lucietta ushered Rebecca and John to a booth in the far corner. They accepted her recommendation to try the evening special of veal parmigiana. They went to the juke box and made several selections and danced a couple of slow pieces. They welcomed the opportunity to hold each other close, but it was warm—no question—it was warm. They returned to their booth and each downed a glass of ice tea . Their dinners arrived and they ate slowly, conversing the entire time. They cooled off somewhat with a dish of raspberry sherbet for dessert. They talked more and then tried to dance another slow one. They were about halfway through the piece when John looked at her and said, "Rebecca, as much as I enjoy holding you close, this heat and humidity make it a real chore to enjoy it."

"I agree." They went back to the booth.

"Beck, you have a long drive home, so we should get moving out of here." They held hands as they crossed the parking lot to get to the Woody. As they approached the car, Rebecca stopped and pulled on John's arm. He looked at her.

She had a devilish grin on her face and said, "How would you like to go swimming and cool off?"

"Where?"

"In the ocean."

"Where in the ocean?"

"I know a place where there's a high sea wall of huge boulders. The road runs on top of the boulders and you can't see the beach from up there. Come on, what do you say?"

"What will we do for swim suits?" he asked.

"Uh … uh … we'll swim in our underwear. You keep your distance from me; do you understand?"

"I understand. Are we sure we want to do this?"

"Yes. I'm about to die from the heat. Come on, you said that we should be bold—this is bold."

"You spoke a parable, girl—bold it is!"

It was dusk as they drove up the coastal road past Monmouth Beach and Sea Bright. The road was on a narrow causeway that had the ocean beach on the right and the Shrewsbury and Navesink rivers on the left. They passed a private beach club on the right and Rebecca said, "Slow down, I think we're getting close." They proceeded at a slow speed and then she said, "There, pull off into that space. Get close to the wall; I'll get out on your side." They parked the car and climbed about ten feet up the huge, brown-colored, cut-stone blocks stacked in tiers to form the causeway and a sea wall. Then they climbed down about twenty feet to get to the beach. It was a lovely crescent-shaped sandy beach. The moon was just a thin sliver and the sky was quite hazy, so it was dark.

Rebecca looked around and said, "I'm going up the beach about fifty yards and strip down to my underwear and then go into the water up to my neck. You stay here and do the same. Turn your back and don't look toward me until you're in the water. I'll call to you when it's O.K. for you to turn toward me. Do you understand?

"Yes ma'am."

They did as agreed. John was in the water up to his neck when he heard Rebecca call, "Its O.K. now." He turned around. She was about twenty yards from him. "This is better than sweltering in that heat and humidity, isn't it," she said.

"I can't argue with that," he replied. They both pushed off and swam with strong strokes out until the water was well over their heads. They swam around for a time, then moved toward shore until they were slowly bobbing up and down on their tiptoes. John held out his arms and moved toward her. She held up her arms and took his hands. They held hands and bobbed up and down as the waves passed under their chins.

"Rebecca, when we first met I never in the world imagined that we would be doing this in a little over two weeks."

"Nor I," she responded. "Maybe it's the time factor we're dealing with. We had better go in now. We'll follow the same procedure only in reverse. O.K.?"

"Roger," John said. They proceeded as planned. John was standing facing south and fully dressed except for his wet under shorts which he held in his hand. Rebecca called, "I'm ready. I'm coming down there, O.K.?" She arrived fully clothed except that she had her wet underclothes balled up in her hand. John held out his hand. She took it, looked at him and said, "John, I don't want you to think that I'm the kind of girl who would do this type of thing with anyone. I've never done this before, and I wouldn't have considered doing it with you if I didn't know that I could trust you completely. Thank you for being a perfect gentleman."

"I believe you, Beck. And I wouldn't have done it unless I knew that I could trust you completely. Thank you for being you." They moved closer. She looked up at him, and their lips met in the softest and sweetest kiss John ever knew. He put his arm around her and drew her closer. Their lips parted and they looked into each other's eyes. They kissed again. They looked at each other, then Rebecca put her cheek against his.

"Oh John, I have a problem—a big problem."

"I hope you have a problem, Beck. I would hate to think that we have the relationship I think we have and you wouldn't be troubled about your engagement and about me. I'll give anything to ease your problem for you." He placed his hand on the side of her face and gently kissed her forehead, then her lips. "Rebecca, I've never met a girl like you."

"John, it's so unfair that we didn't meet earlier. But right now I need help; will you help me?"

"Yes, of course. We'll work it out. Let's go over and sit on the wall." He put his arm around her waist and they walked through the sand toward the huge stone blocks. They climbed up to the second course of blocks and sat on what amounted to a deep stone bench. They sat close and leaned back against the next course of stone blocks which were warm from having been heated by the sun during the day. John took her hand. They kissed. "Beck, I want to be sure I know exactly what you're thinking. Tell me."

"I'm sure you know. I've never met a man like you, and I believe I have a right to know you better. John, I really want to. I don't want to think about marriage to Dick when you've become so important to me. But, there's terrific pressure on me."

"Rebecca, the only thing we can do is to be honest with ourselves and with everyone else. The facts are different now than they were when you became engaged. The facts are different, and the prospects of making a mistake by continuing the engagement have increased tremendously. It's foolish to continue playing the old game when the facts have changed drastically. I recommend that you tell your fiancé exactly what has happened, and tell him that it's wrong to continue the engagement when you don't know if you want to marry him. I'll go with you, but it has to be soon. Tell him that you need time to work this out. I can't imagine that he would want to continue with the engagement if he knows how you feel. I would think he would want you to be certain that you're doing the right thing."

"Dick isn't my only problem and probably not my biggest problem. John, how much time do I have to work this out? What's going to happen to you in the immediate future?"

"Rebecca, the chances are good that I'll go to Korea, but I'm not absolutely certain. I should get my orders within a week or ten days. If I go, I don't know how long I'll be gone. It depends on how long the war lasts. If the Communists kick us out of Korea, I can't imaging that the United States will just quit and come back home—that's not like us. I may be gone a year, maybe two, maybe more. I just don't know, Beck." He squeezed her hand. "Poor, sweet, lovely Rebecca, I've gotten you into a pickle, haven't I." He kissed the back of her hand. She looked at him, forced a smile, and rested her head against his.

"Rebecca, we can't go wrong being truthful. I'll help you any way you want me to; you should not have to shoulder this burden alone. Tell me what you want me to do."

"'Honest John'. You're my 'Honest John'." She kissed him. "You're right, I don't think there's any other way. Let me think about the best way to break the news. Do we have to decide that tonight?"

"No, but we should have it decided by tomorrow afternoon. Now, we had better leave so you can get started home." They kissed and reluctantly went back to the car and drove off. They made plans to meet at noon the next day at Gibbs Hall for the special Labor Day brunch.

✾✾✾

As Rebecca and John worshipped together Sunday morning, on an estate outside Princeton, N.J., Mrs. William R. Hazlet suffered with a mild case of food poisoning which most likely was caused by the catered food that she ate at the outdoor dinner party Saturday night. She told William that she didn't want to remain in Princeton another day feeling as poorly as she did, so they made their apologies and thanked their hosts and left for home shortly after 1100 hours.

✾✾✾

Monday, Labor Day, Grady studied until 1100 hours, then caught the shuttle bus to Gibbs Hall and waited in the lounge for Rebecca. He kept thinking about yesterday and about the decision that they had to make about how to proceed. Noon came and went, but Rebecca didn't arrived. She usually was punctual. Twelve-thirty hours came and went, then 1300 came and went. John was concerned. Has something happened to Rebecca? She should not be by herself out there in the country. If anything has happened to her he would feel responsible for keeping her out after dark. He went to the phone book and looked up her number in the directory and dialed. The phone rang five times, then a woman's voice said, "Hello." It was not Rebecca's voice.

Grady replied, "Hello, may I please speak with June Hazlet?" He figured that he should use the name June rather than Rebecca.

"Who is this?" the voice demanded.

"This is John Grady. May I speak with June, please?"

"She can't talk to you. Don't you call here any more." CLICK.

"Holy Toledo! Who the hell was that?" Maybe he called the wrong number. He checked the directory again. That had to be the Hazlets of Hazlet. Maybe he misdialed. He very carefully dialed again. After four rings the same woman's voice answered the phone.

"This is John Grady. May I please speak with June?"

"You again—I told you not to call here. Now stop bothering us!" CLICK.

"That has to be Rebecca's mother," John thought. "What's she doing there? She's not supposed to get home until later this afternoon. Poor Rebecca, I wonder what she's going through now with her mother? It has to be mighty unpleasant. How can I talk with her?" Grady had questions but no answers. "Maybe Rebecca will call me. Yes, she'll call to explain," he reasoned. He caught the next shuttle bus back to his BOQ.

The remainder of Labor Day was a drag for Grady. He could not get Rebecca out of his mind, and he could not think of a solution to contact her. If he had a car he would drive out there to see her, but her mother probably would call the police if he did. Rebecca's call never came.

CHAPTER 12. (5 SEPTEMBER 1950)

Just before lunch on Tuesday, Class 329 learned that its scheduled class at 1600 hours was canceled and in its place the members would meet in Building 302, the small auditorium where they had their indoctrination into The Signal School. As they left for lunch, Grady asked Kas Korjovic, "What's this class change about?"

"Damned if I know; they didn't tell me anything."

Shortly before 1600 hours, Class 329 assembled in Building 302, and at precisely 1600 hours Major Arthur Bowen walked into the room with a first lieutenant who had a bulging manila folder under one arm. Bowen went to the lectern in front, and the lieutenant took a seat behind him.

"Good afternoon, gentlemen," Bowen said with his customary smile. "As all of you are quite aware, your stay in The Signal School is quickly coming to an end. You will be leaving here for many parts of the world, and you have a number of personal matters to take care of before you leave here. Lieutenant Stills here has a printed sheet with most of your likely personal matters listed and whom you should see to take care of them. You will have time Friday afternoon and Monday to take care of your personal matters. If you absolutely need more time, it can be arranged.

"For all of you going overseas, and even for those of you who aren't, I urge you to be sure that you have an up-to-date Last Will and Testament. The Staff Judge Advocate's office will prepare one for you at no cost to you, so be certain that you stop there. Another important item is your insurance. Review your life insurance policies and be certain that your beneficiaries are the way you want them. If you need to close bank accounts, do it before you leave because it's inconvenient to take care of that matter after you're gone. If you need to store any personal goods, a couple of reliable storage companies are listed.

"One more thing I want to emphasize most strongly: do not leave town owing money to local merchants. You are leaving, but others are staying, and many more will come here. Don't give the army a bad name by being a deadbeat on your debts. Being a deadbeat on your bills will make it more difficult for others in the army to get along with the local people.

Bowen paused, then continued. "Gentlemen, the Department of the Army has issued orders for your duty assignments after graduation. Lieutenant Stills has copies of your orders and will pass them to you. When your name is called, please come forward and receive copies of your orders and the printed sheet that I spoke about. You are dismissed after you receive your orders. That is all I have. I wish you Godspeed and good luck."

"Wow! That was a surprise ," John said to himself. "I didn't expect orders today." He had butterflies in his stomach.

Lieutenant Stills stepped up to the lectern, placed his folder on it, and began calling names alphabetically. Bowen stepped back from the lectern, but did not leave the auditorium. As each officer received his written orders and walked toward the exit, Bowen nodded and smiled to him. John's name was called and he went up and received the paper and his printed orders. As he walked away, Bowen smiled at him and said, "Good luck to you, Lieutenant Grady."

"Thank you, Major Bowen." John was surprised that Bowen remembered his name considering how many student-officers there were in school.

John could feel his heart beating. He walked out the side door and stopped about twenty feet away. He looked at his orders. He had to work his way through them and decipher all the army jargon and abbreviations. Finally he found it—FECOM! In reality, that meant Korea. Actually, the orders stated that he was to report to the Army Port of Embarkation at Camp Stoneman, Pittsburg, California, on 25 September 1950 for transfer to the Far East Command. Graduation would be on 13 September, so that would give him twelve days for leave and travel. John looked up from his orders and his first thought was that he wanted Rebecca to know. But how?

Grady was in a somber mood. He walked back to his room, washed up, and went to dinner. He ate alone, then came back to his room and reclined on his cot. He didn't have to study because the next day his class and several others were going to Sea Girt, N.J., to fire MI carbine rifles on a rifle range. Sea Girt was down the coast from Fort Monmouth, so they would have an early breakfast and an early departure by bus. He thought about Rebecca. Surely she will call. She surely knew that he couldn't get through to her. He fell asleep.

The firing range at Sea Girt was a New Jersey National Guard facility on a rather small piece of land as military reservations go. The target pits were in an embankment that overlooked the ocean, and the firing positions for three different distances were to the west. John scored well and qualified without trouble.

After everyone had fired and the students had policed the area, they assembled down on the beach where a team of enlisted men was to demonstrate the construction and operation of a .30 caliber water-cooled machine gun and an air-cooled .50 caliber machine gun. The students gathered around the guns as the enlisted men went through their explanation of the construction and operation of the guns. The students then went back to the western edge of the beach and sat. The gunners fired the machine guns out into the ocean to demonstrate how machine gun crews operated.

At the conclusion of the firing, the student-officers loaded into buses and returned to Fort Monmouth. Grady went to the mess hall, and then to his room and showered. He wanted to call Rebecca, but he decided that it would be futile. He still hoped that she would contact him. She didn't.

Thursday, 7 September 50, Class 329 would go to Fort Dix, N.J., a recruit training center, to go through the Infiltration Course and the Close Combat Course. They would have an early departure and a long bus ride to Fort Dix. The training at Fort Dix would be the only quasi-realistic combat training that the students would receive, so Grady felt that in view of his orders it would be particularly important to him.

The bus entered the gate at Fort Dix and proceeded through the main part of the post and into a wooded area that had dirt roads. They came to a stop in a small parking area adjacent a dirt lane that led to the Infiltration Course. The men dismounted from the bus and walked to a large cleared area that was the Infiltration Course. The course was one big field of Jersey sand about seventy yards long and forty yards wide. The end of the course where the student-officers were waiting had a log-lined trench that extended across the width of the course. The trench was of the type Grady had seen in pictures of World War I trenches in France. The end of the trench nearest them was open to allow access to it.

The range officer standing on a wooden tower on one side of the course addressed the student-officers over a public address system and told them that they first would go through the course in a "dry run." That is, without live ammunition being fired overhead. They would go through the course a second time with a .30 caliber machine gun continuously firing live ammunition over them. They would return at night and go through the course a third time in the dark, again with the machine gun firing live ammunition over them. The range officer was quite deliberate and specific in telling them that they were to go "over the top" of the trench and hit the ground on their stomachs. They were to cradle their rifles in their arms and crawl across the first twenty-five yards keeping their bodies as close to the ground as they could get them. When they reached a horizontally-stretched net of barbed wire, they were to roll over onto their backs and crawl under and beyond the barbed wire. After exiting the barbed wire, they were to again roll over onto their stomachs and crawl into a fox hole where they would find practice hand grenades. They were to take a grenade and pull the pin, release the handle, then throw it into the ditch about ten yards ahead of them. The practice grenades had tiny concussion devices in them that would go off with a "pop." After that, the students were to hurl themselves into the concluding ditch with an aggressive action.

The student-officers filed into the trench. The whistle blew and they went over the top and hit the ground on their stomachs. The dry run was rather uneventful for Grady except that he had sand all over him and throughout his clothing. The second run with the machine gun firing live ammunition didn't bother him even though he could see the tracer bullets streaming overhead.

The students boarded the bus and went to the Close Combat Course. That course was in a wooded area, and targets in the shape of a human body would suddenly appear from behind fallen logs, trees, bushes, and a couple of log bunkers hidden by bushes. Each officer was issued a fixed number of specifically-colored bullets that he fired at the targets as he walked through the course. The staff manning the course inspected the targets after each small group of students went through the course and recorded the colors of the bullet holes in the targets to determine how many hits an individual made on the targets. Grady scored well but was squeamish about firing at man-shaped targets.

On the return trip to Fort Monmouth, John thought about how he might contact Rebecca but realized that he would get back much too late to even attempt it. He resolved to call her the next day, no matter what. He couldn't understand why Rebecca hadn't called him. At the very least, good manners dictated that she contact him and offer some explanation.

She certainly had manners and good upbringing. He just could not understand.

Class 329 reported to the pistol range at Fort Monmouth on Friday morning to fire the Colt .45 pistol for qualification. The Colt .45 pistol was the official sidearm for army officers, but John didn't like it and hoped that he never would be in a situation where his life depended on him having to use it. It was big, bulky, and heavy. John was a good-sized man, but he couldn't hold the pistol steady enough to get good aim with it. When it came his turn to fire, he struggled with the damn thing but did manage to qualify.

Grady finished at the pistol range by 1030 hours and had the remainder of the day free to take care of personal matters. He went to the pay telephone in his BOQ and dialed Rebecca. A woman's voice answered the phone. It wasn't Rebecca, and it wasn't that other woman whom he presumed to be Rebecca's mother. "Hello, this is John Grady. May I please speak with June?"

"I'm sorry, but she's not in," the woman said in a slight southern accent.

"I really must talk with her." He took a chance. "Is this Sally?"

"Yes. How did you know?"

"Rebecca, uh I mean June, told me about you; she's very fond of you. Sally, please listen to me—I need your help. I'm in the army and I'm going away, and I must talk with June before I leave. Can't you get her to the phone now, or later?"

"I'm sorry, sir, but June and Mrs. Hazlet have gone out of town."

"When did they leave?"

"Two days ago."

"Where did they go?"

"I'm sorry, sir, but I can't tell you that. I have instructions from Mrs. Hazlet."

"Do you have a telephone number where I can reach June?"

"I'm sorry, but I can't give you that either. I'm sorry, Mr. Grady, but I have my instructions."

"When will they return home."

"Mr. Grady, please understand that I can't tell you anything."

"I understand. But Sally, you must do one thing for me. Please tell June that I'm going to Korea. You can tell her that without Mrs. Hazlet knowing, can't you? Please, Sally, I believe June wants to know. Just tell her this one thing, that's all: I'm going to Korea."

"I will try," Mr. Grady.

"Please give her that message, Sally."

"I believe I can."

"Thank you, Sally, I appreciate it very much."

John now understood why Rebecca had not called. She must be a virtual prisoner of her mother. He asked himself, "But Rebecca is a bright and intelligent adult; why does she allow her mother to dominate her so?"

Grady called a local moving and storage company and arranged to have his large, old, heavy suitcase containing his civilian clothes stored in their warehouse. He went to the Staff Judge Advocate's office and had his Last Will and Testament made out. He had no close relatives, so he left whatever estate he might have to the Salvation Army. It was a moot point because he lived from paycheck to paycheck, except for a small savings account. He already had named the Salvation Army the beneficiary of his Veterans Administration World War II life insurance policy, so nothing needed to be done there. So far as he could think, except for arranging his transportation to the West Coast, all his personal matters were in order.

After lunch John went over to the newspaper vending machines and purchased copies of several New York newspapers to look at airline advertisements. He went to his room and looked at the ads. North American Airlines was flying from La Guardia or Newark airports to Los Angles or San Francisco for eighty-eight dollars on a four-engine plane or seventy-two dollars on a two-engine plane. The flights were the one-stop, overnight "Red Eye" flights. Compared with the prices that the major airlines were asking the prices looked good. He would make his reservation as soon as he decided which day he wanted to travel.

Saturday morning, 9 September 1950, John went to breakfast, then he returned to his room and began packing his civilian clothes into his large, old, heavy suitcase so that it would be ready for the storage company on Monday morning. After that he bought a copy of the newspaper and read that fighting on the Pusan Perimeter was characterized by local attacks by each side. The North Koreans continued to bring in reinforcements of men and armor. UN forces were trying to gain some key positions in anticipation of the Communist all-out offensive. He noticed that the New York newspapers printed only the combat causalities from New

York, New Jersey, and Connecticut in the official causality list that they published each day. Previously, the paper had published the entire list of causalities from all the states, but that entire list had become too long.

In other news, President Truman approved "substantial increases" in the strength of the United States forces stationed in Western Europe. Communist aggression in Korea had caused the free world to wake up and face the worldwide threat of Communist expansion. Western European nations, lead by the United States, were taking defensive measures.

Grady decided that since he had no family to visit he would leave for the West Coast after graduation and spend a few days in San Francisco before going overseas. He would save money by staying at the BOQ at Camp Stoneman and commuting into San Francisco. Graduation would be Wednesday, 13 September 1950. He wanted one day to check out of Fort Monmouth at his leisure, so he would make reservations to fly to San Francisco on Friday, 15 September 1950, provided he could get the cheap reservations he saw advertised in the newspaper.

Grady called North American Airlines Monday morning and made the Friday night reservation he wanted. The flight would depart Newark airport Friday night at 2200 hours. The truck from the storage company came at 1030 and took his trunk. He went to the bank and withdrew all but fifty dollars from his account. He left that money in the account as something to draw on when, and if, he returned to the States. By default, Fort Monmouth had become his home. That took care of everything remaining he had to do except for checking out of the post. He enjoyed not having anything to do for the rest of that day, so he went to the post library after lunch and read some magazines and out-of-town newspapers. Late in the afternoon he walked to Scrivner Hall and had a bourbon and soda. It tasted pretty good, so he had another one. He thought about Rebecca. He concluded that both time and Rebecca had run out on him. John went to bed that night feeling freed from Rebecca and at peace with himself.

***

One big event would take place on Tuesday, the last day of classes, and Grady had been apprehensive about it ever since he woke up that morning: final class standings would be announced. The standings were posted on the bulletin board at 1100. Grady was first in academic standing for the third trimester of the course and first in final average for the full course.

He could not believe it—he had accomplished it! He had increased the spread between his average and that of Korjovic who finished second.

Kas came up to John, shook his hand and said, "Congratulations John, you did it. I tried my best to catch you, but you wouldn't let me. Nice going."

They talked for a while, then John said, "Kas, I've enjoyed getting to know you. Take care of yourself and the best of luck to you." They shook hands again.

"The same to you, John."

Graduation was at 1000 hours on Wednesday in building 302. The class sat in the student chairs, and Colonel Willis B. Bottoms, Director, The Signal School, Officers Division, and Major Arthur L. Bowen, Secretary, sat on the stage. Bottoms spoke first and summarized what they had accomplished during the past twelve weeks and addressed what they might expect in the future—Korea being very much the subject of his remarks. Bowen spoke about the responsibilities they had as Signal Corps officers.

Bowen announced that Colonel Bottoms would present each of them a diploma signifying successful completion of the Associate Signal Company Officers Course. The diplomas were awarded in the order of class standing. Bowen called Grady's name first and handed the diploma to Bottoms. John walked forward and Bottoms handed him a rolled-up, printed diploma that had an orange ribbon tied around it. As John received his diploma, Bottoms said, "Congratulations, Lieutenant Grady. Good work."

At the conclusion of the graduation ceremony many of the class members stood outside Building 302 talking and saying farewells. Major Bowen came out of the building with Colonel Bottoms, said something to him, and then scanned through the graduates congregated outside. He saw Grady and walked over to him. All of the young officers talking with Grady saluted and greeted the major as he approached.

Bowen said softly, "Lieutenant Grady, may I see you in my office at 1330?"

"Yes sir."

"What did you do now, Grady?" one of his classmates said.

"They found those crib notes he used throughout the course," another classmate said. They all laughed. They shook hands, said good-bye, and went their separate ways. Most men intended to clear the post immediately and go on leave. Grady went back to his room, washed up, and went to lunch.

Grady walked into Major Bowen's outer office at 1330. The civilian secretary showed him into the major's office. "Lieutenant Grady reporting as ordered, sir," Grady announced as he held a stiff salute.

The major returned the salute and said, "Please have a chair, Lieutenant."

"Thank you, sir."

"Lieutenant Grady, I wanted to talk with you just briefly. I hope I'm not delaying your departure."

"No sir, not at all."

"John, you have compiled a fine record at The Signal School. Academically, you earned one of the highest averages we've seen in some time, and you did well in the field exercises and in the weapons training. You showed promising leadership qualities, and you got along well with your classmates. We always are happy to get young officers such as you. You're Regular Army, John, what are your plans for the future? Do you intend to make the army a career?"

"Sir, right now I honestly don't know. I'm not looking ahead any farther than my assignment to the Far East. I have respect for the army and for the officers whom I've had contact with. In particular, I'm impressed with the competence and dedication of the senior officers. I suspect that I'll be better able to give an answer to your question after a year or so of active duty."

"John, the army can be a good and satisfying career. I've found it to be so. The army needs men such as you, and I urge you to consider the possibility of an army career.

"John, work hard when you go to your next assignment. Because you're a Regular, your superior officers will be watching you. Keep up your hard work and I'm sure you'll do well.

"The Signal Corps is not so awfully big, John, and our paths may cross again. If I ever can do anything for you, please let me know." With that, Bowen stood up and held out his hand. John stood, extended his hand, and shook Bowen's.

John replied, "Thank you, sir, I appreciate very much your interest. I'll keep in mind what you said." While walking back to his BOQ, Grady said to himself, "That was real nice of Major Bowen. He didn't have to do that."

John went over to Scrivner Hall before dinner and sipped a bourbon and soda as he read the newspaper. The big news was that President Truman had replaced Louis Johnson, the Secretary of Defense, with General George C. Marshall. Grady did not like to see his fellow West Virginian, Johnson, leave office, but he knew that General Marshall was a fine man who had done an outstanding job of directing the worldwide U.S. military effort during World War II.

BOOK TWO

CHAPTER 1 . (15 SEPTEMBER 1950)

Grady was up very early Friday morning. In southern West Virginia they call it being "journey proud." That is, being anxious about an immediately pending journey. After breakfast, he bought the morning newspaper and read absolutely startling news from Korea! United States and South Korean Marines had made an amphibious landing in force at Inchon, the port for Seoul, on the West Coast of South Korea. The landing was approximately twenty miles from Seoul and about one hundred fifty miles behind the Communist lines at the Pusan Perimeter. Other South Korean troops made an amphibious landing behind enemy lines on the East Coast. The U.S. Marines were moving out from Inchon toward Seoul and Kimpo airfield, a major airfield outside Seoul. Heavy air and naval bombardments preceded and accompanied both landings. This certainly was a dramatic turn of events. "That Douglas MacArthur is a genius at warfare," John thought.

***

After lunch, John rode the post shuttle bus out to the West Gate and Highway 35 where he caught the Greyhound bus to Newark. As the bus passed through Middletown, he saw the side road that led to Rebecca's house. "Too bad we didn't meet earlier," he thought. "But that failed affair is behind me, and I have other things to think about now."

At the Newark bus station he boarded a local bus to the Newark Airport. He went to the North American Airlines counter and paid for his ticket and checked his duffel bag. The flight was uneventful and long. The stewardess made her announcement about their decent into San Francisco, and the plane flew down the glide slope and made a smooth touchdown. Grady went to the baggage claim area and claimed his duffel bag, then he went to the men's room and washed and shaved. He went out into the terminal and located the Military Assistance desk and learned that an army shuttle bus to Camp Stoneman would leave the airport at 1145 hours.

John wondered whether he ought to go into San Francisco and get a hotel room for a couple of days. But that would add up to a good bit of money, and he could stay at the army BOQ for very little money. He once heard someone say, *Once poor, you always think poor.* John guessed that he always would "think poor." He would get a billet at the BOQ as a transient officer and take a bus into San Francisco each day. He figured that he had more time than money.

About thirty-five personnel of various ranks gathered at the Military Assistance desk at 1145 hours and loaded into a large army bus that headed north in heavy traffic. They arrived at the Stoneman bus terminal and John retrieved his duffel bag. He saw a civilian who appeared to be acting as a dispatcher and went over to him and inquired where he should go.

"You want to take bus number seven," the dispatcher said. "Get off at the fourth stop at the big wooden building on the right. Number seven will be along in ten minutes." Number seven bus arrived and Grady rode it to the fourth stop. He walked up the sidewalk to the entrance of a very large building of the Quonset Hut style. He walked through the vestibule, through another set of doors and into the cavernous interior. A platform about six inches off the floor was on the far side of the hall, and a couple of desks were on the platform. A captain sat at a desk at the front of the platform, and an enlisted man sat at a desk on one side of the platform. Grady went up to the captain's desk which had a nameplate on it, "Captain A.M. Small QC."

"Captain, I'm Lieutenant John Grady. I have orders—"

"Go sign in on that register over there on the table by the wall," the captain interrupted, "then report back to me." Grady signed in and went back to the captain's desk.

"Sir, I want to get a billet at the BOQ until—"

"Lieutenant, you will do what I tell you to do," Small interrupted again. "Give me a copy of your orders." John wondered what was the matter with this guy. Was he trying to prove that he was a tough guy? Grady set his handbag down, unzipped it, and dug out his orders and handed a copy to the captain. Small looked over the orders and told him to have a seat over to one side where there were about one hundred fifty steel folding chairs. He told Grady to wait until his name was called.

"Captain, I don't officially report in until the 25th. I'm here now as a transient."

"Lieutenant, when you log in on my register you're here for duty. Now go have a seat like I told you."

"With due respect, Captain, I have written orders ordering me to report in on the 25th."

"You just reported in," the captain replied with a smirk on his face.

Grady's face became scarlet red, and his reply was slow and measured. "Captain, I have written orders signed by a major general ordering me to report on the 25th. The last time I heard about such things the written orders of a major general took precedence over the oral orders of a captain." With that, John snatched the copy of his orders off Small's desk, picked up his bags, did an about face, and headed for the exit. He was steaming mad as he walked out the front door and looked around. He saw a bus stop across the street, so he crossed over, set his bags down, and waited for the next bus. He didn't care where it was going—he was getting the hell out of there.

He had waited about ten minutes when he saw an olive-drab Chevrolet sedan coming slowly down the street on his right. It stopped on the opposite side of the street about twenty yards from where John was standing. Two husky military policemen stepped out of the car and stood near its front. The one who had been driving was a sergeant first class and the other one was a buck sergeant. The sergeant first class said something to the other man, then they slowly crossed the street to where John was standing.

"Good afternoon, Lieutenant," the sergeant first class said. "Sir, may I please see your orders?"

"Why do you want to see my orders?"

"Sir, Captain Small asked us to look for a Second Lieutenant Grady, and we was wondering if you might be the lieutenant."

"Sergeant, I have nothing to do with Captain Small. I have written orders to report in here on 25 September. I'm leaving here now and reporting in when my orders say to report in."

"Sir, may I please see your orders? I'm ordered to find Lieutenant Grady and take him to Captain Small, and that's what I'm going to do, Lieutenant." With that, the sergeant first class nodded to the buck sergeant behind him and the two of them took positions immediately in front of Grady.

"This is one sweet pickle of a mess," Grady said to himself. He certainly couldn't get into a fistfight with the MPs. No matter how correct he was on the matter at issue with Small, he never could satisfactorily explain a fight with two military policemen. That would be one hell of a way to start an army career!

"Yes, I'm Grady."

"Thank you, sir. Will you please bring your gear and come with us to see Captain Small." The three of them crossed the street, entered the large building, and approached Small's desk. The two MPs stood back as Grady went up to the desk.

"Welcome back, Grady," Small said with a smirk. "Give me your orders and go over there and sit down." John pulled out his orders again, gave a copy to Small, picked up his bags, and walked over to the folding chairs. Small motioned to the two MPs. They had a brief conversation, then one MP took a seat near the exit door at the back of the section of folding chairs.

About half of the folding chairs were occupied. John sat down a couple of seats away from a first lieutenant, Corps of Engineers. The engineer leaned over and said, "Have a little trouble with 'Little Caesar' over there, did you?"

"I don't know what's the matter with that guy. He seems to be power-drunk on his captain's bars," John said. "I'm not even supposed to be here. Who the hell is he?"

"He's a RETREAD, a Quartermaster Corps (QC) reservist called back to active duty. He's trying to make an impression here to show us how tough it was in the old army during World War II, I guess. He has quite a reputation around here. He can't get along with anyone. This is my second day here, and so far as I can see, he's done nothing but cause trouble." The engineer then introduced himself and John reciprocated. They talked.

At 1715 hours the enlisted man on Small's platform made an announcement on the public address system that the men waiting in the chairs would go to the mess hall next door and then report back at 1900 hours with bags and baggage. Grady and the engineer followed the crowd into the mess hall. It was raining lightly. John and the engineer finished their dinners, freshened-up, and walked back into the large hall. Grady noticed one MP trailing behind him and then sitting at the back of the section of folding chairs. At 1900 hours, Small's corporal announced that he would call out a list of names and that everyone called would leave there by bus and travel to Travis Air Force Base to board an airplane and fly to Japan. The corporal called Grady's name and the engineer's along with most of the others waiting in the room. Grady could not believe what was happening to him. He was supposed to be on leave, but here he was shipping out to the Orient! He felt as if he were being Shanghaied. In fact, he was—by Captain A.M. Small QC.

On reflection, Grady realized that he had been just plain dumb to come to Camp Stoneman before the 25th. He could not get away from thinking poor. "So, I would have spent some money if I had stayed in San Francisco," he told himself. "Big deal! What good is money going to be to me where I'm going?" He castigated himself that he should be looking for desired end results and never lose sight of the ultimate goal. Saving a few bucks was not the primary reason he had come to California early. Dumb, dumb, dumb.

At 1930 hours the waiting men lined up and went out a side door, each calling his name to a corporal who checked it off on the detachment list on his clipboard. Grady and the engineer sat together on the bus and talked some. It was raining harder and getting dark. He slept during most of the bus trip. Once inside the terminal at Travis they received instructions from an air force officer on their loading procedure and flight schedule. They took seats and waited. They boarded the plane at 2230 hours, and Grady and his engineer friend sat together. The plane was a chartered United Airlines DC-4, and United pilots and stewardesses made up the flight crew. The plane departed the terminal and taxied to the end of a runway. It then hurled down the runway and up into the rain and blackness of the night. Both John and his friend slept, as did most of the men. They stopped at an air force base in Alaska to refuel the plane. The men departed the plane and ate a hot meal in a nearby mess hall. They soon assembled and reboarded the plane which took off and quickly climbed high above the cloud cover.

***

John's thoughts wandered to what lay ahead for him. He resolved that he would give his utmost to meet the new challenge, and he asked God to give him strength and courage to do his duty. He prayed that if it be God's will that He protect him. Unashamedly, John believed that there was a God and Creator. He had attended church regularly when he was growing up, but mostly because his father attended and expected John to attend. John really didn't think too deeply about God and creation until he was in college after his navy service in World War II. He took a course in Ana-

lytical Geometry and by the end of the term he found that when he looked
at some mathematical equations he could draw the plot, or graph, of the
equation, and he could look at some curves or plots and write the equations. John began to suspect that there was some plan behind this physical
world. When he studied Calculus, he was amazed how physical events
and relationships were explained and investigated by the use of Calculus.
He saw the same thing in physics courses, and even more so in electrical
engineering courses. He came to the conclusion that there was a created
law and order to this universe. He did not believe that human life on earth
was the result of a succession of fortuitous anomalies that had slithered out
of the primordial soup. The formal arguments of *Creation vs. Evolution* were
not important to John. He believed that there was no validity whatsoever
to the proposition that science refutes the notion of a Creator. The more
science John learned the more his belief in a Creator was confirmed.

***

The United Airlines charter landed at Haneda U.S. Air Force Base
outside Tokyo. The entire detachment traveled by busses to the Reception
Center at Camp Drake, also outside Tokyo. The officers were assigned
billets, were told where the mess hall was, and were told to report back
at 0800 in the morning. Grady returned to the Reception Center after
breakfast the next morning. A sergeant called twenty-five officers, including Grady, to the main desk and told them that early the next morning they
would travel south by train to the port of Sasebo. He told them to report
with bags and baggage to that same desk tomorrow morning at 0700.

"I need to get some cigarettes," Grady said to the sergeant. "Where's
the PX?" Grady walked to the PX and bought a half-dozen packs, and
he bought a newspaper to find out what was happening in the war. Up in
the Inchon landing area on the West Coast, marines of the 1st Marine
Division had captured Kimpo Airfield and had reached the Han River
west of Seoul. They were maneuvering for an attack on Yongdungp'o, the
industrial suburb on the western side of the Han. The U.S. 7th Infantry
Division was landing at Inchon.

At the Pusan Perimeter on the East Coast, U.S. forces were shifting
from defense to offense. The 38th Infantry Regiment of the 2nd Infantry
Division had fought its way across the Naktong River and had secured a
bridgehead. The 5th Regimental Combat Team and other U.S. units were

making advances against stubborn and suicidal resistance by North Korean troops. Casualties were high on both sides.

The next morning at 0700, an army bus took John and the group of officers to the train station in Tokyo where they went through a gate and onto a platform adjacent a waiting train. A Japanese railroad trainman led them to a coach, and they stowed their gear on the overhead racks. They sat up for the entire trip to Sasebo.

They arrived at the replacement depot in Sasebo on 21 September. The officers received billet assignments and were informed that duty-assignment processing would begin promptly at 0800 the next day. At the processing the next morning, a sergeant collected the personnel files from the officers and left the room. A short time later, a first lieutenant in the Adjutant General Corps called Grady to an interview booth. The lieutenant greeted Grady outside the booth with a smile and firm handshake and invited him to take the seat in front of a small field desk inside. The lieutenant introduced himself as Tom Winter. He opened John's file and began to read it in silence. Several times he nodded his head slightly and pursed his lips. Winter closed the file, looked at John and said, "Grady, I'm sending you to the Signal Section, Headquarters Eighth Army. They can use a man with your background."

"Where is that Signal Section located?"

"Yokohama."

"That will mean duty in Japan rather than Korea?"

"Right," Winter responded with a smile.

Grady was a little unsettled in his thinking about duty in Japan rather than going over to Korea. That was something he had not previously considered. Grady surprised himself that he said this—it just kind of popped out—but he said to Winter, "Lieutenant, I haven't thought about staying in Japan; the big show is going on in Korea. I didn't get into World War II until it was almost over, and except for several months on a destroyer that was doing radar picket duty in the Western Pacific, I just about missed that war. A number of my friends and the older guys in my neighborhood made substantial contributions to winning that war, and I've always felt a little guilty that I didn't do more. In life we seldom get a second chance; this may be my second chance, so if you can send me to a Signal outfit in Korea I surely will appreciate it." Grady felt kind of silly having said it, but that was how he felt. He figured that he would not pass that way again so he had better make the most of it while he had the opportunity. He didn't want to live the rest of his life thinking that he hadn't done his share.

"Sure, if you want to go over to Korea, I can arrange that. I'll send you to Signal Section, Headquarters Tenth Corps that already is in Korea, and they can put you where they need you. How does that sound?"

"That's fine with me." John wondered if he had done the right thing. "Maybe I'm a fool," he thought. "Still, I'm in the Signal Corps so it's not like I'm volunteering for combat."

Winter addressed Grady, "You'll get transportation over to Inchon as soon as it can be arranged. We'll cut orders for your assignment and you can pick them up downstairs tomorrow morning." That afternoon Grady and others went to a Quartermaster warehouse where they drew the gear that they needed for entering the combat zone. That included a steel helmet and liner, a pistol belt with that damnable Colt .45 caliber pistol, a cartridge pouch, a first aid kit, a canteen, and a mess kit which he hoped he wouldn't have to use (he hated to eat out of the damned things because he was guaranteed to get a case of "the runs" if he hadn't scrubbed it absolutely hygienically clean after eating a previous meal out of it.)

The next morning, the processing personnel told John to stand by until they could schedule him for transportation over to Korea. After waiting for some time, Grady and other officers climbed onto trucks and rode to a pier where they boarded a Landing Ship Tank (LST). Parts of two Engineer companies of a heavy construction battalion already were on the LST. An hour later the ship's crew raised the loading ramp and closed the bow. The LST backed away from the pier, turned, and proceed slowly out the harbor. Two other LSTs joined them, and a navy destroyer appeared and took up an escorting position when they reached open water.

They sailed around the southern tip of the Korean peninsula and were in the Yellow Sea off the West Coast of South Korea when the LSTs reduced speed and began slowly circling. The height of the water in Inchon Harbor varied approximately thirty feet between high and low tides at that time of year, and at low tide a portion of the harbor was nothing but mud flats. The LSTs waited for a higher tide to make their landing.

Those variations in water levels between high and low tides at Inchon were among the greatest in the world and was the reason why no one except General MacArthur ever considered making an amphibious landing there. The North Koreans had not prepared much in the way of defenses at Inchon because they considered that a landing there was unlikely. But MacArthur's boldness and the U.S. Navy's and U.S. Marine Corps's skills at amphibious landings accomplished the near impossible.

An hour later Grady felt and heard the LST's propeller increase revolutions, and they broke out from the circling pattern and headed for Inchon. The ship arrived at the harbor and John saw several LSTs and a couple of cargo ships unloading. He saw the destruction caused by the naval and air bombardment of Wolmi-do Island in the harbor, and of the shore facilities at Inchon.

The LST ran in toward the beach as far as it could go, then its bow opened and its ramp dropped into mud. Grady and the rest of the supernumeraries descended a ladder (a set of stairs) from the upper deck and walked down the ramp. A navy boatswain mate told them to check with the beachmaster on the beach after they were beyond the sea wall. An Infantry major in the group led the way through the mud and over a break in the sea wall that was the result of a direct hit by a large naval shell.

A navy lieutenant commander came out of the beachmaster's tent. The major introduced himself and asked, "Where do we get transportation to Tenth Corps Headquarters?"

"Major, every vehicle on the beach is in use taking supplies forward to the marines and the 7th Division. Tenth Corps Headquarters is up in Ascom City. You can walk or you can hitch rides on trucks."

They hitched rides and arrived in Ascom City where they received directions to X Corps Headquarters. Grady received directions to the Signal Section and set off to find it. It was in the city telephone exchange building. "That figures," Grady said to himself. He passed two sentries in front of the building, walked up a couple of steps, and entered the lobby. A corporal at an army switchboard and another one at a desk made out of equipment packing boxes were on the right side of the lobby. Field wires from the switchboard passed through an open window to the outside.

"Corporal, where can I find the officer in charge," Grady asked the corporal at the desk.

"The colonel is gone, but Captain Walker is in that office across the hall."

John walked across the lobby and through the open door into the office. A sergeant sat at a desk near the door, and a Signal Corps captain sat at another desk on one side of the room.

"I'm John Grady. I have orders to report to Signal Section, Headquarters Tenth Corps," he said to the sergeant.

The captain turned in his chair, looked John over and said, "Come on in, Lieutenant. Come over here and have a seat." The captain rose and extended his hand. "I'm Phil Walker; glad to meet you. Where did you come from, and how long have you been in the army?"

"I've been in the army a little over three months," John replied. "I recently finished the Basic Officers Course at Fort Monmouth, and I just arrived from the replacement depot at Sasebo."

"Let's see your orders and your 201 File," Walker said as he held out his hand.

Grady opened his handbag, pulled out his orders and file and gave them to the captain. Walker gave a quick look at the orders, then opened the 201 Personnel File and read. He liked what he saw.

"We're happy to have you, Grady. We're short-handed around here and sure can use you. This is Sergeant Ballard," he said as he pointed to the sergeant at the other desk. "Sergeant, take the Lieutenant's papers and take care of his billeting for tonight."

Walker looked at his watch and said, "Lieutenant, let's go get something to eat before they close the mess hall. We can talk there." He addressed Ballard, "If anything comes up, come get me at the officers mess. Also, we'll need a Jeep at 0530 tomorrow morning. I want two men riding shotgun, and I want a SCR 610 radio that works." He asked John, "Do you have a carbine?" Grady said "No." Walker told Ballard, "Draw a carbine and ammunition for the lieutenant." John liked Walker's style. Walker was not impressed with his own rank, was informal, and knew what he wanted to do.

Walker and Grady walked about three blocks in downtown Ascom City to an old building that looked as though it had been a warehouse. A field kitchen served hot meals in the interior of the building. They went to the serving line and each took a standard stainless steel mess tray which pleased John because he wouldn't have to use his mess kit. He was surprised at the good quality of the hot meal.

They went to a table made of planks extending between wooden shipping boxes that had Japanese writing on them. As they ate, Walker explained to Grady the situation with the Signal Section, Headquarters X Corps. "Tenth Corps is a bastard outfit made up of the U.S. 1st Marine

Division, the ROK (Republic of Korea) 1st Marine Regiment, the U.S. 7th Infantry Division, the U.S. 187th Airborne Regimental Combat Team (RCT) that just arrived at Kimpo Airfield, plus some miscellaneous units. The U.S. Marines are fully engaged in fierce block-to-block street fighting in Seoul. The 7th Infantry Division has its 32nd Regiment fighting in the southern part of Seoul, and its 31st Regiment is in a blocking position about thirty miles south of Seoul to keep North Korean troops that were down at the Pusan Perimeter from coming north to join in the defense of Seoul. The 17th Regiment of the 7th Infantry Division is unloading from ships at Inchon right now.

"Lieutenant Colonel Ackerman is Commanding Officer of the Signal Section. He's over around Seoul with the 32nd Infantry Regiment, and Major Lamb, our executive officer, is with him. General Almond, commander of Tenth Corps, issued a statement last night that Seoul was captured, and General MacArthur issued the same statement to the press today. The top brass are waiting to make a triumphal entry into Seoul. That's why Col. Ackerman is over there. But the marines still are doing a hell of a lot of fierce block-to-block fighting in Seoul."

Walker continued, "The situation with the 31st Infantry Regiment down south at Suwon is critical. A North Korean armored division is coming up the main corridor to reinforce the Communist defenders in Seoul, and the 31st Infantry has to stop them. Elements of the 187th Airborne Regimental Combat Team and 7th Infantry Division reinforcements are rushing to Suwon.

"We have low frequency radio and VHF radio links from Tenth Corps Headquarters to the marines at Kimpo Airfield and have just gotten a link established with the 32st Infantry on South Mountain in Seoul. The situation with the 31st Infantry down at Suwon is fluid, and I'm going down there tomorrow morning to see what we need to do for them. It's too dangerous to travel at night. You'll go with me.

"Tenth Corps isn't the usual outfit in terms of organization and equipment, and it looks as if we're going to have to provide service right down to the regiments. The marines are taking care of themselves, and we have only to keep the radio and VHF links open to them." Walker didn't talk down to Grady or treat him as if he were a greenhorn.

John asked Walker, "What's the quality of your noncommissioned officers?"

"Pretty good. Of course, most of them don't have combat experience, so we're going to have to work closely with them until they get seasoned. Also, we have to work with the South Koreans, and language is a problem there. You don't happen to speak Korean do you?"

Walker and Grady returned to the telephone exchange building and went into Walker's office. The captain asked Sergeant Ballard, "Did anything come in while I was out?"

"Nothing out of the usual. The lieutenant's carbine and two bandoleers of ammo are there by your desk. Since we're leaving early in the morning, I have the lieutenant's sleeping bag upstairs with you."

"Very good," Walker said. "Only, 'we' aren't leaving in the morning. I want you to stay here and hold down the fort. Do you have two good men to ride shotgun?"

"Ballard looked disappointed. "They'll be ready in the morning. The Jeep will be ready at 0530."

"You're a good man, Sergeant."

"Don't tell me, sir, tell the paymaster. Maybe he'll have something extra for me on payday."

"Sergeant, show Lieutenant Grady our setup here, then show him where he's going to sleep."

"I won't need you tonight, Grady, so you can get settled and get some sack time. I'll wake you by 0430 if you're not up by then." He reached for a stack of messages and orders on his desk.

Sergeant Ballard led Grady through the building showing him the different operating sections of the Signal Headquarters. They went upstairs to a small office in one corner and Ballard said, "You'll be in here temporarily with the captain. That rolled up sleeping bag over there on the floor is yours. The latrine with running water is on the far side of this floor."

Grady went to the latrine and washed the best he could in the absence of a shower, then went back to the room and spread out his sleeping bag. The room was warm so he stretched out on top of the sleeping bag. He fell asleep and awakened just briefly about 2300 when Walker came in.

John awoke by himself shortly before 0430 and found that Captain Walker had already gone. Grady hurried to the latrine where he washed and shaved, then he dressed and put on his pistol belt with the Colt .45. He jammed his steel helmet under his arm, grabbed his carbine and bandoleers of ammunition, and rushed downstairs to Walker's office. No one was there. Sergeant Ballard came in shortly after Grady arrived and said that he expected Walker in about twenty minutes. He advised Grady to go eat breakfast. Grady returned from breakfast, and Walker explained, "We're going to take a radio van and crew and radio relay equipment and team down to the 31st Infantry Regiment at Suwon. Truck and tank traffic on the narrow roads to and around Suwon has torn up the land lines used for telephone and teletype communications, so we're going to make radio the primary communication means. We'll take a couple of extra SCR 610 radios with us. Lieutenant Roland Amory and a couple of crews are going with us."

"It looks as if you've already put in a day's work today," John said to Walker.

"We don't punch a time clock around here; you'll get use to it. Come with me. I want to get this detachment moving as soon as we have enough daylight." Grady grabbed his gear and followed Walker outside to a Jeep parked in front of the building. "You drive," Walker told John. Walker said that he didn't have time to wait for the two "shotguns" to show up, and he would kick ass about that when he returned.

Walker directed Grady to a cleared lot adjacent an industrial building on the edge of Ascom City where they saw a number of Signal Corps vehicles parked. Walker introduced Grady to First Lieutenant Roland Amory, Sig C. There was a radio van and attached trailer of the type that John had operated in the field exercises at Fort Monmouth. Two 2½ ton trucks and a ¾ ton truck also were there. Walker told Amory to call his men around him, and when they assembled Walker said, "I want two men with carbines to ride with me, and I want two people on each of your vehicles riding 'shotgun'. There are reports of guerrillas and cutoff North Korean soldiers throughout the entire area so watch the terrain on both sides of the road. Keep a lookout for freshly-filled holes in the roadway and any place on the ground that looks freshly smoothed over because there might be land mines buried there. Everyone keep on your toes. I'll take the lead and Lieutenant Amory will follow behind the trucks in the ¾ ton. Don't let the trucks bunch up too close. We pull out in five minutes."

Grady was impressed with Walker's leadership. Walker had served in Italy, France, and Germany in World War II, so he had considerable experience in combat zones. He had been in-grade as captain a number of years and should make major before long. He was the senior captain in the signal section.

Walker showed Grady on his map the route they would take. They would follow the Inchon-Seoul highway to the southwest side of Yongdungp'o, the western suburb of Seoul, and then turn south onto the Seoul-Suwon-Taejon highway. Two privates first class came to the Jeep to ride "shotgun." The vehicles pulled out as soon as the light was good. Grady kept his eyes on the road and was not able to see much of the countryside, although it was obvious to him that heavy fighting had recently occurred there. Battle-wrecked vehicles and equipment of both armies littered both sides of the road. Six destroyed North Korean T34 tanks were on one side of the road. He drove through the burned-out town of Sosa. Traffic was getting heavy in both directions.

John had smelled a putrid odor ever since they had left Ascom City. He asked Walker, "What's that odor that's everywhere?"

"That's fertilizer that the Koreans use. They save their human excrement and use it to fertilize their crops. You'll see big crocks near their houses: that's where they store it."

Military traffic was heavy, and progress was slow as they approached the western outskirts of Yongdungp'o. They arrived at the main Seoul-Taejon highway and headed south in traffic that was slow-moving, and at times halted, because elements of the 187th Airborne RCT had priority use of the road as they rushed to Suwon to help stop the North Koreans from coming north to Seoul. The Signal Corps detachment under Captain Walker stopped briefly at 7th Infantry Division headquarters in Anyang-ni and arrived in Suwon in late afternoon. Walker led the detachment to the edge of the Suwon airfield which had been captured five days earlier, and then he departed for the 31st Infantry Regiment headquarters.

Walker came back in about thirty minutes and called Amory, Grady, and the senior non-commissioned officers to a meeting at his jeep. "The situation is this," Walker said as he referred to his map spread out on the hood of the jeep. "Our troops of Tenth Corps have secured the main Seoul-Taejon highway down to the vicinity of these three hills that are on opposite sides of the highway. The North Korean 105th Armored Division occupies those hills in force, as well as the terrain south of there. The 31st Infantry has sent a force around to the southeast to outflank the hills, and they should be on the highway south of the hills and north of Osan by now. They've made contact with a small group of tanks of the 1st Cavalry Division of Eighth Army racing up from the South. Communications aren't good with those forces, and 31st Infantry troops fired on the 1st Cavalry troops coming up because they didn't have radio contact. The 1st Cav suffered casualties. Amory, you take the radio van with its trailer and the VHF relay team around to the southeast on that same flanking route to give the people down there added communications. An escort detail will be here to lead you through. Get ready to move out right away. Grady, you and I will stay here for now."

John was disappointed to miss the linkup of Eighth Army and X Corps which he considered to be an historic event in the war.

Walker told John, "Let's go over to the ComCenter, then we'll grab something to eat." They drove to another part of the airfield where a couple of radio antenna towers and tents were standing. They went inside a tent and John recognized Signal Corps equipment that he had trained on at Fort Monmouth. Walker introduced him to Second Lieutenant Donald Smith and several noncommissioned officers of the 7th Signal Company. "Smitty," Walker said, "show us what you have here." Lieutenant Smith pointed out the equipment they had in the tent and with whom they were in communication. He went to a map on the wall that had a clear plastic sheet over it and showed them the communication lines and links marked on the clear plastic with black marking crayon, just as Grady had done in field exercises at Fort Monmouth.

"Where can we get something to eat around here," Walker asked Smith.

"I was about to go over there myself. Come with me," Smith said. He lead them to a field kitchen in a large tent. They talked about the tactical situation while they ate.

The three officers went back to the 31st Infantry ComCenter to keep in touch with developments. That night they received a communication from Amory advising that his crew had arrived at Osan without incident and was operational. Walker and Grady both slept on the ground in one of the ComCenter tents that night.

Grady arose before dawn the next morning, and after washing and shaving, he went to the ComCenter main tent to see what had happened during the night. Not much had happened on the northern side of the hills. He went to the mess tent for breakfast. Captain Walker came in and sat down and said that he was going up to 7th Division headquarters that morning, but that Grady should stay there. The 31st Regiment was going to assault those hills that morning and he should help Smith if he were needed. Walker said that he would return about noon.

John guessed that Captain Walker was trying to ease him into the war-zone situation as much as possible without giving him any responsibilities right at the start. John didn't like this— he felt that he was ready to take responsibility—but he figured that Walker was sizing him up so that he would know better what kind of assignment to give him. Also, X Corps was a strange outfit at this point, and maybe Walker was feeling his way. Who knows?

Grady stayed at the ComCenter during the morning trying to learn what was going on and how they were going about it. He learned that the assault on the hills would begin at noon. He said to Lieutenant Smith, "Do you think you'll need me here for the next couple of hours? If not, I want to get a look at our assault on those hills."

"Everything is under control here, so go ahead if you want to."

John took his carbine with him and walked out to the road and hitched a ride on a truck that was going to the Seoul-Taejon highway. There, he hitched another ride south. Shortly after they crossed the railroad tracks, MPs stopped them and said that they could not go any farther south. Grady stepped down from the cab of the truck and started to walk south, but MPs again stopped him. "Sorry, sir, but no traffic of any kind can go south of here until further notice."

John could see U.S. troops falling back from the hills. "Are they retreating?" he wondered. U.S. aircraft soon appeared overhead and commenced to dive-bomb the hills on both sides of the highway. The planes made successive bombing runs at the hills dropping both high explosive bombs and napalm. U.S. troops had pulled back from the hills to get out of the way of the bombing. After the planes completed their bombing runs, artillery and mortars laid down a heavy barrage of high explosive shells on the hills. A barrage of white phosphorus shells rained down on the hills, and then our troops began their assent of the highest hill. The North Korean defenders slipped off to the east when the U.S. troops reached the upper parts of the hill. The U. S. troops did not suffer a single casualty in taking the hills. The Seoul-Taejon highway was open!

Captain Walker and Lieutenant Smith were talking when Grady arrived back at the ComCenter. Walker asked Grady where he had been, and John described in detail what he had seen. "That sounds good," Walker said. "Things are in good shape here, so I think you and I will go up to see the 32nd Regiment southeast of Seoul."

Walker contacted Lieutenant Amory and told him to render as much assistance there as he could and to stay ready to move if need be.

Walker and Grady climbed into their Jeep and proceeded north on the Seoul-Taejon highway. Walker had his map on his lap and followed their progress with his finger. They traveled without much conversation, each keeping watch on the road and on the surrounding terrain. They arrived at the village of Kwanmun-dong and took a left fork in the road and headed north toward the Han River. They arrived at Simsa-ri without incident and found the ComCenter. They went in and Walker introduced Grady to the communications personnel. Walker excused himself to go pay his respects to the senior officers of the regiment and to see if they needed anything in the way of communications.

Walker returned and said that General MacArthur was holding a ceremony in Seoul the next day to restore the South Korean government to South Korean President Syngman Rhee. Colonel Ackerman and Major Lamb would be there to work with the civilian press, etc.

Walker continued, "We'll get some chow here tonight, sack in here, then go find the 17th Infantry tomorrow morning. They're newly arrived and we ought to check them out to see if they need anything from us. Let's go eat."

The next morning after breakfast, Grady and Walker caught up on the latest information and set out for the 17th Infantry Regiment located southeast of Seoul. They were advised to be careful because North Korean small groups and stragglers were active throughout the area. They located the 17th Infantry ComCenter and introduced themselves to the regimental officers that were there.

***

(At this place in the events, the reader already has been informed of Walker's and Grady's experiences with a blown fuse in a switchboard at Lieutenant Tim Cavendish's platoon in the 2nd Battalion, 17th Infantry Regiment, at a forward outpost, and how they fought with the defenders of the outpost when it came under attack by North Korean forces. With the coming of dawn, defenders of the outpost removed their dead, treated their wounded,

and regrouped. Walker and Grady helped out where they could, then said their good-byes and left the outpost. They walked back to battalion headquarters, then went to their jeep.)

***

Both Walker and Grady were in deep thought, and they traveled about a quarter of a mile without conversation. Grady brought the Jeep to a stop and asked, "Captain, where are we going?"

"Oh, let's get back to headquarters at Ascom City."

They arrived back at Signal Section, Headquarters X Corps at supper time. Walker said, "Let's wash up and go to the mess hall. Missing meals last night and today has made me as hungry as a bear." They washed up but didn't take time to shave their two-day-old beards or change their fatigue uniforms which were wrinkled, sweat stained, and dirty from their episode at the outpost with Lieutenant Cavendish's platoon. They went through the chow line at the improvised mess hall and turned to go to a table to eat when Walker said, "There's the 'old man.' Come on, I want you to meet him." They walked over to the table and Walker made the introductions. "Colonel Ackerman, this is Lieutenant John Grady; he's been assigned to us." Walker introduced Grady to Major Lamb, the executive officer, and to several other officers. John said hello, and Walker and he took seats.

Lieutenant Colonel Robert Ackerman was tall and husky. He had close-cropped sandy hair with a few gray ones sprinkled about. His complexion was clear and ruddy. He was a handsome man.

Major Morris Lamb was short and considerably overweight. He had dark hair and dark eyes. Lamb looked at Walker and Grady with a displeased look and said, "You two are expected to be more presentable when you come to officers mess. We're not going to throw discipline out the window just because we're over here."

"I apologize, Major," Walker replied. "We've been on the road and in the field for a couple of days, and we haven't had much to eat the last couple of days and didn't want to miss another meal."

"Where have you been and what have you been doing the last couple of days?" Colonel Ackerman asked matter-of-factly.

Walker told him about their trip with the radio equipment to the 31st Infantry Regiment down at Suwon and their visit to the 32nd Infantry Regiment headquarters south of Seoul. He then described in considerable detail their experience with the 17th Infantry Regiment and Lieutenant

Cavendish's platoon. He gave a full account of Grady's actions throughout the attack on the outpost.

"What the hell were you doing down at a platoon?" Lamb challenged. "You know that we don't have any responsibility at platoon level. Are you two trying to be heroes or something?"

"Major, they had inoperable communication equipment and asked us for help. I didn't want to tell a combat unit that I wouldn't try to help them. Lieutenant Grady was able to correct the problem, and the equipment was vitally important in the attack that took place fifteen or twenty minutes later."

Ackerman seemed to ignore Lamb and said, "It sounds as if you two have been busy the last three days. You accomplished a hell of a lot more than we did at that dog and pony show over in Seoul. I guess the ceremony was a historic event, though." He shook his head and said, "That city is really torn up; it's a shame."

They commenced eating and Walker talked with the other officers during the meal. John was chagrined to be dirty and unshaven at his introduction to his commanding officer, but Ackerman didn't seem to mind and seemed not to pay attention to Lamb. As they all stood up to leave, Ackerman walked over to Walker and Grady and said, "Phil, I want to see you in my office first thing tomorrow morning. Try to get some sleep tonight."

As they walked away from the mess hall, John said to Walker, "The colonel seems to be a regular guy, but Major Lamb is another story."

"Colonel Ackerman is a good man. I served with him in Japan before we came over here, and I ran across him in Europe in World War II. But Lamb ... I don't know him. He arrived in Japan just before we shipped out. I think he's trying to make a tough-guy first impression, so maybe he'll settle down as time goes on. Just let him go and don't worry about him; you're doing O.K."

They arrived at the telephone exchanged and went into Walker's office. They met Sergeant Ballard inside the door. Captain Walker asked him, "Do we have showers yet?"

"Yes. Quartermaster set them up yesterday afternoon."

Walker said to Grady, "The war is just going to have to wait. I'm not doing another thing until I get a shower and shampoo. Come on, let's get over there." They arrived at the portable shower unit and stripped off their clothes and threw them onto a pile of dirty clothing. The water was warm and the soap made a good lather. It was sheer luxury! They dried off and each drew an issue of clean underwear, socks, and fatigue uniform. And, the clean clothing was free!

They returned to the telephone exchange and Walker told Grady, "I have some work to do, but there's no need for you to hang around here. Why don't you go up and hit the pad."

***

Walker reported to Colonel Ackerman's office the next morning after breakfast. Ackerman began, "Phil, bring me up to date on our situation here. I've lost contact the last couple of days. My trip to Seoul was a waste of time as far as I'm concerned." Walker told the colonel about the status and condition of the Signal Section, Headquarters X Corps.

Ackerman said, "Tell me about the new lieutenant; is he going to be any help to us? What's his name?"

"His name is John Grady. And yes, I think he'll be a help to us." Walker proceeded to tell the colonel what he knew about Grady. "Sir, if I may make a recommendation, if he can work with me for a couple of days while he gets familiar with Tenth Corps I can get him broken in so he'll be able to assume responsibilities on his own. I believe that once he gets acclimated to our situation here he'll be a real asset."

"I sure hope so. Keep this under your hat, Phil, but I don't know if that Lamb fellow is going to be much help to me. I've spent the last couple of days in close contact with him and he nearly drove me nuts. I'm not sure he understands what he's over here for. Because of that, I'm going to have to rely on you more than I had planned. Stay away from him as much as you can, and I'll keep him busy here with administrative matters. If he doesn't work out soon, I'm going to relieve him. I need an exec. who'll be some help to me."

Ackerman told Walker what he had learned from the generals over in Seoul, and what he wanted Walker to do the next couple of days. "That's it Phil, thanks for coming in."

Walker returned to his office and called for Grady. "John, you're going to work with me before we give you an assignment. Tenth Corps is going into reserve, so things will be quiet for a while. The colonel says that Generals Almond and Walker are concerned about reports of atrocities committed by the North Koreans against South Korean soldiers and civilians and against American GIs. They're forming a joint investigating team comprised of people from Eighth Army and Tenth Corps to look into the situation. We're going to provide communication service for them. I'm sending Lieutenant Amory with a combat photographer and a radio unit to provide the communications for that investigating team, and I want you to go with Avery and give him any help he needs. He's a good officer; you can learn from him. He'll be here at 1000 and I'll brief both of you then."

Captain Walker gave Lieutenants Amory and Grady all the information he had on their assignment to the atrocities investigation team. They were to be in Taejon the next day to join the Eighth Army part of the team. The Lieutenants spent the remainder of the day getting the personnel and equipment ready. John met the photographer and the radio crew. The combat photographer was a sergeant first class who had served in the Pacific Theater during World War II, and he was a real pro. John found Lieutenant Amory to be competent and an easy person to work with.

CHAPTER 2. (1 OCTOBER 1950). STATUS OF KOREAN WAR.

The 7th Infantry Division assembled in the Inchon-Suwon area when X Corps went into reserve, and the 1st Marine Division assembled around Inchon.

The North Korean Army was in a rout trying to get back to North Korea. Several of its divisions were decimated at the Pusan Perimeter when the Eighth Army broke out. Others of its divisions broke up into small units and headed north as best they could. Rapidly advancing UN units bypassed many North Korean units still in South Korea. The bypassed Communists took to the hills and operated as guerrilla bands harassing and ambushing UN units when they could. Some enemy units of regimental size did make orderly withdrawals north beyond the Thirty-eighth Parallel.

The collapse of organized resistance by the North Korean Army was so complete and the UN advance so rapid that U.S. civilian and military leaders were not certain how they should proceed. They could not decide whether or not to cross the Thirty-eighth Parallel in force, and if they did so, how far north to go. (On 30 September 1950, the ROK 3rd Division actually advanced beyond the Thirty-eighth Parallel.) The opinion that ultimately prevailed in the Truman administration was that if the UN forces did not completely destroy the North Korean Army at that time we probably would have to fight them again after China and the Soviet Union rearmed them and perhaps joined them in another attack south. Accordingly, the authorities decided to go all the way north to the Manchurian and Russian borders, thereby destroying the North Korean Army and re-unifying Korea in the process. The authorities would reevaluate the situation if Chinese and/or Soviet Union troops appeared in force in Korea.

This course of action by the United States was undertaken despite the fact that the highest U.S. civilian and military officials had been informed by the Armed Forces Security Agency that the Chinese were massing armies in Manchuria.

✻✻✻

On 1 October 1950, several events of consequence occurred. First, General MacArthur ordered X Corps to load onto ships and make an amphibious landing at Wonson on the East Coast of North Korea. X Corps then would advance westerly through a corridor in the mountains to attack P'yongyang, the North Korean capital. Simultaneously, Eighth Army would attack up the Seoul-P'yongyang corridor to complete a pincer movement on the enemy capital.

The 1st Marine Division was ordered to embark on ships at Inchon on the West Coast, and the 7th Infantry Division and some X Corps support units were to move by trucks across South Korea to the port of Pusan on the East Coast and load onto ships.

Another significant event that occurred on that date was that Chou En-Lai, the Communist Chinese premier, made a speech declaring that China "will not tolerate foreign aggression and will not stand aside should the imperialists wantonly invade the territory of our neighbor." It was reported that India's ambassador to China was told by the Chinese that China would go to war if UN forces advanced north of the Thirty-eighth Parallel. But, General MacArthur convinced the authorities in Washington that this was bellicose saber rattling on the part of China. Despite the information he possessed on the Chinese Army buildup in Manchuria, he believed that China would not intervene in Korea.

CHAPTER 3. (1 OCTOBER 1950)

Lieutenant Amory's group departed at first light on 1 October 1950 to join the atrocities investigating team in Taejon. They had a ¾ ton truck, a Jeep, a radio van and trailer, and two other radios. All in the group except the photographer carried carbine rifles. Although North Korean soldiers were in the hills and were harassing road traffic along the route that Amory's group had to travel, the group made it through to Taejon without trouble. They met the representatives from Eighth Army who included a JAG major (a lawyer), a first lieutenant from the provost marshal's staff, a squad of riflemen from the 2nd Infantry Division, and a small group of hired South Korean laborers. The JAG major briefed them on their mission and told them where they would begin their investigation. He wanted extensive photographic records of anything they found. They had to complete their field work within seven days. The JAG major would write a report on their findings at the conclusion their field investigation.

Those next days were the worst that John Grady had ever experienced. Their first investigation was at the Taejon airstrip where a South Korean civilian guided them to a mass grave. There, the North Koreans had tied the hands behind the backs of about five hundred South Korean soldiers and executed them. The laborers unearthed many of the bodies. The stench of the decomposing bodies was sickening. The combat photographer took photographs of the findings. Grady was standing near the burial pit observing the scene when the photographer asked him to stand closer to the pit and point to unearthed bodies on the ground in order to direct attention to them. Grady complied, holding his breath to avoid inhaling the stench.

The team visited other mass graves around Taejon that same day. When the North Koreans occupied the South, they imprisoned wealthy South Korean landowners and government officials of all levels. When UN forces broke out of the Pusan Perimeter and began to advance northward, the Communists took the prisoners out and executed them. The JAG major estimated that in the Taejon area the Communists executed up to seven thousand South Koreans. Forty American prisoners of war died in that same manner.

Horror scenes abounded. At Sach'on, two hundred eighty South Korean officials and landowners who were locked in the city jail by the Communists died when the retreating Communists burned the jail with the prisoners in it. The investigating team found other inhuman acts committed at Anui, Chonju, Hamyang, Kongju, and Mokp'o.

The team learned that six individuals survived the atrocities: two of them were American GIs. The GI survivors had been tied to South Koreans with field wire and led to an open pit where they all were shot and pushed into the pit and covered with dirt. The two Americans were only wounded and were covered with just a thin layer of dirt which allowed them to get sufficient air to breathe. They poked holes in the dirt to get more air and were rescued by soldiers of the advancing U.S. 24th Infantry Division.

The team realized that in the time allotted they could take only a sampling of the many atrocities committed by the Communist North Koreans. At the end of the fifth day, the JAG major decided that he had all the evidence he needed to establish beyond a reasonable doubt that many atrocities had been committed. The team made a record of other atrocity sites that they learned about but were unable to visit. The major said that he would add an addendum to the report if time permitted additional field investigations. The team returned to Taejon on the morning of 6 October. The photographer stayed with the major to be sure that the film was processed promptly and according to his liking. Amory's Signal Corps team headed north to rejoin Signal Section, Headquarters X Corps. Trucks carrying supplies from Pusan north to the Eighth Army packed the road. Again, Amory's team made the trip without incident, although others on the road that day were not as fortunate.

The team arrived back at headquarters at early evening. Lieutenant Amory said to Grady, "You might as well take off now and get some supper before the mess hall closes. I'll take the vehicles in and see that the equipment is cleaned up. There's no sense in both of us missing supper." John liked Avery. They had become friends during the field trip.

Grady entered the mess hall and saw Colonel Ackerman, Major Lamb, Captain Walker and a couple of other officers sitting at one of the tables. Here he was again—coming to a meal dirty, and there was Major Lamb. John thought about going to another table to avoid them, but he was part

132

of their command, so he should try to be with them. It appeared that they had finished eating and were talking. He went over to the table with his tray and said, "Gentlemen, I've just come in from six days in the field and have not had a chance to clean up. If I won't offend you, may I join you?"

Ackerman pointed to an empty space and said, "Sit down and tell us what happened on the atrocities investigating team."

John settled in on the bench, thought a moment, then gave them a complete, well organized, vivid account of the findings of the investigating team. All at the table listened in silence. When he finished, no one said anything. Finally, Major Lamb said to him, "Lieutenant, what did you learn from all that?" Lamb sounded as if he were a schoolteacher quizzing a secondgrader.

"Major, I learned never surrender to the North Koreans."

CHAPTER 4. (6 OCTOBER 1950)

The Signal Section, and some other support units of X Corps, along with the 17th Infantry Regiment, had orders to pull out for Pusan on Sunday, 8 October 50. Their route would be through the mountainous central part of the country because the main Seoul-Taejon-Pusan highway had been reserved for vehicles carrying supplies from Pusan up to the Eighth Army. The two regiments of the 7th Infantry Division that traveled that same central route through the mountains several days ago had encountered ambushes and had suffered casualties at several of the passes in the mountainous region.

Mobile radio crews were dispersed throughout the line of march. Lieutenant Amory was with one crew in the middle of the 17th Infantry, and Captain Walker and Grady were with another mobile crew toward the rear.

The 1st Battalion, 17th Infantry, set out for Pusan just after first light. Other units joined the line of march in their turns. John was in Captain Walker's Jeep, as was Sergeant Ballard who was driving. They waited over two hours to join the line of march. To John, the number of personnel, vehicles, and equipment seemed awesome, and that was just one regiment and some Corps support groups.

Things went well the first day on the march, but the situation changed abruptly in the early morning darkness of Monday, 9 October. North Korean stragglers hiding in the hills and acting almost simultaneously ambushed the convoy at two separate passes through the mountains. They rained down rifle and automatic weapons fire into the U.S. trucks caught between the walls of the passes. Captain Walker tried to contact Lieutenant Amory but could not raise an answer. He kept trying but still no response. After twenty minutes a corporal from Amory's unit called in an excited state and reported that they had been ambushed and that Lieutenant Amory and Sergeant Cornish were wounded. Lieutenant Amory seemed to be in serious condition.

"Captain, do you want me to go up there and see if we can help?" Grady asked.

"We can't move out of this line; the road is just too narrow; we'll never make it."

"I'll go on foot. It'll take me a while, but someone ought to go up there—they're our people. I can find out what the situation is and call back to you. Can we get the medical unit behind us to send some people forward as soon as possible?"

"All right, you go ahead, but don't do anything foolish; we don't need any more casualties. I'll alert the medics about the ambushes and get some of them up there." Again, Walker noted that Grady had the ability to quickly assess a situation and propose a response. He didn't wait for someone else to act. It was Grady's good fortune that Walker was a mature individual who accepted suggestions from a junior officer.

John grabbed his carbine and bandoleers of ammunition and started out at a trot. He soon became winded and settled down to a fast walk as he moved past the stopped vehicles of the convoy. He was soaking wet with perspiration when he finally arrived at the radio vehicles. Only sporadic rifle shots came from the hills and from the convoy. Sergeant Cornish sat with his back against a tire of a Jeep, and Lieutenant Amory was stretched out on the ground beside his ¾ ton truck. Cornish had a thigh wound and appeared to be taking it well. A bullet had struck Amory in the neck and apparently had passed down into his chest area. John could tell that Amory was in serious trouble. John contacted Captain Walker and described as best he could Amory's serious wound and asked him to get the medics up there as soon as possible. Walker replied that a doctor and three medics already had departed and should be there shortly.

After investigating the entire scene at the ambush area and communicating to Walker, Grady went back to Amory. "How're you doing, Rollie?"

"I don't know, Grady, I seem to attract bullets the way honey attracts bees."

"Is there anything I can do for you now? Captain Walker radioed that medical people are on the way. They should be here soon."

"I am O.K, Grady. You watch your ass, though, those people are still up there on the hills."

The 17th Regiment sent troops onto the hills and engaged the North Koreans. The Communist troops dispersed from the area by late morning, and U.S. helicopters came in and evacuated the seriously wounded. John stayed with Amory until he was lifted out.

Captain Walker talked with Grady on the radio and told him to stay with Amory's unit for the remainder of the trip. The Signal Unit arrived at its assembly area outside Pusan on 12 October 50. Colonel Ackerman attended a staff meeting where he received the latest information on the North Korea invasion. He returned to the Signal Section and called a meeting of all his officers and the senior noncoms.

"All right, pay attention; I've have the latest information on the landing. The good news is that the ROK Army advanced up the east coast of North Korea and captured the port of Wonsan on 11 October. That means that our landing won't be opposed by the North Koreans. The bad news is that Wonsan harbor and its sea approaches and beaches are heavily mined and no landing can take place there until the mines are cleared. The navy has twenty-one minesweepers working to clear the harbor and its approaches, but I don't know how long it's going to take them to clean things up so we can get ashore.

"Over in the West above Seoul, Eighth Army has crossed the Thirty-eighth Parallel and is advancing northward toward P'Yongyang, the North Korean capital.

"I want all signal equipment in this command to be checked and rechecked to be absolutely certain that it's operable. Also, I want you to check that you have all your required spare parts and supplies—I don't want anything left to chance.

"Major Lamb, you're in charge of requisitioning our needed equipment and supplies. All you people get your requirements to the major by 1000 tomorrow. Captain Walker, you check all equipment to see that it is operational and ready for loading aboard ship."

Ackerman made it known that he wanted all officers in his command to have their meals together in the mess tent. It gave him an opportunity to better know his men and permitted him to disseminate and receive information. At breakfast on 15 October, Colonel Ackerman addressed the assembled officers in a solemn voice. "Gentlemen, I've been informed that Lieutenant Roland Amory has died of his wound." All the officers were greatly saddened by the loss of the popular fellow officer. Grady lost a friend.

The colonel also announced that there would be a staff meeting at 1330 at which he wanted complete reports on the status of men, equipment, and supplies. Just after lunch, Ackerman gave Grady some reports to deliver to X Corps headquarters. Consequently, Grady was not at the staff meeting.

Ackerman had a few remarks to open the staff meeting, then he said, "Major Lamb, how do we stand with supplies?" Lamb began his report with a pleased attitude. He announced that he had requisitioned all their required supplies and equipment and had managed to get about ten percent more than they were authorized. He added that winter clothing would be distributed tomorrow, and again he had requisitioned extra clothing.

Ackerman looked displeased and said, "Major, what the hell are we going to do with all that excess equipment. Who's going to carry it?"

"Well, you never know when we might need it," Lamb responded weakly with a forced smile on his face.

"We'll take what we're supposed to and nothing more," the colonel said emphatically. "The roads are poor to nonexistent up in North Korea, and we can't be burdened with anything we don't need. There's one exception to that: we'll take extra socks."

The other staff members made their reports. The headquarters section seemed to be in good shape for the landing.

At the conclusion of the reports, Colonel Ackerman said, "With the death of Lieutenant Amory, we have an open position that needs to be filled and—"

Captain Walker interrupted. "Excuse me sir, I've been working closely with Lieutenant Grady since he joined us, and I believe he can handle that job. He's mature, he thinks well in tight situations, and he has an electrical engineering degree. He was an enlisted man in World War II and gets along well with our enlisted men. I'm confident he can handle the job."

"What the hell do you mean; he just got over here," Major Lamb blurted out.

"How long have you been over here, Major," Ackerman shot back at Lamb. The colonel clearly was agitated with Lamb. The colonel's face was red and blood vessels stood out on his neck. Walker recalled his conversation with the colonel when the colonel had said that he was not sure that Lamb was going to make it and that he might have to relieve Lamb.

Ackerman looked at Walker and said, "O.K., the change is effective immediately. That slot calls for a first lieutenant. I'll put in for his promotion today." As much as anything, Ackerman made the statement about the promotion to "stick it" to Lamb. The colonel was "heaping coals on his head."

"What?" Lamb blurted out again. "He hasn't been in-grade long enough to be promoted."

"Major," Ackerman responded, "you're in charge of requisitioning supplies, you find a pair of silver bars for the lieutenant and get them to me by supper. I'll pin them on him then."

Walker thoroughly briefed Grady on his new job and gave him encouragement. Grady spent most of his time working with the enlisted men.

All personnel received their issue of winter clothing. John was impressed with it.

***

The 1st Marine Division and most of Corps Headquarters sailed from Inchon on 16 October and were at sea. Because of the mines in Wonsan Harbor they could not land and were steaming back and forth off the East Coast of North Korea waiting for the harbor to be cleared. Signal Section, Headquarters X Corps loaded aboard a transport ship in Pusan harbor on 19 October.

Late on 19 October and early on 20 October, U.S. and South Korean troops of Eighth Army fought their way into P'yongyang and secured the city. The captured of the North Korean capital thus accomplished the original mission of X Corps. Accordingly, General MacArthur changed plans and ordered X Corps to march north to the Manchurian and Russian borders instead of marching west to P'yongyang. He ordered 7th Infantry Division to make an amphibious landing at Iwon, North Korea, which was one hundred fifty miles north of Wonsan.

With the new mission of the 7th Infantry Division, its 17th Regiment was to be the first to land on the beaches at Iwon. Authorities expected the North Koreans to oppose the landing. The 17th Regiment would secure the beach at Iwon and then march north to Hyesanjin on the Yalu River which forms the border between North Korea and Chinese Manchuria. The route to the Yalu River from Iwon would be through some of the highest mountains in North Korea, some of which exceed seven thousand feet. The road was hardly more than a cart path through the high elevations.

This change of orders required the 17th Regiment to unload from transport ships in Pusan harbor and reload into seven LSTs in order to make the assault landing on the beaches at Iwon.

The change of plans for X Corps meant a change of plans for Signal Section as well. The generals wanted to have reliable communications with the 17th Regiment because, at first, it would be the unit closest to the Manchurian border. If there were to be any serious trouble with the Chinese, the generals wanted to know immediately.

Colonel Ackerman called a meeting of his officers to explain the new plans. He said, "I'm sending VHF radio relay units to maintain communications with corps headquarters and the 17th Regiment. As of now, Lieutenant Grady will command the VHF crews." Addressing Grady he continued, "You will unload your equipment from the transport ship and load it aboard one of the LSTs as soon as possible. I'm sending a detail of South Korean laborers to go to North Korea with you to help carry the equipment to off-road sites where the antenna towers and radio sets will be placed." (The GIs called the Korean laborers "Choggies.") "The remainder of the Signal Section will stay on the transport and will sail north with the 31st and 32nd Infantry Regiments."

In private, Ackerman told Walker that he wanted Walker to stay with him at headquarters because he had little confidence in Lamb. He also expressed some concern to Walker whether Grady had enough experience to take the VHF teams up to Iwon and to the Yalu River.

Walker said, "Colonel, I think you're going to find that Grady will be able to handle any job you give him. Besides, those VHF crews have good NCOs who know what to do and don't need someone to nursemaid them."

The 7th Infantry Division and corps support units remained in their ships at Pusan about a week until mines were cleared from the North Korean harbors. Grady used this delay as an opportunity to sharpen up his Signal crews.

Seven LSTs carrying the 17th Infantry Regiment and Grady's Signal crews sailed for Iwon, North Korea, on 27 October. Meanwhile, the ROK Capital Division rapidly advanced up the East Coast of North Korea and captured Iwon and the surrounding area. Consequently, the 17th Regiment's amphibious landing would be unopposed.

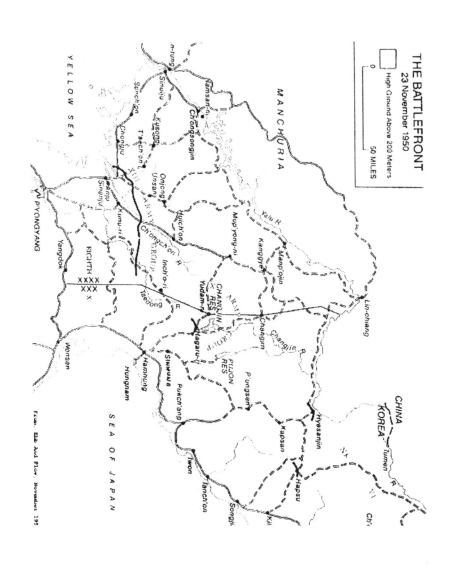

THE BATTLEFRONT
23 November 1950

High Ground Above 200 Meters

0

50 MILES

From: Ebb And Flow, November 195

CHAPTER 5. (29 OCTOBER 1950)

First units of the 17th Infantry Regiment went ashore on the beaches of Iwon on the morning of 29 October 50. Grady's radio teams and equipment went ashore mid-morning.

X Corps headquarters staff and the 1st Marine Division had landed at Wonsan three days earlier and moved north to the industrial city of Hamhung where X Corps established its headquarters.

The 1st Battalion of the 17th Infantry Regiment, with field artillery and combat engineer support, immediately set out on a motor-march for the town of Pukch'ang which was located southwest of Iwon. Fifty miles north of Pukch'ang was the town of P'ungsan where 7th Infantry Division was to establish its headquarters. The South Korean Army already occupied P'ungsan. From there, the 17th Infantry was to head north through the mountains to the town of Hyesanjin on the Yalu River.

Grady's first task was to erect a VHF radio relay station at Pukch'ang to establish communications with corps headquarters at Hamhung. He designated Master Sergeant George Stringer to set up the relay station. John stayed long enough to be sure that he agreed with the site selection. Grady informed regimental headquarters where the site was located and made arrangements for it to receive supplies and support. After the site became operational, Sergeant Stringer had orders to rejoin Grady and the rest of the Signal Corps unit as they followed the 1st Battalion on its march north. Sergeant Horace Atkins was left in charge of the station at Pukch'ang.

***

Elsewhere in North Korea, PLA troops (Peoples Liberation Army—that is, the Communist Chinese Army) hit hard and punishing blows at Eighth Army south and west of X Corps. Even closer, PLA troops attacked South Korean troops south of the Changjin (Chosin) Reservoir which was high in the mountains and considerably north of Hamhung. Captured Chinese soldiers told U.S. interrogators that three divisions of Chinese regulars were in the Chosin Reservoir region. There was little doubt that China had entered the war. However, U.S. civilian and military officials believed that the Chinese commitment was minimal at that time and that their aim was only to protect the retreating North Korean Army to permit it to reach safe grounds in the North Korean mountains or in Chinese Manchuria.

✲

Late on 31 October, Grady's Signal units followed the 1st Battalion, 17th Regiment, into P'ungsan which was held by units of the ROK Capital Division. In the morning, the Signal unit would erect another VHF radio station there. But that night, North Koreans in regimental strength attacked the ROK units on the northern outskirts of the town. The 1st Battalion aided the South Koreans in repulsing the attack. The North Koreans attacked again the next morning. During that day, most of the remainder of the 17th Regiment arrived in P'ungsan and fought off the attacking North Koreans. The battle lasted for most of four days, after which the North Koreans withdrew. The 17th Regiment immediately marched north on foot to the Ungi River.

At the conclusion of the battle north of P'ungsan, Grady's men erected another VHF station on the south side of town. John was not sure that he would be able to establish contact with the station at Pukch'ang. According to what he had learned in The Signal School, the distance was greater than the maximum distance for a good working link. But, he wanted to be near some defended town or village rather than being at a completely isolated site miles from nowhere. The crew erected the antenna towers and tuned the radio equipment. Technical Sergeant Harold Black ("Blackie"), the senior NCO since Sergeant Stringer was not there, aligned the antenna array along the compass reading for Pukch'ong, the relay station south of them. They tried to make contact but couldn't receive a signal. The crew checked everything and tried again—nothing.

John hoped that he hadn't made a mistake by selecting that site. He took his map and compass to a nearby observation point and looked at the mountains south of them and located them on the map. He studied the map for a short time, looked at the mountains, took a compass reading, then went back to the crew. "Sergeant Black, do you see that highest mountain south of us and to the east of our present alignment, align the antenna array fifteen degrees to the east of the present alignment so the radio waves will hit the side of that mountain."

Sergeant Black didn't know Grady very well at that time and gave him a strange look. "Lieutenant, we have line-of-sight propagation at these frequencies, and that mountain is off our line of sight."

"Give it a try Sergeant. We don't have anything with our present alignment." Black shook his head but told the crew to realign the antenna array fifteen degrees to the east. They realigned and again tried to raise Pukch'ong. It worked! Both stations received strong signals.

The crew looked at Grady. John explained: "At these frequencies, you sometimes can get the radio waves to bounce, reflect, or refract, off of topographical features. You never know for sure that it will happen. In this mountainous terrain we may have to rely on it more than once." John learned about that phenomenon in a Radar course that he took in his senior year in engineering school. In that course, he had read reports of experiences in World War II where successful propagation of radar and radio signals occurred in situations that seemed impossible according to textbook theory.

***

The Chinese were playing a strange game in North Korea. After inflicting sharp and punishing blows against Eighth Army and X Corps in the last week of October, the PLA disengaged on 6 November.

***

On 14 November, elements of the 17th Infantry Regiment crossed the Ungi River on an improvised floating bridge in the face of light North Korean small arms fire. The regiment fought its way north and captured the town of Kapsan on 19 November. They were only twenty-three miles from Hyesanjin and the Yalu River. Grady's men set up a VHF radio relay station in Kapsan.

Winter slammed into the mountains of North Korea with the ferocity of a powerful sledgehammer blow. Bitter-cold winds howled in from Manchuria, and the temperature plunged to far below zero, Fahrenheit.

On 21 November, the 17th Regiment traveled on foot over the icy and snow-covered mountain road and entered Hyesanjin. Grady established his last VHF station on a mountainside on the south side of the town and ran landlines into the town from the VHF station.

Grady kept in contact with his units at the other VHF stations and with Captain Walker at corps headquarters on the monitor channel of the

VHF link. Walker advised that he would send additional VHF equipment in a day or two. Grady had planned to go back and make regular visits to his other VHF units he had established along the way, but the icy single-lane road was so bad that he decided not to attempt the trip until things improved. The U.S. Air Force dropped supplies by parachute to the 17th Regiment to make up for the inability of a sufficient number of supply trucks to get through the mountains.

The 17th Infantry Regiment was to attack west from Hyesanjin and join up with the 32nd Infantry Regiment that also was to go to the Yalu. The 17th Infantry tried to move west on the morning of 22 November but became engaged in a stiff fight with North Koreans about seven miles outside of Hyesanjin. The North Koreans fought harassing battles with the 17th Infantry during the following week, thereby keeping them from getting away from Hyesanjin.

Temperatures were far below zero most of the time and frequently fell to thirty-five and forty degrees below zero. The extreme cold seriously affected vehicles, guns, and other equipment, often rendering them inoperable. Frostbite of fingers and toes took a toll on the troops.

Grady's Signal site at Hyesanjin included three canvas tents, an electrical generator, and a relay radio unit that included two twenty-five foot antenna towers. One tent housed the radio equipment, another was used as a warming and sleeping tent for the Signal Corps troops, and the third tent was for the Korean laborers. Supply people from the 17th Infantry brought food and supplies to the bottom of the mountain and the Korean laborers carried them up to the site. Grady and his crew could see about a quarter-mile of the road that ran south out of Hyesanjin. He established his perimeter defense and posted sentries twenty-four hours a day. Sentries spent a maximum of one hour on duty. So far, the North Koreans and Chinese had not bothered them.

✳✳✳

John had a compelling curiosity to see the Yalu River and Manchuria. He decided that he was not coming halfway around the world and get to within a couple of miles of them without seeing them. One morning he went to Sergeant Black and said, "Blackie, put on your going-to-town clothes; we're going to town."

"What do you mean, Lieutenant?" Black was intelligent and hardworking and tended to be on the serious side. He was from Oklahoma and had worked in the oil fields before joining the army. He was younger than Grady and had been in the army four years.

"You and I are going to Hyesanjin to see the Yalu River and Manchuria. You can tell your grandchildren about them." The two of them bundled up and went down the mountain to the snow-covered road and walked into Hyesanjin. They stopped at regimental headquarters where Grady talked with headquarters personnel about their communication situation. Headquarters people were satisfied with the communication link that Grady's men provided. Grady and Black also talked with the officers and noncoms of the 7th Signal Company who were with the 17th Regiment.

Black and Grady walked to the end of the town and stood on a bluff overlooking the frozen-over Yalu River. The Manchurian side of the river valley was flat along the river's shore and there was a village to the right. John saw smoke rising from the chimneys of small houses in the village. He took out his binoculars and looked at the village and saw several civilians walking about, and he saw a Chinese soldier on sentry duty. He passed the binoculars to Black. For some reason, John thought that this was an exciting experience.

❊❊❊

It snowed Thanksgiving morning, 23 November. In their isolated location, and with their menu restricted to field rations, there was no Thanksgiving Day spirit in the VHF crew at Hyesanjin. Later in the day, the sky cleared and the sun offered some warmth, but the temperature remained well below zero. Late in the afternoon, several air force cargo planes flew over the 17th Regiment area and dropped supplies by parachutes.

The next day, a supply truck from Regiment came to the bottom of Grady's mountain, and the Korean laborers went down to the truck, loaded up, and carried up to the VHF installation all the food and trimmings for a Thanksgiving dinner. They had turkey, dressing, mashed potatoes, cranberry sauce, several vegetables, pumpkin pie, and fruit and nuts. By the time Grady's men were able to eat it, the food was stone cold, and for those on sentry duty it was on its way to becoming frozen. But the men appreciated the effort of the army to try to get the dinner to them. What the men appreciated even more than the food was the first mail delivery since they left Pusan. There was no mail for Lieutenant Grady.

Temperatures continued in the subzero range. Grady had never been in such a cold climate. He had two 2½ ton trucks, a trailer, and a Jeep at the base of the mountain. He told the Korean laborers to drain and collect the oil and radiator fluid from the vehicles, remove their batteries, and carry them up the mountain to the warming tent. John knew that at those temperatures the oil became thicker than mud, and a battery lost its efficiency. He didn't want to get caught with immobile vehicles. It would be hard enough trying to get them started even with warm oil and a warm battery. Some 17th Regiment units in Hyesanjin started and ran their vehicle motors every half hour, or every hour, to keep them from freezing. John just did not have enough manpower to have someone trudging up and down the mountain all the time to start the vehicle motors. Putting out sentries twenty-four hours a day was as much as he could handle in addition to the radio duties.

CHAPTER 6. (25 NOVEMBER 1950)

On the night of 25-26 November, wave after wave after wave of Chinese soldiers stormed against Eighth Army, and on the night of 27-28 November other masses of Chinese assaulted X Corps. On the east side of the Chosin Reservoir, several battalions of the 31st and 32nd Regiments of 7th Infantry Division were cut to ribbons by the Chinese. And, the 5th and 7th Regiments of the 1st Marine Division were surrounded on the west side of that reservoir. It was apparent that the Chinese Third Field Army was committed to annihilating X Corps. So far, the Chinese had not hit the 17th Regiment at Hyesanjin. Grady's crew learned sketchy details of the Chinese offensive over their radio channels.

On 30 November, Major General Edward Almond, commanding general of X Corps, ordered the 1st Marine Division and the 7th Infantry Division to withdraw to the Hamhung/Hungnam area on the East Coast of North Korea. The marines and what remained of the battalions of the 31st and 32nd Infantry Regiments up at the Chosin Reservoir would have to fight their way out.

Corporal Ollie Clark, who was on duty in the radio tent, came to Grady in the warming tent and said, "Lieutenant, something's up, you had better come over to the radio tent." John put on his coat and hat and boots and went with Clark to the other tent. They entered the tent and John greeted Corporal Bill Savin who also was on duty. "What's up Bill?"

"I got word from guys in the 7th Signal Company that the entire 17th Infantry Regiment has orders to pull out the first thing in the morning. They're evacuating the entire area. They're ordered to withdraw to Hamhung on the double. The 7th Signal Company will cut their circuits with us at 0200 in the morning."

"Is this for sure?" John said. "They aren't pulling your leg are they?"

"I don't think so, sir. You can talk with them yourself if you want to."

John called one of the officers he had met a couple of days earlier when he and Blackie were in Hyesanjin, and sure enough, it was true.

John asked the officer, "Is there anything for Signal Section, Headquarters Tenth Corps?"

"All I know is that the 17th Infantry has orders to leave."

"Thanks," Grady replied.

Grady and his crews were not actually part of the 17th Infantry. So far as John understood, he and his crew were under command of Signal Section, Headquarters X Corps and received their orders from them.

"Bill, get Captain Walker at corps headquarters," Grady said. Savin raised the Signal Section at X Corps headquarters but was informed that Captain Walker and Colonel Ackerman were somewhere up north and were not now in contact with headquarters. The operator at Corps said that Major Lamb was the officer in charge.

Grady said to Savin, "Well, I don't know what else to do, so I guess I'll have try to contact Major Lamb. Grady felt that he should be extra cautious in dealing with Lamb, so he sat down with a message pad and printed out the following message.

To: OFFICER IN CHARGE, SIGNAL SECTION, HEADQUARTERS X CORPS

From: J. GRADY 1ST Lt SIG C

IN VIEW OF ORDERS FROM COMMANDER X CORPS TO COMBAT UNITS IN NE N. KOREA, REQUEST SPECIFIC ORDERS FOR SIGNAL SECTION UNIT AT HYESANJIN.

John tore off the top sheet from the pad and handed it to Corporal Terry Rogers, the cryptographer of the crew. "Terry, put the proper routing on this, code it, and get it off as soon as you can."

Two and one-half hours later, Major Lamb called back on the monitor channel. Grady answered, "Hello, Major, this is Lieutenant Grady. Major, we need to get orders right away."

"Don't you move your ass 'till you're told to; do you understand?"

"Major, our supported organization has orders, and we should stay with them. And, we have other stations down the line, don't forget."

"You'll do what you're told to do, damn it. Don't you dare desert your post until you get orders to leave. Do you hear me, 'Hot Shot.'" Lamb cut the circuit.

"The bastard," Corporal Savin muttered.

"Get Master Sergeant Stringer down at Kapsan; I want to talk to him right away." Savin put the call through and Grady said, "Sergeant, have you heard about the orders from Corps Commander to our supported organization?"

"Yes sir, I sure have."

"Sergeant, unless you hear from me to the contrary, you and your crew plan on accompanying our supported organization. Do you understand what I'm saying?"

"Yes sir. I was hoping to get that message from someone."

Grady gave that same message to the other stations down the line. "Bill, keep trying to locate Captain Walker and Colonel Ackerman. If you locate them, come get me right away. Tell your relief the same thing. That's the matter of top priority for operators until further notice."

Grady went back to the warming tent, looked in and said, "Sergeant Black, may I see you outside?" Black came out, and John said, "Let's take a little walk." They walked away from the tents and John explained the situation. "One way or another, we're going to get out of here. It'll be with the 17th, or as soon thereafter as we can make it. I'm not going to sacrifice this crew and the ones south of us because Major Lamb and the other 'brass' can't get their act together. Start making plans what you're going to have to do. Stay calm and keep things under control, and don't let the men get excited. Things will work out O.K."

Before dawn the next morning, Charlie Ienfeld came to the warming tent and shook Grady awake. "Lieutenant, the 'Choggies' have gone. I thought you would want to know."

"When did they go?" John said, half awake. "Did they tell anyone where they were going?"

"They didn't tell anyone they were leaving, and no one saw them go. They took food with them, we know that."

"Has anything happened at the sentry posts? Didn't the sentries see them go?"

"No sir, everything has been quiet. The temperature is forty degrees below zero, so it probably is too cold even for the North Koreans and the Chinese."

John went to the radio tent where George Fuller was the operator on duty. "George, have you been in contact with corps? Have you located Captain Walker and the colonel?

"We've been in contact with corps, sir, but we haven't located the colonel or the captain."

"Have you talked with our other stations recently?"

"Yes sir, everyone is operational but cold as hell."

"O.K. George, keep trying."

John ate as he wrote notes to himself about things that he wanted to do and what he wanted Blackie to do.

At the faintest hint of dawn, Grady's men saw a stream of headlights down on the road. The 17th Infantry had started moving south. Someone said, "Running with their headlights on in enemy-infested territory and over that treacherous road, they really are in a hurry to get out of here."

Grady was concerned and angry because of Signal Section's failure to give him orders. He was working hard not to show his emotions to the men. John called to Sergeant Black, and they went into the tent that the Korean laborers had occupied and discussed what they were going to do. John consulted his notes. "Tell the men to get packed and be ready to leave here on a moment's notice. Take nothing that's not absolutely necessary. Each man take his sleeping bag and all the socks he can carry. Be sure that all weapons are clean and functioning. Divide the ammunition among all the men. Take no more than five days of food rations—if we have that much—and every man should have a full canteen of water. Keep the motor oil, the radiator fluid, and the batteries warm until it's about time to go. Detail a couple of men to get oil and batteries into the vehicles before we start down the mountain. Have the backpack radio ready to go and let Chuck Moore carry it. Tell him that he's to stay close to me at all times. If we don't get orders within the next half-hour or so, you can figure on destroying all the other radio equipment and antennas. We just won't have time to cart them down the hill and stow them. Assign men to that task now so that they'll be ready when the time comes. You tell them what to do to be sure that no one will ever be able to use the equipment again. Keep sentries posted until we leave.

"Blackie, we have to be sure that the men are clothed to withstand these temperatures. I'll leave it up to you to be sure that every man wears what he needs. What do you think, should we take a 2½ ton truck and the Jeep, or just the truck?"

"All we need is the truck. I'll send some men down to transfer the gas from the one of the trucks and Jeep into the other truck."

"Blackie, keep your cool and keep the men focused on what they have to do. Give those guys that have stripes on their sleeves responsibilities to get us ready. If you think of other necessary things, go ahead and do them. If we all work together on this we'll come out O.K. Let's get started."

John went to the radio tent and got in touch with Master Sergeant Stringer. "Sergeant Stringer, have you had any orders from corps?"

"I haven't had a word from corps headquarters. Have our friends left yet?"

"Affirmative," Grady said. "Sergeant, I've not received orders from Signal Section, Tenth Corps. If you don't hear from them, do as we discussed yesterday. Your authorization to act is from me. Any questions?"

"I read you, Lieutenant."

Grady contacted the stations at P'ungsan and Pukch'ang and gave them the same message to evacuate with the 17th Regiment.

PFC Stan Obromowitz, the driver of one of the 2½ ton trucks, came to Grady and said, "Lieutenant, that truck has been sitting in these subzero temperatures for days now. I don't know if I can get the motor to turn over even by putting warm oil in it. I was thinking that maybe I could take some blankets and the heater from the warming tent and put it under, or beside, the truck to get that engine block warmed up. If I can't get that engine to turn over, it's a mighty long walk to Hamhung."

"You're right about that, Stan. Your idea sounds good to me. Go to it right away because we'll be leaving soon. Tell Sergeant Black that you have my permission." Shortly thereafter, John saw Obromowitz and two other men start down the mountain carrying blankets and dragging an equipment crate with the heater in it.

Grady's crew was busy with the tasks that Sergeant Black gave them. Things seemed to be going well. John went back to the radio tent and had the operator contact the Signal Section at corps headquarters, but neither the colonel or Captain Walker were there. "Tell them that I need to talk to Major Lamb," John told his operator. After a delay, the operator at corps said, "The major says that he's busy and can't talk right now."

John spit out the words to the operator at corps, "Tell the major that I must talk to the officer in charge of Signal Section. Orders have not been issued in a critical situation, and whoever is in charge will not want that to go down on his record—it may ruin his career. Tell the major that." Grady was livid with anger.

Grady went looking for Sergeant Black. "Blackie, how are we coming along? How much more time do you need before we're ready to leave?"

"Lieutenant, we can be ready to leave in twenty minutes, including the time we need to destroy the equipment. If you're in a hurry, we can make it sooner."

"Good, figure on making it sooner. As soon as everything is ready, I want to say a few words to the men."

The 17th Infantry vehicles continued moving in a slow, steady stream past the mountain where Grady's crew was positioned.

John decided to try one more time to get someone at corps to give an evacuation order. He went to the radio tent and had the operator contact corps. He asked for Captain Walker, but the Corps operator said that Captain Walker was up north near Chinhung-ni. The situation up north was very fluid and they couldn't locate him. John asked for Colonel Ackerman. He was up north with Captain Walker. John said, "O.K., let me talk with Major Lamb. Tell him that it's urgent."

After a few minutes Lamb came on. "I got your smart-ass message, Grady."

"Major, we have to get orders. Things are happening up here, and we still are sitting here."

"What's the matter 'Hot Shot,' are you getting scared to be in a battle zone? You'll stay there until I tell you to leave, do you understand me? The colonel isn't here, and I've not received orders for you to evacuate."

"Major, you're the officer in charge—you issue the order."

"Listen, 'Hot Shot,' don't try to tell me how to do my job. I was in the army when you were still in knee pants."

"Major Lamb, why does the army want us to stay here? Who are you going to send messages to, or talk to? The only people up here are North Koreans, the Chinese, and the twelve of us. Do you know where we are? We're a couple of miles from the Manchurian border. The Yalu River is frozen over, and all that the Chinese have to do to get here is walk across the ice, walk through the town, and they're at our position. Major, it's time for us to leave."

"It sounds to me like you have a yellow streak up your back, 'Hot Shot'. If you desert your post without orders, I'll have you court-martialed so fast it'll make your head swim. I'll see to it that you spend the rest of your life in Leavenworth Prison. I told you before, I haven't received orders yet." Lamb hung up.

John was steaming mad! He walked out of the radio tent to try to hide from the men his anger and disgust with Lamb. "Who would leave a numskull like that in command of anything, particularly when lives are at stake," John muttered.

Just then Stan Obromowitz came running into the compound. "Lieutenant, the 17th Infantry is gone. The road is deserted. They're all gone."

"Get Sergeant Black here right away," he told Obromowitz.

Grady went back into the radio tent and had the operator contact Master Sergeant Stringer at Kapsan. "Sergeant, it's time to do it. Put your people to work. And remember, you're acting on orders from me. Don't allow anyone to accuse you of bugging out. Do you have that?"

"I have it, Lieutenant. I'll see you in you know where."

John called the other stations south of him and gave them the order to act according to their previous conversations.

Sergeant Black came into the radio tent. "You sent for me, Lieutenant?"

"Sergeant, put your wrecking crews to work on the equipment and supplies that we're not taking. We're leaving as soon as they finish their job. Have the oil and batteries gone down the mountain yet?"

"They're leaving now."

"Take all the batteries," Grady said. "We might need a booster to get that truck started."

"I planned to, sir."

The men quickly finished their assigned tasks, loaded up with the supplies that they were taking with them, and assembled in front of the burning remains of what had been the radio tent. Grady addressed them. "Men, good work. We may have an easy ride back to Hamhung, or it might not be so easy. The important thing is that we have to work together to assure that we get there. Keep in mind at all times what it is that we're trying to do. Help each other. We'll catch the 17th Infantry as soon as we can. Moore, I want you to stay close to me with that radio. Let's get out of here. Follow me." They started down the mountain in a group just as it started to snow. They arrived at the truck parking location as Obromowitz and two other men were connecting a second battery to the truck battery under the open hood. The warm oil and radiator fluid already were in the engine, and the heater and blankets had been removed.

"Here goes nothing," Obromowitz said as he scurried around the front of the truck and took his position behind the wheel. He turned the ignition switch. Nothing happened. Obromowitz had a concerned look on his face as he glanced at Grady. He tried again. A groan came out from under the hood. He waited a few seconds, then tried it again. This time, a grunt accompanied the groan, indicating that the crankshaft had turned. Obromowitz shook his head. He tried it again. This time it was definite: the engine had turned over. Not much, but they now knew that the engine was not frozen stiff. On the next try it turned over several times.

"This is good," Obromowitz said, "the pistons are moving." After an extended coaxing from Obromowitz, the engine caught. It ran roughly at first, then settled down to its deep-throated purr.

"Great," John said. "Smash everything you can on the engines of the Jeep and the other truck and push them and the trailer over the hill. Load up on this truck. We'll take turns riding in the cab. The people in the cab are our lookouts. Watch the hills for enemy troops and guerrillas, and watch the road for land mines."

Sergeant Black and Ollie Clark climbed into the cab with Obromowitz, and John and the eight others loaded into the back of the truck. They started out at a cautious speed. New snow covered the road, but outlines of tire tracks from the 17th Infantry vehicles were still visible in the snow. The temperature outside was twenty-five degrees below zero.

Everyone wanted to race down the road to catch the 17th Infantry, but they knew that Obromowitz was doing the best he could under the conditions. Besides, the 17th Infantry probably wasn't making any better time than they were and perhaps even slower progress. They traveled for half an hour at the cautious speed, and then John shouted up to the men in the cab to stop. Obromowitz drove onto a level place in the road and stopped. John climbed out the back and walked to the front of the truck. He said that the men in the back were getting cold and that it was time to switch positions. Black and Clark came to the back of the truck, and two other enlisted men climbed into the cab. Just before the truck took off again, they heard two faint rumbles coming from a distance down the road south of them.

"What was that?" Corporal Bill Savin said, looking at Grady.

"I have no idea. Maybe vehicles in the 17th hit land mines in the road, or maybe they're firing at enemy troops. Or, maybe enemy troops are firing at them."

They traveled at their snail's pace for another half hour and John began to feel that they were making progress and might even catch the 17th Infantry before too long. Minutes later the truck slowed and then stopped. Sergeant Black and John climbed out the back of the truck and went forward to the cab.

"Why are we stopping, Obromowitz?" Sergeant Black demanded.

"Take a look down there, will you."

The road was cut into the side of the solid-rock mountainside, and ahead of them the road went down a slight grade and then curved sharply to the left. A crevice in the rock of the mountain extended up and down the mountainside and formed a steep-sided gully at the curve in the road. A poured-concrete bridge that had spanned the fifteen-foot wide gully was lying askew on the side of the mountain below the road. Combat engineers with the 17th Infantry had blown up the bridge behind the retreating troops.

"Holy Toledo, will you look at that!" John said. "This is what the explosions were that we heard back there when we were stopped on the road. Damn it, I never thought about them blowing bridges behind them."

"I didn't either," Sergeant Black replied.

It was obvious to everyone that this was the end of the road for the truck. Grady, Black, and several other men walked down to the site of the blown bridge and surveyed the terrain to see what their options were. The gully had almost vertical rock sides and was about twenty-five feet deep. If they did get down the near side, they never would get up the far side. As the men talked among themselves, Grady thought about what he should do next. "Sergeant Black, get the other men here." When they assembled, John said, "There is a way across this gully, and we're going to find it. We'll split into two groups: one group with Sergeant Black will look for a way across higher up the mountain, and I'll take the second group and we'll look for a way across lower down the mountain below the road. In each group, keep in sight of each other. Keep in mind the reel of field wire in the truck. It can serve as a rope for us if we need it. Does everyone understand what we're going to do. If not, speak up now." Everyone nodded.

John's group backtracked along the road, looking over the edge to see if there were any way to get lower on the mountain and maybe find a way across the gully. Thirty yards back they found a way to get down to an exposed stratum of rock that looked like a narrow shelf that ran horizontally across the mountain. They carefully worked their way down the icy and snow-covered rocks and rubble to the shelf forty feet below the road. They gingerly worked their way in single file toward the gully. When they arrived at the gully's edge, Corporal Terry Rogers exclaimed, "Damn it, it's no better than up on the road." They looked up and down the mountain for a possible solution but saw none. The group turned around and retraced their steps along the shelf. They were just about to the location where they were to start their climb up to the road when they heard shouting from the other group.

"We can get across up here. Come on."

Grady called out, "O.K. Wait up. Don't cross over yet." They all assembled at the truck and John inquired about getting back to the road after they crossed the gully.

Black said, "There's a mass of rocks and boulders filling the gully up there. There must have been a rock slide that got jammed in the gully. We can pick our way across the boulders to the other side, and even though the mountainside is steep, I think we can descend to the road without too much trouble."

John commanded, "Get from the truck everything that you want to take with you, and don't take anything that you don't absolutely need. Everyone, take your sleeping bag. Sergeant Black, let's take some of that field wire with us. I don't know why, but it may come in handy.

"How are your feet?" John inquired. "Does anyone feel that his toes are getting in trouble from the cold? Can you wiggle you toes? Can you feel them?" Each man indicated that he was all right. They collected their gear from the truck. Black rolled out a long length of field wire, cut it into three lengths, and made three coils that he had three men carry over their shoulders. Chuck Moore brought the portable radio.

Grady told Obromowitz, "Stan, turn the steering wheel on the truck, put it in neutral and release the brake so we can shove it over the mountainside." The truck made a spectacular dive and tumble down the mountainside.

"O.K., let's move out," John called.

Sergeant Black led the way back up the mountain to the pile of snow and ice-covered rocks and boulders. They were cautiously working their way across when Chuck Moore let out a yell. He slipped off a boulder and fell on his back onto rocks ten feet below. Grady and Sergeant Robert Pettit worked their way down to him. He was shaken up and bruised, but he seemed not to have suffered any serious injury. They didn't know if the radio on his back was damaged; they would check it later. With considerable slipping and sliding on the ice and snow, the entire crew made it across the rocks and boulders and back down to the road.

"Good show, men," Grady said when they assembled on the road. "O.K., we have to catch the 17th Infantry, so there's no sense stopping anywhere short of catching them. Lets move out. If anyone gets in trouble from the cold, speak up. Follow me." Darkness fell, the snow stopped, and the temperature dropped. A couple of inches of new snow on the road squeaked when the men walked on it. Several times Grady dropped back along the line of his men to inquire how they were making it and to compliment them on their effort. "Swing your arms," he told the men. "That will get blood to your fingers and keep them from freezing. Wiggle your toes as you walk."

After a long march in the dark they reached the outskirts of the town of Kapsan. They stopped at an abandoned cottage. "Sergeant Black," Grady said, " post three sentries outside. The rest of us are going inside and massage our toes." The men thought he was joking about massaging their toes. He wasn't. He ordered every man to remove his boots and to rub and massage his toes and feet until they felt warm. He removed one of his boots and started rubbing. "Put on a pair of clean socks next to your feet," John said. After five minutes he had massaged both feet and had both boots back on. "Sergeant Pettit, you and Chuck Moore check the radio and see if you can raise the 17th."

"Sergeant Black, switch sentries and bring those men inside and have them massage their feet. Ienfeld and Rogers, check your rifles to be sure they're loaded and operating. We're going to see if it's safe for us to pass through this town. John told them to stay on a back street of the town, and to move quickly past windows and doors of buildings. He led the way into the darkness. The three of them cautiously worked their way through the town and found it to be abandoned, at least as far as they could tell. "Charlie, hurry back and tell the others to come here as quickly as possible because I don't want to lose any more time," he told Ienfeld.

When the remainder of the group caught up to Grady, Sergeant Pettit said, "Lieutenant, the radio is dead. The local oscillator tube and an i.f. amplifier tube won't even heat up, and we don't have any replacement tubes."

"Smash it and throw it away," Grady ordered.

The group proceeded south with Grady again leading the way. It was getting colder—probably the coldest night yet. The bitterly frigid air burned their nostrils every time they inhaled, and the exposed skin on their faces became windburned and raw. Grady kept out in front but occasionally dropped back and reminded them to swing their arms and wiggle their toes. They walked an hour and one-quarter and came upon another blown bridge. There was not much moonlight to see by, but this obstacle appeared not to be as bad as the first one.

"O.K., you know the routine," John said to the men. "Sergeant Black's group will go to the right and look for a crossing place, and my group will go to the left. One man in each group will be a sentry to keep watch with his group while the others look. Savin, you're sentry in my group. Let's move."

Black's group found a relatively easy crossing about one hundred yards to the right. They made the crossing and continued on their way.

John had seen on his map a road junction south of them where the road from Kapsan intersected with the road from Samsu, which was a village up north of them and southwest of Hyesanjin. He wanted to make that road junction by daylight. He would have to push his men, but he figured that this first day while they were relatively fresh would be the time to do it. He hoped to catch the 17th Infantry sometime the next day, and if the 17th encountered opposition from North Koreans or Chinese, it would slow them and he could catch them even sooner.

The group walked in silence except for the squeaking of the dry snow under their boots. They had walked for quite a distance when Sergeant Black came up to Grady and said, "Sir, I believe the men could use a short rest. You're setting a fast pace, and this cold and their heavy clothing are cutting down on their efficiency and they're getting tired."

"O.K. Blackie, we'll take a breather at the first place that looks like it's safe to stop." In another mile they came upon a dried up stream bed that crossed the road. Combat engineers with the 17th Infantry had blown up the short bridge across the stream bed. John stopped short of the blown bridge and said, "We'll take a breather here. Let's go upstream a short distance to get off the road. We can get down into the creek bed to get out of the wind. We'll take five minutes to rest and five minutes to massage feet and toes. Everyone massages—no exceptions."

John was concerned because they were not covering the distance that he had hoped they would—the conditions were tougher than he had contemplated. "Men, keep in mind that this territory up north is the place that we want to get out of in a hurry. So, if we have to shovel coal to make steam, the place to do it is where we are now. Let's try to make as much distance as possible these next twenty-four hours. You have the rest of your lives to rest."

Ollie Clark spoke up, "Let's shovel coal, Lieutenant; I can go without a rest."

"Yeah," Charlie Ienfeld said, "I'll rest when I get to Hamhung." Several others concurred.

Sergeant Black said, "If you don't want to stop to rest, that's fine with me. Let's move it then." The stop and brief discussion had an invigorating effect on the men. John was pleased with them. They crossed the creek bed and returned to the road on the far side. They continued squeaking through the snow for several more hours with no complaints from anyone.

John thought while he was walking, "What should I be doing about our security? We've been lucky not to have encountered any North Koreans or Chinese, but if we do, what will I do?"

He figured that they should reach the road junction in an hour or an hour and a half. Road junctions usually are considered strategic places, and if they would encounter the enemy any place up here, that junction was a prospect. He wished that The Signal School had given him more schooling in small unit tactics. He knew that wishing wouldn't make it so, and he had the responsibility for getting these men to safely, so he would have to use his best judgment and hope that it was adequate.

John looked over his shoulder and called, "Sergeant Black, will you come up here, please." When the sergeant arrived, Grady said, "Blackie, we'll be approaching the road junction soon, and I want to have someone out front of our main group to act as a scout so our crew won't get bushwhacked without a warning.

"I'll get someone out there right away," Black said.

"Let me talk to him before he leaves the group. Relieve the scout every half hour."

PFC Melvin Toller came up to Grady and said, "You want to see me , sir?"

John emphasized that the scout should be out fifty to one hundred yards in front of them and should be especially alert. If there was any question in his mind about anything while he was out there, he was to stop and evaluate the situation. If it looked like trouble, he should come back to Grady as quickly as possible. Toller moved out with a quick pace and took his forward position. The group continued their march for another half an hour without incident. Sergeant Black sent PFC Albert Ramey to relieve Toller at the point position. They walked for another half hour and Black sent Corporal Chuck Moore forward. As he passed Grady, John said, "Moore, you and Ramey hold up when you reach him. Check the situation carefully."

John figured that they were not too far from the road junction and he didn't want the group to go waltzing into the junction as if they are on a Sunday outing. In the dark he could not see enough of the topographical features to determine their precise location on his map.

When the group reached Ramey and Moore, Ramey said, "Lieutenant, something doesn't look right with the road up there. I can't make it out in the dark, but do you see what I mean?" He pointed ahead of them.

Grady said to Sergeant Black, "You and the others stay here and stay alert while Ramey and I go forward." The road there was cut into the rock face of a very steep mountain. It just kind of hung there on the side of the mountain. Ramey and John walked forward to where the road made a turn to the right around the mountain. At the middle of the turn, the roadbed had been blasted off the mountainside by the engineers accompanying the 17th Infantry so as to leave a void space of about twelve feet wide. The mountainside was solid rock and almost vertical above and below the blown-out section of road.

"Not again!" Grady exclaimed. "Those engineers are too damned efficient. Albert, go back and tell the others to come up here." When the others arrived, John said, "Well, there it is. If we can't figure a way to get across that void space, we're going to have to backtrack and find a place where we can climb up and over this mountain. Any suggestions?" John was tired and knew that the men were tired.

The men moved up to the edge of the void space and looked. Buck Sergeant Robert Pettit pushed his way to the front to get a good look. He was just a little shorter than Grady, had a thin frame, dark hair, and an intelligent-looking face. Pettit was the undisputed intellectual of the group. He was the technician who repaired the radio equipment. The operators could set up the equipment, get it on the air, etc., but if anything serious went wrong with the equipment, they had limited knowledge to repair it. Pettit, on the other hand, probed inside the equipment, tested the components and subcircuits, and found and repaired the problems. He was quiet and stayed pretty much to himself. He read magazines and books that the others had little interest in. At Hyesanjin, he took his turn as an operator because he had little else to do, and he also took more than his share of sergeant-of-the-guard duty.

Pettit stared across the void space. "Lieutenant, may I turn on my flashlight to get a look at that hole?"

John looked all around him and said to himself, "Hell's fire, not even a mountain goat could stand on this mountainside let alone hide on it."

"Go ahead, Sergeant." Pettit ran the light beam along what had been the inside edge of the road. He ran the beam a few feet and stopped, a few feet more and stopped, etc., until his light beam had traversed the entire width of the void. John began to see what Robert had in mind. There appeared to be remaining on the inside edge of the former solid-rock roadbed a jagged lip that was three, four, and up to six inches wide across most of the void. The engineers probably could not get their drilling equipment closer to the inside wall when they drilled holes for the explosive charges. The blast blew the roadbed outwardly away from the mountain and the narrow lip remained.

Pettit extended the butt of his carbine outwardly and pushed it along the lip to clean away snow and debris that lay on it. He cleared off about one-third of the lip, then shined his light onto the rock face above and stopped it at a couple of large cracks in the rock face. Now, everyone in the group saw what Pettit was up to.

"Lieutenant," Pettit said, "I don't know about the rest of you, but I can get across that damn thing."

"I think you have something there, Sergeant," Grady said to him. "I'll try it first, but take some of that field wire and tie it around me as a safety line in case I fall."

"No, I'll go first," Sergeant Pettit said in an authoritarian voice, as if to say, "I figured it out, so I get to go first."

John was somewhat amused and said, "O.K. Sergeant, but get a safety line on you before you start." Sergeant Black and another man took one of the loops of field wire and unwound it. They doubled the wire and wrapped it around Pettit's waist several times and tied it, then they stretched out the free end along the road. Other men picked up the free end and prepared to hold it against a possible fall by Pettit. Pettit eased himself onto the lip and looked overhead and placed his gloved hands in one of the cracks. Several men shined their flashlights to help Pettit see. He very gingerly shuffled his boots along the ledge as his body hugged the rock wall. He stopped and tried to clear the rubble from the center section of the lip with his boot. He looked up and moved one hand to another crack. He resumed shuffling along the narrow lip of rock, then repeated his routine of clearing rubble and changing his handholds. No one said a word. Several more sequences of this and he was across. "That a'way to go, Pettit," several shouted.

Pettit called, "Throw my carbine and my sleeping bag and pack over to me." They did, and he cleared the snow and debris on the lip from his side. He called over to them again, "Before you come across, take off your overcoat and throw it over to me so you can get your body closer to the rock. And don't look down—that's spooky as hell." Pettit also recommended that they get another length of field wire to use as a safety line tied to the next person crossing. Pettit would hold the line that was tied to him on the outside of the man crossing and those on the other side would do the same with their end of that line to help hold a man against the rock face as he crossed.

"Good show, Sergeant Pettit," Grady called. "Who's next?"

'I am," Stan Obromowitz said. "Let me get this over with before I turn chicken." In turn, the other men cautiously made their way across the void. Grady was the last one and threw all the remaining gear over to the men on the far side. When he arrived at the other side he grinned and said to the men, "A piece of cake—it'll take more than that to stop this crew!" The men donned their overcoats, re-coiled the wire, put their packs on their backs, and continued down the road as the first faint light of dawn tinted the southeastern sky.

Sergeant Black again sent a scout ahead of the main group. As they walked around the mountain, John dropped back to Sergeant Pettit and said, "Robert, that was a good job you did back there; you saved our butts."

As they continued on the road, there now was enough light for John to see that a valley was out ahead of them. "The road from Samsu probably runs down that valley, and the road junction probably is out there," he said to himself. He called a halt and brought Sergeants Black and Pettit over to look at his map with him. They looked at the topography around them, and then John said, "I think we're right here," pointing to a spot on the map. "And, the road junction is ahead of us in that valley. Do you agree?" The sergeants studied the map, looked around them again, and agreed with John. "I want to skirt around the eastern side of the junction and hit the road again south of it." John referred to the map again, "Let's get off this road here and go down the mountain to the deep ravine that runs westerly. We'll follow it to this north-south ravine that's east of the junction. We'll follow that ravine until we get to where we want to get back onto the road. We'll lose time avoiding the junction, but I believe it's the safest thing to do. Any comments?" There were none. "O.K., when we get to the junction of these two ravines we'll take a breather and eat something."

They went down the side of the mountain picking their way carefully among the rocks and the ice and snow. At the bottom, they followed a dry stream bed to the intersection with the north-south ravine where they settled themselves among some large boulders that sheltered them from view and from the wind. They were one cold and tired group of GIs!

John said, "Massage your feet to get good blood circulation in your toes and inspect them to see if they're O.K. Then, get some food in your stomach. This cold weather eats our energy in large chunks.

"Is it O.K. if I eat before I massage my feet?" Bill Savin asked. "I'll enjoy my food more if I do." They laughed.

"Drink some water also," John advised. The water in their canteens had frozen the previous day when they had carried them on the outsides of their overcoats. They all switched their canteens to inside their overcoats so that their body heat would thaw the ice and keep the water from refreezing.

After the men had eaten and massaged, or massaged and eaten, Sergeant Black changed the sentries and most of the men dozed. John figured that they all needed rest, so he decided to stay there about an hour. They then continued down the north-south ravine and passed east of the road junction. Beyond the junction, Grady sent George Fuller and Albert Ramey up the side of the ravine and across a flat area to the road to check the situation. If everything looked clear, they were to make a call like a crow to tell the remainder of the crew that it was O.K. for them to come up to the road. The road was clear and the men resumed their march south on the road.

Grady estimated that they were about ten or twelve miles from P'ungsan, and if they could walk without interruption, they could make it there in three or four hours. They walked for two hours and he decided that he had been overly optimistic in estimating the progress that they were making. Several times he called a halt to send scouts ahead to check the area ahead of them. They stopped once in a sheltered area to massage feet and hands. The cold was brutal! Shortly before darkness fell, they climbed a low hill and passed to the east of P'ungsan. They returned to the road south of there, resumed their march, and followed the same routine with the forward scout that they had used previously. That routine was the only thing John could think to do.

They soon would be approaching another road junction, the left branch being the one they had come north on from Pukch'ong two weeks ago and the right branch being the one they would take to Sinhung and Hamhung. Grady decided that they should get past the road junction before they stopped for another rest. They continued walking in the dark until he figured that they were in the vicinity of the junction. They left the road and walked across two small frozen rice paddies to the base of a hill and followed it for about a quarter of a mile after they saw the junction. They came to an abandoned farm hut beside another rice paddy, and John decided that they would take their rest there. Sergeant Black posted sentries, and the others went inside and ate, massaged feet and hands, and dozed.

Grady worried about the fact that they had not encountered any civilians. Why? (In fact, many of the civilians headed for the coast when they learned that Chinese forces had entered the area in strength. Earlier, the Chinese told the native North Koreans that if they went to the coast the U.S. Navy would take them to South Korea. The Chinese wanted the North Korean refugees to clog the roads to make movement by the Americans more difficult.)

Grady was even more concerned about the fact that he and his crew soon would be directly east of the Chosin Reservoir where platoons of the 31st and 32nd Regiments had been badly mauled and where the marines had been surrounded. Surely, the Chinese would have forces protecting their eastern flank and that would put them near, or on, the road that Grady was on.

John roused the men and they walked across the frozen rice paddy and met the road again. Shortly after midnight they encountered another blown-up bridge and had to detour around it, losing more time. Grady was more eager than ever to get down the road as far and as quickly as possible, but he tried not to show his concern to his men. He pushed the men during the night and they walked until dawn, taking just one short rest to tend to feet and fingers. Grady knew that if the men's feet became frostbitten and they could not walk, they surely would be trapped behind enemy lines without any hope of getting back to their own lines. If they did get out, John was determined that his men were not going to lose fingers, toes, or feet to frostbite and be cripples for the rest of their lives.

CHAPTER 7. (3 DECEMBER 1950)

At dawn on 3 December, they came to a place where the road made a left turn through a low area in the terrain. Grady told them to get off the road and move into a large complex of boulders that was on the right side of the road. Many of the boulders were separated from each other and the men could get in among them. Grady posted sentries on high ground overlooking the boulders at locations where they had a clear view up and down the road and across a relatively flat field behind the boulders to the base of a hill. After they ate and massaged their feet and fingers, some men dozed. John was tying the laces on his shoepac boots when Stan Obromowitz came running to the edge of the high ground overlooking the boulders and shouted, "Lieutenant, we have visitors coming and they ain't ours. They look like Chinese."

"On your feet everybody!" Grady shouted. "Get your weapons and ammunition."

"Where are they, Stan?"

"They're north of us and coming south down the road, and they have an advance patrol coming down that field between us and the hill. There must be a full battalion of them."

"How far away are they?"

"Three hundred fifty yards, maybe."

John didn't want to be caught holed up among the boulders without any chance to maneuver or to make an effective fight, so he commanded, "Everyone up to the edge of the high ground, and don't show yourselves." They all scrambled up to the high ground. John spread them out along the perimeter of the high ground facing the field and facing north. Obromowitz was correct, it looked to be about a battalion of Chinese, most of whom were marching in formation on the road, but an advance party of about twenty men was sweeping across the field well ahead of those on the road. Most of the PLA soldiers had white outer garments over their uniforms.

"Hold your fire, everyone, and don't move," Grady said in a low voice.

"What in the world are we going to do?" John said to himself. "Twelve

GIs with carbines against an entire battalion of Chinese? But, if they continue straight along the way they're going in that field, they might miss us.
If we keep in our concealed positions, the Chinese on the road possibly
won't see us. Maybe we'll get out of this after all."

Both groups of Chinese continued moving south. As the Chinese in
the field approached, one of them shouted commands and half of them
veered to the left and headed straight for the depression in the terrain
where Grady and his men were deployed. It was almost as if the Chinese
knew all along where the Americans were. The Chinese formation on the
road continued toward them. Grady considered having the men retreat
back to the boulders and try to hide before the Chinese in the field reached
them, but there they would be like trapped rats for the Chinese to dispose
of at their leisure. Surrender was out of the question because Grady had
seen firsthand what North Koreans did to captured GIs, and the Chinese
may be no different.

When the Chinese in the field approached to within fifty yards of the
GIs, Grady shouted, "Fire, fire." A volley of shots went out from the GIs
and several Chinese fell to the ground. Two of Grady's men couldn't get
their guns to fire—the moving parts on the rifles were frozen. One of the
Chinese shouted something and the Chinese went to the ground in prone
positions and commenced shooting and throwing grenades into the GIs.
Several Chinese soldiers started to move around to one side of Grady's
crew, threatening to outflank them. The GIs continued shooting. A whistle
blew and the Chinese stood up and charged at the Americans. The GIs
fired another volley and then most of them broke and ran for the boulders.
Grady and Sergeant Pettit still were at their positions.

"Make a run for it, Robert," Grady shouted. "Dodge and weave. Go,
go!" Somehow they made it back to the boulders. John shouted to his men,
"Reload and get ready." He and Pettit went behind a large boulder near
the left side of the complex while the others sought shelter throughout the
boulders. Several were near the right side of the boulder complex.

A shot rang out above them and a GI let out a moan. John went
around the edge of the boulder and saw a Chinese soldier standing at the
edge of the high ground in the rear and aiming his rifle down into the GIs.
John stepped out and fired his carbine at the PLA soldier who fell and
tumbled down. Just then Chinese soldiers came around both sides of the
boulder complex and began firing.

"Fire! Fire! Fire!" Grady yelled at the top of his lungs. "Everyone, fire, fire!" The GIs began firing. Grady whirled to his left and saw three Chinese soldiers coming around the closest boulder. He fired several shots and two of them fell. The remaining one had a burp gun and was sweeping its fire across the scene. Grady felt as though someone punched him in the left arm. Robert Pettit shot the one with the burp gun. John raced over to the other side of the boulder complex where he saw several enemy soldiers shooting into the rocks. John, Bill Savin and Sergeant Black advanced toward them and eliminated them.

Suddenly, all the surviving Chinese attackers vanished. They had moved past the Americans and joined the other Chinese marching on the road. The PLA on the road never broke formation to attack the Americans and never tried to help their comrades—they just kept marching, as did those remaining up in the field.

"This is absolutely astonishing!" Sergeant Robert Pettit exclaimed when he realized what had happened. "They could have annihilated all of us."

Grady called for Sergeants Black and Pettit. "Check the men right away, and let's get any wounded in among the rocks to get some shelter."

George Fuller came up to Grady and said, "What do we do now, Lieutenant?"

"Come with me, George. We have to get a head count and see how everyone is. Are you hurt?"

"No sir. I don't know why, but I'm O.K., I think."

They came to PFC Albert Ramey who was laying on the ground in the middle of the complex. Grady and Fuller knelt down next to him and saw blood on his overcoat. "Albert, how are you doing here; are you hit?" Grady asked

"I've been hit in the left side above my hip."

John opened Ramey's coat, dug his way through the clothing to bare skin around his waist and found the wound. A bullet had entered the side of his abdomen and exited about five inches away from where it entered. It appeared that it was sufficiently to the side that it probably missed internal organs. At least that was John's guess since he had little knowledge about medical things.

"George, get Albert's medical pouch and tend to that wound. You had first aid training didn't you?

"I had a little first aid in basic training. If I need help, I'll call."

Grady next came upon Bill Savin and Stan Obromowitz who were kneeling over Melvin Toller. When they saw Grady coming , Obromowitz stood up and shook his head, "He's dead, Lieutenant. He's shot right above his eye, and he doesn't have a pulse anywhere." Bill Savin looked up and nodded his head in agreement.

"Are you two all right?" John asked them. They both answered, "Yes sir."

John looked around. Sergeant Black was coming toward him. "Lieutenant Grady, Terry Rogers is dead, and Chuck Moore and Charlie Ienfeld are missing. Ollie Clark is wounded in the left shoulder, but he's walking. Sergeant Pettit is tending to his wound."

"Sergeant Black, go tell Sergeant Pettit to take charge of things here. You and I are going up to where the engagement started. Bring your weapon." Grady and Black walked up the slope to the edge of the field where the firefight began. They heard someone call. It was Charlie Ienfeld. Grady and Black went over to him. He had a wound in his right thigh and was almost too shocked and terrified to speak. A Chinese grenade had exploded beside him, and he had played dead as the Chinese soldiers ran over him on their way to the boulder complex. Several Chinese soldiers had actually stepped on his body as they ran.

"Sergeant, look after Charlie's wound while I look for Chuck Moore." Over to the far left Grady found Moore's dead body with a massive wound in the side of his head. John returned and told Black the bad news.

"Lieutenant, let's get Charlie up. We'll take him down to the shelter of those boulders and treat his wound there." John and Black bent down and began to lift Ienfeld to his feet. When the weight of Ienfeld's body pulled on Grady's arms, a sharp pain shot up John's left forearm and he let Ienfeld drop as he grabbed his arm.

"What's the matter, Lieutenant?" Black asked with alarm.

"I don't know. I got a sharp pain in my left arm."

Black released his hold on Ienfeld and said, "Let me look at your arm." He slowly raised the arm and noticed frozen blood at the cuff of the sleeve, and he saw for the first time a tear in the sleeve of Grady's overcoat. "Have you been hit in that arm?" Black asked.

"I don't know; I don't remember getting hit."

Black said, "Let me get Charlie on his feet. I'll take him down to the boulders. I'll come back for Chuck Moore. John put his good arm around

Charlie Ienfeld and Black slid his left arm around him, and they helped him down to the boulders. When they arrived they found that Sergeant Pettit had improvised a makeshift aid station among the boulders. He had the healthy men take the white outer clothing from the bodies of the dead enemy soldiers and laid them on the ground under the wounded Americans. Pettit found a place for Ienfeld, and he and George Fuller began treating his wound.

Sergeant Black said to Grady, "Lieutenant, let's have a look at your arm." Grady took off his overcoat and his field jacket and rolled up the sleeve of his outer wool shirt. They saw that the sleeves of his inner wool shirt and his long underwear were bloodsoaked.

"Holy Toledo, what the hell happened here?" Grady said. He thought back and remembered the Chinese soldier with the burp gun and the feeling that someone had punched him in the arm, but after that he had been so frightened and angry at the same time, and so busy, that he forgot about it. "How can that be?" he asked himself.

"We'll look at your arm, Lieutenant, when we finish with Ienfeld," Sergeant Pettit said.

When Pettit examined Grady's arm, he found that the bullet had entered the outer side of his arm just above the wrist and exited at the base of the elbow joint. Pettit swabbed both wounds, sprinkled sulfa powder over them and placed compresses over them, but he didn't know what to do about the region between the entrance and exit wounds.

"Thanks, men," John said. He put his garments back on and went to the wounded men to see how they felt and to inquire about the severity of their wounds. He was trying to assess how soon they could get out of there. He told Sergeants Black and Pettit that he wanted to see them over to the side of the "aid station." As John walked over, he felt a strange discomfort throughout his crotch. He discovered that sometime during the shock and fright of the firefight with the Chinese he had involuntarily wet his pants. "Holy Toledo, a grown man ...," John said to himself with humiliation and disgust.

The two sergeants arrived and Grady asked them, "How serious are the wounded?"

Pettit replied, "Ramey's wound in his side is not too bad if we can keep it from bleeding and can keep sulfa on it. Ienfeld's thigh wound really is kind of superficial. A grenade fragment hit him. The layers of clothing probably slowed it down before it hit his leg, and I was able to pick the fragment out. I think that the grenade blast and the Chinese running over him shocked him more than anything. He's settling down now, and I think he'll be O.K. Ollie Clark was hit in the lower part of the shoulder. The bullet is still in him. It's probably painful, but he's taking it well."

"Can they resume the march?" John asked. I want to get out of here as soon as we can. They'll freeze to death if they lay here too long."

"Lieutenant," Black said, "I recommend we wait about half an hour and let those fellows settle down before we take off. We'll get some food and water in them, and maybe the blood at their wounds can clot good and minimize their bleeding. I'm no medic, though, you understand. Besides, let's let those Chinese get down the road before we start."

Pettit nodded his agreement and asked, "What about your arm, Lieutenant."

"My arm is O.K. We leave in half an hour. I don't see how we can take our dead with us, do you? Sergeant Black, collect the dog tags and personal effects of our men and we'll take them with us. Detail men to take the bodies—ours and theirs—and lay them at the edge of the road. Hopefully, someone will find the bodies and can give them a decent burial when the ground thaws. Before we leave, everyone massages feet and fingers. Another thing, when we get back on the road we're going to need a scout behind us as well as in front of us. The Chinese are in the area and they can overtake us from the rear.

"Come with me. Let's take a look at the Chinese soldiers," John said to the two sergeants. They went over to the edge of the boulder complex where two enemy soldiers lay. John stood there looking and said, "They're not wearing gloves; look at the color of their fingers." Their fingers were purple and black. "Their boots look like canvas basketball sneakers," John said as he stooped down and untied a shoe and took it off one of the bodies. There was no sock on the foot, and the toes of the foot were black. "Do you see why we have to keep massaging our toes and fingers to keep them from getting frostbitten. There are going to be a lot a PLA soldiers missing toes, feet, fingers, and hands when this war is over."

It took them longer to get ready than John had hoped, and when they finally were ready, John had them gather around their fallen comrades and he offered a prayer.

The nine survivors returned to the road and continued south. They all were alert and wary now knowing for sure that the enemy was in front of them as well as behind them. They walked in a light snowfall until dark, taking just one short breather for rest and massage. The wounded held up well during the march, but the progress of the group did slow down. John complimented the wounded for their splendid effort.

A chill went through John's body and the hair on the back of his head tingled. For some reason he was uneasy and knew that they ought to get off the road. How did he know? He could not explain how—he just had that strange feeling. A low hill at the base of a mountain was off to the east. He didn't want to climb the mountain, but thought that it would be advantageous to be on the lower hill because it gave them a good view of the road. He gathered the men and told them that they were going to take a rest on that low hill to the east. The healthy men helped the wounded and they all climbed to the top of the hill and over the summit to a flat area with a small grove of coniferous trees. The men settled in among the trees, and Sergeant Black posted sentries to keep the road and nearby hills under surveillance.

John stopped and talked with the wounded men and congratulated them on their good showing on the march. He visited with the others and encouraged them. He settled down and had just dropped off to sleep when George Fuller woke him and said, "Lieutenant, Savin wants you out at the forward sentry post."

John roused himself and walked toward Savin's post. "Good lord it's cold," he said to himself as he shivered. His lungs hurt from inhaling the frigid air. "How much longer can we survive in this deep freeze?" he wondered.

"Yes Bill, what do you have."

"Over on the road—it's a pretty big unit." Both men spoke in soft voices. Faint moonlight shining on the snow-covered ground made enough light that they could make out troops moving on the road. Grady handed his binoculars to Savin who looked through them and then said, "They're Chinese, and most of them are wearing those white sheets like the Chinese that attacked us. They have a lot of pack animals with them."

"Because of our air superiority during daylight hours, the North Koreans move their troops and do most of their fighting at night," Grady said. "It looks as if the Chinese are doing the same thing. The ones who were on the road in daylight and attacked us must have been in an awful hurry to get somewhere. Maybe that's why they didn't stop to finish us off."

"Maybe they also were trying to catch the 17th Infantry," Savin said.

"Maybe. Good work, Bill. Keep those binoculars and pass them to your relief. I want them back when we leave. Let me know if the Chinese get off the road."

John walked back toward the other men and thought to himself, "What a pickle we're in. We're in enemy-occupied territory with only one road out, and now the enemy is using that road. With three wounded we hardly are able to go cross-country over these snow-covered mountains." John continued thinking as he walked. He stopped, turned around, and went back to Bill Savin. "Bill, when that unit on the road passes, stay here about five more minutes and if no other units come down the road, come back to the crew right away." Grady went back to the group and tried to sleep, but his left arm hurt and he couldn't.

Sergeant Black came to Grady and said, "Lieutenant, Savin is back from his sentry post and says that the road is empty now."

"O.K., call the sentries in and get the men together." When everyone had gathered, Grady continued, "Men, you're bright and intelligent—you wouldn't be in the Signal Corps if you weren't—so you know as well as I do that we're in a tough situation. We'll get ourselves back to our lines if we have more determination and more patience than the Chinese have. We're a small group and have an advantage over large enemy units that operate by the book. We have to use good judgment and take advantage of every opportunity that comes our way. It won't be easy, and it'll test our manhood, but I believe we have what it takes to get out. And I wouldn't want to try it with any other crew than you. We're going back on the road and walk until dawn, then we'll see what happens. Remember that the Chinese fight their war at night as much as they can, so be on your toes.

'Speaking of toes, how are your feet? Let's do a quick five-minute massage and then we're off. If you think the massaging is foolish, ask Sergeants Black and Pettit about the fingers and feet of the Chinese soldiers who attacked us this morning. They weren't pretty." The sergeants nodded their heads. Grady quickly massaged his feet and went over and helped Ollie Clark massage his feet and get his shoepacs on. Other men helped the wounded who needed help.

They returned to the road and walked. It seemed that the men walked faster than they did in the afternoon. They walked until the first signs of dawn in the southeastern sky revealed that they were approaching a sharp bend in the road. John did not like sharp bends in the road in enemy territory. He called Stan Obromowitz to him and said, "Stan, we need a safe place to lay up for a while to see what the situation is in daylight. See that low mountain off to our left, can you get up there without being seen and check it out to be sure that there are no Chinese on it? If it's clear for us to get up there, give out a call like a crow. (Grady hoped that crows lived in North Korea.) If you get in trouble and can't get back right away, bark like a dog. Can you do that?"

"Sure, Lieutenant." Obromowitz looked at the topography, then headed for the base of the hill. The remainder of the men sat along the road. They positioned one sentry ahead of them and another one behind them. Charlie Ienfeld's thigh wound was well enough for him to pull sentry duty. In twenty-five minutes they heard a crow call and started up the mountain. It was full daylight when they reached the summit.

"Men, we're going to stay up here an hour, maybe more, so get something to eat and get some rest. Don't allow your feet get too cold. Put clean socks on when you massage your feet. Sergeant Black, post sentries for three hundred sixty degree protection. John found a relatively sheltered place, unrolled his sleeping bag, slipped into it, and slept as soundly as a baby for an hour, then he woke up with his arm hurting him. He stood up, looked around and saw that most of the men were asleep. They had had little sleep these past two days, and they still had a long way to go, so he let them sleep. He made the rounds of the sentry posts— everything was quiet.

He went back and ate some rations and studied his map. He noted that a road junction ahead of them was where a road from the Pujon Reservoir up north joined the road they were on. He wanted to avoid that road junction for sure. Starting at that junction and continuing southwesterly from there might be the most difficult section of road for them. Grady figured that the Chinese would marshal their forces to keep the marines and army units from reaching Hamhung, and he was on the wrong side of those forces.

John didn't know what was happening with the remainder of X Corp. "What a ridiculous situation this is," he muttered to himself. "Here we are a Signal Corps unit and we have no equipment to communicate with anyone. Where did I go wrong?" He figured that he had better start thinking about what they would do the remainder of that day. "Maybe we still are too far north to get involved with the PLA. Maybe we still can use the road." He wished that he had something better to go on than "maybes." He did notice that the mountains there were not as high as they were up north where they had come from. Maybe things would get better. "There's that 'maybe' again," he said as he shook his head.

Grady felt uneasy. He went back to the sentry post that overlooked the road. George Fuller was on duty. "How's it going, George?"

"It's going all right so far. Nothing is happening except that I'm mighty cold. Maybe the sun will come out strong today and we can get some warmth from it."

Fuller saw John studying the landscape and said, "I don't know, Lieutenant, my eyesight isn't the best in the world, but do you see a bridge or something down on the far side of that bend. I can't make out if there's a bridge there or just more rocks."

Grady pulled out his binoculars and focused them on the road in the region of the bend. He looked for some time, then he said, "You look, George, and tell me what you see."

Fuller looked and refocused the binoculars. He was still as he looked, then he pulled the binoculars away from his eyes and said, "Lieutenant, that's a blown bridge down there."

"That's what I think, George." That made Grady's decision about the immediate future easy. "We aren't going down to the road," he said to himself. "We'll go over the ridge of this mountain to its backside, across the saddle to the next mountain, and then go down the far side of that mountain. That will put us beyond the bend in the road and beyond the blown bridge. We'll see what happens next when we get there. It won't be easy for the wounded, but it looks to be the best thing to do. The army didn't promise them a rose garden when they entered service."

Grady went back and roused the men and told them what he had decided. After a quick massage they climbed up the mountain and over the crest and across the saddle to the next mountain. It was difficult and slow going but there were no complaints. About three-quarters of the way down the second mountain they reached a sheltered spot and Grady called a halt for a rest. He and Sergeants Black and Pettit went to the edge of the sheltered area and looked across to the road. A shallow ravine and seventy yards of an upwardly sloping area separated the mountain they were on from the road that was at the base of the opposite mountain. They saw no activity on the road. Grady handed his binoculars to Black and told him, "Take these and look up and down the road and up and down the mountain to see if you see anything." John was not feeling too well: his arm was hurting and he had a headache.

"I don't see anything," Black said. "Here, you see if you can see anything," he said to Sergeant Pettit. Robert took the binoculars and methodically scanned the road and the mountain. He was about to return the binoculars when he said, "Wait … wait a minute … I think I saw something move over there!"

"Where," Black asked.

"Do you see about a quarter way around the curve where there's a recess in the hillside, I think that I saw movement there." Pettit kept the binoculars fixed on that spot. No one spoke. After several minutes of silence, Pettit exclaimed, "There—there it is again. Quick, look."

Black took the glasses and looked where Pettit was pointing. He looked for about a minute, then said, "Yeah, yeah, I see it. It's in that recess. Here, Lieutenant, you look." John took the binoculars and looked. At first he didn't see anything, then he too saw movement at the recess. He continued looking and tried not to breath in order to hold the binoculars steady. "Yes, I see movement over there, but I'm not focusing too well today. Here Robert, take the glasses and see what you can make of it. Sergeant Black, while Robert is looking, you go back and warn the others not to show themselves. You be careful not to show yourself on your way back. Tell them to stay alert and be ready to move immediately."

Pettit resumed his watch and after a short while he said, "Lieutenant Grady, I can see at least two figures over there, and if I had to bet right now I would bet that those figures are wearing GI helmets and overcoats."

"You're kidding," Grady said. He thought a moment, then cautioned, "Even if they are wearing our clothing that doesn't make them UN people. Enemy soldiers or guerrillas could have picked up GI clothing somewhere."

"I understand, Lieutenant. Here, you take a look."

John looked again. "Robert, right now I can't argue with you. Do you have a shaving mirror with you? If you don't, run back to the others and see if someone has a mirror. Hurry." Pettit took off on the double up the mountain to the others. Shortly, he and Black came back with a thin, three inch by five inch piece of highly-polished stainless steel that Stan Obromowitz used as a shaving mirror.

John remembered the survival training that he had in the navy. Survival kits on life rafts included a signal mirror that survivors on the raft could use to signal aircraft or ships if they were lucky enough to see one. Obromowitz's mirror was not a signal mirror because it had no means to aim it, but it would have to do. John took the mirror from Pettit and looked at the angle of the sun and the angle of the recess in the mountain across the way. He held up the mirror and very slowly moved it about trying to get the sun's reflection from the mirror directed onto the recess. Grady said, "Do you see the reflection over there? I don't see it. I don't know where I am. Am I close?"

"I see it," Pettit said. "You're way high and off to the right. Do you see it?"

"Yeah," John said. He moved the reflected light down to where he wanted it. Several times he slowly swept it back and forth across the area where they had seen the figures. He withdrew the mirror and waited. Nothing. He raised the mirror and again swept the reflected light across the recess. He stopped for a short while, then did it again. They waited. Sergeant Black kept the binoculars fixed on the recess. "Hold it—I see a figure. Try your mirror again, Lieutenant. Put it right on that figure; I'll guide you." Together they directed the reflected light onto the figure. The figure darted back into the recess. "Now what do we do?" Black asked.

"We just keep signaling," John replied. "Their curiosity will get to them after a while."

" Sergeant Pettit, get ready to block and unblock the mirror with something to send some Morse code over there. You're in the Signal Corps, you do know Morse code, don't you. We'll hope if they're friendly they can read it. But first, let's wait a few minutes to let them respond to seeing our light.

"Sergeant Black, watch that entire mountainside to see if any people start moving out of that area. If they start coming this way, we may have to get the hell out of here in a hurry. We'll climb back up the mountain and head south along the backside of the ridge."

They waited about five minutes. John was not sure what they should do next. He had to keep the men moving or they would freeze to death, and he figured that they could not wait much longer before they would have to move. His arm was hurting, and he was getting impatient. He told himself that he had to keep his head and not do anything stupid.

"He's back," Black called. "Same place."

"O.K., guide my light back to him," John said. "Robert, get ready to send to him."

"What should I send?" Pettit asked.

"Send USA three times. Do it slowly and distinctly." Pettit waved his mitten back and forth across the mirror to make the Morse code letters. They waited.

"He's disappeared back into the recess," Black said. In a couple of minutes he exclaimed, "There are two of them over there now. Quick, signal them again." Grady and Pettit signaled USA five times.

"They're waving," Black reported. "They both are waving their arms in this direction." "What do we do now?" Pettit asked.

"Send them the word COME," John said. They again directed the reflected light onto the figures, and Pettit sent the message five times.

"If they come out of there and come this way, I'll go down to meet them," John said.

"No you won't, Lieutenant," Black said. "Begging your pardon, Lieutenant, but you should stay up here with the men; they're looking to you to get them out. I'll go and take Obromowitz to cover me."

"He's right, you know, Lieutenant," Pettit said.

"O.K., but let them come far enough so you can make a positive identification that they're our people before you go down there. You and Obromowitz stay separated from each other."

Pettit went back and summoned Obromowitz. Black kept the binoculars on two advancing figures as they crossed the road and started across the sloping area.

"They look genuine to me, Lieutenant," Black said. "Here, you check them out," he said as he passed the binoculars to Grady.

Grady studied the two figures as they cautiously walked across the sloping area. "I agree with you. Still, be on your guard; you never know for sure."

The two figures in GI attire stopped short of the ravine and looked all around them. They were standing about fifteen feet apart, one behind and off to one side of the other. The one in front made a "Come here" motion with his arm. He said nothing. He apparently had not seen Grady and his men yet because he didn't look exactly in their direction when he motioned.

"O.K. Sergeant Black, go ahead. Stan, keep behind him and keep him covered. Don't cross the ravine; make them come to you. We can give you some fire support from up here." Black and Obromowitz moved down to the base of the mountain and slowly approached the ravine. Sergeant Black stopped and motioned for Obromowitz to stop.

"What outfit you from, soldier?" Black called to the one in front.

"31st Infantry Regiment," was the reply.

"Who's your division commander?" Black called back.

"Major General David Barr."

"Who are the senators from Oklahoma?" Black challenged.

"Who the hell but an Okie knows who the senators from Oklahoma are. I'm from California and don't give a damn who the senators from Oklahoma are. Who the hell are you, and what are you doing here?"

"We're Signal Corps with Signal Section, Headquarters Tenth Corps. We were up at Hyesanjin on the Yalu with the 17th Regiment and we missed them when they left. We've had to walk and fight our way out. What are you doing here?

"We were in the 31st Infantry east of the Chosin Reservoir. Our battalion got chewed up pretty bad. We couldn't get back to our people, so we took off cross-country to the east to try to get around the Chinese and get back to our forces."

"How many of you are there?" Black asked.

"There are four of us. How about you?"

"There are nine of us. Where are the rest of your people, and where are you headed?" Blackie didn't want to tell him about the wounded. He was playing his cards close to his chest and didn't want to reveal their weakness.

"We have two more over on that mountain. We have a captain with a broken leg. We're headed south to Hamhung, but since the captain busted his leg we're not making very good progress."

Black said to the stranger, "Come across the ravine—both of you—I want you to talk to our lieutenant." The strangers came across the ravine, and Black pointed up the mountain and said, "Straight up there. Go ahead; we'll follow you up." The group came to Grady and Pettit. Black said,

"Lieutenant Grady, they say they're from the 31st Infantry, and they say there are two more of them over on the mountain."

John introduced himself and asked them some of the same questions that Black had asked. They told him that the soldier in front was Sergeant Art Smith, and the other one was Private Frank Tomilson. They said that they had been traveling for days, mostly cross-country except for short distances on mountain roads, or more like paths. They said that Captain MacDowell had slipped on the ice late yesterday and had fallen down a cliff and broke his left leg. They said that they had a marine with them who's with the captain over on the other mountain.

"How come you have a marine with you," John asked.

Smith answered, "He was with the Marine Corps Tactical Air Controller who was attached to the 31st Infantry when the Chinese hit us. He was with us when we got cut off from the rest of our outfit, so he stayed with us. He was able to read your code. He's a good man."

"How badly is your captain hurt? Can he travel?" Grady was not eager to become involved with the new people and get slowed down any more than he already was.

"It's a break just above the knee. He's in a lot of pain, but he's toughing it out. He's moving with the aid of a branch that he's using for a crutch, but he can't move very fast."

John was not happy to hear that. "Have you run into any Chinese or North Koreans?"

"Not since we left the reservoir area. How about you?"

"We had a firefight with some Chinese north of here.

"Did you take casualties?" Smith asked.

"We lost three killed, and we have three wounded."

"Four wounded," Sergeant Pettit corrected him.

Smith looked at Sergeant Black as if to say, "Why the hell didn't you tell me that before?" Now it was Smith who was wondering whether his group wanted to get slowed down by these people who had four wounded. Although they were countrymen and fellow soldiers, they all knew that they were in a difficult situation and the instinct of self-preservation was strong in them. This is where training and leadership make a difference.

Grady asked Smith, "What kind of setup do you have over on that mountain? Do you plan to spend time there or are you moving on?"

"We don't have any setup at all. We just stopped to let the captain rest.

"O.K., we'll go over to see your captain," John said. "We're going down the road after that and you can join us if you want, but we have to get moving. Obromowitz, go up and bring the men down here right away."

Sergeant Black scanned the road and mountainsides north and south with the binoculars and pronounced that the way was clear. Grady's crew, with Smith and Tomilson, went down the mountain, across the ravine, and up to the recess where they met Captain James MacDowell, Infantry, and U.S. Marine Corps PFC Paul Bloucher. MacDowell was as tall as Grady, was thin, had black hair, and looked as though he was about the same age as Grady. Bloucher was shorter than Grady, was muscular, and had a narrow, serious-looking face. He looked to be about 21 years old.

Grady felt personally responsible for his crew and intended to see to it that he led them to safety, despite the fact that the captain outranked him and normally would assume command of the combined groups. The fact that the captain had a broken leg was the deciding factor in Grady's thinking. "Captain, we're heading down this road until it gets dark. The PLA probably won't be active on the road until dark, and they don't seem to have stopped in these mountains. Then we'll get off the road and see what develops. We're trying to get to Hamhung the best way we can and as quickly as we can. We'll be shoving off right soon. You and your people are welcome to join us if you wish."

"Captain, they have four wounded," Sergeant Smith said. "But they seem to be able to move pretty well, considering."

Captain MacDowell now had to make a decision. He stood up from the rock he was sitting on and said, "Lieutenant, let's you and me go over there and talk," as he motioned to a location away from the other men. John fully expected to be chewed out and the captain would pull his rank on him and tell him what he was to do. The captain hobbled over to the spot, and John followed behind him.

"Lieutenant, we're thirteen men here behind enemy lines in the severest weather the Good Lord has to offer. Let's be honest, it'll take a miracle to get us out of here. I can hardly walk with this broken leg, and if I go with you I'll reduce the odds of the rest of you getting out to practically zero. You take the eleven others and head south. I'll take my chances on my own."

John didn't know what to say. Decision time again. He hesitated a moment, then he looked MacDowell in the eyes. "Captain, you're going out with us. This is your only chance—seize it. We're not going to allow you to slow us down, and it's going to be tough as hell on you, but it'll be a picnic compared to what'll happen to you if you stay here by yourself. That's the end of it. Let's get ready to shove off." As the two of them walked back to the other men, John said, "Captain, we're Signal Corps and don't know much about infantry tactics. We're going to rely on you for that, so stay alert." MacDowell nodded his head. John was taking command, whether anyone liked it or not and whether it was the proper army procedure or not. He felt that the captain had his hands full just moving, and he was not sure how resolved the captain was right now about getting out.

"Everyone on your feet," John said when the two officers joined the men. "We're heading south on the road—immediately. Who'll volunteer to help the captain?" Sergeant Smith and Private Tomilson both said that they would.

"Captain, we've been marching on the road with a scout out in front about seventy yards or so and a scout following up the rear. Do you have any suggestions?"

"That sounds good to me," MacDowell said.

"Sergeant Black, post our scouts."

They returned to the road and the captain hobbled the best he could with his improvised crutch. When he began to fall behind, Smith and Tomilson extended a MI rifle between them and the captain sat on it. They carried him out to the front of the main group and he started hobbling again. The group's progress was slowed, but no one said anything. Some of Grady's men gave Smith and Tomilson relief from time to time. They walked for an hour after darkness even though John knew that it was risky.

***

John was about to look for a place to stop when the forward scout George Fuller came hurrying back and said, "Lieutenant, there's a side road, or really a trail, branching off up there. Do we stay on the main road all the way?"

"I don't know about a side road, George; I didn't see it on my map. We'll look when we get there." They walked farther and saw what looked like a cart path running off to the right of the road. There were no tracks in the snow on the path.

"Let's get off the road right now and see what's up here," Grady said. "We have to rest somewhere. Sergeant Smith, take Bloucher and Obromowitz with you and reconnoiter this trail up ahead. The rest of us will wait up there where we can't be seen from the road." The main group waited while Smith, Bloucher, and Obromowitz walked off into the darkness. Captain MacDowell lay on the ground trying to ease the considerable pain in his leg. Grady checked his wounded men and Captain MacDowell, and all said they were O.K.

Smith, Bloucher and Obromowitz came back and said that they had gone down the cart path about a quarter mile and saw nothing that looked like trouble. They had seen no tracks in the snow. Bloucher reported that up the trail they saw what looked like a large rock overhang that formed a shallow cave up on the hillside. It would be a good place to take a rest. They could see the trail from there, and they would get some protection from the weather.

Sergeant Smith led the group to the rock overhang. It was the most protected spot they had found yet. The softer rocks under the overhang had eroded away about eight feet inwardly to form a twenty-five feet long shelter under the overhang. They were about twenty feet above the trail and could see roughly forty yards of it but not the junction with the road. On the other side of the trail, the ground fell away to a narrow frozen stream bed.

Grady went over to MacDowell and said, "Captain, what do you recommend for posting sentries?" MacDowell recommended that at least one sentry be posted high on the hill and close to the junction with the road so he could see if anyone started to come down the trail. Sergeant Black posted the sentries, and Grady had the remainder of the men massage their feet. John helped MacDowell with his shoepacs and massaged his feet. When the men finished massaging, Grady asked MacDowell if any of his men had medical or first aid training. MacDowell replied in the negative. Grady called to Sergeant Pettit, "Sergeant, let's hold sick call. Check the wounds and dress them, or do whatever you think needs to be done."

With the aid of a flashlight that Bill Savin held, Pettit worked in turn on Ollie Clark, Albert Ramey, and Charlie Ienfeld. He went to Captain MacDowell and felt around the break in his leg. He told the captain that he just didn't know enough to do anything. He gave the captain two APC pills to kill the pain.

Pettit finished with the captain and said, "O.K. Lieutenant, you're next." MacDowell wondered what he was talking about. Grady went over and exposed his arm. Pettit sprinkled more sulfa powder on the two wounds, bandaged them, and said, "Lieutenant, that arm between where the bullet went in and came out is red and swollen, but I don't know what I can do about that. You had better take another sulfa pill."

MacDowell called Grady over to him. "Lieutenant, I didn't know you were wounded. How serious is it?"

"I don't think it's too serious. It's beginning to get sore and stiff, but that's to be expected. We'll be out of here before long; I'll get the medics to look at it then."

The wind turned brisk and snow fell steadily. John didn't know if this were good or bad. New snow might cover their tracks, but it would make their movement tomorrow more difficult. Grady didn't know what to do tomorrow. If the Chinese were in the area, they surely would have roadblocks along the road. He discussed the situation with MacDowell, but they couldn't reach a decision on a course of action. Grady went off by himself and contemplated their situation. No new thoughts came to him.

At daylight the next morning, 5 December 50, the men slowly roused from their sleeping bags. The snow had stopped during the night, and the sky was crystal clear. It was bitterly cold. They ate and Grady had them massage again. He and MacDowell talked again and decided that they could not sit still. They would move out and take their chances. They were studying the map when the sentry who had been closest to the road junction came scurrying to the rock shelter and exclaimed, "Some people are coming up the trail pulling a cart. They look to be Korean civilians."

Grady jumped to his feet. "On you guard everyone. Get your weapons and ammo. Keep concealed. Bloucher and Tomilson, come here and bring your MIs." When they arrived, John said, "Frank, you and Paul go up behind us to the top of the hill, then go over the crest of the hill and proceed toward the road junction. Get into position so you can see the trail. Stay hidden on the hill, but keep the strangers in view until they get here. If you see them taking hostile actions toward us, get off some shots at them. If you hear us shoot, you open up. Do you understand?" They both nodded and went out the far end of the rock shelter and to the top of the hill and over the crest, then they cautiously proceeded toward the road junction.

Grady told the wounded to get to the rear of the rock shelter, and he dispersed the able-bodied men along the twenty-five feet of the shelter and out of sight from the trail below. He buckled his pistol belt with the Colt .45 pistol on it around the waist of his overcoat and took a prone position at the forward edge of the shelter. His rifle was beside him. They waited.

Shortly, a two-wheel cart that had two long handles extending out front came down the trail. Four Korean civilian men dressed in loose-fitting, white winter clothing pulled and pushed the cart. One man was on each of the handles in front, and the other two men were at rear corners of the cart. The cart had rails along the front and two sides, and a large, faded, tan tarpaulin covered the back of the cart concealing what, if anything, was in it. The Korean men at the front of the cart looked down at the ground trying to follow partially-obscured footsteps in the snow, and then they looked ahead and up to the side of the hill. The two men at the rear of the cart continually scanned the entire area. They moved very cautiously.

New snow covered most of the footprints that the GIs had made yesterday, and the Koreans were having difficulty figuring out how many footprints were there and where they went. The men at the front of the cart saw that some footsteps in the snow went straight ahead and that others went off the trail and up the hill. They stopped and conversed and looked around. They didn't know what to make of the tracks.

Captain MacDowell dragged his prone body up to the side of Grady and peeked over to the trail below. He withdrew from the edge and whispered to John, "All males: no women or children—watch out for guerrillas. I don't like the looks of this one bit."

The two Koreans who had been at the front of the cart walked forward, hesitated at the base of the hill, looked around, and then slowly followed the faint footprints up the hill. Their eyes swept back and forth across the hill in front of them. They never took their eyes off the hillside. Obviously, they were hunting. When they were about halfway to the rock shelter, Grady loosened the flap on his pistol holster and stood up. He held out his right arm with the palm of his hand facing them to indicate that he wanted them to stop. They did. He dropped his arm so that his fingers were not far from his pistol. None of the other GIs showed themselves. Grady very slowly worked his way toward the Koreans, always being certain that he had good footing. "Do you speak English?" he asked. They both made big smiles at Grady, muttered something in Korean, and shrugged their shoulders. Each Korean had something like a white poncho covering his outer clothing, and each had moved an arm under his poncho. Grady moved downhill to a position about ten feet in front of them and looking down on them.

Just as Grady was about to speak again, a shot rang out from the top of the hill to his left and there was commotion down at the cart, which also was to his left. In the flick of an eyelash, Grady drew his pistol and shot the first Korean in the head. As his arm recovered from the recoil, he instantly leveled the pistol and shot the second one in the head. His ears rang from the noise of the shots.

"Holy hell, Lieutenant, you killed them!" Sergeant Pettit yelled as he came rushing down to Grady. Just then another shot rang out from the top of the hillside to their left. Then, everything was quiet. Grady looked down at the cart but didn't see any activity. "Obromowitz, come on down here," he called back up to the rock shelter as he continued watching the cart. "Sergeant Pettit, you and Obromowitz search these bodies." Each Korean had an automatic pistol under his white poncho and several Russian grenades in his pockets.

"Look at that, will you," Obromowitz said as he pointed to the feet of the dead Koreans. Both were wearing American GI shoepacs. "How do you suppose they came by those shoepacs?"

"I don't know," John said, "and I don't want to know. Come with me. We're going down to the cart. Be on the ready." They cautiously approached the cart down on the trail. When they were close to it they saw Paul Bloucher and Frank Tomilson approaching from the other side. They made hand signals to each other to indicate that they saw each other. The two groups arrived at the cart and found two dead Korean civilians behind it. A Russian-made AK47 rifle was beside one of them.

"Lieutenant Grady, I saw one of them taking aim on you from behind the cart when you showed yourself," Bloucher said. "I couldn't take a chance, so I did like you told me. After I heard two shots from you people, the other guy was trying to get something from the cart. Again, I didn't think that I could take a chance, so I got off another round."

"You did just right, Paul," John said. "You probably saved us some casualties—one of whom might have been me. Let's see what's under that tarp." Obromowitz and Tomilson pulled back the tarpaulin. There were several bags of rice and boxes of food, a wooden box with Russian writing on it and grenades in it, and several boxes of rifle ammunition. Another AK47 rifle also was there. Several U.S. canteens and pistol belts also were on the cart.

"Leave those things in the cart; we can use some of them," John said. "Place those bodies over to the side of the trail, and let's get back to the shelter." When they arrived back at the shelter, Grady explained to everyone what had happened and what they had found, and then Grady and MacDowell conferred alone. "We have to get moving if we hope to get out of here," John said. "I know it's risky to take to the road, but what alternative do we have? I say we have to risk it. What do you think, Captain?"

"My friends call me 'Mac.' Why don't you call me that," MacDowell said. "John, I can't argue with you. We'll freeze to death if we sit still too long. It's unlikely that any of our people in Hamhung are coming to get us, so we have to get to them."

"O.K., let's shove off as soon as we can. We have some transportation for you and our seriously wounded; we'll use that cart as long as we can."

***

They returned to the main road and proceeded southwest. Captain MacDowell, Ollie Clark, and Albert Ramey rode in the cart. Charlie Ienfeld said that his thigh wound was not serious and that he could walk, although with some pain and a limp. The healthy ones took turns pulling and pushing the cart and serving as the forward and rear scouts. They were making fair progress. They were on the road about two hours when they heard airplanes off to the west, but the planes were too far away for the group to attract their attention.

In early afternoon the forward scout came back and told Grady that there was a house just ahead of them and about one hundred yards off to the right side of the road. The scout reported that he saw no activity up there and there were no tracks in the snow on the trail to the house. John conferred with MacDowell and they decided to send a small patrol up to investigate while the others waited at the beginning of the trail. The patrol returned and reported that the house was deserted. MacDowell asked them if they had entered the house. They replied that they had. MacDowell asked them if they had checked for booby traps. PFC Bloucher said that they had checked and had found none. The Americans went up the trail and entered the house. It was one of the finest Korean houses John had seen. It was a two-story dwelling that might have been built by a wealthy Korean before the Communists took over, or more likely, by a wealthy Japanese when Japan occupied Korea. The house overlooked a large valley between two mountains. The owner probably farmed the valley. The house looked almost like a western house, both outside and inside. There was no furniture in the house, and there were no stoves or heaters.

John told Sergeant Black to post sentries around the area and told the others to get something to eat and to massage their hands and feet. Grady continued, "Men, we have plenty of space here for us to spread out into several rooms, but if we get eight or ten bodies in one room we might be able to raise the temperature in that room a degree or two, maybe even more. Every little bit will help, so let's all sack out for the night in one room. Corporal Savin, find the largest room that we can shut up to preserve any heat that we generate." John felt silly doing this, but he was determined to do everything he could think of to get them back to their own lines. Even if it were silly and useless, he figured that it would do no harm. Savin returned and said, "Lieutenant, there's a large room upstairs that runs the length of the house. It's to the left of the stairs, and we can shut the door from the hallway into it. It has a fireplace, and there are windows where we can see out."

Grady said that they wouldn't have a fire in the fireplace because he didn't want to attract attention, but the room sounded good. John looked at MacDowell with a questioning look.

"I'll make it up the stairs; don't worry about me," MacDowell said.

They went upstairs, turned to the left around the end of a railing at the top of the stairs, and then turned to the right across the hallway and into the room. MacDowell sat on the steps and pushed himself up one step at a time with his good leg.

After the men ate and massaged, Grady said with a grin , "O.K. Doctor Pettit, time for sick call; please check your patients."

John went over to the captain and said, "How's the leg, Mac?"

"I guess I'm no worse off than you are. If you can make it, I can." Both were experiencing considerable discomfort. Grady could not get rid of his headache. Pettit tried to tend to both officers, but with his limited experience he could do nothing more than sprinkle sulfa powder on Grady's wounds and give each of them a sulfa pill from their first aid kits.

Grady and MacDowell talked about tomorrow. Neither had any

bright ideas, so they decided to try to do tomorrow what they had done that day and hope that it worked. Without saying it, both realized that the most difficult portion of their journey was in front of them.

Grady went to Sergeant Black and said to him. "Sergeant, take an inventory and see how we stand on food, medicine, ammo, and socks to see if we have to start rationing our use of them." Black did so and reported that after that day they would be very short of food and just about out of medicine. In a day or two days they would be out of both. Clean socks were good for a couple more days and always could be stretched out more than that.

The weary men settled in. Several already were in their sleeping bags and asleep. Grady went outside and checked with each of the sentries. Everything was quiet. He returned to the upstairs room and crawled into his sleeping bag and fell asleep. Except for waking up several times during the night when sentries changed, he slept soundly.

A majority of the men in the room were awake long before dawn on 6 December. Grady called to Sergeant Black, "Sergeant, change the guards and let the fellows out there come in and get warmed up a little before we shove off. I want to get under way as soon as possible." Just then, Bill Savin, who was on sentry duty outside, ran into the house and up the stairs to the room. "Lieutenant, some people are coming down from the north. They're coming right up here."

"How many?" Grady asked.

"I couldn't make out for sure in the dark, but I would guess that it's half a dozen or so. It looks like a Chinese patrol."

"How close are they?" Grady asked.

"They're out at the edge of the clearing and moving in toward the house. I don't know if they saw me come in here or not. I worked my way around and came in from the back of the house, but they probably see my footprints. Maybe I should have fired on them when I saw them."

"O.K., Bill, close the door and stay here." As Savin closed the door, they heard the front door swing open. Grady turned to the rest of the men and said in a low voice, "Here we go again, men. Open the front and side windows nearest the door. Sergeant Pettit and Savin, each of you take positions on opposite sides of the door and close to the wall. If a grenade comes through that door, scoop it up and throw it out an open window. You have to be quick. We'll shoot through the door to cover you when you go after the grenade. If those two can't get to the grenade, everyone hit the deck."

"Bloucher, you stand near the outside wall to the right of the fireplace and out of the way of the doorway so that if someone shoots through the door you'll be out of the way. If someone starts through that doorway, you nail him. The door is hinged on the side opposite you, so you'll see him as soon as the door starts to open.

"Tomilson, you do the same on the front side of the room. The door is hinged on your side so you'll not see anything until someone gets through the door. You can shoot through the door when you see it start to open. Everyone else, stay in the back of the room against the inside wall and be ready to shoot anyone who comes through the door."

John was concerned for George Fuller and Stan Obromowitz who were outside on guard duty. "They both are bright and have good common sense, so I hope they play it safe," John thought to himself.

John went over to Captain MacDowell who was sitting against the back wall. "What do you think, Mac, are we doing the right thing? This is all I can think of."

"You're doing fine, John; I can't think of anything else. If they try to burn us out, we'll have to go out the windows. That two-story drop to the ground won't be too bad. We can hang from the windowsill and drop from there. We can get covering fire from here and maybe from our two perimeter guards who are still outside." MacDowell seemed willing to have Grady take command here and elsewhere.

Grady took a position between Bloucher and the fireplace. He didn't think he could hold his carbine steady because of his aching left arm, so he sat on the floor with his shoulders against the outside wall. He pushed his buttocks out from the wall and drew up his knees and rested his Colt .45 between his two kneecaps. He figured that he was down low enough to the floor and far enough to the side of the door so that if anyone shot through the door he would be well out of the way.

Dawn was breaking as they waited in silence. John wondered what he should have done different to avoid getting his men holed up like fish in a rain barrel. Maybe he should have posted more sentries. Maybe they should have stayed on the first floor of this house instead of going up to the second floor. Maybe they should not have stayed in the house at all. Maybe he should not be in the army in the first place. Maybe there should not be a war going on. "Hold it fellow," he told himself, "this is not going to get the men out of here. You are going to get them out, and you had better pay attention to business."

A noise occurred outside the door. Sergeant Pettit poked his finger several times in the direction of the door. Everyone in the room checked to be certain that the safety on his weapon was in the off position.

Like an explosion, the door burst open and a figure in the doorway sprayed bullets from his burp gun into the room! Bloucher and Grady fired their weapons at that very same instant. The figure stumbled backward through the doorway and across the hallway and came to rest in a slouched sitting position against the balusters of the stair railing. Grady saw two figures run down the stairs.

A half-dozen shots rang out from outside. Those inside the room waited. They heard no more noise from inside or outside the house. Grady stood up holding his left arm and said, "Sergeant Black, see if we have any more casualties. Bloucher, Savin, come with me." The three of them went to the doorway and Grady took a quick look outside, then darted his head back in. "Cover me," John told them, "I'm going out into the hallway." All three went into the hall. "You two check the other rooms up here. Keep each other covered and don't take unnecessary chances. Wait until Tomilson gets out here to help you." Grady called Tomilson, and the three men set off.

Grady stood in front of the Chinese soldier sprawled against the balusters. He wore quilted coat and trousers, and a narrow red stripe extended around the edge of his coat collar. Grady guessed that he was an officer because he had not seen such a red stripe on any of the dead Chinese soldiers he had seen two days ago. The Chinese officer was alive and looked to be younger than John. He looked up at John, then he looked away in the direction of the burp gun that had fallen to the floor beside him. Grady moved forward and put his boot beside the gun and slid it out of reach. The young Chinese looked up at John with a look that revealed exactly what he was thinking—a haunting look that John never would forget. That quiet, soulful look said, "I don't want that gun. You don't have to worry about me causing you any more trouble: I did a foolish thing and it cost me my life. I lose, you win. I will not get home to see my family. I am dying—alone." John had tears in his eyes. The young Chinese looked at Grady and nodded, then lowered his head. His breathing became fainter—then stopped.

"What a terrible world this is," John thought. "This never should be allowed to happen." He brushed the tears from his eyes with the back of his glove and called to Bloucher, Savin, and Tomilson to check all the rooms on the first floor. He returned to the large room. "Sergeant Black, what are our casualties?"

"Can you believe it, Lieutenant, even with that burp gun he didn't hit anyone. Our shots took him out him before he could pick targets and aim."

"What about that firing outside?" Grady said. "Take a couple of the able-bodied men out to see what's going on. Check our sentries.

"That burp gun didn't miss everyone," Grady said to Sergeant Pettit. "It hit me in the arm. I don't understand how he hit me; none of his other bullets hit anywhere near me. I must have been hit by a ricochet off that stone fireplace. Sergeant, you have more work to do on this left arm."

Pettit came over and looked at the sleeve of his coat. "This one is higher up than the other one, isn't it, Lieutenant?"

"Yes, this one's in the upper arm."

"Take your outer clothing off, Lieutenant, I have to get a good look at it."

Grady pealed off the clothing and exposed his left arm. The bullet had hit him in the inside of the upper arm. Pettit wiped the wound with a piece of gauze and looked at the arm. "I don't see an exit hole for the bullet. It must still be in there."

Captain MacDowell hobbled over and said, "May I see that arm?" He looked at it with a grim face. "How do you feel, John?"

"I've felt better, Mac, but I still can function." Pettit swabbed the wound and tore open a packet of sulfa powder and sprinkled it into the new wound. While he was at it, he sprinkled some on the old wounds. He bandaged all of them and gave Grady a sulfa pill.

"How are your medical supplies holding out," Grady asked Pettit.

" That's it—I'm out. We had better get to Hamhung soon."

Sergeant Black and the other able-bodied men entered the room. "Sir, three of the Chinese got away. They headed back to the north. Fuller shot one, but the other three slipped away."

"Is Fuller O.K.," John asked.

"Yes."

MacDowell spoke up. 'Lieutenant Grady, that was a patrol, which means there are more PLA in this area and they know where we are. Let's get the hell out of here."

"Right you are, Captain. O.K. men, we leave immediately. Sergeant

Black, recall the sentries so they can get back here and get their gear. They hurried down the hill and onto the road in the valley. MacDowell, Clark, and Ramey again rode in the cart.

John was more fearful than ever about traveling on the road in daylight, but because of the wounded they could not leave the road and go cross-country across the hills. Ollie Clark's shoulder wound was getting worse, and the captain could not walk over rough terrain. But the Good Lord was with them that day—they had no more encounters with the enemy. But they didn't cover as much distance as John would have liked. The men were tired and seemed to be losing strength. They came upon one blown bridge, but had little difficulty getting around it. At dark, they left the road and rested for an hour. They walked several hours during the night, then stopped at a secure location to rest, eat, and to massage. Very little food remained. John's left arm hurt every time he moved it, and the headache would not go away.

Grady and MacDowell studied the map by the dim light of a flashlight and tried to plan their day. They figured that they had to be getting close to the rear area of the PLA forces. They finally decided that they just didn't have enough information to make any intelligent plans, so they would go forward, stay alert, and try to make the best of it. What a lousy situation to be in! They did decide to double up on the forward scout.

***

They returned to the road and resumed their march. A couple of hours after daylight they heard aircraft off to the west and saw four planes a couple of thousand feet high and coming in their direction. As the planes came closer, the men saw that they were U.S. Navy or Marine Corps Corsairs. The men waved their arms frantically and shouted at the planes as they approached. The planes passed over them and kept going. The men stopped shouting and their hearts sank. Then, two of the planes made long sweeping turns to the right and one plane circled around and approached Grady's group at a lower altitude. The other plane flew higher overhead and behind the first one. The men frantically waved their arms again, and the lower plane slowly rocked its wings as it flew over the group. The men let out a cheer. The plane gained altitude, joined the overhead one, and both flew off and returned to their aircraft carrier that was steaming in the Sea of Japan off the North Korean coast.

The men talked excitedly. "What do you think they'll do?" they asked Grady.

"Hopefully, they'll report our position to the army. What the army can do, I don't know. We're still behind enemy lines, don't forget. Don't get your hopes up too soon, and don't let your guard down. We're not out yet."

The group resumed their march with renewed spirits. After noon, they heard the faint sound of an aircraft off in the distance. They saw a small speck in the sky, and as the speck grew in size they recognized the plane to be a single-engine U.S. Army L-5 artillery spotter, or observation plane. The men began to wave their arms as soon as they identified it. As the plane passed over them at a very low altitude, the pilot threw out of the window something that had a very long, narrow, cloth streamer attached to it. When it struck the ground, George Fuller ran to it and brought it back to Grady. It was a stone with a note tied to it with string. Grady untied the string and read the hand-printed note. He read it aloud, "GO TO SINHUNG. 7th DIV HOLDING THERE. DO YOU NEED ANYTHING?" (At this time, the retreating X Corps had established a defense perimeter extending outwardly from Hamhung and anchored on the port city of Hungnam. Sinhung was within the perimeter.) The plane made a long, lazy, circling maneuver in the sky.

Grady said to Sergeants Black and Pettit. "Quick, use your carbine butts and print in large letters in the snow the following words: Rx; FOOD; NEED RADIO; PLA-WHERE?

"What else do we need?" Grady asked.

"How about a crutch?" MacDowell asked.

"Why not. Add CRUTCH."

The sergeants scraped large letters in the snow to form the seven words. The plane made two more low-altitude passes over the group, and each time Grady made motions simulating giving an injection and talking on a telephone or a microphone. The plane waggled its wings and headed back in the direction from which it came.

Grady and MacDowell conferred about their next move. "Mac, we have to get medicine for the wounded; we can't take the chance of not getting the supplies. The L-5 pilot has our present location, and he's sure to look here for us. If we continue walking, who knows what we'll find down the road or where we'll be when they come looking for us. I say we stay put and wait. What do you think?"

"That sounds reasonable to me, John."

Grady told the men the options and why he decided to wait for the supplies. He told them, "I don't know how long we'll have to wait, so make yourselves as comfortable as possible." They posted sentries and settled in behind a hill. The men turned the cart over on its side to provide a buffer against the wind, and they rigged the tarpaulin to give them additional shelter. They massaged their hands and feet, then most of the men dozed in their sleeping bags.

Grady and MacDowell sat to one side of the men, and for the first time since they met they had an opportunity to chat. Mac asked Grady about his background, and John gave him a quick summary. John asked the same question of Mac.

"I'm from Great falls, Montana," Mac replied. "I've been in the army over four years now. I received my commission through OCS and thought I'd give an army career a try. I wanted to get away from the small town. My grandfather started a newspaper in Great Falls, and my dad now runs it. I always was known in town as 'Little Jim' or 'Little Mac' because my grandfather and dad both are named Jim. I wanted to get away on my own and be my own man. I thought the army would be a good way to do that."

"Did you go to college?" John asked.

"I went to Montana State two years."

"What was your major in college?"

"Journalism, what else. My dad was hoping I'd join him on the newspaper. He took it kind of hard when I decided to stay in the army. I was sorry to disappoint him."

They asked each other about their present injuries and wounds. Each put up a bold front and said that he was doing all right. In truth, Mac's leg was throbbing and hurt constantly. The wounds in Grady's arm produced a constant and severe pain, and the headache was almost as bad.

In late afternoon the sentry on the hill yelled down, "A plane is coming." The able-bodied men scrambled out of their sleeping bags and ran to the clearing and waited. It was the L-5 again. The men waived their arms. The pilot waggled the wings and came in low and slow and dropped a freefalling bundle when he was over the clearing. Several men hurried out and retrieved the bundle. The plane made two more passes, each time dropping a bundle. The last bundle had a small parachute attached to it. The pilot made a wide turn, rocked the wings, and flew off.

The men brought the three bundles back to the tarpaulin shelter, and Fuller, Obromowitz, and Savin set about opening the two smallest bundles. They contained food, water, medicine, a folded map, and a small amount of rifle ammunition. Sergeant Pettit took charge of the medicine and read the labels to see what he had. Grady took the map and handed it to MacDowell who was sitting off to the side. "Here Mac, see what you can make of this."

Sergeant Black and Charlie Ienfeld went after the bundle that had the parachute attached, thinking that it might contain a radio. It did, and it also contained an aluminum crutch. The bottom part of the crutch was pivoted up and taped to the forked part that contained the handle and the shoulder brace. The bolts that held the parts of the crutch together would have to be undone and the parts reassembled correctly.

Black and Ienfeld inspected the radio. "Shall we fire it up, Lieutenant?" Black asked.

"Let's hear from Captain MacDowell before we do anything," Grady replied. "I want to know where we are relative to the PLA." They all gathered around MacDowell who was studiously reading the map. The captain spoke without taking his eyes off the map. "They've marked in pencil for us our present position and the locations of the PLA forces north and east of Sinhung. They also marked a route for us to follow to keep us off the road. It must be a trail or something through the hills. We can get on it just a short way down this road."

Grady asked, "Did they show where we're supposed to go through the line?

"No, they just marked our route up to the area of the PLA front line."

Grady responded with irritation, "How the hell are we supposed to know where we go through the lines? Do they expect us to flap our arms and fly over them? What incompetence!"

Grady turned to Sergeant Black. "O.K., Sergeant, what about that radio? Does it work?

"Let me turn on the plate voltage and see," Black replied. "What should I send?"

"C. Q. any UN forces," Grady replied.

"C. Q., C. Q., ANY UN FORCES. CUT OFF TENTH CORPS SIGNAL UNIT SENDING. PLEASE ACKNOWLEDGE. OUT."

Black spoke the message several times. They waited. Nothing. "Maybe we're not close enough yet," Black said.

"We'll try later," Grady said. "Sergeant Pettit, what medicine do you have there?"

"They sent more sulfa powder and pills, and some iodine. I also have more gauze bandages and tape, and more APC pills. They sent written instructions that the wounded are to take two sulfa pills immediately and one each three times a day."

"O.K., we'll do that in a minute," John said. "Corporal Savin, what food did we get?"

"More rations. It looks like about two-day's worth. They sent some water, but a couple of the containers broke when the bundle hit the ground, so we'll have to ration our use of it."

Grady moved into high gear. "Sergeant Pettit and George Fuller, take care of the wounded and give them sulfa pills. Sergeant Smith, distribute the food rations among the men. Obromowitz, Tomilson, and Bloucher, strike the tarpaulin and get the cart ready for travel. Savin, get that radio ready for travel. Let one of the wounded who will be riding on the cart keep the battery under his overcoat to keep it from freezing. We'll try again to make a contact when we get to a high elevation south of here. Everyone, be ready to leave as soon as Sergeant Pettit is finished with the wounded."

John went over to MacDowell. "Mac, it'll be dark soon, do you think you can find that cutoff in the dark?"

"We'll just have to, that's all. If we get away soon we ought to get there while we still have some daylight left. Take a good look with me at the terrain on this map to see where we get off the road; we'll have to locate it even if it's dark."

They resumed their march and found their cutoff just as darkness fell. The next hurdle to jump would be finding the trail through the mountains. They located the beginning of it and proceeded up a slight grade. The trail reminded John of the long-abandoned logging roads that he had encountered in the woods in West Virginia when his father and he had hunted rabbits and grouse. The crew walked most of the night. The able-bodied men took turns pulling and pushing the cart with the wounded in it. They had considerable difficulty getting the cart through the snow and ice on the inclined portions of the narrow trail. All the men were tired and worried, but John didn't hear one complaint. Periodically, Grady told the wounded to get out of the cart and walk because he wanted them to move their arms and legs to keep their blood flowing. They easily could freeze to death if they stayed in the cart all the time. They stopped several times to rest and to massage feet and hands.

John's arm was one constantly throbbing pain, and never in his life had he had such a headache. He took his left arm out of his overcoat and field jacket sleeves and held it against his body. He zipped up the field jacket and overcoat, leaving the left sleeve of the overcoat dangling at his side. Maybe the heat of his body would make some of the pain go away from the arm. Or, should he try to keep the arm cold? What should he do? He guessed that the other wounded and Mac also were feeling terrible. "We had better get to the front line soon, and we had better get through the line and get some medical help soon," Grady said to himself. He became frightened every time he thought about how in the world they ever would get through the line.

They trudged on in silence during the pre-dawn hours of 8 December. At first light, Grady saw that the trail ahead of them went through a narrow pass between rock cliffs on both sides. If ever there were an ideal place to get bushwhacked, that was it. He called a halt. "Men, turn back and go around that last bend in the trail so we're out of view of that pass. Move off the trail when we get there. On the double. Let's move." They did so. John said, "Take a rest, eat something, and massage."

John helped MacDowell off the cart and led him behind a rock. He called Sergeants Black, Pettit, and Smith to join them. Grady addressed the four of them, "I'm uneasy about that pass up ahead. We're surely close to the Chinese positions, and they undoubtedly have a secondary line and rear positions, but we don't know if they're marked on our map. I don't want to go through that pass until we've reconnoitered it as best we can. I want two men to go to the top of the hill above us and keep a watch on that pass and on the cliffs and hillsides on both sides of it. Watch them every second. If there's a PLA soldier anywhere near here, I want to know it. Sergeant Black, send Paul Bloucher and Stan Obromowitz up there first. I have a lot of trust in both of them. Here, give them my binoculars. Get them up there right away and tell them not to show themselves.

"Sergeant Pettit, you and Savin see if you can raise any friendly people on that radio. We have to get more information in a hurry.

"Sergeant Smith, you work out a perimeter defense. Check it with Captain MacDowell.

"All of you, keep massaging your feet and hands and see that every man does it, including the wounded. O.K., everyone move."

John and MacDowell were alone. "How long do you plan to wait here?" Mac asked John.

"I don't know. Just as long as it takes to be sure that we can move safely through that pass. Doesn't that pass look ominous to you?"

"Yes it does, but I worry about the men freezing in this weather. We can't stay inactive too long."

"I know that, Mac. This is our eighth day trying to get back to our people, and we're close now. I don't want to lose it all by getting too eager and careless. Do you have any suggestions?"

"No, John, I don't."

Grady went over to Robert Pettit to see if he had raised anyone on his radio. He had not. "Sergeant, this is a poor location. Climb up to the top of this hill near where Bloucher and Obromowitz are and see if you can do any better up there. Don't expose yourself to view from the area of the pass and the cliffs. You had better not get too close to the other guys up there. I'll be up there to join you in a couple of minutes. Savin, you stay down here for now."

John then went over to the wounded and advised them not to stay inactive too long. He talked to all the men, being as positive about their situation as he could. He didn't lie to them or give them any false hopes. He knew that they were as smart as he was, and they already had shown their manhood. He respected them.

Grady then climbed the hill to find Robert Pettit. Pettit saw him approaching and motioned Grady to hurry. John arrived and Pettit said, "I have some guy from the 7th Signal Company, and can you believe it, I don't have the password and he's giving me a hard time. He's not believing anything I tell him. Here, Lieutenant, see if you can get through to him."

John took over. "This is Lieutenant John Grady, Signal Section, Headquarters Tenth Corps. We were operating the VHF station up at the Yalu with the 17th Infantry and got stranded. We've been on the road seven days trying to get back, and we think we're close to your lines. We have thirteen people here behind enemy lines, and we have four wounded and one with a broken leg. We need your help getting back. Check with

Lieutenant Donald Smith of the 7th Signal Company. I met him down at Suwon the end of September. My name is Lieutenant John Grady, and I was at Suwon with Captain Phil Walker. Check with Lieutenant Smith for verification and get back to me at 0830. Can you do that?

"Oh, also, an L-5 plane dropped supplies to us yesterday. It dropped this radio we're using. It didn't give us any password. You can check on that also. Move as quickly as you can, soldier, we don't have any backup batteries for this radio. You call us at exactly 0830—same frequency. Out."

"Will call at 0830 if you check out. Out," came the reply.

Pettit and Grady waited. Pettit ate. Grady was not hungry. Instead, he massaged his feet and hands while he waited.

At precisely 0830 the radio crackled. After initial formalities, the voice on the other end said, "This is Lieutenant Smith responding to a call from a Lieutenant Grady. Who is commanding officer of Signal Section, Headquarters Tenth Corps? Over."

"Lieutenant Colonel Robert Ackerman. Over,"

The voice asked another question. "Signal Section, Headquarters Tenth Corps lost an officer in South Korea. What was his name? Over."

"Are you talking about First Lieutenant Rollie Amory? I was with him on the road to Pusan when he received a gunshot wound. He was ambushed by North Koreans. Over."

"O.K., I believe you. I think I remember Captain Walker and you visiting us at Suwon. What can we do for you? Over."

"Do you know the map that was air-dropped to us yesterday? Over."

"Yes. I checked with the L-5 guys. They verified the airdrop. Over."

"Do you know the route that was marked for us on the map? Over."

"I don't know what was marked on the map. Why? Over."

"They didn't give us specific instructions on getting across the line to our side, and we need help on that. If you don't know where we are, you can't give us directions. I'm talking 'in the clear' and don't know who else is listening, so I don't want to give my position. Find out who marked the map and get him to contact us on the radio. He, or someone else, will have to direct us to a crossing place. Maybe the pilot of the L-5 marked the map. Do you understand—we need specific instructions on where and when to pass through the PLA lines.

"Lieutenant Smith, we have four wounded and one with a broken leg. We need help. Also, will you get in touch with Captain Walker at Signal

Section Headquarters and tell him that you made contact with us and that we need help getting out. Lieutenant, will you contact us every hour on the hour and let us know what the situation is? Over."

"Will do all of the above. Out."

"Robert, you hold on up here since we know we can make contact from this location. I'll send Bill Savin up to give you relief. You tell him exactly what the situation is when he gets here."

Grady then crawled on his stomach in the snow to where Paul Boucher and Stan Obromowitz were watching the pass.

"We haven't seen a thing, Lieutenant," Obromowitz reported. Bloucher was farther ahead with the binoculars pressed to his eyes scanning the pass and hillsides.

"O.K., but don't take your eyes off that area for one second. I'll send some relief for you when I get back down to the trail." Grady crawled back to the back side of the hill and descended to the tail. He informed Captain MacDowell and the sergeants what had transpired up on the hill.

Grady addressed Sergeant Black. "Sergeant, send Savin up there to relieve Pettit, and send relief for Bloucher and Obromowitz."

Grady went off by himself behind a large rock and threw up. He picked up handfuls of snow and put them into his mouth in an attempt to wash the taste of bile from his mouth. He didn't remember ever feeling that lousy. He felt feverish; his arm ached constantly; his head hurt; the exposed skin on his face burned; his fingers ached from the cold; his lungs ached from breathing the freezing air; the insides of his thighs were chapped and raw from having wet himself in the first fight with the Chinese; and his thighs, armpits, and bearded chin had sores on them from clogged pores resulting from not having showered since they left Pusan. He stank. He extended his right arm and braced himself against the rock. He shook his head and thought, "Good lord, how is this going to end? When is it ever going to end? Here we are trying to avoid the Chinese, but they probably can smell us half a mile away!" He straightened up, took a deep breath, and told himself, "Get hold of yourself fellow; it's your responsibility to get your men back, so you had better forget about yourself and tend to business." He went back to MacDowell. "Mac, they say they haven't seen anything yet. If they don't see anything in the next hour to an hour and a half, I think we should get moving. What do you think?"

"I think we should be safe by then. You know how I feel about sitting still."

John replied, "I'll go up to the radio about ten minutes before the hour so I'll be there when the next transmission comes in. I sure hope they have something concrete for us, and I wish to hell I knew what's ahead of us at that pass and on the other side of it."

Lieutenant Smith called again, but he didn't have anything concrete for them and he had not gotten in touch with Captain Walker. He was working on it. Smith would call back on the next hour.

The lookouts on top the hill still hadn't seen anyone at or near the pass, so John called everyone down to the trail and they started for the pass.

CHAPTER 8. (8 DECEMBER 1950)

At Signal Section, Headquarters X Corps in Hamhung, Grady's other crews that had manned the VHF stations in the link to the Yalu River had arrived at Hamhung with the 17th Infantry Regiment, having had very little trouble during the evacuation from Hyesanjin. Colonel Ackerman and Captain Walker had returned from Chinhung-ni up north. The story about Grady and his crew being stranded up at Hyesanjin was circulating in the Signal Section. The enlisted men gave Major Lamb the silent treatment.

Colonel Ackerman heard the rumors and talked to Lamb about the situation. Lamb told him, "I gave orders for all the stations to evacuate with the 17th Regiment, but I couldn't make contact with Grady's station. I guess Grady never received the word and probably didn't know what to do to get his crew out."

Ackerman was distrustful of Lamb, so after Lamb left he called Master Sergeant George Stringer to his office. "Sergeant, you were with Lieutenant Grady on the VHF link up to the Yalu weren't you?

"Yes sir. I had the station at Kapsan, and Lieutenant Grady was up at Hyesanjin."

"When Major Lamb gave the order to evacuate, do you know why Grady didn't get the order?"

Stringer sat back in his chair with a surprised look on his face. "Major Lamb gave the order to evacuate, sir? I never got an order to evacuate from Major Lamb."

"Where did you get your order?"

"Lieutenant Grady gave me my order to evacuate. He said if I didn't get an order from corps I was to shut down and go out with the 17th Infantry. I didn't get an order from corps, so that's what I did."

"Sergeant, did you have radio contact with Lieutenant Grady at Hyesanjin?"

"Yes sir, right up until the time we shut down our station at Kapsan."

"Do you know why Lieutenant Grady didn't leave with the 17th Infantry?"

Stringer was uncomfortable. He wiggled and shifted his weight in his chair.

"Sir, Lieutenant Grady talked several times with Major Lamb trying to get the major to issue an evacuation order, but he wouldn't issue it. I know that I shouldn't have done it, but I patched in and listened in on their conversations. The major threatened Lieutenant Grady with a court-martial if he left his post."

"What happened to Grady's crew? Did they get away from there?

"Sir, Lieutenant Grady told me that his crew was leaving with the 17th Infantry whether or not he received orders from corps. But they didn't come out with the 17th; I don't know what happened to them. There were a lot of good men in that crew."

Ackerman looked Stringer in the eyes and said, "Sergeant Stringer, are you absolutely certain that Major Lamb never issued you an evacuation order?"

"Absolutely certain, sir. And I'm not the only one who knows what happened up there." Stringer looked over his left shoulder, then over his right shoulder, and not seeing anyone else in the room, he leaned forward in his chair and said, "Colonel, trying to get Major Lamb to make a decision is like trying to push a straight string."

"Thank you Sergeant. I may want to talk to you later, but that's all for now."

Ackerman stood up and paced back and forth a few times, then went out to his clerk and said, "Tell Major Lamb and Captain Walker that I want them here right away."

When they had gathered, Ackerman said, "Major Lamb, you told me that you issued the order for the VHF crews to evacuate with the 17th Infantry. Is that right?"

"Yes sir. Why do you ask?"

"Because I have reason to doubt that, and I'm going to investigate it further. In the meantime, you are relieved of all duties, effective immediately. Furthermore, you are confined to your billet except for one hour for each meal. If I find that you lied to me, I'll be taking further action. You're dismissed." Lamb left without saying another word.

Ackerman was silent for some time just staring at his table top. Walker sat motionless in his chair. Ackerman raised his head and told Walker what Lamb had told him and what Master Sergeant Stringer had told him.

He continued, "Right now, I have no reason to doubt Sergeant Stringer; he's a good man. Phil, I should have relieved Lamb a long time ago. I'm afraid that we lost a good crew because of my hesitancy to act." He was quiet for a moment more, then he looked at Walker and said, "Come hell or high water, I'll not have Lamb in my command.

"Phil, you're my new executive officer. I'll get the orders published right away, and I'll get papers moving on your promotion to major. You know the drill here, Phil: I don't need to tell you what to do. Just keep me informed on what's going on and what you're doing—I don't like surprises."

CHAPTER 9. (8 DECEMBER 1950)

Grady's crew moved back onto the trail and advanced toward the pass. They continued their procedure of having two scouts out in front of the main group and one behind. Everyone was alert and watched the pass and the hills on both sides. The forward scouts hesitantly approached the pass, entered it, and walked out the far side. Nothing happened. Grady let out a sigh of relief and felt foolish for having been so squeamish and cautious.

The main group with the cart entered the pass, and as they exited it—instantly—a mass of Chinese soldiers jumped onto the trail with rifles leveled at them! The terrified Americans didn't have a chance to do anything but freeze in their tracks. Grady stood in utter shock! He couldn't believe it—PLA soldiers were everywhere: on the trail in front of them and behind them, on the cliffs beside the trail, and on the hillsides. There was at least a full company of them—maybe more.

"HOLY TOLEDO!" Grady exclaimed. He cursed himself, "Now I've gotten all my men killed! I failed them! We're dying in one gigantic disaster, and I caused it."

Yet—not a shot had been fired.

"They'll tie our hands behind our backs and then shoot us," John said to himself as he remembered the mass executions uncovered in South Korea by the atrocities investigating team.

"Stand still and raise your hands," a clear voice commanded in English as a tall Chinese man strode forward from the mass of PLA soldiers. He was a handsome man with coal-black hair under a fur-lined hat. He had a lean, intelligent-looking face, and he looked to be in his mid or late thirties, or maybe early forties, it was hard to tell. Red cloth stripes ran down the outside seams of his quilted trousers, and he wore a pistol belt with holstered pistol around the waist of his quilted coat. Obviously, he was an officer, and probably a senior one at that. "Who is in command here," he demanded, again in English with scarcely an accent. He continued looking at the individuals in the group of Americans.

One of the GIs said in a weak voice, "Lieutenant Grady is."

John walked forward with his right arm raised and stood in front of the Chinese officer. He was humiliated to be holding his arm up in surrender.

"Who are you?" the PLA officer demanded.

"I'm Lieutenant John Grady, United States Army Signal Corps."

"You have a sorry-looking lot here, John Grady. Where did you come from, and where are you going?" John looked at his group. Indeed, they were a sorry-looking lot. They all had a week's growth of beard, and they had lived in the rumpled clothes they had on for longer than that.

Grady replied, "We're trying to get back to the United Nations lines. We were providing communications up at the Yalu River and got cut off when our troops pulled out of there. This is our eighth day of walking trying to get back to our own people."

"Why are those people riding in that cart?" the Chinese officer demanded as he pointed to the cart.

Grady could not believe that the officer was speaking in near-flawless English. "Those men are wounded. One has a broken leg."

The officer pointed to Grady's empty left sleeve dangling down at his side. "What about you, are you wounded?" Grady nodded affirmatively.

"How did you people get wounded?"

"We were attacked by the Peoples Liberation Army," Grady replied, looking him straight in the eyes.

Grady then looked at the Chinese soldiers who surrounded the Americans. They all carried U.S. MI Garand rifles. "How do your men come to have American rifles," Grady asked, pointing to the nearest Chinese soldier.

The Chinese officer smiled and replied, "Compliments of Chiang Kai-shek." (Chiang Kai-shek was leader of the Nationalist Chinese government on the Chinese mainland before the Communists captured it. The United States furnished him with war supplies and money to fight the Japanese during World War II and to fight the Communists after the war. Chiang Kai-shek and the remnants of his Nationalist Army fled to Formosa [Taiwan] after the communists defeated them on the mainland. Either the Communist Chinese soldiers surrounding Grady had captured the MI rifles when they defeated the Chinese Nationalist forces or they had been in the Chinese Nationalist Army and defected to the Communist and took their U.S.-supplied equipment with them. Many Nationalist soldiers defected to the Communist side. In fact, entire divisions of the Nationalist

Army switched their allegiances to the Communists when things began to go bad for the Nationalists.)

"Your men are well disciplined," Grady said. "We watched this area for several hours and didn't see a thing. How did you do it?"

"I know. We saw you watching this area. My men are old campaigners; they know how to soldier." That was all he revealed.

"Do you have American cigarettes?" the Chinese officer asked.

"Yes," Grady replied. He opened his overcoat with his right hand and tried to reach across to the left pocket of his field jacket. He wasn't making any progress. He looked at the Chinese officer and pointed several times to his left pocket. "Here, they're in this pocket. There's also a lighter in there. Reach in and get them."

The PLA officer reached into Grady's pocket, looking him in the eyes all the while, and pulled out John's Zippo lighter and a crushed pack with about half a dozen cigarettes in it. The Chinese officer straightened a bent cigarette with his fingers and put it in his mouth, flipped up the lighter cover with his thumb, cupped his hands around the cigarette, spun the wheel on the lighter with his thumb to produc a flame, and lit the cigarette. Obviously, that wasn't the first time he used a Zippo lighter. He took a long, deep drag that made the end of the cigarette glow brightly. He exhaled slowly, looked at the cigarette, and said, "Aahh, I miss these." He extended his hand with the cigarette pack and lighter toward Grady to return them.

Grady shook his head. "No, you keep them; I don't think I'll be needing them where I'm going."

"Thank you very much. You are kind," the Chinese said with a smile.

"Where did you learn to speak English so well?" Grady asked.

"That doesn't matter. You get moving on your way," the Communist officer said in a commanding tone as he pointed down the trail.

Grady did not believe what he just heard. He hesitated, almost afraid to speak. "You're turning us loose?" he asked incredulously.

"Your bunch doesn't look too dangerous to me," the Chinese officer said contemptuously. "Besides, we have no means to take care of your wounded, and we don't want any prisoners. We have trouble enough getting along in this weather without taking care of you too."

"You don't want our weapons?" Grady asked, again incredulously.

"No, you will need them where you're going. Now, you go," he said sternly as he again pointed down the trail. He took another puff on his cigarette.

"Move out, men," Grady said. Without a moment's hesitation the Americans started down the trail at a lively pace. Grady's head was swimming. He believed that he must be dreaming this whole thing. The other men looked at him with astonished looks as if to say, "What the hell is going on here, Lieutenant? Is what just happened really real?" *

When Grady was about thirty yards along the trail he stopped, turned around, and saluted the Chinese officer. The Chinese officer stood with his arms across his chest and casually made half a wave with his hand that held the cigarette. "That's the last I'll see of that bunch of rabble," the Chinese officer said to himself.

Grady resumed walking. He believed that in view of his conduct that past week he was not worthy to speak to God, but he said a prayer of thanks to God for delivering them out of the mouth of the fiery furnace. He wondered if he ever would know why.

Not only was Grady severely shaken by their capture at the pass, but he now was more frightened than ever. Would the English-speaking Chinese officer report to other Chinese units the presence of the Americans? The PLA probably had roadblocks at every advantageous location, and John doubted that other PLA units would treat his group the way that last one did.

When he was sure that they were out of sight of the Chinese at the pass, John had his men get off the trail and into a secluded location. It was almost time for the next radio transmission from the 7th Signal Company. And, he needed time to think. For the first time he fully comprehended the extreme gravity of the situation they were in: they were slogging about in the midst of the Chinese Army, and he had absolutely no idea whatsoever how to get through the enemy lines to his own people.

Endnote:
* The above-related capture and release of U.S. servicemen and their encounter with an English-speaking Chinese officer is derived from a report of an incident that occurred during the Korean War. It has been fictionalized in this story.

CHAPTER 10. (8 DECEMBER 1950)

Grady and his crew gathered around the radio waiting for the hour. Lieutenant Smith called on time, and after preliminaries, Smith said, "I have First Lieutenant Williams with me. He's S-2 (Intelligence Officer), and he'll handle you from now on. Good luck."

"Williams here. We're at a disadvantage having to talk in the clear. We can't give exact locations, time, etc., you understand. I'm going to give you some instructions, and you'll have to pay close attention and use your imagination. You do the same when you talk to me. Do you understand? Over."

"Let's try it. Over."

"Can you give me any information where you are? Be careful. Over."

Grady looked puzzled for an answer. MacDowell pointed to the map and ran his finger along the penciled-in route that had been marked for them. Then he tapped a spot on it. Grady nodded to Mac.

"We received a piece of paper with penciled information. We are approximately three-quarters, or four-fifths, the distance along a pencil line. Do you read me? Over."

"Stand by," came the reply. After what seemed like an eternity to the stranded crew, the radio crackled again, "Roger that. Stand by." Another period of silence was even longer than the previous one. "Wilbur and Orville visiting," the voice on the radio finally said. "You squawk in two hours. Out."

Sergeant Pettit made a motion with his hand like a maneuvering airplane and pointed up to the sky. The others nodded in agreement.

"Roger. Out," Grady replied.

Grady wondered if the English-speaking Chinese officer were listening to that radio conversation. If he were, he probably figured out exactly what the situation was. "But, we have to go with it, it's the only game in town," John said to himself.

"George Fuller, you're the timekeeper; let us know ten minutes before our two-hour time limit is up."

Grady's group heard artillery firing in the distance. They didn't know whose artillery it was or how far away it was. John looked on this as an incentive because it meant that they were close to the front and they soon would be out of their pickle.

"Sergeant Black, double the sentries and spread them out; we don't want to miss Wilbur and Orville."

The group went into its usual routine for a rest period. Grady sat trying to get his shoepacs off to massage his feet but was having trouble. Paul Bloucher came over and helped him with the boots and massaged his feet for him.

"Thanks, Paul, I appreciate your help. Where are you from, and how long have you been in the Marine Corps?"

"I'm from Wisconsin, up near Appleton, sir. I've been in the Corps a little over a year."

"Appleton, Wisconsin—you ought to be used to this cold."

"Sir, I've never been this cold in my life. Wisconsin gets cold, but it's like Key West compared to this."

"What did you do in civilian life, Paul?"

"I worked on my parents farm for over a year after I graduated from high school, then I enlisted. I thought that farming in Wisconsin was a tough life, but I'd trade for it in a minute right now. "

"If you need help on that farm, take me with you," John said. They both chuckled. John liked Bloucher; he was a fine young man. Despite being in a different branch of service, he willingly had done everything asked of him, and more.

A freshening wind and low-flying gray clouds heralded a weather change. The sky intermittently spit snow. John hoped that the weather would not interfere with Wilbur and Orville's visit. He did not like not knowing what was going to happen, and definitely did not like being in the position that their fate was in the hands of someone he didn't know. He hoped to hell it wasn't another Major Lamb.

Grady felt lousy. His entire left arm from his shoulder to his fingertips felt as if it were in contact with a red hot poker. He believed that the severe headache was affecting his vision. He had no appetite to eat. He talked with the other wounded and knew that they felt as lousy as he did, but they were toughing it out without complaining. He admired them and was proud of them.

Hours later they heard an airplane motor far away and above the clouds. Without regard to security, Sergeant Black rushed to the radio and raised Lieutenant Williams. He reported, "We hear a high performance bird in our vicinity. Is that our visitor? Out."

"Roger that. Out," the reply crackled.

Shortly, a P-51 Mustang fighter plane broke through the clouds and passed off to one side of them. John was puzzled. Why would they send a high performance aircraft rather than the L-5? The men signaled to the plane, and it climbed back into the clouds. They heard the motor straining as the plane gained altitude. Apparently, the plane didn't have a radio that was compatible with the one that Grady had.

They heard the plane's motor go into a high-pitched whine, indicating that it was diving. The men searched the clouds in the direction of the sound. Suddenly, the plane broke out of the clouds in a steep dive and headed straight for them. It pulled out of the dive and dropped an object with a long streamer on it . The P-51 immediately went into a steep climb and disappeared into the clouds. Savin and Obromowitz ran out and retrieved whatever had fallen from the plane.

MacDowell said to Grady, "The Chinese must be awfully close to us for them to send a P-51 and for it to dive at us like that and climb out in a hurry. They probably couldn't risk sending the L-5. With this cloud cover I don't know how the pilot found us. That's good navigating. If I ever meet that pilot, I'll buy him the biggest drink he ever saw."

Obromowitz handed Grady an olive-drab canister. Grady told him to take the end cap off. Grady reached into the canister and pulled out some papers and a small box. The box looked as if it contained medicine, so he handed it to Robert Pettit. He separated some papers that included a map with markings on it, which he handed to Captain MacDowell. A large twelve inch by eighteen inch glossy print of an aerial photograph showed in considerable detail an area of hilly ground. The photograph had markings and writing on it. There also were two sheets of writing which a quick look indicated were instructions for them. John's eyes were not focusing too well, so he handed the instructions to Sergeant Black. "Here, find out what we're supposed to do.

"Sergeant Smith, see what you can make of this photograph; you might be able to tie it in with Captain MacDowell's map. Work with him."

John hoped that the men didn't notice him sloughing off all the tasks to other people, but he was not seeing too well, and he feared that he might not be too sharp mentally. The fever was working on him.

While others were busy with the new material, Sergeant Pettit came over to Grady and said, "How are you feeling, Lieutenant? They sent us some new kind of pills in that drop; let me give you two of them." Pettit noticed.

In a couple of minutes Grady said, "O.K. men, what do we have? First, Captain MacDowell and Sergeant Smith, tell us what you have on the map and the photograph to get us oriented. Don't get into nitty-gritty details yet, just get us oriented relative to the PLA and our people.

"Sergeant Black, when they're done, you read the instructions. When you get down to the nitty-gritty details, we'll try to follow them on the map and photograph."

The men gathered around MacDowell. He started by pointing out a circled area marked A where Captain Williams thought they were. "Actually," MacDowell said, "we're right here in the forward part of the circled area. Tenth Corps front line is along here," as he moved his finger along a penciled arc on the map. He moved his finger along another line and said, "They probably want us to follow this route from point A to this point marked B. I think we'll move forward and go through the line at this point C. Sergeant Smith's photograph shows the points B and C in good detail. Everyone should study this map and photograph in detail. Memorize them. That should get us ready for the nitty-gritty."

Sergeant Black read the instructions. First, they were warned that the entire trip would be through Chinese-occupied territory and would be extremely hazardous. They were to leave point A at 1800 and follow the marked route to a dry stream bed at point B, arriving there no later than 2100. Extreme caution was to be exercised on this next portion of the route. Captain MacDowell pointed out the route on the map as Black read. From B, they were to stay off the road, conceal themselves and travel forward in the deep stream bed that was on the right side of the road. The PLA occupied the hill that extended forward like a finger on the left side of the road. Again, MacDowell and Smith pointed out the route on the map and photograph, and pointed out the PLA positions on the left side of the road. They were to move along the stream bed five hundred and fifty yards and wait. There would be a demonstration at 2200. Black looked up from the paper with a questioning look on his face. "What the hell are they going to demonstrate?

Captain MacDowell answered, "It's an artillery and/or mortar barrage. They're trying to cover our asses."

Black continued. "At exactly 2210, fifty yards short of the blown up bridge that crosses the stream, we're to go straight up the hill on the right and pass through our front line at point C. The password is 'Missouri,' and the countersign is 'River.' The instructions are to be destroyed before we depart here."

"A piece of cake," Grady grinned. "Sergeant Black, let's go through that once more right now. Do it just as you did it the first time." John nodded to MacDowell and Smith to follow along on the map and photograph as they had done before. Black began to read again. When he finished, John said, "Now, each of you memorize that map and photograph and study the contours of the terrain. Remember, it'll be dark and we have to know exactly where we are and exactly what to look for. We'll go through it together one more time before dark."

John talked with Ollie Clark, Albert Ramey, and Captain MacDowell, the seriously wounded and injured. "You saw on the map and photograph that we're going to travel over some rough terrain where we can't take the cart. From the time we leave here, the whole thing will take us about four and a half hours. These may be the most important and most trying four and a half hours of our lives. If ever there is, or ever will be, a time to dig deep within ourselves to put out our maximum effort, this is it. You can do it for four and a half hours, I'm sure. You have the rest of your lives to be thankful for the effort you make now. What do you say?"

Each said that he was determined to make it. When Grady was alone with MacDowell, he asked Mac if he would be able to maneuver with that crutch in the ice and snow.

"When we get in that rough terrain, I'm going to take this rubber tip off the end of the crutch. I think the bare metal tubing at the end will hold me better on the ice and snow.

"If I slow you down too much, John, I want you to promise me that the rest of you will go on without me. I'm not going to be the cause of the rest of you not making it. Don't put that burden on me."

"I promise you, Mac. I'm not going to allow you to slow us down. I think you have it in you to make it with the rest of us." They went over to the others and studied the map and photograph.

The crew had their third collective reading of the instructions, massaged their hands and feet, ate some rations, and waited for 1800. Complete darkness engulfed them. Snow now fell continuously and the wind was brisk. John thought that this would be to their advantage. It was the dark of the moon, and combined with the falling snow, visibility would be poor for the Chinese. Also, maybe the Chinese would not be so active tonight. At 1730 they tore up the map, the photograph, and the instructions, and buried them in the snow. By the time the snow melted in that place it wouldn't matter if someone found them. Everyone wanted to get started in order to get it over with—one way or the other—so they started early. Surprisingly, John felt better than he had earlier in the day. He figured that the adrenaline was flowing and was pumping him up. He had put his aching left arm through his field jacket sleeve and his overcoat sleeve, hoping he would be better able to balance himself walking over rough terrain in the snow and ice.

They were able to take the cart just a short distance on their march toward point B. Without being asked, Sergeant Smith and Frank Tomilson helped Captain MacDowell. Grady's healthy signalmen helped Ollie Clark and Albert Ramey when they needed it.

The wind intensified and the snowfall became much heavier. Back home in West Virginia it would be called a blizzard. They could barely make out features of the terrain, but so far, they were making it. John felt optimistic because the Chinese could not see them unless they were very close to them, and the heavy snowfall and high wind would quickly cover their footprints in the snow.

Because of the rough terrain over which they traveled, they arrived at the creek bed at point B a little behind schedule. The stream bed was mostly gravel and stones covered by ice and snow. From now on, punctuality was critical. Paul Bloucher acted as the forward scout on this night's march. He waited for the remainder of the group at point B. They rested a few minutes, then Grady whispered, "We go up this stream five hundred and fifty yards and wait for the artillery barrage. Keep low in the stream bed and no noise. Have your weapons and grenades ready. Sergeant Smith, you join Paul out front. Start out now and stop and wait for us when you think you're at the five hundred and fifty yard mark."

Smith and Bloucher moved out and immediately were out of sight in the swirling snow and blackness of the night. Then the main group moved out. MacDowell discarded his crutch because he was afraid that the aluminum would strike the gravel and rocks and make noise. Frank Tomilson helped him as best he could. Mostly, MacDowell clenched his jaw and hobbled.

The main group reached Smith and Bloucher where they thought the five hundred and fifty yard position was. They still had ten minutes until the barrage started.

"Do you see the blown bridge up ahead," John whispered to Sergeant Smith.

"No," Smith whispered. "We can't see very far, and I don't know for sure that we're fifty yards from it. I just guessed. Let me go ahead and check for sure."

"Paul, you go with him. The fifty yard point is just before the stream bed makes a sharp turn to the left."

"Yes, I remember from the photograph," Smith whispered. He and Bloucher started up the stream bed.

In five minutes, Bloucher came back and whispered into Grady's ear , "Sergeant Smith is up at the spot. It's about seventy yards ahead." The main group started out and had gone about halfway when they heard rifle shots up ahead.

Grady said to Sergeant Black in a loud whisper, "Bring them up slowly, and be careful."

"Come on, Paul, let's get up there." Bloucher led Grady at a slow trot up the stream bed. They approached Sergeant Smith who was kneeling on one knee with his side snug against the steep left bank of the stream. Smith saw them and jabbed his hand forward several times, indicating that there was something ahead of them. Grady and Bloucher crouched down behind Smith.

"It must be a Chinese patrol," Smith whispered. "I hope to hell it isn't ours. I got a shot off and they did too." All three of them believed that the U.S. forces would not have sent a patrol into no man's land if they were expecting this group to be coming through the line. It had to be Chinese up ahead. Just then, two shots rang out and the three men heard the bullets go by and hit into the bank of the stream bed.

"That's not an MI or a carbine firing," Smith whispered. "It has to be Chinese." None of the three could see anything ahead of them except swirling snow and blackness.

Bloucher whispered into Grady's ear, "With your permission, sir, I'm going up top, move forward, and drop a grenade on them." He scrambled up the bank and disappeared. Shortly, a grenade exploded. There was a loud moaning and some shouting in Chinese, followed by two rifle shots that sounded as if they had come from an MI.

"Bloucher coming in," he said in a low voice as he tumbled back into the stream bed with Grady and Smith. He stood up and peeked over the top of the bank. He whispered to Smith and Grady, "There were about half a dozen of them in the stream bed. I think I saw three or four figures climb out and run for the hill over on the left after the grenade went off. I got off two rounds, but I lost them in the dark. I can't see anything now, but I can't see very far. "

Sergeant Black and the others came up. Suddenly, a machine gun commenced firing over to the left of the stream bed. They all hunched down in the stream bed and snuggled up as close as they could against the left bank. None of the bullets hit near them. The shooting stopped. They waited. The machine gun resumed firing, and this time the Chinese gunner swept his fire up and down the stream. Grady's men heard bullets hitting the opposite bank. It stopped for a short time, then resumed. In the middle of this burst from the Chinese machine gun, the men heard a rumble of artillery far off to their right. The covering barrage was starting. Artillery shells exploded on the hill to their left. The machine gun stopped firing and the artillery barrage continued.

Grady and Bloucher stood up and peeked over the top of the bank. They could see the artillery shells exploding on the top part of the hill. They also saw a rapid successions of small flashes coming from the bottom of the hill, and they heard bullets whizzing over their heads. The Chinese machine gun crew saw that the artillery fire was directed at the top of the hill and felt safe enough to resume firing. A second series of rapid flashes occurred off to the right of the first ones. A second PLA machine gun had commenced firing.

Grady crouched down in the stream bed and whispered, "Sergeant Pettit, get on that radio and tell them to shorten the artillery fire to hit the base of the hill." Pettit did so. They waited, but the artillery bursts continued on the top of the hill.

Paul Bloucher came to Grady and whispered , "Lieutenant Grady, if we expect to get out of here and climb that hill on our right, we're going to have to do something about those machine guns. If the visibility improves, we could be in worse trouble than we are now. I request permission to go silence them with grenades."

Grady didn't know what to say, or what to do. "Decision time, fellow," that voice inside him said.

"Sergeant Black," Grady called. "When you hear grenade explosions over at the base of the hill on the left, get everyone out of here and get on your way up the hill to our line. Don't worry about the exact time. You have the password, use it. Bloucher and I are going after those machine guns at the base of the hill on the left. Don't wait for us. If we don't catch up with you, tell them up on the line that we're on our way. Who has grenades? Give Paul and me some grenades." Grady and Bloucher loaded their pockets with grenades.

"Let's go Paul."

The two of them climbed up and over the top of the bank. Bloucher had his MI rifle and Grady had his Colt. 45 pistol in its holster. Grady whispered to Paul, "Stay separated. We'll go after the one on the left first. We'll approach it from both sides; you stay on the left." They hurriedly crawled through the blinding snow to the first machine gun. It opened fire in the direction of the ditch. Bullets streamed above the two. They crawled toward the flashes. The machine gun stopped. The two men continued sliding forward on their bellies, but they couldn't see much because of the blowing snow. The machine gun off to their right resumed firing. John figured that they had better make their move fast before the machine gun crews moved their positions. The machine gun on the left opened fire again. Paul and Grady saw the flashes and threw their grenades at the same time. Both men lay on the snow as flat as they could. BOOM! BOOM! They scrambled to their feet and jumped into the gun emplacement. It was a low log barrier over which the gun had been shooting. They arrived behind the barrier at the same time with guns at the ready. Three bodies lay motionless on the ground. Paul picked up the machine gun and hurled it out of the bunker.

Grady pointed toward the second machine gun and nodded to Paul. They crawled through the blowing snow toward the gun. They each threw two grenades when they were within range. The grenades went off—then an even greater secondary explosion went off from the machine gun position.

"Holy Toledo, what the hell was that! Let's move out of here, Paul."

They started running, then Paul grabbed Grady's sleeve. "Lieutenant Grady, the artillery barrage has stopped."

"We can't stay here; head for the stream bed. It'll take the Chinese time to recover," Grady said as he started to run back over the same route they had taken up to the guns. They both arrived at the stream bed and hurled themselves into it. They were exhausted from running through the deep snow.

"Let's not dally here, Paul, let's get up the hill." They went up and over the right bank just as a mortar shell hit and exploded on the top of the left bank. They dove to the ground.

"Are you all right, Paul," Grady called.

"I'm O.K., Lieutenant. Move out."

They stood up and ran for the hill with Grady in the lead. They had taken a dozen steps when mortar shells hit on both sides of the stream behind them. Both men again dove to the ground. They scrambled to their feet and started up the hill. Paul slipped and went down. He struggled to his feet just as a mortar shell hit between the two of them! A blinding flash of light—a thunderous blow struck both bodies—blackness.

Gradually, John gained consciousness. He was laying face down in the snow. He raised his head and blinked his snow-encrusted eyelashes. "Where am I?" He fought drowsiness. His rump felt as though it were on fire. He took the glove off his right hand and felt around. He felt large tears in the seats of the outer pants and the wool pants underneath. His hand became sticky. He put his glove back on and raised himself on his right elbow and looked around. He saw a body laying on the ground below him. With great physical effort he pushed himself down to the body. "Oh, yes ... Paul ... Paul, are you hurt?" No answer. "Paul." No answer. He tried to call again but couldn't organize the effort. Exhaustion overcame him. He lay on the snow ... blackness .... Snow fell on the two motionless bodies.

At 2245, a platoon of the U.S. 17th Infantry Regiment that was holding the line at the top of the hill sent a patrol out into the blizzard to try to find the two men who didn't get through the line with the other signalmen from the Yalu. They started at point C and retraced the route down the hill toward the stream bed. Near the bottom of the hill the point man of the patrol tripped over something in the snow and went sprawling. The patrol found two snow-covered bodies and carried them back up the hill and rushed them to the battalion aid station. One was dead. One was unconscious and barely alive.

The live one was taken to a field hospital where medical people treated him for shock and hypothermia and gave him blood transfusions. He was held at the field hospital overnight because all vehicular traffic had stopped due to the blizzard. The snowstorm ended the next morning. He was taken on a stretcher to a helicopter and flown to an airport at Yonp'o, a town near the port city of Hungnam. He and many other wounded men on stretchers were loaded onto a large airplane and flown to Yokohama, Japan. An ambulance took him to a U.S. Army hospital in Yokohama. He was just another casualty flowing through the medical-evacuation pipeline. In his unconscious state, he knew none of this.

BOOK THREE

CHAPTER 1. (12 DECEMBER 1950)

Three days later he heard mumbling and saw two ghostly figures standing beside him, but they faded away. Fourteen hours after that, John Grady opened his eyes. Everything looked fuzzy gray; his left arm ached; his rump burned; his left foot throbbed; his body hurt; his head felt as though the top were going to blow off; his mind was disoriented; he tried to turn to see his surroundings, but he couldn't move. "Help…. Help me …. Paul, where are you?…. Sergeant Black, Sergeant Pettit, can you hear me? Someone help me."

"There now," a female voice said. "you're all right."

Grady couldn't see anyone; he didn't understand. 'Who are you?" he said as he tried to determine where the voice had come from. He tried to move but couldn't.

"I'm Captain Cheraw, an army nurse. You're all right."

Grady's brain processed the information extremely slowly. "Where is this?"

"You're in an army hospital in Yokohama, Japan. You're going to be all right," she said as she moved to where he could see her.

It took time for the information to register in his consciousness. All he could see was a white blob beside him. "I can't move. Help me."

"You're all right. You're strapped to your bed so you won't hurt yourself and so you won't pull the tubes out." Grady didn't understand.

"You lie still while I put in a call for the doctor." Grady was still for a long time. His vision began to clear somewhat. He realized that he was laying on his side on a hospital bed. He could see another bed not far from his. His head and the back of his neck ached so much that he didn't want to move his head.

The nurse greeted an army doctor approaching Grady's bed. "He's been conscious about twenty minutes now," she said. The doctor read Grady's chart that was hanging at the end of his bed. He placed his stethoscope at several places on Grady's back and listened. He placed it at several places on Grady's chest. The doctor asked several questions, but Grady had trouble answering them. The doctor examined Grady's arm and his buttock, then went to the foot of the bed. Grady could feel him handling his aching left foot.

"What's the matter with that foot?" John asked. The doctor didn't answer. Grady repeated the question.

"I'll talk to you about that later," the doctor said.

"Well, damn it, it's my foot, talk to me now," Grady snapped back. His whole body felt as if it were one huge festering sore and his disposition matched it.

The doctor didn't say anything for a moment, then he cleared his throat and answered. "You have severe frostbite on your left foot. We felt that it was necessary to take immediate action to prevent serious trouble. Your heart is strong, so we went ahead and removed your small toe and two joints from your second toe. If things go well, we won't have to do any more. We'll know for sure in a day or two. Do you understand what I just said?"

"I have the worst headache I ever had in my life," Grady replied. "Can't I get some aspirin?" The doctor said something to the nurse and told Grady that he would see him in the morning. John didn't get a chance to ask him about his aching arm.

In a little while, the nurse brought a small paper cup with some pills in it and a glass of water with a straw. Grady washed down the pills. She checked the tubes going into his body, checked two bottles of clear liquid suspended from a stand beside the bed, and checked a bag hanging below the bed. She made notations on the chart. She returned later and engaged him in conversation trying to judge how alert and rational he was. Grady tried to think about his toes but drifted off to sleep.

A different nurse woke him up early the next morning and gave him pills to swallow. She took his temperature, blood pressure, and pulse rate. She checked the fluids, wrote on his chart, and left. Two hours later another nurse took the bandages off his arm, buttock, and foot, put something on them, and put fresh bandages on them.

"What's wrong with my rear end?" Grady asked the nurse.

"You've been wounded there. Didn't you know that?

"No, I don't remember getting hit there." Grady's mind was fairly clear that morning and he tried to think back. He remembered the events in North Korea, except that he didn't know how he got there in the hospital, and he didn't know if his group made it through the line. He guessed that he was going to live. He didn't know anything about medical matters, but he doubted that they would have amputated his toes if they thought he were dying. He became convinced that he was going to live. He was not going to die all alone as the young Chinese officer did in the house in North Korea. That young Chinese officer's face still was vivid in his memory. John felt exhilarated that he was going to live. He said a prayer thanking God for getting him out alive and asking His forgiveness for his conduct.

Three doctors in long white coats came to his bed. There was the captain who saw Grady the day before, a major, and a full colonel. The captain talked to the other two as they looked at John's chart. John couldn't hear what they were saying.

"How are you feeling this morning, Lieutenant Grady?" the major asked.

"Pretty good, I guess."

The colonel wanted to see the arm. He examined it closely then backed away to give the major a look. The three stepped away from the bed and engaged in conversation which Grady couldn't hear. The captain and major came back and looked at the arm again. The major paid particular attention to the upper arm. To John, he looked like a butcher sizing up a side of beef trying to decide how he was going to carve it.

"Gentlemen, please don't do anything to my arm. I'm a fast healer; give it a chance to heal. I didn't get any attention to that arm for a couple of days, so it might not look too good now, but give it a couple of days and it'll come along. I'm feeling better today."

"You should have had that arm attended to right away," the captain admonished.

"I was up at the Yalu River cut off behind enemy lines. The army didn't hold sick call up there," Grady said with some sarcasm in response to the doctor's dumb statement.

"You're lucky that the Chinese didn't capture you up there," the major said trying to make small talk to cover the captain's remark.

"They did," Grady said, "and the Chinese didn't hold sick call either." The three doctors were silent. The colonel motioned the other two away from the bed and engaged them in conversation. He came back alone to the bed and took his time reexamining the arm closely. He poked it a couple of times with his finger. The three doctors had another conversation.

The colonel came around the side of the bed to where Grady could see him clearly. "Lieutenant Grady, we're not going to do anything to your arm right now. We'll watch it closely, and if it doesn't get any worse in the next two days, we'll send you back to the States where they can treat it."

"Thank you, Colonel." John didn't mention his headache to the doctors.

***

The condition of Grady's arm did not worsen during the next two days nor did it improve. The doctors were satisfied with the conditions of the toes and the wound in his buttock. The doctors released Grady from the Yokohama hospital and he was carried on a stretcher to a large bus-like ambulance with other wounded men and taken to an airport. The wounded men were loaded onto a large medical-evacuation airplane that was fitted out as a hospital ward with bunks suspended one over the other along both sides of the cabin. The plane took off for the United States. Grady knew very little about what happened on the flight except that they landed at Midway Island and at Hickham Field in Hawaii. He was held overnight at Tripler Army Hospital in Hawaii for examination and evaluation and was assigned to an army hospital in the States. Again, he was loaded onto a medical-evacuation plane and flown to Travis Air Force Base, California, where he landed late in the day on 15 December 50.

It had been two months and twenty eight days since he had left Travis on his way to the Orient. On the calendar that was not a long time, but to John it seemed like a lifetime. It very nearly was.

Grady and other wounded men were taken by ambulances to another medical evacuation plane and were flown to McGuire Air Force Base, New Jersey. Bus-like ambulances met the wounded and took them to Valley Forge Army Hospital, Phoenixville, Pennsylvania, not far from Philadelphia. Even though he had slept during much of the trip, John was exhausted when he arrived at the hospital. He had not moved off his side the entire trip. He felt terrible: his head hurt, his arm hurt, his buttock hurt, his left foot hurt, it seemed that everything on his body hurt. After a brief delay at a reception area, he was hoisted onto a gurney and wheeled to a typical hospital room with four beds in it. Orderlies lifted him off the gurney and onto a bed. A nurse checked his tubes and bottles and the bag that went under the side of the bed.

As the nurse was getting him settled, John said, "Nurse, can you give me some aspirin, or some APC pills, or something, I have a king-size head-ache." He was so uncomfortable from the headache that he felt nauseous. Had anything been in his stomach he would have thrown up.

"In a minute," she replied. She left the room and came back in a couple of minutes with a load of supplies. As she was storing them, Grady asked her, "Did you bring the aspirin?"

"I told you, in a minute."

'Well, damn it, why didn't you get them while you were out. My head is killing me; don't you understand that?"

She looked at him but said nothing. She finished her task and left the room. The same nurse returned in a couple of minutes with two pills and a glass of water and a straw. She helped Grady with the pills. She took his pulse, temperature, and blood pressure. As she entered the data on his chart, Grady said, "Nurse, I apologize for my short temper. Thank you for the pills."

She finished entering the data, looked at Grady and said, 'To you, Lieutenant, I am Captain Parker, and don't you forget it." She left the room.

Grady could not move from the position they had placed him in. He worried about his arm: what would new doctors do? He felt as though he were in never-never land—nothing seemed real. He asked himself, "Is this really John Grady in this terrible condition? Is this John Grady who was in a violent war and killed men, was shot, and was captured?" He knew that it was real, and he knew that he would have to deal with it—when he felt better.

***

Captain Parker and a doctor awakened Grady the next morning. The doctor said, "Hello Lieutenant Grady, I'm Major Mott. How are you feel-ing?"

John tried to put up a good front, "I feel pretty good, but as I was telling Captain Parker yesterday, I have a headache."

"Let me have a look at you," the doctor said. He started with the arm and gave it a long and careful examination. He then went to the buttock, and then carefully looked at the toes. He went back to the arm. "You have three bullet wounds here."

"Yes sir, but I was shot only twice. The first one made a hole when it went in and another one when it came out. The second one only made one hole." John then said to Dr. Mott the same things that he had said to the three doctors in Yokohama. That is, about him being a fast healer and that the arm would look better in a couple of days, etc.

"What was it that hit you in the buttock?" the doctor asked.

"I don't know about that one, sir."

The doctor continued his examination. He didn't seem to be in a hurry and talked with John as he examined him. The doctor looked at X-rays that were in Grady's medical file that accompanied him from Japan. "I want a new set of X-rays of the left arm," the doctor said to the nurse. He gave instructions on what medications he wanted Grady to take. He wrote for some time on Grady's chart. When he finished writing he came back to Grady and said, "Lieutenant, we'll keep a close watch on that arm. I'm prescribing some pain killers and some antibiotic pills for you. Your buttock has quite a large wound, but it looks as if it will be all right. Your frostbitten toes don't seem to be critical, and the incisions on the left foot are healing. If we can do anything for you, let us know"

"I'll be a lot more comfortable if I can get rid of this headache." John didn't want to be a whiner, but he had never experienced anything like that.

"We'll work on that."

By 22 December, the condition of Grady's arm had changed very little. It seemed that his mind, emotions, and body had suffered so much trauma that the body could not now deal with the severe injury and infection. Major Mott performed some kind of minor operation on the arm. Grady didn't understand what he did or why he did it. The large wound in his buttock was healing nicely. His left foot still was sore. He could not walk with crutches because both his left foot and left arm were incapacitated. The few times that he left his bed he went by gurney. John had no radio, and because of his severe headache he didn't want to read. He was bored stiff but grateful to be there.

***

Grady made inquiries to the hospital staff about the situation in Korea. They told him that Eighth Army was retreating south after suffering severely punishing blows from the Chinese Army. The Communists had recaptured the North Korean capital of P'yongyang. Eighth Army was trying to establish a defensive line north of Seoul. In Northeast North Korea where Grady had been, X Corps had withdrawn to an ever-shrinking perimeter around the port of Hungnam as its troops evacuated by sea from North Korea.

John was bored to death. He asked to be taken to the lounge where he watched a television news program. The western world was arming itself against threatening moves by the Soviet Union. General Dwight Eisenhower was summoned back to active duty to assume command of North Atlantic Treaty Organization (NATO) troops in Europe. Earlier, President Truman had declared a State of Emergency in the United States. The size of the U.S. Air Force was to double.

There was great concern in the United States about Communist spying and particularly about alleged Communist infiltration of U.S. government agencies. Employees in all levels of government service; college professors and school teachers; corporation executives and employees; movie actors, writers, and directors; and others were being asked to sign statements that they were not now and never had been members of the Communist Party. And, they were reminded that lying under oath was a crime and they would be prosecuted if they were found to have lied. A Commerce Department employee was being prosecuted in Federal District Court for lying under oath that he had never been a member of the Communist Party.

Another item in the television news reported that Communist China was demanding a seat in the United Nations. The United States and its allies opposed it.

***

The hospital was gaily decorated for Christmas and a large lighted evergreen tree was on the lawn in front, but John could not get into the Christmas spirit. Captain Parker came into Grady's room early Christmas morning to go through her usual routine with him. John greeted her with a "Merry Christmas," and she returned the greeting. As she was taking his blood pressure he said to her, "How come you have the duty today, Captain Parker? I would think that a captain would have enough rank to get the holiday off."

"I volunteered to work today. I'm single and don't have a family near, so I took the duty so that some of the other girls could be off."

"That's real thoughtful and kind of you, Captain Parker."

"You don't need to be so formal. You can drop the 'Captain Parker'."

John grinned at her, "I'm only doing what you told me to do. I always follow the orders of a superior officer. "

"Well, you can forget that," she said. John again apologized for his short-tempered remarks to her on the day of his arrival and asked her where she was from, how long she had been in the army, and where she had served. They talked for a while after she finished her routine with him.

Family members visited some of the hospital patients on Christmas Day. Grady had no visitors. The day was long and boring because the hospital was on holiday schedule and not much was happening. Shortly after 1600, Captain Parker came into John's room with some cookies and two coffee mugs. She put a couple of cookies and a mug on his stand. She kept the rest and sat down in a chair by his bed. "Merry Christmas, Grady. I thought that you might like to celebrate the holiday with me."

"Well, thank you, Parker, that's real kind of you." From that time on, they addressed each other by their surnames. Parker said that she also had volunteered to take the duty for the next shift and was taking a break. They talked as they ate cookies and drank the coffee. John found her to be a pleasant and interesting person. She was in her mid-thirties, on the tall side, and slightly overweight. She had dark hair, an attractive face, and was a down-to-earth person. She said that she had been married to an army officer, but the separation caused by their duty assignments to different army posts had caused the relationship to cool, and they divorced on friendly terms. Grady told her very little about himself and nothing about his service in Korea.

Toward the latter part of January 1951, Grady's buttock had healed nicely, and he walked, although gingerly, on his left foot. The left arm was another story. It had improved some, but still was far from healed. Progress seemed to have slowed. John could not use his left arm or hand, and he still had considerable discomfort in the arm. On the bright side, he knew that the threat of amputation had passed. The headaches subsided in intensity, but occurred frequently. Additionally, he took an antibiotic drug orally three times daily and each time it made him feel nauseous. Consequently, seldom did he feel good.

Major James Mott was his primary doctor. John liked him, and they developed a good relationship. John asked him why the arm was not coming along as well as the toes and buttock. The doctor didn't know but said that it probably was just going to take a long time for it to recover. John's slightly elevated temperature indicated that the arm still carried infection. John resigned himself to a long recovery period.

As time passed, Grady and Parker became friends. She treated him as she would a brother. Several times she took her breaks in his room and had a coffee or a Coke while talking with him.

John didn't make close friends with other men in his room. They came and went rather rapidly, and he would just about get to know them and then they would leave the room.

CHAPTER 2. (15 DECEMBER 1950 - 15 JANUARY 1951)

In Korea with Signal Section, Headquarters X Corps.—The Signal Section evacuated by ship from Hungnam, North Korea, and landed back in Pusan, South Korea, just before Christmas Day. Prior to evacuating North Korea, Lieutenant Colonel Ackerman interviewed several of the survivors of Lieutenant Grady's crew from Hyesanjin who made it back through the line. They corroborated Master Sergeant George Stringer's account (a). that Major Morris Lamb did not give an evacuation order; (b). that Lamb told Grady that he was not to evacuate Hyesanjin with the 17th Regiment; and (c). that if Grady did leave without orders from Lamb, Lamb would court-martial him.

Colonel Ackerman kept Lamb under restriction during the evacuation from North Korea, and as soon as the Signal Section became halfway settled at its assembly area north of Pusan, Ackerman initiated general court-martial proceedings against Lamb. In accordance with military law, an Investigating Officer was appointed to investigate the situation and to make a recommendation as to whether a court-martial trial should be held. (The Investigating Officer's role was somewhat similar to that of the grand jury in the civilian justice system.)

Colonel Justin Mannas, Infantry, was appointed Investigating Officer. He conferred with Colonel Ackerman, and interviewed Major Lamb, Master Sergeant Stringer, and some of the survivors of Grady's VHF crew. The assignment as Investigating Officer was in addition to Mannas's other duties, so it took him most of a week to get the interviews, and he had not completed his report. By that time, the Chinese and North Koreans had begun a major New Year's offensive which put UN forces in great peril. X Corps was ordered north to the central sector to try to stem the Communist drive. Mannas told Ackerman that that was not the time to get X Corps senior officers bogged down in a general court-martial and suggested that they abort the court-martial proceeding and issue orders to ship Lamb back to Japan. Reluctantly, Ackerman agreed, and within forty-eight hours Lamb ignominiously returned to Japan for reassignment.

Morris Lamb was sent to a remote electronic "listening station" on the northernmost Japanese island where a crew of Signal Corps specialists listened in on Russian and Chinese communications. The Signal Corps specialists knew their business and did it well. Another major ran the operation, so there was very little for Lamb to do except stay out of the way and count the days.

***

January 1951 was bad for UN forces in Korea. Chinese and North Korean forces mauled UN forces and pushed them to the south. Communist armies captured Seoul for the second time in the war, and UN forces retreated and established a defensive line approximately midway between Seoul and Pusan. Fighting was intense and casualties were high. General Matthew Ridgway, the new Eighth Army commander, had his staff planning for another Pusan Perimeter defense. By the end of the month, however, Eighth Army regained it spirit and composure under General Ridgway's leadership and began inching northward toward Seoul.

CHAPTER 3. (FEBRUARY 1951)

Grady was concerned as to what had happened to the other men in his group in North Korea. He knew that Captain MacDowell was from Great Falls, Montana, and that his father published a newspaper there, so one day he climbed into a wheelchair and went to the pay telephone in the hall. He called telephone information for Great Falls and obtained the office number for James MacDowell. He put the call through and a woman politely answered, "Mr. MacDowell's office."

"This is Lieutenant John Grady calling. I was a friend of Mr. MacDowell's son in Korea. We became separated and I'm trying to find out what happened to him and where he is. Is Mr. MacDowell in? If so, may I speak with him?"

"One moment please."

Shortly, a deep baritone voice said, "Hello, this is Jim MacDowell. Are you the Lieutenant Grady who was with my son Jim in North Korea?"

"Yes sir, I am. I became separated from him and everyone else who was with us. I called to find out what happened to him."

"Yes, Jim told me about you. Jim's in a hospital in California. His femur bone was badly splintered. I spent a couple of days with Jim at Christmas. Where are you, Lieutenant Grady?"

"I'm at Valley Forge Army Hospital in Pennsylvania. Mr. MacDowell, could you give me Mac's address so I can write to him?"

"Jim thinks he might be transferred from the hospital where he is now. He might be gone by the time your letter gets there. Give me your telephone number, Lieutenant Grady, and I'll call you back and let you know as soon as I get the information. I know Jim will be delighted to know you're safe. He told me that he probably wouldn't have gotten back if it weren't for you."

"Mr. MacDowell, Mac got back because he had the guts to get back."

John gave him the number of the pay telephone in the hall. "Thank you, sir, I'm eager to get in touch with Mac to find out what happened to him and the others."

"I know that he'll be glad to hear from you. Good-bye, Lieutenant Grady."

Two days later an orderly came into Grady's room and told him that there was a telephone call for him at the pay phone in the hall. The orderly helped John into a wheelchair and wheeled him to the phone. He handed the instrument to Grady.

"Hello, this is John Grady."

"Hello John, this is Mac MacDowell. Boy, was I glad to hear about you! We didn't know what happened to you. They took us to the rear almost as soon as we made it to our line. I stayed up on the line long enough to get them to agree to send a search party for you and Paul, but then they moved me to the rear. What happened? We heard the grenades."

"Mac, I don't know. I remember that Paul and I took out the two machine guns, but I don't know what happened after that. Tell me about yourself and the others. What happened? What about Paul?"

"I don't know about Paul. He didn't get through the line while I was there. The rest of us made it to the U.S. lines, but we were separated soon after we arrived there. I don't know about the others." Mac told John that he had started writing an account of their experiences in North Korea. John asked him what he was going to do with it.

"I don't know, but I think we shouldn't forget what happened there. I guess that it's the journalist in me. Maybe I have ink in my veins like my grandfather and my dad. I'll send you a copy when I finish it." They talked for twenty minutes. Mac promised to call again next week.

***

Major Mott was not pleased with the slow progress of Grady's arm and called in another army doctor to review his case. The new doctor saw Grady twice a day for four days. The only thing that he could recommend was minor surgery to remove some bad skin that was around the single bullet wound. That was done. Dr. Mott said that sometime in the future he would have plastic surgery performed on the entire arm to make it look better.

***

Mac MacDowell called John on the telephone again and said, among other things, that he had finished writing an account of their experiences in North Korea. He said he had decided to send it through army channels with a recommendation for a metal for John. He told John that, to meet army regulations, he was sending it as commanding officer of the group, although he and everyone else knew that it was John who led them out.

"Mac, why are you doing that? That's all behind us now. I'm not looking for any medal; all I want is to get out of this damn hospital and get back to duty. Please don't send it to the army. Send it to all the men in our group."

"It went out yesterday," Mac replied.

***

By the first of March Grady was getting some movement in his left arm and hand. His temperature was back to normal, but the doctor kept him on an antibiotic drug. He started physical therapy for his arm and hand and slowly began to regain control of them. Grady was beginning to feel optimistic about his recovery. The headaches left him when his temperature returned to normal. Still, the days were long and boring. He quickly scanned *The Philadelphia Inquirer* on Sundays after church services in the hospital chapel, but he seldom had the patience to read a complete article.

***

One day in early March, just before Grady's afternoon physical therapy session, Parker hurried into his room and dumped clean pajamas and bathrobe onto his bed and said, "Someone from Washington is coming to visit you. Get these clean things on as quickly as you can. He's on his way up here."

"What's this all about? Who is it?"

"I don't know. Change. Hurry, and throw the old ones in your closet."

Grady changed, and in a couple of minutes a tall, middle-aged Artillery lieutenant colonel walked into Grady's room. He had a chest full of World War II campaign ribbons on his uniform jacket.

"Lieutenant Grady, I'm Lieutenant Colonel Tom Carter. I'm with the Awards and Decorations Board in the Pentagon. The Board recently received a recommendation concerning you that was initiated by a Captain James MacDowell. I scanned the submission and it kind of caught my interest. The board won't get to it for a while, but I'm on my way to Camp Indiantown Gap on a completely unrelated matter, and since you're not too far out of my way I thought that I would come by and talk to you. We usually don't do this, but as I said, this story kind of caught my interest. Would you mind if I asked you some questions about you and about your experiences in North Korea?

"Sir, Captain MacDowell told me that he was sending something in, but I didn't have anything to do with writing it, and I would just as soon he hadn't sent it. He was supposed to send me a copy of what he wrote, but I haven't seen it. Our experiences are interesting from a historical perspective, but that's it as far as I'm concerned."

"I understand." Carter began by asking John questions about his background. Then he questioned him about the North Korea experience. John was hesitant to say too much, but Carter kept prodding him with questions. Apparently, Mac had written quite a detailed account. Carter wanted to hear Grady's version of the story and took notes as Grady spoke. The colonel had a nice way about him, and they got along well. By the time they finished, Carter had the entire story from Grady, including the days before the Signal Corps crew met MacDowell and his group. But despite Colonel Carter's prodding, John's memory still was a blank about the very end of the experience.

"Lieutenant, tell me again, who all was with you that last night when you went after the Chinese machine guns?"

"Just Paul Bloucher, the marine."

"Where is he now?"

"I don't know, sir. The only one I've talked with since the incident is Captain MacDowell, and he didn't know either."

"Lieutenant Grady, I thank you for going through your experiences with me. We look at the Medal of Honor recommendation closer than the others."

Grady looked at him with astonishment. "Beg your pardon, sir, did you say Medal of Honor?"

"Why, yes, that's what Captain MacDowell recommended, and it was endorsed all the way up to the board. Didn't you know that?"

"No sir, Mac didn't tell me that. Look, Colonel, I don't care anything about a medal; that business in North Korea is behind me, and a medal won't bring back to life the men from our crew who we lost. But I'll tell you what I would settle for: I think that all of us earned a Combat Infantry Badge. I don't know what your requirements are to get it, but in my opinion we fought our way out as infantrymen, even though most of us were Signal Corps, and we sure had combat. So, what else is there?"

"I'll keep that in mind. Thank you for your help, Lieutenant Grady. Good luck to you."

As Colonel Carter left Grady's room and entered the hallway outside, Parker hurried up to him and said, "Colonel, I'm Captain Parker, Lieutenant Grady's nurse. Is there anything we should do, or ought to know about him?" (No one ever accused Mary Parker of being shy and backward.) Carter was amused at her nosiness and told her that Grady had been recommended for the Medal of Honor and that he, Carter, was looking into the matter. Parker told the supervising nurse and Major Mott, and word spread throughout the hospital staff. Two days later, Grady was moved to a private room of his own.

The night of Lieutenant Colonel Carter's visit, Grady telephoned Mac MacDowell. "Mac, a light colonel from Washington was here asking me about our time in North Korea. What the hell did you tell them?"

"I wrote the truth, the whole truth, and nothing but the truth. What did he say?"

"He didn't say anything; he just asked questions. He said the visit wasn't official, that he was passing through and just stopped in, or something like that. Did you recommend me for the Medal of Honor?"

"I did."

"What did you do that for? I'm just a poor slob trying to do his duty, and I didn't do it very well; we lost three fine men up there. They don't get to come home as you and I did. And while I think of it, Mac, why don't you try to find out about Paul Bloucher. You're a writer, write to the Marine Corps; they'll know.

"How is your leg coming along? And, I forgot to ask you, did you get any frostbite?"

"The leg bone is healed pretty well, but that leg is shorter than the other one. I don't know what that will do to my army career. Yeah, I had some frostbite, but nothing too bad. I still have ten toes. Yes, I'll try to find out about Paul."

Grady gained more use of his arm and hand every week. He was impatient to get out of the hospital and felt that he was malingering because he had been there for such a long time.

Grady also was impatient with the situation in Korea. UN forces were slowly pushing the Communist forces back to the Thirty-eighth Parallel, and in some areas, north of the parallel. The Chinese were avoiding major battles. Seoul had been recapture by UN forces, making it the fourth time that control of the capital city had changed hands since the war began last June. But, we were not making a major all-out offensive that would destroy the enemy armies and reunify Korea.

***

During the last week of March, John asked Major Mott how long he thought it would be before he could get released from the hospital.

"John, you're beginning to make good progress now, but I can't give you a definite date. You had a badly damaged arm, and I'm not going to release you until I'm satisfied that you're one hundred percent."

"Major, I've been here more than three months now, and I haven't been out of this hospital once. What are the chances I could get, maybe, a seven-day sick leave?"

"Let me think about it. In the meanwhile, work hard in your therapy and we'll talk about it next week. I'm not making any promises, you understand."

Grady asked Parker, "Parker, I might get a leave in the near future, and I don't have one stitch of a uniform. Where can I get uniforms without paying a fortune?"

"I haven't heard anything about you going on leave. When and where are you going."

"Well, nothing's definite. I asked Major Mott about it, and he said we would talk about it next week. I'm getting stronger all the time, and I'm going stir-crazy in here. I need to get away for a couple of days and get back into the real world."

John became obsessed with getting away from the hospital. He realized that he was not ready for full release and assignment to duty, but he just had to get away. Shortly after arriving at Valley Forge he had filed a claim for the loss in Korea of his personal uniforms and goods, and had received a payment for them. He had opened a checking account in the bank branch in the hospital with the claim money he received. He went to the quartermaster store and bought one olive drab winter uniform, an overseas cap, and a rain coat with a lining. He bought a couple of shirts, ties, shoes, and everything that he thought he would need for a week. He hung them in the closet in his room.

John had not drawn any pay since he had left the States in September. There was little need for money in Korea or in the hospital, so instead of taking his pay each month he allowed it to accumulate on the books. Counting that month's pay, he had seven month's base pay coming. Furthermore, he was entitled to forty-five dollars a month combat pay for the three, and maybe four, calendar months he was in Korea. The knowledge that he had that much money coming to him gave him the boldness to think about buying a car.

Grady worked hard at his physical therapy sessions the next week, and although he didn't have full use of his arm and hand, he really felt good. On Thursday, he asked Major Mott about leave. Mott had reservations about Grady leaving for a week but couldn't find a real good reason to say "No." Consequently, he approved a leave starting at noon on Saturday, 7 April 51, and ending at 1700 on Sunday, 15 April 51.

Dr. Mott admonished Grady, "John, you must keep in mind that you still have to be careful: don't allow yourself to get overly tired; don't try to do too much; get a good rest each day; no alcohol, and eat moderately; and exercise your arm and hand when you get up in the morning. Your fever is gone, but I'll write you a prescription for an antibiotic that I want you to continue taking. You shouldn't have any problem, but if you do, call me." Dr. Mott wrote his telephone numbers at the hospital and his home on the top sheet of a prescription pad and gave the sheet to Grady.

"Major, I can't thank you enough. I thought this day would never come. You've done a tremendous job on me, and I want to thank you for it."

***

Saturday finally arrived. Grady ate an early lunch and signed out at the stroke of noon. He rode a bus from the hospital to a bus station in downtown Philadelphia where he bought a bus ticket for Red Bank, N.J. The bus went north to Princeton where he changed to another bus that went east to the coast. He was nervous, and for some reason, not sure of himself—he had been confined too long. He carefully thought out everything he had to do and paid close attention to everything that was happening. On the bus ride to Red Bank, he thought about how long it had been since he had been at Fort Monmouth. He took the calendar from his wallet and started figuring. He remembered that he had graduated from The Signal School on 13 September and had departed two days later. By his count, he was away six months and twenty-two days.

John arrived in Red Bank late in the afternoon and took a taxi to the BOQ billeting office at Fort Monmouth. He received a room assignment without difficulty—quite different from his experience with Captain A. M. Small QC at Camp Stoneman, California. John had a room to himself because that time of year was not the busy time for the Officers Department of The Signal School. He put away the extra clothes he had brought and hung up one of the towels he had "borrowed" from Valley Forge. He made his cot himself because orderlies were not on duty Saturday night. He stretched out on the cot and rested for half an hour, then went to the mess hall.

He returned to his room and brushed his teeth, then walked over to Scrivner Hall and walked around there looking at all the once-familiar details. He went to the bar and ordered a Coke from a bartender whom he had not seen before. It was a quiet night at the club, and Grady sat alone at the bar conscious of nothing but his loneliness. He finished his Coke, went back to the BOQ, took a pill, and went to bed.

John slept soundly and took his time getting up in the morning. He did some exercises for his arm and hand, then showered and shaved, and went to the mess hall for breakfast. He attended church services at the post chapel and found that there was a new Protestant chaplain whom he did not like as well as the one who had been there last summer. The weather was cold and damp. He put up the collar of his raincoat and stuffed his hands into his raincoat pockets. He stopped at the enlisted men's pool hall and bought a copy of the Sunday newspaper which he dropped off at his room on his way to the mess hall. So far, he had not seen one face he recognized.

John went back to his room and read the newspaper. UN forces were fighting north of the Thirty-eighth Parallel and were pushing forward in measured steps over difficult terrain and against stubborn resistance.

An interesting news item caught his attention. The presidents of Harvard College and Princeton University sharply criticized the government's policy of deferring college students from being drafted into military service. The presidents said, "... boys who can afford to continue their education are given special privileges." Grady agreed. Twice he had left college to go into the service, and he didn't see why the government should defer someone just because he was in college. He became sleepy and pulled back the blankets and slept for the remainder of the afternoon. His evening was no more exciting than his afternoon.

CHAPTER 4. (9 APRIL 1951)

John slept late Monday morning, did his exercises, showered and shaved, and took a pill. He was late and missed breakfast at the mess hall. The weather was cold and cloudy, and a light precipitation that was a mixture of snow and rain was falling. He figured that it was a good day to look for a car since dealers had cars displayed in their indoor showrooms. He wanted to look at the Chevrolet, Ford, and Plymouth dealers. He decided to start at the Chevrolet/Oldsmobile dealer which was on the south end of Red Bank, just across the railroad tracks. He took his time dressing, then went out to the road near the BOQ and caught the post bus that went out to the West Gate. He walked to the bus shelter on Route 35 and caught the public bus to Red Bank. He stepped off the bus opposite the Chevy dealer, waited for traffic to clear, then crossed the highway. He climbed the three steps to the showroom, pulled the door open with his right hand and entered. He didn't have gloves for his hands, so his left hand was cold and stiff.

Grady stood inside the door and removed his cap and shook the snow and rain off it. He looked around the showroom. Five new cars were on display on his left behind the large plate-glass windows that faced the highway. At the left-rear corner of the large room, a man behind the service counter thumbed through a stack of work orders, and a secretary sat at a desk behind the counter. A rubber floor mat extended from the front door straight back to the rear of the room and ended in front of a set of double doors that led to the service area in the rear of the building. The customer-waiting area was on the right side of the floor mat at the rear of the showroom, and Grady saw a woman sitting there on a well-worn, artificial-leather couch reading a magazine.

He walked along the floor mat as he looked for a salesman, and as he approached the waiting area he glanced over toward the woman—he stopped dead in his tracks. She had the magazine on her lap and was looking down at it. She turned a page and continued looking down. She slowly turned another page, and as she did so, in her peripheral vision she saw someone standing there. She looked over and saw him looking at her.

Slowly, she sat up straight. She spread her hands flat against the magazine. She looked as if she didn't know what to do.

"Hello, Rebecca," he said to her in a friendly voice. "Good lord," he said to himself, " I had forgotten what a beautiful woman she is."

"Why ... well ... hello John Grady." She was blushing.

"What are you doing here, Rebecca?"

"Mother bought a new Oldsmobile station wagon and it's due for its thousand mile check-up. Harold has the flu and can't bring it in, so I did. What are you doing here?" She appeared flustered and chagrined.

"I'm thinking about buying a car and came in to look at the Chevrolets."

"John, I'm surprised to see you. If I remember correctly, you said you would be in Korea at least a year. You came back early."

"Yes, they didn't need me over there so they sent me back to the States," he lied.

"Are you at Fort Monmouth again?"

"No. I'm just visiting here for a week while I'm on leave."

"Where are you stationed?" Neither one look away from the other.

"Over in Pennsylvania." John looked over to the showroom but didn't see a salesman. She was saying something, but he wasn't listening to her. His mind was racing. He had a ringing in his ears.

"Rebecca, have you had breakfast?

"No. I only had time for a cup of tea this morning."

"I haven't had breakfast either, and I'm going over to that diner across the highway and get some. I'll be pleased if you'll join me."

She had an expression of uncertainty on her face.

"Come on, grab your coat. Let's get out of here," he said as a smile slowly formed on his face.

At first she was surprised at his commanding voice, then she remembered those words. She smiled and stood up. They went to the coat rack and he helped her with her raincoat. She was halfway into it when she turned partly toward him and said, "You know, John, I was driving down Tinton Avenue the other day and passed the Fort Monmouth golf course and thought about the golf game we played there. That was some time ago, wasn't it. How long has it been since we've seen each other? It must be nine months, at least."

Grady did some quick arithmetic in his head adding days to the time he had been away from Fort Monmouth. "It was seven months and two days ago."

She looked at him with astonishment. "How does he know the exact days?" she wondered. She kept looking at him, then slowly she said out loud, "Seven months and two days?" He nodded his head. She wondered, "Has he been counting the days?"

She resumed putting on her raincoat and tied a scarf around her head. They went outside and stood under the overhang getting ready to make a dash through the rain and slush to the diner across the highway. She looked at him and said, "Seven months and two days?" He smiled and nodded.

They set out at a fast pace first crossing the highway and then going across the railroad tracks to the diner. They went inside, shook off the rain, took off their raincoats, and slid onto opposite seats at a booth toward the far end of the diner. A waitress came to their booth and handed John two menus and asked, "Coffee?"

"I'll have hot tea, please," Rebecca said. Grady nodded "Yes." Grady held one menu in his right hand and extended the other one in his left hand toward Rebecca. The menu dropped from his left hand. He tried to pick it up, but the fingers were cold and stiff and wouldn't function to get under the menu. He fumbled with it until Rebecca reached out and picked it up.

'You seem to have trouble with your left hand, John, did you hurt it?"

"Uh ... well ... yes ... yes, when I came back to the West Coast from overseas I was getting into a taxi cab and the driver shut the door on my hand. It's a little stiff and sore, but it'll get better." He lied to her again, but he told himself that it was none of her business. He probably would never see her again, so it didn't matter.

"Ouch, that hurts just to think about it. Have you seen a doctor? Maybe you broke something in your hand."

"Yes. Nothing is broken."

They studied the menus, and when each seemed to have made a decision and looked up, John said, "I take it that you live in this area now." She nodded affirmatively. "And, your husband commutes to New York on the train?"

Rebecca looked down at the place mat in front of her. She was blushing. She didn't say anything at first, then she looked up at John with a solemn face and said, "I'm separated from Dick. I'm living at home with my parents." She continued looking at John, but said nothing more.

"How long have you been separated from your husband?"

"It's been five weeks now."

"Well, gee, Rebecca, ... I'm sorry to hear that." They looked at each other. She looked as if she were one unhappy woman. She wondered what he was thinking.

Then John said, "No, I'm not, Rebecca—I'm not sorry your marriage broke up."

Her face turned red. She looked at the place mat again. She collected her thoughts and said, "John, I can understand that you're not sorry. I treated you badly, and you don't owe me anything."

John's eyes narrowed, he had a puzzled look on his face, and he leaned forward in his seat. "Now, just a minute; hold the phone. Do you think I'm happy because you've had an unpleasant and probably a traumatic experience with your marriage? You're not reading me right; I didn't mean that at all." The waitress brought the tea and coffee and took their orders. John waited until the waitress was gone. "Rebecca, please don't think I take delight in seeing you suffer an unpleasantness. That's the farthest thing I had in my mind, believe me."

"John, I'm embarrassed at the way I ended our relationship. I would expect you to have strong feelings about that."

"Rebecca, you didn't listen. Now, you listen to me—get this straight in your head. When I left Fort Monmouth, I accepted the fact that it was all over between us. Then, I became so busy in Korea that I didn't have a chance to think about you. You have no idea how consuming it is of one's attention, energies, and emotions to get caught up in a war. I don't say this in a pejorative sense, Rebecca, but I quickly got over you. The truth is that I remember you as a fine person, and I have no ill will toward you."

"What about the seven months and two days, " she asked.

He grinned at her. "I'm quick with math. I'm an engineer, don't forget. Besides, two days ago I was figuring out how long I had been away from Fort Monmouth."

Both of them were uncertain how to deal with their unexpected meeting. The waitress brought their orders and they began eating in silence. After a while, John stopped eating and said to her, "Rebecca, I told you that I'm not angry at you. That certainly is true, and to be absolutely frank

with you, the reason I said I'm happy your marriage broke up is that ...
maybe ...well ... well, if I ever want to see you again, then maybe it'll be
easier to see you if you're not happily married. Do you understand what I'm
saying? Rebecca, I never in the world ever expected to see you again, and I
haven't really thought about you for months. When I saw you this morning
it surprised me and I just got all mixed up. Forgive me for my clumsiness.
Do you understand what I am saying? Do you believe what I'm saying?"

Rebecca had stopped eating while he spoke. She replied, "Do you
remember that I once called you 'Honest John'? Yes, I believe you, John."

They continued eating, then John had to ask a question. "Rebecca,
don't answer this question if you don't want to—just tell me to mind my
own business—but I was wondering why your marriage came upon hard
times?"

She took a deep breath and looked John in the eyes and said, "I found
out that Dick had a mistress. Not only that, but he had her before we were
married. As soon as I learned it I left him and came home." Her humili-
ation was apparent. "As far as I'm concerned, the marriage is irrevocably
ended. I'm using my maiden name, and I'm having nothing more to do with
him except divorcing him. I truly believe that God considers the marriage
ended, regardless of what the law says."

"That's too bad, Rebecca. That's why he was away somewhere else on
some weekends and holidays last summer."

She looked at him with a horrified look. "John, did you know? Why
didn't you tell me?"

"No, no, I didn't know, but I had suspicions. If it had been I
who...."

John smiled at her and said, "You've changed you hair style." It was
longer than it had been last September, and she had braids on each side of
her head that met in the back.

She was pleased that he noticed. "Do you like it?"

"No. I like it the other way better."

"Honest John."

John continued the conversation, "What are you doing with yourself
now that you're home again? How do you spend your time?"

She looked chagrined. "I really don't do too much. I just ...." She
shrugged her shoulders. She tried to smile, but couldn't. She looked and
acted like a whipped dog whose spirit was broken.

John looked out the window. The rain had stopped and the sky was beginning to show some blue. "Rebecca, I haven't been in downtown Red Bank for some time, and I was thinking about walking up there and walking around town. Why don't you join me. The weather is clearing, and the walk will do us both good. What do you say?"

"Thank you, John, but I have to get the station wagon."

"The station wagon will wait. They'll hold it for you."

""Don't you want to look at the cars in the showroom?"

"I'm in no rush. Come on, grab your coat. Let's get out of here." John stood up and held her raincoat for her.

"John, I really can't."

"Yes you can. Now, put your coat on." She reluctantly stood up and slipped into her coat. John put his coat on and they went to the counter and he paid the bill. They crossed the highway and headed toward the center of town. A new weather system was moving up the coast from the South, and fresh, warmer air was blowing in. John tried to make small talk as they walked. Rebecca was polite and responsive, but she was not the old Rebecca that she had been last September.

John asked her, "Have you been riding much since you've been home?"

"No, not yet." They walked on.

"What was Korea like, John?"

"A poor country ravished by a brutal war. The people are suffering terribly. I didn't see any pretty towns such as Red Bank. We are really fortunate in this country. I wish all the people in this country could understand what a very special thing we have here."

They entered the main part of town where the small shops were located. They moved from shop window to shop window looking at the merchandise on display. Rebecca frequently looked to see if anyone were watching them. John noticed it and politely said to her, 'Rebecca, if you're uncomfortable being with me in public, we can go back to the car dealer."

She was embarrassed and touched his arm with her hand. "I'm sorry, John, forgive me. Let's continue; I'm all right." They sauntered down the street, turned the corner and came to a small park with benches. John was getting tired and said, "What do you say we sit for a while?"

They sat several feet apart on the bench, and John asked her, "Are you still doing volunteer work at the hospital?"

"No, I haven't gotten back to it, but I intend to."

They talked, both somewhat guardedly as they tried to conform their conversation to this unforeseen meeting. Yet, they were not uncomfortable in each other's company. Apparently, a mutual respect remained that they could build upon should events take that turn.

They were quiet for a while, then Grady said, "You know Rebecca, I can't get over the fact that we ran into each other this morning. As I told you, I never expected to see you again, and I never would have looked for you. It's kind of an odd thing that I'm at Fort Monmouth at all. I had never been in that car dealership in my life, had you?"

"No, I hadn't either. Harold always takes care of those things."

"Speaking of Harold, did Sally give you a message from me when I left Fort Monmouth for overseas?"

"Yes, she did," Rebecca said with an apologetic look.

John saw her look and said, "Rebecca, you don't need to feel bad about what happened between us in the past. I told you that I quickly got over it, and from my standpoint it probably was for the best while I was overseas. Let's both wipe the slate clean. Can we?"

She nodded affirmatively. "That's kind of you, John. Most men wouldn't be as forgiving. Thank you." He could see that she needed a morale boost. She really was at an emotional low. She was vastly different from the upbeat, good-natured Rebecca that he knew last summer. He didn't know what he could do for her.

"Do you want to start back?" he asked.

They resumed their leisurely walk. John saw the Molly Pitcher Inn down the street. "You know, I've never been in the Molly Pitcher. Have you?" She said that she had. "Let's have some lunch in there today. I really am enjoying seeing this town—this country. I want to see the Molly Pitcher. Come on, I don't want to do it by myself; it's no fun to eat alone."

"John, I have to be getting home. Mother will wonder what happened to me."

"What are you going to do when you get home? Nothing—right? The car will sit in the garage when you take it back—right? I'll bet that the Molly Pitcher has a telephone in there so you can call your mother and tell her that you're having lunch in town." He grinned at her. "Live boldly."

"Oh, John ... all right" They went into the lobby and Rebecca went to a phone booth and made her call. John looked around the lobby. Very nice, he concluded.

Rebecca returned and John asked, "Is everything all right?"

She understood why he was asking. "Everything is fine. John, I had a big breakfast; I'm not really hungry."

"This is a lovely lobby," he said. "We can sit here a few minutes and then go into the dining room for a little something—just enough to hold body and soul together."

She smiled at him. They found two comfortable chairs and talked longer than either one thought they could. They went to the tastefully-decorated dining room where a hostess seated them and gave them two large menu folders and said that a waitress would come to take their orders.

John surveyed the dinning room and said, "This is nice; I'm enjoying this. In fact, I've enjoyed the entire morning. Thank you, Rebecca."

"I've enjoyed it too. You know, I have a confession to make. This is the first time I've been out with anyone, male or female, other than Mother, since I came home five weeks ago."

John was quiet for a while, then he asked her, "How old are you now?"

"I'm twenty-three. Why?"

"You have, maybe, up to three times that many years of your life yet to live. They can be fruitful, exciting, and fulfilling years. Rebecca, it's time for you to accept the fact that the marriage didn't work out and get on with your life. You're an intelligent and resourceful person. You should work hard to get yourself back into a confident frame of mind and start living a useful life. I'm not criticizing you, Rebecca, I imagine that a marriage breakup is a wrenching emotional experience, but if that's the worst thing that ever happens to you in your life, you'll be a very lucky girl."

Her face was expressionless as she looked at him. "John, I know deep inside me that what you say is true, but it just isn't as easy to do it as it is to say it. There's a lot of hurt that I have to get rid of. But I appreciate very much your concern; it's nice to know that someone is trying to help.

"John, I don't want to talk about my marriage any more. Can we leave it out of our conversation?"

The waitress came and took their orders.

"You want to leave out of our conversation all talk about your marriage? Sure, we can do that. I'll tell you what, we'll chop out of history the months from mid-September 1950 to 9 April 1951." He made two chopping motions and a sweeping motion with his right hand as he spoke. "We'll resume history from that night last September when we both stood on the beach without any underwear on. Do you remember that?" He grinned at her.

She looked shocked. She looked around to see if anyone had heard him.

John continued grinning, "Yes, the two of us standing on that beach without any underwear on."

"Oh, John," she admonished, as she looked around again. He burst out laughing. She had to laugh too. "John, you make it sound naughty."

"There's nothing naughty about two people standing on a beach without any underwear on." They both laughed. The waitress brought their food and they made occasional small talk as they ate. John suggested that they return to the lobby.

Rebecca looked at her watch. "I have to get back to the Oldsmobile garage, don't forget. What about you looking for a car?"

"Don't worry about that; I'll take care of it." They went into the lobby and found two comfortable chairs and talked some more. After a while, Rebecca said, "John, I just have to be going. I'm leaving." When they stood up, John said, "Rebecca, why don't you stay in town and have dinner with me tonight. If I go back to the post, I'll have to eat by myself in the mess hall where I don't know anyone, and I'll have a lonely meal and a lonely evening. You don't want that to happen to me do you?" He grinned at her as he spoke.

"John, I can't stay any longer."

"How would you like some Italian food for dinner? I know a good Italian restaurant in Long Branch. Do you think you can find it again? But, it might be a little cool for a swim afterwards. Come on, Rebecca, it's time to come out of your cocoon."

She looked at him for some time. "John Grady, you've not changed one bit. All right, but I'll have to call home right now. Here, hold my coat." She started toward the phone booth.

"Wait, Rebecca." He went up to her and said, "Rebecca, I don't know what you told your mother about lunch, but I recommend you tell her that you're with me, and that you've been with me all day. I don't want to play a cat and mouse game again. You ought to consider that before we finalize our plans for dinner tonight."

Rebecca looked at him with a serious face, but said nothing. She turned and went to the phone booth and was gone for quite a while. She returned to where John was sitting and took the chair next to him. He looked at her with a questioning look. She made a slight smile and said, "O.K."

"Did you tell her that you're with me?" She nodded. John wondered how O.K. it really was.

"John, I'm glad that you said what you did about not playing games again. I agree. One reason I enjoy your company is that I always know where you stand. You ought to know where I stand. John, I do enjoy your company, but I don't want to get involved with you or with any other man. I've had enough involvement with a man to last me for a long time." She paused, then continued, "I have to confess that I really don't have any close friends. For some reason, I can talk with you, and I trust you. If we can continue as friends I would like that, but if you have something more in mind, I'm not ready for that and we shouldn't continue seeing each other."

John was pleased that Rebecca had clearly expressed her feelings. That was the Rebecca he remembered. "Rebecca, what you propose is fine with me. I understand how you feel, just so long as you don't stay in your cocoon. And I don't believe I'm ready to get involved with anyone just yet." Here, John was tempted to tell her the truth about what had happened to him and about his present situation—but he didn't. "I don't know how my present assignment is going to work out, and I don't know what my next assignment will be or where it will be. I have a lot of uncertainties in my immediate future, so what you propose is fine. Who knows, we may never see each other again. In the meanwhile, I enjoy your company and I'll be proud to be considered your friend."

They walked back to the Chevrolet dealer, and while Rebecca took care of the bill for the Oldsmobile, John looked at the Chevys in the display room. When she finished they went outside to the station wagon.

"Here we are again," John said. "you're driving your car and I'm sitting here like a bump on a log. I feel like a lush. When I get a car, I'll repay you for your kindness. I want you to know that I really appreciate it."

"That's what friends are for," she said, smiling at him. John thought that she was reminding him about their agreement and that he should remember to play by the rules.

They drove over to Long Branch and drove through town and stopped at the beach to kill time. She found the restaurant on the first try. He congratulated her. They went inside and sat at a booth—a different one from the one that they had occupied last September.

"Thanks for coming, Rebecca, this is considerably more pleasant than having supper in a mess hll with a hundred guys I've never seen before."

They had a relaxing meal, and she drove him back to Fort Monmouth. Before he stepped out of the station wagon he said, "You know Rebecca, I've never bought a car before, and I don't want to mess up on this first one. You have good taste and good judgment, why don't you come with me tomorrow when I look. I respect your opinion, and I'll appreciate your help. What do you say?"

"John Grady, you're up to your old tricks. I thought we had an agreement to be just friends."

"Rebecca, I'm not trying to make a move on you. I'm here alone, and you said that you have no close friends, and I'm not kidding that I would appreciate your input on selecting a car. That's not incompatible with friendship, is it? And, to be truthful, Rebecca, I think you need to get out of your house and start living a normal life. You should not waste any more of your life. Please pardon the sermon."

Rebecca was silent. "He probably is right that I should get out of the house more," she thought. "Maybe he does want my help. If I can't trust John Grady, who can I trust?" She looked at him and said, "All right, John."

"Good, I'll meet you at the diner across from the Chevy dealer tomorrow morning at nine o'clock and we'll have a bite of breakfast before we start. O.K.?"

"That's fine, John."

"Thank you for a nice day, Rebecca. Good night."

Grady returned to his room and contemplated the happenings of the day. He never expected to see Rebecca Hazlet again—and, she being separated from her husband. He tried to decide whether or not it was good that he met her again. Getting involved with her seemed to be a complex situation. First it was her engagement, and now it was her marriage breakup. Did he want to get mixed up in that type of situation again? But, if she ever gets her life straightened out .... Well, they were going to be ' just friends,' and she certainly needed a friend right now. He would see what happens.

He reminded himself that his first priority was to get well and return to duty. He would not allow Rebecca Hazlet, or anyone else, distract him from that goal. He took a pill and went to bed.

John awoke Tuesday morning, did his morning exercise routine, and went to the officers mess for a cup of coffee to wash down an antibiotic pill and to get his caffeine fix. On his way back to his room he stopped at the BOQ Billeting Office and asked to see their Fort Monmouth telephone directory. He found the number for Arthur Bowen, Lieutenant Colonel, and wrote it on a slip of paper which he put into his wallet. "Major Bowen has been promoted, I see."

He brushed his teeth, then took the post bus to the West Gate and Highway 35 where he boarded a public bus to Red Bank. It all was familiar to him: he had done this same thing many times prior to going overseas. But somehow it now seems different to him. He felt as if he were a different person from that young second lieutenant he was just seven months ago. Indeed, he was different—he had left in North Korea whatever youth he had taken there.

Rebecca arrived at the diner and greeted him with a smile and a warm hello. They went to a booth, studied the menus, and placed their orders. She seemed more at ease and not at all the doleful Rebecca that she was yesterday. "What's our schedule for today?" she asked cheerfully.

"I want to go to the Chevy showroom first, then to the Ford and the Plymouth dealers. I'm not sure what I want, so please don't hesitate to speak up. I'll appreciate the benefit of your good judgment. As I told you yesterday, I've never done this before. I'm just a poor hillbilly from West Virginia who happens to have a few buck in his pocket at this time."

"Hillbilly my foot," she replied with a grin.

They left Rebecca's Woody at the diner and walked across the highway to the Chevrolet dealer. John engaged a salesman and told him what he had in mind. The salesman took him to a green, four-door Chevy on the showroom floor and explained all the comfort features to him. John inquired about the engine and about the price. When he heard the price he said, "What are the prices on the two-door models?" He looked at Rebecca and said, "I don't like this green color. What do you think?"

She asked the salesman, "What other colors do you have?" He brought a brochure and showed color samples to both of them.

"That maroon looks nice, don't you think?" Grady said to Rebecca.

She agreed. He explained to the salesman that he wanted to look at Fords and Plymouths, but that he might be back. Before they left, John wrote down on a sheet of paper the prices of the four-door and two-door models. The salesman gave John his business card.

Rebecca drove them to the Ford dealer, then to the Plymouth dealer, where much the same procedures took place as at the Chevy dealer. John was getting tired. "I want some time to digest all this information we've collected on the various cars. Let's get some lunch. I liked the Molly Pitcher Inn where we ate yesterday; let's go back there."

They had a pleasant lunch, and after discussing the features of the various cars they had seen, John concluded that he wanted a maroon Chevrolet. "How does that sound to you?" he asked.

"John, I think you should get what you really want."

"You're right. It's no fun living with our regrets or our mistakes."

"I know all about that business," she replied while looking down at her hands on her lap.

"We can't cry over spilt milk, Rebecca. We have to get on with our lives and make the most of them that we can. God expects us to do our best."

"You're right, John, and I'm working on it. Thank you for your help."

They departed the Molly Pitcher Inn and drove back to the Chevrolet/Oldsmobile dealer. The salesman who waited on them earlier saw them enter and arose from his desk to meet them.

Grady said, "I've decided that I want the maroon one."

"Will that be the four-door or the two-door?" the salesman asked.

"I'll take the two-door."

Rebecca was standing behind John as he spoke to the salesman. "John," she called to him softly. He turned and went to her. "John, I think you'll like the four-door model better. You'll have friends going places with you, and it'll be much more comfortable having four doors rather than making grown men climb around the front seat to get into the back seat."

John studied her face as he thought about what she had said. He didn't want to spend the additional money, but he concluded that she was right. He also concluded that he had never seen a more beautiful woman.

"Rebecca, you're right.

"Make that the four-door model," he told the salesman.

The salesman led them over to his desk and offered them seats. He looked through a notebook that contained data on the dealership's inventory of cars. He looked up and said, "We don't have a maroon four-door in stock, but we do have that green one on the floor and a tan one. I can have you in one of them tomorrow."

John looked at Rebecca. Rebecca asked the salesman, "How long will it take you to get a maroon one?"

"I can have one here in ten days to two weeks."

Rebecca looked at John and said, "I know you're disappointed, but why don't you wait and get what you really want."

He was disappointed because he had planned to drive the car back to Valley Forge. On the other hand, he probably could talk Major Mott into giving him a weekend pass to come over to Red Bank to get the car when it comes in. And, it might provide an opportunity to see Rebecca again. "O.K., I'll wait for the maroon one." John signed several papers and gave the salesman a fifty dollar deposit.

The two of them walked out the front door of the dealership and John stopped. "I never feel good about spending money, but I feel good about buying that car, thanks to you. You are some kind of girl, Beck." She remembered that phrase. She smiled and blushed. Grady was in an expansive mood. "Let's celebrate. Let's go over to Scrivner Hall and have a drink. Then, how about going down to the Berkley-Carteret and have dinner? Again, we have to rely on you for transportation. What do you say?"

Rebecca was silent for a moment, then she smiled and said softly, "John Grady, this pattern sounds familiar; we've been through this routine a number of times since we first met. I told you yesterday that I don't want to get involved with anyone. We were together all day yesterday and most of today, and that's enough for right now. I respect you, John, but I really mean what I said."

"I respect your feelings, Rebecca. If you feel that I'm putting pressure on you, then we shouldn't do it. Thanks for your help. I appreciate it." He held out his hand to shake hers.

She thought maybe he was offering a final and concluding good-bye. Deep inside her she knew that she didn't want to completely terminate their renewed relationship, whatever there was of it, so she quickly said, "But, I would like to help you celebrate the purchase of your new car. I'll pick you up at your BOQ Thursday night at 6:30 and we'll go to dinner. I know a good place to celebrate."

Now he really didn't understand what she was doing, but he wanted to see her again. "That's thoughtful of you, Rebecca. Thursday is good with me."

"Come on, I'll drive you back to Fort Monmouth."

"No, thanks. I'll take the bus back."

***

John arrived at the BOQ and stopped at the pay phone inside the entrance. He retrieved Colonel Bowen's telephone number from his wallet, dropped a nickel into the coin slot, and dialed.

"Lieutenant Colonel Bowen's office."

"Good afternoon. This is Lieutenant John Grady, and I'm an acquaintance of the colonel. I recently returned from Korea, and I wonder if I might stop by for a few minutes and pay my respects to the colonel. Tomorrow or the next day will be fine for me."

"Lieutenant Grady, just a moment please." She came back in twenty seconds and said, "The colonel said he'll be delighted to see you. Will 1100 tomorrow morning be satisfactory?"

"Yes ma'am."

Wednesday morning, John went through his usual early-morning exercise routine. After breakfast he rested on his cot and tried to mentally prepare himself for his meeting with Colonel Bowen, but his thoughts wandered. He felt uneasy and dissatisfied with his present situation. He always tried to be in control of his life, but he didn't feel that way now. He was not completely healed, and he didn't know how long it would take. His recovery was largely in the hands of others and he didn't like that, but there was nothing he could do about it. He wondered if his arm would be strong enough to qualify him for full duty, or would he have a crippled arm? And, he didn't have the slightest idea where his next duty assignment would be.

Then, there's Rebecca. She's an intelligent woman, but why does her life get so messed up? He felt that he was fighting his emotions about her. He wanted to be practical and sensible about her, not emotional. He tried to convinced himself that his interest in her was for reasons other than the fact that she was a beautiful woman. They had agreed to be friends, but he wondered if he were being honest with himself, and with her, about how he felt about her.

John arrived at Bowen's office exactly at 1100. The sign on the door read, "Lt. Colonel Arthur L. Bowen, Deputy Director, The Signal School." The civilian secretary ushered him into the inner office. Bowen rose from his desk, smiled, walked around the desk and extended his hand and said, "Hello, Lieutenant Grady, it's good to see you again. Thank you for stopping by."

"Thank you, sir, it's nice to see you again. And congratulations on your promotion."

"Thank you. And are those silver bars on your shoulders? You have been promoted?"

"Yes sir. I happened to be at the right place when they needed someone to fill a slot."

"Let's see, you graduated from The Signal School in September, and you've already been promoted. That's splendid." Bowen seemed genuinely pleased to see Grady and was pleased to see that he had been promoted. It made Bowen feel as though he had placed a bet on a racehorse and his horse had won the race. "Please have a seat, John." Bowen pointed to a chair in front of his desk. He sat in another chair in front of the desk and moved it so that it faced Grady.

"Well John, tell me what you've been doing since you left here in September. You were ordered to FECOM, correct?"

"Yes sir, I was."

"Are you assigned back at Monmouth? What are you doing now?"

That was exactly what Grady was afraid of. He didn't want to go any further. "No sir, I'm just passing through here. I'm staying only a couple of days."

"Where are you stationed? What are you doing?" Bowen kept boring in. He was going to get his answers. He didn't do things by half measures.

John could see no alternative. "Actually, sir, I'm stationed at Valley Forge Army Hospital. I have a seven-day pass and decided to come over and see this area again."

"What are you doing at Valley Forge? John, are you a patient there? Have you been injured?" Bowen showed genuine concern. He stood up from his chair and went to the door of his office and said to his secretary, "Mrs. Stokley, please hold my calls; I'll return them later." He came back to his chair and looked at Grady with a beckoning look as if to say, "Come on man, tell me."

John tried to answer Bowen's questions without getting too detailed, but the colonel kept prodding. They talked for twenty minutes, and at the end, Bowen had highlights of Grady's experiences, both in Korea and his recovery in the hospital.

"John, what are your most vivid recollections of Korea?"

"Without question, first was the cold weather in North Korea. I can't describe it; you have to be there and experience it. I never have experienced anything as brutal, and there was no escape from it. Second, I guess that it was being captured by the Chinese and then immediately being released. Either that or our first firefight with the Chinese. So much happened in a short time span it's hard to sort it out right now. Then, there were the atrocities committed by the North Koreans against the South Koreans and the American GIs." John told him about the atrocities investigating team that he and Rollie Amory accompanied.

"Tell me John, do you feel that your training in The Signal School prepared you for what you experienced in Korea?"

Grady thought for a moment. "Well, yes and no, Colonel. As far as the communications equipment is concerned, yes, I was familiar with the equipment and felt well prepared. I have an electrical engineering degree and that helped. Where I felt deficient was in small unit tactics and maneuvering. We were behind enemy lines for more than a week, and as I mentioned, we had several encounters with the enemy. I felt inadequate in protecting the men and in trying to get them safely through the enemy-held territory. I wished that I had the know-how that I saw a young infantry platoon leader display in South Korea." John then told him about the afternoon and night that Captain Walker and he had spent with Second Lieutenant Cavendish's platoon under attack on the outpost south of Seoul. "He knew what to do and seemed to know what to anticipate. I believe that was his first combat experience, so he had to get that knowledge in training."

Bowen was silent for a while, then he said, "John, your experiences are rather unusual for a Signal Corps officer. My guess is that few, if any, Signal Corps officers will ever experience what you experienced. Our training time is limited in The Signal School, and I don't think it would be fruitful to devote any more time trying to prepare our officers to handle the situations that you experienced behind enemy lines in North Korea. Incidentally, from what you told me, I think you handled the situation very well.

"Do you know when you'll be released from the hospital? Do you know where you'll be assigned when you're released?"

"No sir, I don't know the answer to either of your questions. I hope I'm nearing the end of my hospital stay, but it depends on how quickly I heal completely.

"Where would you like to be assigned when you're released?"

"Sir, I would like to come back here to Fort Monmouth and take the next course in The Signal School. In any event, I would like to stay in the States until I'm absolutely certain that my health is back to one hundred percent. One thing I know for sure is that I don't want to go where it's very cold." They both chuckled.

Bowen looked at his watch. "John, it's lunch time, will you join me for lunch?"

"Yes sir." They walked to the officers mess and had a leisurely lunch.

The officers mess was buzzing with the news that President Truman had relieved General Douglas MacArthur of all his commands and duties. General Matthew Ridgway was appointed to replace him, and General James Van Fleet was named to replace General Ridgway as commander of Eighth Army.

When they finished eating, Grady said, "Colonel, I've taken too much of your time already; I should leave now and let you get some work done today. I've enjoyed seeing you again, sir."

"It was good seeing you, John. Please come by and see me if you get back here again."

✻✻✻

Grady went to the newspaper vending machine and bought a newspaper to read about the MacArthur firing. Differences between MacArthur and the Truman administration about how to fight the Korean War were public knowledge for some time. On his own initiative, on 24 March MacArthur issued a statement addressed to the Communist Chinese that was both taunting and threatening. He proposed that the Chinese end the fighting on terms that would realize the political objectives of the United Nations, and he told them that if they didn't accept the offered terms they would suffer an imminent military defeat. This statement incensed the Chinese, the Truman administration, and the UN allies.

What apparently precipitated the dismissal at that particular time was a 20 March letter from MacArthur to Massachusetts representative Joseph Martin, the Minority Leader of the U.S. House of Representatives, which Martin read on the floor of the House. MacArthur wrote in the letter that the United States should give first priority to Asia rather than Europe in combating Communism. He further wrote that Chinese Nationalist troops on Formosa should be allowed to mount an attack against Communist Chinese troops on mainland China. That act would considerably expand the war in Asia, but the Truman administration already had set the policy that it would try to confine the conflict to the Korean peninsula. Truman said that he was relieving MacArthur because MacArthur "was not able to give his wholehearted support to the policies of the United States Government and of the United Nations."

The dismissal news was a real shocker to Grady. He remembered how impressed he had been with MacArthur's bold maneuver in September 1950 of landing X Corps at Inchon, and John was proud to have been part of that operation even though he had missed the initial landing.

John also read in the newspaper that the American Red Cross had issued a special appeal for blood donors. Casualties were heavy in Korea and blood supplies were low.

The paper contained a short item about the suspension of a Department of the Navy civilian explosives expert on the grounds that he was a security risk. Senator Joseph McCarthy had earlier named him as a Communist. U.S. Senate and House committees were holding hearings on national security and alleged Communist infiltration of government departments and agencies.

***

Grady was tired. He fell asleep and awoke in time for supper. While he was eating he decided to go to the bible study class at the Methodist Church. After the bible class, he arrived back at his room quite tired and wondered why since he hadn't had much physical exertion that day.

John slept late Thursday morning. He did his exercises and the remainder of his morning routine and was late for breakfast in the officers mess. He rode the post bus out to the West Gate and had breakfast at the diner just outside the gate. He didn't have any plans for the day, so he rode the post bus back to the post library. He read several newspapers about the MacArthur firing, and then went to lunch at the officers mess. He wasn't hungry and didn't eat everything on his tray. He went back to his BOQ and took a nap. When he awoke he looked at his watch and though about getting ready to meet Rebecca at 1830.

Rebecca also was thinking about the coming evening. She had to admit that her life had brightened since she met John Grady on Monday. She admitted to herself that there wasn't any other man she would enjoy being with right now. Rebecca told herself that she shouldn't get serious with him, but at the same time she didn't want him to go away—not again. Maybe she should say something to let him know.

John waited for Rebecca outside his BOQ. She was on time, and as they drove off Grady asked her, "Where are we going for this celebration?"

She smiled at him, "This is a special event, so we're going to the Shadow Brook."

"Oh my, that's an expensive place." He had heard of the good reputation of the restaurant, but he had never been in it. It was too expensive for a lieutenant's pay.

"This is my treat," she smiled at him. "I made the reservation and tonight is on me."

"Now, hold the phone. If I take a girl out, I expect to pay the tab."

She looked at him and smiled, "You're not taking me out tonight; I'm taking you out."

"Rebecca, this is not right."

"It's right if we say it's right. Please, John, I want to do this. Won't you grant me this favor?"

"Rebecca, you make it very difficult."

"John, let's put our difficulties behind us—all of them. Let's just enjoy the evening."

"I don't like it, but if you absolutely insist, I'm not going to fight you any more about it. It is most unusual, though." After a pause he continued, "Then, come to think about it, our entire relationship has been unusual from the very beginning, hasn't it."

"Yes, it has been unusual, John, but we remain friends. That's important."

They drove down a long, winding driveway to the Shadow Brook restaurant which was situated in an estate-like setting. An attendant came to park the car for them and they went inside. They sat at a table in a corner of the room. Grady looked around the elegant dining room. A violinists, a cello player, and a piano player softly played chamber music in an alcove on one side of the room.

"This is nice, Rebecca, you made an excellent choice. And, you look very nice this evening."

"Thank you, John." Rebecca was in a cheerful, talkative mood. For the first time since their second meeting she was more like the Rebecca he remembered. She made John's spirits rise out of the somber mood he had been in earlier in the day.

There was a wide selection of entrees on the menu, and John selected salmon and mashed potatoes to be sure that he could handle them with just a fork in his right hand. Rebecca ordered a lobster and drawn butter.

"John, when are you going back to your camp?"

"I'm leaving Red Bank Sunday morning."

"What are you going to do until then?"

"I have no plans, except that I'm going to New York on Saturday to see the matinee of the New York City Opera."

"Oh, what's being performed?"

"Madam Butterfly."

"Where did you get your ticket?"

"I don't have a ticket."

"You don't have a ticket; how are you going to get in?"

"I'll get in. Ever since we played classical music in the high school band I've wanted to see an opera. This is my first chance and maybe my last one for a while." He didn't invite her to go with him.

The dinner and evening went exceedingly well for both of them. They didn't talk much as they drove back to Fort Monmouth. When Rebecca stopped the Woody in front of his BOQ, she shut off the engine and turned to him. "John, I'm indebted to you. I was in a terrible funky state when I returned home. I didn't have ambition to do anything, and the worst part of it was that I didn't have anyone to talk with. You've admonished me to quit feeling sorry for myself, to get out of my cocoon, and to get on with my life. You're right, and I believe I'm starting to make some progress. These last couple of days I've felt the best I have since I came home. Thank you, I'm fortunate to know you." She looked at him and smiled and said, "And I've enjoyed being with you this week."

"I'm glad that you feel that way." Both were silent for a time, each

271

wanting the other to say something. Eventually, Grady said, "You made it clear that you don't want to get involved with me in anything more than what I think they call a Platonic relationship where we're 'just friends' and nothing more. I can live with that, but you know, Rebecca, tonight I made an observation. Tonight we shared a warm and delightful evening—kind of the way we did last September. I felt as if the two of us were in our own little world set apart from the rest of the world for a couple of hours. I'm trying to figure out if that's the way 'just friends' interact with each other. I don't think so. What do you think?"

Rebecca didn't respond to him for a long time as she looked straight ahead through the windshield. She turned and looked at him with a pleading look. "Can you give me some time, John? I have more work to do to get myself over the depression that has overtaken me, and I have to go through a divorce proceeding. I need time to get those things behind me. I'm afraid you won't like me the way I am now, and I don't want that. Believe me, I do enjoy being with you, but for the present can we do it the way we agreed without again losing contact with each other?"

"Sure, if you insist."

"Am I going to see you again before you go back to camp?" she asked.

He hesitated, then looked at her. "Do you want to go to the opera on Saturday?"

Despite what she had just told him, the words escaped from her mouth, "I thought you would never ask."

Grady was tired and went directly to bed after he left Rebecca. He awoke during the night with an uncomfortable feeling in his left arm. He thought that he probably was laying on it and had caused a restriction in the flow of blood. He rolled over onto his back and tried to go to sleep, but he couldn't. He got up and exercised his arm, thinking that exercising would get the blood flowing in the arm and get rid of the uncomfortable feeling. He put on his socks and shoes, obtained an aspirin from his kit, and went to get water to wash down the aspirin. He went back to bed and fell asleep after an hour.

John slept late Friday morning and awoke feeling tired. He went through his morning routine and didn't finish until long after the mess hall had closed. Going out to the West Gate diner seemed like too much trouble, so he skipped breakfast. He walked over to the laundry and picked up clothing that he had taken there several days ago. On the way back to his BOQ he bought several newspapers which he read until time for lunch. He didn't care for the lunch, so he left part of it on his tray.

***

Grady went back to his room and continued reading the newspapers. Eighth Army was cautiously moving north in pursuit of withdrawing North Korean and Chinese forces. Enemy forces were making scattered defenses everywhere along the line, but they were avoiding major battles. Air reconnaissance and signal intelligence revealed that the Chinese were bringing fresh forces to assembly areas north of the Thirty-eighth Parallel, and the North Koreans were reorganizing their forces in that area. The UN command anticipated a major spring offensive by the Chinese and North Koreans. UN forces hoped to establish their main line of resistance along and above the Thirty-eighth Parallel.

The Chinese and the nations of the UN that had troops in Korea wanted to find a way to stop the fighting, but each side wanted to have a decisive upper hand on the battlefield before talking about a cease-fire. So far, neither side could achieve that goal with the resources they were willing to commit to the war. U.S. Generals Ridgway and Van Fleet were told that they could not expect to receive major reinforcements. Consequently, the fighting and killing continued.

***

John became sleepy, so he crawled into bed and took a nap. He awoke in late afternoon with a slight headache. He took an aspirin, dressed, and went over to Scrivner Hall for a Coke. He didn't know anyone there. He didn't want to go to the mess hall for dinner, so he ate a hamburger and drank a glass of milk at the Scrivner Hall grill. He walked around the club after he ate, but still didn't see anyone he knew. He went back to his room, brushed his teeth, took a pill, and went to bed.

CHAPTER 5. (14 APRIL 1951)

John awoke Saturday morning in time to do his morning exercise routine and eat breakfast in the mess hall. He swallowed two aspirins before
he left for Red Bank to meet Rebecca. They met on the station platform
and boarded the train to New York City. They took a taxi from Pennsylvania Station to the opera house and stood on the sidewalk in front of the
entrance. The box office was in the lobby, inside the locked entrance doors.
People were gathering on the sidewalk, and a tall man in a gray felt hat
had a couple of tickets in his hand and was working his way through the
crowd hawking the tickets. John went over to him and asked, "Do you have
tickets for this afternoon's performance?

"Yes, they're good seats in the front of the balcony."

"What do you want for them?"

"Twenty five dollars each."

"That's too much. Thanks anyway."

The crowd on the sidewalk grew larger and several more scalpers
worked the crowd. John checked with them, but they all wanted more
money than he wanted to pay. The lobby doors opened and the crowd on
the sidewalk flowed into the lobby. Rebecca and John worked their way
through the crowd to the box office and inquired about tickets.

"We're sold out for the matinee today," the woman behind the glass
responded.

Grady and Rebecca went back outside where only about half a dozen
people remained. They were looking at people on the sidewalk when a
well-dressed, middle-aged woman walked up to Rebecca and asked if they
were looking for matinee tickets. "Yes we are," Rebecca quickly replied.

"I have season subscriptions, but we can't make today's performance. I
have two tickets in the first mezzanine, and I'm asking eighteen dollars for
each one. Are you interested?

Rebecca and Grady responded in unison, "Yes we are." John pulled
his wallet from his hip pocket and held it in front of him. As his right hand
reached in for the bills, the wallet slipped out of his stiff left hand and fell
onto the sidewalk. He cursed and reached down and picked it up with his

right hand. He straightened up and cradled the opened wallet between his left arm and his chest as he reached in with his right hand and took out the money. Rebecca noticed but said nothing. He received the tickets and they hurried into the lobby. John purchased a libretto and they headed for their seats. Well, it turned out that the seats were front row, center, in the first mezzanine. When they were seated, Rebecca squeezed John's arm and said, "Aren't these wonderful seats. Aren't we lucky."

They hastily read the translation of the first act in the libretto. Then the house lights dimmed, the orchestra played the overture, the curtain rose, and the opera began. When the house lights came back on, Rebecca looked at John with a pleased look. "Wasn't that wonderful?"

"Yes. They're good actors as well as good singers; I didn't expect that." They read the translation of the second act sitting close together with shoulders touching.

When the opera was over, they walked down to the sidewalk in awe of the performance they had just seen. "Thank you for coming, Rebecca, it was more enjoyable sharing it with you."

They went to the Astor Bar in the Hotel Astor on Times Square and enjoyed the lively atmosphere generated by the young and middle-aged adults that filled the room. They both had Cokes. They walked a couple of blocks east to a quaint German restaurant that had blue and white checkered tablecloths. They ordered German favorites and then sat back and talked. John marveled that he never had trouble talking with Rebecca. Before Rebecca, he had to force himself to keep a conversation going with a woman.

"John, how is your left hand? I noticed that you had a little trouble getting money out of your wallet. Is your hand getting any better? Should you have it looked at again?"

John thought that maybe it was time to tell her about his arm and what had happened to him. He thought about it, but he really didn't want her to know—not yet—it was not time for her to know, so he lied again. "It's just badly bruised. It'll take time for the soreness to go away."

They had a pleasant dinner, then headed for Pennsylvania Station to catch the 7:20 p.m. train to Red Bank. Not long after the train left Penn Station John asked, "Are you warm? I think it's warm in this coach."

"No, I'm quite comfortable."

Grady stood up and took off his Ike jacket and put it on the overhead rack. Shortly thereafter, he felt perspiration running down the small of his back, and he began to feel nauseous. He asked Rebecca, "Is that German dinner agreeing with you?"

"Yes it is. Are you feeling all right?"

"I don't know. Excuse me a minute." Grady walked down the aisle to the restroom at the end of the coach. He went inside and threw up. He really felt lousy. He waited a while, then washed his face and hands and washed out his mouth with soap and water. He returned to his seat.

Rebecca watched him as he walked up the aisle. "John, you don't look well. You're ill, aren't you."

"I've felt better. Maybe that dinner didn't settle very well," he lied again. He was certain it wasn't the dinner that was causing the trouble—his left arm told him that. A short time later he became chilled and couldn't control his shivering.

'Oh John, you are ill. Is there anything I can do?"

"Rebecca, I'm sorry to spoil your day; we've had a nice time up until now."

"Don't worry about me; it's you we have to worry about." They didn't talk too much during the remainder of the train ride.

Before the train arrived at Red Bank, Rebecca said, "John, you should have a doctor look at you. I'll take you to Riverview Hospital."

"No, thank you, Rebecca, that's thoughtful of you, but I'll take a taxi to the post."

"You will not take a taxi: I'll drive you!" They stepped off the train and went to Rebecca's Woody. Not long after they left the train station, John said, "Rebecca, you had better drop me off at the post dispensary. I'll give you directions." When they arrived at the dispensary Grady said, "Thank you for a wonderful day, Rebecca. You had better be getting home."

"I'm not leaving you here; I'm going in with you." She brushed aside his protestations and parked the car.

As they walked through the front door together, John saw a nurse at a desk over to the left and some chairs in a waiting area to his right. "Rebecca, please wait while I talk to the nurse over there. I'll be right back." Rebecca sat down and Grady walked toward the nurse, a captain in the Army Nurse Corps.

"Good evening, Captain, I'm John Grady. I'm a transient here at Fort

Monmouth, just spending a couple of days on a pass. I'm a patient at Valley Forge Army Hospital where I've been treated for some combat wounds. I'm afraid I'm having some trouble with them right now. I feel like I have a high fever, and I had the sweats and the chills this evening, and I've thrown up. I don't feel too well, and I wonder if you have a doctor here who might take a look at me."

"I'll call Captain Abrams who's on duty tonight. Come with me."

"Wait a minute." John turned and looked at Rebecca. She immediately left her chair and briskly walked over to him.

"Rebecca, a doctor is going to look at me. There's no need for you to stay here any longer, so why don't you go home before it gets any later. Thank you for everything. I'll call you the first thing in the morning."

"John, I am not leaving here until I know what's wrong with you," she said resolutely. "You go ahead; I'll wait here."

The nurse said, "Lieutenant, you come with me. Miss, you have a seat and I'll let you know as soon as the doctor examines him." The nurse led Grady to an examination room and told him to have a seat. She came back in five minutes and took his temperature, pulse rate, and blood pressure. His temperature was one hundred and four degrees. Captain Abrams came into the room and John explained the situation to him. The doctor looked at his arm, his buttock, and his toes, and asked him what medications he was taking. Abrams told John that he should stay at the dispensary overnight, and tomorrow the duty doctor would contact Valley Forge and talk with Dr. Mott. That sounded reasonable to John.

John said, "A young lady is waiting for me in the waiting area. I want to talk with her."

"You come with me. I'll send the nurse to talk with her," Abrams said.

John said very emphatically to Abrams, "I don't want her to know that I have wounds. I want the nurse to know that before she talks with my young lady. Do you understand that? Abrams conveyed John's message to the nurse.

They put John in a private room at the far end of the dispensary. Abrams told him that he would give him the same antibiotic drug that he had been taking and that the duty doctor would check him the first thing Sunday morning. Shortly, a nurse came in with an antibiotic pill and a glass of water.

Meanwhile, the first nurse went out to the waiting room and told Rebecca that the doctor had recommended that Lieutenant Grady be held overnight in the dispensary. She told Rebecca that they would not know anything more until tomorrow morning, so she should go home now and call tomorrow to inquire about John's condition. Reluctantly, Rebecca went home.

At 0630 Sunday morning Colonel Jeremy Woodson, commanding officer of the dispensary, arrived at his office and read the status report of the events of Saturday afternoon and night. Woodson was six feet four inches tall, was skinny as a rail, had dark hair, and a pointed nose. He was slightly stooped and looked like Abraham Lincoln. He had been in the army since before World War II and was serving in the Philippines when the Japanese attacked Pearl Harbor and the Philippines. He was captured by the Japanese and was on the Bataan Death March. He spent the remainder of World War II in a Japanese prison camp trying to keep American prisoners of war alive. He was an excellent physician and a no-nonsense soldier. He was exceptionally dedicated, as evidenced by his presence at the dispensary on Sunday morning.

When Colonel Woodson saw the report on Grady and the notation that he was suffering from combat wounds, he immediately called for the duty doctor and the two of them visited Grady. Woodson introduced the duty doctor and himself. "What seems to be the trouble, Lieutenant." Grady went through the explanation of the wounds in the left arm and how the infection had been difficult to clear up. Grady continued, "Colonel, it feels now as it did several months ago when the infection was bad. I thought we had it licked, but now I don't think so."

Woodson inquired about the other wounds, and Grady told him he thought that they had healed cleanly. "Let's have a look," Woodson said. He and the duty doctor made a thorough examination.

"Who is your doctor at Valley Forge?" Woodson inquired. Grady told him, and Woodson replied, "I don't know him, but I'll be talking with him as soon as I can raise him.

"I want a complete set of X-rays on that left arm," the colonel said to the duty doctor. "While we're at it, let's have X-rays of the buttock wound and the toes on the left foot. Call me when they're ready."

"Yes sir," the duty doctor said. "The X-ray people won't be in until 0800, but this being Sunday, they might be a little late."

"If they're late, I want to know about it," Woodson replied. The doctors left the room.

Grady was dejected. "What a fine pickle this is," he lamented. "Four months of treatments on this arm and what do I have to show for it? I'm almost back to where I was when I arrived at Valley Forge. And Dr. Mott and Parker probably will be furious with me for conning them into giving me leave." He lay on his bed dozing and trying to think what was going to happen to him. He didn't know how long he had been in that half-conscious state when he sensed the presence of someone in the room. He opened his eyes.

"Rebecca, what are you doing here?"

"John, I had to see how you are. How are you?"

"What are you doing here? Did you stay at the dispensary all night?"

"No. I went home, but I didn't sleep very well. I had to find out how you are. How are you? What's happening?"

"Two doctors looked at me earlier this morning, and I'm going to be X-rayed later this morning."

"How do you feel?"

"I've felt better. Rebecca, I don't know if you should be here. Maybe you should go home. I'll call you when I know something. Thanks for coming."

"No," she said resolutely. "I'm going to church later, and I'll wait with you until it's time to go to church." They talked.

In ten minutes two orderlies came into the room pushing a gurney. One of them said, "Lieutenant, we're going to put you on this gurney and take you to the X-ray department. They're going to X-ray those wounds in your arm and they—"

Rebecca's eyes became as big as saucers. Her jaw dropped. "Wounds in your arm?" she blurted out. She thought a moment, then exclaimed, "John, you were wounded in Korea, weren't you! That's why you came home. That's why you're sick. You lied to me about your hand! You have lied to me all week! Oh John, how could you? You of all people. 'Honest John' my foot. You're no different from the rest of the men—you all lie to me!" She began to cry.

Grady flipped his hand several times at the orderlies motioning them to leave the room. They left.

"Ah, Rebecca, I did lie to you, and I apologize, but I didn't want you to know. I didn't mean to hurt you."

"John, I never expected that you would do this to me. Just when I need a friend the most, you lied to me just like all the rest. A great friend you turned out to be!" She sobbed heavily. She fumbled in her purse for a tissue.

"Rebecca, I apologize. I just didn't want you to know. I never lied to you about anything else, and I will never lie to you again. You have my word—for whatever it's worth to you. Rebecca, we can't allow it to end like this."

Grady scooted his body to the far side of the bed and smoothed the sheets on the near side of the bed. He patted the bed with his right hand. "Rebecca, come over here and sit on the bed. I want you to know why I lied to you. It was not right, and I'm sorry, but I want you to know. Please, Rebecca, before you leave, I want you to know." He patted the bed several more times. He looked at her and forced a smile.

She wiped her eyes and slowly walked over and sat on the edge of the bed with her body half turned toward him.

"Beck, I was wrong to lie to you, and I understand your anger. When we first met at the Chevrolet dealer, I assumed that you were happily married and we would never see each other after that. Getting wounded and being hospitalized has been a very personal thing for me, a private thing; it's no one else's problem and it's no one else's business. I thought that since I never would see you again it was none of your business. So I lied to you. I was wrong to do that.

"Then, after we spent some time together, I wanted to tell you … but yet … I didn't want you to know." He hesitated before continuing. "Rebecca, listen to me—listen very carefully. If anything good ever happens between us, it has to be solely because of Rebecca Hazlet and John Grady. It can't be for any other reason or it'll be no good: it won't last. I don't want you feeling sorry for me because I'm a wounded soldier. I don't want your sympathy. When I recover and the sympathy is gone, if sympathy is all there is to our relationship, it surely will die. If it lives, it'll be because of you and me and for no other reason. Do you understand what I'm saying, Rebecca? Do you understand why I didn't want you to know?

"Beck, you say that you need a friend, well … I'd like to be your friend, if you'll have me, even if nothing ever happens between us. You can be assured that I never will lie to you again. I'm flat on my back and can't help you now, but I'm going to get over this as fast as I can." They were silent. Then he said, "Don't forget this, Beck, God is here to help you. You don't have to wait until I heal or until you get over your depression. He's ready now, and He'll accept you just as you are, depression and all.

"Now, there are some tissues in the box on the stand over there. Take a couple of tissues and wipe those pretty blue eyes and give your nose a toot."

She went over to the stand and took several tissues, wiped her eyes, blew her nose, and regained her composure. Grady again patted the bed with his hand. She came back and sat on the edge of the bed.

"Rebecca, if you were to accept me as your friend right now, I would say this to you. You are a bright and intelligent woman, you have a good disposition, you get along well with people, and you are accommodating to people—probably to a fault. Rebecca, you cannot allow other people to control your life. You have to seize control of your life and live it. Don't let someone else live it for you. That may be hard to do in your situation, but you have to be tough. I didn't say unkind, I said tough.

"Beck, when I find myself in a difficult situation or in a new situation that I've never faced before, I ask myself this question: 'How do I want this to end up?' It usually is easy to answer that question. Then I work as hard as I can to bring about that end that I want, and I don't allow anyone to distract me from achieving that end. It seems to work. You know, Rebecca, many people never ask themselves that first question. They just take whatever each day hands them and they live with it. You'll be at a great advantage if you ask yourself that first question, and then work as hard as you can to see that it ends up as you wish. And, you have to be tough. You have to seize control of your life, and you have to be tough."

Both were silent. He placed his hand on hers and held it tightly. "Beck, both of us have taken our licks these past months. Your marriage ended up on the rocks, and I got my butt kicked around pretty good in North Korea. You say that you need a friend, well maybe I also could use a friend. Rebecca, I've been in hospitals for something like the last fifteen or sixteen weeks—I've lost count—in Japan, in Valley Forge Army Hospital in Pennsylvania, and now here at Monmouth." Rebecca's eyes widened again. "And, you know what, Rebecca, except for army people on business, you're the only person on the face of this earth who has visited me in the hospital. I find it's kind of nice to have someone visit. Thank you."

She had tears in her eyes again. "John, I didn't know. Oh John, sixteen weeks in the hospital, why that's—"

"There you go," he interrupted. "No sympathy! I don't want you feeling sorry for me. Now, do you understand what I'm talking about?"

Bursting into the room came army nurse First Lieutenant Emily Colbert. The orderlies followed her. "What's the holdup here; you're due in X-ray." She saw Rebecca sitting on the bed with tears in her eyes. "Oh, I'm sorry, but Lieutenant, you have to get going; Colonel Woodson is waiting for the X-rays of your arm. The colonel is very thorough and also wants X-rays of you foot and that wound in your buttock."

Rebecca stood up and backed away from the bed. "Wound in your buttock and your foot? John, you didn't tell me about them." She started to cry again.

"Rebecca, I didn't lie to you about them. They're healed; they're clean; there's no reason to talk about them." The orderlies transferred John to the gurney as he was talking. They started pushing the gurney through the door and into the hall. As John passed Rebecca he held out his right arm to her and said, "I didn't lie to you about them; there's no reason to mention them. I didn't lie to you, Rebecca."

Lieutenant Colbert saw that there was a problem, so she said to the orderlies, "You go ahead and take him. I'll catch up to you."

"Mrs. Grady," Colbert said, " your husband will be all right. Colonel Woodson is on this case, and he's a fine doctor. You have a seat here." Colbert looked at her watch. "I'll be off duty very shortly. You stay here and I'll come back and we'll have a talk."

Emily Colbert came back in ten minutes. "Let's go to the nurses' lounge and have some coffee." They went to the lounge and Colbert asked, "Do you take your coffee black or with milk."

"If you have tea, I'd prefer that."

"Yes, I can do that." She handed Rebecca the tea and fixed herself a coffee and sat down next to her. "Mrs. Grady, I take it from the conversation I heard that Lieutenant Grady didn't tell you about his wounds. Is that the problem?"

Rebecca blushed. "I'm not married to Lieutenant Grady. I'm Rebecca Hazlet. John and I are friends. But, yes, he didn't tell me about his wounds. He told me he hurt his hand in a car door. He told me nothing about being wounded in Korea, and I was absolutely shocked to learn that he was wounded."

"Rebecca, don't be too hard on him for not telling you about his wounds. Some men don't want to talk about their injuries. There probably are several reasons for that attitude, but whatever the reason, it happens. Accept it. He needs some tender loving care now, not confrontation. Lieutenant Grady didn't rest much last night, so the doctor probably will prescribe a sedative for him when he comes back from X-ray. There's nothing you can do here right now. Where are you staying? Give me your telephone number and I'll keep in touch with his situation and call you sometime this afternoon to let you know how he is."

"I live near here. Thank you very much for talking with me." Rebecca wrote her telephone number on a slip of paper and gave it to Emily Colbert.

Dr. Mott did not have the duty that weekend, and Valley Forge Army Hospital had trouble locating him Sunday morning. When they finally did locate him, he called Colonel Woodson at Fort Monmouth. They discussed the situation and decided that the best thing would be to get Grady back to Valley Forge as soon as possible.

At 1600 Lieutenant Colbert called Rebecca and told her that Valley Forge Army Hospital wanted Lieutenant Grady back there and had sent an ambulance to take him back. The ambulance departed Fort Monmouth twenty minutes ago. Lieutenant Grady was sedated and was resting comfortably.

"Thank you for calling, Lieutenant Colbert, I can't tell you how much I appreciate it."

"Call me Emily"

"All right, Emily. How can I contact Valley Forge Hospital to find out about him?"

"I'm in my room right now and don't have access to their number, but just get Valley Forge's telephone number from telephone information. When you call, ask where Lieutenant Grady is in the hospital, then ask to have your call transferred to the nurses' station there. Call during the day and talk to the nurse who's assigned to him."

"Emily, I can't thank you enough. Good bye." (Mid-afternoon on Monday, a dozen red roses were delivered to Lieutenant Emily Colbert at the Fort Monmouth Dispensary with a note of thanks from Rebecca Hazlet.)

CHAPTER 6. (15 APRIL 1951)

Grady arrived back at Valley Forge Army Hospital in early evening and immediately received antibiotics orally and intravenously.

Mary Parker came into his room early Monday morning. "What the hell happened to you? What did you do on your pass?"

"I didn't do anything that I wasn't supposed to do. I did exactly what Major Mott told me to do. I didn't drink, I rested, and I took my pills."

"How did you spend your time; you had to do something for seven days?"

"Well, I looked at cars, and I put a deposit on a new Chevrolet. I had lunch and dinner a couple of times with a girl I knew before I went overseas and just happened to meet in Red Bank. And, we went to the opera in New York Saturday afternoon. We were coming home from the opera when I began to feel bad. The rest of the time I stayed on the post."

"Ah ha. Were you fooling around with that girl?"

"Knock it off, Parker!" Grady responded sternly. "She's not that kind of girl."

"Oh, pardon me," Parker said with great flair. "She must be some kind of girl for you to get your dander up like that. I want to meet that girl."

Major Mott came in later in the morning and John went through his explanation of what he did and didn't do on his pass.

Mott said, "Colonel Woodson from Fort Monmouth sent over with you in the ambulance the X-rays of your arm that he had made there. He thinks the X-rays show infection in the bone in the arm. I looked at the pictures this morning, and I agree with him. I checked your earlier X-rays and they don't show any indication of bone infection."

"Well, how did the infection get there, Major? How can it take hold and flare up like that with so much antibiotic drug in my system?"

"I can't answer that right now, John. I'm going to take a blood specimen and a urine specimen from you and have them analyzed to see what they show. Meanwhile, I'm going to stuff you with antibiotics to try to get to the infection."

"How much of a setback does this mean for me? In time, that is."

"I can't answer that, John."

Talk about *deja vu*, Grady had it in spades. Here he was again wearing a hospital gown, flat on his back, an intravenous needle in his arm, a splitting headache, and alone.

Grady thought that maybe he now had an answer to why he had accepted the Regular Army commission rather that a Reserve commission. He thought that because he was a Regular he was not as likely to be discharged from the army before he was certain he was one hundred percent healed. He didn't want to be discharged from the army and then have complications arise from his wounds and have to go to a Veterans Administration hospital for treatment. He figured that he would get better treatment at an active army hospital such as Valley Forge that routinely treated many wounded soldiers. He didn't know if that were true, but for the first time he was able to convince himself that he had made the correct choice on his commission.

Grady did take time to drop a note to Colonel Bowen thanking him for his time and again saying that he had enjoyed seeing him. He mentioned that the infection had flared up again and that his discharge from the hospital would be delayed. He also dropped a short letter to Mac MacDowell telling him about his delay in getting out of the hospital.

***

Parker came into Grady's room at lunch time on Thursday and said, "General MacArthur is going to speak before a joint session of the Senate and House of Representatives in a few minutes. They have it on the TV in the lounge if you want to see it." Grady made his way with his rolling bottle stand to the lounge which was crowded with patients and some staff who could get off duty.

Truman's firing of General MacArthur was the biggest news story in a long time. When the general left Tokyo on 16 April, Tokyo time, a quarter million Japanese lined the streets bidding him good-bye as his motorcade traveled to the airport. Japanese dignitaries, the diplomatic corps, and General Ridgway were at the airport to see him off. One hundred thousand people were at the airport to greet him when he landed in Hawaii. When his plane landed in San Francisco, thousands overwhelmed the police and rushed his airplane. A half-million welcoming people lined his route to his hotel that night. A like number were in the downtown area the next day when MacArthur was there. Nothing like this had been seen before. When he arrived in Washington, D.C. in the first hour of Thursday morning, more than ten thousand people were at the airport to greet him.

Whether or not people agreed with MacArthur, many agreed that his address to the joint session of Congress was a stirring event. He concluded his address with this statement:

The world has turned over many time since I took the oath on the Plain at West Point, and the hopes and dreams have long since vanished. But I still remember the refrain of one of the most popular barrack ballads of that day which proclaimed most proudly that *Old soldiers never die, they just fade away.*
And like the old soldier of that ballad, I now close my military career and just fade away—an old soldier who tried to do his duty as God gave him the light to see that duty.
Good-bye.

There was not a dry eye in the lounge or among many of the millions who listened and watched throughout the country.

A half-million people crowded downtown Washington, D. C. to see and cheer him that day.

MacArthur next went to New York where he was greeted with the largest event ever seen there. New Yorkers gave him a Ticker Tape Parade that lasted over six hours. Authorities estimated that seven and one-half million people lined the parade route, and that over two thousand tons of paper showered down on the MacArthurs as they passed by. The event was even bigger than the victory parade for General Dwight Eisenhower when he returned home after the victory over Nazi Germany in World War II.

***

Except that his headache was not quite as bad, Grady didn't see much improvement in his condition after the first week back from leave. One afternoon in the middle of the second week he was sitting in his chair leaning forward with his right elbow on his right knee and his forehead resting in the palm of his hand. His eyes were closed. Parker came into the room with a box of chocolates intending to offer him some. John didn't move when she came in.

"Are you all right, Grady?"

At first, he didn't move, then he slowly straightened himself to an erect sitting position and said, "Parker, I'm damned tired of not feeling well. I think it'll never end."

"Well, here, have some chocolates. They ought to cheer you up."

"Thank you. Where did you get them?"

"Oh, I have a secret admirer. Take another one for later." They talked for a while. Parker shook her head after she left the room. She had not seen him so dispirited since he first came to the hospital.

At the end of the second week back from his leave, John noted just a slight improvement in his condition. Dr. Mott seemed concerned at the slow progress. Grady certainly was concerned.

John received a short reply note from Colonel Bowen saying that he had enjoyed seeing him again, and that he was sorry to hear about the setback in his recovery. It was the first personal letter that Grady had received since he entered active duty. It made him realize how isolated his life was.

The third week back from leave was a carbon copy of the previous week. On the morning of Saturday, 5 May 51, Parker came into Grady's room. "Parker, what are you doing here on the weekend?" he asked.

"I switched duty with someone. You're going to have a visitor. Here, put on these clean pajamas and robe."

"Who is it?"

"Just do as I say. You don't have much time."

John had learned how to deal with Parker's bossiness: ignore it. He thought maybe the lieutenant colonel from the Pentagon Awards and Decorations Board might be stopping to see him again. Grady really wasn't in a mood to talk with him, and he already had given him all the information he could. He changed pajamas and robes and waited. Nothing happened. He sat dozing in the large chair in his room when a knock on his door startled him awake. A head with a bright smile peeked around the door and said, "May I come in?"

"Holy Toledo! What in the world are you doing down here?"

"I came to visit my friend in the hospital. May I come in?"

"You had better come in here." He pushed himself to a standing position with his right arm and went over to meet her. He held out his right hand to her. She took it between her hands. "What a pleasant surprise. Rebecca, you look great. Here, let me take your coat. Or, uh, you can hang your coat in the closet there. I can't believe this. Why didn't you tell me you were coming?"

"Why didn't you contact me after you came back here?" She still had the bright smile on her face.

"I don't have any good news to report, and I've been waiting for some good news. Here, please have a seat." He offered her the seat that he had been sitting in. He sat on the edge of the bed close to her.

"You look fine, John." That was a white lie. He had lost weight and his complexion was pasty.

He was delighted. He looked at her, smiled, and said, "You've changed your hair style."

"Yes. You said that you liked it this way better." She wrinkled her nose at him and said, "I do too. Oh John, I have so much to tell you. But first, tell me about you. How are you?"

He wasn't about to lie to her; he'd had enough of that business. "The doctor says I have some infection in the bone in my arm. No one understands why, but there it is. I'm taking antibiotics and they're doing a little good, but quite slowly. The buttock and foot are healed and clean. End of report. Now, what do you have to tell me?"

"Well, do you remember the nurse Emily Colbert at Fort Monmouth? I had given her my telephone number and she called me a couple of days after you left there and said they had learned that you had been staying in the BOQ and had some clothes and things there. She wanted to know if they should send them over here, or did I want to pick them up. Well, I went over there and she took me to the BOQ office and we picked them up. I took them home, and Sally and I washed everything we could. I have everything in the car. Your shaving things are there also. And, Sally baked some cookies for you. They're in the car, too. I'll go down and get them later."

"Rebecca, you are some kind of girl, you are."

"Well, what are friends for?"

They talked for a while, then John said, "Let me show you where I do my walking in the hospital." Grady took her first to the nurses' station where Parker was busy entering data onto record cards. "Captain Parker," he called to her. She looked up, then arose and went to the counter opposite him.

"Captain Mary Parker, this is Rebecca Hazlet. Rebecca and I went to the opera together." He told Rebecca, "Captain Parker is my Florence Nightingale."

With an expressionless face, Parker said, "Miss Hazlet, it's nice to meet you."

Rebecca replied with a serious look, "It's nice to meet you, Captain Parker."

John showed her the places in the hospital where he usually walked to each day but was careful not to take her near the wards where the seriously wounded men were. They went to the lounge on his floor where visitors and patients met.

"Now, tell me what else you have to tell me," John said as they sat in adjacent chairs.

"Well, do you remember what you told me when I was sitting on your bed in the Fort Monmouth Dispensary—about taking charge of my life, about being tough, and about thinking about how I wanted a situation to turn out and then working to make it turn out that way? Well, that evening I wrote those things in a notebook and thought about them. I often look at that notebook, and I've been trying to do the things that you told me. You know what, I believe they work. I've told myself that I'm in charge of my life, and I already feel better about myself and about other people. I've asked myself how I want a couple of my situations to end up, and I know what I want to do about them. And, I've started volunteer work at Riverview Hospital again, and I'm thinking about going back to school next September. John, thank you so much for that information and insight. You're a real friend."

"That's great, Rebecca, I'm happy for you. But, have you also remembered what else I told you when you were sitting on my bed?"

"What's that?"

"I told you I don't want you feeling sorry for me and I don't want your sympathy. Have you also remembered that? I hope you didn't come down here to see me because you feel sorry for me."

She looked into his eyes and said, "Yes, I remember. I've thought about it a lot, and I have that situation under control."

They talked for a while, then John said that he should go back to his room because it was time for his pills. They were walking down a hall toward his room when Rebecca said, "John, I've been watching you walk, and I can't detect any limp at all. I thought that because of your missing toes you might have a limp, but you don't."

They took a dozen more steps, then John halted and looked at her with a suspicious look. "Hold the phone. How do you know I have a couple of toes missing? I didn't tell you that. All that was said at the Fort Monmouth Dispensary was that they were going to X-ray the foot. Whom have you been talking with?"

Rebecca bit her lips and had an expression on her face that said, "Don't make me squeal on someone."

"I smell a rat, and I think I know who she is," John said.

A short time after they arrived back in John's room, Parker came in with a small paper cup with two pills in it. "It's time for your pills, Lieutenant Grady," she said in a business-like manner.

"Parker, you have a big mouth," Grady said to her.

"Who me? Whatever are you talking about?" She turned toward Rebecca with a smile and winked at her. As she left the room she said over her shoulder, "How did you like the chocolates, Lieutenant Grady?"

John looked at Rebecca and asked, "Did you send her those chocolates?"

Reluctantly, Rebecca nodded.

"How much did you talk with her, and what all did she tell you?"

"I've talked with her several times a week since you've been back here. I wanted to talk with you, but I thought that you should call me if you wanted to talk with me. John, do you really want to know what she told me? Does it matter?"

"No. I won't insist."

They talked more. At noon, an orderly came into the room with two food trays and announced, "Captain Parker said to bring two trays today."

"Welcome to army chow" Grady said to Rebecca. "Have you ever eaten out of one of these partitioned trays?"

"No, this is exciting." She chattered while they ate. That was the Rebecca that John remembered. That was the genuine Rebecca. After lunch they again walked in the hospital. They were delighted to be with each other. They went back to the lounge on John's floor and talked more. "Rebecca, you had better be going on your way. You should get home before it gets dark."

"I'm not going home today. I'm spending the weekend with my uncle Ted. He lives outside Bucktown and it takes no time at all to get there. I don't need to leave until later this afternoon, if that's all right with you."

"Did the sun come up this morning? Of course it's all right. I didn't know that you have relatives in this area."

"Yes. Uncle Ted lives in the Gregory family home where Mother and he grew up. He's the only uncle I have, and I love him dearly.

They talked more, then Grady said, "It's pill time again. I had better get back to the room." They returned to the room and waited.

Parker came in with the pills and gave them to Grady, then she said, "Miss Hazlet, Lieutenant Grady should get a little rest now, why don't you come with me and we'll let him rest." She looked at John and said, "Get on the bed and rest for half an hour."

Rebecca said she would go out to her car and get John's clothes and shaving equipment. Parker was due for a break, so she and Rebecca first went to the cafeteria for tea and coffee. After talking with her on the telephone a half-dozen times these past weeks, and after their very brief meeting that morning before Rebecca went in to see John, Parker enjoyed getting to know Rebecca. She liked her and understood why Grady was interested in her.

Grady was on top of the covers with his eyes closed when Rebecca returned to his room. She stood at the side of the bed looking down on him. He sensed her presence and opened his eyes. She smiled at him. They didn't speak, but they were communicating. Grady swung his legs over the side of the bed and stood up. They spent the remainder of the afternoon completely unaware of the hospital and everyone else in it.

When it was time for Rebecca to leave, she said, "What are you doing tomorrow?"

"I'll be right here waiting for the meals to be served and waiting to take my pills. That's about it. Things are pretty quiet around here on Sundays."

"May I visit with you again tomorrow?

"That would make it a very special Sunday. Why don't you come at 1000. We can talk some, then go to church services in the chapel at 1100. Are you leaving for home tomorrow?"

"No, I'm staying with Uncle Ted tomorrow night. I'm driving home Monday morning."

"Wonderful, we'll have the remainder of the day together.

"By the way, Rebecca, does your mother know what you're doing down here?"

"Yes she does. I've taken charge of my life, just as you told me to do."

Sunday was a special Sunday for them, although they did nothing special. Before she left, Rebecca said that she would visit him again in two weeks.

***

Doctor Mott had attended a medical conference at Jefferson Medical College on Friday and Saturday, and at lunch there he talked with a couple of doctors about treating infections. Mott mentioned Grady's case, and one of the doctors recommended a new antibiotic drug that he had prescribed with success. Mott spoke on the telephone with a doctor on the medical staff of the drug manufacturer, and he, Mott, decided to try it on Grady. Mott expected to receive a shipment of the new drug in a couple of days. The new antibiotic arrived Wednesday afternoon, and it was given to Grady immediately. By the following Monday, Grady and Dr. Mott noted improvement in John's condition. It was the first significant improvement since Grady returned to Valley Forge from Fort Monmouth. On the following Friday, Major Mott told John that he could resume physical therapy on his arm on Monday.

***

Grady was feeling so much better that he put on a uniform Saturday morning. It was the first time that he wore a uniform since coming back to Valley Forge from his leave. He still had limited use of his left hand and had to have someone button the cuff button on his right shirt sleeve.

Rebecca arrived at midmorning on Saturday looking elegant, as usual. John met her outside his room. She was surprised and pleased to see him in his uniform instead of hospital attire. "Oh John, how wonderful, you're making progress. Soon I won't have to visit my friend in the hospital." She came into the room and placed her purse on the stand and turned to John and said," You really look good, John." They stood looking at each other for a long time.

Grady reached out and took her two hands in his. "Rebecca, I promised to be truthful with you. Now, about that 'just friends' agreement we made—"

She interrupted him. "I know what you're thinking, John; it isn't working out for either one of us the way I planned, is it."

293

"I lost that battle, for sure, during your last visit." They moved closer to each other until their foreheads touched. They didn't speak, and they didn't move for some time.

Finally, Rebecca said, "Let's sit down; I have something to tell you." She sat in the large chair and John sat in a straight chair facing her. She took a big breath and said, "John, I know that you haven't been in condition to do anything about the Chevrolet that you made the down payment on, so I took the liberty to stop in and talk with the salesman. I told him that you were in the hospital and asked him to hold the car. The car came to the dealership later than he promised, so he said that he would hold it for you. I was in there this week and told him that you wouldn't be getting out of the hospital for a while, and he said he couldn't hold it any longer. I know you wanted that car, so I bought it for you and—"

"You what!" Grady exclaimed as he popped up from his chair.

She flinched back in her chair and pleaded, "Oh John, please don't be angry. I knew you wanted it, and I didn't want you to get out of the hospital and not have it."

"Well, give me the coupon book so I can take care of the payments. Did you have to pay anything more than the fifty dollar deposit that I put down? Did you take title in your name?"

"I don't know what you mean, John; they didn't give me any coupons. Yes, I'm listed as owner, but the salesman said that it can be transferred to you any time."

"If you didn't get a coupon book for time payments, did you pay cash for the car?"

"Yes, wasn't that all right?"

"Well, it has to be O.K.—it's done. Where did you get the money to pay for the car?"

"Both my grandmothers left me legacies, so I have some money of my own. My father manages the money for me, and I told him that I needed it."

"Well, I'll pay you back, of course, but it'll have to be in installment payments because I don't have that much cash. And, I'll pay you the going rate of interest. Where's the car now?"

"It's outside. I drove it down so you would have it here."

"How are you going to get home?"

"Uncle Ted is driving me back Sunday morning. He wanted to visit with Mother anyhow."

John stared at her with a troubled look, then a smile broke out on his face. "You are some kind of girl, you are. Thanks."

"You aren't angry with me, then?"

"I was shocked and surprised at first, but no, I'm not angry. I just find it hard to believe that you would do something like that for me. That's quite a commitment on your part—in several ways. Come on, let's take a walk." He took her to the hospital library where he obtained a copy of *The Philadelphia Inquirer* and turned to the automobile section. They looked at the advertisements for new cars to determine what the going interest rates were for new-car loans. They went to the reference section of the library and selected a small book that had tables of loan payments for a range of interest rates and various principal amounts of loan. Grady asked Rebecca how much cash she paid the Chevy dealer. They looked in the tables and came up with the amount of money that Grady would pay Rebecca each month for three years.

As they sat at the library table talking, John asked her, "Rebecca, I know that we agreed not to talk about your marriage, but I'm kind of interested in what's happening in your divorce. Do you mind talking about it?"

"No, I don't mind. I believe you should know. My father took me to see a divorce lawyer in New York City, and I gave him all the information. He said he would start divorce proceedings right away."

"How long ago was that?"

"Oh, that was about two weeks before you and I met the second time.

"John, I want to tell you something about the background of why I married Dick."

"I think I've figured out why you married him."

"You don't know the whole story, and I want you to know it. I couldn't have told you this story before now, but after what you told me at the Fort Monmouth Dispensary and what has happened to us recently, I have to be honest with you and discuss it with you.

"I have to go back a number of years. My family lived in the same house with my grandparents—I told you that before. The whole family was very close. We had dinner together every night in the large dining room, and Grandfather presided at the head of the table and directed the conversation. It was wonderful. We talked about everything and everyone. My sister and I were encouraged to take part in the conversation with the adults, and I read the newspapers and magazines so I could follow the conversations and so I could join in. Both my grandparents died within a short time, and we moved into the main part of the house. Then, I went away to boarding school, and in a couple of years my sister went to college."

"What's your sister's name?" Where did she go to college?"

"Her name is Elizabeth; she's named after my mother. We call her Liz. She went to Wellesley

"Well, in Liz's third year in college she somehow started dating a fellow who waited tables in a sandwich shop in Wellesley. When Mother heard about it she hit the ceiling. She told Liz that she was not up there to date someone like that, and if she didn't stop it she would have to come home. Liz was furious with Mother. She came home one holiday and the two of them had a terrible argument. Liz left home, dropped out of school, and she and the fellow went to Maine and have been living together up there in a trailer on a plot of land in the country. They didn't get married.

"She doesn't communicate with Mother at all. I call her on the phone once in a while, but she's still quite bitter. I find it difficult to talk with her—and we used to be close, too. Daddy still manages her legacy, but I think their only contact is about Liz's money.

"Daddy was angry with Mother and said that she forced Liz to leave. He and Mother started quarreling, and Daddy didn't come home very much for almost a year. He lived most of the time in our apartment in Manhattan—the apartment has been in the family ever since I can remember. Anyhow, my close-knit family fell apart. No one was happy. Gradually, Daddy started coming home more, but our family life just wasn't the same.

"For some reason, I forget why, I started seeing more of Dick. I think that my mother and his mother thought that it would be wonderful if we got married. I told you last September that our mothers were college roommates. Truthfully, I really wasn't exactly thrilled with the idea. I'm sure you knew that—you had to know. But I was afraid that if I resisted the idea then Mother and I would get into an argument as she and Liz did and that Daddy would get involved and then the entire family would fall apart for good. My family has meant so much to me that I just couldn't face that prospect.

"You know what happened when Mother found out that I was seeing you. John, I lacked the courage to take charge of my own life. I see that clearly now, but look at what I did by not having the courage. I'm ashamed of myself for what I did and for what I didn't do.

"When I returned home after I left Dick, I felt that my life was worthless. I was so shamed and humiliated I couldn't look in a mirror. Fortunately, I met you again, and I believe the worst is behind me and that I'm going to survive this whole mess. If it weren't for you, I don't know how I would get through this."

"Beck, what's your relationship with your father?"

"We get along all right, but I don't feel close to him anymore. He doesn't talk to me much since I came back home. I think he's afraid that he'll say the wrong thing to me. He seems uncomfortable in his own home. Things are so different now. I never imagined they could be this way.

"That's a long story to tell you how I messed up. John, I believe I learned a lot from my bad experience, and I'm convinced that the future is going to be better. I'm working on it every day."

"I'm sure it will be," he said as he squeezed her hand. "Keep your vision on the future, not the past."

They spent the day in their own little world at the hospital. They went outside and looked at the maroon Chevrolet, and they took several long walks on the hospital grounds. They held hands whenever they could. John told her that officers were not supposed to hold hands in public.

Before Rebecca departed, John said, "Beck, I have to get out of this place. I feel as though I'm losing part of my life being here. I'm improving rapidly now, and I'm going to try to target a date for my discharge from here. I don't know where I'll go when I leave here, but wherever it is we're not going to lose contact with each other."

"John, we can't allow that to happen again."

CHAPTER 7. (21 MAY 1951)

When Major Mott visited him Tuesday morning, John said, "Major, I believe you've found the magic bullet with that new drug you're giving me. I'm feeling much better, my temperature is normal, and I'm back at physical therapy, so do you think I can be released from here in a couple of weeks?

"John, I'm pleased to see that you're making good progress, but I can't put a definite date on your release. Don't forget what happened when you went on leave; I'm not going to allow anything like that to happen again."

"Major, I want to get back to duty as soon as I can."

"I understand that, but I'm not going to take a chance."

That Saturday John received a letter from Colonel Bowen at Fort Monmouth saying that he had not heard from John for several weeks and was anxious to learn how his recuperation was progressing. He asked if John knew when he would be returning to duty? John smiled and shook his head and said, "That Colonel Bowen is something else." John was pleased and appreciative that Bowen had taken an interest in him. He decided to wait a couple of days before replying to Bowen because by then he might know something more definite about his release.

John's health continued to improve through the next week. He continued to work hard on strengthening his arm at therapy sessions and in his room. He could see that his biceps had grown in size and that his stomach was flat and muscular. His left arm felt the best it had since he got hit.

Major Mott said, "John, it's time for us to think about the cosmetic surgery on your arm."

"What's that, Major?"

'Your arm was badly shot up, and we operated on it several times, so we need to do some plastic surgery on it to make it look better. You don't want to go through the remainder of your life with it looking like that."

"What's involved, Major?"

"We'll do a skin graft: take skin from another part of your body and use it to cover the badly damaged areas on your arm."

"When will you do that? Will it mean that I have to stay in the hospital longer?"

"We can do it later this week or next week, depending on the schedule of the plastic surgeon. It will extend your stay here."

"Will the operation have any effect on the functioning of my arm?"

"No, John, it's strictly cosmetic."

"Do I have a say in this?"

"Yes, of course. Why?"

"Major Mott, I want to get out of this hospital and get back to duty. I don't want to extend my stay in the hospital one day longer than absolutely necessary. And to be honest about it, for the rest of my life I probably will want to wear long sleeve shirts to cover the arm even if I have the operation, don't you think so?"

Mott contemplated Grady's question. "Yes, you probably will want to."

John was quiet as he thought, then he said, "Major, I decline the cosmetic surgery."

✱✱✱

The first week of June, Grady received a long letter from Mac Mac-Dowell. It had a postmark from Great Falls, Montana, and the envelope had the name and address of a Great Falls newspaper. Mac reported that his leg had healed fairly satisfactorily but it was shorter than the other one and he had a limp that he just could not hide. It did impede his running, etc., and the medical people would not certify him for full duty. He could see that his army career was over, so he took a medical discharge with a thirty percent disability.

Mac wrote that at first he had some trouble adjusting to civilian life, but he now was doing fine. He was working at his family's newspaper and was rather enjoying it. His father had given him a long leash to cover in depth a couple of municipal construction projects, and some of the facts that he was digging up were making some prominent people in town uncomfortable.

Mac informed John that he had written to the Marine Corps about Paul Bloucher. The marines replied that Paul had died in North Korea on 8 December 1950 as the result of enemy action. The specifics were unknown. Mac also learned that Sergeant Art Smith and Private Frank Tomilson had gone back to the 31st Infantry Regiment, and so far as he knew, they still were in Korea. Mac knew nothing about the Signal Corps men who were with them in North Korea.

Learning that Paul Bloucher hadn't made it back to the line alive hit Grady hard. He sat down and wrote an account of all he could remember about Paul's activities with his crew. He particularly detailed Paul's actions that last night when the rest of the group made it back to U.S. lines, how Paul had gone out of the creek bed and dispersed the Chinese patrol from the creek, and how he had volunteered to assault the machine gun emplacements so the others could make the last dash to safety. Grady mailed it to MacDowell and asked him to send it to the Marine Corps with a recommendation that Paul be awarded a medal for heroism. His parents should know that Paul was a hero, so Grady asked Mac to make a nice printed copy of his account and send it to Paul's parents who lived somewhere outside Appleton, Wisconsin. Grady told him that a good newspaper man ought to be able to find the address. John wrote a cover letter addressed to Paul's parents and asked Mac to include it.

***

Monday morning, Dr. Mott told John that he might think about 23 June as a possible release date from the hospital. John was overjoyed. That night he called Rebecca and told her the news. She was so delighted that she choked up. Grady worked hard at his therapy all week, and on Friday Major Mott said that he had made the 23 June release date official. He said that the hospital administrative personnel already had forwarded the information to the Department of the Army, and Grady could expect orders for his next duty assignment any day now.

John again found that waiting for orders was a tension-filled experience. He had no idea where his next assignment would be. He had been in the army a year now, but he had been in the hospital half of that time, so he knew that the army might send him anywhere in the world—even back to Korea. Because of that, John was intensely interested in what was going on in Korea.

Some of the bitterest fighting of the war now was taking place. Over a quarter of a million Chinese and North Korean troops launched a major Spring Offensive on 22 April and forced back U.S. and South Korean forces anywhere from twenty to thirty-five miles. The main thrust of the drive was in the western sector with Seoul as the initial objective, and the ultimate goal was to drive UN forces into the sea. UN forces stopped the drive on the outskirts of Seoul, and by the end of the month the Communist forces withdrew to just about where they had started.

The Communists refurbished and strengthened their armies and began a second phase of the Spring Offensive on 16 May. In that earlier phase of that offensive the Chinese had had a great advantage in manpower, but the U. S advantage in fire power from artillery and aircraft had overcome the Chinese manpower advantage. Consequently, the Chinese and North Koreans decided to launch the second phase of their Spring Offensive in the Taebaek Mountains in the central and eastern part of the country where conditions were less favorable to the UN forces. Again the Chinese and North Koreans made initial advances, but because of heavy losses the offensive ran out of steam. U. S. and South Korean forces counterattacked and the Communist armies withdrew north of the Thirty-eighth Parallel, leaving the opposing armies pretty much in the positions they held prior to the Spring offensive. UN casualties were high. Chinese casualties were horrendous.

***

Grady received his orders on Thursday. He was ordered to The Signal School, Fort Monmouth, New Jersey, to attend The Company Grade Officers Course. He couldn't believe it! He had wished for it but never really expected it. John smiled. He suspected that Colonel Bowen might have had a hand in this. He sat down and wrote a short letter to Bowen giving him the facts, as if he didn't already know.

That night John called Rebecca and told her the good news. After she heard it she was silent. Then, in hardly more than a whisper she said, "Thank the Good Lord. My prayers have been answered. When will you be here?"

"I'm leaving here after breakfast on Saturday, 23 June. I report in at the post on Monday, 25 June. Can you meet me at the Molly Pitcher for lunch on Saturday?"

"Of course."

John saw Major Mott for the last time on Friday, thanked him profusely, and told him that he always would remember what he had done for him.

John obtained a pass to go out that night and took Parker to dinner at a nice restaurant. He thanked her for all the nursing that she had done for him. He told her, "Probably more important than the nursing was the fact that you were a friend. I think I would have gone nuts if you hadn't been there to talk with and share some time with. Thanks."

"You're welcome, Grady. I have mixed emotions about you leaving. I'm happy that you're leaving healthy, but I'll miss you. I don't know why it is, but I feel almost as though we've been family."

John was awake and packed before breakfast on Saturday morning. He said a prayer thanking God for seeing him through that ordeal. He ate, signed out on the hospital register book, and put his bags into the trunk of the car. He turned and looked at the hospital and thought about the condition he was in when he arrived there. He said "Thanks" to everyone involved, slid into his maroon Chevy and drove off.

BOOK FOUR

CHAPTER I. (23 JUNE 1951)

John arrived at the Molly Pitcher Inn before Rebecca did and took a seat in the lobby. When she arrived and saw John, she broke into a bright smile and almost ran to him. "John, I can't believe I have you home at last. I'm sorry I'm late, but it took me longer to get ready than I expected. I wanted to look nice for your homecoming."

"You succeeded," John said. They held hands and walked to the dinning room. They sat down and John said, "It's great to be with you, Rebecca. I can't think of a better way to spend my first hours out of the hospital." They talked while they waited for their meals and could not take their eyes off each other.

As they ate, Grady said, "What do you want to do the remainder of the day?"

"I want to be someplace where I can be alone with you; somewhere where we can feel free."

"Would a walk on the beach fit that description?"

"If it's a lonely beach."

"How about going out to Sandy Hook and walking south from Fort Hancock? When we walked there last September we didn't meet anyone on the beach. We both will have to change clothes, and I'll have to get a room at the BOQ. If I get to your house by three o'clock, will that be too late to start?" She said that it was not.

"Grab your coat. Let's get out of here," he said, grinning at her. They stood up and walked toward the cashier.

She was waiting for him on the front steps of her home when he drove up. "Come in, John, I want you to meet my parents." That surprised him. He turned off the ignition and followed her into the house. Mr. and Mrs. Hazlet were sitting on a screened porch reading when Rebecca and John entered. The Hazlets stood to meet them. Mrs. Hazlet was not as tall as Rebecca. She had blond, neatly-fashioned hair that probably was colored. She had clear skin and blue eyes and was an attractive woman. John could see that Rebecca resembled her. She was a little overweight, but her dress was tailored to hide it fairly well. Mr. Hazlet was as tall as Grady and had black hair that was lightly flecked with gray at the sideburns and temples. He was not fat, but he didn't look trim or in shape—the look of the typical busy businessman who was getting older. He wore horn-rimmed eyeglasses. He was a nice-looking man.

The introduction and responses were proper, brief, and reserved, especially from Mrs. Hazlet. Rebecca immediately said that they had to be on their way. Grady said that he had enjoyed meeting them. Rebecca and John returned to his car, and as they drove off John said, "It was nice of you to introduce me to your parents, but I was a little surprised that you would do it considering the history of our relationship."

"I've taken charge of my life now. I want them to know you, and I want you to know them. Thank you for being gracious."

They arrived at Fort Hancock and walked to the beach. It was a perfect day with clear blue sky, a nice breeze on the beach, and temperature in the mid 80s. They walked slowly, each with an arm around the other's waist.

"John, did you think that we ever would see this day?"

"There were times when I wouldn't have bet money on it. There have been so many obstacles—yet, so many coincidences, and so much good luck that I have to believe that there must be something special intended for us."

"You said that in that first letter you wrote to me. Do you remember?"

"I don't remember saying it in the letter, but I know that I felt it because it caused me to do some strange and bold things."

✳✳✳

Monday morning Grady officially logged in on the register at Russell Hall and reported in at The Signal School, Officers Branch. He was assigned to a class that would begin its studies on Monday, 9 July. Until then, he was required to report in each morning to the office, but otherwise he would be free. That almost amounted to two weeks leave. Not bad duty!

John walked to Lieutenant Colonel Bowen's office and asked his secretary if he might see the colonel for a very brief visit. The secretary remembered John and said that she was sure the colonel would want to see him. She ushered him into the inner office.

"John, how nice to see you," Bowen said as he rose from his chair and extended his hand.

Grady shook his hand and said, "It's good to see you , Colonel. I apologize for dropping in without an appointment, but I was in the area and decided to come in."

"Good, I'm glad that you did. Please have a seat. How are you feeling? Are you fully recovered?"

"Yes, sir, I'm fully recovered, and I'm feeling fine."

"I'm happy to see you back at Monmouth," Bowen said.

"I'm happy also, and very fortunate to be here. I'm deeply indebted to those who had anything to do with getting me here." John looked at Bowen and gave him a knowing smile. Bowen didn't reply to that statement. They talked for a short time, then John excused himself and went back to his BOQ.

In his free time, John shopped the local banks for the best loan rate. He borrowed the amount that he owed Rebecca on the Chevrolet and paid her the remainder of the debt he owed her.

***

The big news at the beginning of July was that on 30 June 1951 General Ridgway, UN forces commander, had broadcast a message to the Commander in Chief of Communist forces in Korea inviting him to meet to discuss a cease-fire in the fighting. The Communists had suffered appalling losses of men and materiel in their Spring Offensive, and the UN civilian and military authorities hoped that the Communists would be in a mood to stop the fighting. The Chinese and North Koreans promptly agreed to meet to talk about cessation of military action and proposed that the two sides meet between July 10 and 15 at the town of Kaesong, near the Thirty-eighth Parallel. Kaesong was in South Korea, but currently was in an unoccupied zone between the opposing armies. General Ridgway didn't trust the Communists and feared that if a cease-fire were immediately implemented they would build up their forces for another offensive. He believed that UN forces held the upper hand on the battlefield and recommended to authorities in Washington that fighting continue while cease-fire talks were conducted. The Truman administration accepted this condition, as did the Communists. Lower-ranking officers of the opposing forces held a first meeting at Kaesong on 8 July 1951 to make arrangements for a meeting of senior officers two days later.

Grady had mixed emotions about a cease-fire at that time. He wanted the killing to stop, but we had not defeated the enemy army as we did in World War II.

***

Rebecca had decided to go back to college—to Rutgers, in New Brunswick, N.J.

"What about your major," John asked her ?

"Daddy's business interests me, and I've talked to him about it. I'm going to major in economics and finance, and I'm going to try to schedule all my classes on just a couple of days in the week so I can live at home and commute to New Brunswick on those days. I don't want to be too far from you. If I need to stay overnight in New Brunswick for any reason, I can get a hotel room."

Grady was in Class C 109 in the Signal Corps Company Grade Officers Course. Some subjects in this course were repetitious of the matters covered in the Basic course, but there was considerable new material. He resolved to study hard because he knew that the men in this class most likely were making the army their careers and every one of them would be trying to make the best record he could.

His billeting was in the same BOQ area that he had been in last summer, but in a different building. He had requested, and had received, a room on the first floor rather than the second floor of the building. His roommate was a young second lieutenant just out of college who was taking the Basic Officers Course. They didn't have much in common, and John didn't see much of him.

John saw Rebecca on Friday nights. They often went to the movies, either on post or in Asbury Park. They were together all day on Saturdays and frequently went dancing on Saturday nights at Gibbs Hall or at the Convention Center in Asbury Park when a big-name band was performing there. They attended bible study class on Wednesday nights at the Methodist Church. They went to church services together on Sunday mornings and had Sunday lunch together.

Their respect and affection for each other deepened the more they were together. Grady never had experienced anything like this. For years now he had been independent and in control of his emotions, and in a way, it scared him that someone could have such command of his emotions as Rebecca did. He could not help himself; she had become an important part of his life. But, a lingering question festered deep in his subconscious mind as to whether he was in over his head in dating a girl from a wealthy family. Perhaps *thinking poor* was ingrained in him.

On Tuesday, 14 August 51, grades and class standings were posted for the first four weeks of school for Class C 109. John Grady stood first in his class. He now was more competitive and combative about his class position than he had been in the Basic Course last summer. That number one position was his and no one was going to take from him!

***

On his way back to his BOQ after classes that day, he saw that a large billboard-type sign had been erected in a corner of Greely Field, the parade grounds, so that it was quite conspicuous from the main road that ran through the post. It had to do with General Lawrence's safe driving campaign. The sign was in the form of a chart showing the monthly tally of traffic accidents involving Fort Monmouth personnel. The month was divided into three ten-day periods which formed the first column on the chart. In the next column adjacent each ten-day period was the number of accidents that Lawrence considered acceptable. In the third column was the number of actual accidents. The acceptable and the actual accidents were totaled at the bottom. The post newspaper had previously carried an article about Lawrence setting a limit on the number of accidents that he would accept, and he warned that sterner measures would follow if that limit were exceeded.

***

The cease-fire negotiations in Korea were getting nowhere. The sole issue discussed thus far was where the cease-fire line would be drawn. The Communists insisted that it be the Thirty-eighth Parallel. The U.S. position was that it should be at the present battle line, which was almost entirely in North Korean territory. Late in August the Communists walked out of the negotiations. The war continued unabated.

The Communist forces had substantially fortified their positions. In prior fighting they had taken heavy casualties from UN artillery. They learned a lesson, so they significantly increased their own artillery and mortar units. UN forces suffered as a result of it. General Van Fleet conducted limited-objective attacks against the dug-in Communist forces. The fighting was difficult and costly, with limited success.

The U.S. Army instituted a rotation system whereby a soldier who had spent approximately twelve months in Korea was "rotated" back to the United States. In Grady's opinion, this depleted from the combat units the seasoned campaigners who had learned the lessons of war, thereby diminishing the effectiveness of U.S. forces.

***

In the second week of September, General Lawrence announced to all commands at Fort Monmouth that the number of August traffic accidents had exceeded the number that he would accept. Most of the accidents had occurred in the enlisted ranks and in the officer ranks below the rank of captain. Accordingly, a post order was issued that on 20-23 September, except in cases of extreme emergency, all military personnel below the rank of captain were prohibited from driving a private vehicle. The only exception was that on Sunday, 23 September, those restricted personnel were permitted to drive to and from church.

***

On a Saturday evening in mid-September, Rebecca and John studied their respective courses in the Hazlet library. Around 2200 they concluded their studies and discussed many things. Rebecca said that she was impatient and discouraged at the slow pace of her divorce proceeding. John asked her where it stood at present.

"I really don't understand what's going on. Daddy said that he would work with the attorney as much as possible to relieve me of the burden and unpleasantness, but I don't see anything happening. Daddy says that I have to be patient. Shouldn't something be happening? You've been to law school; you should know something about it."

"I have no way of knowing. If you think it would help, I'll speak with your father."

"Would you, please."

"I don't want to do it tonight, but give me his business address and telephone number and I'll contact him when I have in mind what I want to say to him. I've been wanting to get to know your father."

"Please do it soon."

When he returned to his BOQ that night, John composed a letter to Mr. Hazlet saying that because Rebecca and he had been seeing each other quite regularly, he would like to get to know Hazlet. He also said that Rebecca didn't understand what was going on in the divorce case and had asked him to see if he could find out for her the status of the situation. John recommended that he meet Hazlet at the Red Bank train station Friday night and they could talk during dinner at the Molly Pitcher Inn. John offered to drive him home after dinner. He posted the letter at the Red Bank post office on his way to pick up Rebecca for church Sunday morning.

After bible study class Wednesday evening, Rebecca told John that her father was a little miffed at John's letter, but he would meet John on Friday evening. She said that her father said that he felt guilty about Rebecca's marriage to Dick and her ensuing agony. He said that he never really cared much for Dick and regretted that he had not talked to her about him before the wedding. Since she was seeing that soldier regularly, he felt that he should get to know him and his background before she again did anything drastic. He said that he no longer was going to be passive about his daughters' male companions. He had remained silent while both daughters had disastrous experiences with men. He wasn't going to allow it to happen again.

After classes on the Friday of his pending meeting with Mr. Hazlet, John polished his cordovan wing-tip shoes, showered, shaved, put on a white button-down collar shirt, tied a blue regimental-stripe tie into a full Windsor knot, and put on his dark gray flannel suit. He waited on the Red Bank station platform as the 6:32 train pulled in. He spotted Mr. Hazlet getting off the club car and went to him. "Mr. Hazlet, I'm John Grady. It's nice to see you again." Mr. Hazlet looked at him as if he had never seen him before. John said, "I'm parked out in the parking lot; we can go this way." They walked to the car in silence. As they drove the short distance to the Molly Pitcher Inn, Mr. Hazlet gave a long look at John and said, "I was expecting to meet someone in an army uniform; you look like a Wall Street banker. You kind of surprised me."

They arrived at the Molly Pitcher and were promptly seated. The waitress brought menus. Mr. Hazlet ordered a Johnny Walker Black Label and water, and John ordered a bourbon and soda.

John began the conversation. "Mr. Hazlet, I thank you for meeting with me, and I hope you don't feel that I'm butting into your affairs. Rebecca has had a lot of hard knocks this past year and—"

"Rebecca? Are you talking about my daughter June? Who are we talking about here?"

"Yes, June, excuse me." John smiled. "I call her Rebecca because to me that name seems to fit her personality better than June. It might sound kind of crazy, but it seems more natural to me. As I was saying, Rebecca had a tough time with her marriage and suffered quite a shock to her confidence and self-esteem when it broke up. But she's doing a wonderful job getting over it. Now she wants to get the divorce proceeding moving and over with. She said that you were handling the matters with the attorney, but she doesn't understand what's going on. She asked me if there were anything I could do, and I said that I would talk with you."

"What's in this for you?" Hazlet asked. He looked and sounded suspicious of John.

John thought before he answered that question. "I have respect and affection for Rebecca, and I'd like to see her free of an unpleasant situation that has given her a lot of misery. And, she's been very kind to me and I'd like to reciprocate her kindness."

"How has she been kind to you?" Hazlet asked.

John didn't know what to make of that question. Didn't he know that Rebecca spent weekends visiting him in the hospital? Didn't he know that Rebecca bought his car for him when he was in the hospital? "Why is he playing games?" John wondered.

"Sir, I was in a hospital for a number of months and Rebecca visited me several weekends and talked on the phone with me a number of times. She went considerably out of her way to visit me, and I greatly appreciate it. It made a big difference to me. She paid for my car when I was in the hospital, and she took care of it until I could take over." John looked at him. "Don't you know those things, Mr. Hazlet?"

The waitress brought their drinks. They both took sips.

"Yes, I remember June mentioned that she visited a friend at the Valley Forge Hospital. You were in Korea?

"Yes sir."

"What do you want from me?"

John smiled at him and tried to answer in a friendly manner. "Only information. Where does the divorce proceeding stand? What has your attorney done so far? What is he asking for in the divorce? What position is Dick taking? What is the anticipated timetable for the proceeding?"

The waitress came to take their orders. John ordered a steak, well done, and mashed potatoes. Hazlet ordered a sea bass and a baked potato and told the waitress to bring him another scotch and water.

"I found June a good divorce lawyer. He's filed the papers in court, and he tells me that things are going on schedule."

"Specifically, what does he tell you that he's been doing after he filed the initial pleadings?"

Mr. Hazlet thought for a minute, then replied, "Well, he hasn't said anything specific, just that things are on schedule."

"Has he told you what the schedule is?"

"No, he hasn't." Hazlet finished his first drink.

"Do you know what Dick's position is?" John asked.

"We haven't heard from Dick, as far as I know."

"He had to answer the pleadings. What did he say in his answer?"

Hazlet was getting the impression that he was not talking with an empty-headed kid. This Grady fellow looks and acts as if he knows what's going on and what he's doing. Hazlet's attitude toward Grady began to change. "Well, I guess I don't know. It's beginning to look as if I haven't kept up with this as I should have. The lawyer sends his statements every month and I pay them. I have to assume that he's doing his job."

Grady took a sip of his drink and hesitated before he spoke again. "Does the lawyer know your financial situation?"

Mr. Hazlet narrowed his eyes and looked at John as he contemplated that question. The waitress brought his second drink. Hazlet immediately took a sip. He pursed his lips and said, "Yeah, he probably does. Why do you ask? What are you thinking?"

John again tried to be friendly and helpful. "Mr. Hazlet, I respectfully suggest that maybe it's time that you and Rebecca scheduled a status meeting with the attorney to have a thorough review of the case. Get answers to the questions that I asked you. Satisfy yourselves that you know everything that's going on and what will happen in the future, and when. Get copies of the papers filed in the case. He's working for you; make him show you what he's doing for you. You should do it soon."

Both were quiet. Hazlet realized that John's comments made sense. "We've never had a divorce in the family before; this is not my specialty. I've been unusually busy lately with a couple of closings and haven't had a lot of free time. I guess I shouldn't have assumed that the lawyer would automatically handle things without me checking. I think your suggestion is good. We'll do that."

Their meals were served and they talked as they ate. Hazlet wanted to know more about Grady, so he asked John about his family. After John told him about his family and spoke with admiration of his father, Hazlet asked him, "How are you and June getting along?"

"All right, I think. I enjoy her company; she's an intelligent and interesting person."

"What does she think of you?"

John thought before he answered. He smiled at Hazlet and said, "With due respect, sir, you should ask her that question."

Hazlet smiled and said, "Fair enough."

John wanted to say something about Rebecca's relationship with her family, but he didn't want to offend Hazlet. But, if he didn't say it, who would? He tried his best to be low key and friendly. "Mr. Hazlet, Rebecca has had a tough time about her marriage break up. She's felt rather lonely and could have used a lot of support from friends and family. She's told me that she doesn't have any really close friends, and she hasn't told me this herself, but reading between the lines I get the impression that she hasn't received all the family emotional and spiritual support that she might have received. Like I said, Rebecca is an intelligent and interesting person. I believe that if you spend time with her and showed interest in her life you would enjoy her company and she would enjoy yours. She has a lot of respect for you." John was afraid that he might have gone too far. That was pretty strong stuff for a stranger to tell a father about his relationship with his daughter. John took a sip of his drink.

Hazlet didn't say anything in response, and John didn't say anything further. They had just about finished their dinners when the waitress walked past their table. Mr. Hazlet asked her to bring the check. He looked at John, pointed to John's drink, and said, "Aren't you going to finish your drink?"

"No sir, I've had enough. I'm driving, and my commanding general doesn't like for his people to get mixed up in car accidents."

Hazlet decided that he liked John Grady. He seemed to be more sensible than any of the men either daughter had brought around the house. He wished that he had not drunk all those highballs here and on the club car. He was afraid that he might have made an ass of himself earlier in the conversation.

They drove back to the Hazlet estate. "Come in," Hazlet said. "June will want to know what happened." They entered the door and she appeared almost immediately. She had a concerned look on her face. "Everything is all right—relax," her father said with a grin. "He can tell you about our evening. I'm going up to take a shower. John, I'll see you before you leave tonight."

John gave Rebecca an account of everything that had occurred during the evening, except for his last comment to Mr. Hazlet about taking more interest in his daughter and spending more time with her.

"Thank you, John, I knew I could count on you. How did you get along with Daddy?

"Fine. He was suspicious at first, but I guess that was to be expected. After all, he didn't know me from Adam. After we talked a while, he was open-minded and friendly. I enjoyed having dinner with him."

Rebecca and John went to the library and talked more. Later, Mr. Hazlet knocked on the half-open door and said, "Anyone for ice cream?" He came into the room carrying a tray with three dishes of ice cream and said, "John and I didn't have dessert with our dinners, so I thought you might want some."

"You've discovered my main weakness," John said to him. The three of them sat and talked as they enjoyed their ice cream. Mr. Hazlet said that he and Rebecca would talk with the divorce lawyer next week. They finished the ice cream, and Hazlet collected the bowls and started for the door.

"Thank you, Daddy, that was lovely."

As Grady drove back to his BOQ that night he thought about the fact that Mrs. Hazlet had not made an appearance, not even when Mr. Hazlet brought the ice cream.

Rebecca went with her father on Tuesday to the lawyer's office in midtown Manhattan, and Mr. Hazlet asked the lawyer the type of questions that Grady had asked of him. The lawyer was indirect in answering most of the Hazlets' questions, but he did reveal that Dick was opposing the divorce. It soon was obvious to them that the lawyer had done practically nothing since he filed the initial paper. He could not satisfactorily justify his billings to Mr. Hazlet.

Rebecca and Mr. Hazlet both were dissatisfied with the lawyer's performance and left his office with the desire to have nothing more to do with him. "What are we going to do now?" Rebecca asked.

"I'm going to call Charlie Jardine. He does a lot of legal work for me.

He's not a divorce lawyer, but he might be able to recommend one. I should have talked with him before."

Jardine highly recommended divorce attorney Dave Able and put Hazlet in contact with him. Able said that he wanted to talk with Rebecca before he made a decision to take her case. He made an appointment for her to see him Thursday of that week. Rebecca went to New York City and met with Dave Able. He agreed to take her case and said that he immediately would contact the present attorney and would file a motion in court for the change of attorneys. He said that he would start interviewing the prospective witnesses whose names Rebecca had given him.

***

On Friday afternoon, 5 October 51, the members of Class C 109 received their orders. Grady was ordered to Headquarters, Signal Corps Center and Fort Monmouth, New Jersey. He couldn't believe it—he was staying at Fort Monmouth!

John called on Rebecca at her home Friday night. She met him at the door and said, "John, come in, I want to tell you about my meeting with the lawyer yesterday. She was happy and in a good mood. They went to the library and she said, "Come over to the couch, I want to tell you about it." She gave him a detailed account of her meeting. She was optimistic that things would start happening now.

With a straight face, Grady said, "I have some news too. We received our orders today." Rebecca's eyes opened wide and her body went stiff. He broke into a smile and said, "I'm staying at Fort Monmouth." Rebecca's body went limp and she collapsed against him. He put his arm around her.

"Oh John, The Lord is good to us. Good things happen to me when I'm with you." They decided that they didn't want to go out that night, so they stayed in the library and talked about what they would do in the coming months. Later in the evening, Rebecca wanted a fire in the fireplace, so John built a fire with the kindling and split logs that were in a box beside the fireplace. They sat on the couch, held hands, and watched the flaming logs. After a while, John stood up to stretch his legs and went over to the fireplace and stood with one foot on the raised hearth and a hand on the mantle as he looked into the flames. Rebecca remained on the couch with her legs drawn up under her.

A knock came on the partially-open door and Mr. Hazlet said "May I come in?"

"Sure, Daddy, come in" Rebecca called.

Hazlet entered carrying a tray with three glasses and a bowl of popcorn. "Can I interest you in some of this?" he said.

"Why Daddy, how thoughtful of you."

"I'll put it on the table over here. June, get the coasters and pull up the chairs." Hazlet sat at the end of the table and Rebecca and John sat on opposite sides of him. Hazlet put the bowl in the middle of the table between them, handed Rebecca a glass of Coke, and handed John a tall glass with ice cubes and a dark-colored drink in it. "Here, try this" he said to John.

John took a sip of the drink. It was bourbon and soda—good bourbon. "This is smooth; it must be from your private stock," he said. Mr. Hazlet smiled. They talked and munched popcorn. When they had finished, Mr. Hazlet put the empty glasses and bowl on the tray, arose from the table, and left the room. Rebecca and John returned to the couch.

The first two days of school the next week were devoted to taking care of personal matters and winding up academic affairs in The Signal School. Graduation would be on Wednesday. Final grades were posted on Tuesday and Grady finished number one. Graduation on Wednesday was much like the graduation from the Basic course. Colonel Bowen attended as a spectator and warmly congratulated Grady after the ceremony was over. Without Grady telling him, Bowen knew that John had orders for Fort Monmouth.

Immediately after graduation, Grady made application for billeting in Craig Hall, the new red brick BOQ. The facilities and furniture there were vast improvements over those in the BOQs that John had lived in thus far. Only officers permanently assigned to Fort Monmouth were eligible to live in Craig Hall and there was a waiting list to get in.

CHAPTER 2. (15 OCTOBER 1951)

Monday morning at 0800, John reported in at Headquarters, Signal Corps Center and Fort Monmouth. The captain who processed him assigned him to 9404 TSU, Signal Corps Center Troop Command. Troop Command housed, fed, and trained the enlisted men who were students in The Signal School. It took care of everything except the technical schooling of the men. Troop Command sometimes was referred to as The Student Regiment, or just The Regiment.

Troop Command regimental headquarters was several streets over from John's BOQ and was a one-story rectangular building of the World War I "temporary" vintage. Grady reported in to the regimental commander's adjutant Captain Francis Cole, a tall, freckle-faced redhead. He welcomed Grady in a friendly, easy-going manner, and the two of them entered the regimental commander's office. John stood before the colonel, saluted smartly, and said, "Lieutenant Grady reporting for duty, sir."

The colonel returned the salute and reached for a chart and some papers on the side of his desk. He studied the chart and papers, then looked up to John and said, "Lieutenant, I'm assigning you to be company commander of Company K, 3rd Battalion. I'm short of company-grade officers, so I can't give you an executive officer. You're replacing Captain Brobach who has orders for FECOM. Major Stemple is your battalion commander. Good luck."

Grady saluted and left the room with Captain Cole. When they were outside the office, Cole motioned for Grady to have a seat at his desk and asked him, "Have you commanded a company before?" John replied "No." Cole talked him through the procedure that John should follow in taking over command of Company K, told him what reports he needed to file with regimental headquarters, and told him where K Company was located. John thanked Cole for his help.

Company K was located in an older part of the post where the buildings were the "temporaries" built in the First World War. In that section of Fort Monmouth, there were eighteen of the older buildings arranged in two rows, with several drill fields spaced throughout the area. The area was even less attractive than the BOQ area where John lived.

Grady located Company K, parked his car, and entered the building. He went into the first sergeant's office and introduced himself and said, "I would like to see Captain Brobach." The sergeant knocked on the captain's door and told him that Lieutenant Grady wanted to see him. "Show him in," Brobach said.

Grady saluted, introduced himself and said that he had orders to take over Company K.

"I know, Captain Cole just called and said that you were on your way over here. Welcome, and have a seat." They talked briefly about what they had to do to change command.

John said, "Captain, before we get started, I think that I ought to pay my respects to the battalion commander.

"Yes, that's a good idea. I'll have the company clerk call over to see if he's in his office." The call was made and the major said for Grady to come over immediately.

Major Stemple cordially greeted Grady and invited him to sit down. The major looked to be in his late thirties, was thin, had a thick head of shiny black hair, and a pleasant-looking face. He called to his clerk to bring two coffees. He asked Grady about his previous assignments in the army. Grady told him that he had been to Korea, but didn't tell him that he had been wounded and hospitalized. Stemple talked about many things as they drank their coffee. He didn't seem concerned about the conversation going on for an extended time, or about Grady taking over Company K. He seemed to be happy to have someone to talk with.

John went back to Company K after lunch and talked with Captain Brobach who said that he needed to get everything transferred by the end of the day tomorrow because he was leaving the day after that. John said that if it was O.K. with Brobach, he, John, would take charge of things to the extent necessary to get the transfer completed. Brobach agreed and John called the first sergeant, the duty sergeant, and the company clerk into the office and told them, "I regard my job and all of your jobs to be extremely important. The men in this company soon might be in a combat zone and it's our duty to make them as ready as possible to meet that situation. I look forward to working with you. Where's the supply sergeant?"

First Sergeant Perry said that the supply sergeant was in the low building across the street. Grady dismissed them and walked across the street with the folder under his arm that contained an inventory of all the government property issued to the company, and the company property that belonged to Company K itself and not to the government, if that distinction could be made. Grady walked into the supply room and introduced himself to Technical Sergeant William Lipscomb and explained what he was doing. Lipscomb was an old-timer and understood the drill. Grady pulled out inventory sheets that had such things as rifles, blankets, sheets, pillows, etc.

"Sergeant, how do you stand with your issued supplies?"

"Sir, we can account for everything we're charged for."

"That's good. I'll spot check a couple of items." Grady would personally assume accountability for, and financial responsibility for, all the equipment and supplies that the company possessed. More than one army officer had been driven to financial ruin because of his failure to exercise control and accountability for supplies and equipment that he was charged with. (Of course, losses and damage occurring in combat were different.)

Grady counted the rifles in the armory room, and counted several other items in the supply room—they all tallied with the inventory sheet. He just did not have time to check everything that he really should have. In a large measure he was forced to rely on the integrity of the supply sergeant and that of the officer he was replacing. John signed for Company K on Tuesday evening and gave Captain Brobach a "clean bill of health" on the transfer.

Grady was busy the first couple of days just getting familiar with the situation and the personnel. He tried to get to know First Sergeant Charles Perry. A good first sergeant can make life much easier for a company commander, and he found that Perry was good.

John's days were long and busy. The work was challenging, but after the first month he felt that he was getting the feel of it. His good news was that his name came up on the waiting list to move into Craig Hall BOQ. He loaded all his gear into his car and moved in one evening. The new facilities were a real improvement, and his bed was larger and more comfortable than the old metal army cot he had been sleeping on. He went to the PX and bought an eight-tube Emerson radio to listen to news and music. He felt that he was living in the lap of luxury.

***

John's return to a duty assignment with troops made him feel that he was back in the army, and it peaked his concern about what was going on in Korea. On 25 October 1951, the Communists returned to the peace talks. At General Ridgway's insistence, the talks now were held at Panmunjom instead of at Kaesong. The two sides still argued the location of the cease-fire line. General Ridgway wanted the Communists to give up Kaesong in exchange for some territory along the present battle line, but only on the condition that all other issues be settled in one month. The communists refused. After acrimonious negotiating sessions, the U.S. relented and agreed to a cease-fire line. All other issues were to be settled by 27 December. Negotiations began on the means for enforcing the cease-fire and on the exchange of POWs.

The American public was weary of the war and wanted it to end. Our battlefield casualties continued. U.S. forces suffered twenty thousand casualties just during the time the two sides negotiated the location of the cease-fire line.

CHAPTER 3. (8 NOVEMBER 1951)

Three weeks before Thanksgiving Day, an order came down from General Lawrence that a special safe-driving class should be held in each company the next week to sharpen the troops' driving skills in anticipation of the coming holiday season when many of the men would be driving home on holiday leave. A packet of educational material accompanied the order. John studied the material and held the class for Company K on Wednesday afternoon, 14 November 1951.

Grady was in his office after inspection on Saturday clearing off his desk in preparation for leaving for the weekend. The telephone rang and the company clerk came to John's door and said, "Sir, it's the provost marshal's office." John spoke into the phone on his desk, "Lieutenant Grady speaking."

" Sir, this is Sergeant Lapman of the MP Detachment. Private First Class Wayne Griffith of K Company was involved in an automobile accident off Highway 1 near New Brunswick. Sergeant Miller and I are going over to investigate it. We'll pick you up in 10 minutes. Good- bye, sir." The MP didn't ask John if he wanted to go; the MP told him that he would be picked up.

John didn't know Private First Class Wayne Griffith. In the short time that Grady had been there, he had learned the names only of the very good ones and the very bad ones. Griffith was neither. Grady asked the first sergeant about Griffith and learned that he had a weekend pass that weekend.

John called Rebecca and said that something had come up and he would not be able to see her until much later in the day. He would call her as soon as he was free, which might be in three or four hours. They were planning to go to Gibbs Hall to a dance that night, and John said that he would be free by then.

Grady was waiting outside the barracks when the olive-drab Plymouth sedan pulled up. Technical Sergeant Miller introduced himself and invited Grady to sit in the back seat. Buck Sergeant Lapman was driving. Grady asked them what had happened and if anyone had been injured in the accident.

Sergeant Miller answered, "We don't know very much about it yet. The only thing we have on it right now is directions to the accident scene. Injuries were not mentioned."

"Where did you get your information?"

"The New Jersey State Police. We have a good working relationship with them."

"Do you do this for all accidents involving Fort Monmouth personnel?"

"All that we learn about, and we learn about most of them."

They drove beyond highway US 1 and onto a state highway. They clocked four and one-half miles, then turned onto a one-lane gravel road that ran westerly through farmland. They came upon the accident scene in a wooded section of country. Two New Jersey State Policemen were there talking to one man near a damaged pickup truck. A soldier stood by an older model Dodge that had a badly-damaged front end.

Grady walked up to the soldier and said, "Are you Wayne Griffith?" The soldier replied affirmatively. "I'm Lieutenant Grady, your company commander."

"Yes sir, I know."

"Are you hurt?"

"No sir, I'm all right."

"Have you talked with the state troopers?"

"Yes sir."

"What happened? What are you doing back here?" Grady did not smell alcohol on Griffith's breath.

"I was going to buy a pistol from a man who lives on a farm up ahead when that pickup came at me at high speed and hit me. I didn't have a chance to get out of his way on this one-lane road."

"How did you know about this farmer?"

"I read his ad in the newspaper and talked with him on the telephone." John didn't know whether or not to believe him.

The state troopers came to Griffith and told him that his car was not operable and it would have to be towed to a garage. They gave him the address and telephone number of the garage. Griffith went to his car and pulled out his weekend bag. The MPs stayed about twenty minutes longer talking to both drivers and making measurements at the accident scene.

"What are you going to do now?" Grady asked Griffith.

"I don't know. I guess I'll have to get back to the post somehow."

"Come with me. You can ride back with the MPs."

When they arrived back at Company K barracks, Grady asked the MPs when he could see their report. They said that it would be in the provost marshal's office Monday afternoon.

John drove over to the provost marshal's office late Monday afternoon and asked to see PFC Griffith's accident report. It was a good report, but was inconclusive about the cause of the accident because the parties told conflicting stories and there were no other witnesses. Grady had no reason not to believe Griffith who alleged that the pick up truck approached him at high speed and made no attempt to stop or to avoid him on the one-lane road.

At 0930 Tuesday morning, Grady received a telephone call from his battalion commander Major Stemple. "Grady, the two of us and PFC Wayne Griffith are to be in General Lawrence's office in Russell Hall at 1600 this afternoon. I'll meet the two of you there."

"Well, it has hit the fan," Grady thought to himself. " The general is on his safe-driving crusade." Grady told the first sergeant to have Griffith report to him in his Class A uniform at 1530 that afternoon.

Grady and Griffith entered the general's aide's office and were ushered into General Lawrence's office. Major Stemple already was there. John approached the general's desk, held a salute and said, "Private First Class Griffith and Lieutenant Grady, Company K, reporting as ordered, sir."

The general looked at both of them, then addressed Griffith, "Well, what happened Saturday?" Griffith began describing what had happened. The general began writing something on a pad of paper on his desk and seemed to be paying very little attention to Griffith. When Griffith finished talking, General Lawrence looked up at him and said, "You want to kill yourself in a car? I'll send you someplace where you can get yourself killed." He ripped off the top sheet of paper that he had been writing on and handed it to Grady saying, "Take this to G-I" (Personnel). He said to Major Stemple and PFC Griffith, "That will be all for you two." The general looked at Grady again and said, "You come back here and see me after you deliver that message." The three of them saluted and walked out of the general's office. In the hallway outside, John said to Stemple, "Major, can you take Griffith back to the company area with you?" Stemple agreed and he and Griffith walked away.

As John climbed the stairs to the G-1 office on the third floor, he read the general's message on the sheet of paper: "Send PFC Wayne Griffith, Company K, Troop Command, to FECOM—immediately." Lawrence's initials were scribbled at the bottom of the message. "Holy Toledo," Grady exclaimed. He delivered the message and returned to General Lawrence's office.

The general immediately challenged Grady. "Lieutenant, I put out an order that a safety meeting was to be held in all units last week, then one of your men goes out and has an accident on Saturday. Did you hold a safety meeting?"

"Yes sir, we had it on Wednesday. I conducted it myself, and I followed closely the safety material that was distributed to us. We had a very good meeting, sir: the men were attentive and responsive."

"Well, they couldn't have been paying too much attention or your man wouldn't have had an accident three days later."

"With due respect, sir, I've seen the MP report and it's inconclusive as to the cause of the accident. Unless you have information in addition to the MP report, sir, you have no reason at this time to assume that my man was at fault. With due respect sir, do you have additional information?" Grady knew that he was sticking his neck out, but he felt a responsibility to stick up for his man.

"No, I don't have additional information, but I have the responsibility to see that these men get out of Fort Monmouth alive. Lieutenant, until you become a senior officer you won't understand what command responsibility is."

That last statement hit John right between the eyes. Blood rushed to his head and he saw red. He slammed his open hand on the general's desk as he leaned forward toward the general and almost shouted at him, "Don't you lecture me about my lack of command responsibility and tell me about the command responsibility of senior officers. I assumed my responsibility and got twelve men out from behind the Chinese lines while your senior officers were safe and sound behind our own lines and didn't have the sense or guts to give an evacuation order that a jackass would have known to give. Don't you lecture me. I carried out my responsibility and got my men out—all but four of them who were killed. You go lecture your senior officers and tell them what their responsibilities are to the men who serve under them."

General Lawrence was flabbergasted. When Grady's open hand smacked on the desktop, the general jerked back and his body went stiff. His legs went straight out with only his heels touching the floor, and he held on to the arms of his chair with both hands. No one had ever spoken to him that way. He never imagined that he would ever hear someone speak to him like that. He didn't know what to do first, or what to say.

Grady realized what he had done. He straightened up, threw his head back, blinked his eyes and exclaimed to himself, "H-o-l-y T-o-l-e-d-o!"

"General, I beg your pardon, sir, I meant nothing personal to the General, but you hit a raw nerve in me with your statement. A senior officer left my unit out on a limb behind enemy lines in North Korea while he was safe and sound. It took a week, but I led our men out. I assumed **my** responsibility; **he** didn't. General, I didn't mean to be disrespectful to you, and I apologize for my strong reaction to your statement, but like I said, sir, you hit a raw nerve in me."

Lawrence looked at him and John looked back, wondering if the general would call the MPs and put him under arrest. Slowly, Lawrence sat up straight in his chair and put his hands on his desk. In a low voice he said, "Lieutenant, that will be all. You're dismissed." John saluted and left.

Grady went out to his car and sat. He could not believe that he did what he just did. He knew that there could be dire consequences. He would not care so much about leaving the army, but if he left he wanted to do it on his terms rather than getting kicked out. He returned to K Company and told First Sergeant Perry that he was leaving for the day.

Grady went to his BOQ. What should he do? He couldn't think of anything. He washed and went to the mess hall, but he ate only half his meal and left. He went back to his room and stewed some more. He needed to talk with someone. Rebecca was the only one he wanted to talk with. He called her and said, "Beck, I need to talk with someone, and I'd like to talk with you tonight. Can you spare half an hour? I can come right out. It's important to me"

"It sounds important. Well, yes."

John arrived and they went to the library. "Thanks, Beck, I won't take much of your time. I'm in kind of a pickle, and sometimes it helps to talk with someone about a problem. Sometimes you see things more clearly when you talk about them." He told her about blowing up at General Lawrence, and told her some of what he had said. He didn't reveal to her that he had been cutoff behind the Chinese lines for a week, but merely told her that he had been left in a dangerous situation.

She asked him, "How serious is it to talk to the general that way. Can you get in trouble?"

"Well, I could be court-martialed for being disrespectful to a superior officer, and for conduct unbecoming an officer. Or, I could be forced to resign my commission for the good of the service. At the very least, I could get a lousy efficiency report that would doom my career." He repeated, "I don't care so much about leaving the army, but if I do leave I want it to be on my terms and not theirs."

"What's the general like?"

"I don't know him. He must have something on the ball to have been promoted to major general. But he's very resolute in his ways on this safe-driving matter—he's a fanatic about it." John then told her about the general sending Griffith to FECOM despite the fact that he didn't know whether Griffith was at fault.

"What did he say to you after you blew up?"

"Nothing. He just dismissed me."

"If you already apologized to him, what else can you do? Would it help to put your apology in writing?

Grady considered it. "Maybe it'll help; it can't hurt. I'll do it and hope for the best. Thanks for the suggestion, Beck. I'll quit bothering you now and go back and put something on paper."

The Hazlets were flying to West Palm Beach the next evening to spend ten days there. "I'm going to miss seeing you this weekend," Rebecca said.

"I'll miss you too, Beck." They held hands as they walked to the front door.

Grady went to his room and wrote the best apologetic letter he could think of. Wednesday morning he gave the letter to his company clerk to deliver to Russell Hall, then he became busy and forgot about the incident for a while.

After lunch he received a telephone call from Colonel Bowen asking him how things were going in the company. "It's keeping me busy, but I enjoy it. I think I'm beginning to get the hang of it."

"That's splendid" Bowen replied. "John, do you have plans for Thanksgiving Dinner?"

"I'm planning on having Thanksgiving dinner in the mess hall."

"John, Mrs. Bowen and I will be pleased if you will join us for Thanksgiving Dinner at our home. Won't you come?"

"Gee, that's nice of you, Colonel, but, isn't it kind of late to tell Mrs. Bowen that she'll have a guest for Thanksgiving? I don't want to put her to a lot of trouble."

"It'll be no trouble at all. Her sister and brother-in-law will be here, so one more will be no trouble. We'll be happy to have you join us." John accepted the invitation.

Up until Wednesday evening, Grady had heard nothing more from General Lawrence or Russell Hall about him or about PFC Wayne Griffith.

***

On Thanksgiving Day, John wore a civilian suit, white shirt, and regimental stripe tie to Major Bowen's home. Grady was poor, but he did possess one valued asset—a good civilian wardrobe. One year in college, his roommate in the fraternity house was a fellow who had flown in the Eighth Air Force during World War II. The roommate had been shot down over Germany and had been fortunate enough to parachute from his falling plane. He had been captured shortly after landing on the ground and had spent over a year in a German prisoner of war camp. He had a big frame, but he was thin when he was liberated from the POW camp and discharged from the service. The roommate was from a well-to-do family that owned several coal mines in Southern West Virginia, and when he arrived home he splurged and bought five new suits. After several years of living the good life in college, the roommate had put on considerable weight and could no longer wear the five suits. The suits fit John, so the roommate gave them to him and he had worn them ever since.

Colonel Bowen introduced Grady to Mrs. Bowen and to the in-laws. Mrs. Bowen was short and trim. She had black hair and a pretty face, and her demeanor was quiet and gracious. The in-laws were friendly. It was an interesting and enjoyable afternoon and evening for John. He said nothing to Bowen about his trouble with General Lawrence.

***

The following Thursday morning it came. The general's aide called Grady and told him to be in the general's office at 1130. "This is it," John said to himself. "Well, I'll go back to law school and finish up. I hope I'll get an Honorable Discharge, but maybe not."

John saluted the general with the statement, "Lieutenant Grady reporting as ordered, sir."

Lawrence flipped him a return salute. "Sit down, Lieutenant." The general had a couple of file folders in front of him. He didn't say anything right away, then he looked at John and said, "I received you note of apology, Grady, and I accept your apology. I've looked into your record, and I've talked to some people about you, and I think I understand why you got so steamed up about that remark I made. It was an inappropriate remark to you, but I had no way of knowing that you're a combat veteran. Why aren't you wearing campaign ribbons?"

"Sir, I just have never worn any. I'm not sure what I'm entitled to wear."

"Find out. Put them on.

"Lieutenant, after our conversation last week I reread the MP report on your man who had the car accident. Did you read that note that I had you carry up to G-I?"

John hesitated, then he confessed, "Yes sir, I did."

"Well, I've rescinded it. The boy will stay in school.

"Grady, I like the way you stood up for your man. A commander who won't go to bat for his men isn't much of a commander in my book."

The general looked at his watch and said, "I'm going home to lunch, and I want you come with me; I want to talk to you."

John was in a state of mild shock at the turn of events. He went there expecting to be cashiered—sacked—booted out—and now here he was going to lunch with the general.

The general's residence was a large, attractive, red brick, Georgian-style home with neatly manicured grounds that looked down colonels' row, a tree-lined, divided avenue with attractive two-story red brick quarters on both sides. Grady followed the general into a side door off the driveway. Mrs. Lawrence greeted them with a warm smile, and the general introduced her to Grady. She was an attractive, warm, and outgoing woman. The three of them went to a sitting room and talked for a short while. A steward, a middle-aged, black enlisted man wearing a starched white coat, came to the door of the room and softly announced that lunch was ready. Mrs. Lawrence led the way to the dining room. Three place settings were at one end of a large dining table. The general helped Mrs. Lawrence into her chair, and the men took their seats. Lunch began with soup and continued with several more courses, all served on fine chinaware. John was impressed—generals live a good life. Mrs. Lawrence and the general kept the conversation moving and kept John involved in it. They covered a number of subjects in their conversation and didn't talk about the army. After desert, Mrs. Lawrence said, "If you gentlemen want to have a smoke, I'll excuse you."

"Good" the general said. "Come on, Grady, let's go out to the sun room." They arrived there and the general said to John, "Go ahead, light up if you have them. Excuse me for a minute." He left the room. He returned in five minutes and sat in a large leather chair, opened a humidor, took out a large cigar and lit it. Grady lit his cigarette. The general blew a cloud of smoke into the air and said, "Grady, I asked you over here because I wanted to talk to you, and I wanted Mrs. Lawrence to meet you. My aide's tour of duty with me will be up in the near future, and I'm looking for a replacement. A couple of names have been suggested to me, but I haven't been particularly impressed with them. I wonder if you've ever thought about an assignment as an aide?" Lawrence then told John some of the duties he might expect to perform as his aide. He continued, "I told you this morning that I've looked at your record and have talked with people who know you. Based on your record and the brief contact that we've had, I think that we can work together—if you can control that Irish temper of yours," he said with a smile. "What do you think?"

"General Lawrence, I'm honored that you would consider me for such duty, but I've never given a thought to such a thing."

"I know, I'm dropping this on you unexpectedly. Now, don't feel that you're obliged to take this assignment because I don't want someone who won't be happy working with me, and I'm not going to force anyone to take it. Think about it and give me your answer by noon tomorrow. Let's get back to work."

John thought about it that afternoon and night. It probably would be interesting duty, but he thought about his future career in the army, if he stayed in. He needed experience as a commander, and he now was at the right place to get it. Besides, General Lawrence's style was that of a butcher with a meat ax rather than a surgeon with a scalpel. Being this general's aide probably would result in making some enemies, and he might meet those enemies later in his career. Grady was afraid that if he hitched his wagon to Lawrence he would have a tiger by the tail. He had the feeling that he should decline the offer.

Grady called the general's office the first thing Friday morning and made an appointment for 1000. When Grady entered the general's office, the general arose and closed the door into his aide's office. Lawrence returned to his chair and John told him, "Sir, I've given a lot of thought to this aide assignment, and I find that I must respectfully decline the general's kind offer. I have the assignment right now where I need to be to get command experience. I'm afraid that if I take the aide's job for a couple of years I might never get another chance for good company-grade command experience. I enjoy working with the men, and I feel that I can do some good working as a company commander."

The general thought for a moment, then said, "All right, Grady, I respect your decision. And from your career point of view, it might be the right decision. I still have to fill this job, so don't tell anyone that I talked to you about it."

CHAPTER 4. (1 DECEMBER 1951)

Grady's thoughts were centered on what he was doing a year ago. A year ago his crew destroyed their VHF station at Hyesanjin, North Korea, and headed out to catch the 17th Infantry Regiment. He sat at his desk in his BOQ and wrote a day-by-day summary of what happened those first eight days in December a year ago. He was in a somber mood. His conscience anguished over the memory of killing enemy soldiers. They kept appearing in his mind. He still could see the face of the young Chinese officer who burst into the room of the house in North Korea and then died slouched against the stair railing.

In Korea at that time, some of the hardest fighting of the war was going on at locations in The Iron Triangle such as The Punchbowl, Bloody Ridge, and Heartbreak Ridge. We occupied those positions, but we paid a high price in casualties for what geographically were small-scale operations. Both sides were conducting limited-objective attacks from well-fortified defense lines.

***

John called Rebecca early Sunday morning to welcome her back home from Florida. He asked her if she were going to church. She answered, "No, we arrived home late last night, so I'm going to skip church today." John said that he would be out to see her after church and lunch. She met him at the front door and whisked him into the library. He held out his two hands and took hers and drew her close. His forehead met hers. They stood there for a brief moment, then Rebecca abruptly pulled away, and with flushed cheeks and her hands on her hips she said with obvious annoyance, "John Grady, I have to wonder about you sometimes."

"What's the matter? What did I do?

"You didn't do anything—that's what's the matter. I've been away from you for ten whole days and all you do is touch my forehead with yours. We've been going together for seven months now and you haven't kissed me once, and except for when we dance you've scarcely laid a hand on me. I wonder if you really care about me, that's all."

He looked at her for some time while he collected his thoughts, then he said, "Rebecca, you have to understand my background. I grew up in a socially conservative family in West Virginia, and attended a conservative Methodist church. There, the marriage institution was highly respected and unless it were properly ended one way or another, married men and women were restricted in their relationships with the other gender. Beck, I'm a product of that environment and it still influences my thinking. I can't eliminate from my thinking the fact that you still are married to someone else. I've gone as far as my conscience will allow me."

He moved in close to her and wrapped his arms around her. "But you listen to me, girl; the day your divorce becomes effective I'll be all over you like stink on a polecat."

She had a confused look on her face, then a smile, then she burst out laughing. "'Stink on a polecat'—where in the world did you get that expression?"

"That's the way we hillbillies talk."

She took his hand and said, "Come on Stinky, let's take a walk outside." She told him what she had done in Florida, and then she said, "Oh, John, I almost forgot. What happened with the general?"

He told her about his meeting with the general and about going to his home for lunch, but he didn't tell her about being asked to be the general's aide. They stayed outside until it began to get dark. On their way back to the house John said, "Call that divorce lawyer and find out what he's done. Keep the pressure on him."

Rebecca had studying to do, so John departed when they returned from the walk. As he walked to his car, Rebecca called, "Good-bye Stinky."

***

On Monday, 17 December 51, General Lawrence issued an order that, effective 15 January 52, military personnel must wear at all times all authorized campaign ribbons and all awards and decorations ribbons, fatigue uniforms excluded. Enlisted personnel could obtain their authorized ribbons at the Post Exchange at no cost to them, but officers must obtain their ribbons at their own expense. Grady figured that he knew the genesis of that order.

The officers mess held a semi-formal Christmas dinner-dance on Saturday, 22 December, at festively-decorated Gibbs Hall. Rebecca wore an attractive mid-length dress that evidenced taste and class. About half the men wore their "pinks and greens," the winter dress uniform, but John wore a conservative civilian business suit. Many of the men were company grade officers in the same general age bracket as Grady. The officers of Troop Command congregated at adjacent tables for dinner, and John introduced Rebecca to many people he knew. After dancing began, the Troop Command officers moved their tables closer together and had a lively and friendly evening. Rebecca enjoyed it and was popular with others, including the women—she never had trouble attracting the attention of men.

The Hazlets were flying to Florida Sunday morning and would not return until Saturday, 5 January 52, so Rebecca suggested that they leave before the dance ended so they could spend some time alone before she left for the holidays.

***

John spent much of the holidays at Company K. He gave the company noncommissioned officers as much time off as possible. He attended Christmas Eve church services at the Methodist Church.

He wondered how his friends in X Corps were spending their Christmas in Korea. Over there, both sides continued the limited-objective actions. Tough fighting for individual hills took place with high casualties on both sides. And, the truce talks in Panmunjom were stalled again, this time on the issue of POW exchange. The United States insisted that the North Korean and Chinese soldiers and civilians held in UN POW camps be given the opportunity to decide whether or not they wanted to be repatriated to the Communist side. In the case of Chinese POWs, that meant that a POW could elect not to be repatriated but to be released and go to Formosa. In the case of Korean POWs, they could choose to be released and stay in South Korea rather than being repatriated. The Communist negotiators would have none of that business. They insisted that all Chinese and North Korean POWs be returned to them. (The Geneva Convention had no provision for giving POWs an option about being repatriated. But the U.S. remembered that at the conclusion of World War II when soldiers of the Soviet Union who were held prisoners by Germany were repatriated back to the Soviet Union, many of them were either executed by the Soviets or sent to prison camps in Siberia because their political thinking might have been influenced by their German captors, and additionally, Soviet soldiers were not supposed to surrender! The U.S. wanted to avoid a repeat of that kind of treatment for the North Korean and Chinese POWs.)

CHAPTER 5. (17 JANUARY 1952)

Regimental Adjutant Captain Cole called Grady on the telephone on Thursday and told him to be in the regimental commander's office at 1500.

"What's up, Captain?"

"Can't say now. Be on time."

John entered regimental headquarters at 1500 and walked up to Captain Cole's desk. Cole looked up from his work and said, "Good, Colonel Stump is waiting for you." The two of them entered the colonel's office where Stump was sitting behind his desk. Major Stemple was standing beside it and had a slight smile on his face. John approached the colonel's desk and said, "Lieutenant Grady reporting as ordered, sir."

"Lieutenant Grady, I have several communications here from the Department of the Army concerning you." Stump looked down at papers on his desk and read the following.

In accordance with the provisions of Army Regulation 600-8-22, First Lieutenant John H. Grady, Sig C, USA, is entitled to wear the Purple Heart decoration with two Oak Leaf Clusters as a result of wounds received in combat operations in North Korea in December 1950 against an enemy of the United States of America.

Stump looked up from the papers and said, "Congratulations, Grady." John wondered why the colonel was congratulating him for getting wounded.

Stump looked down at the papers again, flipped the top sheet over, then looked up at John and said, "Grady, there's more here, but I won't read the rest of it verbatim. It says that you also have earned the right to wear the Combat Infantry Badge (CIB) for sustained personal combat action against enemy armed forces in North Korea in December 1950. Congratulations." Stemple and Cole also congratulated him.

Stump again looked down at the papers, flipped over the second sheet and read to himself from the third one. He looked up at John and said,

"Lieutenant Grady, you've been awarded the Silver Star Medal for 'Gallantry in Action Against an Opposing Armed Force.' Congratulations. I won't present the medal and decorations to you today because General Lawrence will present them to you at a ceremony in Russell Hall next Tuesday at 1100. You may invite guests to the ceremony if you wish. Lieutenant Grady, I'm proud to have you in my command." The colonel stood up and shook John's hand. Stemple and Cole also shook his hand and congratulated him. Stump said that was all he had at that time. Grady left and went back to Company K.

John sat in his office and pondered the matter of the awards and decorations. If he could, he would prefer to forget the entire experience in North Korea and the medal and awards as well. In reality, hardly a day or night went by that he didn't have some thought about Korea. He also wondered why the medal had been reduced from the Medal of Honor to the Silver Star. The lieutenant colonel from the Awards and Decorations Board who visited him in the hospital said that the Medal of Honor recommendation had been endorsed all the way up to the board. John wasn't offended, though, because he really felt that what he did was carrying out his command responsibility and for that he didn't deserve the Medal of Honor or the Silver Star. (Unknown to Grady, the act for which the Metal of Honor is bestowed must be verified by at least two eyewitnesses. Paul Bloucher, the marine who didn't make it back across the line, was the only other one who witnessed the attack on the two machine gun emplacements on that snowy night.)

Grady wondered about inviting guests. He should invite his battalion commander, and he wanted to invite Colonel Bowen. Should he invite Rebecca? He didn't want her to think that he was glorifying war, and he really didn't want her to know about the details of what happened to him over there. On the other hand, they had become close and maybe she should know at least some of the facts. Maybe that could be a way for her to find out some of the facts since the formal citation probably would contain some of them. He would have to think more about it.

After lunch he made appointments to see Major Stemple and Colonel Bowen. Stemple said that General Lawrence already had extended an invitation to him, but he appreciated John's thoughtfulness. Bowen was pleased to hear about Grady's awards. He said that he had heard rumors but had not learned the specifics. He thanked John for the invitation and said that he would attend the ceremony next Tuesday.

Rebecca and John attended bible study class on Wednesday night. He still had not made up his mind about inviting her to the ceremony. After class they drove their cars to the parking lot behind Riverview Hospital that overlooked the Navesink River. Rebecca parked her Woody and slid in next to John in his car.

"Rebecca, I think that things have gone well with us recently, and I'd like for them to continue. How do you feel about it?"

"John, do you have any doubts that I feel the same way? You must know that I do."

"Beck, I want to share with you what's going on in my life, just as I want to be a part of what's going on in your life. Something is going to take place on the post next week that involves what happened to me in Korea. I haven't told you very much about it up to now, but maybe it's time I did. It was an unpleasant experience that I would prefer you didn't know about. But, in view of our feelings for each other, I don't want to withhold from you something that was a major event in my life. I'm not proud of what happened over there, and I would give anything if it could have been avoided, but it was a war. Beck, war is terrible and shouldn't be glorified under any circumstance. The army is giving me some recognition of my service in Korea at a ceremony next Tuesday, and they told me that I can invite guests. I'm thinking that maybe ... well ... well for you to know me better you might want to attend. If you don't want to, I certainly understand. I don't know if I'm doing the right thing ... it might be dumb for me to be asking you. Beck, I just don't know. I feel like a different person when I'm with you. I've never had these feelings for a girl before."

She could tell that this was an important event for John and that he was having trouble with it. "John, if this involves something important that happened to you, I want to know about it."

"Beck, it involves a side of me that you don't know and things that you never have seen or imagined. You should understand that and be prepared for it. If we're just good friends, or even very good friends, don't come."

"John, we're more than very good friends. I want to attend that ceremony." John told her about the arrangements for next Tuesday, and told her that he would be unable to drive out to her home to pick her up before the ceremony. He told her to park in the parking lot nearest the West Gate and he would pick her up there and drive her to Russell Hall in his car.

Tuesday morning began cold and drizzly. The temperature was just above freezing, and as the morning progressed, the drizzle turned into a constant rain. John met Rebecca in the parking lot and they drove to Russell Hall. They went to a large conference room on the second floor where the ceremony was to be held. A lectern was at one end of the room and about two dozen neatly-aligned folding chairs were facing the lectern. A large conference table had been pushed to a back corner of the room. Post Sergeant Major Reimer was present making sure that everything was in order. Major Stemple came in, and John introduced Rebecca to him. Colonel Stump and his regimental staff came in. Colonel Bowen entered the room, and John took Rebecca to meet him. Bowen was interested to see what kind of girl Grady was dating.

At the appointed time, General Lawrence and his aide entered the room with a half- dozen more officers of his staff. Bowen escorted Rebecca to a seat and sat beside her. The general took a standing position to one side of the lectern and directed John to stand in front of him.

A young-looking first lieutenant who was aide to the G-I went to the lectern and placed a folder and several small boxes on it. The lieutenant read the recitation that Colonel Stump had read about John being entitled to wear the Purple Heart with two Oak Leaf Clusters. The lieutenant was very dramatic reading the recitation—too dramatic Grady thought. The aide then took a box to General Lawrence and took the Purple Heart medal out of it and handed it to General Lawrence. The general stepped up to John and pinned the medal on his blouse.

They went through the ceremony for the Combat Infantry Badge. The lieutenant then began the recitation for the Silver Star. Here, he was more dramatic and flowery than previously. The citation commended Grady's leadership in leading his group to safety from deep behind Chinese lines. The recitation was longer than John would have liked, and went into considerable detail about the various actions and firefights that his group had in North Korea. It mentioned the subzero temperatures and the killing of Chinese soldiers and North Korean guerrillas. It described in detail the incidents of the last night when the crew crossed over to the U.S. lines. The recitation asserted that, despite being twice wounded, Lieutenant Grady had placed himself in great peril by attacking and destroying two enemy machine gun emplacements so that the remainder of his group could safely pass to friendly forces. It stated that in that encounter Lieutenant Grady again was severely wounded and later was recovered unconscious in no-man's land. (The recitation didn't mention Paul Bloucher's action against the machine gun emplacements or the group's capture and release by the Chinese.) When the lieutenant finished his flowery and dramatic reading, John wanted to punch him in the mouth.

As General Lawrence pinned the Silver Star metal on Grady, the general said for all to hear, "If I had anything to do with this award I'd be pinning the Medal of Honor on you."

The officers and Sergeant Major Reimer congratulated John and then went for refreshments that were on the table in the back of the room. Bowen and Rebecca came up to him. Bowen shook his hand and said, "You're a fine officer, John." Bowen departed and the two of them were alone. Rebecca looked at him with teary eyes. She said nothing. John took her behind the lectern, and with their backs to the others he handed her his handkerchief. She wiped her eyes and smiled at him. They joined the others for refreshments. John talked with several officers, and Rebecca talked with a different group of officers that included General Lawrence. Lawrence tried to learn as much about her as he could. He was impressed with her, and it didn't surprise him that John Grady dated a bright girl.

The reception ended and John led Rebecca out of Russell Hall. He was chagrined and angry at the way the lieutenant made such a dramatic show of the event. John said nothing to Rebecca as they walked in the rain to his car. They drove in silence to the parking lot. He parked his car next to Rebecca's, turned to her and said, "That damned pipsqueak doesn't know the first thing about what he was doing or saying. Rebecca, I apologize for subjecting you to that. I never should have asked you to come; it was a mistake.

"You don't belong here, Rebecca; you shouldn't have anything to do with me. You're a good and decent person, but I'm filthy. I have blood and sin all over me. Get away from me as fast and as far as you can. Go find yourself an Ivy Leaguer, marry him, raise children, and forget that you ever knew me. You deserve something better than this filthy sinner.

"Look at this." John raised his arms and looked around. "What can I offer you? Nothing. Here we are sitting in the rain in a hot, steamy car, and I have no decent place to take my best girl. Go find yourself someone respectable—you're too fine a person to be stuck with me. And you can forget that I called you 'my best girl.' You can do much better than me."

Rebecca said nothing. She took his hand and held it. After a while she spoke softly to him, "I am your best girl. And you're my hero."

"Don't you say that," he snapped back at her. "I'm not a hero. I'm a sinner who's going to have to pay for his sins, and you don't want to be near me when the day of reckoning comes. Get as far away from me as you can and forget that you ever knew me."

"John, you're in the army. You were in a war that the Communists started. It wasn't your choice."

"Do you think that matters? Do you think that makes it O.K. with God? You heard them today—I killed people—do you know what that means? I'm filled with sin, and I can't wish it away. I can't say that it doesn't matter because I'm in the army. Rebecca, you had better go home; you don't belong here with me."

Rebecca sat there a moment, then reached into her purse and pulled out her car keys. She slid out of John's car and went to her's.

Later that week, both the *Asbury Park Evening Press* and the *Long Branch Daily Record* printed a short press release from the Fort Monmouth Public Affairs Office about First Lieutenant John Grady receiving awards and decorations for his service in Korea.

Grady didn't go to bible study class Wednesday night, or to church on Sunday. He didn't contact Rebecca during the remainder of that week, or during the weekend, and he didn't call her the next week either. He again stayed away from church. He went about his work in Company K without enthusiasm.

Late on Friday evening of the third week after the awards ceremony, Rebecca telephoned John at his BOQ. "Hello, John, this is Rebecca."

"Why are you calling?" he challenged her. "I was hoping that you had taken my advice and were staying away from me."

"And I was hoping that you'd be back to your senses by now. I haven't heard from you and I'm worried about you. John, I need to talk with you."

"What about?"

"About you. John, I've talked with Pastor Lowe at the Methodist Church. He flew a bomber in World War II, you know, and I've made an appointment for you to talk with him Saturday morning at 10:00 o'clock."

"Why in the world did you do that? Rebecca, what do you think you're doing?"

"John, please talk with him. He might know what's troubling you. He faced the same things you did."

"Like hell he did. He was up twenty-five or thirty thousand feet where he couldn't even see people on the ground. He never had to look people in the face and fight them. Rebecca, you just go about your own business and leave me alone—you'll be better off.

She snapped back at him assertively, "John Grady, you listen to me, and you get this into your head. I'm not going away and marry some Ivy Leaguer and forget about you. I did that once, if you remember, and it didn't work. I know what I am doing, and I want you to meet me at 9:45 tomorrow morning at the Methodist Church. Do you hear me?"

John had never heard Rebecca speak in such a firm, authoritarian manner before. He didn't answer her.

"Do I have to drive to Fort Monmouth and get you in the morning? John, you need help, and you need a friend. I'm more than a friend to you, and I'm going to help you. When you helped me I wasn't as stubborn about it as you are now. Why can't you be sensible about this? This is not like you, John. Now, either you're coming to the church on your own or I'm coming to your BOQ to get you. Which will it be?"

What should he do, tell her to go away or give in to her? Decision time, fellow. He had to admit that she was right about one thing: he really didn't feel like himself. He has been moping around as if he were lost ever since the awards ceremony. "Maybe she's right," he conceded to himself. Furthermore, would he ever know another woman who would do this for him? His better senses told him, "Wake up, dummy, do you know another Rebecca Hazlet?"

"All right, Rebecca, I'll meet you in the church library at 9:45 in the morning."

Rebecca was bright and beautiful when they met Saturday morning in the sun-lit church library. John gave her a sheepish smile and said, "Beck, you're some kind of girl." They talked briefly before John went into the pastor's office. Rebecca said that she would wait in the library and told him to come get her when he was done.

John knocked on the pastor's door, and The Reverend Martin Lowe told him to come in. Lowe was in his late thirties. He was taller and heavier than Grady. His brownish hair was beginning to get thin in front. As a result of John having attended the pastor's bible study class before and after he went overseas, John knew him, but not real well. Lowe greeted him with a handshake and offered him a chair.

Pastor Lowe took the initiative in the conversation. "John, Rebecca showed me a newspaper article about you receiving decorations for combat service in Korea, and she told me that you had been wounded and hospitalized. She said that you apparently are having a moral struggle with yourself about your actions in combat. She suggested that because I flew in combat I might be able to help. I'll be glad to talk with you about it, if you want to. I don't know that I have answers for you, but sometimes it helps to talk. What do you think?"

"Thanks, Pastor Lowe—"

Lowe interrupted, "Let's not be formal. Call me Martin, or Marty."

'O.K., Marty. I always thought that I was fairly strong emotionally and spiritually, but the combat experiences have kind of unsettled me recently. My crew and I were cut off behind the Chinese lines in North Korea, and we had to walk and fight our way out. We lost some of our people, and we killed some Chinese and North Koreans, some quite close up.

"The bible says: *Thou shalt not kill.* I killed people. I committed a sin— many times. I know of nothing in the bible that says that God gives me a dispensation because I'm in the army. I feel that I'm carrying a huge, bloody, dirty, and sinful burden on my soul. That's about it."

Lowe was thoughtful for a moment, then he spoke. "John, I never was in close combat, but I have had to deal with the concept of killing people in war. I was a bomber pilot in the Pacific, and toward the end of the war we flew to the Japanese home islands. We were assigned to bomb military targets in the cities, but from the high altitudes we flew we knew that our bombs would not always land in the target area. Some days the target area was under complete cloud cover, but we still dropped our bomb loads. We had no idea where those bombs hit. We never saw it, but we figured that we killed civilians inside and outside the target areas.

"Yes, your concern has been, and is, shared by many men who served. John, I don't have a stone tablet from God with the answer chiseled in it, so all I can do is tell you how I've dealt with the problem. I'm of the opinion that there comes a time in the history of the world when forces of evil must be resisted. If a force of evil chooses to extend its sphere by force of arms, then force of arms must be employed to counter it. I believed that in World War II this country was justified in the use of force of arms.

"In Korea, the Communists North invaded South Korea. From what I read, they inflicted harsh and cruel treatment on military and civilian people alike. One has to consider the effects of Communism on the bodies and spirits of men and whether this is an evil that must be opposed by force for the good of mankind. Personally, I believe that Communism is an ungodly concept that must be resisted by force when it becomes the armed aggressor.

"John, I'm not convinced that you and I sinned. But keep in mind that even if we did sin, we have the promise that God will forgive us if we are truly sorry and repent. John, I find prayer to be very important. Now, I don't know if I have been any help to you."

"All those things have passed through my mind, Marty, but I keep wondering if I'm not kidding myself. Am I telling myself: *Sin boldly, that grace may abound?* That's phony. Is that what I'm doing?"

"I don't think so, John. Remember, if we did sin, the message of the New Testament is that Christ came to save sinners. If you truly repent and became a child of God in your faith, I'm confident that you will be forgiven. Don't forget that God forgives us, not because we deserve it, but because He loves us. But, there's no way I can prove it to you, John; that's what faith is all about."

"Marty, thanks for sharing your thoughts with me. I appreciate you taking the time to talk with me." They shook hands and John returned to the library.

Rebecca was sitting at a table reading a book and looked up when John entered the room. He walked to the table and sat down on the side opposite her. They looked at each other, but neither said anything. Finally, John spoke. "Rebecca, events these last couple of weeks have brought to a boil some concerns of mine, and as a result of everything that has happened I have learned a very valuable thing. If I didn't already know it, I learned for sure that Rebecca Hazlet is a loyal, unselfish, kind, and wonderful person whom I am privileged to know. Thank you for everything you have done for me. And, I apologize for the sharp remarks that I made to you.

"The pastor and I talked some about our experiences, and he said some things about my concerns that might be helpful to me. Thanks for arranging the meeting."

"John, I also learned some things these past weeks. I'm glad that you invited me to that ceremony because I learned some of the things that you and other men have gone through in a war. I should know those things about you.

"John, this past week I thought about something that you said to me the day we met the second time. You said that if my marriage breakup were the worst thing that ever happened to me, I would be a lucky girl. After hearing what you experienced over there, I understand what you meant by that statement. You were right, I am a very lucky girl, and I will try never to forget it."

CHAPTER 6. (11 FEBRUARY 1952)

Grady received a telephone call from Colonel Bowen. "John, Mrs. Bowen and I were talking about you over the weekend, and she said that it has been a while since we had you over to our house. She suggested that we invite you for dinner Saturday evening. And, I was thinking that if you still are courting Miss Hazlet, we'd like for her to join you. I enjoyed meeting her at your award ceremony."

"Thank you Colonel, that's very kind of Mrs. Bowen and you. Yes, Rebecca and I still are seeing each other, and I don't know of any engagement she has for Saturday night, but I'll not be able to contact her until tonight. I'll do that and confirm with you later tonight, if that's all right with you."

"That's fine, John. I hope you both can make it. I intend to wear civilian clothes, so please feel free to do the same."

The Bowens were gracious hosts and made Rebecca and John feel at ease. After everyone seemed relaxed with each other, in a very tactful way John told the Bowens that Rebecca was married but was in the process of getting a divorce, and he explained why. He told them that he knew Rebecca before she was married. The Bowens seemed to accept this. As the evening progressed, they found Rebecca to be delightful.

During dinner, Colonel Bowen mentioned something about the awards ceremony, and Rebecca said to him, "Colonel Bowen, that ceremony had a depressing effect on John. It reminded him of unpleasant experiences in Korea and again raised questions in his mind about the morality of what he had to do over there in fighting the Chinese and North Koreans. How do you professional soldiers deal with the matter of morality of war?"

"That's a matter that many of us face in our careers, so I'm not surprised that John is struggling with it. In my case, I believe that America has been the defender of justice and liberty, and without her active participation in recent wars the world would be in a far worse condition than it now is in. Because totalitarian nations have been the aggressors in waging war, we have been forced to engage them in combat. I don't know any other way to counter them to preserve freedom and decency in the world. I'm proud to be part of the instrument that is at the forefront in keeping the world from sliding into subjugation to totalitarian nations.

"As to the morality of it, I believe we must preserve societies where morality, religion, and value for life can live and flourish. I don't see that it is immoral to try to preserve those qualities. I don't know any other way to preserve them when they are attacked by armed aggression than to defend them with arms.

"I'm not a philosopher or a theologian, so my simple explanation is the best I can offer. John, I have always admired Benjamin Franklin. He was a self-educated man who was a scholar, a successful businessman, a statesman, a philosopher, and an ardent patriot. He also had a strong personal religious faith. He served in the militia in his early days, and as you know, strongly championed the war for independence from Great Britain. I have a copy of his autobiography and letters which I'll lend you to read. Maybe it will be some help to you."

"Thank you, Colonel, I'd like to read it."

Rebecca helped Mrs. Bowen clear the table and stack the dirty dishes. John and the colonel went to the living room and talked about the war and about John's present duties. Rebecca and John left in about an hour. All enjoyed the evening.

After taking Rebecca home, John returned to his BOQ room and retrieved the pint of bourbon that he kept buried deep in his footlocker and mixed himself a tall drink of bourbon and water. He sat in his easy chair with his feet resting on his bed and reminisced about his experiences in Korea and mulled over in his mind what Colonel Bowen and Reverend Lowe had told him. He concluded that some wars were necessary when sufficient provocation existed; that wars were not won by sunshine patriots; that wars were won by killing enemy soldiers; that when his country was at war he should do his part to assure his country's victory; that if he, and others like him, didn't do their duty in the face of the enemy, who would? He realized that he had to do what he did in Korea and that he would just have to act like a man and live with it. He was chagrined that he had acted as he had after the award ceremony, and he was ashamed that he had treated Rebecca as he had.

CHAPTER 7. (25 FEBRUARY 1952)

Several weeks later in Company K, Grady received a telephone call from Captain Cole, the regimental adjutant, telling him to come to regimental headquarters. When Grady reported, Cole asked him, "Grady, you have some legal background, don't you?"

"I have two years of law school, that's all."

"Colonel Stump is setting up a legal section in Troop Command to handle the less serious military justice matters. He wants to keep them in the regiment rather than sending them over to the JAG office. Captain Masters, a Signal Corps officer in the regiment, is going to head it up. He's a lawyer, a RETREAD, called back to active duty from the Reserves when this war broke out. We've located two enlisted men who were in law school when they were called to active duty and who will be clerks in the legal section. I'd like for you to help out if and when you're needed. You'll keep Company K since this legal business shouldn't take too much of your time. How does that sound to you?"

"Good, so long as I don't have to give up the company. But Captain, I'm a little surprised that the colonel would want to set up a legal section. It sounds like a duplication of what the JAG office is supposed to do."

"Well, the colonel feels that he wants to take care of his own dirty laundry in Troop Command, so to speak." (Unknown to Grady at this time, Colonel Stump was an "Empire Builder," and having his own legal section enlarged his empire and bestowed more power on him, the emperor. Besides, Stump didn't get along well with Lieutenant Colonel James, the Staff Judge Advocate, and he would just as soon not have to deal with him any more than he absolutely had to.)

Cole took Grady to a small office on the far side of regimental headquarters and introduced him to Captain Lester Masters. "I'll leave you two to talk" Cole said.

The legal section began operation, and in the first six weeks John handled several summary courts-martial trials. They were minor disciplinary matters, and John gave sentences of extra duty to the offenders.

Of course, Lieutenant Colonel James learned of the bootleg legal section at regimental headquarters and was incensed that Colonel Stump was infringing on James's domain of military justice. He called Stump on the telephone, and in as nice a tone as he could muster for the occasion he asked Stump what he was doing and why. Stump also mustered a pleasant sounding voice and gave James a sugar-coated explanation. Although Stump was a full colonel and outranked Lieutenant Colonel James, James was feisty and said that the JAG office had the responsibility of administering military justice on the post and that the legal section in Troop Command would disrupt the orderly administration of military justice. Stump disagreed.

***

Matters were going well in K Company. The routine with the troops included a work session each Thursday evening during which the troops gave the barracks a thorough cleaning from top to bottom to get it ready for Saturday morning inspection. Having it Thursday night rather than Friday night assured that all the men in the company would participate in the cleaning since weekend passes began at 1700 on Friday.

One Thursday after the troops returned from school, First Sergeant Perry came to Grady's door and said that Private Burton wanted to speak with him. "Send him in," Grady said. Burton came in and saluted. He had a husky build, ruddy complexion, and blond hair. Grady recognized him, but he had not had prior personal contact with him. "Stand at ease Burton. What can I do for you?"

"Sir, about the work details cleaning the barracks on Thursday nights, a couple of us in the company were wondering if you would excuse us from them. It's O.K. for the others, sir, but we're college men and we don't think we ought to be doing things like that. You being a college man, sir, we knew you would understand."

Grady had to wait and settle down before answering. "Burton, you're in the United States Army the same as the other men in Company K. You have the same responsibilities that the other men in the company have to keep your living environment clean and healthy. I know of no other organization, except possibly for a trapeze act, that requires more cooperation and mutual effort than an army unit, and that mutual effort applies to everyone in a training unit in garrison as well as to a unit in a war zone.

"If you serve in a communications crew in a combat zone, you must be an integral part of that crew to assure that the crew accomplishes its mission. Other lives depend on your crew doing its job. You can't sit on your ass and expect that the other members of the crew who didn't have the privilege of going to college will do their work and yours too. If your position is attacked by the enemy, do you expect the non-college men to defend it while you sit by and watch or hide in a foxhole? Burton, when the Chinese and North Koreans come after you they don't ask if you're a college man. I'm disappointed in you and your college men; I would think that college men would have figured out by now that they have responsibilities to fellow soldiers and to their organization. Your request is denied, and you tell the other college men exactly why I denied it. Now, you hold it right there a minute, Burton.

"Sergeant Perry," Grady called, "will you come in here please." When Perry entered, John asked him which company noncommissioned officer would be on duty during the work session later that night. Perry replied that Sergeant Johnson would be on duty.

Grady looked Burton straight in the eyes as he spoke. "Sergeant Perry, Private Burton here will be working very hard in the work session tonight to show his fellow soldiers that he's man enough to pull his own weight in this man's army. I want Sergeant Johnson to watch carefully to see how well Private Burton works, and I want the sergeant to report to me the first thing in the morning and tell me what a fine job Private Burton did."

"Do you have any questions, Private Burton? Dismissed."

Grady thought about the men in his group in North Korea and how they all had worked, cooperated, and sacrificed for the benefit of the group. A far cry from the attitude manifested by Burton and his "college men." At the next Troop Information Program in the company, Grady talked to the men about duty and responsibility of a soldier. In his talk he used as examples a couple of the incidents that he had seen and experienced in North Korea.

Speaking of Korea, the fighting and peace talks seemed interminable. The UN negotiators told the Communists that of the great mass of POWs that the UN held, less than half had elected to return to the Communist side. The Communists were outraged and walked out of the truce talks. Communist POWs rioted in several UN POW camps.

Meanwhile, the simmering feud between Colonel Stump of Troop Command and Lieutenant Colonel James, the Staff Judge Advocate, about the bootleg legal section in regimental headquarters ratcheted up a notch when James requested a meeting with General Lawrence to discuss the matter. Stump was not invited to the meeting. James argued every logical reason he could think of why the legal section in Troop Command should be shut down and the operation moved to the JAG office.

General Lawrence really wanted all courts-martial to be handled in the JAG office. He didn't remember why he gave Stump permission to set up the bootleg operation—Stump undoubtedly had sold him a bill of goods. The general told James to draw up a plan for the consolidation of the two operations, get the plan to him in a week, and send a copy to Stump. James wrote up a plan whereby the legal section at Troop Command would immediately terminate operations and all personnel associated with it would be transferred to the JAG office and be under James's command. Stump was incensed. He wrote out an alternative plan for the continuance of the legal section in Troop Command and forwarded it to General Lawrence. In his scanning of Stump's report, Lawrence noticed that Lieutenant John Grady was doing work in the legal section of Troop Command.

CHAPTER 8. (SPRING-SUMMER 1952)

Rebecca informed John that her divorce attorney had told her that the divorce would be effective as of 25 July, and she told John to make no plans for the night of 25 July because she was planning a celebration dinner for the two of them at the Shadow Brook restaurant.

When that momentous evening arrived, Grady drove to the Hazlet home and rang the bell. Mr. Hazlet answered and showed John into the house. He said that Rebecca was a little late, so they went to the parlor and talked until Rebecca came down. She arrived bright and cheerful. Mr. Hazlet excused himself and left the room. Rebecca and John grinned at each other. He moved to her and embraced her. They kissed with a passion that finally was free to be manifested. "Oh, Stinky," she purred.

Rebecca had made all the dinner arrangements with the Shadow Brook restaurant and had ordered everything from soup to nuts. She had even ordered a bourbon and soda for Grady. He said to her, "Beck, I feel as though we've stepped into a new world."

"John, I apologize for putting you through so much trouble, and I thank you for sticking it out."

"I knew that it would be worth it."

Several weeks later, Grady was at the Hazlet's home on Saturday evening for a date with Rebecca. Mr. Hazlet talked with them, and before Rebecca and John left the house he said, "John, I haven't seen much of you lately. Why don't you come for dinner next Saturday evening. I'd like for you to join us."

"That's very kind of you, Mr. Hazlet." John looked at Rebecca. She had a surprised look on her face and nodded to John to accept the invitation. "I'm happy to accept your invitation."

When they were driving away in the car, Rebecca said, "I didn't put him up to that invitation; he did that on his own."

The evening of the dinner at the Hazlets, John wore a dark gray, single-breasted suit that had a faint light gray stripe in it. It was one of his favorite suits. He wore a white shirt and regimental stripe tie and had a high polish on his cordovan wing tips. Mr. Hazlet mixed drinks on the screened porch before dinner. Rebecca had her usual Coke. The conversation went well between Rebecca, Mr. Hazlet and Grady, but Mrs. Hazlet's participation was minimal.

Sally came to the door and announced that dinner was ready. Mrs. Hazlet led the way to the dinning room. John helped Mrs. Hazlet into her chair, and Mr. Hazlet helped Rebecca. Mrs. Hazlet sat at the near end of the table, and Mr. Hazlet at the far end. Rebecca was in the middle of the table on her father's right side, and Grady sat opposite her. As they were eating, John had the feeling that Mrs. Hazlet was sneaking looks at him, expecting him to show poor table manners. In fact, he had excellent table manners. His parents insisted on them when he was growing up, as did his fraternity in college. Even the party boys in the fraternity used good table manners. If a fraternity member became lax in his manners, the older members let him know that such conduct was not acceptable in their dining room.

Midway through the main course of brisket of beef, Mr. Hazlet mentioned that Mrs. Hazlet and he were going to spend two weeks at their home in West Palm Beach the latter part of August and the first part of September. He said that it was not the best time to go to Florida, but he was having a new roof put on the house and a heating and air conditioning system installed, so he wanted to be there while the work was being done.

Without meaning anything in particular, John commented, "You certainly have some impressive addresses: Manhattan, Hazlet, N.J., and West Palm Beach."

Mrs. Hazlet immediately said, "Is that why you're sniffing around here?"

Mr. Hazlet snapped back in a loud whisper, "Elizabeth!"

Everyone was silent. Rebecca and her father looked at John. They didn't know what to say. John looked down at his plate and sat motionless. Slowly, he placed his napkin on the left side of his plate; he placed his fork across the center of his plate; and he moved his knife across the plate and placed it beside the fork. Still looking down at his plate, he slowly pushed his chair away from the table, raised himself to his full height, and stepped behind the chair and pushed it toward the table. Keeping his hands on the back of the chair, he nodded his head toward Mr. Hazlet, and without looking up said, "I thank you for your kind invitation for dinner this evening, but it's not appropriate for me to remain in a home where I'm not welcome." He looked at Mr. Hazlet and Rebecca and said, "So, I shall say good evening." He walked toward the dining room door.

Mrs. Hazlet spoke to no one in particular, "Well, I have never had anyone walk away from my table."

"Elizabeth, be quiet," Mr. Hazlet commanded.

As John passed through the dining room door, Rebecca called, "John, wait!" She excused herself from the table and hurried to catch up to him. As they walked toward the front door she said, "Oh John, I apologize. Please don't be angry with me."

"You don't need to apologize, Beck, it wasn't your doing. And I'm not angry with you. Now, I must be going."

"Wait, I'm going with you." They went to Grady's car. He started the motor, then looked over to her and shook his head. They drove to the iron entrance gate in silence. Before they opened the gate, Grady put the gear shift into neutral and said to her, "Beck, here we are again, I get myself into trouble and you're here sticking with me. You're some kind of girl. Thanks."

She leaned over and kissed him on the cheek. "Where are we going?"

"I don't know, where do you want to go?" They drove to the high cliff at Atlantic Highlands and looked out over Sandy Hook Bay at the lights of Staten Island and Brooklyn.

"Beck, I don't know why it has to be so difficult for us. I thought that our troubles were behind us, but now this pops up. I bring you trouble."

"John, you haven't been the source of the troubles we've had; you know better than that. Sometimes I think I should move out of the house and get an apartment. That would take care of our troubles."

He reached over and pulled her close. "That might get me into trouble."

Rebecca and John went to church the next day, then went to lunch. Rebecca gave him a note from her father apologizing for the event last night.

Grady continued to call on Rebecca at the Hazlet home, but he would not enter the house. He waited for Rebecca at the door.

CHAPTER 9. (16 SEPTEMBER 1952)

Grady walked out of the provost marshal's office at 0800 after completing his turn as JOOD (Junior Officer of the Day), a duty assigned to junior officers to be nominally in charge of affairs on the post when the OD (Officer of the Day) and other senior officers were not on duty. The duty ran from 1700 in the evening until 0800 the following morning and came up every five or six months for a junior officer permanently assigned to the post. As John walked in front of Russell Hall on his way to the JAG office, General Lawrence's car drove up and stopped. The general stepped from the back seat and started toward the front steps. Grady saluted and said, "Good morning, General."

Lawrence flipped a return salute, took a couple of steps forward, then stopped and turned toward John and said, "Grady, I'm glad I bumped into you; I've been wanting to talk to you about something. Come up to my office." When they arrived at the general's office, Lawrence offered him a chair and immediately started talking.

"Grady, I understand that you're doing some work in that legal section of Troop Command. Stump and James are having a tug of war about that legal section and have dumped it onto my lap. Military justice matters belong in the JAG office, so I'm going to move everything over there. I have some things in mind that I want to do, and I want to know how things are handled by the JAG office. At times, James can be an independent-minded cuss, and he doesn't always see things as I do. I want someone there I can trust and who knows what's going on. Grady, I'm going to transfer you permanently to the JAG office, and I want you to stay on your toes over there."

"With due respect, sir, what about my company? Also, sir, I'm not sure I understand what you have in mind for me in the JAG office. Are you planting a spy, so to speak?"

"You'll get a replacement to take over your company. You've been there about a year, right? That's enough time for a guy like you to learn that job. I gave you a choice when I asked you to be my aide, but this time you don't have a choice."

"Now, as to what you'll do in the JAG office, I didn't say I wanted you to spy on anyone, but I do want to know what's going on. Those damn monthly reports are virtually worthless to me. How am I expected to make decisions when I don't know the facts and the reasoning behind actions taken."

Grady was uneasy about what the general wanted him to do. Why does he want to know the details of what is going on in the JAG office? "General, I don't want to work in a situation where I can't be honest and up front with the people I work with. Am I correct that I'll have no problem in that regard?"

"You'll have no problem so far as I'm concerned."

"Thank you, General, I'm glad to know that." John felt that the general had more in mind than he just revealed. "When will the transfer take place, sir?"

"Soon, but don't tell anyone yet. I want Stump and James to hear it from me first."

***

John didn't tell anyone about his pending change of assignments, not even Rebecca. He commenced to get his affairs in order for transfer of Company K. He went to Sergeant Lipscomb, the supply sergeant, and told him that it was time for yearly inventory. He told Lipscomb to inventory everything on the books and if so much as a straight pin were missing he wanted to know it. Grady said that he would get Lipscomb some help, and he wanted it completed in five days. John brought the Company Property Book and the Company Punishment Book up to date, and he told First Sergeant Perry to have all routine reports ready for his signature the day before they were due.

Several days later, Sergeant Lipscomb came to John's office and reported that everything was going well with the inventory except that he had discovered that seven pistol belts were missing. Lipscomb could not explain it and said he was sure that they were there the last time he counted. Grady thanked him and dismissed him, then he called Sergeant Everett Johnson, the duty sergeant, to his office. Johnson was an old-timer who knew the army and its ways inside-out.

"Sergeant Johnson, the supply sergeant tells me that we're seven pistol belts short. Do you think you can do something about it?"

Johnson seemed almost bored. "I'll look into it, sir."

Three days later, Grady passed Sergeant Johnson in the hallway outside the first sergeant's office. Johnson said rather casually, "Oh, sir, about that shortage of pistol belts, we've made up the shortage."

"Thank you, Sergeant." The matter was closed. Grady didn't ask him where he got the pistol belts or how he got them—he didn't want to know. The army's most innovative and efficient supply operation had just scored another victory. John had no pangs of conscious about this off-the-books mode of supply requisition. The army hardly could function without a little of this ingenuity going on.

***

In Korea, General Mark Clark replaced General Ridgway in May 1952 and experienced some of the frustrations that General Ridgway had endured. General Ridgway replaced General Eisenhower as Commander of NATO forces in Europe when Eisenhower left the army to run as the Republican candidate for president.

Nothing of significance was happening at Panmunjom except that the two sides held infrequent meetings to make charges and tirades against each other. The UN walked out of the meetings in October when the Communists rejected a settlement proposal from the UN.

Rebecca and John frequently discussed current events. They both felt frustration at the stalled Korean truce talks and discussed the possibility that John could return there.

The presidential campaign between Dwight Eisenhower and Adlai Stevenson was heating up. Big issues were the alleged Communist infiltration of the State Department and the Defense Department under Democrat administrations, and the unresolved war in Korea. Democrats closely scrutinized General Eisenhower's World War II record and ranted against Senator Joseph McCarthy.

***

Grady received a call from Captain Cole to attend a meeting at regimental headquarters the next morning at 0900. John asked, "What's up, Captain?"

"The transfer of the legal section to JAG is going to be discussed. Colonel James will be there."

"Oh, when will the transfer take place?" Grady had heard nothing about his replacement for Company K.

"That's one of the things to be discussed."

Attending the meeting for Troop Command were Colonel Stump, Captain Cole, Captain Masters, and Grady. For the JAG office were Lieutenant Colonel James, First Lieutenant Robert Plusser, a JAG officer, and Colonel James's civilian secretary who had her stenographer's notebook open and half a dozen sharpened pencils at the ready. Stump presided and formally, and stiffly, welcomed the JAG people. He and James engaged in a dialog about the matter that John found hard to follow. Obviously, considerable discussion had preceded this meeting, but John knew nothing about what had gone on beforehand. James's secretary recorded the conversation in shorthand. That annoyed Stump, and he looked at James and said, "Is it necessary for her to do that?" James smiled and replied, "I'm sure you want a record of this meeting so there'll be no later confusion about what was said."

James argued for an immediate transfer of the entire legal section, but Stump insisted that they wait until the legal section worked its way through its present backlog of work. Eventually, Captain Cole proposed that the transfer be done gradually. Someone from Troop Command would go over to the JAG office immediately to prepare the way for the remainder of the section, then others would follow in coming weeks. That seemed to be the best that the two colonels could get out of the situation, so they agreed to the compromise. James wanted to know who would come over first. Stump looked at his people at the table and said, "Lieutenant Grady will go over immediately." John was surprised, but with a little thought he saw what Stump was doing. John spent only a very minor portion of his time with the legal section and he was its least important member, so his absence from the regimental legal section would have no effect on its operation. Stump intended that Grady would come back to Troop Command when the remaining people of the legal section went to the JAG office. (Stump didn't know that General Lawrence wanted Grady in the JAG office.)

At the conclusion of the meeting, Stump said to Grady, "Lieutenant, you go back to the JAG office with Colonel James." Grady had no idea what he was to do or how long he was to stay once he went there. John walked with the JAG people the four blocks to the JAG office, and once inside the building James said to Lieutenant Plusser, "Introduce the lieutenant to our staff." The colonel then went into his office and started working on a pile of papers on his desk. Plusser made the introductions, but John couldn't remember the names of the secretaries or the other JAG officers. He did remember the name of Sol Solomon, a civil service employee and the only civilian attorney in the office. Sol had prepared John's Last Will and Testament before John had gone overseas.

Neither Plusser or John knew what to do after the introductions were made. Plusser pointed to an empty desk at the end of a row of desks along the front part of the building and said, "Why don't you sit there for now until Mr. Klingen, our warrant officer and office manager, gets back. He was here this morning, so I expect he should be back soon." The office was warm, so John asked where he could hang up his Ike jacket. Plusser pointed to a coat rack at the far end of the room. John hung up his jacket and returned to the desk where he sat doing nothing. Warrant Officer Clarence Klingen came in and looked around the office. He saw Grady, but did nothing. Klingen sat down at his desk and immersed himself in papers.

Grady became irritated, and at 1155 he left the desk and went to Klingen and introduced himself and said that he had come over from Troop Command as part of the transfer of the legal section. He asked Klingen what he should be doing. John's shirt had no indication of his rank on it nor any of his decorations and ribbons, so Klingen had no way of knowing who Grady was or what his army experience was. Klingen pointed to the empty desk that John had just come from and said, "You go back there and have a seat at that desk. I'll tell you later what you're supposed to do."

"Mr. Klingen, you people don't know what the hell you're doing here. You fought to get the legal section over here and now that I'm here you don't know what the hell to do with me. I have a company to run in Troop Command, and I'm going back to my company now. I'll be back here at 0900 tomorrow morning, and if you have something for me to do I'll stay until noon, then I'll return to my company. If you have nothing for me to do in the morning, I'll immediately return to my company." With that, John turned and walked to the coat rack to get his coat and cap. Klingen came out from behind his desk and was about to say something to Grady who then was putting on his jacket. When Klingen saw the Combat Infantry Badge, Purple Heart, and Silver Star ribbons, as well as other campaign ribbons on Grady's jacket, he returned to his desk and sat down. As John walked out the door, Klingen said, "See you in the morning, Lieutenant Grady."

John was at the JAG office at 0900 the next morning. Mr. Klingen warmly welcomed him and showed him to the desk that he had occupied yesterday. Laid out on the desktop was a new yellow pad of paper, several sharpened pencils, a stapler, a staple remover, a box of paper clips, a new copy of the *Uniform Code of Military Justice,* and the record of a general court-martial case.

"Lieutenant Grady, I'm trying to get you set up here, but Colonel James hasn't told me what your assignment will be. While you're waiting, you might want to browse through the *Uniform Code of Military Justice,* and I've pulled the file on one of our general courts-martial cases that you might want to look through. Captain Berisford tried that case; you might find it interesting. If I can do anything else for you, please let me know."

"Thank you, Mr. Klingen, I'll look through these things." John opened the court-martial file and began reading.

A short time later, a middle-aged JAG officer walked past John's desk on his way to the latrine. He nodded to Grady as he walked past. On his return, the JAG officer stopped and said, "I don't know if you remember me from yesterday—you met a lot of new people—but I'm Terry Berisford. Are you going to be with us permanently?" He chatted with John and asked him about his background and his army experiences. Captain Terence Berisford was of medium height; he was trim looking; he had light brown hair; he had a few freckles on his nose and cheeks; and he wore army-issue, metal-frame eyeglasses. Berisford was soft-spoken and was quite precise in his choice of words. Every statement out of his mouth was a grammatically-correct, properly-edited English sentence. He looked and spoke like a college professor. Berisford was a World War II veteran who had remained in the Army Reserves after that war and was called to active duty when the Korean War broke out—he was a RETREAD. In civilian life he was a trial lawyer in a large law firm in Chicago. While stationed at Fort Monmouth, he lived in West Long Branch in a rented house with his wife who worked in the Customer Relations Department of the New Jersey Bell Telephone Company in Asbury Park. He had no children.

"I'm reading the record of one of your cases right now," John said.

"Which one is that?" They talked briefly about the case, then Berisford excused himself. John was impressed with him. At noon, John put his office supplies away and returned to K Company.

Shortly after John arrived at the JAG office the next morning, Colonel James came out of his office with a piece of paper in his hand and walked to Grady's desk. "You're the new Post Claims Officer," James said as he dropped the paper onto John's desktop. He walked back into his office. John picked up the paper and read an order from Fort Monmouth Headquarters appointing First Lieutenant John H. Grady Post Claims Officer. "Is this General Lawrence's order transferring me to the JAG office?" John wondered. "Hold the phone one damn minute! I haven't been relieved from command of K Company," Grady exclaimed to himself. He went to Colonel James's office and knocked on the door. The colonel told him to enter.

"Sir, does this order transfer me from Troop Command to the JAG office?"

"That's what's intended, and that's the way I read it."

"Sir, I have command of a company in Troop Command, and I haven't been formally relieved of that command. On the books, I still have responsibility for that company and all government and company property of that company. If this order is interpreted as transferring me here, I'm left in limbo with regard to my company."

"That sounds like a Troop Command problem. Go talk to Troop Command about it."

John left the room without saluting. He was not going to get hung up on a meat hook on the transfer matter. If he had to, he would go to General Lawrence. "He got me into this pickle, and I think he's man enough to get me out of it," John said to himself. John told Mr. Klingen that he was going to regimental headquarters and then to Company K.

John went to regimental headquarters and to Captain Cole's desk. Cole was not there. As John looked around for Cole, Colonel Stump came out of his office. Grady saluted and said, "Colonel, may I speak with you a few minutes about this move to the JAG office?"

"What is it, Grady?"

"Sir, when I arrived there this morning, Colonel James gave me these orders appointing me Post Claims Officer." John handed the order to Stump who hurriedly scanned the paper and handed it back. "Sir, he says that these orders transfer me to the JAG office, but I've not been relieved of my command of K Company. As far as I can see, I'm still responsible for K Company and all its property until I get a formal release."

"Damn it, Grady, why did you allow yourself to get into this mess?"

"With due respect, Colonel, I didn't cut these orders, and I didn't volunteer to go to the JAG office. Sir, I assumed that when you sent me over there—"

"Damn it, Lieutenant, don't you know that you can't assume a damn thing in this man's army." Both were silent. Stump shifted his weight and looked uncomfortable. "Well … it's not your fault, Grady; you're caught in the middle. Let me see those orders again." John didn't understand the "caught in the middle" statement. Stump reread the order and had to concede that James had gotten ahead of him on this one. He had sent Grady over there just as a temporary holding measure. He never intended to lose his decorated Signal Officer. "Come into my office, Grady." Stump sat at his desk contemplating the matter, and Grady stood silently in front of his desk.

"Grady, I understand your concern about not being relieved from command of your company. I'll ask James to hold off on the execution of this order. I'll go to the 'old man' if he gives me any trouble. Meanwhile, I'll have to find a replacement for you. I'm short of company-grade officers, but I'll find someone in a couple of days. You stay here; I'll call James now."

Stump dialed a number on the telephone. "Colonel, this is Erwin Stump. Listen, I want to talk to you about Lieutenant Grady who I sent over there. You and I have put him between a rock and a hard place." Stump repeated the situation that Grady was in and said that if James would hold off on that claims officer order for a week, he, Stump, would have a replacement to take Grady's company and then Grady could be cleared from Troop Command. James liked the situation that Stump was asking him for a favor, so he graciously agreed.

***

Rebecca and John went to a dance at Gibbs Hall Saturday night. They arrived a little late, and on their way to a table they passed Terry Berisford and his wife sitting by themselves. Terry greeted John and extended him an invitation to join his wife and him. John accepted the invitation and introduced Rebecca. The two couples talked while they waited for John's order of two Cokes. The Berisford's were drinking scotch and water.

The two couples talked and danced throughout the evening and exchanged partners for one set of dances. Both Terry Berisford and his wife were quiet-mannered and refined, well-informed, and good conversationalists. Rebecca and John enjoyed their company.

At one point in the evening when the ladies excused themselves and went to the powder room, John asked Terry about Colonel James—what kind of person and what kind of officer he was.

Terry thought a moment, then said, "At times he's very sharp and competent, but at other times he does some odd things. Sometimes he tends to get excited. When he really wants something, he's like a bulldog until he gets it. I imagine that he's a good defendant's lawyer. He knows the army and military justice well, and overall I guess that I would have to say that he does an acceptable job—nothing exceptional, but acceptable. He doesn't seem to have many friends on the general's staff, and he doesn't seem to try to make friends. On the other hand, his wife is lovely and is an outgoing person. She's very active in the officers-wives organizations.

"James has been passed over once for promotion to full colonel. If he's passed over again, he'll have to retire. His promotion to full colonel will be considered again by the promotion board in six to nine months, I believe."

Rebecca and John wanted some time to themselves, so before the dance concluded they excused themselves and left. John drove to a lonely road not far from Gibbs Hall. Rebecca told him about her classes at Rutgers, and he told her the details of his move to the JAG office.

Grady spent Monday and Tuesday getting his affairs in order in K Company, and on Wednesday a captain recently rotated back to the States from Korea arrived to take over the company. At reveille formation on Friday morning, Grady said good-bye to the troops and wished them good luck. The transfer went smoothly, and by late Friday Grady was relieved of command. He personally thanked each of the noncommissioned officers for their hard work and their loyalty. He stopped at the 3rd Battalion office and thanked Major Stemple for his help and support.

***

Grady reported at the JAG office Monday morning at 0800. Mr. Klingen showed him the claims office and again introduced him to Sylvia Thompson, the secretary in that office. Sylvia was a single woman in her mid-fifties. She had faded blond hair that was turning gray, and she was tall and slender. She had worked in the claims office for twenty-one years and had seen many claims officers come and go. To her way of thinking, it was her claims office and the army officers assigned as claims officers were visitors passing through.

Sylvia asked Grady if he knew anything about claims work. He said "No." She told him that the *Federal Tort Claims Act* governed their claims work. Grady spent the remainder of the day studying the statute and the army regulations relating to it. The next morning he began working on a claim.

CHAPTER 10. (10 NOVEMBER 1952)

Colonel James came into Grady's office and handed him a paper. "Lieutenant, you've been appointed Assistant Trial Counsel on one of the prosecuting teams. You'll work with Lieutenant DuPre." John read the Fort Monmouth Headquarters order appointing DuPre and him a prosecuting team for general and special courts-martial. John immediately went to DuPre's office to find out what he would have to do as an assistant trial counsel.

First Lieutenant Paul DuPre was shorter than Grady and had dark hair. He seemed studious and business-like. John talked with him about his duties. They then asked about each other's background. DuPre was from Maine and had a decided down-East accent to his speech. He was married. He had graduated from Yale Law School and had practiced law in a firm in Portland, Maine, for a year and a half before joining the JAG Corps. He had been in the army over a year and didn't intend to make the army his career. Except for three months at the JAG School in Charlottesville, Virginia, he had been at Fort Monmouth trying cases.

DuPre told Grady that there was nothing for him to do until they were assigned a court-martial case, at which time he would brief Grady more thoroughly.

A week later, Paul DuPre came into Grady's office with a file under his arm. "John, we have a case to try that involves a second lieutenant who is accused of stealing a pistol from a gun shop in Long Branch. Here's the file, look it over, then come to my office and we'll discuss it."

John read through the file. The defendant was Second Lieutenant Carl Pullman, a recent graduate of Officers Candidate School (OCS). He had finished second in his OCS class and had compiled a fine record during his eleven months in the army. He was twenty-two years old and unmarried. Allegedly, he had gone to the gun shop to purchase a pistol in anticipation of receiving orders to Korea. (Some officers purchased their own pistols to use in place of the big, clumsy Colt .45 caliber army issue.) The allegation against him was that he looked at the gun, then asked the shop owner to see another one. The owner placed the pistol on the counter and went to the back room to get another one. While the owner was in the back room, the lieutenant hurried out of the shop with the pistol tucked into his inside jacket pocket. The owner ran out and apprehended him and called the police. The Long Branch police arrested the lieutenant and turned him over to military authorities. First Lieutenants Mike Turner and Lloyd Albert from the JAG office were the defense counsel and assistant defense counsel, respectively.

John went to DuPre's office with the file. DuPre said, "I've talked on the telephone with the gun shop owner to get his story and he has agreed to testify as a witness in the court-martial trial. I want you to serve this subpoena on him at his gun shop because I don't want him to get cold feet and not show up. This is a general court-martial, so wear your pinks and greens to the trial."

On the day of trial, two military policemen escorted Lieutenant Pullman from the post stockade to the courtroom. He was of average stature, and he looked lean and in good physical condition. His black hair was trimmed and neatly parted; his "green" blouse was pressed; his "pink" trousers had sharp creases running down the legs; and his brass was shining. He looked sharp. He sat between Mike Turner and Lloyd Albert at the defense counsels' table on one side of the courtroom. DuPre and Grady sat at the trial counsels' table on the other side of the room, and members of the court-martial board sat behind a long desktop on an elevated platform at one end of the courtroom. Chairs for spectators were at the opposite end of the room. The board members used a small room located behind their courtroom seats to deliberate on guilt or innocence and on the punishment to be given a guilty defendant.

A general court-martial trial had a law officer who acted somewhat as a judge in that he instructed the board and ruled on matters of law. For that trial, Captain Roy Milliken from First Army JAG sat as law officer. The president of the court-martial board was a lieutenant colonel, and the remainder of the board was composed of two majors, three captains, and three first lieutenants. All board members were Fort Monmouth officers.

Precisely at the appointed time, Grady arose from his chair and went to the board and handed each member a typed sheet of paper that set forth the charges and specifications against Lieutenant Pullman. John returned to his seat, the law officer made a statement, and then Paul DuPre began his opening statement. After defense counsel Mike Turner completed his opening statement, DuPre called the gun shop owner to the witness stand. The owner told his story to the board, and he identified Lieutenant Pullman as the man who took the gun out of his shop. Paul asked the gun shop owner if he had given Lieutenant Pullman permission to take the gun out of the shop.

The owner replied, "No. It's my policy that I don't allow customers to take guns out of my shop. Once in a great while, I'll allow someone I know well to take a gun to test fire it. But when I do that I make him sign a form that says he's borrowing it to test it and that he'll return it in seventy-two hours cleaned and in proper working order.

Paul asked the owner if Lieutenant Pullman had signed such a form.

"No, because I didn't lend the pistol to him; I had never seen him before in my life. I would never allow a stranger to take a weapon out of my shop. He skipped out with it while I was in my back room."

Mike Turner then took the floor and cross-examined the shop owner. The cross-examination was fruitless.

DuPre rested his case, and Turner called Lieutenant Pullman to the witness stand. Pullman testified, "I told the store owner that I wanted to take the pistol back to Fort Monmouth to test fire it on the pistol range to see if I liked it. He said that it was all right with him."

Paul DuPre cross-examined Pullman. "Lieutenant Pullman, do you have a receipt, an authorization form, or anything in writing giving you permission to take that pistol off the premises of the gun shop?"

"No sir. He said I didn't need anything."

Grady didn't believe Pullman. He couldn't help but compare Pullman with Lieutenant Cavendish, the platoon leader on the outpost south of Seoul. Cavendish also was a second lieutenant and an OCS graduate. Cavendish had displayed leadership, responsibility, and bravery in commanding his platoon in defense of the outpost against attacks by North Korean troops. In Grady's opinion, Pullman was the antithesis of Cavendish.

DuPre and Turner delivered their closing statements to the board, Turner emphasizing Pullman's fine record prior to that incident. The law officer Captain Milliken gave his instructions to the board, and the board retired to the room behind them to deliberate. John congratulated Paul for a job well done.

The board returned in twenty minutes, and everyone in the courtroom rose to his feet. The defense counsels and the defendant stood before the board. The president of the board announced that the board had found Lieutenant Pullman guilty of all charges and specifications.

The law officer announced that the board now would consider the punishment of Lieutenant Pullman. Paul DuPre leaned over to Grady and whispered, "We won't say anything here. The board already looks mad." DuPre announced to the board that he had no statement to make.

Lieutenant Turner stood before the board and spoke of all the matters that he could think of in way of mitigation and extenuation, such as Pullman's youth, his excellent record in OCS, his love of the army, his desire to make the army his career, this was his first time in trouble, etc. The board retired to the back room and deliberated on the punishment. It returned in ten minutes and sentenced Lieutenant Pullman to a dishonorable discharge, forfeiture of all pay and allowances, and confinement to a penitentiary at hard labor for six years. Pullman showed no emotion when the sentence was announced. Two MPs escorted him back to the post stockade.

DuPre and Grady thanked the gun shop owner for his cooperation and assured him that he had contributed to the administration of military justice at Fort Monmouth. The shop owner was shaken by the six-years prison sentence that the board had handed out. He said that a civilian court might not have given Pullman six years since he was so young and he hadn't actually gotten away with the gun.

DuPre replied, "He was an officer. The army doesn't like thieves in its officer ranks."

***

Several weeks later, Colonel James walked into John's office with a handful of papers and said, "Lieutenant Grady, a young officer has been caught in a motel with a woman not his wife, and the general wants him to resign his commission for the good of the service. You prepare a suitable resignation letter for the lieutenant to sign."

John read through the papers and learned that the lieutenant was a ROTC graduate from Arkansas and a student in the Basic Officers Course. He and the woman had checked into a motel on Highway 35 between Eatontown and Asbury Park. The owner of the motel was an elderly woman who frequently wrote to General Lawrence about the conduct of his troops. She had written in prior correspondence that the general was training soldiers at Fort Monmouth, but his soldiers were bringing women to her motel to put them through their basic training and she was getting tired of it.

The night that the lieutenant checked into the motel with the woman, the owner called Fort Monmouth and complained. The military police went to the motel and confronted the lieutenant. The general saw the MP report on the incident and decided that he had to do something to set an example.

John wrote out several drafts of a resignation letter, then settled on one and had Sylvia type it. He took it to Colonel James for his approval. James said, "Good, take this down to General Lawrence's office tomorrow morning at 1000. The general will have the lieutenant there at that time."

Grady arrived at the general's office the next morning and showed the letter to the general. "Good, wait here," the general said. Grady stood to the side of the general's desk. The accused lieutenant arrived at the aide's office and was ushered into the general's office. He saluted and announced that he was reporting as ordered. The general looked at him and said, "Lieutenant, I'm not naïve enough to believe that you're the only officer in my command who's shacking up, but you happen to be the unlucky son of a bitch who got caught. Now, you sign this letter resigning your commission or I'll have to bring court-martial proceedings against you for conduct unbecoming an officer and for bringing disgrace upon the army." Lawrence pushed the resignation letter across his desk and handed the lieutenant the pen from his desktop pen holder.

Without saying a word, the lieutenant stepped forward and signed the letter. The general said, "All right, you're dismissed." The lieutenant left the room.

The general said, "Grady, you stay here. Sit down there." The general asked him how things were going for him in the JAG office.

"Good, General. I'm finding things interesting and different from everything else I've done in the army."

"Grady, what does the JAG office think about my safe driving campaign?"

"General, I haven't heard comment about it in the JAG office. There was general grousing on the post about that four-day driving ban some time ago, but that's all I've heard."

"Has Colonel James said anything to you officers about my authority to impose the driving restriction?"

John wasn't sure what the general was fishing for. "No sir, I haven't heard the colonel say anything about it."

"Good. That will be all, Grady."

John enjoyed working in the JAG office. He was learning new things, the people were friendly, and the atmosphere was relatively informal. Everyone except Colonel James was called by his first name. Except for the colonel, Captain Terry Berisford, and Warrant Officer Clarence Klingen, the other JAG officers were about John's age and most were recently married.

Another Signal Corps officer had recently reported for duty in the JAG office. He was Second Lieutenant Wilbur Mullins, a recent graduate from the Signal Corps Basic Officers Course. Mullins was just about as tall as Grady, had broad shoulders, a thick chest, and long arms. He had coal-black hair and a fair complexion. Mullins was a member of the Idaho bar and went by the name "Willie." Willie's family owned a large potato farm in Idaho, and Willie tried to play the role of a poor, dumb farm boy. In truth, his family was worth considerable money, and Willie had been an excellent student and had been on the law review staff in law school. He was "dumb like a fox." Willie was assistant defense counsel on a defense team that John had not opposed as yet.

Thanksgiving was coming up and Rebecca was going to West Palm Beach with her parents. Grady spent most of Thanksgiving weekend on post. He spent some time with Willie Mullins and found him to be quite enjoyable. Willie had a good sense of humor and was intelligent and thoughtful. John invited him to eat Thanksgiving Dinner with him in the mess hall, and they went to Asbury Park to a movie on Friday night. John caught up on his reading during the weekend. Rebecca was on his mind much of the time.

***

Grady's thoughts also went back to Thanksgiving two years ago when he was freezing his butt off up at the Manchurian border in North Korea. He shivered just thinking about it.

As for the present, John was of the opinion that the attitude in this country was such that the war in Korea seemed not to be in the forefront of the thinking of most people unless a family member was serving in the military over there. John couldn't help but contrast that situation with the way it was in World War II when the war was foremost in the minds of just about everyone.

In the fighting in Korea, the opposing armies were standing toe to toe slugging at each other. Neither side made great territorial gains, but casualties were high in bitter fighting on hills such as Old Baldy, Bunker Hill, Sniper Ridge, T-Bone Hill, and Pork Chop Hill. Authorities in Washington told Eighth Army that it could not expect reinforcements with which to launch a major offensive and that its mission was to inflict the maximum enemy casualties at a minimum cost to its own forces and without jeopardizing its battlefield position. In plain English, Washington had settled on a bloody stalemate.

The cease-fire negotiations were going nowhere.

CHAPTER 11. (1 DECEMBER 1952)

On 1 December 1952, Fort Monmouth headquarters distributed copies of a new Post Regulation No. 219 to all commands at Fort Monmouth. The new regulation would go into effect on 1 January 1953. It stated, in effect, that all military personnel assigned to Fort Monmouth would operate their private motor vehicles in a safe and prudent manner and would have their vehicles under control at all times so as not to cause injury to persons or damage to property. Violation of the post regulation would subject the offender to disciplinary action under Article 92 of the *Uniform Code of Military Justice*. The regulation went on to say that a military person whose vehicle was involved in an accident that caused injury to a person or damage to property was required to immediately report the accident to the Fort Monmouth Provost Marshal.

Grady read the regulation, then read Article 92 in his copy of the *Uniform Code of Military Justice*. The applicable part of Article 92 read as follows:

Article 92. Failure to Obey Order or Regulation
Any person subject to this chapter who—
(1) violates or fails to obey any lawful order or regulation;
(2) ....
(3) ....
shall be punished as a court-martial may direct.

John reread Post Regulation 219. It didn't expressly state that an auto accident must occur on-post for the regulation to apply, nor did it say that the military person must be on duty at the time of the accident. If that were so, it meant that an accident could occur at any time and at any place on the face of the earth and the military person involved would have to report it to the provost marshal and possibly subject himself to court-martial. John wondered about that. He walked back to Captain Terry Berisford's office.

"Terry, have you seen the new Post Regulation 219 about auto accidents?" Terry said that he had seen it. "As I read it," John continued, "an automobile accident could occur at any place in the world and at any time and the military person would be subject to possible court-martial. Do you read it that broadly?"

"Yes, John, it looks wide open to me."

"Did the general get a legal opinion from this office before that regulation was issued?"

"I haven't heard that such a request has been in the office, and I haven't seen anyone working on that issue. I've seen nothing in the Reading File on it."

"What do you think, Terry, will the general try to extend its enforcement to accidents off-post on off-duty time?"

"I wouldn't be surprised."

"Well, I'm surprised that he would issue such a regulation without seeking advice from Colonel James."

"James won't do anything to interfere," Terry said.

"Why not?"

"This automobile accident business is Lawrence's pet project—he's fanatical about it. Colonel James wants a good efficiency report from the general in hopes that he'll be promoted to full colonel and won't have to retire, so he isn't going to do anything to get in the general's way and make him angry. The general knows that and will push James to the wall."

"Thanks Terry, I appreciate your input." John now understood things better. General Lawrence wanted all the legal matters in the JAG office because he knew that Colonel James would not likely interfere with anything that he, the general, wanted to do. Grady also understood why the general wanted him in the JAG office. The general said that he didn't want a spy in the JAG office, but he really did. He certainly was interested to learn from Grady if Colonel James had said anything to the JAG officers about his safe driving campaign. At the very least, if a problem arose for the general he wanted Grady to tell him. John thought that he now understood the general well enough to be sure of that.

"What a fine pickle this is," John said to himself. "Not only was I a pawn in the feud between Colonel Stump and Colonel James, but now the general wants me to be his stool pigeon in the JAG office to cover his butt on his eccentric schemes." Grady resolved to be his own man on both matters.

The Hazlets were back home in New Jersey the first week of December. Rebecca called John late Thursday night saying that she was home. Grady told her that he had missed her. They made arrangements to go to the post movie Friday night and then to Scrivner Hall.

Grady hurriedly ate his dinner Friday evening, showered, dressed, and rushed to the Hazlet's home. The night was cold and crisp. Rebecca met him at the door and they eagerly embraced and kissed. They drove to the post theater and stood in a rather long line that extended across the front of the building. They had much to tell each other and were engaged in conversation. Rebecca began turning and trying to get behind John. He was wearing civilian clothes, so there was no indication of his rank. He noticed that a number of the GIs in line were looking at Rebecca.

She said, "John, I'm uncomfortable here, let's leave." He agreed, and they walked toward his car. He smiled at her, took her hand and said, "Men wouldn't stare at you if you weren't so good looking."

She blushed. "John, you've never said that to me before."

"I didn't because it's not important. That's not why I think so much of you. I'm attracted to you because you're kind, unselfish, loyal, morally and intellectually honest, intelligent, an exceptionally good conversationalist—and most important of all—you're the only girl I know who'll go out with me." He grinned and put his arm around her waist. She gave him a shove with her shoulder.

They went into the club and John hung their overcoats in the cloak room. Rebecca went to the ladies room to comb her hair, and when she returned they went to one of the tables in the back of the lounge. There was no waiter service, so John went to the bar and ordered two Cokes and a basket of snacks. They talked, sipped their drinks, and nibbled on the snacks. They were delighted to be together again. They finished their drinks and snacks, and John went to the bar to get refills. As he left the bar with his refills on a serving tray, he saw General Lawrence and his aide, both in civilian clothes, leaving one of the meeting rooms. As they approached, John said, "Good evening, General."

"Hello, Grady. What do you have there?"

"A couple of drinks and snacks, sir."

"Who do you have with you?" the general asked as he looked around the room. "Are you with that attractive blond you had at your award ceremony?

"Yes sir, Miss Hazlet is with me. Do you care to join us?" John didn't know if he were out of order in inviting the general; he did it just to try to be polite.

"Why, yes, I could use a nightcap."

"I'll see you Monday morning," the general said to his aide. John and the general walked to the table.

"Rebecca, you remember meeting General Lawrence at the award ceremony."

"Good evening, General, it's nice to see you again."

The two men sat down. The general looked around and said, "How does a fellow get a drink around here?"

"General, I'll get one for you at the bar. What will you have?"

"I'll have a scotch and water." John departed for the bar, and when he returned to the table with the general's drink, Rebecca and the general were having a good laugh about something.

"General, what brings you to the club tonight?" Grady asked.

"The Board of Governors of the Officers Mess is having a meeting tonight about trying to save its liquor store, and they invited me over to see if I would help them lobby to keep it. The private liquor store owners in this area have written to the local congressman and to the Secretary of the Army complaining that the Officers Mess liquor store is unfairly competing with them, and they asked that the Officers Mess liquor store be shut down. The board wants me to contact the secretary and the congressman and ask them to back off. Before we had our own liquor store we had to go over to the officers club at the Earl Naval Ammunition Depot to get a decent price. Why the navy can have a liquor store and we can't, I don't understand." The general was very cordial and kept the conversation moving. He asked Rebecca what she was doing and about her family. They talked a while, then Rebecca excused herself to go powder her nose. John didn't want to be left alone with Lawrence.

"Grady, what do you think about the new Post Regulation 219 on safe driving?"

"General, on its face the regulation reads as though it applies to off-post driving during off-duty hours as well as on-post driving. Do you intend it to cover both?"

"Of course I do. The men are in the army off-post as well as on-post, aren't they. My responsibility for them doesn't end when they drive out the gate. What do the JAG officers think about it?"

"Some were surprised at its breadth. Do you have a precedent for that broad of a coverage?"

The general snapped right back at John, "Of course I have a precedent—it's called command responsibility. You know about command responsibility don't you Grady? The Army gave you a medal for it. What does Colonel James have to say about it?"

"I haven't heard the colonel comment on it, sir."

Rebecca returned to the table and the general turned on his charm and continued the conversation without again mentioning the regulation. He finished his drink, said that it was nice to have seen them both again, and left the club.

Grady knew that the general had obtained the information that he was looking for, but John believed that he had not been a stool pigeon.

✿✿✿

Rebecca and John finished their Cokes and left the club. John drove through the Main Gate, through Little Silver, along River Road in Red Bank, onto Highway 35, and turned off onto the county road leading to the Hazlet estate. He pulled through the Hazlet's front gate and turned off the car engine. John slowly turned to her and said, "I'm about to say something that may make a fool of me."

"What do you mean?"

"Rebecca Hazlet, I'm so head-over-heels in love with you I don't know if I'm coming or going. I can't get to sleep at night because I can't get you off my mind. I walk around the post daydreaming about you and wake up somewhere and don't know how I got there. I walk out of the mess hall and have no idea what I ate because I was thinking about you all the time I was eating. I can't wait to be with you, and I don't want to leave you when I'm with you."

Rebecca looked at him with wonderment. Her eyes became teary. "Oh John, I have waited so long to hear you say that. I've been in love with you for months and months, and I was afraid you would never say it." They embraced and joined in a warm, passionate kiss.

"Beck, you had to know I love you."

"I hoped, but I needed to hear you say it. Why did you say that you might make a fool of yourself?"

"I was afraid that I would declare my love for you, but then you would tell me that you don't feel that way. I can't believe that someone as wonderful as you can be in love with me."

"Nonsense. John, you'll never know what a wonderful moment this is for me. You've been my hero for a long time, and I love you with a love I've never known before. For you to tell me that you love me is my dream come true."

***

John went alone to Christmas church services on post, and had Christmas dinner with Willie Mullins in the officers mess. He met Rebecca at the Hazlet home at 1500. They walked around the property and exchanged small gifts. They had agreed not to exceed fifteen dollars for the cost of the gift.

"John, I don't like us having to stay outside when you visit me at home. It's time for me to get an apartment; we're missing the opportunity to spend some precious time together."

"Beck, it's not going to do your reputation any good for me to be seeing you in your apartment, and I don't want to have to face the temptation of being alone with you in an apartment. I don't think that's the solution to our problem. Be patient; this too shall pass."

They went to a New Year's Eve party at Gibbs Hall. There were many young officers there with their wives or dates. John knew a number of the officers from Troop Command, and a couple of the JAG officers were there. The event was well planned, and Rebecca and John mixed with the group and enjoyed themselves thoroughly.

***

In the middle of the second week of the new year, Paul DuPre came into John's office with a new file and said, "John, we have a general court-martial case for desertion. Look it over, then we'll talk about it."

The defendant was Private Lloyd Jacobson from Camden, New Jersey. Jacobson was absent from the army for nine and one-half months and was apprehended by the FBI and returned to Fort Monmouth. Jacobson had a full-time civilian job in Camden when the FBI arrested him. Private Jacobson was twenty-one years old and had been in the army a little over a year before he left. He had not served overseas. He was a high school graduate, was married, and had no children. Before he left, Jacobson had been a member of the 3901 Service Company, Signal Corps Center and Fort Monmouth.

John went into DuPre's office and discussed the case with him. Paul said, "It looks like a straightforward desertion case to me. He left the army, was gone nine and one-half months, had a job on the outside, and there's nothing so far to indicate that he ever intended to return to the army. John, I'd like for you to go down to the 3901st and talk with Captain Hardy, the company commander, to see what he might know about the man and his situation. Someone said that Jacobson might have been in trouble with the civil authorities. See if you can find out anything about that. By the way, the defense counsel for this case will be Bob Plusser. Willie Mullins will assist him." John telephoned Captain Hardy and made an appointment to be at his office at 1400.

Personnel on the post commonly called the 3901 Service Company the "Thirty-nine-Oh-First." The 3901st was not a Signal outfit and was not part of Troop Command. It was made up of truck drivers, many types of unskilled laborers, and men who did menial work on the post. Misfits gravitated to the 3901st. Most men in the company were privates or privates first class, despite the fact that they had been in the army for several years—some, for many years. The 3901st had more courts-martial than any other unit on the post. JAG officers called it the "Thirty-nine-Oh-Worst."

John arrived at the 3901st and was shown into the captain's office. He had never met Captain Hardy, although he had heard about him and had seen him on the post. Captain Roger Hardy was tall and husky. His blond hair was cut in a crew haircut, and he had bushy blond eyebrows. He was an Infantry officer who had fought in World War II with the 1st Infantry Division in North Africa, Sicily, the Normandy landing, France, and Germany. He was of the opinion that if you have not served in the 1st Infantry Division you have never really soldiered. He wore the 1st Infantry Division patch, the Big Red One, on the shoulder of his right sleeve.

John looked at the captain and smartly saluted and said, "Lieutenant Grady reporting to Captain Hardy for the requested meeting, sir." Admittedly, Grady was "putting on the dog" to show Hardy that you don't really have to serve in the 1st Infantry Division to know how to soldier. Hardy was not expecting a spit-and-polish entry from someone in the JAG office (those Legal Eagles aren't real soldiers, are they?), and when he saw Grady's ribbons and decorations on his blouse, his face lit up—he was impressed with the whole show. He smiled and offered Grady a chair.

John explained that he wanted to know what kind of soldier Jacobson had been; did Hardy know of any reason why Jacobson left the army; any problems he had before he left; did Hardy know anything about his wife, his family, or his home life in Camden, N.J.

Hardy replied, "The kid was kind of an intense kid and was uptight much of the time. His wife was sick and lost a baby prematurely, and she never seemed to be well after that. I gave him more weekend passes than he was entitled to so he could be with her. She went to the hospital one time and I gave him a ten-day leave to be with her. I did about all I could for him without getting him, and me, in trouble because of all his absences. He worked in the motor pool and he was always asking them for time off. He left one weekend and never came back."

John asked Hardy if he knew anything about Jacobson's civilian life or about him being in trouble with the civil authorities.

"No, I don't know anything about that."

"Do you have any information that would indicate that he intended to come back to duty? Did he ever contact you or anyone in the company while he was absent?"

"No."

"Thank you Captain, it was nice to meet you. We'll be in contact with you again before the trial." Grady stood up, saluted, and left.

A couple of days later, Colonel James and Paul DuPre came into the claims office and told John that the assistant defense counsel Willie Mullins was going over to Camden, N. J., to a police precinct station to talk with a Camden Police Department detective about Lloyd Jacobson's past history. James wanted someone from the trial counsel team to be there, and John was elected.

"What do you want me to do over there?" Grady asked DuPre.

"Just listen to know what they find out. I want to know as much as they do. Don't be afraid to ask questions."

The next morning at 0730, an olive-drab Plymouth sedan from the motor pool was at the JAG office. Willie and John slid into the back seat, and Willie handed the driver a slip of paper with the Camden precinct station address on it. The driver found the precinct station, and the two lieutenants stepped out of the car and approached the station house.

The building was a three-story brick structure that had been built at the end of the last century. The exterior of the building and the windows were drab and dirty with a half-century of accumulated smoke and soot. Grady opened one of the two large wooden front doors and the two men walked into a very large room that was poorly lighted by the feeble rays of sunlight that managed to get through the dirty windows. The ceiling was at least twenty feet high and was formed of embossed metal sheets which also looked as though they had not been cleaned since installed. The wooden floor was empty except for a desk sitting on a raised platform located fifteen feet to the left of the front door. A bald-headed police sergeant behind the desk wore a dark-blue shirt with epaulets on the shoulders and a shiny badge on his chest. On the far side of the room there were several closed doors about ten feet high with frosted glass in the upper half. A name of a police officer or detective was painted on the opaque glass of each door.

When the two army lieutenants came into the room, the desk sergeant straightened up in his chair, smiled, and said, "We don't get army officers walking in here every day; what can I do for you gentlemen?"

The two officers walked over to the sergeant's desk and Willie said, "Hello, sergeant, we're looking for Detective Lieutenant Ronald Lance."

Continuing his smile, the desk sergeant said, "Lieutenant Lance is not here right now, but I expect him any time. If you care to wait, you can have a seat in those chairs on the side there." Between the front door and the desk sergeant's desk was a low railing with a half dozen chairs on the near side of the railing. John and Willie went over and sat. Ten minutes later the front door burst open and a thin, wiry man with scraggly, faded blond hair, and wearing an unbuttoned rumpled trench coat and rumpled civilian suit walked briskly across the room. He had a weathered face and looked to be forty-five or fifty years old.

The desk sergeant called out, "Lieutenant Lance, these two gentlemen are here to see you."

The man stopped, turned sideways and looked at the two army men. "Yeah," he uttered arrogantly, "what do you want?"

"Sir, I'm Lieutenant Mullins from Fort Monmouth and this is Lieutenant Grady. We'd like to talk to you about Private Lloyd Jacobson who comes from this neighborhood. Do you know him?"

Lance looked back and forth at the two of them, then said, "Yeah, I know the son of a bitch. Come to my office." He went to one of the office doors that had his name painted on it, took out a set of keys, selected one, and unlocked the door and walked in. Without speaking, he motioned to two chairs in front of a desk. The army men sat down. Lance sat down in a swivel chair behind the desk, took a cigarette from his shirt pocket and lit it with a wooden match that he lit with his thumbnail, rocked back and forth a couple of times as he looked at the two army men, then said, "So, what's the son of a bitch done now, raped his mother?"

"You know Private Jacobson?" Willie repeated.

"Yeah, I know the ____ ____!"

"Has he been in trouble with the police?"

"The ____ ____ has been in trouble half his life." Willie asked Lance several more questions, and in answering them it seemed that every other word out of Lance's mouth was a foul cuss word. To Grady, it seemed that Lance was trying to impress Willie and him with the fact that he, Lance, lived in a tough world. John knew all about living in a tough world and wasn't impressed.

The conversation continued and Lance began to get the impression that these guys knew their business. He stopped the foul language and started to respond more directly to their questions. Lance told them, "I never actually arrested Jacobson for a crime. When he was a teenager he ran around with a couple of hoods who I did arrest and who were convicted of crimes and sent to prison, but I was never able to get the evidence I needed against Jacobson. And believe me, I tried." Lance continued, "He seemed to have settled down since he married, but I still don't trust the son of a bitch, and I still kept a watch on him."

Lance confirmed that Jacobson's wife was ill much of the time, and he added that a doctor had diagnosed cancer in his widowed mother. Jacobson was the sole support for them both. Lance said that he didn't know that Jacobson was absent without leave from the army. John found that hard to believe since Lance made it his business to know almost everything else about Jacobson. After several more questions from both of them, Willie and Grady thanked Detective Lance for his help and left his office. They nodded to the desk sergeant and thanked him as they walked to the front door. The experience with detective Lance left a "bad taste" in John's mouth.

John made notes about the interview with Detective Lance on the drive back to the post and briefed Paul DuPre when he returned. Then he said, "Paul, this kid has major problems in his life and court-martialing him is not going to take care of his sick wife and mother. If these conditions had existed before he was drafted, he might have qualified for a hardship deferment. Can't the army do something for this kid other than send him to prison?

DuPre thought for a moment, then said, "Let's go talk to Colonel James. You know the facts, you tell him." The two of them went into the colonel's office, and John gave the colonel the factual background. He repeated the statement that if the conditions had existed before Jacobson was drafted, etc. He asked the colonel if they couldn't do something other than court-martial Jacobson.

The colonel didn't answer right away. He worked his lips several times, then he said, "General Lawrence is the convening authority, I'll talk to him about it."

The next day before lunch, Colonel James called DuPre and Grady to his office and said, "I talked to the general this morning about Private Jacobson and told him what Lieutenant Grady reported to me about Jacobson's present situation. When I asked the general if we might consider some alternative course of action, he told me , 'Absolutely not. Other soldiers are performing their duty and are getting shot at and getting killed in Korea. Jacobson had a duty to perform and he ran away from it. I'll never excuse that conduct.'"

Before they left the colonel's office, the colonel said, "Lieutenant Grady, you have all the facts in this case, and it seems like it won't be difficult, so you try it."

John said, "Colonel, I've had just two years of law school, and I'm not a member of the bar. This is a general court-martial."

"That's all right, Lieutenant DuPre will be there with you if you need help. You go ahead and try the case."

John wasn't sure he knew how to interpret the colonel's remarks. Did the colonel have confidence that he could do the job or was he hoping that John would botch the job so that Jacobson wouldn't be convicted of desertion?

John studied everything he could about the crime of desertion. He read all the desertion cases he could find in the military justice reports and journals, and he felt confident that he knew what he was doing. He prepared a set of instructions to the court-martial board which he would give to the law officer, and he wrote out a list of questions to ask Jacobson should defense counsel Bob Plusser put him on the witness stand.

On the day of the trial, two MPs escorted Private Jacobson into the courtroom. He was a good looking fellow with slightly curly sandy hair and a ruddy complexion. He had broad shoulders and a thick chest, and he looked strong and muscular.

The MPs left the courtroom, the members of the court-martial board took their seats, and the trial began. The Law Officer made his opening statement to the board, as did John and Bob Plusser. John then introduced Morning Reports from the 3901 Service Company listing Private Jacobson absent without authority. Grady called Captain Hardy to the stand and interrogated him about Jacobson's absence, about whether he had given Jacobson permission to be absent, about how long the absence had lasted, etc. He asked Hardy if Jacobson had contacted anyone in the 3901st during his absence to indicate that he intended to return to duty. Captain Hardy replied in the negative. He asked him if anything had occurred during the absence that might indicate that Jacobson intended to return to duty. Again, Hardy replied in the negative.

Grady then introduced into evidence an affidavit from Private Jacobson's former civilian employer stating that Jacobson had been a full-time employee during most of the period that Jacobson was absent from duty. (Plusser and Grady had a conference telephone conversation with the employer before the trial. Plusser agreed to the use of the affidavit rather than having to subpoena the employer to appear in person at the trial.) John did everything that he could to cover all elements of the crime. He rested his case.

Plusser had not told the trial counsels whether or not he was going to put Jacobson on the stand to testify, and John was anxious to see what he would do. Plusser did call Jacobson to the stand and asked him a number of what John thought were innocuous questions. Plusser then announced that he had no further questions. John was surprised because Plusser hadn't solicited testimony about Jacobson's wife and mother. Grady didn't see how Jacobson's testimony helped his case. And, by Plusser calling Jacobson to testify he had opened Jacobson to cross-examination by trial counsel.

Grady took the floor and asked Jacobson several questions about him leaving the army and about him getting a full-time job while he was away.

Jacobson was truthful in his answers even though they put him in an unfavorable light. John then asked the crucial question, "Private Jacobson, did you intend to return to the army?" Without hesitation Jacobson replied, "No sir." John believed that Jacobson's truthful answer assured his conviction for desertion. He turned to the board and told them that he had no further questions.

Trial and defense counsels made their summaries, and the law officer instructed the board. The board retired to the back room to deliberate and soon returned with a guilty verdict. John and Paul had talked while the board was out and had decided that they would not argue for a stiff sentence. John told the board, in effect, that the punishment was up to them, considering the circumstances of the case. He figured that Plusser would bring out the "circumstances of the case."

Plusser addressed the board and rambled rather ineffectively. Grady expected him to bring before the board the matters of Jacobson's ill wife and cancerous mother in an effort to show extenuating and mitigating circumstances, thereby trying to get a light sentence for his client. Plusser didn't bring Jacobson back to the stand to testify on those matters, and didn't even mention them! At the very least, Plusser could have obtained an affidavit from the wife's doctor attesting to her illness and an affidavit from the mother's doctor attesting to her cancer.

The board brought back a sentence of a dishonorable discharge, forfeiture of all pay and allowances, and five years in prison at hard labor. Jacobson was shocked at the sentence.

Bob Plusser was the wrong guy in the wrong place to be defending peoples' freedoms. He had graduated from a top-rated law school with high marks, and he had been awarded the Order of the Coif. Plusser thought that he was brighter than the other lawyers, which might have been true, but he somehow had the idea that the practice of law was easy for the gifted. He didn't understand that practicing law the right way was hard work.

Until recently, the MPs who brought a defendant from the stockade to the courtroom for trial sat in the back of the courtroom until the trial was over, then escorted a convicted defendant back to the stockade. The defense counsels complained to Colonel James that the presence of MPs in the courtroom during a trial was prejudicial to the rights of a defendant because it might cause the board members to think that everyone expected the defendant to be found guilty and the MPs were there to take him off to the stockade. James agreed and said that no MPs were permitted in or near the courtroom unless they were witnesses. As a result of that ruling, and since there was no telephone in the courtroom, the practice was established that the assistant trial counsel was responsible to take a convicted defendant to regimental headquarters where he would telephone the provost marshal and tell him to send the MPs to escort the prisoner to the stockade.

Accordingly, after Jacobson's sentencing, Grady opened the drawer in the trial counsel's table and brought out the loaded and holstered Colt .45 pistol and pistol belt that he had placed there before the trial. He buckled the pistol belt around his green coat and went over to Lloyd Jacobson. "Private Jacobson, you and I will walk over to Troop Command headquarters where I will call the provost marshal who will send MPs to take you back to the stockade. I'll walk behind you all the way over there. Let's move out now, and we'll walk at a normal pace."

The two of them left the courtroom and began walking toward Troop Command headquarters four blocks away. The street that they were walking on passed by the end of the parking lot of the BOQ area where John formerly lived. There were many parked cars in the lot. Grady was about a step and a half behind Jacobson as they entered the area at the end of the parking lot. All of a sudden, John had a strange feeling and a chill went through his body. He was certain that Jacobson was going to make a dash for freedom by running through the parked cars. Instinctively, John flipped open the flap on the pistol holster and decided that if Jacobson made a break for it he would have to shoot him. He would shoot for his legs. John immediately took several quick steps forward and came up to Jacobson's right shoulder—the shoulder nearest the parking lot. Jacobson's head snapped over to his right, and when he saw Grady within easy reach of him—instantly—Jacobson's shoulders and chest sagged and the tenseness went out of his body. The chill left Grady's body. They walked the remainder of the way to regimental headquarters without incident. Grady made his phone call, and the MPs came and took Jacobson back to the stockade.

John and Paul discussed the case later that afternoon and lamented the fact that Jacobson didn't get a proper representation on the sentencing matter.

As John entered the JAG office a few minutes before 0800 the next morning, Paul DuPre greeted him with, "Did you hear about Lloyd Jacobson?"

'No, what about him?"

"Lloyd Jacobson tried to escape from the stockade early yesterday evening. He went on K.P. duty in the stockade mess hall when he returned from the trial, and while everyone else was busy serving the evening meal to the stockade prisoners, he slipped out the back door of the mess hall, climbed over the nearby fence, and ran into the marsh and woods. A guard in the mess hall discovered that he was missing and sounded the alarm. The entire military police detachment turned out and went into the marsh and woods after him. They caught him in about forty minutes and brought him back to the stockade. He's in maximum security now."

John was not surprised. He was absolutely certain that Jacobson had intended to try to escape yesterday on their walk from the courtroom to regimental headquarters. John said to DuPre, "The poor guy is really messed up; he could have been killed in that escape attempt."

In the next couple of weeks, DuPre and Grady tried several soldiers who had car accidents in violation of Post Regulation 219. Of course, they were convicted. The convictions were not gratifying experiences for DuPre or Grady.

CHAPTER 12. (WINTER 1953)

At mid-morning on one crisp winter day, Grady received a call from the provost marshal's office saying that a government vehicle from Coles Signal Corps Engineering Laboratory had an accident with a civilian vehicle on Tinton Avenue several miles west of Gibbs Hall. The caller said that two MPs were leaving to investigate the accident, and since it may involve a claim against the government, did the lieutenant want to go along? Grady replied affirmatively.

They arrived at the accident scene which was on a curve in the highway in a rural area, and sure enough, a government vehicle was involved—it was a twenty-five ton army battle tank! A civilian automobile with its front end crushed flat was sitting in the middle of the highway close to the tank. A Signal Corps photographer who also came with the MPs began taking pictures.

John and the MPs went over to a state police vehicle where two New Jersey state troopers were talking with the male driver of the crushed civilian car and his young son, both of whom were sitting in the back seat of the police vehicle. They both seemed shaken up, but there were no visible signs of injury to either one. The state troopers told the man that an ambulance was on the way and would take him and his son to Riverview Hospital in Red Bank for examination.

One of the troopers asked the man, "Are you sure you're all right, sir? Do you need any first aid now?

"I don't think so," the man replied.

Three civilians with somber faces were standing beside the tank. John assumed that they were laboratory employees, so he walked over to them and introduced himself. Two men were electronic engineers who worked at Coles Signal Corps Engineering Laboratory, and the other one was the civilian tank driver who also worked at Coles. One of the responsibilities of Coles Signal Corps Engineering Laboratory was to develop radio equipment for the army. The engineers told John that they had installed an experimental radio in the tank and then drove the tank west on the highway to see how far they could go and still have good communication with a base radio back at the laboratory. They said that they were returning to the laboratory when the accident occurred.

The tank driver told John that the tank was moving eastwardly and entering the curve when two cars traveling westerly approached the curve. Suddenly, the trailing vehicle that was traveling westerly pulled out and tried to pass the other car in the middle of the curve despite the fact that two solid white lines ran along the middle of the highway. The passing car got halfway around the leading car and ran smack into the tank. The left track of the tank passed over the left half of the car hood and the left fender. Half of the hood, the left fender, the engine, and the left front wheel were smashed against the concrete highway. The passenger area of the car showed only slight damaged.

An ambulance arrived and took the man and his son to Riverview Hospital.

John went over to the MPs who were talking with a second man who was the driver of the first car that was moving westerly. The MPs questioned him about the accident, and he confirmed the story that the tank driver told. The second man said, "I can't imagine what he was thinking about. There's a double solid line on the highway and he pulled out to pass me right in the middle of the curve. He's lucky he didn't kill himself and his boy. But what was that army tank doing on the highway?"

The JAG office had a complete set of the New Jersey statutes in its law library, and the first thing Grady did when he returned to the office was check the New Jersey motor vehicle laws. What he found didn't please him because he learned that the Coles Laboratory people should have notified the state police before they took the army tank onto the highway, but they hadn't done that. The police would have provided an escort vehicle for the tank had they been notified.

Grady then went to a commentary on New Jersey tort law. He learned that New Jersey followed the *proximate cause* rule on torts rather than the *comparative negligence* rule. That meant that a jury or court would look to see what really was the cause of the accident and would not try to assign relative degrees of fault between the two parties. West Virginia also followed the *proximate cause* rule, and John had studied two semesters of tort law in law school and was familiar with the rule and its application. John believed that the real cause of the accident was the action of the driver of the second car pulling around the leading car on a curve where he could not see what was coming in the opposite direction. The fact that the tank should not have been on the highway without an escorting vehicle was not the *proximate cause* of the accident and should not make the government liable, in the absence of other negligent acts by government people. Grady spent the next day writing a report on the accident. He obtained the military police report and the photographs of the accident scene and put them all in a file to await further action on the matter which he was sure would come.

CHAPTER 13. (WINTER 1953)

After attending bible study class on Wednesday night, Rebecca and John made plans for their weekend. Rebecca said that she had volunteered to work at Riverview Hospital on Saturday and would be tied up until 4:00 p.m. She suggested that she change from her hospital uniform to her street clothes at the hospital, then she would drive over to Fort Monmouth to meet John and they would go to dinner.

They met at 5:00 o'clock at Scrivner Hall. John wore civilian clothes. Rebecca said that she had put a big run in her stocking while getting out of her car and didn't want to be seen in public with the run. John told her that the PX sold women's stockings. They could go over there and get a new pair, then come back to Scrivner Hall and she could change stockings in the ladies lounge. She selected a pair of hose at the PX, and John showed his I.D. card and paid for them. They were walking toward the exit when John stopped abruptly and pulled Rebecca to a halt. She looked at him. He was staring at a soldier in uniform who was staring back at him.

"Robert!"

"Is that you, Lieutenant Grady? Lieutenant, I heard rumors that you made it, but I never heard any more and I was never sure." Sergeant Robert Pettit came up and hugged Grady. Rebecca and several GIs watched. "Lieutenant, I wasn't sure. I can't believe I'm seeing you again."

"You made it through the line all right?" Grady asked.

"No trouble. What happened to you?"

John saw several people watching them, so he took Robert by the arm and took Rebecca by her arm and moved them to an area of the PX where there were no customers.

"Rebecca Hazlet, this is Sergeant Robert Pettit. Robert and I were together in North Korea."

John and Robert quickly exchanged questions. Robert said that he had been back at Monmouth for two weeks taking an advanced course in The Signal School. John told him what he was doing. Grady looked at Rebecca, then back at Robert and said, "Robert, Miss Hazlet and I are going to dinner shortly; won't you join us? I want to hear what you've been doing and about the other men. Are you free?"

Robert had a questioning look on his face and pointed back and forth between John and himself. "What about the two of us going to dinner together?" Robert was referring to the military custom that officers and enlisted men usually don't socialize together.

"We've eaten together before haven't we; I don't see why we can't again. Come with us, but we're going to make a stop at Scrivner Hall before we leave."

John drove to a small, nice restaurant in West Long Branch. Rebecca and he sat on one side in a booth, and Robert sat on the other side. They ordered, and the two men talked.

"Tell me, what happened to the others," John said.

"Well, when we arrived at the line, they took us back to the battalion CP. Captain McDowell talked with the officers for a while, then he, Ollie Clark, Charlie Ienfield, and Albert Ramey were taken to the aid station. Albert wasn't too good, and the captain was in a lot of pain—worse than before. I never saw them again nor heard anything about them. Sergeant Black, Bill Savin, George Fuller, Stan Obromowitz, and I went to Hamhung and rejoined the Signal Section at headquarters. We evacuated from Hungnam on an LST and landed back at Pusan. By the way, Colonel Ackerman sacked Major Lamb: he sent him back to Japan. I expect you're happy to hear that. Tenth Corps went onto the line almost immediately, and I was transferred to Eighth Army. It was kind of nasty for the next six months, but I never experienced anything like we had it in North Korea. Then I was promoted and transferred to a repair depot back in Japan. I had good duty there.

"What about you Lieutenant, what happened after you and Paul left us. We heard the grenades. That's when we left the creek, just like you told us to do."

John was hesitant to talk in front of Rebecca. "Paul and I took care of our business and returned to the creek. I don't know much about what happened after that, except that somehow I got wounded in the butt."

"What about Paul?" Pettit asked.

Grady slowly shook his head from side to side, then quickly spoke before Robert or Rebecca could ask any more questions. "I've been in contact with Captain MacDowell. His leg healed, but he says he has a bad limp, so they gave him a medical discharge. He's working on his family's newspaper in Montana and says he's happy."

"You know, Lieutenant, I still wake up at night with the sweats thinking about the Chinese jumping us at that pass. How about you?"

John nodded his head, then cut his eyes toward Rebecca and pursed his lips. Robert got the message and dropped the subject.

John told Rebecca, "Robert is a skilled electronics technician, and he was our medical person over there. He tended to the wounded, and I'm grateful to him for what he did for me."

"I didn't know what I was doing, really."

They talked some more, then John had to excuse himself to go to the men's room.

Pettit asked Rebecca, "Ma'am, are you and the lieutenant serious?" Robert could read the way the two interacted with each other. That question surprised Rebecca, and she wasn't sure how much she wanted to reveal to him. He saw that she was hesitant to answer, so he backed off. "Excuse me, ma'am, that's none of my business; I shouldn't have asked. But if you are, you have yourself one heck of a man. I'd serve with him anywhere in the world. I figure I've already been to hell and back with him—a frozen hell, that is."

'Robert, what was it you were saying about the Chinese?"

"Ma'am, Lieutenant Grady doesn't want me to talk about that. Has he told you what happened to us in North Korea?"

"I know a little about it, but not much about the details."

John returned and the conversation changed. They ate and then Robert said that he had better get back to the post. They exchanged telephone numbers and agreed to get together soon.

CHAPTER 14. (WINTER 1953)

Several weeks later, Colonel James came into John's office with a handful of papers. "Lieutenant Grady, a man has sued the government because our tank ran over his car with his boy and him in it. The Unites States District Attorney in Trenton is handling the case and wants a report on it. You know about that accident don't you?"

"Yes sir."

"Take these papers and send him what he wants." John read the papers. A complete copy of the complaint that was filed in United States District Court was included. The man not only sued the government, but he also sued the tank driver personally. The man alleged physical injury and mental suffering to himself and to his son, as well as the total loss of his car. The complaint alleged negligence on the part of the government and the tank driver for having the tank on the public highway and for operating it in a negligent manner.

John read the letter from the U.S. Attorney. In essence, he wanted Fort Monmouth to do the investigation and produce all the available evidence and witnesses they could. John believed that the man driving the second car was at fault and that he and his attorney shouldn't collect money from the taxpayers. John felt a challenge and set to work immediately. He reread his earlier report and the MP report on the incident. He looked in the telephone directory for the telephone number and address of the district office of the New Jersey Highway Department. It was in Freehold. He called the number and asked to speak with the highway engineer who was responsible for the section of highway that was five to ten miles west of the Coles Signal Corps Engineering Laboratory. His call was transferred to an engineer, and John identified himself and asked if he could come over and talk with the engineer about getting some information on a section of road. The engineer agreed to meet with John at 1330.

On his drive to Freehold, John drove through the curve where the accident occurred. He had a pad of paper and a pen with him and recorded exact odometer miles from several landmarks to the curve so that he could identify exactly where it was. He arrived at the district office and was directed to the engineer's office. John explained in detail what the situation was and said that he would like to obtain a blueprint of the section of highway where the accident occurred. John showed the engineer the odometer readings he had recorded. The engineer studied them and said, "That looks like it might be Section 49." He went to a cabinet and pulled out a folder of large mechanical drawings, each one of short sections of highway. He folded back several sheets, then he spread out on a drawing table one drawing that showed a road curve and the approaches on each end of it. Many measurements and distances were on the drawing. John and the engineer studied the drawing and checked John's recorded distances and agreed that the drawing showed the curve that John was looking for.

John copied all the highway department numbers and letters that identified that particular drawing and section of highway. He copied from the drawing the distances, radii, and reference points that he thought he needed. He then drove to the Post Engineer's office at Fort Monmouth. All personnel in this office were civilians. He spoke with the supervisor and told him about the lawsuit and what he was doing and what he needed. The supervisor took him to a room where a draftsman was sitting at a drawing table and told the draftsman to help the lieutenant. John again explained everything and showed the draftsman the data he had on the section of highway. The draftsman looked at the data and said that he could give John the drawing he needed. John asked him to make three copies on sheets as large as he could get on his drawing table.

John immediately called Coles Signal Laboratory and talked with the tank driver and asked him if he had any data on the dimensions of the tank. The driver said that he had the army manual on the tank. John told him to bring it over right away. The driver arrived at the Post Engineer's office and explained to the draftsman exactly where the tank and the car were on the highway at the time of the accident. He showed the draftsman the drawing and the dimensions of the tank, and John told the draftsman to draw the tank to exact scale and location on the drawing of the highway and then show the automobile where the tank driver said it was when it hit the tank.

John talked more with the tank driver. He was a civilian in his late thirties or early forties. He was a slow, deliberate speaker and a believable person. He had been a sergeant in the Army Tank Corps during World War II and had spent almost all of his service time at Fort Knox, Kentucky, as an instructor teaching soldiers how to drive tanks. He frequently drove the tank at Coles Laboratory when engineers tested radios. The U.S. attorney couldn't ask for a more competent tank driver or a better witness.

John went to Riverview Hospital the next day to see if he could look at the medical records of the man and boy involved in the accident. He didn't expect that the hospital personnel would allow him to see the records, but he thought he should try. He went to an important-looking woman behind the main desk in the lobby and explained in full detail who he was, what he wanted, and why. To his surprise, the woman directed him to another office on the ground floor. He walked to the office and entered. A counter was inside the door of the room, and the remainder of the room contained stacks of shelves loaded with file folders. Two women were working at a table behind the counter. One looked up and came to the counter when John entered. She looked to be in her early twenties, was blond and attractive, and she wore the same kind of gray uniform, white stockings, and black shoes that Rebecca wore when she volunteered there.

"May I help you," she said with a very friendly smile.

"Yes ma'am. I'm Lieutenant John Grady from Fort Monmouth. I'm the Post Claims Officer, and I'm investigating an automobile accident involving an army tank and a civilian automobile occupied by a man and child who were brought here for examination after the accident. The man has sued the government, and I'm trying to collect evidence for the government about injuries to the man and his son." John gave the names of the man and boy, and the date and approximate time that they would have been admitted, and asked if he could see their medical records.

The young woman never stopped smiling at him while he spoke. When he finished she said, "What did you say your name is." John repeated his name.

"Do you know June Hazlet?"

"Yes. She and I date."

"I thought your name sounded familiar."

"You know June?"

"Yes, she volunteers here too. We work together sometimes." She continued looking at John and continued smiling. John waited. After a long pause she said, "What is it you want, John?" Grady explained the whole thing to her again. She wrote down the names and date on a slip of paper and walked into the stacks. She came back with a big smile on her face and a folder in her hand. She placed it on the counter and stood there smiling as John looked through the papers in the file.

He learned that an emergency room doctor had examined the man and child and had found no injuries in either one. They were released from the hospital immediately after the examinations. The hospital bill was sixty-five dollars and was paid by an insurance company. John quickly copied down the doctor's name and his statement that was on the record card about the findings of the examination. He copied down the name of the insurance company and the number and date of the payment check. He closed the folder and handed it back to the young woman.

"What's your name, ma'am?"

"Judy Stephens."

"Thank you very much, Judy, you've been very helpful. I'll tell June that we met."

When the drawings of the highway curve and vehicles were completed, John had the tank driver check them for accuracy, then he wrote a comprehensive report tying everything together and sent it to the United States District Attorney in Trenton.

✸✸✸

The world learned that Joseph Stalin, the despotic dictator of the Soviet Union, had died in the first week of March. Uncertainty and uneasiness arose in the free world in anticipation of who would succeed him and what the successor's intentions would be regarding communist expansion and the Cold War.

CHAPTER 15. (APRIL 1953)

Rebecca told John that the Hazlets were going to attend spring stee-plechase events in Camden and Aiken, South Carolina, then they were going on to West Palm Beach for a week. She asked him if there were any way he could go with them. He said that there wasn't a chance.

They attended a dance at Gibbs Hall on the Saturday night before Rebecca was to leave for the South. She looked especially lovely, and she felt soft and warm in his arms as they danced. At the conclusion of the evening, John parked the car in front of the Hazlet's house and escorted Rebecca to the front door. They kissed. John took hold of her arms and said, "This last year and a half that we have been going together has been the most delightful period of my life. I never imagined that I would ever meet a wonderful girl like you—I didn't know that one existed. Beck, I don't want to live the remainder of my life without you; will you marry me?"

Rebecca stared into his eyes. Her eyes became watery, tears formed. She bit her lower lip and had a pained expression on her face. "Oh John, I've dreaded having to face the day you would say that."

He looked at her with astonishment! He let her arms drop and he stepped back. He felt as if she had hit him smack in the face with a baseball bat. "Well, pardon me, Miss Hazlet, I guess I've gone too far; I guess I've been playing out of my league." He turned and walked to his car.

She recovered enough to say, "John, wait."

He climbed into his car and drove off.

Very early Sunday morning a telephone call came for Grady at his BOQ. He refused to take it. He told himself, "Damn it, I should have known that I didn't belong in the world with rich people." All he could think about was that she had done it to him twice now. The first time he overcame it without any trouble at all, but this time it hurt. It hurt real bad. He didn't like to lose at anything, and seldom did, but this rejection by her was a kind of loss he had never experienced. It was more than humili-ation—and he certainly felt that—it was the dashing of his dream for his future life. He was in a somber mood and spent the most of the next day in his BOQ reading newspapers and parts of a couple of books. He followed the war in Korea. He thought that maybe he should volunteer to go overseas, maybe back to Korea to finish the job there. Or, maybe to Europe. Yes, Europe would be interesting. He called Sergeant Robert Pettit and they went to dinner.

Junior army officers were required to maintain their weapons proficiency and periodically were ordered to go to the rifle range to shoot the rifle for qualification. It had been more than a year since John had been to the range, and he received orders to go on Tuesday, 7 April. He reported in his fatigue uniform to the warehouse where he drew his equipment for the day. Three buses filled with officers went to the rifle range at Sea Girt, N.J. John qualified, but didn't score as well as in previous trips because his left arm was unsteady in supporting the rifle.

Upon return to Fort Monmouth around 1745, Grady turned in his gear at the warehouse and walked to his BOQ. As he approached the front door, he saw Rebecca's Woody in the parking lot. She saw him and got out and stood at the side of the car.

"What in the world ... ?" he muttered to himself. He figured that he still had some pride left and that he ought to be civil, so he slowly walked over to her.

He nodded and said in a flat tone, "Hello, Rebecca."

She had a serious look on her face. "Hello, John."

"I thought that you were going to be down South for two weeks."

"I came back—obviously. John, we need to talk. I've made reservations for dinner; will you go with me?"

"I don't know that we have anything more to talk about. I think you said it all."

With irritation she replied, "John Grady, at times you can be as stubborn as a mule. We badly need to talk and I've invited you to dinner, now are you going to go? I don't want to have to stand here in this parking lot to talk with you."

John looked at her for some time, then said. "All right, but I need to shower. Can you wait twenty minutes?"

"Of course I can," she said impatiently. "We'll be late for the reservation I made, so I'll go to Scrivner Hall and make a telephone call to have them change the time. You hurry."

"Yes ma'am."

John came out of his BOQ wearing his single-breasted gray flannel suit, a white shirt, and a black knit tie. He thought that the black tie was appropriate.

"Where're we going?" he asked.

"Shadow Brook. Come on, get in." She drove.

"How long have you been waiting?"

"About two hours. I called the JAG office and they told me that you wouldn't be there today but probably would be at you BOQ late in the day." They talked very little. He realized that by taking her car she controlled his coming and going. He wondered if she had that in mind. She probably did. She's no dummy, and she seemed resolute.

They sat at a table in the back of the dining room, and the string ensemble was playing chamber music—same as last time. A waitress came and asked if they wanted to order drinks. Rebecca asked for hot tea. Grady ordered black coffee.

"No bourbon and soda tonight?" Rebecca said with a smile.

"No."

They couldn't get a conversation going, which was something unusual for them. After the tea and coffee came, Rebecca said, "John, it didn't dawn on me until after you left what I said to you on the porch. I have something to say to you, and please let me say it.

"The events at Camden and Aiken are always filled with entertainment and parties at people's country estates. Our family looks forward to going there and seeing old friends, and I usually enjoy our time there. This year I didn't.

"Our house in West Palm is in a compound with other houses owned by friends who have been there for many years. We spent an evening with several other families when we first arrived, and there were two single men there about my age. We've known each other ever since I can remember. The more I was with them the more I regretted that I wasn't with you.

"I talked with Daddy that night about our situation, about the statement I made to you, and how you responded. I asked him— "

"Excuse me for interrupting, Rebecca. All that is very interesting, but I've been doing some thinking this past week and I've concluded that I've been wrong in courting you. We're from two different worlds. You belong in Aiken, Camden, West Palm Beach, Manhattan, etc., and I belong in the army. Your mother was right, I shouldn't try to sniff around in your world.

"Rebecca, it's good that we didn't go any further. I tried my best to court you with sincerity, but as I said before, I was shooting too high. I'm through trying. I quit. In fact, I might just quit in a lot of things.

The waitress brought their meals and they began eating in silence. John kept his eyes on his plate. Periodically, Rebecca looked at John. Midway through the meal Rebecca put her fork on her plate and pushed the plate away from her. She folded her hands and placed them on the table in front of her and leaned forward.

"John Grady, look at me. I don't care what happens between us, but I don't ever again want to hear you say that you quit. You're not a quitter. God gave you the talents to be a leader, and He expects you to use those talents. You've been a leader in everything you've done, and you're not going to quit now. John, you're honest, a good person, a spiritual person, an achiever, a leader. God gave you those talents to serve Him and His world. You're not allowed to quit just because I hurt your feelings."

Rebecca brought her plate back in front of her, picked up her fork, and picked at her food.

John continued looking at Rebecca. "What kind of woman is this?" he said to himself. He thought about how she had matured since they first met, about her loyalty to him in various situations, their previous apparent complete compatibility, and now this speech she just made. "Yet, she rejected my marriage proposal," he told himself.

They continued eating in silence. Rebecca again placed her fork on her plate and leaned forward. "John, I said something a couple of minutes ago that isn't true. I said, 'I don't care what happens between us.' What happens between us is the most important thing in my life right now; that's why I'm here. John, I need you, and you need me, and whether or not you want to admit it right now, we're in love beyond description. You **are** going to spend the rest of your life with me, and I'm going to be the best wife for you that this world has ever seen."

"But Beck, when I asked you to marry me, you said that you dreaded hearing me say that."

"John, I didn't say that I wouldn't marry you. What I meant by that statement was something completely different from what you thought I meant."

"What did you mean?"

Rebecca looked around them. "I don't want to talk about it here. I will later."

They continued looking at each other. John thought, "She's absolutely right: I do need her. What is my life going to be like without her? She's been right about everything she said tonight." A faint smile started on his face and began to grow. She smiled back.

They said in unison, "Grab your coat, let's get out of here."

They stood up and started for the exit. John said, "Wait, we forgot the bill."

"It's taken care of."

"You've thought of everything tonight, haven't you." She gave him a shove with her shoulder. They went to the car, and Rebecca told him to drive to the parking lot behind Riverview Hospital.

"Beck, forgive me. When I thought that you rejected me, I lost it. You mean so much to me that I just couldn't handle it. Now, what did you mean by that statement you made when I asked you to marry me?"

She was silent for a long time, then she turned to him and asked, "John, have you ever had a sexual experience?"

The question surprised him. That was the first time they had raised the subject. He answered, "No."

"I knew it," she exclaimed as she pounded her fist against his chest in anguish. "Don't you see?" she said with tears in her eyes. "You come to me pure, but I can't come to you pure. Don't you see? Oh John, I'd give anything if I hadn't been married—anything. I love you so, you'll never understand how it makes me feel. That's what I meant when I said I dreaded the day you would ask me to marry you. I was sure you were pure, and I knew that I couldn't come to you pure, and I dreaded having to face that truth when you mean so much to me. Do you understand?"

He drew her to him and kissed her. "Rebecca, your marriage is behind us. Let's forget it forever. We're going forward together and never looking back. You're right, Beck, we do need each other. You straighten me out every time I get my head all mixed up. Our relationship is synergistic."

"It's what?"

"Synergistic. Together we're more than the sum of each of us alone."

"That's true, John."

He gently kissed her lips. "Tell me again what you said about me living the rest of my life with you. I want to hear it again."

"Beck, let's not say anything about getting married until we've decided when and how we're going to do it. This is our business and I want us to control it, not other people. Is that all right with you?"

"I want it that way, too."

"Beck, I told you in our first telephone conversation before we even met that there was something special meant for us. Now, do you believe it?"

"Yes, but you said it in that letter you wrote."

"I don't think so."

She turned on the interior light in the car and fumbled for something in her purse. She pulled out an envelope and handed it to him. "Read it."

He tilted the envelope up to the light. It was his handwriting. It was that first letter that he had written to her. He looked at her, then pulled the letter from the envelope. Something fell onto his lap as he pulled the letter out. He read the letter, nodded his head and said, "You're right."

He searched for the thing that had fallen onto his lap. He picked up a folded newspaper clipping from the *New York Herald-Tribune* and unfolded it. It was a photograph of an American soldier at a partially-open mass grave in South Korea pointing to exhumed bodies. The soldier was looking down and his face was almost obscured by shadows and the steel helmet that he had on. The caption under the picture did not identify the soldier, and even John could not recognize himself in the picture. John stared a long time at the picture of that horrible scene that was burned into his memory. He remembered that sickening stench. Without looking up he said, "I didn't know that this was published." He looked up at her and asked, "How did you know?"

"I knew."

"You had these all the time?"

She nodded.

He replaced the letter and the clipping into the envelope, handed it back to her, and said, "You came loaded for bear tonight, didn't you."

"I didn't intend to go home empty-handed."

On a Saturday night soon thereafter, Rebecca and John went to a movie in Asbury Park. They stopped at a cafe for a snack and then drove to the Hazlet estate and stopped inside the iron gate at the entrance. They embraced and kissed. They became more passionate the more they kissed. They felt that their love was overwhelming them. They broke apart and sat silently. Rebecca straightened her hair and looked at him. "John, it's time we get married; we've waited long enough."

"I was about to say that. And we had better make it soon because I don't know how much longer I can keep away from you. Can we make it next week? What do we need: a marriage license; a physical exam; a blood test; or what? " They discussed what they needed to do, and agreed that they would go together Monday morning to get a marriage license and whatever they needed in connection with it.

"John, I want to call my sister Liz to ask her to come to the wedding. This is something special, and I want her to be part of it. And I would like Sally and Harold Scott to be there; they're part of the family. Do you mind?

"Of course not. I'd like to meet Liz, but how are you going to work it out with your mother?"

"I don't know, but it's time that nonsense ended. John, can you get some time off for a honeymoon?"

"I'll talk to Colonel James as soon as we finalize the date. I haven't had leave since I left the hospital, so I ought to be able to get some time off.

"When shall we tell Mother and Daddy?"

"As soon as possible. How about if I come out here tomorrow morning around 0930 and we tell them together?

"John, I can't get married, go on a honeymoon, be a wife for you, and still stay in school. I'm going to withdraw right away. What do you think?" He concurred.

"Beck, we have to find a place to live, and it's not going to be with your family—I can assure you that."

"We'll just have to find our own place, that's all. What about the married officers' quarters where Mike Turner and some of the others live?"

"There's a waiting list for them. Besides, I don't know if I want to live on post. Let's think about that."

At 7:30 Saturday morning Rebecca called her sister in Maine. "Liz this is June. How are you?" They chatted for a while, then Rebecca said, "Liz, I'm going to marry the most wonderful man in the world, and I want you to be here for the wedding. Only the family will be at the wedding. Please come, it really is special—not like the last time—this is forever. I want you to meet him; he's the army officer I told you about at Christmas. Won't you please come."

"What does Mother say about you marrying an army officer?"

"We're going to tell her and Daddy later this morning. But it doesn't matter what she says or does, we're going to get married as soon as we can—next week if we can work out the details."

"Next week? You aren't fooling around, are you."

"I've never been as sure of anything in my life. Please come, Liz, I want you to be part of it, and I want you to get to know John. I know you'll like him."

Liz was silent for a moment, then she said, "You know, Sis, I just might come. I've been thinking lately that maybe I ought to get out of here and start doing something useful with my life. What do you think Mother will do if I show up?

"I don't think she'll do anything. I really believe she's sorry for what happened, but she can't bring herself to do or say anything about it. She and John don't get along either. He won't even come into the house. He picks me up at the front door and leaves me there at the end of a date. I think she's sorry about that too, but it's not in her to say 'I'm sorry.'"

"He doesn't get along with her either? He can't be all bad. I want to meet him.

"How's Daddy?"

"He's fine. We've been getting along exceptionally well—just like old times. And, he likes John. Please come, Liz. Daddy and I'll work on Mother and everything will be all right."

"Sis, call me as soon as you set the date. I'll let you know for sure then. Congratulations, and I hope this one works."

Grady arrived at the Hazlet home a few minutes before 0930. Rebecca took him into the library and they agreed that John would talk first. Rebecca brought her parents to the library where they sat on the leather sofa.

John said, "Good morning Mrs. Hazlet, Mr. Hazlet. Rebecca and I want to tell you that we're going to marry. We know each other well, and we're certain that it's the right thing for us to do. We'll be married as soon as we can arrange it. We plan to have a simple marriage ceremony in the Red Bank Methodist Church with Reverend Lowe performing the ceremony. We very much would like for both of you to attend. We'll find an apartment in the area and will live there, at least for the immediate future. I hope that you and I will have a cordial relationship. I'll be pleased if we do."

John looked at Rebecca. She said, "That pretty much says it. We both know this is the right thing for us to do. I've never been as happy in my life."

Mr. Hazlet stood up from the couch, went to Rebecca and kissed her on the cheek and said, "Congratulations, Junie, I'm happy for you." He went to John and grasped his hand in both of his and said, "Congratulations, John, I'm happy to know that June and you will be together."

Mrs. Hazlet went to Rebecca and kissed her on the cheek. She was choked up and couldn't speak. She went to John and shook his hand and nodded her head. She had tears in her eyes. She and Mr. Hazlet then left the room.

"How did it go?" John asked Rebecca.

"It went well. They've been expecting it, I'm sure. Now, let's look in the newspapers and see what apartments are for rent."

When they completed looking through the list of want ads, John said, "Let's call Marty Lowe and tell him what we have in mind and ask him if he will perform the ceremony." John called and Lowe said that he would be out of town at the annual conference the next weekend but would be available the following Saturday. John asked him to hold that date for their ceremony at 11:00 o'clock in the morning. Lowe said he wanted to talk with them after bible class Wednesday night.

Rebecca and John then took turns making telephone calls about a couple of apartment prospects. They made appointments to see three that sounded promising.

Mrs. Hazlet came into the library at 11:30 and said, "John, won't you stay and have lunch with us? We'll be eating in about half an hour."

"Thank you, Mrs. Hazlet, that's kind of you."

She smiled and left.

Rebecca came to John and put her arms around him. "It looks as if the ice jam might be starting to break up."

At lunch, Mrs. Hazlet spoke up, "John, I apologize for the remark that I made to you several months ago. I've regretted it ever since, and I hope you will forgive me for it."

"Yes ma'am I do, and I hope we can put the incident behind us."

Mrs. Hazlet continued, "You're welcome in our home, and I hope you'll get to feel that it's home to you as well."

Rebecca spoke to her mother, "Mother, I very much want Liz to come to our wedding. While we're mending broken fences, can you and she mend the broken fence between you two?"

Without looking at Rebecca, her mother said in a soft voice, "I would be happy to see that."

"Mother, that's wonderful. May I tell Liz that?" Her mother nodded.

Mr. Hazlet looked delighted at the turn of events. He asked Rebecca and John if they were going to take a honeymoon. John said that it would depend on whether he could get leave, but he thought he would be able to get it.

Mr. Hazlet said, "If you want to use the West Palm house, you're welcome to it. This is a nice time of year down there. And, if you want to use the Manhattan apartment, you're welcome to it also. You can use them both if you want to."

Rebecca said, "Thank you Daddy, we'll decide when we find out if John gets leave."

That afternoon Rebecca and John looked at an apartment in Fair Haven, and two in Long Branch. They didn't like any of them.

On Monday, John took a couple of hours off work, and Rebecca and he obtained the application for a marriage license. Wednesday night they talked with Pastor Lowe and made arrangements for the wedding. It would be the Saturday after next, 9 May, and would be the simple marriage ceremony in the Methodist tradition.

Rebecca said that she wanted to call Liz right away with the definite date. They drove back to the Hazlet home and went into the library where Rebecca made the call. "Liz, the date for the wedding is definite; it's May the ninth, a week from Saturday. Why don't you come a couple of days early so you can get to know John."

Liz said she was uneasy about meeting her mother.

"Liz, call Mother and tell her you're coming and that you're looking forward to the two of you getting along in the future. You don't need to discuss who was at fault in the past. I know that Mother wants to heal the breach; she told me that."

Liz said that she would call, and unless something nasty happened when she talked with Mother, she definitely would come for the wedding.

Grady went into Colonel James's office on Thursday morning and told him that he was getting married and ask if he could get two weeks leave, starting the Friday before the wedding. The colonel congratulated him and consented to the leave and said that he would have orders made up. The news spread through the JAG office and everyone congratulated John.

John visited Colonel Bowen's office that same morning. They warmly greeted each other. John said, "Colonel, you remember Rebecca Hazlet whom I've been dating for some time, well, we've decided to get married. The wedding is Saturday a week. We're having a small private wedding with only her family there. I wanted you and Mrs. Bowen to know."

Bowen had a big smile on his face and congratulated John. "She's a fine girl, John. I know you both will be very happy. Thank you for sharing your good news with me. Mrs. Bowen will be delighted to hear the news."

**

A local plumber was at the Hazlet home making the plumbing hook-ups for a new kitchen sink. Rebecca was in the kitchen telling Sally that she was getting desperate because John and she had not found an apartment they really liked. The plumber overheard the conversation and said that his wife and he had just completely redone the upstairs apartment in their home and he would be happy to show it to Rebecca if she were interested.

"Where's it located," Rebecca asked.

"In Middletown, just off Highway 35. It's no more than ten or fifteen minutes from here. Do you want to look at it?"

"Sure. I have to find something suitable in the next couple of days or we're in trouble."

"As soon as I finish here, I'll take you over and you can look at it."

Edmund (Emmie) Miller, the plumber, drove his truck to his house, and Rebecca followed in her Woody. He went into the downstairs of the house to get the key for the separate outside entry door to the upstairs apartment. He led the way up the stairs to the apartment. It was freshly painted, and the furniture in the living room was either new or newly re-upholstered. The kitchen was bright and cheery, and the stove, refrigerator, and sink were new. The bathroom was small but modern. The bedroom was a good size, and the closet space was adequate. It was the nicest apartment Rebecca had seen since they started looking.

"Mr. Miller, it's very nice. May my fiancé look at it this evening?"

"No problem."

Rebecca called John and told him the news and gave him directions to the apartment. They went through the apartment, and she asked him, "What do you think?"

"Let's go for it. If it doesn't work out, we'll find something else." They went downstairs and John made inquiry about the terms and conditions of the lease. He told the Millers their wedding and possible honeymoon plans, and said that they would not actually move in until they returned from the honeymoon.

"No problem," Emmie said. Grady wrote out a check.

That night Rebecca and John decided that they would go to West Palm Beach on their honeymoon.

✳✳✳

Despite the arguing and tirades that had characterized the cease-fire negotiations in Panmunjom, on 20 April 1953 the UN and the Communists began the exchange of their sick and wounded prisoners of war. The UN returned more than eight times the number of prisoners the Communists did.

CHAPTER 16. (MAY 1953)

Liz arrived at the Greyhound bus station in Redbank late Wednesday afternoon. Rebecca met her and drove her home. She had long, raven-black hair and fair complexion. She was as tall as Rebecca, but now outweighed her by twenty pounds. Rebecca and Mrs. Hazlet were surprised at her weight because she always had been trim and athletic looking, as Rebecca was. Liz had a pretty face despite the double chin. She wore bib overalls over a gray sweatshirt. Ever the rebel!

Mrs. Hazlet kissed her on the cheek, patted her shoulder, and said, "Welcome home, Elizabeth." The Hazlets had an intimate family dinner and evening together on Wednesday evening.

Mr. and Mrs. Hazlet had invited John to have dinner with the family on Thursday night and to stay overnight. He arrived at 1830 wearing a civilian suit and carrying a suit bag of clothes. Rebecca immediately introduced him to Liz who was pleasant but reserved. Rebecca showed John to his room where they embraced and kissed.

Mr. Hazlet arrived from work and served drinks in the large parlor. The conversation moved along but didn't get serious on any subject because no one wanted to present an opportunity for an argument to arise. Everyone enjoyed dinner and the remainder of the evening.

John was an early riser, and was up and showered by 0530 the next morning. He put on a blue oxford cloth shirt and maroon regimental stripe tie, gray flannel trousers, and his tan tweed sport coat and went to the library. He was sitting in a large armchair reading yesterday's newspaper when Mr. Hazlet came into the library and greeted him with, "Good morning, John, you're getting an early start today. I want to talk with you a few minutes before the others get down here, if you don't mind. John, let me first say that I'm happy that Rebecca and you are getting married. I welcome you into our family, and I hope you'll feel that you're a part of our family. John, I'm not privileged to have a son, but if I had a son, I'd be proud if he were like you. I've heard you speak with admiration of your father, and I know that I can't take his place, but I hope we can have a good family-type relationship.

"Now, this 'Mr. Hazlet' business—we have to find something better than that. I don't expect you to call me 'Dad,' or something like that, but why don't you work on it and come up with something less formal.

"You and Rebecca are starting out from scratch and there are many things you'll need and will want to do. I want you to take this—it might come in handy sometime." He reached into his shirt pocket and handed John a folded check. John opened the check—it was for $5,000!

"Mr. Hazlet, you're very kind and most generous, but I can't accept this from you. I make a salary that we can live on, and although Rebecca won't be living in the manner she's accustomed to, she knows that and is willing to accept it. Thank you anyhow." He handed the check back to Mr. Hazlet.

"Now John, I'm not inferring that you can't support Rebecca. I just want you two to have a little nest egg in case you want it or need it some day."

John noticed that Mr. Hazlet was calling her Rebecca, not June. "Mr. Hazlet, I appreciate your thoughtfulness, but I really can't accept it."

"John, I can't force you to take it, but I'll see that Rebecca gets it. I manage some money that she inherited; I don't know if she told you that. I'll add this to the money that I manage for her."

"Yes sir, she told me she inherited from her grandmothers and that you manage it for her. That's her money and it's to remain hers in case she needs it. So long as I'm able to provide for her she'll just hold on to it and save it for the day when she may need it." John grinned at him and said, "My line of work can get hazardous at times."

"Did she tell you how much her inheritance is?"

"No sir."

"I've been looking for you two," Rebecca said as she entered the room and kissed her father on the cheek and John on the lips. "Liz said she'll be down in a few minutes. Let's have some breakfast." She looked at John and said, "Mother is a late sleeper." They went to the dining room, and Sally set large plates of breakfast foods on the table. Liz joined them and was rather quiet during breakfast. The four of them finished eating, then went to the sun room. Mrs. Hazlet joined them there.

Liz said, "Mother and Daddy, may I talk with you?" John looked at Rebecca and motioned his head toward the door. Rebecca said that they were going to the library. Liz told her parents that she had decided to leave

Maine permanently, and if they thought that they could put up with her, she would like to remain at home until she got herself back on track. Both her parents kissed her and implored her to stay.

Friday evening, the five of them sat down to a fine dinner at the Hazlet home. Before they began eating, from his chair at the head of the table Mr. Hazlet said to the others, "I don't know that there ever has been a happier occasion in this house. We have a loved one return, and we welcome a new member into the family. We truly are blessed; let us say grace and offer our thanks."

Later that night, Rebecca and John lingered long at the front door as he departed. They embraced and didn't want to part. "This is the last time I have to leave you at the end of the day," John said.

Saturday morning, John loaded his bags into his car and drove to the church. He and Marty Lowe talked as they waited for the Hazlets. The Hazlets and the Scotts arrived and John greeted them and introduced them to Reverend Lowe. The Hazlets and Scotts sat in the second row in the center section of pews. There were no other guests in the sanctuary, and there was no organist for the service.

Rebecca wore a conservative dress. She and John stood before the pastor as he read through the marriage ceremony. They each said "I do," and the Pastor said, "I pronounce you man and wife." Rebecca and John turned to each other and smiled. Rebecca said, "Look out world, here we come!"

BOOK FIVE

CHAPTER I. (MAY 1953)

Rebecca and John spent their honeymoon at the Hazlet's West Palm Beach home and had little contact with anyone else. Those days were the most marvelous days that two people ever experienced. Their love and respect for each other leaped to a new height that they never imagined existed. They agreed that God intended them to be together and had guided them through adversities and diversions to get them where they now were.

They were eager to set up their apartment, so they changed their airline reservations and flew home a day early. They arrived at the Hazlet home about 2000 and were warmly greeted by the family. John and Rebecca moved into their upstairs apartment at Emmie Miller's house the next morning.

Monday morning, Rebecca followed John to the post to get her Woody registered with the provost marshal and to obtain a commissary card so she could buy groceries there. But first, John took her to the JAG office and introduced her to those people she had not previously met. When John introduce Colonel James to her, the colonel was particularly cordial. They chatted for a short time, then the colonel invited them to his quarters after work the next day to meet Mrs. James and to have coffee.

Rebecca and John called at Colonel James's quarters after work on Tuesday and were cordially received. Mrs. James was pleasant, outgoing, and down-to-earth. During their conversation, Mrs. James learned that Rebecca played golf and bridge and invited her to play with the officers' wives. They played bridge on Wednesday and golf on Thursday. Rebecca thought that she couldn't say no to the wife of John's boss, so she accepted the invitations and thanked Mrs. James.

John arrived home after work Wednesday evening and asked Rebecca how bridge went that afternoon. "What an afternoon!" Rebecca said as she rolled her eyes. "Many of the ladies were colonels' and majors' wives, and I was almost afraid to talk for fear I'd say the wrong thing."

"Did you enjoy it at all?"

"Yes, I did. Those gals are some bridge players; I learned things from them today."

The next evening John asked her how golf with the ladies went. "Pretty well. I was a little nervous at first, but after a couple of holes I settled down.

"What kind of golfer is Mrs. James?"

"She's good. There are some good golfers in that group. Mrs. James invited me to play in a foursome with her next Tuesday. The other two gals who will be in that foursome were the top finishers today.

"Oh, also, the women talked me into volunteering at the Thrift Shop next week. The officers' wives run it and sell second-hand uniforms and things and use the money for charity. I'm beginning to feel like I'm in the army."

***

Courts-martial for violation of Post Regulation 219 were keeping the trial teams in the JAG office busy, and uneasiness continued among the JAG officers about prosecuting soldiers for accidents occurring off-duty and off-post. The trial team of DuPre and Grady handled many of the prosecutions.

At 1650 on a Friday afternoon, Colonel James's secretary came into John's office and told him that the colonel wanted to see him in his office. The colonel said, "Lieutenant Grady, a new class for the JAG School is forming, and I've submitted your name to The Judge Advocate General in the Pentagon. They said that the class is not full yet, and if it isn't full by the time classes are to begin, they'll allow you to attend."

"That's nice of you Colonel, but I don't have a law degree, and I'm not admitted to the bar."

"That's all right. I'll let you know, but I won't know until the class is about to begin."

John didn't know what to think. He had never even thought about attending JAG School because he was a Signal Corps officer and wasn't a member of the bar. He didn't think it was a real possibility, regardless of what Colonel James said. After he arrived at home that evening and changed into casual clothes, he sat in the kitchen while Rebecca prepared dinner and mentioned to her that Colonel James had told him that there was a possibility that he might go to JAG School for three months.

Rebecca stopped what she was doing and declared, "I'm going with you. Where is it? When?"

"It's such a remote possibility that we really don't need to worry about it. I'm a Signal Corps officer, and I can't transfer to the JAG Corps because I am not a member of the bar, so I don't see why the army would spend the money to send me."

"Where is the JAG School?

"It's in Charlottesville, Virginia. It's in the same building as the University of Virginia Law School. All the JAG officers in the office have been there. The next class starts 15 June and runs for three months."

"That's a little over a week. I can be ready."

"I said it's a remote possibility. It would make more sense for the army to send me overseas right now. That way they would get at least a year's overseas duty out of me before my four-year tour of duty is up."

"Wherever you go, I'm going if I possibly can."

"You know, Beck, if they do send me to JAG School, I'll have just nine months left in my tour of duty when I finish. It's unlikely they'll send me overseas with just nine months left, so if I do go to JAG School it means that we won't be separated."

She looked at him with an earnest face and said, "John, I don't want to be separated from you. I don't know how army wives endure it when their husbands go off to war or go overseas without them. They're brave women."

Colonel James called John into his office at 1130 Wednesday morning and told him that he had just received word that the class at JAG School was not full and that John had been accepted. School would begin next Monday. "Lieutenant Grady, Lieutenant Albert will take your place as Post Claims Officer while you're gone. After lunch you show him what you're working on, and then you may go home and start getting ready to leave. I'll see to it that your orders are cut right away. Hopefully, you can pick them up tomorrow. Good luck to you."

Rebecca was at Gibbs Hall to play bridge with the officers' wives, so John called the manager's office at Gibbs Hall and asked them to have Mrs. Grady call her husband at the JAG office. He went to Lloyd Albert's office and told him what the colonel had told him, and that he would go over the claims work with Albert at 1300. Grady called Colonel Bowen and told him the news. He said that he would clear the post tomorrow, and if he could he would stop by and say good-bye. He began making a list of things that he needed to do on post and at home before leaving for Charlottesville on Friday morning.

Rebecca returned John's call, and he said, "Beck, we're going to JAG School. Classes start Monday, and I want to leave here Friday morning because we have to find a place to live in Charlottesville. Have you started to play bridge yet?

"Oh John! No, we're just getting ready to eat lunch."

"Can you get away now, or do you think you should stay there and play?

"I'll leave after we eat."

"You'll have to tell the Millers that we're leaving. We'll settle with them when I get home. I'll be home about 1430."

John arrived at the apartment in the middle of the afternoon. Rebecca had clothes laid out on the bed and had some boxes on the floor. They embraced and Rebecca said, "John, this is happening so quickly; I don't know what to take."

"Take the minimum of what you think you can get by with for three months.

"Is it all right if I take my golf clubs and tennis racket?"

"Sure. Have you told your folks?"

"Yes. Mother invited us for dinner tonight and tomorrow. I called Daddy to be sure he wouldn't be late tonight.

"John, when I told Millie that we were leaving for three months, she asked me what we intended to do about the apartment. I told her that we would have to give it up. She said that if we were sure that we would be back in September they would hold it for us and we wouldn't have to pay rent for July and August. Isn't that wonderful of her. I told her I'd have to talk to you."

"O.K., go ahead and tell Millie to hold the apartment while we're gone, but we should pay at least one-month's rent while we're gone. That way they'll loose only one-month's rent."

Thursday morning after picking up his orders, Grady stopped to see Colonel Bowen for a few minutes. Bowen wished him well and said that he was looking forward to seeing him in three months.

John arrived home and finished loading the maroon Chevy. They cleaned up and drove both cars to the Hazlets. Rebecca parked her car in the garage and told Liz that she should use it whenever she wanted. The family had a pleasant dinner and evening together. Rebecca and John thanked the Hazlets for everything and departed early.

Rebecca woke up a little after 0400 in the morning and whispered, "Are you awake?"

"Yes. Let's leave now. We can stop for breakfast after we've driven a couple of hours." They dressed and left the house as quietly as they could.

They made the trip without incident and arrived in Charlottesville in late afternoon. John looked in the telephone book yellow pages for a real estate agent and called one and made an appointment for the first thing Saturday morning. The third apartment they looked at was a small one-story brick cottage about forty yards behind a large old residence in a nice section of town. The cottage had been the quarters of slaves who had worked in the residence a century or so ago. It had been remodeled into a modern apartment that was quite nice. It was small, but it could do for three months. Rebecca liked it, so the agent took them to the big house to meet Mrs. Perkins, the owner. Mrs. Perkins, a widow in her late seventies, lived alone in the large house. She liked the Gradys and agreed to rent the cottage to them.

The Gradys went to the supermarket that afternoon and bought staples and groceries. Sunday they went to church, had lunch, then went over to the University of Virginia campus and located the law school. They also saw the serpentine brick wall and the cottage that Edgar Allan Poe occupied when he was a student there.

Monday morning, John put on a fresh khaki uniform and tie, but he didn't wear his ribbons or CIB. Rebecca drove him to school. The class of sixty men was larger than John had expected. Orientation and indoctrination consumed the first two hours of the morning, and among the materials they received during indoctrination was a packet of information on the local area and its attractions. At 1000 the class took a break. As John was leaving the classroom, a senior officer called him aside and introduced himself as Lieutenant Colonel Hendrix, Assistant Commandant of the JAG School. He asked Grady to come with him to his office. John followed him down a hall to a small office. The colonel sat behind his desk and offered John a chair in front. In a serious tone of voice Hendrix said, "Lieutenant Grady, welcome to the JAG School. Lieutenant, as you know, the requirement to be a JAG officer is that one must be admitted to practice before the highest court of his state. You're not a member of the bar, and you haven't completed your legal education. We don't take students with your background, but because this class was not full, and because First Army made persistent requests for special consideration, we made an exception. We've never done this before." Colonel Hendrix then said slowly and emphatically, "You should understand that you will have to keep up in your work or you will not be allowed to stay. I want you to understand that clearly from the beginning. Do you have any questions?"

"No sir." Grady stood up, saluted, and said, "Thank you, sir." He walked out the door and down the hall. "Well, that was quite a welcome to the JAG School," he said to himself.

John didn't tell Rebecca that evening what Colonel Hendrix had said to him, but he did tell her that he was going to have to spend an awful lot of time studying and asked her to be patient with him. He gave her the packet of information on the local area that he had received in the morning indoctrination and asked her to look through it. Rebecca read through the material in the packet while John studied.

John finished studying, and Rebecca fixed them Cokes and showed him some of the material that she had read. She handed him one printed sheet that offered to army officers enrolled in the JAG School a three-month associate membership in Keswick Country Club. The club had a golf course, a swimming pool, tennis courts, and a clubhouse with dining room. The price was reasonable for a country club and for a junior army officer.

"John, this looks interesting. I'd like to check it out tomorrow. What do you think?"

"Sure, go ahead."

Rebecca told John about Keswick Country Club during lunch the next day. She had gone out to the club after dropping him at school in the morning, and the membership secretary showed her the facilities. She liked what she saw. "John, I can't sit here in this apartment all summer; I really believe I can get a lot of use out of it."

"I think you're right. Go ahead and sign us up."

Grady had no trouble getting involved in the subjects in school. He knew the army well; he had been on a trial team and had tried cases himself; he had been a claims officer; and he knew what went on in a JAG office. Many of the class members had just come into the army and knew very little about the army or about military justice or military affairs. John figured that because the other students had one more year of law school than he did didn't give them an advantage over him.

Rebecca signed them up at Keswick Country Club and began playing golf with the ladies. She played several times and regained her old form. Some of the better golfers invited her to play with them during the week, and she played tennis with some of the women she met. She usually swam in the pool after golf and tennis. She mixed well with many of the women, and they liked her. That led to several weekend social invitations for the Gradys.

The instructors in JAG school frequently gave "pop" quizzes. Consequently, John never could ease up on his studies. One morning during the third week of classes, the students noticed that one of the class members was absent. He had not done well on the quizzes and tests and was dropped from the class.

✳✳✳

John followed the war in Korea the best he could in the limited free time he had. In the cease-fire negotiations in Panmunjom, the parties finally worked out a cease-fire agreement that both sides could live with. Most people received the news with a sigh of relief that the killing and suffering finally would end. There was one notable exception—Syngman Rhee, the crotchety old president of South Korea. He bitterly opposed any cease-fire that did not provide for the reunification of North and South Korea under his government. He threatened to have the South Korean Army continue the fight against the Communists even if the UN signed a cease-fire with the Communists. To disrupt the situation, Rhee had South Korean guards open the gates of a Prisoner of War camp and allowed over twenty thousand Communist prisoners to escape. The escapees simply melted into the South Korean population. In retaliation for Rhee's attitude and conduct, the Communists launched a large-scale offensive against that sector of the UN defensive line held by South Korean troops. The South Koreans suffered heavy losses and lost ground. Other UN forces came to the rescue of the South Koreans and stabilized the UN defensive line. The United States told Rhee that if he didn't cooperated in the peace effort the UN countries engaged in the fighting would sign a cease-fire with the Communists and would withdraw all their forces and aid from South Korea. Rhee dropped his opposition.

✳✳✳

Grades for the first four weeks of JAG school classes were posted, and two more students were dropped from the class that day. Grady stood third in the class.

***

After two years of frustrating negotiations with the Chinese and North Korean Communists, a cease-fire agreement was finally signed. The fighting stopped at 2200 hours on 27 July 1953 with the opposing armies facing each other across a demilitarized zone, most of which ran through former North Korean territory north of the Thirty-eighth Parallel. Grady was thankful that the killing ceased, but he was displeased that the war ended without a clear-cut defeat of the opposing forces. His feeling at the end of this war was quite different from the proud and satisfied feeling he had experienced at the conclusion of World War II when we had achieved the unconditional surrender of Germany and Japan. On the positive side, however, he reasoned that we had stopped Communist aggression in Korea and were aroused to resist Communist attempts at expansion elsewhere.

John thought about what the armistice meant to him and to his future. He had less than a year remaining in his four-year tour of duty. Now that the fighting had stopped, did he want to stay in the army beyond his four-year obligation? The situation in Europe was tense and dangerous, and maybe he had a duty to stay in the army while the threat existed. On the other hand, he now had served during two wars, so maybe it was time to finish his education and get on with his life. He would decide that issue once he finished JAG School.

The second month's class standings were posted, and Grady had moved up to second place in the standings. Studying and sitting in class were trying on his patience, and he had to exert his maximum self-discipline to keep at his school work. When the final class standings were posted, Grady again stood second in the class. He was disappointed, but the important thing to him was that school was over.

The graduation ceremony was held in the auditorium of a near-by university building at 1000 on 16 September 1953. Rebecca attended, as did family members and friends of some of the other students. The men in JAG school wore their dress uniforms, and for the first time that summer Grady wore his ribbons and decorations. The Judge Advocate General of the Army, a major general, delivered the commencement address.

Driving back to their apartment after the commencement ceremony, Rebecca said, "Congratulations on finishing second in the class."

"Beck, in most endeavors in life, no one cares or remembers who finished second."

They arose early the next morning and were on the road for New Jersey at daybreak. They drove for twenty minutes, then John pulled over to the side of the road and stopped.

"Why are we stopping?" Rebecca asked.

"I don't want to go back home yet. You're the most important person in my life, but with the pressure of school and all the studying that I had to do this summer I feel as though I haven't spent much time with you. Before we get back to the rat race at Monmouth, let's get lost somewhere down here for a couple of days—just the two of us."

"Where will we go? What'll we do?"

"I don't know. The Valley of Virginia is beautiful and so is the Shenandoah Valley and the Eastern Panhandle of West Virginia. There are some pretty little towns in those places and there are some interesting things to see. Let's go exploring."

She leaned across and kissed him. "I love you. It's exciting being married to you.

***

The Gradys arrived at their apartment in New Jersey Sunday afternoon and unpacked the car. Rebecca called home, and her mother invited them to supper. The Hazlets greeted them warmly and asked many questions. They all had drinks on the screened porch. Rebecca did most of the talking and told them of the interesting summer they had, what she had done while John was in school, and that John had finished second in the class. It was evident to the Hazlets that Rebecca was exceedingly happy.

When John finished his drink, Mr. Hazlet said, "John, let's go inside and let me freshen that drink for you. They arrived at the liquor cabinet and Mr. Hazlet said to him, "John, it's good to have you two back; we missed you. I've never seen Rebecca more buoyant and exuberant. I take it that things are going well with the two of you."

"Yes sir. I don't know how things could be any better. Rebecca is a wonderful person, and I'm fortunate to be married to her."

"Well, you both are fortunate. Do you need anything? Is there anything I can do for you? I feel that I want to do something for you two."

"No sir, there's nothing we need; we're getting along fine.

"Well, it's good to have you back."

CHAPTER 2. (21 APRIL 1953)

John was in the Fort Monmouth JAG office before 0800 Monday morning, and everyone greeted him warmly. The guys wanted to know how he had done in JAG school and were impressed when he told them that he had finished second in the class. John went to Colonel James's office and paid his respects. The colonel asked John about the summer and how he had done in school. The colonel told him that he wanted him to take over the claims office again and that he again would be an assistant trial counsel and work with Paul DuPre.

Grady left the Colonel's office and scanned the outer office. He hadn't seen Willie Mullins yet. He went to Willie's old desk and it looked to be cleared out and unused. John went to Warrant Officer Klingen and said, "Clarence, where's Willie Mullins? I don't see him."

"Willie's on special assignment up at Russell Hall. It's a classified matter, and I haven't talked to him since he left."

That night John asked Rebecca if it would be O.K. for him to invite Willie Mullins over for dinner some night next week. He told her, "I like Willie. He's a bright guy and has a good sense of humor. He's on special assignment away from the JAG office, and I haven't seen him yet."

Rebecca replied, "Go ahead and invite him." John called Willie at his BOQ and invited him over for dinner next Friday evening. Willie gladly accepted.

During his first week back in the office, John worked on a court-martial for violation of Post Regulation 219. It involved an off-post, off-duty, minor fender-bender automobile accident between two privately-owned cars. There were no personal injuries. The defendant was a red-headed, freckled-faced sergeant first class in his late thirties or early forties. John read the file and concluded that the other driver probably could have avoided the accident as well as the sergeant could have.

The sergeant's wife and his two young children were in the courtroom for the trial. To have a defendant's family in the courtroom was new to Grady. They were dressed in very modest-looking clothes. The young daughter looked to be about ten years old and was the spitting image of her father, freckles and all. Her plain dress was a size or two too large for her. She and her younger brother looked scared and had looks on their faces that said, "What are you going to do to my daddy?"

Paul DuPre tried the case and obtained a conviction. The court-martial board sentenced the sergeant to a one-step reduction in rank and a monetary fine of thirty dollars.

That court-martial and the entire Post Regulation 219 matter greatly disturbed Grady. He didn't want to live his life doing that sort of thing. When he returned to the JAG office he went to Terry Berisford's office and said, "Terry, are you busy right now? I'd like to talk with you a few minutes."

"Sure, John, come on in." Grady went into the office and pulled the door closed behind him.

"Terry, I've just witnessed, and was part of, an event that I find quite disturbing. We just court-martialed a sergeant first class for a minor off-post auto accident he had in his own car that he might, or might not, have been responsible for. He was reduced in rank one step and fined thirty dollars. He's married and has two kids. It's hard enough for the married enlisted men to get along on the salary the army pays them, and here it is fining him thirty dollars and reducing his rank and salary because of an extremely minor happening. Outside in the civilian world it would amount to little more than a minor claim with the insurance company, and at most, a minor traffic summons. Here in the army, the sergeant's career is affected and his monthly salary is reduced. His family will suffer for something that doesn't amount to a hill of beans. This isn't what all of us are in the army for.

"What are things like this doing to make an army career attractive to men in the enlisted ranks? This man obviously has been in the army for a number of years and has achieved a senior enlisted rank, and on the salary the army pays him he can't offer his family much more than a modest life. Now it does something like this to him—as if he had committed a criminal act. Is this going to make him want to stay in the army? If it were I, I immediately would be looking for employment outside the army.

"Terry, has anyone ever questioned this Post Regulation 219? When a man reports that he's been involved in an accident he's almost assuring that he'll be convicted in a court-martial. Besides, almost all of these accidents occur off-post. Has anyone ever put this whole matter up to examination?"

As John was talking, Terry gently rocked back and forth in his swivel chair and slowly tapped his fingertips together. Terry didn't reply immediately, then he said, "Since I've been in this office, I don't know of any investigation or official opinion on the legality or propriety of Post Regulation 219. John, look at the situation realistically. The general is a fanatic on this safe driving campaign; he can't see anything but the statistics on automobile accidents. I told you before, Colonel James wants a good efficiency report from the general in hopes that he'll get his promotion to full colonel. So, he's not going to do anything to invoke the displeasure of the general, and you can bet he's not going to challenge Post Regulation 219. The members of the courts-martial boards are career officers who don't want to invoke the general's displeasure either, so they give him the convictions of those who have auto accidents. No one cares to look at what's happening to people like your sergeant who was court-martialed today.

"John, it will take a lot of guts for someone to step up and challenge the general on this matter. If anyone does, it'll be a lonely and uphill battle that he could easily lose. It hasn't happened yet, but who knows, some day it might."

"Terry, what about this security business and the alleged Communist espionage in the Signal Corps Engineering Labs? I'm reading newspaper reports about accusations by McCarthy and his people about espionage in the labs., but they haven't shown any firm evidence yet. I don't know whether or not they're credible."

"John, all I know about that is what I read in the newspaper."

They both sat in silence for a moment, then John said, "Well, thanks for your time, Terry."

"Any time. Listen, John, the wife and I are going out to dinner Thursday night. How about you and your bride joining us."

"That sounds good to me. I'm sure Rebecca would enjoy it. "

***

Friday night Willie Mullins came over to the Grady's apartment for dinner. Rebecca had Sally talk her through the steps of preparing a meat loaf dinner with baked potatoes and creamed corn, a menu suggested by John. Willie and John talked over beers while Rebecca prepared dinner.

"Willie, what's this hush-hush business you're involved in? No one in the JAG office knows what you're doing."

"Well … uh … what I'm doing is supposed to be classified, and I haven't talked to anyone in the JAG office about it. But, I feel I need to talk with someone. John, I trust you not to repeat anything I tell you."

"O.K. Willie, I won't"

"This all started last summer when you were away at JAG School. General Lawrence called Colonel James and said that he wanted to use me for a special project that would require full-time duty for six or eight weeks."

"Willie, I didn't knew that the general knew you well."

"Yeah, I've had several conversations with him in his office. He's called Mike Turner and me to his office several times when he had the impression that we were defending courts-martial defendants too vigorously. He espoused his philosophy that all courts-martial defendants should be found guilty and given the maximum sentence. If the sentence were to be reduced because of mitigating or extenuating circumstances, then he, as convening authority, would reduce the sentence. He said that's the only way to maintain discipline among the troops.

"Mike told him that it was our duty as army officers and as lawyers to give the defendants the best defense we could, and if the general wanted us to do something less in defending them, then he should put it in writing as an order. Of course, the general would never do that, but he made it clear that he's a major general and we're lieutenants and what he thinks and does is correct. During those sessions I corrected the general's misconception of a couple of legal principles. I guess he thinks I know what I'm talking about.

"Anyhow, I went down to see the general and he said he wanted me to review the security files of civilian employees from the Signal Corps Engineering Laboratories who were suspected of being national security risks.

"How many employees have been suspended from their jobs?" Grady asked.

"It started with a single one last summer, and now it's up to twenty-some, or thirty-some, I forget the exact number, but I have eighty-two security files that I'm reviewing. Many of those eighty-two people are under suspicion but have not actually been suspended from their jobs.

"John, the thing that's troubling me is that I've gone through all the files once, and I've made an abstract on each one, and I honestly have to say that I can't find that any one of those people has been involved in subversive activities or is a disloyal American."

"Willie, why were those eighty-two people considered to be security risks in the first place? Who designated them as risks?"

"I don't know. The files were there when I arrived at the G-2 office (Intelligence) to start reviewing them."

"Was Senator McCarthy involved in designating them security risks?"

"I don't think so. I believe that was done before McCarthy became interested in Fort Monmouth. I think he just latched on to an ongoing investigation here at the post because it possibly involved communist influence or communist sympathizers in sensitive classified military work."

John asked, "What are the general's views on the alleged communist activity and influence in American society? I've never heard him say anything on that subject."

"You haven't?" Willie responded somewhat surprised. "Well, you've been away for a while, so maybe that's the reason. I would say that, if anything, he's more of a fanatic on it than McCarthy is."

"I interrupted you, Willie, go on with your story."

"As I said, so far I haven't seen anything about communist activities or sympathies on the part of any of the employees. The connections to communist activities and sympathies are most tenuous. You might not believe this, John, but one case involves an individual whose neighbor reported that the employee had in his personal library the book *War and Peace*, by Tolstoy. Based on that alone, it was stated in the FBI report that the employee had a bias for Russian literature and Russian things. Hell, I have that book in my room, and I'm a loyal American army officer with a Secret clearance.

"Another case involves a young woman who has never had any connection with anything or anyone remotely considered to be subversive. The evidence against her is that a number of years ago her father gave a five dollar donation to some organization of which he was not even a member. Several years after the donation was made, the organization was added to the U.S. Attorney General's List of Subversive Organizations (Attorney General's Black List). The girl had nothing to do with the father's donation or with the organization, and the father was never accused of being a communist or a communist sympathizer."

"Willie, it's hard to believe that anyone with common sense would consider things like that to be subversive and constitute a national security risk."

"Well, there's something more I need to consider, and I'm going to go through all the files again looking for it. A person can be a perfectly loyal American but still be a security risk. For example, if a loyal scientist in the engineering laboratories has access to classified information and he has a grandmother living behind the Iron Curtain, Russian agents might contact him and say, 'Either you cooperate with us and give us classified information that you have access to or we'll send your grandmother to a work camp in Siberia.' That would put the scientist in a tough situation. That's legitimate grounds for classifying someone, even a loyal person, a security risk. I have to check the files for things like that."

"Is there anything common to the suspended people?

Willie thought for a moment, then answered, "Well, I would say that for some of them there is. A number of them are Jewish people from New York City who went to CCNY (City College of New York). The atom-bomb spy Julius Rosenberg went to CCNY, and some of the suspended people were there when Rosenberg was. Some visited Rosenberg's home, but the files don't say why. Maybe they were there studying with him. Others merely knew him, or had classes with him. And don't forget that Rosenberg worked at Squires Engineering Laboratory."

"Then, Rosenberg is the common thread," John said.

"For some of them, I think so. As I see it now, it's guilt by association. But, as I said, I have to look through the files again for potential subjects for coercion."

"What are the suspended employees saying about the charges against them?" John asked.

"So far as I know, they haven't been told what the charges are against them."

"Are you getting pressure from anyone to make findings one way or another?"

"No. No one is bothering me. The general told me when I started that the final determination would be mine. He'll make permanent the suspensions of those that I consider security risks and will lift the suspensions of those I consider not to be risks."

"Well Willie, you certainly are getting some interesting and important jobs. Think what you'd be doing if you were in a large law firm in civilian life. You'd be carrying the bags for the senior members of the firm and trying cases in Justice of the Peace courts."

"You're right about that; we're getting good experience. And furthermore, I've learned a valuable lesson from this."

"What's that?"

"I'm never going to join any organization of any kind unless I absolutely have to. I joined the American Bar Association when I was admitted to the bar, but when my membership comes up for renewal I'm not going to renew."

"Why not?"

"John, you should see those files I'm reviewing. Some of them are full field investigations by the FBI. They contain information on everything you have ever done and every organization you have ever been associated with in any capacity. They contain interviews with your neighbors, with your junior high school teachers, your high school teachers, your coaches, and your college professors. They have lists of your school activities and organizations, your social and political activities, if any, what church you go to, if any, and whom you associate with. From now on, I intend to be as invisible as possible.

"Well, thanks for listening, John. I have some tough decisions to make in the near future, and I felt like I needed to let off some steam to reduce the pressure."

CHAPTER 3. (8 OCTOBER 1953)

The Permanent Investigations Subcommittee of the U.S. Senate Government Operations Committee began five days of closed hearings at Fort Monmouth to look into the alleged espionage in the U.S. Army Signal Corps Engineering Laboratories. The subcommittee had degenerated into a one-senator subcommittee: Senator Joseph McCarthy. McCarthy and his chief legal assistant Roy Cohn had reputations of being abusive and intimidating to witnesses and of passing incorrect information to the press concerning a witness's testimony before the subcommittee. Other Democrat and Republican subcommittee members objected to McCarthy's style of operation and had stopped attending the meetings, hearings, and other activities of the subcommittee. Thus, being unchecked, McCarthy and Cohn did as they pleased. Democrats in the senate engaged in verbal attacks against McCarthy from the safety of the senate floor and to the press. It seemed like common sense to Grady that if the subcommittee members objected to McCarthy's tactics and behavior they should attend the subcommittee meetings and hearings and take actions to check McCarthy and Cohn. For some reason they were not doing that. Grady didn't understand politicians.

Newspaper, radio and television reporters closely followed everything that McCarthy did and said about the alleged espionage problems at the Signal Corps Engineering Laboratories. They freely reported McCarthy's statements and accusations without trying to independently verify them. The New York newspapers had a field day reporting on the McCarthy hearings at Fort Monmouth and on hearings he held a week or so later in New York City.

McCarthy summoned a number of the Fort Monmouth suspended civilian employees to testify before the subcommittee. At the conclusion of a day's closed session, reporters crowded around McCarthy and he issued wild and sensational statements about the national security dangers in the laboratories. The newspapers had front page headlines such as the following: The Situation At The Laboratories Has All The Earmarks Of Extremely Dangerous Espionage; It Looks Like It Might Be Worse

Than Just A Security Leak; Army Radar Data Reported Missing—German Scientist Reports Having Seen Microfilmed Copies Of Monmouth Documents In East Germany; Important Witness Breaks Down Under Cross-examination And Agrees To Tell All He Knows About Espionage Rings; Rosenberg Called Radar Spy Leader—Ring He Set Up May Still Be In Operation At Monmouth Laboratories; Espionage In Signal Corps For Ten Years Is Charged.

On several days McCarthy promised the reporters that tomorrow's sensational testimony would expose the entire espionage ring and would name the names of the spies. Rumors circulated that the witnesses were harassed and intimidated. Grady noticed that McCarthy's repeated pronouncements of a great disclosure of espionage that was to occur "tomorrow" never occurred. But that didn't bother the reporters. They eagerly awaited more statements from McCarthy and rushed them to their editors who published them.

Those unsubstantiated accusations against laboratory employees bothered Grady. He wanted to talk with Willie Mullins about the accusations that McCarthy was making since Willie had told him that he, Willie, had found no evidence of disloyal activities in the employees' security files that he had reviewed. John decided that he wouldn't bother Willie since Willie was not supposed to discuss with anyone what he was doing. But Grady suspected that someone was lying, and he would bet his next paycheck that it wasn't Willie Mullins.

***

Late Friday afternoon, Grady received a telephone call from General Lawrence's aide telling him that the general wanted to see him in his office immediately. Grady dropped the work he was doing and headed for Russell Hall. He reported to the general and sat in the chair in front of the general's desk. "Grady, I need you next Tuesday. We have some 'visiting firemen' coming here, and I want you to stay near me to help me keep my damn mouth shut and keep me out of trouble. I'm not sure that my aide is as sharp as you are about some things. I know that you're not afraid to speak up to me, and I want someone with some legal background who understands what's going on. The newspaper and TV reporters who'll be there won't be as suspicious of you as they would if I had a JAG officer tagging along with me. I don't want to be any more conspicuous than I have to be, and I don't want to say anything that the reporters will paste all over the front pages of their newspapers and report on the six o'clock news. I want you to stay close to me and be sure that I don't say or do anything indiscreet in front of the dignitaries, or do or say something that will draw the reporter's attention to me. Don't be afraid to speak up to me—although you never have been. Do you understand?

"Yes sir. General, who are the 'visiting firemen' and what are they going to do?"

"They are Senator McCarthy and his assistant Roy Cohn; the New Jersey Senator; the local Congressman; the Secretary of the Army; a legal counsel in the office of the Secretary of the Army; and, The Chief Signal Officer from the Pentagon. We're going to make an inspection tour of Evans Signal Corps Engineering Laboratory down at Belmar. Colonel Crawford, the director of Evans Laboratory, will lead the group through the facility. I'll let Colonel James know that you'll work for me on Tuesday. Wear your pinks and greens and wear your decorations and ribbons. Be here in my office at 0800 Tuesday. Any questions?

"No sir, I understand. I'll be here Tuesday at 0800." Grady saluted and left the office. He understood the general's concern about putting his foot in his mouth in front of that group, not to mention reporters. John thought to himself, "The Secretary of the Army and the Chief Signal Officer are his bosses, and with all the national publicity that Fort Monmouth has received about employee suspensions and the McCarthy espionage investigation the general undoubtedly feels that he's living under a microscope." Indeed, he was. "He's a strange man," John thought. "He can be brash, arrogant, and even reckless at times, yet now he's showing the good sense to guard against his weaknesses."

John told Rebecca about his meeting with the general and the inspection tour with the dignitaries on Tuesday. She responded, "John, for some reason I don't have a good feeling about the general. That man is going to get you into trouble yet. You be careful."

Grady spent Saturday afternoon in the Hazlet's well-stocked library reading their newspapers, news magazines, and other current-events publications to be sure that he was up to speed on what McCarthy was doing and what was happening in the U.S. Senate and House of Representatives. He asked Mr. Hazlet what he knew about the New Jersey senator and the local congressman. Hazlet knew them both personally and told John what he knew about them. John read Sunday's edition of *The New York Times* from cover to cover.

Tuesday morning, Grady was at Russell Hall before 0800. At 0900 the Secretary of the Army and his legal counsel arrived. Shortly thereafter, McCarthy and Cohn arrived. The general introduced Grady to everyone, but no one paid attention to him. That was fine with John; that's what the general wanted.

General Lawrence announced the itinerary for the day. The New Jersey senator and the congressman would meet them at Evans Laboratory, as would the laboratory director. The Secretary of the Army, Senator McCarthy, The Chief Signal Officer, and himself would ride down to Belmar in the general's limousine. Cohn, Grady, and the Secretary's legal counsel would ride down in another army car. John noted that he and the general would not ride together. He hoped that the general would be on his good behavior during the ride.

Colonel Crawford, Director of Evans Signal Corps Engineering Laboratory, greeted them when they arrived at the laboratory, as did the senator and congressman who had arrived earlier. The colonel directed them to a conference room and gave them a short talk on the mission of Evans Signal Corps Engineering Laboratory. He emphasized the secret radar development work that was going on there, explained what the tour would include, and told them what to look for at a number of places. Crawford continued, "Because of the secret and sensitive nature of the work being done here, we have strict security measures, as you might imagine. It's our standing policy that no one is admitted to the restricted areas of the laboratory who does not have a 'need to know.'" With all the notoriety that Fort Monmouth had received about its security measures recently, the colonel was making sure that the visiting dignitaries would be impressed with the security measures in effect there. Colonel Crawford concluded, "Accordingly, it has been determined that only the two senators, the congressman, the Secretary, The Chief Signal Officer, and General Lawrence have the requisite 'need to know' to join the tour today." He looked at Cohn, Grady, the Secretary's legal counsel, and a man from Evans Signal Lab., and said, "Gentlemen, you may make yourselves comfortable in the reception lounge until we return."

The headquarters building of Evans Signal Corps Engineering Laboratory was a two-story red brick building that had been a private girl's school before the government acquired the property. To the left side of the front entrance foyer was a small area with a counter where several reception people worked. The reception lounge was in an alcove in the rear of the entrance foyer and included some overstuffed chairs, a couch, and a coffee table.

The entire group walked to the entrance foyer and the colonel showed the lounge to the four who would not enter the laboratory. The dignitaries continued through the foyer and into the restricted area of the laboratory.

Cohn's jaw was set and his eyes were narrowed. When the dignitaries were out of earshot, he complained about being told that he didn't have a need to know and intimated that that amounted to a declaration of war, presumably referring to the subcommittee verses the army. The Secretary's counsel advised Cohn to take it easy. He explained that Colonel Crawford was under a lot of pressure because of the allegations of espionage in the Signal Corps laboratories, and as a result of that he was trying to impress the big shots with the security measures.

Grady was astonished at Cohn's reaction. "This is the guy who's the ramrod in McCarthy's investigations?" John asked himself. He couldn't believe it.

Grady didn't say anything, and the other men paid no attention to him. The more Grady thought about it, he could not figure out what General Lawrence was doing. He thought to himself, "The general said that he wanted me to stay close to him during the day, but then he put me in a different car than he was in, and now he goes into the laboratory and I stay out here. How does he expect me to help him?" Grady had to wonder if things just didn't work out as the general had planned, or did the general change his mind, or is the general 'losing it'? John didn't know, but he realized that it was a bad situation when he had to be suspicious of his commanding general's motives, actions, or competence.

The dignitaries returned in a little over an hour, and the entire group returned to Fort Monmouth's main post where they had an elegant lunch prepared by army cooks. After lunch the dignitaries in the group went their separate ways. General Lawrence told Grady to come back to his office with him.

The general directed Grady to a chair, then he smiled and asked," How is that good-looking wife of yours?"

John smiled back and replied, "Rebecca is fine, sir."

"Is married life treating you all right?"

"Yes sir, things are going very well."

"Good, good, I'm glad to hear it." They looked at each other, but neither said anything.

Lawrence pursed his lips, then said, "Grady, I don't know why I keep getting involved with you." He hesitated, but yet, he seemed to want to talk. "I guess maybe it's because you're the kind of young officer I wanted to be but never was. You've excelled in school, in combat, in commanding your company, and you've married a bright and attractive girl. I always had visions of doing what you've done, but I never had the chance. The army has kept me behind desks in staff assignments ever since my graduation from West Point. I couldn't get away from them, and the good lord knows that I tried. Maybe I was too good at what I was doing."

"Well General, I'd say that your career has been quite a success. Few officers ever get to wear two stars on their collar. That's an exceptional achievement."

"I have been fortunate, but that doesn't change what I said." The general casually shook his finger at Grady and said, "But, I will say that I can match you in one category: I married a good woman. She's been my greatest asset throughout my career."

"Indeed, she is a fine lady, General. I enjoyed meeting her when you invited me to lunch at your quarters."

Again, both were silent. To John, the general appeared to be a lonely man reaching out for friendship and companionship, but because of his position and his pride he was unable to completely let loose.

"How do you think the day went today?" the general asked.

"General, I can't answer that. I was away from you most of the time, so I don't know what went on. May I ask a question about today?"

"Go ahead."

"Sir, you asked me to stay close to you to help you if you needed it, but I was never in a position to get near to you. I wonder why you wanted me to accompany you today."

Lawrence didn't answer right away. Then he said, "You really are an up-front guy, aren't you Grady. You say what's on your mind."

"General, I don't mean to be disrespectful to you, but today was kind of unusual in view of what you told me last Friday. General, we both are trying to do our jobs, and I think we can function better if we know what the facts are."

"You're right about that, Grady. About today—don't worry about it."

They both were silent, then the general said, "Well, that's all for today, Grady. You can get back to work."

Grady stood up, saluted, and said, "By your leave, sir." He went back to the JAG office, but he didn't get much work done. He thought that maybe he should not have asked why the day didn't work out as the general told him last Friday. He sensed that the general was under stress and couldn't open up. He again wondered if the events occurring at Fort Monmouth were getting to the general and whether the general was starting to buckle under the pressure. John also was troubled about what he saw Cohn do today. He asked himself, "What's going on here? Is it I, or is it they?"

When John returned home that evening he told Rebecca what had happened that day. "Beck, I believe your feeling about General Lawrence might be right. I thought I knew him, but now I don't understand him at all. I feel that I ought to try to help him if I can, but he makes it difficult, and I don't know why. I'm just going to stay away from him if I can." John then told her for the first time about the general asking him to be his aide. "Something inside me told me not to take that job. I'm thankful I didn't."

CHAPTER 4. (25 OCTOBER 1953)

On a cold, rainy, and blustery Sunday night in late October, Rebecca and John were snug on their couch watching a program on the TV set that came with the apartment. At Fort Monmouth, rain blew in sheets across the desolate parade ground and along the dark streets and roads. A lone, dark-colored Pontiac sedan slowly drove down a deserted street and came to a stop in front of the provost marshal's office. A man wearing a civilian felt hat and a long army raincoat with the collar turned up got out of the car on the driver's side, and leaning against the blowing rain, walked to the provost marshal's office. He entered and stood inside the door, then reached under his raincoat and pulled a white handkerchief from his hip pocket and wiped the rain off his army-issue, medal-frame eyeglasses.

The MP sergeant behind the raised desk at the far side of the room sat up straight and said, "Yes sir, may I help you?"

The man put his eyeglasses back on, returned the handkerchief to his hip pocket, walked up to the desk, and said, "Yes, Sergeant, I'm Captain Terence Berisford, and I've had an automobile accident."

The desk sergeant recognized Captain Berisford and knew that he was a JAG officer. The sergeant opened a side drawer in the desk and pulled out a notebook. He laid it open on his desk, flipped some pages, and looked up at Captain Berisford. "Yes, Captain, where and when did the accident occur?"

"Sergeant, I told you that I had an accident. That's all I'm going to tell you."

The sergeant was perplexed: this is a JAG officer; he knows the routine here. "Captain, you're familiar with Post Regulation 219. I have to take down all the information on the accident."

"Sergeant, Post Regulation 219 requires that I report the accident to the provost marshal. I've reported it."

"I know, sir, but we take down all the information about the accident. That's our standard operating procedure. The Captain's familiar with that, I'm sure."

"Sergeant, I've reported the accident as I'm required to do. I'm in full compliance with Post Regulation 219. Good evening, Sergeant." With that, Terry Berisford turned and walked out of the provost marshal's office, walked through the rain to his car and drove off.

***

Colonel James had a useful procedure in the JAG office. Each morning, copies of most non-classified and non-confidential correspondence, orders, memoranda, opinions, reports, etc., that were generated or received in the office the previous day were placed in a manila folder called the Reading File. The first thing each morning, the Reading File was circulated among all the officers who were required to immediately read it and pass it along without delay. By means of the Reading File, all officers knew what was going on in the office and on the post and could benefit from the work product of fellow officers. The first item in the Reading File each morning was the provost marshal's report of the events in his jurisdiction that occurred the previous day and night.

Early Monday morning Grady came out of his claims office and saw three of the officers congregated around Paul DuPre's desk reading something on his desk. They all had concerned looks on their faces. John went over and saw that they were reading the provost marshal's report in the Reading File. John looked over shoulders and began reading about Captain Terence Berisford's experience at the provost marshal's office the previous night.

DuPre said to Willie Mullins, "Go get the Post Regulations." Willie went to the library and brought back a large notebook. DuPre opened the notebook and turned pages until he found Post Regulation 219. They all read it in silence. Mike Turner said, "All it says is that the individual is to report the accident to the provost marshal—period."

Grady walked to Terry Berisford's office and gave him a thumbs-up sign and said, "Let me know if I can do anything for you." Terry nodded.

No one in the office discussed Terry's situation during the remainder of the day. Colonel James said nothing to anyone and he didn't call Terry into his office to discuss it.

At exactly 0800 Tuesday morning General Lawrence called Colonel James on the telephone. "James, what about Berisford's position on Post Regulation 219?"

"I haven't talked with him about it, General."

"No, damn it, I mean does he have a valid position on the matter? Will his interpretation hold water?"

Colonel James badly needed to be in the good graces of General Lawrence in hopes of getting a good efficiency report from him, but James did exert his independence at times. His present feeling was that the general had his people in Russell Hall draw up Post Regulation 219 without the advice or approval of the JAG office. That action had offended James both professionally and personally. Having to prosecute soldiers for violation of that regulation only rubbed salt into the wound. Only now, after a flaw in the regulation had surfaced, was the general coming to the JAG office for advice.

"General, Captain Berisford has complied with the requirements of Post Regulation 219."

"Thank you."

Colonel James leaned back in his chair and contemplated the situation regarding Post Regulation 219 and about his prior silence in the matter. First of all, he had to admire Terry Berisford for having the guts to stand up to the general. But Terry was a RETREAD—his career was not on the line. Still, if James had it to do all over again, he would raise hell about the regulation. He initially believed it to be faulty on several grounds, but he let it pass without commenting. Every court-martial for violation of that regulation burned his conscience. In the back of his mind he always suspected that some day there would be a Terry Berisford to challenge the regulation. And, what about all those men already court-martialed?

Wednesday morning Grady saw Clarence Casey come in the front door of the JAG office and turn to the right and walk down the aisle toward the end of the building. John stepped out of his office and watched Clarence stop outside Terry Berisford's office, say something, and then enter Terry's office and pull the door closed.

Clarence Casey was in his late thirties, was tall and thin, and locks of his straw-colored hair stuck out from under his gray felt hat. Clarence was an enigma to Grady and to just about everyone else at Fort Monmouth who knew him. They all knew that he was in the Criminal Investigation Division(CID) of the army, but they never knew what he was doing. Since Grady had been in the JAG office, Casey had come in a number of times to see Colonel James or Sol Solomon. When he entered someone's office, he always pulled the door closed behind himself. He usually wore civilian clothes, most often a light-colored salt-and-pepper wool suit and the gray felt hat, but once he came into the office wearing the uniform of a sergeant first class. John once saw him on the post wearing a captain's uniform. Clarence would not tell anyone what his rank was. He was friends with John's secretary Sylvia and usually stopped in the claims office to see her before he left the building. John would say to him something like, "Hello Clarence, what brings you to the JAG office?" Each time Clarence would smile and say, "Oh, nothing." John asked Sylvia what his rank was and what he did, but she didn't know either. Clarence took delight in remaining a mystery man. He looked and acted somewhat countrified, but that did not mean that he was not a good investigator. He had the nose of a bloodhound and the tenacity of a bulldog.

Grady went to Terry Berisford's office at lunch time and said, "Do you want to go to the officers mess for lunch?" "Sure," Terry replied. During lunch, John didn't ask Terry about his situation except for one question when he asked, "Does the general have his hounds out?" Terry nodded in the affirmative. John said, "My offer stands."

A military person or civilian employee at Fort Monmouth was required to register his vehicle with the Fort Monmouth Provost Marshal in order to obtain a sticker that permitted the vehicle to be regularly driven and parked on the post. On the registration form, the applicant was required to show that the vehicle was insured by giving the name of the insurance carrier and the name of the insurance agent. Terry Berisford had his car insured through a local insurance agent Roy Long in Asbury Park and that information was on file in the provost marshal's office.

Thursday morning, an olive-drab army sedan pulled up in front of Roy Long's office, and Clarence Casey, dressed in his salt-and-pepper suit, stepped out and went into the office. He asked to see Roy Long and was shown into Long's office. Clarence introduced himself and said, "Mr. Long, I'm investigating an accident involving the car of a Captain Terence Berisford who's stationed at Fort Monmouth. That car is insured by you. Can you tell me about that accident and may I see your accident report on it?"

Roy Long was tall and thin, had sandy-colored hair, and wore rimless eyeglasses. He smiled politely and said, "Mr. Casey, I regard my client's insurance business as confidential, and I don't release any information without permission from my client. I've received no such authorization from Captain Berisford. Sorry."

Clarence persisted. "Has Captain Berisford or his wife filed a claim with you for damage to a vehicle they have insured with you or for injury or damage that they might have caused to other people or to other property?"

Mr. Long smiled again and said, "I'm sorry Mr. Casey. Now, if you will excuse me, I have business to attend to." Clarence thanked him and left the office. Roy Long wrote out a short note, put it in a plain envelope that he addressed to Captain Terence Berisford and gave it to his secretary and told her to mail it that day. (In talking with Mr. Long about the accident, Terry Berisford warned Long not to call him on the telephone because he suspected that his telephone line might be tapped.)

That same day, Clarence Casey went to the business offices of the New Jersey Bell Telephone Company in Asbury Park and asked to speak with the supervisor of the Customer Relations Department. He was shown into the office of Mr. Julian Howard. Clarence introduced himself and said that he was from Fort Monmouth and was investigating an automobile accident involving an automobile registered to a Captain Terence Berisford whose wife worked in Mr. Howard's department. Clarence asked Mr. Howard if he knew anything about an accident involving the Berisford family, and if he did, would he please tell him about it.

Mr. Howard did not take kindly to an army investigator coming to the New Jersey Bell Telephone Company to pry information from him about one of his employees' private life. Mr. Howard told Clarence, "I don't have such information, and I wouldn't tell you if I did."

Clarence was undeterred. "I'd like to talk to Mrs. Berisford, please."

Julian Howard bristled. "That is completely inappropriate. Mr. Casey, if you have no business with the New Jersey Bell Telephone Company I believe that our conversation is over." Clarence knew that he had struck out, so he left the office.

Later that day, Clarence Casey called on the Berisfords' landlord and asked him if he knew anything about the Berisfords being in an automobile accident. The landlord was no help to Clarence.

Monday morning, General Lawrence summoned Terry Berisford to his office. Terry entered the office, held a salute and said, "Captain Berisford reporting to the general as ordered, sir."

"Berisford, you've covered your tracks very well, but come hell or high water I'm going to find out about your automobile accident. Now, do you want to tell me about it?"

"Sir, I have met all the requirements of your Post Regulation 219. That's all I have to say on the matter."

"Well, when I find out—and I sure as hell will—I'll have something to say on the matter; you can bet on that. You're dismissed."

Everyone in the JAG office knew that Terry had gone to see the general. No one said anything to him when he returned. In about twenty minutes, Grady walked up to Terry's office and stuck his head in the door and said, "Do you have a minute, Terry?" Terry motioned him to come into his office. John asked him, "How are you and the wife holding up under the strain?"

Terry made half a smile and said, "We're making out all right."

"Is there anything I can do for you folks? I don't want you to think that you have to shoulder this burden alone. I'll be happy to help in any way I can."

"Thanks John. If I need your help I'll let you know."

"Terry, Rebecca and I would like for you and your wife to come over to our apartment for dinner some night this week. I promise we won't talk about Post Regulation 219 or General Lawrence."

"John, that's kind of you, and I appreciate it, but my wife and I both have been followed by the general's investigators, and if they report that I was visiting you it probably wouldn't be good for your career. You're Regular Army, and you don't need to get mixed up with me."

"Terry, I'm not concerned with that."

"That's all right, John, thanks just the same. Maybe some time later."

***

An order came down from post headquarters requiring all officers of the command to attend a classified meeting on national security. Two identical sessions would be held in theater No. 2, the theater where the first-run movies were shown. Warrant Officer Klingen split the officers in the JAG office into two groups. Grady was in a group with Mike Turner, Willie Mullins and Klingen. On the day of the classified meeting, John and his group walked from the JAG office down to Theater No. 2. Each man was checked off on a roster when he entered the lobby of the theater. The theater was completely filled by the starting time of 0900. Colonel Berl Thompson, G-2, began the meeting by announcing that the meeting was classified and that nothing about the contents of the meeting was to be disclosed. He announced the agenda of the meeting and then introduced Lieutenant Colonel August Hollman who had just returned from duty in Germany and would talk on the subject, Communications and Electronic Surveillance on the Fringes of Soviet-Occupied Eastern Europe. Hollman gave a very interesting talk about the activities of the Signal Corps units that monitored communications of the Soviet Red Army and other Communist armies in Eastern Europe. John was surprised at the audacity of the U.S. forces, but was pleased to know that they were monitoring the Soviets. The talk was well received, even by the lawyers from the JAG office.

Next, Hollman played an audio tape of a U.S. Army radio transmission in Morse code that the Soviets had electronically jammed. It was just a cacophony of weird noise to everyone in the audience, but Colonel Hollman said that trained Signal Corps radio operators could make out the Morse code message through all the noise that the Soviets were putting out. Really amazing!

General Lawrence was next on the agenda. In his customary style, he strode to the lectern and without notes began to talk. His theme was: The Security of The United States in the Face of Communist Espionage and Subversion.

He first spoke about the suspension for security reasons of civilian employees from the Signal Corps Engineering Laboratories. He said that the army had the right to suspend them without telling them what the charges were against them. He made the analogy that an insurance company had the right to deny insurance coverage to an applicant without telling the applicant the reason for the denial. Grady thought that it was a poor analogy.

The general said that he had no objection to using wire taps in the investigation of criminal and subversive activities. John noted that the general did not qualify the statement by saying "court approved" wire taps. He wondered if the omission were intentional or inadvertent.

Next, the general said that he was favorably impressed with Senator Joseph McCarthy's investigations of subversive activities. Lawrence asked the rhetorical question whether communists and communist sympathizers were dismissed from the U.S. State Department, from the U.S. Department of Defense, from colleges and universities, and from Fort Monmouth before McCarthy began his campaign? The general then stated his approval of President Eisenhower's order that permitted the firing of any government employee who took the Fifth Amendment and refused to answer questions about his past or present activities.

Lawrence then made the statement that he believed that many of the colleges and universities in the large metropolitan cities of the country had on their faculties Communist sympathizers who fostered communism in this country. He specifically mentioned City College of New York, Columbia University, Harvard, Yale, University of Chicago, University of Michigan, and Massachusetts Institute of Technology. He said that especially he didn't trust lawyers from the large Eastern law schools.

The general expressed his displeasure with the reporting of several newspapers such as the Asbury Park Press, The Washington Post, and the New York Post.

Grady thought that the general was rambling. His talk was not as well organized as past talks that John had heard him give. He remembered the general's actions and conversation the day the dignitaries made the inspection trip at Evans Signal Corps Engineering Laboratory. "Is the general loosing it?" John wondered.

Colonel Thompson concluded the meeting with the reminder that the meeting was classified.

On their walk back to the JAG office, Willie Mullins asked Grady, "What do you think about the general's remarks?"

"Well, as to some of them, if I were commanding general I wouldn't announce them in front of hundreds of people."

"Right," Mike Turner said. "I went to two of those universities that he called communist influenced. I guess I ought to apply for a transfer out of here before the general finds out."

"He probably already knows," Willie chuckled. "That's why he calls you to his office to lecture you about your vigorous defenses in courts-martial trials."

Grady really was surprised at the general's remarks. He wondered if something were physically or mentally wrong with the general. A man in his position should not make remarks like that.

Several days later, local newspapers published the gist of the generals remarks at the "classified" meeting.

※※※

The U.S. Army had been reducing its active-duty manpower ever since the United Nations signed the cease-fire with the Chinese and North Koreans on 27 July 1953. Many Reserve and National Guard units and individuals called to active duty at the beginning of the war were being released from active duty and returned to civilian life.

Not long after General Lawrence first called Captain Berisford to his office, he summoned him a second time. The general sat behind his desk and held a sheet of paper in his hand and said, "Berisford, you're a Reservist, and this paper I have here in my hand says that you're eligible for release from active duty, but you're not going anywhere until you tell me about that automobile accident. Now, are you going to tell me about it?"

"General Lawrence, I've told you all that I'm required to tell you."

Lawrence pounded his fist on his desk. "Well, by god, you are not leaving this post 'till you do, and I don't care how long that takes. Dismissed."

✳✳✳

That same afternoon Clarence Klingen distributed to each officer in the JAG office a communication from General Lawrence addressed to all officers at Fort Monmouth. It stated that each officer in the command must read the new book *The Rosenberg Case: Fact and Fiction*, by Rabbi Dr. S. Andhil Fineberg, published by Oceana Publications. The communication stated that the book was available for purchase in the PX and that each officer must read the book and sign the attached certificate certifying that he had read it. The signed certificate was to be returned to the post adjutant no later than 15 December 1953. Grady went to the PX after work and purchased his copy of the book. He arrived home that evening with the book in his hand. Rebecca asked, "What's that you have?" He explained the situation to her, and after dinner he read several chapters out loud to her. He left the book home during the day, and Rebecca finished reading it before he did. They discussed it evenings after dinner.

"Do you think the Rosenbergs were guilty?" she asked.

"Yes. I have to go with the judicial system." John picked up Rabbi Fineberg's book and searched through it until he found the passage he wanted. He read it to her.

The Rosenbergs had a trial by a jury of their peers. Conviction was by a unanimous vote of the 12 jurors. The sentence was appraised seven times by the U.S. Court of Appeals and upheld. The case came before the Supreme Court seven times. Repeatedly, the case went to the White House. President Eisenhower concluded there was no basis for clemency. There were 27 months of legal review.

John added, "Judge Kaufman was on the bench for the trial. He's a respected judge."

"John, I had no idea of the extent that the communists were involved in the demonstrations and agitations to free the Rosenbergs and to obtain clemency from the death sentence. Did you know that?"

"Not really. To be truthful, I didn't follow the matter that closely. I was recovering from my own encounter with the Communists in North Korea. Also, I guess I was self-centered in my school work and in my other duties—and, concentrating on you. But, it should teach us a lesson that the Communists can muster worldwide action for their causes while we in the U.S. go about our own business. We have to stay alert or they'll run over us."

"It's scary to think that they can raise that much agitation in the United States," Rebecca shuttered.

"If you will recall, not all the agitators were dedicated Communists," John replied. "There were many different kinds of people involved. Some were just against the death penalty. You remember that the Rabbi pointed out that a couple of well known scientists spoke out on the Rosenbergs' behalf. They probably were not communists or communist sympathizers, but just people who had soft feelings and were duped into following a cause. They didn't take the time or effort to investigate the matter thoroughly. Sometimes intelligent people become intellectually lazy."

"Do you think there are Communist spies at Fort Monmouth now?" Rebecca asked.

"I don't know for sure, but if there are, Joe McCarthy hasn't found them. I'm coming to the belief that he's a dangerous man. He's an attorney, and he was a judge, but he has no regard for personal rights. It's too bad, too, because we need people to fight Communism, but he's as bad as the communists when it comes to the truth and to smearing and abusing people. Before I found out much about him, I thought that he was sincere. I now find that hard to believe."

CHAPTER 5. (13 NOVEMBER 1953)

Sylvia called in at 0800 Friday morning and told John that she was not feeling well and would not come to work that day. John went to Warrant Officer Klingen and said, "Clarence, Sylvia just called and said that she's taking a sick day today. I have a couple of claims reports that I want to get out; can one of the other secretaries give me some help today?"

"You're in luck, John. Captain Berisford has taken leave today, so his secretary Helen is free. I'll send her in to you in a few minutes."

John explained to Helen what he wanted her to do. He showed her the material that he had worked out in draft form and said that there was a standard format for the final report. Grady told her, "I'll get one of our old reports from the files and you can use it for your guide." He went to Sylvia's file cabinet and started searching through the file folders for a suitable example. While looking, he came across an old correspondence file that he had never seen. He continued looking and found a suitable report for Helen to use as a guide. He gave the report to Helen and then pulled the old correspondence file that he had just found and took it to his desk. He quickly leafed through the carbon copies of memoranda and letters that a Captain Agee and a Major Balfour had generated during the year 1950. He had never heard of either man. He went back to the beginning of the file and examined the papers more closely. The memoranda related to military affairs and military justice matters and most were addressed to the Post Staff Judge Advocate. It appeared that Colonel James must have arrived in the JAG office some time after March 1950.

The title on one memo caught Grady's attention, so he pulled it from the folder. It was dated 9 March 1950 and was addressed to a Staff Judge Advocate that John did not know—undoubtedly James's predecessor. The title was, POST COMMANDER'S JURISDICTION OVER ACTS COMMITTED OFF-POST BY POST MILITARY PERSONNEL. John read and reread the title. "Holy Toledo! What in the world is this?" He quickly read the memo. Then he reread it slowly and analyzed it as he would a court opinion. It was a well-composed memorandum that had army military affairs and military justice opinions cited to support each conclusion reached. A paragraph of the memorandum commanded John's attention. He read it several times. It stated that in answer to the question recently posed by the post commander, it has been ruled that, in the continental United States, absence unique or extraordinary circumstances, a post commander lacks jurisdiction to control, restrict, or to impose conditions on the operation of a private vehicle that is operated by a military person outside a military reservation during the military person's off-duty hours.

Thoughts immediately raced through Grady's mind. He wondered who was post commander on 9 March 1950? Was this memo, or the conclusions in it, ever delivered to or communicated to that post commander?

John went out to Warrant Officer Klingen and asked, "Clarence, when did General Lawrence assume command of Fort Monmouth?"

'I don't know, but I'll find out if you need to know."

"I'll appreciate that, Clarence; I need to know."

A short time later, Klingen came into Grady's office and told him, "Russell Hall says that General Lawrence assumed command of Fort Monmouth on 17 January 1950."

"Thanks, Clarence."

That afternoon, John called Rebecca and told her, "Beck, I have some work to get done and I'll be late getting home, so don't wait supper for me." He lingered in his office that evening until everyone else had departed. He took the memo on a commander's jurisdiction to the office library. He carefully reread the memo, then went to the books in the library and read all the military affairs and military justice opinions cited in the memo. He spent two and one-half hours reading opinions, regulations, and laws, and making notes and copying citations. His training at JAG School was invaluable in helping him know where to look for what.

There was no question about it—the authorities made it clear that, in the absence of unique circumstances, a post commander in the continental United States lacked jurisdiction to court-martial military personnel in his command for ordinary-type private-vehicle accidents occurring off-post on off-duty time. That means that Post Regulation 219 is illegal!

Good lord! Grady felt that he had a tiger by the tail. Now that he had this information, what was he going to do with it? He was concerned about his own situation knowing that he had participated in convicting soldiers for violating Post Regulation 219. He was ashamed of himself for having been disturbed about prosecuting people for violating Post Regulation 219 but never researching the issue. The answer was right there in the reported opinions for anyone who cared enough to look. Why didn't he look? There was no excuse for not looking. Why hadn't the other JAG officers researched it?

John wondered about the memo? Did General Lawrence see the memo? Does he know about its conclusion? Has Colonel James seen it or does he know the contents of it? Has Terry Berisford seen the memo? Is that why Terry has taken his stand? But Terry said that he knew of no research on the issue. John had to believe Terry. And, what about all the men already convicted of violating Post Regulation 219?

Grady had a knot in his stomach. He leaned back in his chair and lit a cigarette and tried to decide what he should do. He had to do something, and soon, but he was completely without inspiration as to what it should be. He finished his cigarette and decided that he would go home. He folded the memo and his notes and slipped them into the inside breast pocket of his uniform jacket. He returned the books and materials to the library shelves and left the office.

He dreaded having to face Rebecca. She considered him to be her hero, and here he was someone who had prosecuted men for offenses that they should not have been prosecuted for, and he had gone along with it without making the effort to research the issue. Some hero he was! Rebecca was at the top of the steps to greet him with a smile and a kiss. She asked, "What are you working on that's taking so much time?"

"Oh nothing. I just wanted to research something while no one was there to disturb me."

"Have you eaten?"

"No, but I'm not hungry. I think I'll have a drink and maybe some snacks. That's all I want right now." He fixed himself a bourbon and soda and came into the living room and sat on the couch. Rebecca tried to engage him in conversation, but he wasn't doing much to keep it going. She knew that something was bothering him and it had to be something important because he handled most things without getting disturbed.

"Can I do anything to help?" she asked. They knew each other well, and she knew that he was troubled, and he knew that she knew.

He smiled at her. "Thanks, Beck, not yet. I have to sort out some things. I'll tell you about it when I know what to do." He took a few sips of his drink, then stood up and paced back and forth between the kitchen and the living room. He seemed unaware of her presence. After considerable pacing, he came over to her chair and leaned down and kissed her. "Thanks for being patient, Beck." He went back to the couch and thought some more. A voice within him kept telling him, "It's decision time, fellow." He remembered hearing that same voice several times in North Korea—a chill went through him at the memory. He asked himself, "How do I want this thing to end up?" The answer was easy. "I want to see Post Regulation 219 rescinded, and I want restitution made to the men who were court-martialed under Post Regulation 219. O.K., how are those things going to happen?" He decided that he had to disclose the matter to as many people and authorities as necessary to get the results. He decided first to talk to Terry Berisford about his findings. The memo and his research ought to be of benefit to Terry.

Grady figured that General Lawrence certainly knew about the memo since March 1950, but he subsequently went ahead with Post Regulation 219 with the belief that Colonel James lacked the guts to oppose him. That's why the general wanted all the courts-martial, and Grady, in the JAG office—he wanted as much advance notice as possible in the event James ever summoned up enough nerve to say or do something about it. "The general used me, and in more than one way," Grady told himself. "First, he wanted me to be his stool pigeon in the JAG office, and secondly, I was on a trial team that prosecuted men who had accidents in violation of his Post Regulation 219." Grady thought about it and concluded that he had no one to blame but himself. "If I had done my homework and researched the issue in the very beginning when I first became troubled about it, things might be different today," he told himself. He could not get out of his mind all the men who had been court-martialed for violating Post Regulation 219.

As a matter of pride, he was going to let Lawrence know that he had found the memo and had verified to his satisfaction that it was a valid legal opinion. He also wanted the general to know that he knew what the general's game was, and that the game was over. That seems like a nutty idea, but he was going to do it.

He also would tell Colonel James what he had found. James probably knows what's in the memo, and he has to know that the game is over.

Grady realized that if the general didn't rescind Post Regulation 219, then he, Grady, would have to pass the information on to First Army and/ or to the Judge Advocate General in the Pentagon in order to get some action. Or, maybe the congressmen and senators of the convicted soldiers should know what had happened to their constituents. That ought to get some action. He resolved that he was going to see this thing through to the end even if it meant the end of his career—and it very well might. It would not be easy for a first lieutenant to take on a major general and win.

He felt better now that he had decided what he was going to do. "Beck, come over and sit beside me; I want to tell you what's been bothering me." He went through the entire history of the matter and explained to her what had happened since Post Regulation 219 became effective, and what had happened that day. He told her what he was going to do and what the possible consequences to him might be.

She kissed him on the cheek. "I'll back you all the way. Just tell me what you need me to do for you."

"You're some kind of girl, you are. I need you to keep loving me."

At 0700 Saturday morning, John telephoned Terry Berisford at his home. Terry answered the phone with a sleepy voice.

"Hello Terry, this is John Grady."

"John, my telephone may be tapped. My wife had the telephone company check, but I can't guarantee that it isn't. You might not want to talk to me."

"Terry, I won't say anything now, but it's important that I talk to you as soon as I can. Are you free this morning for me to come over there?

"John, I told you before, you shouldn't associate with me these days."

"Terry, it doesn't matter now. I need to talk with you, and I'll appreciate it if you give me half an hour."

Terry was silent for a while. For John's sake, he didn't want John to get mixed up in his troubles. But he respected Grady and considered him a level-headed person. If Grady thought that it was important to talk with him right now, there must be a reason. "John, you should understand that my house probably is being watched, so your visit here will be known."

"Terry, it doesn't matter now."

Terry wondered why Grady was saying "it doesn't matter now." He had said it twice. "All right, John, when do you want to come over?"

"As soon as possible. I'm ready to leave here now."

"All right, come over now. Do you know where I live?"

"No."

Terry gave him directions.

Grady found Berisford's house on a quiet street of modest homes. The house was a one and one-half story bungalow with siding of large bluish-gray shingles in need of paint. The upper half-story overhung the large front porch, and the wide, shingle-covered pillars that supported the overhang kept the front porch and the front room of the house in subdued light. Grady knocked, and Terry opened the door and welcomed him. Berisford had on a pair a gray flannel trousers and a gray sweatshirt, and he hadn't shaved yet. "Let me take your coat. Have a seat," Terry said. His wife came into the room and greeted John and asked about Rebecca. She said to the two men, "Would you fellows like some coffee?"

"Sure," Terry said. She served the coffee and left the room.

John began, "Terry, what I'm going to tell you is for your information. I'm not soliciting any action or cooperation from you, but I thought the information might be of interest to you. You can do anything with it you want, or you can do nothing with it.

"You know that I've been troubled about us prosecuting men under Post Regulation 219." John told him about finding the memo the previous day and what he had found in his research. He then pulled the folded memo from the inside pocket of his sport coat and handed it to Terry. Both men were silent as Terry read it. Terry handed it back to Grady without comment.

John told Terry why he believed the general knew what was in the memo when he issued Post Regulation 219. For background information, he told Terry about the general transferring him from Troop Command to the JAG office in hopes of having a spy in the JAG office even though John told him that he would not be his spy.

He told Terry what action he had decided to take. "I now think I'll try to get an appointment to see General Lawrence Monday morning. I know him well enough that I think he'll see me without knowing what it is I want to see him about. Even if he didn't know before that Post Regulation 219 is unlawful, he'll know now. If he continues with Post Regulation 219, higher authorities will not look kindly on him for continuing when he had legal advice that his actions were wrong.

"I then will talk with Colonel James about the situation. He's been good to me, and I owe it to him to tell him what I'm doing. If any corrective action results from my initiative, it probably assures the end of the colonel's army career. But he made his decision on how he wanted to deal with Post Regulation 219 and now his day of reckoning has arrived.

"If I don't get positive action from the general in a couple of days, I'll go up the chain of command to First Army and/or the Pentagon. Realistically, I expect I'll have to do that. I intend to tell the general and the colonel that I'll do that. That's about it, Terry. I don't know if this information will be of any use to you, but I wanted to run it past you before it hits the fan."

Terry was silent. He took a sip of coffee. "Would you like some hot coffee; this is cold?" John nodded. Terry picked up both mugs and took them into the kitchen and came back with hot coffee. He sat down and sipped his coffee. Grady sipped his. Neither man spoke.

Terry took another sip of coffee, put the mug down, and said, "What you propose is bold action, John."

"I can't think of any other way to attack the situation than to meet it head on. Terry, I'm ashamed of myself for having done nothing up until now. I have to do something."

"Maybe you won't have to."

"What do you mean?"

"John, I don't know if you know it or not, but I took a day's leave yesterday."

"Yes, I know. Helen did some typing for me yesterday. Do you remember me telling you that's how I came across the memo?"

"Yes. Well, yesterday I went up to First Army Headquarters on Governor's Island and talked to the Inspector General of First Army. I told him about General Lawrence's Safe Driving campaign including his four-day restriction on driving for everyone below the rank of captain. I showed him a copy of Post Regulation 219 and told him about the number of courts-martial we are having under it, many of which are for accidents off-post during off-duty hours. I told him about my problem with the general and the fact that he's holding up my release from active duty because I won't tell him about my accident. I told him how the general and his investigators are hounding my wife and me. The Inspector General called in First Army JAG people and we talked with them. It was decided that the Inspector General and some JAG people will come down to Fort Monmouth to look into the matter of Post Regulation 219 and the courts-martial under it. They also are going to do something about the general holding up my release from active duty. They'll be down next week or the week after.

"John, I can't tell you what to do, but why don't you hold off on your plans until you see what comes out of First Army's investigation. You might get the result you want without sticking your neck out. I'm leaving active duty, so it doesn't matter that I'm the one who upsets the general's apple cart. You're staying; there's no reason to put your career in jeopardy if you don't need to. What do you think?"

Grady never expected anything like this. He didn't know what to make of it. He sipped his coffee and didn't say anything while he evaluated the situation. "Terry, what are the chances that First Army will do something about this. I worry that if I carry out my plan, will the army protect it's own, so to speak? Will the army do nothing to the general but make trouble for me? After talking with them at First Army, did you get a feel for how they're going to approach this matter?"

"John, I'm of the opinion that First Army is going to be objective about it. They asked me what kind of man Lawrence is. They knew about his recent comments about Communists on college faculties. And apparently, there is more going on here about security matters in the Signal Corps Engineering Laboratories than we know about. First Army is watching Lawrence."

"What did First Army JAG people think of Post Regulation 219?"

"Their initial reaction was that they didn't like it, but they said they would research it. Your memo and research could be helpful to them if they need it.

"John, my recommendation to you is to sit tight and see what happens."

They sipped their coffees in silence. Finally, Grady spoke. "Terry, right now I'm inclined to take your recommendation. If you hadn't done what you did and I went my route, I probably would have to go to First Army. So, you're at least two steps ahead of me. I'll wait and see what happens. If First Army doesn't do anything as a result of your visit, I'll take a different route.

"Terry, I'll be on my way now. I hope your efforts are successful, and I wish you success in getting released from active duty. If I can help you in any way, let me know. You can be sure that I won't discuss with anyone what you told me this morning, and I know you'll treat my information the same. However, I will have to tell Rebecca because I told her that I would make my move on Monday. She'll have to know why I'm not starting it on Monday. She won't tell anyone.

"I have a favor to ask of you, Terry. I don't want this memo to be on me when I leave here. If your house is being watched, as you suspect, someone might stop me on my way home. This is the only copy I have, and I don't want the general to get an advantage. Can you mail it to me?"

"I understand. Sure, I'll mail it."

"Thanks. Mail it in a plain envelope. Maybe you had better address it to my wife. Use her maiden name and send it to her parents' home." John gave him the name and address.

CHAPTER 6. (NOVEMBER 1953)

At exactly 0815 the following Thursday morning, the Inspector General of First Army and the Inspector General from the Pentagon walked into General Lawrence's aide's office, introduced themselves, and said that they wanted to speak with General Karl Lawrence. They introduced themselves to Lawrence and told him that they wanted to talk with him about Fort Monmouth Post Regulation 219.

At precisely the same moment that the Inspectors General walked into General Lawrence's aide's office, a lieutenant colonel and a major from First Army JAG walked into the Fort Monmouth JAG office and told Warrant Officer Clarence Klingen that they wanted to speak with Lieutenant Colonel James. They told James that they wanted to discuss with him the courts-martial that had been conducted for violation of Fort Monmouth Post Regulation 219.

It was not long before everyone in the JAG office knew that there were visitors from First Army JAG in Colonel James's office. Grady was surprised that the visitors had come so soon. He didn't expect First Army to do anything for a couple of weeks, if then. He didn't say anything to anyone. Terry Berisford said nothing.

The visitors were in James's office for over an hour. After they left, James remained in his office with the door closed for twenty minutes. He came out and called a meeting of the entire office staff, both military and civilian. When everyone had gathered in the conference room, James spoke. "You all know that I had visitors this morning. They were from First Army JAG, and they were interested in our enforcement of Post Regulation 219. They want to review all courts-martial trials that we have held in the last eighteen months. Mr. Klingen, you will pull all the files and trial records and make them available to the officers from First Army. They will begin reviewing them Monday morning. Have three desks available for them to work on. I want everyone to cooperate to the fullest extent with the First Army people. Give them anything they ask for." James assigned one of the civilian secretaries to be available to provide them secretarial service if they needed it.

Clarence Klingen spoke up. "Colonel, a clarification, please. You said they were investigating trials under Post Regulation 219, but you told me to pull all the files and trial records for the last eighteen months. Do you want me to pull all of them or only the ones under Post Regulation 219?"

"They want to see all the special and general courts-martial cases that we have tried in the last eighteen months regardless of what the charges and specifications were. The enlisted men here in the office will help you. If you have to work through the weekend to get everything ready, then you will do so. I want to know by Saturday noon how you are progressing.

"To you officers who are serving as trial counsels and defense counsels, you will not hold any new trials of any kind until notified otherwise. That is all."

In the afternoon, Grady learned that the Inspectors General had visited General Lawrence that morning. To say that General Lawrence and the Fort Monmouth JAG office were "on the carpet" would be putting it mildly! That evening John told Rebecca what had happened. She listened intently to every word that John told her.

"John, are the JAG officers who tried those cases in trouble? Are you in trouble?"

"I don't know, Beck. We're junior officers following orders. But that's a pretty feeble excuse, and it wasn't a successful defense for Nazi officers in the Nuremberg Trials after World War II. I don't know how First Army and the Pentagon will deal with us.

"This is a bad situation for the general and for all of us in the JAG office. It's a hard way to learn, but it has taught me a lesson. I was troubled with Post Regulation 219 for a long time, but I did nothing about it. I stayed dumb and complacent while we court-martialed men for violating that regulation. Those men lost at least some of their rights, their freedom, and their money, and now some of us in the JAG office may have a day of reckoning coming because of our complacency. That should teach us that unless we're diligent about everyone's rights and freedoms, all of us will suffer adverse consequences of some kind. Beck, if I ever forget that lesson, you remind me. O.K.?"

"Should I continue playing bridge with the officers wives? What should I say if they ask me questions?"

"Go ahead and play if you want to. Tell them the truth about what you know, except that you shouldn't say anything about Terry Berisford going to the First Army Inspector General. I promised him I wouldn't disclose that to anyone but you. And don't say what I found out from that memo or what I intended to do. That doesn't leave you much to say, does it."

The following morning, a notice from post headquarters arrived in the JAG office advising that Post Regulation 219 was suspended, effective immediately.

Rebecca and John spent the weekend talking about the situation. They both were restless and concerned.

Monday morning when John arrived in the JAG office, army officers from First Army already were there working. Two JAG captains were at desks reading trial records. The lieutenant colonel who was there last Thursday was at another desk reading records. Grady introduced himself to the First Army officers later in the morning. They were cordial and showed no animosity.

Mid-morning on Wednesday, Lieutenant Colonel Sayer, the JAG Lieutenant Colonel from First Army, came into Grady's claims office and ask if he could talk with him. Sayer asked Sylvia to leave the room, and he closed the door when she left. Grady was apprehensive.

"Lieutenant Grady, Captain Berisford tells me that you've done some research into the legality of Post Regulation 219 and that you were going to do something as a result of it. Is that correct?

"Yes sir."

"What kind of information do you have?"

Grady told him about the memo he had found and about his research on the subject.

"May I see what you have."

"Sir, the memo is here in the files, but my research notes are at home. My notes are not too well organized, so I don't know if they'll be of value to anyone else."

"May I see the memo?" Grady went to the file cabinet and pulled the file and found the memo. Sayer read it. "Does your research support the conclusions reached in this memo?"

"Yes sir, right down the line."

"I want to see your research notes; bring them to the office tomorrow. We also have done some research on the matter, but I would like to see what you have. This memo looks good."

"I think it is, sir."

Sayer stayed in Grady's office and talked with him. He asked John about his background and prior service, and asked how a Signal Corps officer earned the Combat Infantry Badge. Grady was as brief as possible. After Sayer left, John thought that the conversation had gone well, but he still didn't know how he stood with First Army and the Pentagon.

With all courts-martial trials suspended, Grady, as Claims Officer, was the only Fort Monmouth officer in the JAG office who stayed busy.

The First Army men completed their review in eight working days and returned to Governors Island. They would write a final report and forward it to First Army Headquarters.

In mid-December, orders came down from First Army Headquarters declaring that Fort Monmouth Post Regulation 219 was null and void, *ab initio*, and was rescinded in its entirety. The order also said that all courts-martial based on violations of Post Regulation 219 were null and void and were rescinded. Full restitutions were to be made of ranks and of all fines and penalties assessed against defendants for alleged violations of Post Regulation 219. And, records of those courts-martial, of any confinements, reductions in rank, fines, or penalties of any kind whatsoever resulting from those courts-martial were to be expunged from the personnel records of the former defendants. The Fort Monmouth JAG office was responsible to accomplish the above in the next forty-five days.

Colonel James assigned Warrant Officer Klingen, Lieutenant Mike Turner, Lieutenant Robert Plusser, the enlisted men in the office, and three secretaries to carry out the restitution order. Other personnel would be added if needed. That was a formidable task because some men prosecuted under Post Regulation 219 now were stationed at other Stateside army posts, others were overseas, and some had been discharged from the army.

The orders from First Army contained nothing regarding officers in the Fort Monmouth JAG office who had prosecuted the courts-martial cases. Still, Grady was chagrined; he had never been in that type of a situation before.

Captain Terence Berisford received orders to report to Camp Kilmer, N.J., for release from active duty.

After everyone had a chance to contemplate what the First Army orders meant, John went back to Terry Berisford's office and congratulated him on receiving orders for release from active duty. He told Terry, "Your

action blew the lid off the whole matter of Post Regulation 219. Congratulations, and thanks. "When do you go to Kilmer for separation?"

"Next Monday. And now that this ordeal is over, what do you say we
take the wives out to dinner this weekend?"

"That sounds great to me."

Several officers from the JAG office were at lunch in the officers mess
when Willie Mullins said that he had heard comments in his BOQ that
some senior officers on the post were blaming the JAG office for getting
Fort Monmouth and General Lawrence into trouble with First Army and
with the Pentagon over the Post Regulation 219 matter. They said that
it was the JAG office's responsibility to advise the general on the illegality of Post Regulation 219 but it had dropped the ball. They said that if
the general had known that it was illegal, none of the trouble would have
occurred. Terry Berisford and Grady were present at that lunch but said
nothing.

When the men returned to the office after lunch, Terry asked Colonel
James if he could make a statement to the office staff. Everyone gathered
in the conference room. Terry told them that he had gone to the First
Army Inspector General and alerted him about Post Regulation 219. He
said that everything that occurred in the First Army investigation resulted
from his visit to Governors Island, and that no one else should be blamed.
He did not go into the illegality of the regulation, or into Grady's finding
the memo, or into the probability that Colonel James and the general knew
from the beginning that the regulation was illegal. Word spread throughout the post that Terry Berisford caused all the trouble. But still, the JAG
office and the people who worked there were in disfavor with a number of
military people on the post.

There was one further fallout from the Post Regulation 219 matter.
Lieutenant Colonel James was notified that he again had been passed over
for promotion to full colonel. That meant that he must retire. He took the
news stoically and discussed it with people in the office. He would retire
effective 15 January 1954.

Colonel James let it be known in the office that he would be liberal
in granting leave during the coming holidays to officers not involved in
the restitution project. Grady had been riding emotional highs lately as
a result of the Post Regulation 219 matter, the First Army investigation,
and McCarthy's civilian-employee security investigation, and he wanted to

relax. He was getting along well with Mr. and Mrs. Hazlet and with Liz, and he was looking forward to a family-centered holiday season. It had been a long time since he had enjoyed one. He applied for a seven-day leave starting on Thursday, 24 December 1953. Colonel James immediately approved it. Willie Mullins requested, and was granted, the same days as Grady.

CHAPTER 7. (21 DECEMBER 1953)

"Beck, I got the leave: seven days starting on the 24th. What do you want to do on our first Christmas together?"

She put her arms around him and kissed him. "Anything you want to do. What's your pleasure?"

"I'd like to relax and take it easy, if that's O.K. with you. I'd like to just enjoy the holiday season. My father enjoyed the Christmas holidays. We always had a nice Christmas tree and plenty of candy and cookies, even in the depths of the depression when we had very little money."

"What about Christmas? Mother and Liz asked me what we're going to do. Mother invited us to spend Christmas eve and Christmas day with them if we don't go somewhere. Do you want to do that?"

"Yes, I'd enjoy that."

"I was hoping you'd say that. This'll be the first year in a long time that my family will be together for Christmas, and with you there it'll be extra special."

Rebecca and John went to the Hazlets' home for dinner on the night of the 23rd. After dinner Mr. Hazlet and John brought the Christmas tree into the house and set it up. Everyone joined in decorating it. As they sat admiring their efforts, W.R. (Mr. Hazlet) said to Rebecca and John, "Why don't you stay here tomorrow night. We can be up early Christmas morning to open presents."

"All right, that will be nice. Thank you," John replied.

On the 24th, Rebecca and John arrived at the Hazlets before lunch with a shopping bag full of presents for the Hazlets and the Scotts. They had a leisurely lunch and an afternoon of just socializing among themselves. It was just what John needed to unwind.

Liz had made a good adjustment to her role as the prodigal daughter and had been doing volunteer work at Riverview Hospital and at the public library. She had lost considerable weight and was a very attractive woman. She and John were alone for a short time during the afternoon. John said to her, "Liz, you look great, congratulations. Do you have any plans for your immediate future?"

"Yes. I've been accepted at the University of Pennsylvania. I'm going down after the holidays to start the second semester. They're transferring all of my credits, so I can get my degree in three semesters."

"Terrific. What's your major?"

"Economics. They have a good department there, and I'm thinking about going to grad school at Wharton, so a degree from there won't hurt."

"Sounds good, Liz, I'm happy for you. Good luck.

Everyone in the house was in a good mood and they had a delightful roast beef dinner. Mrs. Hazlet wanted to go to the Episcopal Church for Christmas Eve services, so they all went with her. The weather was cold and rainy, but it didn't dampen their Christmas spirits. They returned to the Hazlet home and had eggnog and cookies before retiring.

John thought back to Christmas 1950 when his Christmas gift was assurance that he would not lose his left arm.

Grady was up early Christmas morning and went downstairs. Liz also was up early and made them coffee. Mr. and Mrs. Hazlet came down shortly thereafter.

"Why Mother, what are you doing up so early?" Liz said. "This is some kind of record for you."

"I don't want to miss anything," her mother said. She was delighted to have the family together for the holidays. They drank coffee and talked.

Mr. Hazlet suggested, "What do you say we have some breakfast. Sally has made my favorite breakfast cake."

"Let me go get Rebecca," John said. "Let's have a nice family breakfast together." He left them and went upstairs.

Mr. Hazlet said to the others, "Did you hear what he said? 'Let's have a nice family breakfast.' I'm delighted he feels that he's part of the family."

Liz spoke up, "He may be the best thing that's happened to this family in a long time."

Her mother replied, "No, the best thing that has happened to this family in a long time is that you returned home."

"Why Mother, that's the sweetest thing you've ever said to me. Thank you." She went over and kissed her mother on the cheek.

John returned and said, "She's getting dressed. She'll be right down."

They ate breakfast, and then the Scotts joined them and they all gathered around the Christmas tree and opened gifts.

Rebecca and John wanted to take a walk but it still was raining. The family talked about what they would do for the remainder of the day and for the remainder of the weekend. Mr. Hazlet spoke up, "The weather here is not going to be good for the next couple of days, so let's all fly down to West Palm Beach and spend a couple of days in warm weather."

The others were surprised at the suggestion and had to think about it. Liz spoke up first. "That's a great idea, Daddy. Can we get reservations this late?"

"Tomorrow is Saturday—no one will be traveling tomorrow. Liz, see what you can do to get reservations for us.

"John, I assume that's all right with you."

John didn't know about that. It was the end of the month, his checking account was near rock bottom, and he wasn't going to allow Rebecca to pay for it. "Well, I don't know, it's the end of the month and—"

"Nonsense, this is on me. This is a family Christmas present. How long can you stay?"

Rebecca came over to John and said, "John, let's do it. Who knows, this may be the last time the family will be together for some time."

"All right. I have to be back on duty on the 31st, so Rebecca and I will have to leave there next Wednesday."

Liz said, "I probably should come back with Sis and John to get ready for school. I want to get settled at Penn before classes start."

"That's fine too," Mr. Hazlet said. "Liz, go call the airlines and see what reservations you can get us. We can leave early tomorrow morning. Very little business will be transacted between Christmas and the New Year, so there's no sense in me going to the office. Mother and I will return on the 3rd. "

Very early the next morning they all crammed into John's car and drove to the Newark airport. They arrived in West Palm and took a limousine to the Hazlet's beach home. They unpacked, then Liz and her mother took their West Palm car to the supermarket.

The weather was warm with just a slight breeze blowing. After lunch, Rebecca and Liz said that they were going swimming and talked John into joining them. He had a problem—the Hazlets had never seen his bad left arm or his foot with the missing toes. He went to his room and put on his swimming trunks, then put on one of the long-sleeve sport shirts that he had brought with him. He kept the long sleeves rolled down. He wore sneakers that he had brought with him.

The family walked onto the beach, and Mr. Hazlet set up aluminum folding chairs and a beach umbrella for Mrs. Hazlet and himself. Rebecca and Liz had beach towels to lay on. Mr. and Mrs. Hazlet sat while the girls and John went to the water's edge. Liz and Rebecca waded into the water up to their knees. "How's the water temperature?" John called. Rebecca put up a brave front and said, "Not bad." The girls slowly worked their way into deeper water. Liz was the first to make the plunge into the water. She swam about and called for Rebecca to join her. She did and the two of them swam for a short time. They both came out and dried off with their towels. They confessed that it was cold, but "not too bad after you're in for a while." The family talked and enjoyed the warm sunshine.

John said to Rebecca, "Let's take a walk up the beach." They walked up the beach about one hundred and fifty yards and stopped. He took off his sneakers and shirt and waded into the water. Rebecca joined him. They swam for a while, then came out of the water and dried off. He put on his long-sleeve shirt, but he didn't want to put his sneakers on his sandy feet. They walked back to the others, and they all basked in the sun and talked. John kept his toes buried in the sand.

After a while Rebecca said, "I want to take a shower."

"I'll go with you," John said as he picked up his towel and sneakers.

As John and Rebecca walked toward the house, Liz noticed their footprints in the nearby sand and called, "Daddy, come look at this." Hazlet stood up and went to where Liz was standing. She pointed to the sand and said, "Look at John's left footprint. What do you think?"

"I would say that he has toes missing, wouldn't you?"

As Rebecca and John were about to enter the house, he looked back and saw Liz and her father looking at the footprints. That night in bed John said to Rebecca, "Did you see your father and Liz looking at our footprints in the sand? They might have noticed my missing toes. It's kind of awkward having to hide my wounds from them. They probably think I'm weird wearing sneakers and a long-sleeve shirt on the beach."

Rebecca responded, "Why don't you just go ahead and show them your wounds and get it over with. You don't want this to go on for the rest of our lives."

"Maybe you're right."

The next morning after breakfast, the family was sitting on the verandah looking at the ocean and talking. Rebecca and John sat in chairs on one side of a coffee table. Mr. and Mrs. Hazlet sat on a wicker couch on the opposite side of the table, and Liz was in a wicker chair next to the couch. When a lull came in the conversation, John said, "I noticed that you were looking at my footprints in the sand yesterday. Rebecca and I talked about it, and maybe it's appropriate that I no longer hide my wounds from you. They aren't a pretty sight, but as Rebecca said, maybe we should get this behind us. What do you think?"

"Whatever you want to do, John," Mr. Hazlet said.

"Well, O.K. I think you know that I was in North Korea in winter where the temperatures were far below zero and frostbite was a constant danger. I tried hard to prevent it, but somehow my toes became badly frostbitten. Army doctors in Japan amputated my small toe and two joints of my second toe on my left foot." Grady took off his left shoe and sock and showed them his foot. "It really is no problem to me now." The Hazlets were silent.

"I was shot twice in my left arm. I wasn't able to get it properly treated for a while and it became infected which caused some problems." He stood up and removed his long-sleeve sport shirt and showed them his arm. "It's not very attractive, and I'll try not to expose it to you, but if I swim with you, for example, it'll be difficult to conceal it."

The Hazlets had serious looks on their faces, but said nothing.

John was putting his shirt back on when Rebecca said, "Well . . .."

He turned his head to her and asked, "Well, what?"

She had a devilish grin on her face. "Well, don't stop now—go ahead and finish."

"You think you're pretty smart, don't you," he said as he grinned back at her.

Grady turned to the Hazlets and said, "What your smart aleck daughter, and sister, is referring to is that I also have a wound on my buttock, but I'm not going to drop my trousers to show it to you."

"I'm with Sis—don't stop now," Liz exclaimed with a broad smile on her face.

"Liz!" her mother scolded. They all laughed.

The family had a restful and enjoyable four and one-half days. Liz, Rebecca, and John arrived home on the evening of 30 December. Rebecca commented that it was nice to be back in their little apartment.

CHAPTER 8. (31 DECEMBER 1953)

Grady was in his claims office before 0800 on Thursday, 31 December, looking through the correspondence that had accumulated while he was away. Willie Mullins came into his office and asked him what he had done on his leave. A few minutes later, Clarence Klingen walked in and said, "I'm glad I caught the two of you together." He handed each of them a sheet of paper and walked out of the office.

"Well, I'll be damned," Willie said. What they were reading was an order from Headquarters, Signal Corps Center and Fort Monmouth that transferred both of them from the JAG office to 9404 TSU, Signal Corps Center Troop Command, effective 1 January 54. They looked at each other.

"I guess Colonel James has seen this order," Grady said.

"Probably so, but I'll find out." Willie went out to ask Clarence Klingen, but he was not at his desk. The two men walked to Colonel James's office and knocked on his door.

Grady spoke first. "Colonel, I presume you've seen these orders transferring Willie and me to Troop Command."

"Yes, John, I have. I don't like to lose either of you, but Troop Command has been after you two for some time. They claim they're short of Signal Corps company grade officers for the student regiment. I've been able to keep you here up until now because we've been busy, but things have slowed down since Post Regulation 219 was rescinded, as you know, so the regimental commander has won out on both of you."

Grady spoke again. "Colonel, the transfer is effective 1 January, but that's a holiday, and then the weekend follows. I don't know what they want us to do about reporting in for duty. Will it be all right if we go over to Troop Command for a short time to find out what they want us to do?"

"Yes, certainly, but come back here because I want you to tell Mr. Klingen where you stand on the work you're doing so someone else can pick up on it without any trouble."

Troop Command had a new commander Lieutenant Colonel Alfred Keuper. John didn't know him. And almost the entire regimental headquarters staff was new to him. He asked Willie, "What do you know about the regimental commander and his staff?"

"I don't know much about him. He's a bachelor, or divorced, and lives in my BOQ. I get the impression that he likes his liquor, and I kind of think he has a short temper. But I really don't know him; I've stayed away from him."

'O.K. Willie, straighten your tie, comb your hair, and let's go over there and get it over with." They walked over to regimental headquarters and reported to the regimental adjutant Captain Leighter. Grady introduced Willie and himself and told Leighter why they were there.

"Oh yes, we've been waiting a long time for you fellows."

"Captain, our orders are to report in tomorrow, but it's a holiday, and then we have the weekend. Do you want us to report in tomorrow? If not, when?"

The captain leaned back in his chair and said, "The old man is on leave for the holidays, so why don't you two report in at 0700 Monday morning."

"Very well, sir. Thank you." Grady and Mullins saluted and returned to the JAG office. Grady spent the remainder of the working day making a detailed docket of all his work on hand so the next claims officer could pick up where he left off. At 1600 he said his good-byes to those who were in the JAG office.

John arrived home, kissed Rebecca, and announced, "I have some news. I've been transferred from the JAG office back to Troop Command, effective tomorrow, but I don't report in until Monday morning."

Rebecca looked at him with a worried look. She contemplated what he just said. "Is that good or bad? Is it because of the Post Regulation 219 business?"

"I don't know what assignment I'll get, so I don't know if it'll be better or worse. Willie Mullins also was transferred. We were the only Signal Corps officers in the JAG office, and Colonel James told us that Troop Command has been trying to get us for some time."

"John, this is dumb—just plain dumb. You spent three months at JAG school and just returned in September, and now they're taking you out of JAG work. What a waste."

He smiled at her, "That's the army."

Mullins and Grady were at regimental headquarters at 0700 Monday morning. The adjutant was not at his desk and the colonel's door was closed, so John and Willie sat on a bench outside the colonel's office. The colonel's door opened five minutes later and out strode Major Roger Hardy, the veteran campaigner with the First Infantry Division during World War II. As a captain, Hardy had been company commander of the 3901 Service Company that had so many courts-martial. He had been promoted to major and now was commander of 1st Battalion in the student regiment. Because he had had so many courts-martial in the "Thirty-nine-Oh-Worst" and had worked with the JAG officers, he knew John and Willie.

Hardy stopped in his tracks when he saw Grady and Mullins sitting there. John and Willie stood up and saluted. "Major, congratulations on your promotion," Grady said.

Hardy nodded his head and said, "What are you guys doing here?"

"We've been transferred to Troop Command. We're reporting in," Grady replied.

Hardy wheeled around, reentered the regimental commander's office and pulled the door closed. Grady and Mullins looked at each other. Several minutes later the door opened and Major Hardy reemerged. He walked up to the two sitting officers, pointed to Grady and said, "You're Company Commander of Company C, 1st Battalion." He pointed to Mullins and said, "And you're Executive officer of Company A, 1st Battalion." Without another word, Hardy walked off.

John said to Willie, "We still have to pay our respects to the regimental commander." John knocked on the door frame and a voice said, "Enter." Both officers entered, saluted, and announced that they were reporting for duty.

Lieutenant Colonel Alfred Keuper was of average build. He had sandy-colored hair and a flushed complexion. The colonel went directly to the point and told them what their assignments were. He looked at Grady and said, "I don't have an executive officer for you." That was it—the meeting was over. Grady's impression was that Keuper was a cold personality, and maybe, not real sure of himself.

The 1st Battalion was located at a far corner of the post in new barracks that were only a year old. The enlisted students in the battalion had a long march to and from their classrooms in The Signal School. Each company of the battalion had its own large barracks, and there was one large mess hall for all three companies of the battalion. It was attached to the rear of Company C barracks, and the battalion commander was responsible for the battalion mess. The battalion office was in Company B barracks.

Grady made a brief stop to formally pay his respects to Major Hardy, then he went to C Company and met the present company commander Captain Vincent Moore. Moore had done a good job with Company C. He was as tall as Grady, had a muscular body, dark hair and dark eyes, and a full dark mustache. Moore had orders for duty in Trieste, a current hot spot in the confrontation between the Soviet Union and the U.S.

Moore informed Grady, "The first sergeant is not in the company area right now, and the duty sergeant is in the hospital, but if you want to get started with checking inventory you can start with the supply sergeant. The noncommissioned officers in the company are good, and the first sergeant is exceptionally good. If you want to take off your blouse, you can hang it on the clothes rack there in the corner." Grady hung his "Ike" jacket next to Moore's, and the two of them went to the supply room in the basement of the barracks where Moore introduced Grady to Staff Sergeant Gerald Bond. Moore left them, and Grady told Bond how he was going to go about the transfer of command.

Grady resolved to be as thorough as he possibly could. They counted inventory until late in the afternoon. They took a break, and Grady returned to the company commander's office. The first sergeant was back in his office, and Moore called him in and introduced him to Grady. Master Sergeant Oskar Champolis was first sergeant and went by the name of Sergeant Champ.

Moore said, "Sergeant Champ, this is Lieutenant Grady. He's just finished a tour of duty in the JAG office here at Monmouth." John didn't have his Ike jacked on, so he wore no indication of rank and no ribbons. The first sergeant seemed unimpressed and was thinking that he would have to spoon-feed this legal eagle to teach him what the real army was like.

John returned to the supply room in the basement and worked with the supply sergeant until 1800. "Sergeant Bond, let's call it a day. I'll see you tomorrow morning at 0700 and we'll continue." Grady went upstairs and entered the company commander's office. Moore was not there, but Sergeant Champ was over at the clothes rack looking at Grady's jacket. Grady stood watching Champolis inspecting his ribbons and decorations. "Sergeant Champ, can I help you?"

"Uh … uh … I was just looking at The Lieutenant's ribbons. I recognize the CIB, the Purple Heart, and a couple of the others, but I don't know this one, sir."

"That's the Silver Star, Sergeant."

"Very good, sir, thank you. I didn't know that The Lieutenant was decorated." From that time forward, Sergeant Champ was as helpful as he could be. He indeed was an excellent first sergeant. He never addressed or referred to Grady as "you," or as "Lieutenant," or as "Lieutenant Grady"; he always addressed Grady in the third person: "The Lieutenant."

The transfer of command went smoothly. The first thing Grady did after that was to go to the Fort Monmouth Dispensary and visit his duty sergeant Technical Sergeant Bruce Stuart. Stuart and his wife had an argument at their home and she stabbed him with a butcher's knife. The wound was deep, but the knife had missed vital organs. Grady introduced himself and asked Stuart if there were anything he needed or wanted. Stuart said "No" and appeared to be chagrined. John wished him a speedy recovery and said that he was looking forward to working with him when he returned to duty. Grady visited Stuart twice each week until he returned to duty. John remembered what it was like to be in the hospital.

Being a company commander required considerably more time at work than the 0800 to 1700 hours he had worked at the JAG office. Not having an executive officer meant that John had no one to share the officer-type duties with. And, with the duty sergeant in the hospital, it meant that Grady and the first sergeant had to cover everything between the two of them. One fortunate thing for Grady was that they had a battalion mess hall that the battalion commander was responsible for. When John had Company K, he was responsibile for his own company mess hall.

Company C had three hundred and twenty-three enlisted men, making it the largest company in the battalion, and it was the only company in the battalion that did not have an executive officer to assist the company commander.

**

General Lawrence had suffered a setback in his safe driving campaign by the revocation of Post Regulation 219, so he directed his energies to other endeavors. He said that he had the responsibility for the spiritual well-being of the troops in his command as well as for their physical well-being, so he scheduled a Spiritual Renewal Week for personnel on the post. During that week, spiritual renewal was the topic for the Troop Information Program (TIP) and units received nondenominational literature for use in the TIP. General Lawrence scheduled a lecture series for all personnel of the post for three successive nights of that week, and he engaged three leading theologians of the Catholic, Jewish, and Protestant faiths to be the speakers. John was impressed that all three men were nationally prominent in their respective faiths.

The lectures were held in the post gymnasium at 1930 hours each night for three consecutive nights. Precisely aligned rows of folding metal chairs filled the entire gym floor and all were occupied even though attendance was voluntary. The Gradys attended the first night. John wore civilian clothes, as did most officers and many enlisted men. John pointed out to Rebecca that Major Hardy was sitting two rows directly in front of them. Hardy kept looking around at the people in the audience to see who was there, but he didn't turn far enough to see the Gradys.

The speaker the first night was a Protestant minister who was head of the Presbyterian Church. He was a noted speaker and writer whose views on various subjects were often sought and published. In his introductory remarks to the military audience, the minister mentioned that he had served as a chaplain in the First Infantry Division in World War I. He had an excellent talk, and Rebecca and John were impressed.

The next morning Grady took some papers over to battalion headquarters and stopped in to say hello to Major Hardy. John had gotten to know Hardy fairly well as a result of working with him on courts-martial cases and found that, at times, Hardy could be a baffling person. Most days Hardy showed intellect, professionalism, pragmatism, class, and culture. On other days, John thought that he was gruff, unrefined, or irrational. Grady liked him, and he liked Grady, but Grady never knew which Roger Hardy was going to show up on a given day—the intellectual, sophisticated and polished Roger Hardy or the unrefined and irrational Roger Hardy.

John entered the major's office and they exchanged greetings. Hardy immediately challenged him, "Where were you last night? I didn't see you at the Spiritual Renewal Meeting."

"I was there. I sat two rows directly behind you and your wife. You wore a gray flannel suit and a navy and silver regimental striped tie. What did you think of the minister's talk?"

"He's a liar."

"What? Major, he's a man of the cloth. He's one of the leading theologians in the nation. Why do you say that?"

"Because the man is a liar."

"What did he lie about?"

"He said he was in the First Infantry Division in World War I. I've never seen him at a First Infantry Division reunion. If he had served in the First Infantry Division he would have been at the reunions and I would have seen him."

"Major, not every veteran attends reunions."

"If he served in the First Infantry Division he would have been there."

John realized that it was the rough, irrational Roger Hardy who showed up that day. John excused himself and returned to C Company.

On subsequent nights, Rebecca and John attended the talks by the Jewish rabbi and the Catholic priest. Both were excellent.

General Lawrence's Spiritual Renewal Week stirred up the faith in some people and stirred up the imaginations of others. Sergeant Champ came into Grady's office a couple of days after Spiritual Renewal Week and said, "Three men from the company want to talk to The Lieutenant." "Send them in," Grady said. Three soldiers came in and saluted. Grady told them to stand at ease.

Private Sidney Wasserman was the spokesman for the three of them. "Sir, in view of General Lawrence's emphasis on spiritual renewal, the three of us are asking permission to attend religious services that Rabbi Green will be holding here on the post."

"Why are you asking me for permission? You don't need my permission to attend religious services."

"Sir, Rabbi Green will hold them here on the post on Thursday nights if enough people will come. But that's the night for cleaning the barracks for inspection, so we need to be excused from the work session."

John could not believe it. It was the same type of game that the "college men" in Company K had tried to pull on him to get out of cleaning the barracks.

"Isn't Friday night the night for your traditional services? Why can't you go to services on Friday night?"

"Sir, the nearest temple is in Long Branch, and we would have to go there."

"Do any of you have a car here on post that you can drive to Long Branch?" Two of them answered that he had a car.

It was obvious that they not only wanted to get out of the Thursday night work session but they also didn't want to spend their Friday nights going to the synagogue.

"Gentlemen, your request is denied. I'm disappointed in you." He gave them the same type of lecture that he had given the "college men."

***

On a Wednesday afternoon in early February, John received a call from Lieutenant Colonel Robert Hollander, the Post Staff Judge Advocate who replaced Colonel James. Hollander asked John, " Do you remember an investigation that you conducted when you were in this office involving a tank from Coles Signal Laboratory running over a car out on Tinton Avenue?"

"Yes sir, I do."

"Well, that case was tried in Federal District Court in Trenton two weeks ago and the government won the case; the plaintiff got nothing. I received a letter from the U.S. Attorney commending this office for the fine investigative report that you submitted. I thought you would like to know that the U.S. Attorney appreciated your work and that the government won the case."

"Thank you for letting me know the outcome of the case, sir. I believe the jury reached the right verdict."

***

That night John talked with Rebecca about some of the fine people he had met in the army. "Beck, I don't want to lose contact with some of them. I'd like to see more of Robert Pettit. Do you think we might invite him for dinner sometime soon?

"Go ahead. Just give me ample warning so I can plan a suitable dinner."

Grady contacted Pettit and invited him to come out to the apartment on Friday evening. Pettit accepted and said that he had his own car now and could drive out. He arrived Friday night in civilian clothes, and the two men warmly greeted each other. They had a beer and talked about their experiences in Korea, current events, and their respective assignments. Robert said that he had completed his course in The Signal School, had been promoted to sergeant first class, and was assigned as an instructor in the enlisted men's branch of The Signal School. Rebecca had a nice meal, and they all talked until late in the evening.

The next day John asked Rebecca, "Do you think we could handle asking Colonel Bowen and his wife over for dinner some evening soon? He's been good to me, and they've invited me, and us, to their home. I'd like to try to repay their kindness."

"That'll be fine with me, they're interesting folks, but do you think it'll be all right for a lieutenant to invite a lieutenant colonel?"

"I think so. He's a regular guy, and we seem to get along all right. I think the difference in ranks won't matter to him. However, I don't know any other lieutenant colonel I would feel right about inviting to our home. And, I think we don't need to worry about our humble abode. He was a lieutenant once; he'll understand."

The Bowens accepted John's invitation, and the four of them had an enjoyable, relaxing evening. Arthur Bowen told Rebecca and John that he had just been informed that he soon would be promoted to full colonel and would attend The Army War College at Carlisle Barracks, Carlisle, Pennsylvania, for a ten-month course. (The army selects its best and brightest senior officers to attend the Army War College to prepare them for leadership at the highest levels. Bowen was on a fast track to his first star.) He seemed pleased and humble. John was not at all surprised at Bowen's elevation and heartily congratulated him.

CHAPTER 9. (FALL/WINTER 1953-54)

In 1953 and early 1954, Grady sometimes felt that world tensions were almost at the breaking point. Both Communist China and North Korea were arrogant and unfriendly, and the U.S. was fearful that the Communists might again attack in Korea if they believed they enjoyed an advantage. The Soviet Union had managed to install puppet governments in the nations of Eastern Europe and had slammed down an Iron Curtain at their borders with Western Europe. The Soviet Union and its satellite nations of Eastern Europe had large, well-equipped armies poised behind that Iron Curtain. The Communist nations were extremely active in espionage throughout the free world. Russia had detonated the dreaded hydrogen bomb in August 1953, and the western nations believed that Russia was able and willing to resort to an atomic first strike if they believed it to be to their advantage. Russia appeared to be on a course of Communist domination of the world, and fear of Communist aggression was on the minds of most Americans. John could not remember such worrisome concerns since the early days of World War II when the American public anguished over an unbroken succession of defeats such as the attack on Pearl Harbor; the fall of the Pacific Islands of Wake, Guam, and the Philippines to the Japanese; and the landing of Japanese troops on Attu and Kiska Islands in the Aleutian chain of Alaska.

It was in this prevailing emotional environment that Senator Joseph McCarthy operated, and he was a master at exploiting it to the fullest. One of McCarthy's most vociferous and notorious campaigns against alleged Communist infiltration into our government involved a dentist from New York City named Irving Peress. Peress was inducted into the army as a dentist in October 1952 with the rank of captain. Peress alleged in his induction papers that he had never been a Communist. In a later loyalty questionnaire, Peress wrote "Federal constitutional privilege" in answering a question whether he had ever belonged to an organization that advocated the overthrow of the U.S. Government. At first, no one in the army noticed his statement. In fact, Peress had been a Communist. Later, his Communist past was discovered and Army Intelligence had him under surveillance. A year later, in a routine administrative matter that promoted many army dentists, Peress was promoted to major. He served at Camp Kilmer, New Jersey, performing routine dental duties.

McCarthy went on a rampage. He wanted to know why this Communist dentist had been inducted into the army. He alleged that there were Communists in the army who had inducted him, and Communists in the army who had promoted him to major. McCarthy's cry became WHO PROMOTED PERESS. The press gave front page coverage to McCarthy and his tirade. His popularity in the nation was high.

McCarthy became emboldened and openly criticized President Eisenhower and his administration on foreign policy matters. Particularly, McCarthy advocated that the U.S. pressure its allies to prohibit trade with Communist China, a position that Eisenhower did not favor. And, McCarthy blatantly tried to subpoena officials and records of the Department of Defense. High officials in the Eisenhower administration held a meeting and concluded that McCarthy's actions presented a challenge to the separation of powers between the executive and legislative branches of government. So, the administration quietly put out word that Department of Defense personnel should not cooperate with McCarthy and his staff.

McCarthy called Major Peress before his one-man subcommittee on 30 January 1954. The army had warned Peress not to cooperate with McCarthy, and he didn't. Additionally, Peress invoked the fifth amendment protection against self-incrimination and would not answer questions about his prior Communist activities. McCarthy was angry and kept up the cry WHO PROMOTED PERESS.

On 18 February, McCarthy called before his subcommittee Brigadier General Ralph Zwicker, commanding general of Camp Kilmer, New Jersey, where Peress was stationed. General Zwicker had been a combat commander in World War II and had been awarded the Silver Star, among other decorations. Zwicker, too, had been told not to cooperate with McCarthy. McCarthy was adamant in trying to find out who promoted Peress, intimating that Zwicker had done it. McCarthy became incensed at Zwicker's lack of cooperation and told him, among other derogatory remarks, that he was "not fit to wear that uniform."

McCarthy's impudent handling of General Zwicker before his subcommittee did not settle well with many Americans, and it angered General Matthew Ridgway, the noted World War II commander, former commander of Eighth Army in Korea, former Far East Supreme Commander, former NATO Commander, and now Chief of Staff of the Army. General Ridgway immediately issued an order to the army that army officers should not respond to McCarthy's summons to appear before his subcommittee.

Another major issue in the confrontation between McCarthy and the army was the matter of Private G. David Schine, the bachelor scion of a wealthy family that owned hotel and movie theater chains. Schine was a close friend of Roy Cohn, also a bachelor, and held the title of unpaid chief consultant to McCarthy's subcommittee. In mid-1953 it looked as though Schine was going to be drafted into the army. He and Cohn tried to obtain for him a direct commission as an officer, but the army declined to commission him. Schine proposed to the Secretary of the Army that he become a special assistant to the Secretary instead of being inducted into the army. Schine was drafted into the army as a private in early November and went to Fort Dix, New Jersey, for his basic training.

Cohn made telephone calls to the Secretary of the Army and to the Counsel to the Secretary of the Army seeking special privileges for Schine while he was in basic training. Cohn and McCarthy continually tried to get Schine assigned to New York City where he allegedly would be available to assist McCarthy's subcommittee. Schine did receive some special privileges during the early part of his basic training but they subsequently were stopped. When the special privileges ended, Cohn became belligerent with Department of the Army personnel and threatened retaliation. (John Grady knew none of this, but it was similar to the threats that Cohn issued against the army the previous October at Evans Signal Corps Engineering Laboratory when he was told that he did not have a "need to know" and was prohibited from joining the tour of the laboratory.)

The counsel to the Secretary of the Army compiled a thirty-four page report on the activities of Cohn, McCarthy, and McCarthy's staff to obtain special treatment for Private Schine. In the second week of March 1954, that report was "leaked" to the press. It was a sensation in newspapers throughout the nation.

At the urging of the Eisenhower administration, Republican senators implored McCarthy to dismiss Roy Cohn from the subcommittee. McCarthy refused.

The formerly-absent members of McCarthy's subcommittee began attending meetings to try to resolve the Army-McCarthy situation which had gotten out of control. Democrat subcommittee members wanted to make McCarthy and the Republican administration look bad in retaliation for all the statements that McCarthy and others had made about the lax national security measures of former Democrat administrations. Politics was dominating and foretold a calamitous outcome for the affair.

On March 16, with all members present, the subcommittee voted to hold public hearings on the Army-McCarthy matter. Democrats insisted that the hearings be televised, believing that if the public saw McCarthy in action it would damage his image and the reputation of the Republicans. The Republicans opposed televising the hearings. The subcommittee's final vote was for televising the hearings.

***

Fort Monmouth had received considerable uncomplimentary national publicity in recent months because of the alleged espionage in the Signal Corps Engineering Laboratories. The Chief Signal Officer, the commanding officer of all the Signal Corps, decided to come up from the Pentagon to make an inspection visit to Fort Monmouth. It was announced that the visit was to boost the morale of the eleven thousand troops and the eleven thousand civilian employees at Fort Monmouth, but Grady suspected that the Chief Signal Officer really was trying to find out what the hell was going on at Fort Monmouth.

General Lawrence was no dummy, and he prepared a busy schedule for the Chief Signal Officer to keep him as occupied as possible with mundane matters. The schedule included a full parade on the parade grounds on Saturday morning and a formal reception and dinner at Gibbs Hall on Saturday evening. All companies in troop command would march in the parade. Only senior officers in the grade of major and above, and their ladies, were invited to the formal reception and dinner.

Saturday parades usually were not held during the winter months when the drill field was wet and muddy, so company commanders had only four days to drill their companies in preparation for the special parade for the Chief Signal Officer. Grady reviewed his *Drills and Ceremonies* field manual and drilled the men each of the four days from the time they returned from school until the evening meal.

It was the custom at Fort Monmouth parades that a judging committee of senior officers selected what they believed to be the outstanding company that marched in the parade that day. That company was awarded the commanding general's guidon: a special orange-colored pennant having a gold fringe and mounted on a staff. The outstanding company proudly carried the general's guidon wherever it marched.

Saturday morning, Grady had the men of C Company gather in the courtyard outside the barracks five minutes before they were to march to Greely Field. The men were in their wool winter uniforms, their trousers were bloused into their combat boots, they had orange scarves about their necks, and they wore highly polished helmet liners on their heads. Grady addressed them. "Men, you look good. We're going to spend the next hour or so going through an exercise for which you are well prepared. Other companies in the parade also are well prepared. The company that will look the best in the parade will be the company that can devote special attention to the task at hand for no more than three to five minutes as they approach and pass the reviewing stand. Why go down there and go through the motions and not be the best—anyone can do that. Company C is not just anyone. If you stay keenly alert and concentrate for at least five minutes on what you know you have to do, we'll win the general's guidon. Isn't it worth five minutes of concentration to be the best? I want to be number one; how about you? Concentrate for five minutes and we'll do it. What do you say?" The troops responded in an enthusiastic manner. Grady had them form up in the street in their place in the 1st Battalion formation. At the appointed time, the battalion marched to Greely Field and took its assigned position on the side of the parade field opposite the reviewing stand.

The Chief Signal Officer and General Lawrence inspected the assembled companies of Troop Command while standing in the back of a glistening jeep as it slowly drove in front of the companies. The generals completed their "trooping of the troops" and then mounted the reviewing stand where they took their places among assembled dignitaries and guests.

From the reviewing stand came the loud command, PASS IN REVIEW. The army band struck up a march tune and stepped out and made a right turn and marched to the end of the parade ground. It then made two left turns and advanced up the parade ground and passed in front of the reviewing stand. Successive companies of Troop Command followed the band up the parade ground and toward the reviewing stand. As the 1st Battalion approached the reviewing stand, the line of march slowed down.

The band was supposed to march a short distance beyond the reviewing stand then make a two hundred and seventy degree maneuver and come to a halt facing the reviewing stand. When the band began to make its turn, it encountered a large muddy spot which caused the band members to slow down. That caused the following companies of Troop Command to slow down, and by the time Grady's Company C approached the reviewing stand, forward progress was halted and his men had to march "in place." It is extremely difficult for a large body of men to march "in place" for very long without loosing its cadence and getting out of step.

Grady realized what was happening, and when his company could not move forward he turned around and silently, but with great emphasis, mouthed the cadence count "left - right - left- right - left - right ...." His back was to the reviewing stand, and although it was not routine that he turned around at that time, the officers on the stand understood what he was doing. On their own initiatives, the platoon sergeants in C Company took up the cadence count in soft voices that only the men in the company could hear. Grady turned around and faced forward again. Consequently, the men of C Company never got out of step, while companies ahead and behind them did get out of step. When the company ahead of them finally moved out, C Company smartly moved out without ever missing a step. The judging officers on the reviewing stand saw that and commented on it among themselves.

All companies of Troop Command passed in review and returned to their original positions on the far side of the parade ground. There was a slight delay while the judging officers conferred among themselves and then with General Lawrence. The senior officer of the judges came to the microphone of the public address system and announced, "Today, the winner of General Lawrence's guidon for excellent performance is . . . Company C, 1st Battalion." He then gave the command, "Company commander and guidon bearer Company C, front and center."

A low murmur came from the men of Company C. Grady and his guidon bearer marched together to the front of the reviewing stand and stood before General Lawrence and his aide. Grady smartly saluted and said, "Company C reporting as ordered, sir."

The general's aide handed the guidon to the general, and the general extended it to Grady. "Grady, your company did a good job of marching in place in front of the reviewing stand. It shows good training. Congratulations."

Grady received the guidon and handed it to his bearer. He saluted and they both did an about-face and marched back to C Company.

At the conclusion of the parade, 1st Battalion marched back to its barracks. Grady had C Company gather around an entrance to its barracks and he stood on the steps and addressed them. "Congratulations men, you can be proud of yourselves for a job well done. Keep in mind the lesson that we learned today. Decide what you want to do, then work harder and smarter than the other fellows and you'll be winners. I'm proud of you. Dismissed."

Grady went inside and talked with Sergeant Champ and the other company noncommissioned officers. All were in a good mood. The telephone rang and the company clerk answered it. It was for The Lieutenant. It was General Lawrence's aide. "Lieutenant, in view of your company winning first place in the parade today, General Lawrence has invited you to attend the reception and dinner tonight for the Chief Signal Officer at Gibbs Hall. Pinks and greens are the uniform of the day, and you should bring your wife."

Grady telephoned Rebecca and told her that they were going to the reception and dinner tonight. When he arrived at home, he explained why they had been invited and told her that it was a major official and social event in the life of the post.

John and Rebecca arrived at Gibbs Hall and saw on one side of the reception room a group of people congregated in the vicinity of a long table that had several punch bowls on it. On the other side of the room, newly arrived people were passing through a reception line that included the Chief Signal Officer and his wife and his aide and General Lawrence and his wife and his aide.

John preceded Rebecca in the receiving line. When John came to General Lawrence, the general extended his hand and shook Grady's. He pulled Grady in front of the Chief Signal Officer and said, "General, I want you to meet an outstanding young Signal Officer. This is Lieutenant Grady. His company won first place in the parade this morning. He was wounded in fighting in North Korea and was awarded the Silver Star for gallantry in action. He also finished first in his class in The Signal School. He's the kind of young officer we need in the Signal Corps."

The Chief Signal Officer extended his hand and said, "It's nice meeting you, Lieutenant Grady." After John and Rebecca had passed, the Chief

Signal Officer said something to his aide who took a pad of paper from his inside breast pocket and wrote something on it.

The Gradys walked to a punch table where they received cups of punch, and then they talked with several other couples. The reception line concluded and the two generals worked the crowd, each going independently from group to group meeting people and making small talk. General Lawrence saw the Gradys and made his way to them. (He seemed to like to talk with Rebecca whenever he had the chance.)

The Gradys were talking with the general when a portly major came up to them, stuck out his hand and said, "Good evening General, I'm Major Morris Lamb. I've just returned from duty in the Far East." Lamb turned to John, extended his arm and hand to him, and said, "Hello Lieutenant Grady, it's nice to see you again." Lamb turned his head to General Lawrence and said, "Lieutenant Grady and I served together in Tenth Corps in Korea."

Lamb kept his arm and hand extended to Grady, but John stood rigid and didn't attempt to shake Lamb's hand. The general and Rebecca looked at John. His face was red and his jaw was clenched. Neither Grady or Lamb said anything to each other.

Finally, Grady addressed General Lawrence. "By your leave, General, Mrs. Grady and I will be leaving now. Thank you for your invitation. It was thoughtful of you; I appreciate it." He took Rebecca's arm and they walked out of Gibbs Hall. The entered their car and drove away. John did not speak during their drive home. Rebecca didn't either. One of Rebecca's fine traits was that she respected John and didn't force him to talk when he didn't want to. She didn't know everything that happened to him in Korea, but she knew enough to suspect who that portly major was.

They arrived at their apartment and changed their clothes. Rebecca fixed them sandwiches and milk, and they sat at the kitchen table eating their sandwiches. "Beck, I'm sorry. I know that I embarrassed you this evening, and I apologize. I know that what I did may be considered inexcusable, but I just could not remain in the same room with that man. He's the cause of three men getting killed and four others getting wounded. I know about forgiveness, but I'm not strong enough right now to forgive that man for what he did. I'm going to have to live with that sin until I grow enough to be able to forgive him—I'm going to have to work on it." John shook his head. "And to think that someone like that remains in the army. Doesn't anyone care?" John told Rebecca the details of his experiences with Major Lamb in South Korea and when he was up at Hyesanjin on the Yalu River.

Monday morning at 0800 Grady received a telephone call at Company C from General Lawrence—not from his aide but from the general himself. "Grady, come to my office." That's all he said.

John entered the general's office and reported. Lawrence looked at him and pointed to a chair in front of his desk.

"Do you want to tell me about it?" the general said.

Grady knew what the general was talking about. He really didn't want to talk about it. He sat there not saying anything and thinking.

"Grady, I know a little about what happened to you in Korea, and I know what you said about a superior officer leaving you stuck behind enemy lines. Is that overweight major who came up to us Saturday night the officer who got you trapped behind the lines?"

Grady looked at the general and nodded his head.

"What's his name?"

"Morris Lamb."

The general wrote it down. "Grady, you've proved to me about every way you can that you're a fine army officer. I've never had reason to doubt your ability, your honesty, or your concern for the army. You've always been up-front with me and said what's on your mind. If that major is unfit, I want to do something about it. I want to hear from you why you think he caused you to become trapped behind enemy lines."

John remained silent—he was formulating a plan. He knew that he was pushing beyond where he had a right to venture, but he proceeded. "General, may I make a recommendation to you? There's a Sergeant Robert Pettit here on the post who was with me in North Korea and who was in our crew trapped behind the Chinese lines. He knows all about Major Lamb. Sergeant Pettit is an instructor in The Signal School; he's extremely intelligent; a resourceful and hard-working soldier; and a truthful and honorable person. I respectfully suggest that you first talk with him about our experiences with Major Lamb in North Korea. You know very well that Major Lamb evokes strong emotions in me, so it might be better for you to first talk with someone else. I'll talk with you after you talk with Sergeant Pettit. That way you can better evaluate what I say and can determine whether or not I'm unreasonably emotional about Major Lamb."

Grady paused for a moment, then continued. "General Lawrence, the army grants direct commissions to outstanding noncommissioned officers who would make good commissioned officers. I believe that Sergeant Pettit would make an excellent commissioned officer. It's my opinion that the army would benefit greatly by commissioning him. He's top-notch in electronic technology, and intellectually he's smarter than most of us. Although he had no medical training, he tended our wounds during our struggle to get back to our lines, and there wasn't a thing he wouldn't do to help his fellow soldiers. And, he's a fighter. If the army is looking to find good officers, I recommend that you do something to commission Sergeant Pettit. And, he doesn't need to go to OCS."

Lawrence looked at John for some time. He rotated his swivel chair around, stood up, and slowly walked away from his desk. He looked out the windows behind him at the flagpole and the Main Gate, then he returned and sat down. He shook his head and said, "Damn you, Grady. Why in the hell didn't you accept my offer to be my aide? We could have worked together. O.K., I'll talk to your Sergeant Pettit, but I still want to talk to you about that major."

"Grady, how long have you been in-grade as a lieutenant?" John told him.

"That will be all."

The general called John to his office again on Friday morning. "Grady, I've looked at Major Morris Lamb's 201 file, and I talked to your Sergeant Pettit. He told me about Colonel Robert Ackerman who was your commanding officer in Korea. I had my aide track him down and I talked to him. Do you remember him?"

"Of course, sir. How is he, and where is he now?"

"He's fine. He's a full colonel stationed at the Pentagon. Grady, I think I understand fully why you feel the way you do about that Lamb fellow. Ackerman told me that he didn't want Lamb in his command, and he told me why. Well, I don't want him in my command either. He's on his way out of the army. He can resign his commission or he can face that court-martial that Ackerman put off."

"General, what do you think of Sergeant Pettit?"

"I liked him, and he has a solid background. I sent him up to G-1 for an interview and told them to see if he can qualify for a direct commission. It might help his chances if you write a letter of recommendation for him. Send it to me and I'll put an endorsement on it."

"I'll do that right away, sir. I thank you for taking the trouble to initiate that action on Sergeant Pettit."

CHAPTER 10. (APRIL 1954)

Now that the U.S. Senate Permanent Investigations Subcommittee had agreed to hold televised hearing on the Army-McCarthy dispute, both the Department of the Army and McCarthy were preparing their cases. The army engaged Mr. Joseph Welch, a prominent and respected Boston attorney, as its chief counsel for the hearings.

In the first week of April, Grady received a telephone call from the G-2 office in Russell Hall telling him to immediately come to that office. He entered the G-2 office and met Sol Solomon, the civilian attorney from the JAG office, and Colonel Berl Thompson, the post G-2. Grady liked and respected Sol and warmly greeted him.

Colonel Thompson spoke to Grady. "Lieutenant, as you know, the army and Senator McCarthy are having a showdown hearing, and the army is collecting its evidence. You were present at Evans Signal Corps Engineering Laboratory on 20 October 1953 when Roy Cohn, you, and several others were denied access to the laboratory. Is that correct?"

"Yes sir."

"The Department of the Army wants a statement from you as to what transpired while you, Roy Cohn, and others waited in the reception area at Evans while the generals and other dignitaries made the inspection tour of the laboratory. They're particularly interested in Roy Cohn's statements. Sol here will help you put the statement in proper written form. Lieutenant, you will regard what you do here as classified. Do you understand that?"

"Yes sir."

The colonel directed Sol and Grady to an unoccupied office and told them to work there.

Sol said, "John why don't you tell me what happened with Roy Cohn down at Evans that day." John gave him an account of what happened and what Cohn and the Secretary of the Army's counsel said.

"That sounds good to me," Sol said. "You know how to prepare a statement of this kind, just write what you told me." John wrote out his statement on three sheets of ruled paper from a yellow pad and gave it to

Sol who read it and said, "Looks good. I'll take it to the colonel to get it typed." Sol returned shortly, and the two men talked about the people in the JAG office and what was going on there at the present time. It seemed to be taking a long time to get just three handwritten sheets typed.

Colonel Thompson returned with four typed copies of John's statement and handed three of them to Grady. He said, "Here, sign this original and two carbons." John placed the original copy on the table in front of him and gave one of the carbons to Sol for him to read. John finished reading first. With an expressionless face, he leaned back in his chair and waited for Sol to finish. When Sol finished, he looked at John and raised his eyebrows.

Grady said, "Colonel, this is not what I wrote." The statement had been softened considerably when it came to the part where Cohn made threatening statements about the army. It completely changed the impact of what had happened there.

"This covers the event sufficiently; go ahead and sign it," the colonel said in a commanding voice.

John and Sol looked at each other. From the look on Sol's face it was obvious that he didn't expect anything like this to happen. John put his hand on the original copy, spun it around, and pushed it across the table toward the colonel. He looked up at the colonel and said, "This is someone else's statement, not mine. I won't sign this statement, Colonel."

The colonel stood glaring at Grady. He then looked at Sol, and when Sol didn't say anything, the colonel picked up the papers and walked out of the room.

"Sol, who all is involved in this matter? Is General Lawrence involved?

"The general is involved in most things that happens on this post, you know that. But, I don't know any more than you do about who looked at and changed your statement. You stay here; I'll be right back." Sol left the room. Grady lit a cigarette and stood up and paced back and forth in the room. He was alone in the room for half an hour.

Sol and Colonel Thompson returned to the room together. Thompson placed an original and two copies of a typed statement in front of Grady. He said nothing to Grady. John looked at Sol. Sol nodded his head slightly. Grady read the statement. To the best of his recollection, it was exactly what he had written. He reread the original, then looked at the carbon copies to see if they were exact duplicates of the original. They were. John signed the three copies and Sol notarized them and returned them to Thompson who immediately left the room.

John and Sol both looked at their watches. "Sol, it is almost quitting time for you. There's no need to go back to the JAG office. You undoubtedly did a lot of talking, so come with me and I'll buy you a beer to quench your thirst."

"That sounds good to me. Where do you want to go?

"Let's get off the post. Do you know that small café in Eatontown? It's quiet, and I think they serve beer. I'll drive us over in my car. Come on."

They arrived at the café and ordered beers. John was eager to talk. "Sol, you know I want to know what happened and who was involved, but if you feel you're not at liberty to tell me, I understand."

"First of all, the general was not there. It was Thompson and his deputy, Major Dodge. Sergeant Major Reimer was there, too. I was surprised, but Reimer was quite vocal in the presence of the colonel. They didn't want your statement to make Cohn look bad—they all support McCarthy. They made several more attempts to water down your statement. I figured that they had orders from the Pentagon to get a statement from you, so when I told them that I know you pretty well and it would have to be your original statement or none, they gave in."

"It doesn't surprise me that they all support McCarthy," Grady said. "I doubt that they could work for the general very long if they didn't support McCarthy.

"Sol, have you been with the general much lately?"

"Oh, a fair amount of time. Since he had trouble with his driving campaign he seems a little more inclined to ask for legal advice. On some things he seems to want a civilian attorney rather than a JAG officer."

John asked, "Have you noticed any change in the general's emotional or mental state over the last six months or so?

Sol thought about John's question. He took a sip of his beer. "Now that you bring it up, he seems to be lonelier and more withdrawn than he was before. I get the impression that he believes he's fighting the battle for the survival of America almost by himself. He's an intelligent and dedicated man, but you know John, his zealousness impairs his judgment. For example, he doesn't see McCarthy and Cohn for what they are. He thinks they're sincere, just as he believes he is. And, he's isolated from objective thinkers; he's surrounded by yes-men on his staff—the whole bunch of them are sycophants. Why did you ask that question, John? Do you have reason to think there's been a change?"

"Yes I do. I agree with you that he seems to be a lonely man. I also agree that he feels that he's alone in fighting the battle for the survival of America. And maybe he's beginning to think that he's losing that battle. That Post Regulation 219 debacle was a major setback for him, as are the allegations of espionage in the engineering laboratories. He undoubtedly feels that he's carrying a heavy burden. Some people snap under those conditions."

John continued, "I feel that I should be doing something to help him. He seems to want to be friendly, and except for an incident or two, he's been good to me. But honestly, Sol, I'm afraid to get too close to him these days."

CHAPTER II. (APRIL 1954)

During the first week of each month, the Deputy Regimental Commander inspected the barracks of all companies in Troop Command and rated the companies on the cleanliness and orderliness of the barracks, on the keeping of company records, and on supply accountability. At precisely 0800 on 1 April 1954 the brand-new Deputy Regimental Commander Major Charles Ocher entered the barracks of Company C, 1st Battalion, and announced that he was there for the monthly inspection. Thus, Grady's Company C was the first company in Troop Command to be inspected in April. Grady wondered why he was first. Was someone in the regiment trying to make it tough on him because of what went on in the JAG office when he was there?

Major Ocher came into Grady's office and they talked for a short while. Grady didn't know Ocher, and it seemed that Ocher was trying to impress Grady with his importance and was talking down to him. The two of them began the inspection tour of the barracks. They started in the basement with the supply room and the supply records. They were in excellent condition, and Ocher had nothing to say. As Grady followed Ocher out the door of the supply room, he gave the supply sergeant a thumbs-up sign for a job well done. Ocher and Grady walked through the day room and the other rooms on the first floor. Everything looked good.

They went to the second floor where most of the men slept and where their latrines were located. Things looked good around the bunks and lockers. They entered the latrine. The plumbing fixtures were bright and shiny, the mirrors were spotless, and the floor was clean. Major Ocher stepped into the shower room and wiped his hand across the wall. He looked at his hand and made an unpleasant face. "Soap scum on the wall. This shower hasn't been cleaned," he said as he made a note on his clipboard.

Grady wiped his hand across the shower wall and worked his fingers over a slight residue that clung to his hand. The residue was gritty, not slimy or sticky. "Sir, this is not soap scum, this is scouring powder left on the wall after the men scrubbed the wall. Not all of the scouring powder was rinsed from the wall."

"It's soap scum," Ocher said with authority.

"I beg your pardon, sir, I was an enlisted man in the navy and I cleaned many a 'head' in my day, and I know that this is scouring powder."

"It's soap scum. Let's go back to your office." Ocher next inspected the Company Property Book and the Company Punishment Book. They were in good order and up to date. Grady and Ocher sat in chairs in front of the desk. Ocher looked over his inspection sheet and began to speak. "Things looked fair, just fair. I inspected the outside area before I came into the barracks and the area around the garbage cans of the mess hall needs to be cleaned up. That, and the soap scum on the shower walls gives you two demerits."

"I beg your pardon, sir. The mess hall is a battalion mess; the battalion commander runs the mess hall. I don't have responsibility for it or authority over it."

"Well, it's in your general area. If you see something that needs attention, you should clean it up."

"Also, sir, I know that what's on that shower wall is not soap scum. It's scouring powder that remained after the wall was cleaned."

"It's soap scum. You're going to have to learn how to soldier in this army, Grady."

"Sir, that scouring powder on the wall of the shower was purchased by the enlisted men out of their own pockets because some staff officer at regimental headquarters didn't budget enough money to purchase supplies to keep the barracks clean. And, we don't have enough light bulbs to fill all the light sockets in the barracks because there are not enough light bulbs available from regimental supply. Major, maybe congressmen and senators would like to know that because of foul-ups by regimental staff their constituents who are enlisted men at Fort Monmouth have to purchase cleaning supplies and light bulbs out of their own pockets. And maybe it's time the senators and congressmen found out." Grady was angry and was in no mood to take crap from a stuffed-shirt major.

Ocher glared at Grady and said, "The inspection results will be posted at regimental headquarters next week." He arose from the chair and left the room.

✸✸✸

The following Monday, Sergeant Champ took reveille-formation duty, and John arrived at Company C a little before 0700. Sergeant Champ immediately came into his office and said, "The Lieutenant should know that Private Allan Gilbert was absent from reveille formation this morning. I talked to his buddy and he told me that Gilbert is AWOL. They went to New York over the weekend and Gilbert told his buddy that he wasn't coming back."

"Do you know where he is now? Is he still in New York?"

"I don't know. His buddy Private Williams didn't tell me if he knew where he is."

"What do you know about Gilbert?"

"Not much. He's a rich kid, I understand. His family is in the banking business in Kansas City. He's doing well in school, so apparently he's smart."

"Sergeant Champ, as soon as the troops get back here for lunch, bring Private Williams in here. I want to talk with him."

At 1210 Sergeant Champ and Private Williams came into Grady's office. Williams was a nice-looking soldier who appeared to be a little younger than most men in the company. He seemed a little uncomfortable being in the company commander's office.

"Williams, stand at ease. Do you know where Private Gilbert is right now?" Williams was hesitant to speak. "Williams, Private Gilbert is AWOL only one day now. That's not too serious an offense. If we can get him back now, he'll not be in too much trouble, but the longer he stays away the more trouble he'll be in. You'll be doing him a favor by getting him back as soon as possible. If you know where he is, tell me and I'll go get him right now."

Private Williams shifted his weight from one foot to the other. Sergeant Champ and John waited. Williams bobbed his head and said, "Sir, we stayed at the Roosevelt Hotel in New York over the weekend. I left late Sunday afternoon, but he said he was staying. That's all I know, sir."

"Did he tell you what he was going to do?"

"No sir."

"Why didn't he come back with you? He's doing O.K. in school; is he in any kind of trouble anywhere?"

"He just gets crazy ideas sometimes. Nothing in particular was bothering him, as far as I know. He just said he was getting tired of the army routine and wanted to get away for a while."

"Did he have money on him?"

Private Williams smiled. "Allan Gilbert always has money on him."

"Thank you, Williams. If you think of any additional information that will be helpful to get Gilbert back, tell me as soon as possible. That's all."

Grady said to Sergeant Champ, "You and Sergeant Stuart stand by. If I can locate Gilbert we're going up to New York to get him." Grady called telephone information and obtained the telephone number of the Roosevelt Hotel in New York. He dialed, and when someone answered he introduced himself and asked to speak with the manager.

"Hello, sir, this is Lieutenant John Grady from Fort Monmouth, New Jersey. I'm a company commander here at Fort Monmouth, and one of my men is absent without leave and is reported to be registered in your hotel. If I can get hold of him right away his absence won't be too serious, but if he stays away for any length of time it could get serious for him. If he's at your hotel, I want to come up there and get him as soon as I can and return him to duty. Sir, will you please tell me if Private Allan Gilbert is registered at you hotel?"

"Let me check." After a short wait, the manager came back on the line. "You're out of luck, Lieutenant. Allan Gilbert checked out of the hotel at 10:50 this morning."

"Did he leave any forwarding address? And, if you can, will you please tell me how he paid his bill?"

"Just a moment." The manager came back on the line and said, "He left no forwarding address. He paid his bill with a check on the Farmers and Merchants Bank of Kansas City, Missouri. That's all the information I have."

"Thank you very much, sir, I appreciate your help. If he registers in your hotel again, would you please have your people call me immediately." Grady gave him his office and his home telephone numbers.

"Sergeant Champ, do you know anything else we can do?"

"The Lieutenant has done everything I can think of right now. I'll talk to some of the men in the company to see if I can get any more information."

Late Tuesday afternoon Grady had a telephone call from Major Charles Ocher, Deputy Regimental Commander. "Lieutenant, this is Major Ocher. You have a Private Allan Gilbert who is AWOL."

"Yes sir."

"Do you know who he is?"

"I understand he's from Kansas City."

"Yes, his family owns banks there. They're a wealthy and influential family. I'm from Kansas City, and I know all about them. His father is very prominent in politics at the local and state levels. You call his father and tell him the trouble his son is in, and tell him to get his son back to duty as quick as he can. The son is a spoiled kid. Tell his father to close his son's checking account so he won't have money to throw around to support his AWOL."

"Major, if the father closes the boy's checking account without the boy knowing it and the boy continues writing checks, he'll be writing bad checks. He already is in enough trouble without also being guilty of passing bad checks."

"Those kind of people think they can do anything they want to. You do as I told you. Call his father."

John found it hard to believe that a man who had achieved the rank of major in the army would be acting the way Ocher was acting. "Major, if you want me to contact his father to tell him to close his son's checking account, you put it in a written order and send it to me."

Ocher was silent for a short time. "Grady, you don't understand what trouble that boy is in."

"Major, I understand very well. I worked in JAG and prosecuted men for AWOL and for desertion."

Ocher was silent. Grady felt that he now had the advantage. "Major, if you want me to tell his father to close the checking account, send me a written order."

Ocher didn't reply immediately. "Well ... no, but you write him a letter and tell him what trouble his son is in. Those people think that they can get away with anything. Send me a copy of your letter. Do you understand?"

"Yes, Major. Good-bye."

Grady obtained Allan Gilbert's home address from the boy's records and wrote a letter to his father explaining the situation to him, and telling him what he, Grady, had done so far. He explained what the consequences of continued absence could mean, and asked the father to try to contact his son and urge him to return to duty as soon as possible. Grady made the letter as informative and friendly as he could under the circumstances. He told the father that he would do all he could to try to get the boy back to duty. Grady sent a blind copy of the letter to Major Ocher. He heard no more from Ocher on the matter.

Rebecca and John sat in their living room after supper that night. John was quiet and not responsive to Rebecca's conversation. She knew that his mind was on something else. She stopped talking and began reading *The Saturday Evening Post.*

John sat motionless for twenty minutes, then said, "Beck, what would you think if we get out of the army in June?"

"I'll be happy to know you'll not be sent overseas and that we'll not be separated. What are you thinking?"

"I'm thinking that it's time for us to move on. More and more I'm getting the feeling that I'm not a career soldier. I believe I've done my duty and fulfilled my military obligation to my country. The truce seems to be holding in Korea, and I believe the war there is over, at least for the foreseeable future. We're getting stronger in Europe, and I think the Russians don't want to risk a nuclear war any more than we do. I can stay in the reserves and be available if they need me in the future.

"What would you think about us getting out of the army and going back to school and finishing up? Money will be tight, but with the GI Bill we ought to be able to make it. I'm assuming that West Virginia University Law School will accept me for the third year. They might feel that a four-year hiatus is too long and may want me to repeat some previous work to get up to speed. I won't go back there if they want me to do that.

"Beck, would you want to get your degree there while I finish law school?"

"I haven't thought about going back to school, but it would be a good chance while you're finishing. What do we need to do?"

"The faculty is very strict at the WVU law school. I wouldn't feel safe just writing a letter and asking them to accept me for the third year—not after a four-year absence. I would rather appear in person and plead my case. I'll try to get a pass for a couple of days and we can drive over to Morgantown. I'll write the dean and request an appointment to meet with him, or with whomever he wants. Let's shoot for Thursday, 22 April—before they get involved with final exams, graduation, etc. You can do the same with the business school. You should write for transcripts of your grades from all the schools you attended. Get as many credits transferred as you can.

CHAPTER 12. (APRIL 1954)

The week after the Gradys decided to leave the army, John received a call in his office that the battalion commander wanted to see him. John walked over to Major Hardy's office. His door was closed, but his clerk said, "The major is ready to see you, Lieutenant, just walk in." John knocked on the door and opened it. All the 1st Battalion officers were gathered in the office.

"Come in, Grady," Major Hardy said. He and most of the other men had smiles on their faces. "Come over here," Hardy said as he motioned John to come over to his desk. When he arrived at the desk, Hardy reached down and picked up a small box, opened it and showed it to John. The box had a pair of captain's bars in it.

"Congratulations, Captain Grady. I'm privileged to be the one to present these bars to you. Put them on; let's see how they look."

Grady really was surprised. He hadn't given a thought to promotion since his decision to get out of the army. He thanked the major, took off his Ike jacket, removed the silver lieutenant's bars, and pinned on the captain's bars. He put his jacket back on, and the other officers applauded. John thanked them all. The major announced that they would go out into the larger room and have coffee.

During their conversation over coffee, Major Hardy said, "Have you men heard about General Lawrence?" No one had heard anything new about Lawrence. "Well, he went down to Walter Read Army Hospital in Washington for his annual physical and they say that they found some problems. He's to stay there for further tests. No one knows how long he'll be there. A new general is coming in as a temporary replacement."

One of the officers asked, "What's the nature of the general's problem?"

"No one knows for sure. Someone said they thought it was a liver ailment."

John and Willie Mullins walked together on their way back to their respective companies. Willie said, "It looks like the army has finally run out of patience with the general. I doubt that we'll ever see him back here again."

"I believe you're right, Willie. It had to come some day, and I'm kind of surprised that they didn't get him before now. He's been living on borrowed time, and he knew it."

"Yes. I expected him to get the ax after the Terry Berisford incident."

"I did too. And if it hadn't been for the fact that the Communist spy scare was going on in the engineering laboratories at that time, I think he would have been relieved then.

"Willie, I've been wanting to talk to you for some time; why don't you stop in my office for a few minutes before you return to your company. Do you have time?"

'Sure, I can spare a few minutes."

John closed all the doors into his office and said, "Willie, I know you're not supposed to talk about the engineering laboratories security work that you were involved in, but that matter has gotten to the highest levels of government and it's involved in the Army-McCarthy hearings. Don't answer this question if you think you shouldn't, but do McCarthy and Cohn have any genuine espionage facts relating to the engineering laboratories? Do they have anything that you didn't have in the files that you reviewed?"

" No. They don't have anything more than I saw in my files. They're using the same material I had. I didn't find any subversive activities, and they haven't shown us anything concrete, have they? They're blowing smoke. I don't trust either one of them. Maybe security measures in the labs did need to be tightened up, but not this way." Willie and John talked for a while longer, then Willie said that he had to be going.

Shortly after Willie left John's office he called John on the telephone. "Guess what, John, I just received orders to report to Camp Kilmer for discharge. I go over next Tuesday."

"Willie, congratulations. What do you say that you, Rebecca, and I go out to dinner tomorrow evening. Rebecca hasn't seen you in a while, and she enjoys your company as much as I do. We both want to see you again before you leave."

Grady received a prompt reply from the West Virginia University law school setting an appointment with the academic committee for 3:00 p.m. on Friday, 23 April 1954. Rebecca received a reply from the WVU business school several days later offering an appointment for 10:00 a.m. on Friday, 23 April 1954. Grady applied for, and was granted, a four-day pass that included Wednesday through Saturday, 21-24 April. John didn't tell anyone at Fort Monmouth where he was going.

"Beck, I'm thinking about doing something I'm not sure I will be proud of."

"What's that?"

"Well, I absolutely have to be admitted as a third-year student. I'm thinking about wearing my pinks and greens and my ribbons and CIB to the appointment with the academic committee. If I can appeal to their patriotism to get from them what I want, then I just might do it. Will I be wrong to do that?"

"No, absolutely not. You left there to go into the army, and you fought in the war and suffered a lot because of it. You shouldn't be penalized because of that. They should be reminded of it."

"I intend to remind them of it. I've prepared a short outline of my four years since I left law school. I set forth everything I've done, and I emphasize the legal work that I did in the JAG office. I've made copies of my diploma from the JAG school, and I intend to give each member of the committee a copy of the entire outline."

***

Friday morning, 23 April, Rebecca and John walked to her appointment in the School of Business at West Virginia University. Her interview lasted for over an hour, and when she came out she explained, "I met with the department head, and he assured me that they will accept me and said that I could graduate in two semesters if I took eighteen hours of credits both semesters. I told him I would, and he told me the courses I'll have to take. So, I'm all set."

They had lunch and went back to the Morgan hotel. John changed into his uniform, and they walked to the law school and entered. John showed Rebecca the law library and said, "You can sit at one of these tables and read a newspaper from the rack over there while I'm with the committee."

John went into the office of the dean's secretary and greeted her. She had been there for years and years and greeted him by name. She told him that the academic committee was meeting in the dean's office. The door to the dean's office opened, and the dean invited John to enter. In addition to the dean, the committee included four professors, all of whom John had classes to before he left for the army.

The dean began the conversation. "Mr. Grady, we received your request for admission as a third-year student and your request to meet with me and/or the committee. We're glad to see you back here. Now, what can we do for you."

"Sir, I thank you and the other professors for meeting with me. My four-year tour of duty in the army is coming to a close, and I believe it's time for me to complete my legal education. I've lost four years time, and my concern is that you won't allow me to resume my studies as a third-year student but might require me to take some refresher courses before my third-year studies begin. I'm confident that I'm ready and able to handle the third-year studies. I've prepared a resume of my activities these past four years so that you might judge my qualifications." Grady handed each of the committee members a copy of his resume and the copy of his JAG school diploma.

"You'll see that I was engaged in legal work for over a year, and I was quite fortunate to have attended the Army Judge Advocate General School. I've been a claims officer handling administrative and tort claims against the government, and I've prosecuted military criminal cases in special and general courts-martial. I believe that I've had considerably more practical legal experience than the average student who enters the third year of law study."

When John concluded, the committee members read through his resume. The dean spoke up next. "Are there any questions for Mr. Grady?" There were none. "Mr. Grady, if you will wait outside, we'll have an answer for you shortly."

In five minutes the dean called John back into his office. "Mr. Grady, the committee unanimously agreed that you should resume your studies in the third-year class. We look forward to seeing you in September." The members of the committee wished him well.

❈❈❈

The Gradys had dinner and retired early. They left Morgantown early Saturday morning, and during their drive across the Pennsylvania Turnpike they listened to news reports about the Army-McCarthy hearings that had started on Thursday. Supposedly, the issues to be determined were whether McCarthy and his staff improperly had sought favorable treatment for Private G. David Schine, and whether the army tried to blackmail McCarthy regarding the matter, as alleged by McCarthy and Cohn. The proceedings started out acrimoniously and continued that way. The proceedings no sooner commenced before Senator McCarthy interrupted with his often-intoned phrase, "Mr. chairman, a point of order."

Now that the television cameras were running, all members of the subcommittee showed up and acted as if they were learned sages who had nothing at all to do with allowing the McCarthy and Cohn excesses to occur. The acting chairman of the committee Senator Karl Mundt was weak in maintaining order and direction, and the proceedings took on the aura of a circus. It was embarrassing to the country.

***

John worked on his letter of resignation on Sunday afternoon after church. He also wrote a letter to Colonel Bowen telling him that he was resigning his commission, effective 5 June 1954, and would return to law school. John had his company clerk type his resignation letter the first thing Monday morning. He signed the letter and told the clerk to take it to battalion headquarters which was the first stop on its way up the chain of command. He put his handwritten letter to Colonel Bowen in the outgoing mail box. Within fifteen minutes Major Hardy called John on the telephone and told him to come to his office immediately. As John entered the door, Hardy challenged him, "Grady, what the Sam Hill do you think you're doing? I won't forward this letter. What's bothering you? Why didn't you come to me to talk about it?"

"Major, nothing in particular is bothering me; I just think it's time for me to move on and finish my legal education. The war is over and the army is releasing a lot of people from active duty; the army doesn't need me."

"You're wrong. The Communists still are a threat to us in Asia and in Europe. You're an outstanding officer, John; we need officers of your caliber and they don't come along every day. Here, you take this letter back and think some more about this resignation business. You come to lunch with me today and we'll talk about it."

"With due respect, Major, I have thought about this a lot, and Rebecca and I have talked about it a lot. We both intend to go back to school to get our degrees. And, I'll remind you, sir, regulations require you to forward that letter up the chain of command."

Major Hardy stared at John. "Grady, I'm going to hold on to this letter. I have to go to a meeting at 1100, but I'll be back here by 1215. You be here and we'll go to lunch. Do you understand?"

"Yes sir."

Major Hardy and Grady had lunch at a table by themselves in the battalion mess. Hardy argued, pleaded, and cajoled John, but John stood firm on his decision. Finally, Hardy said, "John, I don't want you to leave the army, but I have to respect your decision. I'll forward your letter."

Thursday evening the telephone rang in the Gradys' apartment. Rebecca answered it. "Hello—Why, hello Colonel Bowen, how are you and Mrs. Bowen?" Rebecca looked at John and motioned him to come to the phone. John grimaced. She exchanged a couple of pleasantries with Bowen, then handed the phone to John.

"Hello Colonel, how are you, sir?"

"Hello John. I received your letter, and I must say that I'm not happy to hear of your decision. In view of your recent promotion to captain I was hoping that you would find it agreeable to stay in the army. John, I hope your decision is not irreversible."

John wondered how Bowen down in Carlisle, Pennsylvania, knew about his promotion. He explained to Bowen why he had arrived at the decision. He continued, "Colonel, I can never thank you enough for your friendship and for the favors you did for me. They've had a significant influence on my army career, and on my life. And Colonel, if all the army officers I've come into contact with during my tour of duty were like you, I might not be taking this course of action."

"But John, I have plans for you." Both men were silent for some time. "John, if I come up to Monmouth to talk with you will you be open to reconsider your decision?"

"Colonel, Rebecca and I have thought this through, and we're committed to this course of action. I appreciate very much your interest and concern, but my decision is firm. Colonel, I intend to join an Army Reserve unit after I leave active duty, so I'll be available if I'm ever needed again. But for now, my mind is made up to go back to law school."

CHAPTER 13. (APRIL 1954)

The Army-McCarthy hearings were the sensational event in the nation. John was particularly interested in them because of his contact with McCarthy and Cohn during their Evans Signal Corps Engineering Laboratory visit, and because of what Willie Mullins had told him about the espionage investigations at the labs. Much of the nation watched the daily live telecasts. The hearings dominated the newspaper headlines, the editorial pages, and the evening TV news. Fort Monmouth and General Lawrence frequently were the subjects of discussion. It was obvious to all that the Democrats on the subcommittee were out to destroy McCarthy, and in the process the Republican party and the Republican administration. Equally apparent was the fact that the chairman Senator Mundt and the other Republican members of the subcommittee were trying to protect McCarthy and their party. Grady listened, but he didn't hear anyone ask the subcommittee senators of both parties where they had been the past three or four years while the McCarthy and Cohn excesses were going on. Those senators were members of the subcommittee and had responsibilities to the nation, but they were AWOL from the meetings and hearings of the subcommittee. Had they been military officers they could have been court-martialed for dereliction of duty.

Nor did John hear anyone expressed concern about the Fort Monmouth civilian employees who had been wrongly accused of being security risks and suspended from their jobs. John noted once again that it was the nation and those "in the ranks" who suffer when those in high places failed to assume their responsibilities. He would take to his grave the scars that proved it.

The Gradys and the nation learned of McCarthy's and his staff's devious and dishonest tactics. During Secretary of the Army Robert Stevens's testimony, McCarthy introduced a photograph showing only the secretary and Private G. David Schine standing together. Apparently, Stevens was looking at Schine and smiling at him. McCarthy alleged that the photograph showed that the secretary and Schine were good friends, so there was no need for Cohn and McCarthy to pressure the secretary to extend favors to Private Schine.

The next day the army introduced the authentic photograph that showed not only what was in McCarthy's photograph but additionally showed a senior army officer and another man standing with Stevens and Schine. This authentic photograph showed that Stevens was looking and smiling at the senior army officer and not at Schine. The McCarthy people had cropped the true photo to eliminate everyone but Schine and Stevens. Thus, McCarthy was caught in an attempt to present a false impression. Upon questioning, no one on the McCarthy staff could explain why the cropped photograph rather than the original had been introduced in the hearings.

Sol Solomon called John on the telephone one day during the hearings. "John, Roy Cohn is supposed to take the stand in the Army/McCarthy hearings tomorrow, and they might get into his conduct during his visit at Evans Lab. Maybe your affidavit will be used. We have a TV set in the conference room here at the JAG office. Why don't you come down tomorrow afternoon at 1400 and watch the hearings with us."

"Sol, thanks for the invitation. I don't have anything scheduled for tomorrow afternoon, so if nothing comes up I'll be there."

John took care of his business the next morning, and after lunch he told Sergeant Champ that he was going to the JAG office. John greeted Sol and his old friends in the JAG office, and the ones who were not busy went into the conference room at 1400. When the hearings finally began and Cohn took the stand, the special counsel for the subcommittee Ray Jenkins began questioning Cohn. The questioning did indeed get to the matter of Cohn's conduct at Evans Signal Corps Engineering Laboratory. Jenkins asked Cohn if he had made a statement to the effect that he was declaring war on The Department of the Army when he was denied admittance to the laboratory on October 20, 1953. Sol looked over to John and nodded his head.

Cohn testified that he didn't have a recollection of what he had said that day. Jenkins tried several times to get Cohn to state what he had said that morning, but each time Cohn professed not to be able to remember what he had said.

Sol said to the people in the conference room, "Now, watch this."

Jenkins tried once more, but again Cohn said that he couldn't remember. Jenkins moved on to something else in the questioning.

Mike Turner asked Sol, "What are we supposed to watch?"

Sol answered, "Jenkins undoubtedly has, or knows of, an affidavit from John Grady stating very specifically what Cohn said. I don't know why he didn't introduce it. I would have used it. John, would you have used it?"

"Yes, I would," John replied.

Paul DuPre asked John, "What affidavit did you make? How are you involved in this?"

Sol Solomon spoke up and explained about the visit of all the dignitaries to Evans Signal Corps Engineering Laboratory, why John was there, what Cohn did and said, and explained about Grady being called down to Russell Hall to make the affidavit. Sol said that a civilian employee of the labs also had made an affidavit to the same effect. Grady had not known that before.

John had seen enough of the hearings. He excused himself and said that he had to get back to Company C.

The spectacle taking place in the U.S. Senate had a disturbing effect on John. Questions repeatedly surfaced in his mind, "Is this what I fought for in Korea? Is this what so many of us suffered and died for over there? What are these politicians contributing to make this country great?" Grady felt used by these people. He never before had felt so cynical about his government. He didn't mention his feelings to Rebecca or to anyone else.

***

McCarthy wanted to call General Lawrence as a witness in the hearings to support McCarthy's allegation against the army that Lawrence was relieved of his command of Fort Monmouth because he had cooperated with McCarthy in the espionage investigations at Fort Monmouth and had made statements supporting McCarthy's actions. The Department of the Army gave General Lawrence a direct order not to testify in the hearings. If the general disobeyed that order and appeared as a witness, he would be subject to court-martial.

General Lawrence was in a state of limbo. He and his wife Grace were in temporary quarters at Fort Myer across the Potomac River from Washington, D.C., and he had infrequent medical appointments at Walter Reed Army Hospital. As they watched the Army-McCarthy televised hearings, Lawrence contemplated the fact that Generals Reber and Zwicker had testified for the army, but he was prohibited from testifying. He told his wife, "Gracie, the army and the country have no more need of me. I've devoted my life to the army and have done my utmost to carry out my command responsibilities. I've saved an untold number of soldiers from killing themselves in their cars, and what thanks do I get? The army has changed; the country has changed. They just don't care any more, and they're going to cause us to lose it all."

CHAPTER 14. (MAY - JUNE 1954)

The following Tuesday at noon, Grady received a telephone call from Sergeant Robert Pettit. "Captain Grady, you started something that's coming to fruition this Friday. You put my name in for a direct commission, and I learned this morning that it went through. They're going to commission me at the Signal School office at 1000 Friday morning. Sir, if you can make it, it will mean a lot to me if you will be present."

"Congratulations, Robert. You bet I'll be there." John attended the ceremony and warmly congratulated Lieutenant Pettit when it was over.

Grady invited Pettit over to his house for dinner that night. While Robert and John sipped beers waiting for Rebecca to finish her dinner preparation, John said, "Robert, I have some news. I've decided to resign my commission and go back to college to get my law degree. I've concluded that I'm not a career soldier and that I shouldn't delay any longer. I have respect for the army and for many of the people, like you, that I've been associated with these past four years. But I don't think that I can do a good job in the army if I am not convinced that I'm doing the right thing for Rebecca and me."

"Captain Grady—"

Excuse me for interrupting you, Robert, but forget the "captain" business and the "sir" business when were not on duty. We're friends; call me John."

"Thanks ... John ... , it seems strange to call you by your first name. I'm sorry to hear that; I was hoping that some day we might serve together again. You're a good officer, and you've been an inspiration and an example to me and to others. But, if you think that resigning is thing for you to do, then I guess you should do it."

"Robert, knowing that you've been commissioned somehow makes it easier for me to leave. I know that you'll do your usual good job."

***

The following Monday morning Grady received orders to report to Camp Kilmer on 4 June to begin processing for release from active duty.

He had mixed feelings. He had no doubt that he should return to civilian life, but he had respect for the army and was proud of his service the past four years. Besides, had it not been for his army tour of duty he would not have met and married Rebecca.

A replacement officer came to take command of C Company. Major Hardy invited all the battalion officers over for a farewell get-together for John late in the afternoon of his last day in the battalion. Hardy had the battalion cooks bake and decorate a special cake, and they had an urn of coffee. The officers regretted to see Grady go, but they were good friends and for a going away gathering it was rather lively.

While the men were talking, Major Hardy's clerk came to Hardy and said in a low voice, "Major, you have a telephone call that you'll want to take." Hardy excused himself. The battalion officers continued talking and mixing. Hardy slowly walked back into the room with a somber look on his face. The battalion officers stopped talking and looked at him. Hardy stopped in the midst of them and looked down at the floor. He looked up, cleared his throat and said, "I have just been informed that Major General Karl Lawrence has taken his own life. That's all the information I have." Hardy turned and walked out of the building. The battalion officers quietly drifted away. The room was empty.

John left the battalion area and drove to Russell Hall where he signed out on the Fort Monmouth register for the last time. He walked through the front door and down the steps of Russell Hall just as the MP detachment began the evening Retreat ceremony of lowering the American flag on the tall flagpole near the Main Gate. The bugle call for the ceremony sounded on the public address system. Grady faced the flag, came to attention, and held a salute. The flag slowly descended the flagpole as the bugle call continued. Grady's eyes became misty. His four-year tour of duty flashed through his mind. The bugle call ended, and Grady smartly finished his salute. He walked to his maroon Chevy, slid onto the driver's seat, and drove home to Rebecca.

Made in the USA